JOURNEY
— FOR —
REVENGE

TOM RENK

authorHOUSE®

AuthorHouse™
1663 Liberty Drive
Bloomington, IN 47403
www.authorhouse.com
Phone: 1-800-839-8640

First published by AuthorHouse 6/22/2011

ISBN: 978-1-4567-5502-7 (e)
ISBN: 978-1-4567-5503-4 (dj)
ISBN: 978-1-4567-5504-1 (sc)

Library of Congress Control Number: 2011904305

Printed in the United States of America

To Karen, Courtney, Michael, Kate
and my parents, Ralph and Peggy,
for always motivating me to truly
accomplish what I set out to do!

PREVIEW PAGE

Meredith sat there sipping his steaming coffee when he heard that bastard's name on the TV hanging from the ceiling. He looked up and stared at the monitor. Bin Laden had surfaced again and it was being shown on the evening news. As Meredith watched, his anger and frustration grew, to the point he involuntarily squeezed his paper coffee cup so tightly, the liquid shot straight up in the air, all over his hand and the table.

At that moment Michael Pappas walked up. "Bill, hey relax buddy, don't let that son-of-a-bitch get to you." Michael looked over his shoulder at the TV above him and gave a one-finger salute to the bearded man filling the screen.

Bill looked up at the words being directed at him by name and saw Michael standing there, still in his police uniform. He looked back down at the table and realized he had coffee all over his hand, and his hand was burning from the hot liquid.

"He is a son-of-a-bitch," he growled. "And my blood pressure is already shot. Hell, I'm on three medications now." And with that he calmed down, grabbed a wad of paper napkins and began mopping up the milky coffee spreading over the tabletop.

Eventually Meredith looked up at the policeman and said, "I'm glad you can join us for a change Michael, you haven't been around for a couple weeks. Have a seat."

With that welcome, he went back to mopping up the mess. When he had pushed the liquid around awhile, he looked out the window and seemed lost in thought, so Michael just sat there quietly.

"You know," Meredith said to no one in particular as he stared out the window. "If I could, I'd personally kill that bastard with my own two hands. I can't believe they can't find him and take him out."

Everyone knows what they were doing on Tuesday, September 11, 2001.

I was driving to work in downtown Chicago, listening to a 24-hour news station, when the first reports of an airplane hitting New York's World Trade Center came across the airwaves. The initial report suggested an awful accident had occurred in Lower Manhattan, and because of the catastrophic collision of plane and building, there was definitely going to be substantial loss of life.

When I got to work, I parked in the garage and walked past the restaurant and bar in the lower level walkway. A crowd had gathered around the bar, which wasn't even open yet. Everyone was staring at the television mounted on the wall. I was drawn in, and then spent the rest of the morning watching a horrific terrorist act unfold.

This is a story about that day, the aftermath, and how some of the victim's surviving family members band together to cope with their grief and sorrow. Their journey starts that September morning and ends in an act of ultimate revenge and retribution for the many innocent lives lost that fateful day.

BOOK I - TERROR

8:25 am. 93rd Floor, WTC

Will showed up for his first staff meeting in the conference room on the 93rd floor a few minutes early, and began introducing himself to the other early arrivers. They were for the most part all young and confident in their dress and stature; they exuded an aggressiveness that was certainly a reason for part of the investment firm's success. He began to realize his path to the top might take a bit longer than he originally thought it would; he obviously would need to exceed their efforts.

Precisely at 8:30 am the boss walked in with two underlings trailing behind him. He sat down and everyone else immediately quieted down and took their seats. Jamie White, the floor Investment Sales Manager, offered his usual 'pump up the team' words of wisdom for a Tuesday morning, because the markets had experienced a typical rollback the day before. He hoped that would turn around today. Suggesting some sales themes for the day, he then rolled smoothly into introducing the newest addition to the firm, William Meredith III, to the assembled traders and investment managers. He quietly hoped the new addition would encourage some work ethic improvements to his charges.

Jamie White explained how Will Meredith would be carrying on some long-standing family traditions, first started over a century ago in London. He shared background information about Will's father being a legend in financial circles, just as his grandfather, and great grandfather had been in the London financial markets. Meredith was mortified that all this attention was being focused on him.

Jamie asked Meredith to stand up and give the assembled staff a short bio of his background, his schooling, and his hopes for the future. William knew this was coming because his father had told him it was kind of a right of passage, that all new investment managers had to do it, and that it was no big deal. Everyone in the room had gone through the same thing.

So he stood up, tugged his jacket down and decided he'd get this hazing requirement out of the way quickly at the front of the room. He walked around the long table parallel to the windows.

He opened with a variation of his interview speech, which had helped him to get here, but he wanted to keep the overall presentation relatively short. As he was reviewing his past and schooling, he began to notice a couple of people sitting at the large conference table facing the windows were staring out into space, ignoring what he had to say. That seemed rude but they had gone through this exercise many times, so he chose to ignore it. They weren't going to intimidate him; he kept on speaking about his hopes for the future with the company.

Then more of the group of traders facing north started fidgeting in their seats and a few made whispered comments as they poked their seatmates. The general state of the audience disintegrated. No one seemed to be listening.

William paused for a moment. Then the others seated at the table with their backs to the window, started turning around, and they too started murmuring.

What the hell was going on, he thought? Why couldn't these jerks at least give me a couple minutes of attention?

Suddenly a young woman started screaming, jumped up from her chair, and ran out of the conference room. The others just sat there with their mouths open gaping into the bright morning light. William was now pissed!

Being at the end of the room where the drapes were, William didn't have a clear vision of what they were all looking at out the 93rd floor window. He wondered what could be so damn important that everyone was so transfixed, completely ignoring him on his first day on the job. He took a couple of steps forward, around the corner of the conference table and looked to his right…

His first reaction was, "What the hell?" His brain could not make sense of what he was seeing. A huge object was filling his entire field of vision and seemed to be hurtling towards the building. His mind couldn't comprehend because he knew they were on the 93rd floor…what the hell was out there? And way up here?

He tried to focus on the large object, and when his mind finally realized what it was, it plowed right into the conference room, and exploded right in front of his eyes… It was 8:46 am.

→ ←

8:40 am 14ᵗʰ Floor, North Tower

Pasha and Mina gathered the children for some early morning exercise in the building's day care center facility on the 14ᵗʰ floor. They were going on a short field trip to the lower level of the building to see how donuts were made in the coffee shop. Pasha liked these kinds of field trips because the children got some exercise and she learned things too.

Most of the 20,000 people working in the two buildings were already in their offices. The lower level would not be as congested and it would be easier to keep an eye on the children. When they went on excursions later in the day, during coffee-break times, the hallways and retail centers downstairs would get very crowded. The children would get scared with all the people rushing about. 8:45am was the perfect time to schedule the excursion. Pasha and Mina had the ten children, including their own, hold hands. The biggest kids were on either end of the line with the smaller children in between. Both women walked on either side of the little group to keep them organized and together.

They left the day care facility and headed down the hall and around the corner to the elevators. The cars were very efficient in this building and upon hitting the button, which Pasha knew she must do or every child would scream that it was their turn, the car arrived almost instantly. They loaded the ten children into the car and she pressed sublevel 2.

Just as the two doors closed there was a terrifying, loud screeching impact sound that reverberated throughout the building and echoed loudly within the elevator shaft. There was a couple seconds of horrific shaking of the car within the shaft. The grating sounds continued to rumble, and were unlike any sound they had ever heard before. Mina felt the elevator shudder and the building tremble as all the children started screaming. She reached for the elevator 'open door' button.

As she did, the lights within the elevator flickered a couple times and then went out for good. The children continued screaming in the dark and Mina tried to calm them down as Pasha tried to feel for the open door button on the board in the corner. Just then the elevator started moving from the 14ᵗʰ floor but it did not go down as they had requested it to do. Instead the elevator started climbing and they felt as if it was gaining speed.

The children were screaming even more now, creating a frightful situation in the complete darkness. The elevator continued to rise and as it did they heard additional loud exploding sounds and high wind velocities blowing around the elevator car as they hurtled upward. The car was shaking and stuttering but continued to climb floor after floor.

In the darkness Pasha, Mina and the children had no idea how high they were ascending. Still searching for the control panel, she felt her way to the phone box below the panel. She would call for help and they would come and get them all. Just as she grabbed the phone from the box, she realized that the elevator was beginning to slow down to make a stop.

As it came to a stop, the elevator doors automatically opened, to a flaming wall of super heated gases generated by thousands of gallons of aviation fuel burning at 4,000-degrees Fahrenheit. The exploding wall of terror rushed into the elevator cabin seeking oxygen, the fuel it so desperately needed.

➜ ⬅

9:02 am. WTC, South Tower

Dennis Shanahan had been right about feeling something unusual 15 minutes earlier. Shortly after he had felt the jolt, which actually shook the entire building, the security intercom system reported a serious fire in the North Tower of the World Trade Center. The tinny-sounding announcer had initially recommended leaving the buildings, and then a short time later had come back on the PA system advising people to remain in the South Tower, as there were safety concerns for people exiting the Tower because of falling debris. Everyone was advised to remain in their offices for the time being until safe passage could be established out the south side of the World Trade Center.

Many office workers were uncomfortable with that command, especially those who had been in the buildings 8 years earlier when a terrorist attack had occurred. Many people decided they were going to leave the building regardless. Some wanted to see what all the commotion was about.

Not easily ruffled after 25 years in the FBI, where he was trained to follow the rules, Dennis remained at his desk. He tried to work but found himself drawn to the extraordinary view to the south and the Statue of Liberty. Sitting at his desk he gazed out the window when something caught his eye in the southwest sky, out over the Hudson River. It was a flash of sunlight reflecting off something. He tried to identify what he'd seen and continued to stare at the strobe like effect. Then he recognized the light was actually the sun reflecting off a large jet aircraft making a sweeping left turn towards Manhattan.

His eyes focused in on the large aircraft as it slowly continued its turn over the New York Harbor and the Statue of Liberty. He presumed it was making an approach to either La Guardia on his left, or making a wide turn heading for Kennedy out on Long Island. But at the altitude it was turning at seemed awfully low. Dennis thought that if the pilot got much closer the plane might actually clip a building in Lower Manhattan.

He sat at his desk watching this odd approach continue as the seconds ticked off. The plane finished its turn with its wings dipping and rising as if the pilot was trying to level out. In these maneuvers he actually squared up on a direct path to the South Tower. Dennis thought, he must certainly see one of the tallest buildings in the world right before him.

Like watching a horror movie film clip, he sat there mesmerized by the sight of the incoming plane. He could not take his eyes off of it and wondered if the pilot had a heart attack. The plane was going to hit the building!

He could not move from his chair as the craft closed the distance. By the time he truly realized the plane was flying right at him, it was too late. The Jet aircraft traveling at over 280 miles per hour slammed into the building. It was 9:04 am.

→ ←

Four hours earlier.

5:15 am. Tuesday, Greenwich Village

William Meredith, III reached for the digital alarm clock as it went off. He debated hitting the snooze button, but remembered the new job was starting this morning, and that was too important to be late for.

He was finally on his way. Today, he was starting his journey as an investment banker just like his father, William Meredith II and his Grandfather, William Meredith before him. While they had both made their marks in London's financial markets, he would make his name and fortune on Wall Street across the Atlantic. He knew he had a lot to accomplish if he was to live up to the family name. That was why the job was so important. It was the first step in making his Father proud. That was his goal. It was time he got the ball rolling.

His parents divorced about 15 years ago. As a young boy, he survived having to share his parents, going back and forth, week in and week out. In retrospect, he felt like his parent's marital problems had made him a stronger person. After the divorce, was finally settled, he went to live with his Father, which surprised Will because he was still unaware of what his Mother had done, or not done, to cause such a court decision.

His father raised him in the south of England just miles from the Cliffs of Dover, about an hour south of London. They lived in a turn of the Century country home, with lush surrounding gardens and a pine forest on the 25 acres. The home was immediately adjacent to a still somewhat functional 14th Century castle that figured prominently in English history. It was even on the tourist circuit and occasionally had Royal Family events on its grounds. Life was good for Meredith and son, and together they prospered.

His Father taught him how to be respectful and resourceful, how to make money and how to help those who could use a helping hand. His Father was good at what he did. So much so, that while Will was still a boy his Father had been knighted by the Queen for all his charitable works. While this charitable work had been important, Will thought it was for his Dad's uncanny ability to make money in the stock market, and then to invest in all sorts of international companies. That was what made people really take notice.

William Meredith had major holdings in shipping, in electronics firms, in major grain commodities and in the foreign financial markets. His wealth had grown so that it probably did rival the Queen's.

The senior Meredith became a role model for everyone in the financial and business world in London and across the UK. Because of his willingness to share his fortunes with many charities throughout England, he had become a favorite of the Royal Family. Through all this he had taught his son to always share in their good fortunes and that was now a part of William's nature. And that would all start this morning once he made some money on his own.

Then one day, Sir William Meredith II surprised all of England and the financial world when he announced that he was retiring at the ripe old age of 50. He decided he and his son would take the considerable wealth he had amassed, and relocate to the United States to live the good life. He announced that he wanted to become a gentleman farmer, and raise racehorses in upstate New York. And that's what he did.

William and Will pulled up stakes and headed west to America, settling in New York State less than 50 miles north of Manhattan. Since moving west, they had built a new life for themselves, had applied for U.S. citizenship, and made many new friends in the States. His reputation as a good man had preceded his travel across the Atlantic and he and his money were gratefully embraced and accepted.

Raising thoroughbred horses had agreed with his Father and he took to it with a vengeance, over the years producing some strong runners at the New York state tracks. It was a new challenge and he took to it with the same zeal that he had approached life back in England. While they lived less than two hours north of Manhattan, his Father insisted he was a dirt farmer, and not a financier.

So now it was Will's turn to carry the Meredith name forward. The challenge awaited him just like it had for his father and Grandfather; it was just a different field of play. He had breezed through Harvard with an undergraduate degree in Business Administration and had just graduated from Wharton with a Masters in International Finance. The Wall Street financial institutions took note of his background, his family pedigree, and his grades and he quickly received a number of corporate finance offers. He was on his way as the best and brightest of the Meredith clan.

No, he decided, he couldn't take another 10 minutes of shut-eye. Today, his quest to make both his Father and Grandfather proud started. He had no intention of ever being a farmer, or a racehorse breeder.

Will jumped out of bed, took a quick shower. He dressed with a bright blue shirt and conservative striped tie, and a dark blue pin stripe suit. He headed for the door, locked up his loft on West 10th and University Place in the middle of Greenwich Village, jumped on the elevator, and was on the street in a matter of minutes.

He headed south through Washington Square Park, which was deserted so early in the morning except for a few street people and a couple of drunks sleeping off last night's revelry. At the Fourth Street subway station he caught the early morning A train on the Blue line, heading south. He quickly passed through four stations to its end point. Up out of the subway, he crossed the wide stone promenade and entered his new workplace. He wanted to be at his desk on the 93rd Floor of the World Trade Center ready to go when the boss showed up.

→ ←

5:25 am - Brooklyn, NY

Across the East River in Brooklyn, Elena Veronin rose from her sleep before the alarm sounded, quietly easing herself out of bed. This was her routine every morning no matter how late she had gotten to bed. Her inner alarm clock told her when it was time to get up, and more importantly, she didn't want to disturb her husband Josef. He would be up soon enough.

Elena quickly showered, brushed her teeth and took her blood pressure pills. Her hair was short enough that it dried quickly. She couldn't understand why so many women wanted such long hair, spending extra hours each morning drying and primping. She was able to simply take a towel to her head, give it a vigorous rub, then drag a brush through it and be on her way. Her hair was graying a bit at the temples, but it was still thick and luxurious and that's all that mattered. Her husband loved her just the way she was. That was why she loved him, because he accepted her as she was.

She continued her morning routine trying to be as quiet as possible. She threw on a simple white blouse and skirt knowing her work outfit would cover almost everything.

Elena had a long commute to her job in the city, using a variety of transportation. These transfers often made it difficult to get to work on time because the timing was easy to throw off with an accident, a broken down or faulty bus, or a late running train, so she liked to start early.

She lived in a pleasant 2 bedroom flat at the corner of 91st Avenue and 121 St. just a few blocks from the Aqueduct Raceway. Quietly out the door, she walked two blocks north, and caught an MTA Bus that paralleled Kew Garden Road all the way to the train station. Once there, she worked her way through the early commuters lined up for trains on the platform to catch the 6:35 to Grand Central Station.

Then she would switch to the Green Line # 4 train that would take her south to the Financial District in lower Manhattan. At the Fulton Street subway stop, the escalator brought her back to the surface next to St. Paul's Chapel, just a few blocks east of her job.

While the first part of her trip had been above ground with a bus, the remainder of the commute was mostly underground until she came out of the subway and saw the Church built in the 1760's. As she exited the station, she noted the morning rush seemed a bit lighter than usual for a Tuesday, perhaps because the day was predicted to be absolutely beautiful. A lot of people would be taking a sick day to play hooky rather than waste what was left of summer.

Elena always liked seeing the peace and quiet of the Chapel, with its famous cemetery plots in the middle of this massive city surrounded by some of the tallest buildings in the world. It was nice to see this solitude with all the chaos that surrounded it. It reminded her that even this great city once had a humble beginning. She walked across the large marble WTC Plaza and under the huge steel globe of the world. As she always did, she looked up to the spot in the Ukraine where she and her husband had first come from many years ago, to make their life in America. It had been a good decision and now they were as American as you could be.

She cut between two of the largest buildings in America and entered the Marriott Hotel through a side door, designated for employees. As she walked past the back entrance security office, she said hello to Joe Wolfe, the security guard who was sleeping behind the desk. She was sure he had been sleeping there almost all night, as was his habit when he pulled the graveyard shift. Luckily, he would be going home at 8:00 am. He could enjoy the day.

While security was not a major issue today, she remembered back eight years ago when there had been a terrible bombing directly below her building. No one had slept on the job for years after that incident.

Islamic terrorists had detonated a huge truck bomb in the World Trade Center basement parking lot, so large that it had blown a huge crater in the Hotel's main ballroom, which sat between the two World Trade Center Towers.

The bomb caused considerable damage to the WTC; its HVAC systems sending smoke and fire into the two main towers and hotel. People had evacuated the buildings, and the ensuing fires, running down the fire exits covered in dust and soot from the bomb blast. A number of people had died from the attack, and many were injured in the ensuing turmoil trying to escape the horrific event.

After that terrible day, the WTC buildings and Hotel were shut down for days. The vast hotel ballrooms were shut down for months because of all the damage from below. That was when security also became a major focus. The Hotel and the building management hired numerous security experts to look at the buildings defenses, hired a retired FBI terrorism expert to be Chief of Security, and made everyone take numerous classes on security. All employees got involved in the process, except maybe Joe, the back door security guard. It looks like he forgot most of his lessons.

"Good morning Joe, what do you know?" she chuckled, proud of her use of American slang. "It's going to be a beautiful day, but you look as if you're going to sleep through all of it."

Joe looked up and raised an eyebrow, "Good morning, darling, you always brighten my day. Listen Elena, you're going to have your hands full today, we have a full house."

"I like keeping busy, it makes the day go faster, and I hate just sitting."

"Not me, this chair was meant for me. You have a great day. Just make sure you stay away from all those grabby men with that legal convention that's in-house. I want you all for myself!"

She laughed and proceeded down the hall through the back of the house, through the kitchens, and up to the second mezzanine floor. She walked down another hall past the freight elevator and turned right into the room marked Housekeeping. Elena headed for her locker and froze for a moment when she saw all the balloons, cards, and streamers decorating her grey cubicle.

Then it hit her for the first time that morning, it was actually her birthday. She was turning 40 and becoming an old lady. Well, enough about that she thought. She put on her maid's apron, went into the housekeeper's day room and checked her floor assignment for the day.

With her seniority she had drawn the rooms on the top two floors, most of them suites and concierge rooms. While it would be a long day there were less overall rooms for her to clean. Hopefully, she had a neat and caring overnight crowd, and no sex parties or rock bands. She packed her work cart with more than she thought she would need and headed for the freight elevator. The 33rd floor would be her home for the day and up there it would allow her to work mostly undisturbed by all the hotel management.

→ ←

5:45 am. Williamsburg, Brooklyn

Michaela Jameson literally bolted up in bed as she did almost every morning, not needing an alarm clock. She called it her first exercise of the day. The morning was her personal time, and she loved the peace and quiet before her world turned into daily chaos. She had even named her dog, Morning, to celebrate her special time. The name could be problematic when the dog got out late at night and she had to chase after her calling out her name. The neighbors all thought she was one of those crazies starting the day a wee bit early. But she loved her perfectly spotted Dalmatian. Every day she wished she could take the pooch to work with her, just like when old firehouse photos showed the regal spotted dogs sitting on the front bench seat of the fire wagons next to the driver.

She was one of New York's finest, and her 12-hour shift at the Old #15 Station would start soon enough. She ran down the stairs to the kitchen and decided to enjoy her first few minutes of solitude before all hell broke loose in this city of millions. She started some drip coffee, got the morning paper off the stoop and let Morning out the back door to wander around in the small fenced yard. In her small courtyard, she did her jumping jacks, sit-ups and push-ups to get the blood flowing. Michaela liked the way she looked, strong enough to put up with all the station guff, yet feminine enough to turn heads when she wasn't in all her gear.

As a Paramedic/firefighter she was assigned to bus # 1011 and seemed to draw every lousy call in Manhattan. At least it felt that way last week. She had missed two dates with Michael, her boyfriend and lover of three years, because of all the emergency calls backing up into the evening. The paperwork alone kept her working late both nights. While her boyfriend understood, because he was a New York cop, it made for a rotten love life.

Michael Pappas was a hunk; he was a Greek god that turned heads wherever he went. Michaela first eyed him in a police and fire fighters hang out, when she was still back in basic training. After meeting him through a mutual friend, she found he was a cop in training at the Academy and would be graduating and moving on to six months of field training. They dated in their free time and after graduation they were assigned to different parts of the city, but they each found time to get together, and for six years had been a couple.

Michael had originally come from Greece as a child with his immigrant parents. As a young boy he had developed his muscles working on his Father's fishing boat in the Adriatic Sea. He had learned the ways of the sea before he could ride a bike and he was proud of his past heritage. While he was now land based chasing bad guys for a living on the streets of New York City, he still cherished his days at sea and had vowed to show Kayla what the Greek Islands were all about. He was in love and not afraid to tell anyone. They would soon be picking a wedding day and then perhaps a honeymoon in the Greek Islands.

At 7:00 am Michaela got dressed in her work blues and headed for the station. She lived right across the East River from Manhattan near the Williamsburg Bridge in a three-story walkup. Michael lived just a couple miles away but their schedules rarely matched for any kind of joint commuting. She jumped on the Brooklyn # 39 bus and took it all the way west across the bridge to Delancy and Mulberry Streets in Little Italy.

She wished she could afford to live in that area, but the rates were way too high and she didn't have the benefit of any rent control. At least it only required one bus route and with her FDNY blues on, no one ever gave her any grief along the way.

When she got to the House, she checked in, dumped her personal stuff in her locker, caught another cup of coffee in the kitchen and walked into the Captain's office.

"Morning boss… for after Labor day it's still almost summer out there. It can't really be mid-September. I hope this lasts for another month. What's on the list for today?"

"Hey, Michaela, glad to see your pretty face, and the rest of you for that matter, I always like it when you come sashaying in here."

Michaela just ignored the comment and plopped down in the only chair in the room. Captain Tony Speciale was a rotund Italian in a mostly Italian firehouse. He was a standup guy, who just let those many years of men-only firehouses cloud his mind every now and then when he did run into a female. He was a straight shooter who let her pull her own weight. But he also kept the guys in line, kind of like a father figure. She appreciated the gesture but also felt she could take care of herself if she needed to.

The captain continued, "It's pretty quiet at the moment, nothing left over from last night and the weekend. Thank God, it's been a tough couple of days."

"Tell me about it, I think I ran through two miles of tape in the bus. I can't keep it in stock." Michaela responded as she looked at the day roster on the Captain's door.

"With three major fires this weekend, I'm just glad we got everyone out and had no injuries. Let's enjoy the peace while we can, I'm sure something will ruin it in a New York minute." the Captain said. He pointed towards the roster, "Engines 34 and 42 will be doing hydrant flushing on Broadway and Grand for the first few hours, until we catch something better to do. You can tag along and make yourself useful until the calls start stacking up."

"You got it, boss. Let's hope we have a quiet day for a change. We could use it."

Michaela went into the kitchen and found her partner in crime, Sean Michaels, buttering toast to go with his eggs, and reading the morning paper. She quietly joined him at the large table. He said nothing.

Sean was a transplanted Irishman with sandy red hair who was somewhat out of place in Little Italy with his strong accent. The thought cracked her up every time she saw him. She had already eaten something and didn't want to lose her girlish figure so she just got a second cup of coffee and waited for him to finish the paper. Not that he would have shared any breakfast with her. Not in this house. He wasn't the sharing kind.

Once he finished his New York Post, he looked up and finally said hello. They both cleared the table and went downstairs to check their supply inventory in the paramedic wagon. The night crew was supposed to set up the vehicle for them before they left, but that never happened, and when it did everything was in the wrong place. Both knew that would be an issue when they had bleeders in the bus and were scrambling, so they took the time to re-organize everything, all the while swearing at the night crew. Once satisfied, they gave a quick blast of the siren telling the Captain they were pulling out and moved into traffic to join the fire crews already out on Broadway. It would just be another day in paradise.

→ ←

6:15 am - Brooklyn

In the same room that Elena had vacated just an hour earlier, the alarm clock finally went off. Josef instinctively reached for the other side of the bed to touch Elena, and realized that she was gone already. He knew she had already snuck off so he could sleep a bit longer and he was angry with himself because he had wanted to wish her a Happy Birthday and give her the present he had purchased. It was a beautiful gold necklace that would look great on her pretty 40-year old neck. He would have to come up with a new idea for delivery of this necklace

He jumped out of bed and thought it may have to wait until she got home that evening. But as he showered he thought about how he might give her the birthday gift since he had overslept. Maybe he could take her out to dinner and give it to her there. That was it. He would call that famous restaurant next door to her building and make a reservation to surprise her with dinner at the world's tallest restaurant.

He raced through his morning routine because he had an important meeting at work. As one of the key translators in eastern European languages at the United Nations, he would be translating an important meeting concerning global warming issues in the General Assembly.

His specialty was the many Russian dialects, as he had originally come from the Soviet Union in southern Russia, from the Ukraine, an independent country now. He still had relatives in Russia and he talked to them regularly to maintain linguistic proficiencies and to stay abreast of the old country.

Now that Russia had so vastly changed and improved communications, they were truly becoming an integral part of the western world. He knew that it was time to visit the family back home. He even had a brother-in-law, Elena's brother, who was a famous General in the army of the new Russia, had served in Afghanistan with distinction, and was moving up in the ranks. He was currently posted in Novorossiysk, in southern Russia, at a very secret military base near the Black Sea. Josef made a mental note that he and Elena should look him up the next time they went home, as the old soldier was close to retiring.

He left the house less than 30 minutes later and almost traced the same path that Elena had taken into the city an hour earlier. He believed that he could still smell her perfume in the train, although in his heart he knew it could not be the same car as that train was probably on its way to Jersey by now. But he liked to think about her, the most beautiful woman he had ever seen. He was a lucky guy and would tell her so tonight.

Once he got to Grand Central Station he stepped off the train into a sea of commuters flowing into the City. He exited the massive station on the Lexington Avenue side of the building, walking straight east, down three long blocks towards the East River, to 1st Avenue. This was a wealthy part of the lower east side.

As he walked east he could see the United Nations buildings rising up ahead on the River. He always marveled that he had gotten such a great job in this international building, in a place that was supposed to be bringing peace to the world. Perhaps today peace will blossom all over the world, he thought.

Then, as he crossed First Avenue, he approached the many layers of security in front of the UN building, and was brought back to the reality the world was still a very dangerous place. Here, on the perimeter of this massive white structure dedicated to world peace and harmony amongst all nations, there were reinforced concrete traffic barricades meant to stop a dump truck, police cordons and screening checkpoints that had to be passed through to enter.

At the main employee entrance, his shoulder bag was thoroughly checked and screened, and a guard gave him a light frisking as he did every day. He wondered what had happened over the last ten years since the cold war ended? Back then everyone thought the world was actually moving towards peace and tranquility. Now it seemed to be in even greater turmoil, with all sorts of third world skirmishes, and nasty terrorist attacks occurring around the world. At least in America, and New York City, the war on terror was mostly an abstract foreign issue. He hoped it would stay that way for a long time. He loved his new home as a peaceful refuge from all that was ugly.

He took the elevators directly to his small office on the 25th floor on the west side of the building. Crossing the hallway to look out the senior translator's window, he leaned out with his cheek touching the window. He could just see the World Trade Center twin towers to the south and thought about calling the Restaurant in the building to make his wife's birthday reservation, but realized 'Windows to the World' wouldn't be open for at least another hour or two. He would have to call later.

→ ←

6:00 am. Portland Airport, Maine

The passengers walking into and through the Regional Airport were groggy, as most people would be when they are up before the sun appears in the east. At this very early hour the airport was still mostly empty, being a smaller regional hub that only had a few flights feeding into the East coast major cities. The only passengers arriving at this hour were catching commuter flights to Boston, New York and Philadelphia, where they would board other larger planes for distant destinations.

There was just a small security detail monitoring the single entrance to the commuter gates. At this early hour security was taking a pretty casual approach to checking passengers because they personally knew most of the regular commuters.

"Good Morning Jim. Where are you off to this week? Somewhere warm I hope?" the policeman behind security asked.

"Morning Jeff, Let's see, today, I'm heading to Detroit, and I doubt it'll be very warm at all. Whatever weather I see there today, you'll get here tomorrow, so I'll call if it's bad. With luck maybe I'll bring some decent weather home with me on Thursday."

"Then I hope you get good weather. Next week, the wife and me are going to Phoenix to visit the grandkids, so at least I'll get some nice heat there." He waved the man through and said hello to the next person in line who he also recognized. The few security guys on duty were going through the motions.

In the midst of this trickle of passengers, a couple of eastern European or South Asian travelers shuffled through the process. Their clothes blended in and they were quiet and polite waiting for their turns in the security line. Once through, they gathered their minimal belongings and moved down the corridor. One went off to get coffee while the other person found a quiet corner away from other people and studied his travel documents.

New England Air called the flight right on time and the boarding process went quickly as there were only 19 passengers making the 25 minute flight to Boston.

The plane taxied out to the primary commercial runway, and after getting clearance from the control tower, it dashed down the runway and was airborne in a matter of minutes. The flight went due south and turned east for final approach into Boston Logan Airport right on time.

→ ←

6:45 am. Hoboken, NJ.

Uri Navroz liked to get up early every morning just like when he was a sailor. In the old days when he awoke he would immediately go to an upper deck of the ship to look out over whatever vast sea or ocean he was on. He would breathe the salt air deeply in and out, and then his workday would begin. Now that he was a just another landlubber, he had to settle for a quick walk to the roof of his building for that shot of fresh air. On the roof he could see the Hudson River and the water calmed his nerves and made him feel good. The smell in the air was not so much ocean, as it was river water, but he felt he could still smell the salt in the air.

Every morning offered a new day and he felt that this would be a good day. He was a proud old Egyptian sailor who had gone to sea at a young age and spent most of his life there. He had crewed and served as a deck officer on many ships, and thought of the sea as a broad highway serving the entire world. As a young man he had dreamed about far off places, and as a sailor he had been to most of those places. He had visited ports-of-call all over the world, and seen every backwater industrial port on the high seas, hauling whatever shipping consignments needed to be delivered.

Over thirty years at sea, he had called on ports throughout the Indian Ocean, the Mediterranean from Gibraltar to the Suez Canal, from the Greek Islands south and west to the shores of Tripoli. He had even plied the Black Sea running Russian military shipments to and from Sevastopol, and run from pirates in the Indonesian Straits. In all those years he had learned how to navigate the seas like the back of his hand, but now he rarely thought of it as a pleasant experience and was glad to be landlocked for a change. He had experienced his fill of lousy captains, pirates, gunrunners, drunks and thieves. He was no longer a seaman; just the opposite. Now he worked high in the sky in an entirely different field. Now he was a proud old man who washed dishes for his son.

His pride and joy was his son Ali, who had talked him into retiring from the sea to come to America, the land of opportunity. Ali had brought him to New York City, the capital of the world according to his son.

Ali had gotten him a job that did not require sea legs but still occasionally challenged his balance. His son was the Day Manager of the

Windows to the World Restaurant, the tallest restaurant on the top of the World Trade Center. He was now paid more than he had been paid at sea for 30 years, even though he was cleaning and washing dishes for a living.

But most important, he was with his son's family in America living the American dream. He emptied his chest and took another deep breath tasting for the ocean's salt air. Then he went back down the stairs, and started to prepare for work.

→ ←

6:56 am. 32nd & 11th Avenue

Osama needed to be at the 36th Street garage on the west side, just a block from the Javits Convention Center, by 7:00 am to take the taxi from Malik, his brother, who worked the nightshift with yellow cab number 1949. Together they sub-leased the cab from the medallion owner and kept the vehicle in motion and service almost constantly. The two Pakistani brothers even had two other drivers who shared with driving when they took an occasional day off. If they could just keep this taxi moving for three more months they estimated they would have the money to buy the medallion from the current owner, who was too sick to drive anymore. That would be a turning point in their adventure in this new country.

After switching seats with his brother, Osama drove around the corner and four blocks south to 32nd St. between 10th and 11th Avenues to his family apartment. It was across from the rail yards and close to one of the many bus terminals, and the New Jersey Tunnel entrance. It was not the safest part of the city but it offered a tiny space above a garage that they could afford. Osama and Malik and their families shared this space with another family from Pakistan.

Pasha had the children outside and waiting in front of the first floor boarded up garage entryway. She and the children would become his first fare of the day and he always gave them a good rate, free and off the clock. He liked driving the family to Pasha's job because it was his best fare of the day. The children jumped in, with 7 year-old Vispy jumping in the front seat and little Sonji, age 4, in the back with his mother.

It was a relatively short trip to the Financial District down the West Side Highway skirting the Hudson River. He made a left at Albany Street and then turned onto Washington St. next to a series of huge buildings.

He joined the long taxi line waiting for fares that were coming out of the station with trains from Hoboken and Newark across the river. Pasha and the children jumped out and waved goodbye to their father as they walked in the shadows of the two huge buildings.

For Osama, another day had started in a peaceful paradise. As he waited to move forward in the taxi line he thought about Pakistan and the suffering he and his family had experienced for many years.

The Mullahs had condemned him and his brother for allowing their wives to work, for selling the infidels music and electronics, and for not sending Vispy to religious school. It had been non-stop with the religious mullahs and militias ramping up their persecution daily.

He'd finally grown weary of the constant abuse and had packed his family off to hide in the northern mountains of North Waziristan where his family had originally come from. He found refuge with distant relatives in Walai, a small village in the mountains in the unruly tribal areas between Pakistan and Afghanistan. It was pretty much straight west of Peshawar, but up in the mountains and light years away from anything remotely modern.

His brother's family also joined him and initially they were at peace as they kept to themselves. But then the local tribe leaders noting the new faces, started to pay more attention to them. And the persecution started all over again.

So he and his brother decided to make a dramatic change for the sake of their families. Having read and seen so much about America through their business dealings and selling tapes and videos, they decided that was the only place that would offer peace and security to their families. It would also allow them to again start up their electronics store.

Months passed as they tried to find a way to get to America. They first tried to go to India but that was difficult, as they had to cross all of Pakistan and ran into all sorts of government scrutiny. So they changed their direction and went back to the Indus River, near Peshawar. The Indus is a major river running north to south from the mountains all the way to Karachi and the Arabian Sea. The river was the major highway of commerce within Pakistan since the few roads and highways in the mountains were barely passable and minimally safe for travelers.

For an exorbitant fee they were allowed to stay below deck in the sail locker and only came out at night for fear of being spotted. In Karachi they quietly made inquiries at the shipping docks and found a tramp steamer captain that was willing to take them aboard for more than half of all their money. Luckily the captain had liked his CD player and Malik had brought along a bunch of CDs to sweeten the deal.

He thought the captain would take care of them. Instead they were put to work cleaning and serving the rest of the crew for the duration of the trip. But the ship was on its way to the Mediterranean and Marseille, France and they were on the ship moving towards their goal.

Four weeks later they were in Marseille, first hiding on the docks, and then in alleys in the French city, trying to figure out how to get to America. They found some work in a backwater bar washing dishes and began to save up some more money. In asking around they were told to go to the city of Calais on the English Channel. Situated in this northern industrial port city, there were supposedly numerous refugee camps that had developed over the years, housing thousands of illegal immigrants, all trying to gain passage to Great Britain, which offered better social benefits and job prospects than other EU countries.

Since 2002 thousands of immigrants had made their way to England, by boat, ship and rail and had often passed through these refugee camps.

Over time the camps had developed into distinct ethnic groupings because of language, religion, customs, and the terrors of travel in people-trafficking circles. They were advised they would find Pakistani and Iraqi refugee camps that could help them to arrange passage to Britain and maybe even America.

Osama and Malik worked hard to save their dishwashing money and eventually bought second-class train passage to Calais. Upon arrival they found the encampments just as reported, spread out in the coastal grasslands and forests west of the port city. They wandered about from one immigrant encampment to another until they entered the so-called 'Jungle'. This was an Afghan/Pakistani enclave patched together beside a rutted farm road. While most refugees were intent on passage to Britain, they asked about passage to America and were told that too was possible.

In a few weeks they were pointed to a ship getting ready to depart for America to New Jersey, which they were told was close to New York City. Again they offered their services as stewards and paid dearly for the job but they were on their way. They had finally found passage to America, and arrived with just the shirts on their backs.

Once in America, they found no welcome, and penniless they did the only thing they could find to do, and started driving cabs for someone else who owned the vehicle and medallion. Each night they earned a few dollars an hour. But it was a start and their original dreams were still alive. After a year they had saved enough to wire money to their families and obtained persecution visas to live and work in America. The families loved America as it had given them personal freedom and a chance to see their children grow up and prosper. Now they hoped they might see their children even attend the University when they were older. Life was indeed good and getting better each day.

→ ←

7:10 am, Logan Airport, Boston

The small commuter prop plane was waved into its normal yellow marked spot on the tarmac right on time. As soon as the left side propeller had spooled down enough, the planes hatch opened and transformed into a set of stairs for the departing passengers. Each person quickly disembarked and walked the short distance across the tarmac to the lower level doors of the waiting room.

Once inside the two men gathered for a moment to get their bearings and then took the escalator to the main passenger terminal above. They had come in at Gate 2-A close to the central terminal access point. As they came upstairs they found themselves next to the security checkpoint for all the American Airlines gates.

But they were on the secured passenger side of the security checkpoint, having passed through their security check in Portland, Maine. They would only have to go through the process again if they had to change terminals. Luckily for them, their next flight departed from the same Terminal just a few gates away.

The two foreign looking men walked to the flight board and verified the gate for their next flight. They also covertly acknowledged three other travelers that were milling about in another small group just across the hallway. As soon as they verified the gate for their next flight the two small groups broke up and went in different directions; a few for a restroom, another for coffee and the others to buy some magazines for the next flight.

In less than fifteen minutes, American Flight # 11 was announced. It was a non-stop long haul to Los Angeles, with a scheduled departure of 7:40 am. It was a relatively light passenger load with only 81 passengers and flight crew of nine on board. The light load was due to the early morning departure time.

The flight attendants got everyone seated and comfortable and then they went through their pre-flight safety presentation. The pilot came on the intercom speakers to say they had a beautiful morning for flying without a cloud in the sky. He advised that they would be leaving on time and without strong headwinds would be in Los Angeles before the scheduled arrival.

The five Middle Eastern travelers settled in different aisle seats in First Class, Business, and Coach slyly turned around to look at one another and nodded their commitment. The plane taxied and was wheels up at 7:59 am heading west for Los Angeles.

→ ←

7:20 am, Upper Westside

Dennis Shanahan ducked into the coffee shop on 11th Avenue and W. 77th St. on the west side of Manhattan. He stopped to grab his usual donut and a cup of black coffee, and to say hello to the store's proprietor, Bob Bohlor.

As he grabbed a copy of the New York Times, he said, "Morning Bobby, how's it going? It looks beautiful out there. Wish I didn't have to work today. Maybe we could play a round and I could make some money off of you."

The store proprietor smiled and reached over the counter to shake hands, "Dennis, you're not good enough to win any money off me, and heck, you don't play as much as I do. I've already played 73 times this season and I'm trying to hit 90 rounds before the snow flies. You really want to try and take my money? If you do, I'm in."

Dennis added two sugars to his coffee and whistled, "90 rounds? Don't you ever work past 10:00 am? I'll wait until I have the time to practice a bit and then I'll whip your ass."

"That's what your supposed to be doing now, your retired! But heck, you seem to be working even harder than before you retired. What's up with that, I hope it's worth it?"

He paid for his donut and coffee and put his change in his pocket for the subway. "It is Bobbie, it is, and I like staying involved. I couldn't just go belly up. They'll have to bury me in this black suit.

"I don't look good in black, that's why I like my apron," Bob grabbed the apron for emphasis, "I can even wear my plaid golf pants underneath and people think it's part of the uniform."

Dennis smiled and said, "Since I left the Bureau, I'm just trying to keep the old mind sharp. And all these years of wearing out shoe leather is finally paying off. I'm making more money now than when I was chasing bank robbers, and the work is a heck of a lot easier. I'm heading down to an investment firm that wants me to do background checks on their key employees. It pays top dollar and I'll get a free lunch to boot."

"Hey, when you going to bring that beautiful daughter of yours around again. She did a great job on all the posters she made for the shop, and it helped bring in all sorts of people. Say hi for me, and tell her to give me a call."

Dennis waved at his friend and headed out the door and down the street to the 79th St. Subway entrance. He wolfed down his donut to free up a hand because he knew the train would be crowded with commuters heading downtown. On the platform he thought about his daughter Katherine and the great business she had built for herself in Manhattan.

Kate was a successful graphic designer and freelanced for a whole multitude of businesses from Madison Avenue all the way down to Wall Street. In the last five years she had added all sorts of quality graphic professionals, including calligraphers, printers and marketing designers. He was proud of her, and was especially pleased when she had helped out Bobby in his small deli shop. The signage was much improved.

He took the #1 Redline Train south and it was crowded as usual. He stood all the way to the Times Square - 42nd Street platform. He squeezed his way through the crowd and out the door just before it closed. He walked west through the tunnel to 8th Avenue to catch the Blue line A Train heading south where he finally got a seat. His mind wandered with the passing subway stops and he thought about his 28-year career at the Bureau. He was second generation FBI.

His father, Edwin Shanahan had been the child of Irish immigrants. As a young man he had become an agent with the Bureau of Investigation way back in the 20's. Dennis was just a baby back in 1926 when his father, five years on the job, had been gunned down on a stakeout on the south side of Chicago searching for a known car thief. When Edwin confronted the criminal the bad guy got the drop on him and shot him dead. He had his personal five-shot revolver with him, but it was no match for the firepower the bad guy had used. He died on the spot leaving a wife and young toddler to fend for themselves.

He became the first agent ever killed in the line of duty. The agents back then were not sworn federal officers and they had no official police powers. They were not even authorized to carry a weapon. Because it was J. Edgar Hoover's first agent ever killed in the line of duty, he took a personal interest in the case and made sure that Winnie, Dennis's mother, was taken care of by the Bureau in the ensuing years. J. Edgar made it a point to stay in touch with the family as Dennis was growing up.

After Shanahan's death, it bothered Hoover enough that he went before Congress, and petitioned to have his national police agents formally designated as federal officers. He asked that they have full police powers, and be authorized to carry weapons. Eventually he got what he wanted, and the Agency became the Federal Bureau of Investigation.

Many years later after World War II, the FBI was authorized to expand the size of the Agency because of the growing menace of Communism. Normally the Bureau required applicants to be attorneys as a basic requirement. They needed to understand the law and abide by it. But the demand for new agents was so great that the law school requirement was waived. Dennis, just out of college, after having served in the Air Corp during the war, filled out an application and sent it to Mr. Hoover.

About the same time he applied for the Bureau, the criminal that had shot and killed his Father some twenty-years earlier, had completed his sentence for murder and was getting out of prison. There was some concern in the Bureau that if Dennis were brought into the Agency he would have a license to look up his Father's killer. But J. Edgar personally reviewed the case and gave approval for him to join the Agency.

Normally after agent training was completed at Quantico, Virginia, a new agent was sent to some small backwoods FBI office to get his feet wet for one year before a more regular assignment was given. This policy was designed to allow an agent to work through his rookie mistakes, and learn from them, before he moved to a more permanent assignment and location. Again, J. Edgar weighed in on the situation and had Dennis assigned to Springfield, Illinois, which was only a couple hours away from Chicago and his Mother, Winnie.

A year later, after working out all those first year kinks, Dennis was re-assigned straight to Chicago and started his career chasing bank robbers. And there were lots of them then. He remembered one case that always made him smile. In the 50's and 60's the FBI's Chicago Office was in the Federal Building on Dearborn St. Every Friday morning the agents would receive their weekly paychecks and most of them would go downstairs to the bank in the lobby and deposit their pay. One Friday, with many of Dennis' fellow agents standing in various lines at the tellers windows, they heard a guy in the front of the line announce 'this is a stick-up'.

About twenty agents were in line and they all drew their weapons and surrounded the guy. When he turned around, he had 20 guns pointed at his head and he wet his pants. Dennis always loved telling that story. Most times bank robberies weren't that comical.

Dennis went on to be assigned to the Organized Crime Unit of the Chicago Field Office and he spent twenty years chasing 'made' mobsters and bad guys. He worked all the vices, found out where the back room gambling dens were and learned how to skip-trace people trying to disappear, He learned how to follow the money and he put a lot of the mob guys away.

It was the legal system that made the job difficult. He would collar the bad guys and they would lawyer up, and get the best defense that money could buy. These guys were well insulated and difficult to prosecute. The cases took years of preparation and testimony to work their way through the legal system. Dennis had spent a good quarter of his career in federal courtrooms testifying against these guys. Even when he had retired, he had been called back as an expert case witness many times a year.

A few months after his retirement Dennis had received a call from the SAC, the Special Agent in Charge in Chicago, asking if Dennis still had his father's original five shot revolver. He was advised they were creating a new Memorial for all the agents that had been killed in the line of duty.

Dennis had intended to leave the weapon to his daughter Katherine. But they talked about the honor and both agreed the weapon should be displayed in the Memorial and shipped it to the Chicago FBI Office. They were invited to attend a dedication ceremony and the new building's largest Conference Room was designated the Edwin Shanahan Conference Room at the ceremony.

In addition, a large Memorial Wall, called the 'Martyr's Wall', was dedicated recognizing all the agents who had died in the line of duty. Edwin Shanahan was the first name and photo on the display. Dennis had been proud of the traditions that his father and he had set over the past 40 years.

He looked up and caught a passing subway sign showing that his station was the next stop. Once the train stopped he exited the subway car at 8:10 am and climbed the stairs looking up and verifying he was just a block from the World Trade Center. He always thought the buildings were very striking and imposing, especially when you looked at them as you came out of the subway at their base. The Twin Towers soared up as if they were touching the sky.

He walked the block west and crossed the Plaza, past the six-story high world globe and went into the South Tower. He took the escalators up to the Elevator floor, went up one set of elevators to the transfer floor and switched to another for the trip to the Investment firm on the 82nd floor. He thought about how great the view would be on a clear day like today and hoped they would give him a workspace near a window. Maybe even on the Statue of Liberty side of the building so he could see the tourist boats going back and forth out to the Statue and to Ellis Island where his family had started their American journey.

At 8:25 am the elevator stopped at the 82nd Floor and he saw his destination just across the hallway. It was a big firm with investment offices spread out on four different floors. While the foyer entrance was an interior business space he could see bright light radiating from the adjacent hallways on both sides of the reception area.

He opened a large, ten -foot high glass door and stepped into the huge, modern foyer. Dennis checked in with the receptionist and she checked her records to see that he was scheduled for the day and where he was being assigned. She directed him to his workspace for the day pointing him down the hallway on the left. Dennis was very pleased when he went down the hallway and ended up in a beautiful office facing south and looking down on the Statue of Liberty.

He set his briefcase on the floor next to the desk and walked to the window to admire the view. Before him he had an unobstructed view of New York Harbor, Ellis Island, the Statue of Liberty and in the distance the Verrazano Narrows Bridge. He stood there for a few minutes taking in all of the beauty from this vantage point, and then he suddenly remembered they were actually paying him to do background checks on employees. He reluctantly turned from the massive floor to ceiling window and went to his temporary desk. He dug out his small laptop computer, fired it up and started his workday. This would be a great day, he thought, staring out the window at the sights below.

A few minutes later, as he pulled up a background dossier on a key Vice President in the firm he heard a tremendous roar and what he took to be a violent shaking of the building. He swore the building shook and he wondered if it was an earthquake. It was 8:46 am.

→ ←

Tora-Bora, Mountains of Afghanistan

The tall gaunt man sat silently with his hands crossed in his lap on a large hand woven rug waiting for his followers to sit. It was like he was in a peaceful trance. The robed men milling about the room started to arrange themselves in a wide perimeter and sat on the floor of the non-descript house at the base of the mountains east of Kabul, near the border with Pakistan.

This was a clandestine meeting of the Mujahedeen leadership and the Taliban warlords from all over the region. These were the fighters who waged holy jihad on the many infidels that had been coming to their lands for centuries. Their grandfathers had fought with the British for over a century, and their fathers had fought the Soviets for years eventually pushing them out in defeat. Now their children were fighting the Americans and the western world. All any of them had wanted was to be left alone to tend their land, their crops, their customs and families. They all believed they did not need any governments to administer them. They could take care of themselves just as they had for the last 1,000 years.

Once the group had settled down and had all been introduced and welcomed, tea was offered and distributed in the ways of the mountain tribes. A rotund bearded man with spectacles finally raised his voice and called for order. This was Ayman al-Zawahiri, in a prior life an Egyptian Doctor, but now the number two leader of al Qaeda, second only to Osama Bin Laden, who sat to his left silently watching the group of Islamic leaders.

These two men had joined forces in 1998. Zawahiri had originally been the leader of the Egyptian Islamic Jihad. Osama bin Laden had started his holy war efforts in Saudi Arabia, in the Sudan, in Yemen and had spent years in Afghanistan. Now they had combined forces and were waging war on the western world. They commanded al Qaeda terrorist activity all over the world.

"We have asked you to join us this evening because we may not have another chance to be together for a long time. Soon we will strike the infidels in their hearts and in their minds." The assembled warriors murmured, but waited for more.

"When we do strike, the American infidels will seek revenge like the hornets that fly in the fields. They will chase us and attack us. They will try to kill us all. What will happen in the near future, I cannot say at this time, but when you hear of it, you will know of what I speak. You will know when we have struck the Satanists. And there will be dancing in the streets of the Arab world! Praise Allah!"

The assembled leaders responded with equal fervor chanting Allah's name with abandon as if they were now in a trance. They looked at one another seeking more information; they spoke quietly to one another and nodded their heads accepting what Zawahiri had announced, even though they had no details. They were excited that something important was finally happening and they were pleased to be a part of it.

The silent bearded man with the white turban raised his hand and spoke for the first time.

"We have been fighting in your holy land for over 20 years against these interlopers. We have fought side by side next to your fathers and your sons. We have fought the enemies as one. First we fought the Soviets to a standstill, ironically with the help of the Americans, and that politician Charlie Wilson. And we forced the Russians out, making them limp home broken and defeated, even though we took tremendous losses."

He continued and spoke with a soft voice and calm that placed an even greater trance on all those listening. Everyone strained to hear what he was saying.

"Now we have a new challenger in the United States, and we have united again to fight the Americans who wish to impose their democratic government and religion on us. They try to take away our natural resources and our crops, and break our faith in Islam. But they will fail! As Ayman has said, soon we will strike them so hard that they will not believe what they see. When we do this, we will have our hands full when they seek their revenge. Thus, we must be ready."

He waved his hand in a broad arc across the room. Each man seated around the prayer rugs felt the heat radiating from his hand as it passed by. They followed the arm in a trance.

"Because of this coming act of terrorism, we warn you to be careful and protect to your families. They will be coming after all of us. We suggest that you leave your homes for the time being, and go into the hills, to the caves, as the Americans will come looking for all of us. They will reign down missiles on our heads and many will die. But many will live if we prepare well. Then we will fight another day. May Allah be with all of you and with your families."

Osama bin Laden stopped speaking and bowed his head in prayer. The room was silent and everyone bowed their heads following the leader.

After a minute of prayer, Zawahiri took command of the meeting again and suggested that they would meet again after the terrorist act was completed, at some new location. They would then plan future acts of jihad. He asked everyone to not speak of this meeting and to return to their villages and fellow tribesman. Everything would change soon.

After the meeting broke up and all the guests had departed, bin Laden and Zawahiri, along with their most trusted soldiers and body guards packed their few belongings and took what they needed to survive on the mountain trails and went off into the night.

The travelers stayed clear of the more direct dirt roads and went off to the mountains. They followed the almost invisible burro trails that had been carved out of the mountains over the centuries. Slowly working their way up the mountainside, they followed the winding switchback trails that were all but invisible unless you were from the region. The terrorists crossed the summit in the pitch black, and then slowly descended the other side. In daylight they would burrow into one of the hundreds of caves gouged out along the trails and wait for nightfall to continue their journey. They would cross two more peaks before arriving at their planned destination.

A series of caves had been dug into the mountainside many years ago, and unless you were standing in front of one of the entrances and knew what you were looking for, it would have been invisible to the naked eye. This was where the mountain people lived. Hundreds of such caves existed throughout the mountains. For centuries they had protected their inhabitants from the hot summers, the very cold winters and the invaders that came from other lands.

While the camouflaged entrances were hard to recognize, once you entered the small entrance gap, the rock face would open up to relatively high ceilings and large, well carved rooms. Inside one of these cave entrances, you would find a labyrinth of connected tunnels carved into the rock. Even larger interior rooms were hollowed out within the mountain. In these rooms there were oil lamps, large rugs, cots and bedrolls, small tables and cooking areas that could house a large number of people.

This small band of travelers settled into their new temporary home and waited for word from the outside world. A few trusted cohorts were back in Kabul and over in Peshawar, Pakistan waiting to hear the news from the western world. Upon hearing they would bring the news up the mountain to the masterminds that had conceived the diabolical plot.

→ ←

7:45 am Over Cincinnati, Ohio

It was a clear cloudless day and you could see for miles. The Bombardier Global Express Jet, with a tailfin # 3497, was heading due east, and the early morning sun was pouring directly into the cockpit windows and down the aisle where William Charles Meredith II sat having a light breakfast. The custom jet aircraft was an ultra-long-range model that could make a 6,200 nautical mile trip without refueling, at a cruising speed of 488 kts.

The sleek jet could carry 10 people comfortably not counting the flight crew and was configured for single seating in the cabin. When converted to its sleeping layout it offered four single and one double bed for the trips to Europe and beyond. It had all the bells and whistles and was equipped with SATCOM for phone fax and data transfers. It was a very comfortable craft for a wealthy financier.

William Meredith reached for his satellite phone and dialed his son's cell phone as he looked down at the Cincinnati skyline from 32,000 feet. It didn't look like much from up here but he could clearly see the Ohio River snaking its way right through the middle of downtown and he could make out all the pedestrian walkways that connected the various downtown buildings and hotels. He wondered why urban planners had decided that enclosing all the walkways in glass and concrete made any sense when you had a glorious day like today to walk around outside.

He was returning from a quick trip to see some horses run their early morning workouts at a Kentucky horse farm, and decided he should wish his son well on his first day at the new job. The phone only rang once.

"Good morning, Son, I hope you've started moving this fine morning?"

"Hi Pop," Will said as he kept walking towards his new building. "Yeah, I'm almost at work, just crossing the Plaza. Where are you, you sound as if you're in a tunnel?"

"I'm about 32,000 ft. above you. Actually, not above you, I am still in Ohio but flying home right now. We should be at Teterboro Airport easily by 9:00am. I was in Louisville this morning to see some early morning training. I have my eye on a two-year old filly that could be a great runner. You should see her bloodlines. But in all fairness you should know that if I buy her, I'll have to forgo any inheritance for you."

He stopped at the door and looked straight up at one of the world's tallest buildings, with an exact twin next door. As he opened the door he said, "That's OK, I can make it on my own. I don't need your money, or is it Grandfather's money that we are talking about? That's where you got yours isn't it? You certainly didn't earn it all by yourself did you?"

"All right, enough tit-for-tat. I called to say good luck today. Polish your shoes and keep your mouth shut. Listening may be a new challenge for you but that's how you make money on Wall Street. "

"I got it Dad, I've been listening to you all these years. I'm looking forward to listening to someone else for a change, anyone else!" Will said mockingly.

"Laugh if you want, but if you're smart you'll listen to what everyone else is saying and then figure out the best course for yourself. If you listen well, you can jump on great buys before they happen. Just don't let on that you have great ears."

"I'll do that, but mostly because I'm unsure what they'll have me doing to start. Probably getting coffee and lunch for the big guys, but as you said that's where I can do that listening." He stepped into the elevator. "Well, I'm here, so gotta' go."

"Go get them Tiger. How about dinner tonight? We can talk about how the first day went? I'll meet you at the Club at 6:30, we can have drinks and talk shop."

"That's fine, I may need a drink by then, I'll see you there. Have a safe flight." The elevator closed and started rising in the north Tower of the World Trade Center.

Will Meredith took the elevators to the transfer level and then took a central bank elevator to the 93rd floor. As he exited he walked directly into the large waiting room of his new firm, covering three entire floors of the North Tower of the WTC.

He found he had beaten his new boss to work according to the receptionist. So he went to find some more coffee, the rocket fuel of investment banking. He found his new office quickly because he had taken a job with a class investment firm and his nameplate was already mounted on the wood paneled door. Entering the interior office, he found a well lit square room with light sand colored walls, perhaps meant to calm the nerves in this crazy financial world. The large door opening allowed some natural light to drift in from the window office across the hall. He found that if he stood in his office doorway, he could look through that office and out over the Hudson River and see all of Newark and Hoboken.

Sitting at his desk he decided to dress it up so that it would look like he'd been there a while, strategically placing some work materials in front of him. He also had some financial reports to look like he'd been studying. He took the Wall Street Journal and rolled it with the name of the publication prominently visible. And he took out a photo of his father and grandfather standing in the financial district in London.

He was ready for his first day on the job. At 8:05 his boss walked by noting he was already present. He didn't really look into the office, but said there would be a staff meeting in the north Conference Room at 8:30 am, and not to be late.

→ ←

7:55 am -Taxi Line, WTC

Osama Tarkan's taxi moved to the front of the queue to pick up his first fare of the day. It was a gentleman in a well-cut dark suit with a large leather satchel. He looked to be in a hurry, jumping in the cab, and asked to go to a Times Square Hotel to deliver some important documents, get signatures, and then come back again. Saying he didn't have time for a messenger service, he asked if the cabbie would be kind enough to wait for him and bring him back, adding he would make it worth his while.

Osama readily said yes and pulled away from the curb. Traffic was heavy as it was every morning going north. Being slow going Osama decided it was time to practice his English. He liked to carry on conversations with his rides as it helped him to learn how to be a true American. He asked the gentleman what he did in the big building they had just left.

"I'm an investment banker with Serafino & Jeffries," the guy responded and looked out the window towards the Hudson River.

Osama reached back and slid the divider window to one side so that he could hear and talk to the gentleman. Most people didn't like to talk with him so when he found someone whom he thought might talk; he tried hard to make conversation. Perhaps this man was a good one that would allow him to practice his language skills.

"Sir, you have ever handle money and stocks from Pakistan?" Osama asked earnestly. "My home country has grown large in few years, we have impact finally on the world," Osama said proudly conversing with this obviously wealthy gentleman.

"I don't think I've handled any Pakistani stock transactions but you are definitely right, Pakistan has certainly been increasing its presence in the world. I am actually an Iranian immigrant myself although I have been over here for more than 20 years. I came here after the Iranian revolution when all those students captured the American Embassy in Tehran and took all those hostages."

"Sir, I do not know of this Iran attack? Were you hurt, Sir?"

The man eyed his driver and wondered if this middle-eastern man would react to his once having been in the Middle East. Over the years he had learned to guard his background because people always seemed to have an opinion about everything. But he decided why not talk and pass the time as traffic was not going anywhere fast.

"I supported the Shah who was the King of Iran at the time. Radicals threw him out and banished him from the country, so as a supporter I had to lay low and get out of the country once the Ayatollah took over. Those weren't good times and I came here to start all over again. I took my family to Italy first, and then on to America. We almost had nothing but the shirts on our backs, but this was the land of opportunity so we decided to begin a new life here. This is a good place to be. What did you do in Pakistan before you came here?" the man inquired.

"I know this story well, this is how I come to America too. I had problem too, but in Pakistan. But is same story I think. I was owner of shop in Peshawar, my brother and I sold electronics that we brought from China and Thailand, sometimes even Sony American, VCR's and cameras. But the Mullahs say we do work of devil and make young people think bad thoughts about America and the devils. They, how do you say it, prostitute me, and make life hard and harder, for me and family."

"I think you mean they persecuted you for your beliefs, prostitute is another thing altogether," the man said.

"Yes sir, that is a word that I know but I mix up. My brother, his family was so too persecuted. So we leave home and go up the mountains and they persecute us there too. That was not a good thing also. So we decide to go to America, the place to be and start new. It took much time, but then we bring our families on same path." With a big smile in the mirror he added, "To America and New York."

"Well, I'm glad you made it. It kind of reminds me of my circuitous route many years ago."

"What is circusious?" Is that curious, because we were curious of what we find here. The land of opportunity, but I cannot find a job, so I drive a yellow car."

"No, sorry. Circuitous means it was a difficult way to get where I was trying to go. It sounds as if you had a circuitous route as well, first out of Pakistan, then through the mountains, and then here. I left Iran because of the crazy ideological zealot students and their religious fanaticism was driving me out. When I got here, I started with nothing and now I am on pretty solid financial ground. It is the land of opportunity. But here in America they applaud your entrepreneurship and encourage you to do whatever you want to. So why are you still driving a cab?"

Osama turned off the West Side Highway at west 47th Street and headed east. "My English is yet not good, I drive taxi to make dollars and to speak American and to learn from the people who will help me be good citizen. My wife, I, and my children, are loving it here. She works in your big building too, on the 12th floor at a children school. They are a care center. Do you know it?"

"No, I'm afraid not, I'm up on the 89th Floor in the North tower. We have three floors up there and employ all sorts of immigrants. I guess that's why they call it the World Trade Center."

As they pulled up to the New York Sheraton and Towers on 7th Avenue, the man handed Osama three $20 dollar bills through the glass window and said if he would wait the ten minutes, there would be another $60 in it to run him back to his office. Osama gladly said yes, and told him he would be around the corner and went for hot tea at the deli on 7th and 48th.

➤ ⬅

8:15 am. Broadway and & 48ᵗʰ Avenue

As he waited for his fare to return, Osama looked over at the souvenir and electronics shop that was on Broadway. It had a huge sign that said 'David Letterman Show' and when he saw two dark skinned men emerge and start pointing at the window displays, he wondered if these men owned this very large shop. Could their names be Letterman? If so, they obviously had made a good business for themselves and had a great sign to show where they were. This would be his story very soon.

In 15 minutes the man was indeed back in the taxi and handed him another $60 asking to go back to Lower Manhattan. He said that his wife was waiting in his 89th floor conference room to sign additional documents completing a major real estate transaction. They had just bought a beautiful brownstone on the Upper East Side that was costing them an arm and a leg, but they were committed to living in Manhattan and his current position would support such a mortgage. The deal was about to go down and then they would be celebrating.

Moving through heavy traffic on the way back down to lower Manhattan, he again got on the west side highway, and struck up the conversation to learn more from the man. Osama asked him, "What the 'arm and leg' means, as I do not understand? I think money is to be used, yes?"

The passenger laughed and realized that he shouldn't have used such an American slang in this situation. The man explained himself better and Osama thought this was a good man. Many passengers did not like talking to drivers, especially a driver from the Middle East. But this man was different.

"So, sir, you are important bank person?" he asked to get the conversation started again. "I am hoping one day I will have invest money to save and make more money from it."

"In America you can do anything that you would like to do, and no one will prevent you from improving your lot in life. So you should work hard and save what you can."

Then noticing the drivers family picture on the dashboard he pointed to it through the glass divider and said, "Hard work will allow you to send those beautiful children to good schools and give them a better chance at a great life in America. How old are they."

Osama brightened at the question, smiled at the photo that was worn and tattered and said, "Vispy is a big boy now, and the little one is Sonji. They are good boys, they listen to their mama and I. Thank you very much sir for kind words that is my true dreams, I work for them and save some each day, but soon much more. Can you tell me how I make money grow?"

They continued their journey south on the Westside Highway. Off in the distance they could see the World Trade Center Towers looming over all the other buildings on the southern tip of Manhattan.

→ ←

8:14 am. American Flight 11

American Airlines Flight 11 had passed through 26,000 feet on its way to a cruising altitude of 29,000 feet southwest of Boston. It would shortly be leaving the Boston ATC, air traffic command center, and would be picked up by the next ATC west.

At that very same moment another jet aircraft was taking off from Boston's Logan Airport. It was United Airlines Flight # 175 also flying non-stop to Los Angeles. Both airlines had similar flights at this time of the morning because it gave their passengers a full workday on the west coast. It too had five foreign passengers on it led by Marwan al Shehhi. He quietly sat in business class and read the Sky Mall Catalog through his metal-rimmed glasses, silently mocking the bourgeois spending these Americans needed in their daily lives.

On the American Flight # 11 about 20 minutes ahead of the United Flight #175, the two passengers sitting in row 2 got up from their seat and casually moved forward into the flight attendant bay adjacent to the cockpit. As they entered the tight work area, they pulled out box cutters from their pockets. They silently surprised the two attendants and quickly subdued them by stabbing them with the sharp instruments. They took the cockpit key from the head flight attendant and opened the lock gaining entry to the cockpit before anyone knew what was happening.

Once inside the cockpit the two hijackers stepped forward and calmly stabbed the two officers at the flight controls from behind. The pilot and co-pilot slumped in their seats never knowing what had hit them. Their lifeless bodies were dragged from their seats and dropped in a heap in the back corner of the cockpit near the flight crew jump seat.

At this same instant, the other three Middle Eastern passengers in Coach sprang into action and started forward. They yelled they had a bomb and sprayed mace at everyone. This caused an immediate reaction on the part of the passengers. One man jumped up when the hijackers ran by and they stabbed him in the neck and chest causing instant panic on the part of everyone.

One of the men came all the way forward and walked into the cockpit, observed the carnage and calmly climbed into the left chair, the pilot's seat, and took control of the plane. He ignored the blood that was smeared all over the seat and started looking at the instruments as if he knew what he was doing.

A flight attendant in the rear of the plane sat in the back row and pulled out the air phone built into the seat in front of her. She called the American Airlines Reservations Office in North Carolina and advised that Flight 11 had been hijacked. This information was patched through to the American Operations Center in Ft. Worth, Texas. As none of the hijackers had noticed her doing this she started giving a play-by-play description of what was happening.

Once the hijackers had gained full control of the flight, the new pilot started a slow wide turn to the south and began descending from 26,000 feet at a rapid rate. All efforts by the Boston ATC and American Airlines Operations to talk to the pilot were ignored. The eastern sun blazed into the fuselage windows on the left side of the aircraft as it headed south towards New York City and Kennedy International Airport. It was 8:30 am.

→ ←

8:35 am. On Broadway in Soho

The FDNY fire crews had been working their way down Broadway between Houston and Canal Streets, moving from fire hydrant to fire hydrant. Michaela was on the forward wrench crew, hopping from one hydrant to another working her way down the wide Avenue. It was her job to open up the hydrants and start the flush. She would uncap the hose coupling on the side and open each hydrant with a hard pull of the wrench. This would allow the water to free flow into the street and gutter.

Half the hydrants flushed water that was brown and dirty, but still maintained a strong flow. That was why they were doing these tests. To make sure good pressure was still there and the rust was occasionally flushed out. The process caused a temporary mess but would insure if the hydrant were needed, it would produce solid water pressure. If they identified a bad hydrant it was documented and a city crew would come out to fix or replace the unit.

She liked this job because it gave her some exercise and she liked to kid the rest of the crew about the male and female parts of the hydrant and hose couplings. It was all very stimulating.

Just then Michaela heard an unusual sound that started rumbling and then turned into a louder noise and continuous roar. At first she thought they had blown a hydrant cap and had a real pressure gusher, roaring into the sky. But the sound was actually coming from higher above and was echoing through the concrete canyons of Manhattan.

She looked up just in time to see the huge belly of a large airplane go roaring overhead less than fifteen hundred feet in the air, like a gigantic bird soaring between skyscrapers. She stood motionless and stared at the amazing sight, realizing that many parts of Manhattan had buildings that would be higher than the plane passing overhead.

Quickly calculating, she figured it must have just missed the Empire State Building on 34th and 5th Avenue. It then occurred to her that the jet must have been in big trouble. She wondered if it could make it to the water south of Battery Park. She turned to yell to the rest of the crew two hundred feet away, but they too were staring at the incredible sight. Plus they couldn't hear her because of the jet engine noise booming down the streets.

Turning she looked around and saw every person on the street was also staring into the sky above them as this huge plane roared south. From her vantage point on the east side of the street she watched until the height of the buildings got in the way and she could no longer see the craft.

Just a few seconds later she heard a massive explosive sound of impact, as if a truck had just barreled into a bus at high speed. It was a metal-to-metal grinding sound that reverberated through the streets echoing off the buildings. While it was difficult to categorize the sound, her instincts told her the plane had not made the river. It had just hit a building in Lower Manhattan. She glanced at her wristwatch and noted the time as 8:46 am. The morning had just gone from perfect to crazy in a New York minute!

→ ←

Lower Manhattan, Westside Highway

Traffic was slow going south towards the Financial District. It encouraged conversation because no one was going anywhere. Ralph Behar reached into his breast pocket, and pulled out a gold embossed business card and handed it to Osama through the now open divider window.

"You look me up when you have some capital to invest and I'll show you how to make a bundle. I like an entrepreneur when I see one. I'd like to help you get those kids to college."

Osama thanked the man and took the card through the window, fingered the edges for a moment and then pocketed it.

"Mr. Ralph Behar, it is pleasure to meet you. I am pleased you choosed my taxi. I am always ready to make your car service on time Sir."

At that moment, Osama heard a tremendous crack, and looked around out the window. It sounded like the boom of the jets that flew over Pakistan in the war with India, so high you couldn't see them, but you could hear them as they cracked the sound barrier. The sound echoed through the streets bouncing off the buildings as if there were some tremendous machine grinding itself through steel and concrete.

The impact sound was indescribable, almost like a massive gas explosion. It put the fear in Osama, who looked around to see what was happening. He looked at his passenger in the rear view mirror and saw he was confused by the horrendous sounds as well. The pigeons on the street jumped into the air startled by the ungodly noise and flew in circles joined by hundreds of other birds flying in circles. The sounds kept booming off the buildings back and forth around the cab. Almost like an echo.

Everyone around them on the street and in other cars and taxis were as confused as they were. They were all trying to comprehend what was happening. The direction of the deafening noise was unknown, but Osama and Ralph Behar knew it was not a good thing. They looked at each other questioning 'what the hell'? Everybody else had the same puzzled look. No one could orient where the sounds were coming from. No one thought to look up and to the south.

→ ←

8:47 am Westside Highway

Osama and the businessman were now only fifteen blocks from the World Trade Center on the Westside Highway, but traffic was stopped dead in the street going nowhere. With horns blaring people were getting out of their vehicles and staring off to the southeast. Osama could not see what they were looking at because of the immediate buildings in front of him.

Since traffic was parking lot still, both he and his passenger got out of the taxi and walked a couple cars forward to a parking lot fenced area on the left. A number of people had gathered to look at whatever was causing the backup.

When they got t o the gap in the buildings the view opened up to the south, and they followed everyone's gaze looking at the World Trade Center. They saw a huge gaping hole in the building about three quarters of the way up the North Tower of the World Trade Center. It was smoking and on fire!

It looked like something had crashed into the building and that something looked suspiciously like a very large airplane. A rough outline of a plane's fuselage with large extended wings could be seen etched into the glass walls of the World Trade Center. The black smoke and fire silhouette was large and circular in the middle and tapered to knife- edge extensions on each end. If it was a plane, it had hit a number of different floors in the North Tower of the World Trade Center.

Both men stared at the building. They were equally shocked and terrified as they thought about the safety of their loved ones in the building just ten blocks to the south. They stood there rooted to the spot unable to move yet knowing they had to.

Glancing at one another, they raced back to the taxi and climbed in. Ralph Behar jumped into the front passenger seat without thinking and Osama piled into the drivers' side, fumbling for his keys. The car started but there was nowhere to go as the entire street was packed with vehicles. Ralph pointed to the sidewalk. Osama needed no further encouragement and jumped the curb, landing nose first with the front bumper grinding on the sidewalk. He straightened the vehicle and took off south, honking to warn people to get out of the way.

Other cars began to follow their example. Both the road and sidewalks quickly became impassable as more and more people jammed up the street all trying to move south and see what was going on. Everyone was gaping at the World Trade Center, which was on fire. As the two men tried to move forward in the cab, they were both silent and lost in their thoughts about loved ones that were in the World Trade Center. They had to get there and save them from this horrible accident.

→ ←

8:47 am - Lower Manhattan

The New York City Emergency Control Center is buried in the basement of Police Headquarters, and the large secure room could be mistaken for a fortress. It controls all police, fire and emergency call activity within the city and boroughs, maintaining continuous contact with police squads and personnel.

The main call center room is a massive theatre like space with various levels all facing a three-story solid wall of monitors and sector maps of NYC that stretched from one end of the room to the other in a large semi-circle. From almost any vantage point the staff could see area maps, subways, traffic patterns, crime statistics and people throughout New York, and the entire Tri-State region.

These dedicated workers monitored computer screens, working phones tied into the 911 Emergency System, processing thousands of calls each day. The 100 plus people on duty Tuesday morning were keeping up with call volume.

Then at 8:44am. A call buzzed announcing that an airplane had just flown directly over Manhattan so close you could almost touch it. Immediately dozens of other call lines lit up. They answered by saying, " 911, How may I help you?"

Almost every phone in the Center had rung at the same moment. It took only a moment for staff to understand they had a major problem on their hands. The look of alarm was on everyone's face as they heard the call messages coming in. A large jet aircraft just crashed into the North Tower of the World Trade Center almost three-quarters of the way up the building. The building was on fire and smoke was pouring out of all the floors near the crash site.

The dispatchers in the room immediately turned to alert their supervisors, to advise they had an important call on their board, and then realized that the operators next to them had identical calls coming in from all over lower Manhattan.

In a New York minute the big monitors charting calls and locations crashed, shutting down the entire board because it could not handle the incoming traffic volume. Then the lights flickered out in the whole room. A few moments later back up systems kicked in and the callboards all lit up again as new calls flooded the system. Every phone in the building was flashing. They were inundated with callers all reporting the same thing. The World Trade Center was on fire!

At the same time, local Police Precincts across lower Manhattan started receiving calls. The firehouse phones lit up as well. Patrolmen in 1st shift squad cars and those on foot patrol, had people running up to them to report a calamity. Something big had just happened and the city of New York was in big trouble.

→ ←

8:48 am. On Broadway Avenue

Michaela had heard the screeching metal on metal grinding sounds that came from the south and tried to figure out what the airplane must have hit. She and her partner ran back to their vehicle and jumped on the radio, but communications were all tied up and she could not get through. She could see the other firefighters doing the same thing in the two fire trucks just up the street. They were all wondering what they should do, return to the house and await orders, or just head for the accident? If the plane did hit a building it would require all the assets of the entire NYFD Department.

Just then the engine claxon on the roof of the fire truck went off and a general alarm came over the radio advising of a major high-rise blaze in the North Tower of the World Trade Center. The tinny voice seemed frazzled and advised it was an immediate five-alarm call, and additional assistance was being requested from across the river.

All units were instructed to immediately report to the scene and assemble for further instructions. They were told Chiefs were on the way and would take command on the scene. This was a big one.

Michaela and her partner quickly closed the fire hydrant they had been working on and threw their gear in the back of the bus, and started moving their rig south on Broadway. Traffic was heavy and many of the cars had people hanging out of their windows looking skyward. Cars were pulling over to get a better look. Michaela flipped on the siren and lights, and started hitting the horn buzzer to clear a path.

As they wound their way through traffic, cutting over to the on-coming lanes to gain ground, they both thought about what lay ahead. High-rise fires were the worst kind because the fire could spread quickly and would be difficult to fight. Fire is a relentless climber consuming everything in its path. It could go up, down and sideways with all the burnable fuel that would be found in a typical office building. And this one was in one of the world's tallest buildings that had a daytime population of over 20,000 workers. It was not an apartment fire with a hundred people spread out on twenty floors, this was the World Trade Center with thousands of workers spread over 100 plus floors in one of the two identical towers.

This would be a fireman's nightmare and no good was going to come from it. They knew how to deal with such fires but this one could be catastrophic because it was so tall and so filled with office workers. This was going to be worse than the 1993 terrorist attack. It was going to be a long day!

→ ←

8:47 am. WTC Marriott Hotel

Elena had been working on her second suite of the day when she heard a roaring sound get louder and closer, and then felt a tremendous jolt as if someone had swung at the building like it were a punching bag. Her first thought was an earthquake had occurred. Leaning over the bed fluffing pillows she lost her balance, fell onto the bed and then rolled to the floor. The room door slammed shut violently from the concussion. She lay there between the two beds for a moment trying to comprehend what just happened. Then the lights in the room went completely out.

"What the hell" was all that came out of her mouth. She thought for a moment and then it registered; maybe terrorists were bombing the hotel again, like in 1993. She jumped up and ran to the window to see what she could see drawing back the drapes which offered her some light in the room. But the suite was on the south side of the hotel and all she could see was the South Tower of the World Trade Center and the Statue of Liberty out in the River.

People were looking out the windows on almost every floor that she could see, but they were not all looking in one direction, or at any one thing. She was confused and still not comprehending what had happened.

Just then the hotel emergency claxons went off in the hallway and then the room emergency speaker alarm started blaring an automatic message in three languages. It advised guests should sit tight for the time being. Further information would be forthcoming in a few minutes once the situation was evaluated. Something had indeed happened.

Elena next went to the door and dutifully felt the wood door for the heat that might be coming from a fire in the hallway, just as she had been trained in many fire drills. There was no heat, so she decided to open the door and see what was happening in the hallway.

But the door would not open as if it were locked or jammed. This was not good, she thought, and backtracked into the room going for the phone on the desk, but it too was not functioning. She tried turning the TV to see if the hotel was making any announcements on the hotel channel but again the electric was not functioning.

She grabbed her cell phone and called the housekeeper's office downstairs, but the circuits were busy and she was asked to try again. Next she dialed Josef and that too was a bust. The message advised all the circuits were busy at the moment and that she should try again.

➔ ←

8:55 am – On Broadway heading south

The various fire engines and paramedic squads headed south, with lights and sirens blaring, as fast as they could on Broadway, which was a wide multi-lane street. But they ran into all sorts of traffic problems with people having abandoned their cars in the roads to gape at the burning building to the south. In less than five blocks they were joined by a couple other fire units from the lower east side, Little Italy and Chinatown, and then again by units from Soho and Tribeca. By the time this convoy got to the Courthouse and City Hall, the combined noise from all the sirens and horns was deafening, and people were looking over their shoulders realizing their cars were blocking the fire crew's access.

In a matter of minutes many of the abandoned cars had been driven off the street and up on the sidewalks so that the fire truck convoy could get through. Everyone was beginning to realize that they were witnessing a very serious calamity.

Michaela's paramedic bus and rest of the convoy turned off Broadway at Vesey Street and cornered at Trinity Place on the north east side of the World Trade Center Plaza. They saw that all sorts of other emergency vehicles were converging on the site and pulling into any available space near the Plaza.

They parked their vehicle near St. Paul's Chapel, a historical church that was dwarfed by the many huge buildings around it. Michaela and her partner Sean climbed down from their rig and simply gawked. They had to look straight up to see where the plane had hit the building, almost three quarters of the way up, perhaps as high as 85 stories up. The smoke and fire was shooting out from the floors above and below the point of impact. It was a hell of a hot fire with all that airplane fuel feeding it.

The Plaza was littered with broken glass and all sorts of building debris, with paper floating down from the building like fluttering birds. Across the Plaza you could see a whole wheel assembly section smoldering near the massive fountain and World sculpture that was a prominent feature of this plaza. It must have sheared off when the plane hit the building. She thought about how lucky it was that no one was standing beneath it when it came hurtling down from that height. Or were there people crushed underneath?

Firemen immediately started suiting up in their full fire gear and began dragging out hose sections, battle axes, extra air bottles, flashlights and other safety gear, for what they knew would be a long and difficult day. Michaela and Sean grabbed their paramedic travel bags, which they had just packed an hour earlier, as they would certainly be finding injured coming down from that inferno.

Various fire crews reported to the first Battalion Chief they found on site, advised which station houses they were from, and what equipment and capabilities they had on their rigs. They all instinctively knew the trucks wouldn't matter much in a fire like this, this would be a hedgerow battle, fighting the spreading fires from floor to floor, office to office, doing search and rescue and knocking down hot spots. They knew they were going in and up, and asked for their assignments.

Just then they heard screams and saw people pointing skyward. Standing south of the World Trade Center Plaza, they looked up as the South Tower Building exploded in a massive fireball. Glass and building materials came raining down upon the crowds that had gathered. Large pieces of metal were cascading down the building when all of a sudden a large black and silver object struck the ground with a thunderous wallop and bounced to a standstill just a hundred yards away.

Everyone sucked in their breath and stared at the object. As the dust cleared it became recognizable as another wheel assembly from a large aircraft with eight black tires and all sorts of hydraulics and metal framework. Another jet aircraft had hit the South Tower.

→ ←

9:01 am. United Nations Building

Josef was working through some rather tedious Russian translation documents for an upcoming Security Council meeting when he heard a commotion down the hall. He heard voices calling out to other people in the language sections near him. He looked up from his document and saw that people were moving towards the windows in the Manger's offices on the north side of the building facing midtown.

He first tried to ignore the commotion but gave up when he heard someone exclaim, "Oh my God" for the second time. He too moved to his Manager's Office and joined the three people already looking out the large plate glass window.

"What are you all looking at? Do we have another demonstration going on?" he asked as he arrived at the window on the 25th floor. He had an unobstructed view of almost everything west and noted nothing amiss. He leaned into the window to look down to street level but saw no demonstrators. As he looked at the guy next to him, he realized he was looking southwest.

Other workers were also pointing to the far southwest and as Josef leaned into the glass and looked that way he saw one of the World Trade Center Towers was enveloped in smoke, and that a good amount of fire could be seen belching from multiple floors.

Then someone shouted, "Look, there's another plane over the Harbor and it's heading towards the building that's on fire! Oh my God, it's crashing into the other Tower!"

Josef reacted just as all the others had, and mouthed the words "Oh my God," He stood there with his mouth agape and realized that was where his wife was at work in the Marriott Hotel, between the two Towers. He turned and ran to his desk for his cell phone and screamed that he was leaving the building.

→ ←

9:10 am. North Tower of the WTC

Most of the firefighters received orders to see the Chief taking command in the Lower Lobby level of the North Tower. When Michaela got there, the Chief knew her because of her father. He also knew she was a Paramedic, so he asked her to set up a triage area below one of the escalator banks to wait for the injured being brought down the stairways.

Michaela and Sean began setting up inside because of all the building materials and shattered glass raining down outside made that an unsafe place to be. They would stabilize the injured and then transfer them to ambulances waiting outside by going out the south doors to the Plaza and then through the Marriott to the south.

They commandeered a bunch of folding tables from a display in the Lobby and set up their equipment and waited. Then across the hallway she noticed that her boyfriend Michael had arrived with his partner and they were assembling with other patrolmen. She saw the Police Captain was directing him and three other Officers to the north stairwell. She yelled across to him and waved with a soul-searching look on her face.

Michael returned the wave when he saw her, but had to keep moving as they were trying to stay ahead of other firemen lugging heavy equipment up the stairs. He waved again and disappeared into the stairwell. He was thankful she had drawn paramedic duty in the lobby, because he didn't like what he was seeing as he had entered the building. She would be safer down here and that is where he wanted his girl. This was not going to be a good day to be firemen or police. But he had a job to do and he was going to do it.

→ ←

9:10 am Greenwich and Chambers Sts.

The cabdriver and Ralph Behar gave up trying to get closer with the taxi and abandoned the vehicle on Chambers at Greenwich St. They were possessed with terror in their minds, Ralph because his wife was in his office on the 85th Floor of the North Tower, and Osama because his wife and children were in the same building at the daycare facility on the 14th floor. Both started running towards the building that was billowing smoke and fire. They had the same thoughts of their loved ones in the horrific scene in front of them. Ralph pulled out his cell phone as he ran and hit his wife's speed dial. The call rang through to a message that announced circuits were overloaded and to try again. He tried the number again with the same result and continued running south.

By the time they got to Barclay Street, a block north of the World Trade Center Plaza, a newly formed police line stopped them. The police had already set up a perimeter to give the arriving fire equipment some room to maneuver. They were not allowing anyone other than authorized personnel beyond that point. Ralph and Osama stood at the police line and stared south at the horrific sight. Behar tried his cell phone again and got the same message.

Both of them searched the crowds of people streaming north looking for their loved ones. People were terror stricken and running in all directions. The word chaos was an understatement.

→ ←

9:16 am Teterboro Airport approach

William Meredith II had dozed off prior to landing and was wakened when his pilot yelled back for him to come forward fast. When Meredith got there, pulling the curtain aside, he could see they were landing from the north with New York City on the left. As he looked at the city spread out before him he could see massive amounts of smoke pouring out of lower Manhattan. "Oh my God, Ryan, what happened?"

The pilot kept his eyes forward and said, "As I called Air Control for landing instructions, I heard radio chatter saying a large jet aircraft had just hit the World Trade Center. Ground Control confirmed and gave me a 'Heads Up' telling us to land immediately. And he said now, or they'll shoot us down!"

With that the pilot turned and looked at Meredith who just kept staring at the smoke cloud billowing into the sky from the south.

"He said what?"

"They want us down, ….now." He held up his hand and spoke into his headset, "This is Global Express #3497 ------- on direct approach, R-27, coming in hot. I'll be on the ground in one."

"You are clear to land #3497. Proceed directly to far end of main and clear quickly. We have additional planes directly on your tail coming in fast. Clear the runway ASAP."

"Roger that, wheels down, in 30 seconds."

The pilot and his passenger looked at one another and then back again at the smoking World Trade Center in the distance.

They landed a moment later and after taxiing back to the Charter Terminal Building, Meredith opened the plane's hatch himself and was jumping down the five steps before they chocked the plane's wheels. He ran for the Jet Airways lounge and noticed people were running about and that there seemed to be all sorts of commotion on the tarmac as planes were bunching up. He entered the lounge and headed straight towards a crowd of people huddled around a single television set. They all looked horrified and shaken and he joined them to see what was happening. He needed answers.

What he saw over someone's shoulder was a hand held camera showing the World Trade Center in the south of Manhattan with a large gaping hole in the building about two-thirds of the way up. Both Towers were on fire and clouded in dark smoke.

"What the hell happened," was all that came out of his mouth as he stood there gaping at the television screen.

A bystander sitting in front of the TV stated, "An airplane just flew straight into the WTC building about 30 minutes ago. And then a second plane followed and hit the South Tower just 10 minutes ago."

"What do you mean a second plane hit the Tower? How can that possibly be?" Meredith asked incredulously.

"That's all we know. Look for yourself." The bystander pointed to a new image on the screen. Both buildings were engulfed in flames shooting out windows. The smoke rose straight up 4,000 feet and then drifted south and east.

Meredith quickly recognized that the outline of the hole in the North Tower was indeed that of an airplane. Having just deplaned himself, he stared at the outline a moment and then realized that a very large airplane had hit the building. He couldn't tell what had happened to the South Tower because it was completely enveloped in smoke and fire half way up with smoke blocking any clear view.

Then his shock registered further when he realized that he was looking at the north face of the World Trade Tower. He thought to himself '*Wasn't that about where Will Jr. would have been on his first day of work?*'

"Oh my God!" was all that came out of his mouth. He reached for his phone and started dialing. Just then Ryan Younger his pilot walked up. Meredith told him to get a car and wait out front, that he would be right out. The pilot took one look at the television and ran for the door.

→ ←

9:20 am – Hoboken, NJ

Uri Navroz walked out of the back bedroom at his son's large apartment. He was getting ready to go to work. He lived across the river in Hoboken with his son Ali who had left for work even earlier that morning.

Ali was the Day Manager for Windows to the World Restaurant, on the top floor of the World Trade Center. He always went in early to beat the rush hour crowds. He was supervising the early set-up for the luncheon crowd.

As usual his son had left the TV tuned to the Today Show, which he watched as he wolfed down his breakfast before departing. As he reached to turn off the set he noticed the Today Show had a picture of the World Trade Center Building on screen. As it registered what he was seeing he noticed the two buildings were engulfed in a dark, thick smoke, and that some of the floors below the top were actually on fire.

He sat there a moment to comprehend what he was seeing and then reached for the phone. He called his son's cell phone and got a busy signal and it went to message.

"Ali, are you there, please pick up and let me know you are safe. Please call." He hung up and immediately called again, this time the main number of the Windows Restaurant. There was no ringing and no message. The phone line was not working. He called his son's cell phone again and got the same result.

Just then his phone rang and he stabbed at the call button. It was his son.

"Father, have you seen what has happened? Our building is on fire and we are engulfed in smoke up here on the top. I can't even see out the windows. Don't come into work as I think we will be closed for a while."

"Ali, the TV says you were hit by a big airplane in the North Tower and that a second airplane just hit the South Tower. The buildings are actually burning, you have to get out of there, now." That was all Uri could think to say.

"We tried going into the Stairwell but the smoke pouring up the stairs was so thick we could not even see. We shut and sealed that stairwell. The other stairwell is the same way. They won't be available until they vent the smoke so we may be stuck here for a bit. We even tried going to the roof, but the smoke is so thick up there you couldn't tell it was daylight out. I think we are better off waiting for them to put out the fire. Where is the fire anyhow?"

Uri looked at the TV and reported that it looked like the plane hit about two-thirds of the way up on the north side of the building.

"They are reporting on TV that the plane hit about the 90th Floor, but it is really burning and flames are shooting out the windows. You have to get out of there!"

"That means the fire is at least ten floors below us. That's actually good, because we're probably safe up here. Hopefully, they will get it under control quickly and then we'll get out. I'll tell everyone here to relax, and not open any windows, ha. They'll get us out soon enough. Stay in contact and I'll keep you updated. I'm going to let the kitchen crew use my phone now, because they don't have any. I'll call again in a few minutes."

That was the last time Uri heard from his son.

→ ←

9:37 am Lobby of the WTC

Michaela and Sean were getting frustrated because while thousands of people were streaming past them, few needed medical attention other than some smoke inhalation and twisted ankles from running down the stairwells. The Chief saw that was the case as well, and decided another paramedic crew should get up into the Towers as preliminary reports were that there were more serious injuries up there.

The two paramedics grabbed their fire gear and go-kits and headed up the north stairwell fighting the steady flow of people coming down. There were two lines basically jammed into the stairwell, with emergency personnel going up, and office workers streaming down.

As they went higher in the stairwell they ran into more and more people with blackened faces and injuries, but these folks were mobile enough to keep moving and get to help in the lobby. Michaela and Sean kept moving up to get to the people who needed paramedic assistance. As she continued her climb step by step, she wondered where Michael was in the building. She prayed he was safe and hoped she would see him again.

→ ←

9:40 am -12th Floor Transfer Lobby

Michael Pappas was pulled off the upward flow of police and firefighters on the 12th floor to help deal with the various groups of people stuck in elevators at a transfer level. As they started popping open the doors to the 16 elevators on this level, they found that some were indeed stuck on the level, while others had risen up to the next transfer point. Up towards where the fire was located.

As they pried open the doors they found terrified office workers who were grateful to be alive and rescued. All of the passengers had been traveling up from the Lobby level when the building groaned loudly and shook dramatically, the lights flickered and the elevators stopped. Then the elevators re-started on auxiliary power and automatically took off to the next floor transfer point. But once they had gotten there, the elevator doors would not open and the occupants found themselves stuck within. Then the lights went out again. They tried the phone inside, but they would not function. Then the screaming started. They had no tools to pry open the doors.

So when the police and fire finally popped the doors, the passengers were beyond grateful and thanked everyone in sight as they made their way to the stairwells to join the exodus going down. Michael and the firefighters moved to the next bank of elevators.

After finishing the elevator rescue efforts on the transfer floor Michael and his team were ordered out of the building as a similar problem was being experienced in the South Tower. As he went down the stairs he wondered where Michaela was.

→ ←

Book II – Sorrow

September 12, 2001 - Lower Manhattan

Smoke and dust covered the entire southern portion of Manhattan and drifted south out over the Statue of Liberty and east towards Long Island. As you looked at the images of the southern tip of Manhattan you knew that there were 60 and 70 story buildings hidden in the billowing clouds of smoke and it was hard to comprehend what you were actually seeing.

The fires in the blocks surrounding the World Trade Center were still being extinguished, and search and rescue personnel with dogs were climbing all over the WTC site to see if they could find survivors. The problem was that the devastation had been so horrific; they were not even finding body parts, much less live people who had survived the devastation that could not be described. A day earlier there had been 20,000 people working in all these buildings associated with the World Trade Center. This morning there was just death and rubble.

On this morning after the tragedy, there were constant images being sent out on television screens across America and the World. There were spools of video footage being played over and over again. Live cameras were aimed south from mid-town buildings, and from the New Jersey shoreline looking across the Hudson River, to capture the post-apocalypse death and destruction that had occurred on what would become known as 9-11.

There was no regular programming on television this morning after. The New York morning news and the Today Show commentators were talking but they looked as if they did not know what to say. There was no scripting for the morning shows. They were just projecting the images over and over, and re-spooling tapes that no one could believe they were seeing. The TV anchors and field reporters were standing as close to the rubble as they were allowed to be, winging it, many of them passing along stories as they heard them on the street. All of them were at a loss for words to describe the absolute devastation that had turned southern Manhattan into a war zone.

Beyond New York and America's borders, the rest of the world was also tuned in with much the same incredulous shock, except in the Middle East. That part of the world reported people were dancing in the streets, as if they had just won a war.

What those celebrating did not comprehend was this cowardly terrorist act would awaken the anger and wrath of Americans, just as another sneak attack had done on December 7, 1941 at Pearl Harbor.

The images told the story but those images were beyond belief. There were photos of demolished buildings, crushed cars and large fire engines strewn about like discarded toys in a playroom. There were frozen images of people covered in soot, crying tears of dust, walking aimlessly as if they were grey zombies.

There were photos of firemen sobbing with grief, of people holding pictures of loved ones still missing, and of people wandering about on soot covered streets. The images could not convey the sense of loss the people of New York were feeling. No one could comprehend what had just happened.

Repeating television clips showed endless streams of New Yorkers walking shoulder to shoulder over the many bridges leading out of Manhattan, trying to escape the terror and find a way home.

In Union Square and many other parks all over Manhattan impromptu information boards were springing up as messages to and from people were posted, looking for people that were lost, or at least not yet located, in this unspeakable tragedy.

At the hospitals in Manhattan long lines of people were waiting for word about loved ones that may have been brought there. Everyone carried a cell phone hoping it would ring with the message they wanted to hear. They needed to know that their husband, their wife, their child, their son or brother, their sister or aunt had been located and was safe from these horrors. But they were not getting that call.

Everyone stood around in disbelief! September 11, 2001 would go down as another Day of Infamy!

→ ←

Late September 2001

The days following 9-11 were seared into people's minds. People in Manhattan were stunned and found it difficult to function. For hundreds of thousands of people across the country, the shock was apparent on everyone's faces, as they watched the endless stream of video on television, over and over again. People couldn't fathom words to speak about the horror. Their work suffered, their families suffered.

The exceptions were the New York City civil servants, the police and fire personnel, the doctors and nurses and healthcare providers. They had a job to do. And they did it well helping the City to pick itself up and get moving again. There were massive clean up efforts being organized to deal with the destruction. At the same time people recognized that ground zero was a death zone and that thousands of people were interred in the rubble.

Immediately after the attack, these civil servants, spent hours searching first for survivors, and then for the remnants of bodies snuffed out by the heinous terrorist attack. Those close to the WTC site, the firemen and public works employees were in the hole pulling twelve-hour shifts, from sunup to sundown. Most of them refused to leave, because their brothers and sisters were yet to be found. Hundreds of police and fire personnel had perished in the buildings destruction. They had run into the building, while all the office workers were pouring out.

The estimates of the dead changed hourly, daily, and weekly, as people didn't return home, couldn't be located in hospitals, or were identified in the rubble of the excavations. In a matter of days the count exceeded 2,500 people dead, or missing and presumed dead. Many people had disappeared, perhaps in the vaporization of the buildings as each floor pancaked into the next, floor upon floor, in an ear-splitting roar and a cloud of dust that turned day into night all over southern Manhattan.

In the days and weeks following the terrorist act, loved ones of the 9-11 victims wandered the city, visiting hospitals, checking daily posts and lists of those still missing and those identified. They distributed posters and pictures of their loved ones in the parks and on the walls of Manhattan buildings. It helped them feel as if they were doing something. And they cried a lot in anguish for the loved ones that would be with them no more.

Within hours of the collapse of the World Trade Center multiple levels of federal government agencies began arriving in New York. They slowly began the process of examining how such devastation could have occurred and who was to blame. In hours they had determined that this was a well-planned terrorist attack beyond anyone's comprehension.

These agencies set up numerous command centers all over Manhattan. The FBI and various security agencies commandeered almost half of the Sheraton Hotel on 48th and Seventh Avenue as their base of operations to try and make sense of this terrorist act.

The FBI and National Security Council dissected the tragedy from every angle, and tried to unravel what had actually taken place. They started to piece together the size and scope of the horrific terrorist act that targeted the World Trade Center, the Pentagon, the White House and the United States Congress.

The initial emphasis went to determining how such a horrific act could have taken place, and who could have orchestrated it. The United States security agencies assembled and began the painstaking process of examining evidence, pointing fingers at possible culprits and laying blame on all sorts of people, agencies, governments, and individuals.

At the same time other agencies began to deal with the human factors of missing loved ones. Whole companies of people had perished in the building collapse, and these companies started setting up assistance centers to help the surviving families. It quickly became clear that people were not coping well with what had happened, they could not comprehend how to deal with it, and they didn't know how to act or what to do to move on.

Recognizing the horrendous effect this would have on the victim's families, social agencies and mental health caregivers at all levels began assembling teams to assist with helping people cope with the catastrophe. Psychologists and psychiatrists immediately saw the need for counseling and support. Healthcare professionals were needed to help these people and victims deal with their sense of loss and help them cope with what had happened. This devastation and loss of life was unprecedented in America.

➤ ⬅

October 2, 2001 Midtown Manhattan

Dr. Peter Hensley reviewed his voice messages that had come in since the prior evening. A tall lanky man, he took notes standing at his office window looking down on Times Square. He already knew what would be on the tape and he dreaded listening because he knew he could not offer the comfort and solace that the callers were looking for. But he had volunteered his services for counseling victim's families; it was his way of trying to assist people through this crisis.

He had initially volunteered his services on that first night of 9-11, at his primary practice hospital on Manhattan's west side, because he couldn't get home to Long Island that night. There had been no commuter trains that night and he felt that he could be useful in helping people cope with the tragedy. One day led to another, and then he stayed at the hospital for the whole next week, sleeping on cots that had been set up for all personnel.

These healthcare workers were dealing with all sorts of physical and mental trauma, some from victims but most from the many firefighters and policemen that were coming in to deal with cuts and scrapes as they dug through the rubble. He saw their profound sense of pain and anguish, having lost their partners, fellow firefighters and friends in the destruction of the World Trade Center.

They were exhausted but refused to give in. They wanted to go back to work again. These burly cops and rock hard firemen were walking around like zombies talking to themselves, and then would just start crying or collapse from fatigue. It was the sight of these tough-guys, curling up and openly crying that had moved him to action. He knew he had to help them and all the victims of this mind-numbing tragedy work through the ordeal.

So he had called his wife to say he was safe, and stayed at the hospital for days. On breaks he would watch the daily television news, which was a 24-hour constant feed on the 9-11 destruction. In these reports he noted other health agencies were assembling healthcare teams to deal with the psychological effects of this tragedy, noting the victims families were trying to cope and handle the situation, but didn't know where to turn for such help.

Dr. Hensley took up the challenge along with hundreds of other healthcare professionals and together they organized world class counseling teams to assist in this grieving process. They set up a counseling network hotline number that was broadcast throughout the city on all the TV news shows, and started posting flyers at all the bulletin board outlets that had been set up in the major parks in the city.

From the numbers of people calling in, the hotline number was quickly overloaded and the city stepped in to assist, offering its 3-11 Call Center to deal with the many calls coming in from the Tri-State area. In this manner more callers were handled and referred quickly to professional counselors. The initial counseling teams available quickly filled up and even more counseling teams were assembled from the Tri-State region to take the increasing call volume.

The assignment teams started placing individuals in like groups so they would take some comfort in having similar situations present in the room when they met. Spouses who had lost a husband were directed to certain groups, firefighter losses were assigned to special groups, police to others, and major business personnel like the investment houses where whole floors and staffs were missing and presumed dead, were directed to other counseling groups. They felt that like people would be able to help one another deal with their grief and anguish.

In the assignment interview process it quickly became apparent there were many foreign-born or naturalized citizens that were surviving victims as well. Early on it was reported that over 300 people from seventy foreign countries had died in the terrorist attack. In the weeks after 9-11, many of these foreign-born and more recently naturalized citizens had a rough go of it, especially if they were Middle Eastern. People were angry about the attack and lashing out at anyone thought to be a foreigner.

To deal with this difficult issue, a new counseling group category was created to bring these type individuals together. Dr. Hensley was asked to head up this group as he had an international background and spoke two languages. He accepted the assignment and began sorting through the lists of potential patients. Hundreds of people who worked in the WTC had international backgrounds, which made sense since it was the World Trade Center that had collapsed.

He began building a series of counseling sessions with these special victims as they were referred for counseling. In a matter of days he had filled up five international counseling sessions that would meet twice a week.

As he unloaded the answering machine he found that another seven people had heard about his new category of sessions and wished to participate. They too had lost loved ones in the 9-11 terrorist act. He recognized his work was cut out for him, just as it was for hundreds of other healthcare professionals all over the Tri-State region.

→ ←

November, 2001 Manhattan

Manhattan had changed in the months after the terrorist attack and to a certain extent the City had lost its zest for life. The city that never slept seemed much quieter and more subdued. Every day there were somber reminders of the tragic event. There were many funerals all over Manhattan and the surrounding communities, constantly reminding everyone about 9-11.

Police and firemen's funerals took place, day in and day out, with their fellow officers turned out in dress blues, bagpipes wailing, and processions snaking through the city. People lined up on the streets to honor the fallen hero's. These same kinds of processions and memorials occurred in the many boroughs of New York City and across the rivers in New Jersey and Long Island. It was as if the wind had been sucked out of the people of New York.

Since the tragedy, New Yorkers had gone back to work, but there was no joy in their eyes. People were constantly reminded of the collapse of the WTC buildings, seeing tributes to those who had fallen, and crossing paths with the tireless workers who worked with the rubble looking for the people missing and unaccounted for. All of lower Manhattan south of 14th Street was still cordoned off so that the Police, fire and investigative personnel could do their work. People living and working within this police zone had to cope with the stench of death, tons of dust and unbelievable destruction.

During this difficult time multiple levels of local, county, regional, state and federal government agencies took the lead and jurisdiction over the expansive WTC site. These agencies built a huge presence in the city, as they sorted through the sordid details of this tragic assault on America.

People would watch as these government convoys drove back and forth from the WTC site dealing with the many issues that came with six square blocks of total devastation. Every day hundreds of dump trucks went to and from the site hauling away the remains of the buildings to a controlled site where every truckload was carefully searched for evidence, body parts, and identifications. The teams dealing with this search function made every effort to handle the process with reverence and dignity to show respect for the fallen victims.

In the weeks after this assault, evidence pointed to al Qaeda as the planners of the terrorist act, which was to have been even bigger than it ended up being. Planes had also been hi-jacked to attack Washington, DC and one had actually crashed into the Pentagon in the same manner the two commercial jets had flown into the World Trade Center that fateful day. The Pentagon attack had killed hundreds of military and civilian workers adding to the death toll and horror of 9-11.

Shortly after that fateful day there were a number of videos showing Osama bin Laden and Al Qaeda taking credit for this ruthless act. These tapes were shown on all of the television stations both here and abroad.

The rest of the world stood with the United States in deploring these savage acts. Sympathy and support was received from all nations even the countries that would be classified as having strained relationships with the U.S.

Osama bin Laden became a pariah and the sworn enemy of the United States and western world. He was deemed the most heinous of terrorists and instantly became the Hitler of this 21st Century. He became the focus of America's anger and frustration. In the weeks following 9-11 the federal governments rhetoric ratcheted up as people demanded justice and revenge. This unspeakable act could not be left unanswered. It was not the time to turn the other cheek; it was the time for action.

The U.S. military establishment geared up for a fight and federal covert agencies began the process of ferreting out who the perpetrators were. There was a universal call for justice from every corner of the planet. President Bush swore that he would take on the enemy wherever they might appear or wherever they were hiding. He declared war on terrorism and began gearing up for that war. Countries that had harbored such terrorist activities in the past were forewarned and targeted to eradicate this kind of crazed activity. America was going to war on terrorism and no terrorist would be safe from the reach of America's wrath.

→ ←

December, 2001 Dr. Hensley's Office

The Christmas season was in full force and the retailer's shop windows heralded the season of joy and peace on earth, but you couldn't tell that from the faces of the people on the street. They went about their business, but there was no joy in their eyes, no bounce in their step. There was a gray pall hanging over the city.

William Meredith II opened the door to the psychiatrist's office and went in even though his mind was telling him to walk away. It had taken him a couple months to get this far in dealing with the loss of his son. He had privately struggled at home and tried to deal with his sense of loss, anger, and the desire to do something about it for weeks. He had moved out of the city, retreating to his ranch north of Manhattan. He spent time with his horses, and tried to normalize his life.

His friends had said the right things, they had offered comfort and supported him through this agonizing ordeal, but he just wasn't able to move on yet. All the money in the world was not helping him cope with the senseless loss of his son.

So he had decided to try another approach. He'd read about all the counseling that was going on throughout the city in the newspapers and seen stories on television. His first reaction had been what good would talking about the tragedy do, but as he read more articles he found that talking about his loss and getting his feelings out in the open could be therapeutic. He had finally called the 3-11 number to seek out some counseling. They had been very supportive and asked a few interview questions. Based on his responses it was suggested he give a Dr. Peter Hensley a call to see if he could join one of his on-going counseling groups.

As he entered the Office he heard some foreign dialects being spoken by other people sitting in the waiting room, and right away the hair on his neck stood up. In the past three months he had begun to hate foreigners, all of them, even though he was a foreign-born himself. But he bit his lip and calmed himself walking to the desk. After checking in he sat quietly in the waiting room.

The Doctor's inner door opened and a tall man in a three-piece suit stepped out and scanned the people sitting in the office.

"Good evening everyone, shall we get started?" As he scanned the waiting room he saw a new face and asked. "Mr. Meredith? Welcome," He offered a friendly handshake. "I'm pleased that you could join us. Come on in and I'll introduce you to the rest of the group."

Everyone filed into the inner office and quickly grabbed favorite chairs that were fanned out in a broad irregular circle. Meredith quietly waited for everyone to find the seat they wanted, and then spotted an empty one on Dr. Hensley's left. He presumed that was for him and quietly sat down with his hands clasped in his lap.

"Everyone, this is William Meredith, and he lost a son on 9-11." He looked at Meredith and said, "May we call you Bill?" Meredith nodded yes but didn't say anything more. He was still ready to bolt for the door, as he didn't think this could possibly help make the hurt go away.

"Bill, everyone here has lost a loved one to the 9-11 tragedy, just like you. They have experienced the same hurt, anger and frustration that I'm sure you are experiencing every day since this horrible event took place. I'm guessing that your feelings are constantly spinning in your head, and you can't sleep, as you wrestle with what took place. And you're probably trying to comprehend how someone could plan such a thing to harm innocent human beings."

William Meredith listened and realized that the Doctor had covered all the thoughts that were locked in his mind 24-hours a day. He again nodded and continued listening.

"These are all natural thoughts, Bill, everyone here has had them. We try to get together twice a week so that we can help each person deal with these questions, and heal at the same time. We're pleased you have chosen to join us. There is no need for you to say anything until you are ready to do so. We understand, and we want to help you,…. and we want you to help us."

With those words of support, Meredith relaxed a bit and thought that he would stick this out at least for the first session. He was pleased that he didn't have to jump right into the conversation like you had to do at an AA meeting. He didn't quite know what he would want to say, other than death to the bastards that turned all their worlds upside down. He relaxed a bit getting more comfortable with not having to say anything. He could just sit and listen to what the others were saying about their sense of loss. Maybe he could learn something and finally get a good night's sleep.

After two hours of listening to the others he had learned something about himself and the others in the room. They all cared about the people that had been taken from them in the terrorist act. He realized that they were just like him in that sense, and he observed one other major similarity. They too were foreign-born, or children of naturalized citizens like himself, and others were in NY on work visas, and a couple maybe even illegally. But they were all dealing with a profound sense of loss. Maybe, he thought, this would be therapeutic and worthwhile.

➜ ➴

February 2004

Two Christmas' had come and gone, along with a couple of New Year's, each heralding a new year and a new start. New York was slowly working its way back to normal. That is, if you ignored the continuing 9-11 reports, the postmortem analysis, the blame game and the constant news reports about the evil perpetrator, Osama bin Laden.

William Meredith was now part of his healing group and he actually believed the sessions were a good thing, one that was leading him out of his sorrowful state. He even had come to like the many people who were in his group. There were even two Pakistani brothers who had grown on him. While he had lost his son, they had both lost their wives and young children.

Mina and Pasha Tarkan had worked at a day care facility in the North Tower and were lost in the rubble along with their three children. The two cab drivers were absolutely crazed and distraught because they had come to America to get away from all the terrorism and repression.

Then there was the Iranian businessman, Ralph Behar who had worked in the World Trade Center at an investment firm. By a stroke of luck, although he did not think so, he was out of the building that morning, but his wife Kathleen had been sitting in his office, and had probably been killed when the first plane struck.

There was an older gentleman, a ruddy, weathered Egyptian, Uri Navroz, who had been a sailor all his life, until coming to America to see his son. That son had been a manager at the Windows to the World Restaurant at the WTC.

There was a NY cop of Greek heritage, Michael Pappas, who lost his fiancé, a NYFD paramedic named Michaela Jameson. She had been in the building that fateful day. He'd been there too, but he'd been ordered out of the building before the collapse.

The group was diverse with representation from all over the globe. There was a Russian translator named Josef Veronin, who worked at the U.N. and lost his wife Elena in the Marriott Hotel collapse under the weight of the Twin Towers falling on it.

Then there was graphic designer of Irish descent, Katherine Shanahan, who lost her immigrant father in the South Tower. He had been a decorated FBI agent (retired) who worked security in the private sector. He was in the wrong place on that fateful Tuesday.

And there was Courtney Ranker, whose husband had died in the building across from the World Trade Center when the explosion blew out all the windows in buildings for blocks around. She was a German born, naturalized citizen who had been a Chemist working for the ATF. Her job had involved all sorts of terrorist work in analyzing bomb making materials, and trying to determine bomb origins, chemical trace, and such. She had worked on the Oklahoma City bombing and had been sent to Saudi Arabia when the embassy compound had been bombed years before. When the 9-11 destruction killed her husband she lost her will to work for the government and now worked for Dow Chemical in Manhattan.

Meredith noted that everyone assembled in this little group had experienced profound loss and was trying to deal with it. Perhaps together they would all come to grips with their losses. Maybe this was a good thing for him to get involved in.

He often remained quiet and listened to the assembled group, and what Dr. Hensley said to help with the healing process. He quickly realized there were many stages of grief and the group could be at different stages in the tragic journey. Some were remorseful, some angry, while others were just plain lost. He was now participating as much for himself as for the others. They had become his support team and he was theirs. Together they were dealing with their personal tragedies.

William Meredith was still in the anger stage of grieving, he just couldn't shake it off. He passed through the shock and disbelief phase rather quickly. Initially, he had a hard time believing his son was actually gone, on the very first day of his financial career. He fixated on the fact he had spoken to his son a matter of minutes before the plane crashed. The newspapers had said the jet flew directly into the north face of the WTC on the very floors his new investment firm was located. He hoped his son's death had been quick, and not drawn out in the firestorm that followed.

He thought about the next phase of grieving, the so-called yearning phase, Dr. Hensley had called it. It was a phase where he would experience intense feelings of loss for his son, an emotion that brings on a yearning, a longing to re-connect, to make up for things not said, to try and re-establish a relationship that has been lost. This stage of grief stays with you a long time, even when you move on to other phases of grieving. And once you were in this yearning phase, you could still get thrown back to the first stage and start all over again.

As Dr. Hensley explained it, the stages of grief were like an endless, macabre, merry-go-round that kept taking the rider/survivors in a circle, forcing them to revisit and rehash everything they had already experienced. They would ride this horrific merry-go-round, going round and round until they all found a way to move on.

Psychologists generally agreed that the anger phase typically sets in at about five months after the loss, and the good doctor found that his group arrived at about that time. But in this stage they stayed for a long time. They were angry with the terrorists, and bin Laden, the mastermind, but they were also angry with their own government for not seeing it coming, and now in the aftermath, for not doing anything to avenge the loss of 3,000 loved ones. That anger consumed them.

→ ←

2004, Federally Administered Tribal Areas, Pakistan

The Federally Administered Tribal Areas, often called FATA, are a loose-knit assembly of six frontier regions that are part of the western mountains of Pakistan. The area is dominated by Pashtuns, who have their own languages and their own laws. They have lived in these mountains for thousands of years. These regions are relatively independent provinces that still have elected representatives that sit in Pakistan's Parliament, Ironically, the laws that Parliament approves mostly does not affect these tribal regions. Even if the laws did apply it was doubtful they would be enforced. These tribal areas are governed by Frontier Crimes Regulations, which gives the various tribes' independence and autonomy with their citizens as long as they take responsibility for the actions of their people.

In recent years the Taliban has made itself at home in these lands doing almost anything they please forcing their religious and political beliefs on all of the tribes that inhabit this mountainous region. They closed schools, burned DVD and CD shops, attacked hashish dealers and harassed women. They were the law in this wild-west part of Pakistan.

It was in these Tribal areas that Osama bin Laden and al Qaeda moved to, after being chased out of the mountains of Afghanistan by the Americans following 9-11.

While the distance was only 100 miles at most, and in most places just miles, the al Qaeda organization found safe-haven in these mountains because the Tribal leaders and elders left them alone. And the Pakistani government looked the other way as a means of keeping the peace in these lawless lands. While the government was generally aligned with the U.S. and gained millions of dollars in aid and military hardware, they drew the line at allowing American troops to enter and chase al Qaeda across the border in Afghanistan. Thus it was a safe-haven for those being chased.

Osama bin Laden and his followers had come to this area after 9-11 when the heat was on. They had disappeared into the mountainous region and were said to be hiding out in the hundreds of caves that dotted the mountain trails. The land was rough enough that there were few roads, and only uncharted trails crossed these border regions between Pakistan and Afghanistan. It had been this way for thousands of years.

At first, the same caves that they had fought the Russians from were the al Qaeda sanctuaries. As time passed these caves were improved and dug out to provide more space and comfort to the searing summers and the severe cold of winter. They became working bases of operation in which the al Qaeda planned future attacks and trained their converts to wage jihad on the western world.

But this too changed when America ramped up their efforts on the war on terrorism. Fighting from Afghanistan and making headway with the Pakistanis to wage war on the terrorists within their lands, the United States made it difficult for Osama bin Laden and his leaders to stay in one place in their mountain hideaways.

Inside one elaborate cave, a small group of elders sat on prayer mats in the smoky air that drifted endlessly back and forth in the shadows.

"I am afraid that we must think about moving on from here to a safer location. I fear that they are closing in and eventually the Pakistanis will cave in and let them attack us without pre-warning us." Zawahiri said this to the tall man seated close to the fire.

Three other men sat there quietly staring at the fire, breathing in the heat that warmed them, and lit the interior of the cave. They were fifty feet laterally into the mountainside, and as such, the fire generated great heat and light, but also the thick fumes that would not clear as quickly as they would like.

The elder suffered the most as he rarely left the caves to breathe fresh air. He could not leave the hideout because of his very identifiable height and stature, which would be easily recognized even on the mountain.

While the Americans had used satellites for years to search for these terrorists, the leaders of al Qaeda were still somewhat free to roam the mountainsides at night to change their locations and move their fighters and weapons. But in recent days, the Americans were using new tracking devices, heat-seeking devices, and newer un-manned planes that could do their searching. They were called drones and could fly for many hours over certain areas, so high up you could not see them or hear them. They were equipped with cameras, and mapping programs, and were equipped with night vision, and infrared capabilities. It was becoming unsafe to venture out even at night for fresh air.

"I agree Ayman, we must think about moving again or they will find us and we will not be able to take the battle to them anymore. But what would you suggest that we do? Where can we go that they will not continue to hound us?"

"I have been thinking about that for some time Osama. I think we must get off this mountain, and move far enough from here to throw them off. I believe they are getting closer and I don't think the Pakistani ISI will be able to protect us anymore. I have been looking down the mountain and closer to the cities so we can blend into society. I think we must find a more traditional house, one that could offer us some comfort and security."

"I would settle for some fresh air. But moving to a house would be nice as my behind would like to rest on something other than a rock for a change. But can we have security in such a house? Will they track us there too?"

"We would not choose a big house or anything that would draw attention to us. It would be simple but it would allow us to get away from these fires that are consuming our lungs. It is as if we are smoking the Americans cigarettes."

"So be it. Let us make plans and we will go. But tell no one other than us four for the time being. The next question is how we will get there without those infernal airplanes seeing us and killing us?"

"I have thought of that as well, Osama. With your tall body and my rotund belly, we do make fine targets for the Americans. Thus, I think from here down the mountain we will have to play dead. Then we could have some burros move us down the mountain on a cart in daylight."

"Sometimes I think I am dead already. What do you mean by cart? If I am to be dead, perhaps I will see the virgins during the trip."

"My thought was that we would have some wooden coffins built, four, I think. Two of them will be for us, and then two more for placement on top of our coffins. That way the satellites will just think that more al Qaeda or Taliban have been killed on the mountaintop and are being taken for burial."

"You are a genius Doctor, sometimes I feel as if I am already dead, so this would be an appropriate way to go. But how will we breathe if we have dead bodies above us?"

"The lower boxes will have breathing openings so we live to fight another day, my friend. And then we just ride down the mountain and once on the road, we will go to our new home, perhaps in a hearse. It will be bumpy and slow, but I think we will beat the Americans at their own games."

"We shall do so. Tell me of the house. Where will it be and can we work from there?"

"I think we must go most of the way down the mountain to the edge of Baggem, still in the Territories. There are good roads there and people move about freely. I have found a house on the outskirts of a small town that also has some neighbor houses in the area. We would blend in with our neighbors, and if we do not cause any disturbances, no one would even know that we are there."

He realized that Osama was interested in making the change sooner rather than later. So he pressed on. "The house I have in mind has a high perimeter wall around a courtyard to keep the animals inside. It will also keep people outside. The courtyard has some trees that will provide cover from the air so those planes that fly day and night cannot see us."

"Ah, the thought of fresh air seduces me. I am tired of breathing the fumes. I will die before my time if I continue to live in this cave. Let us make plans and go soon."

" I am pleased you agree with the concept. Could I suggest an even bolder move? We have complained about this damp cold mountain weather for years. We have not been in warm weather year around since our days in the desert. I think it is a perfect time to move even further away, perhaps to a city, and disappear right out in the open."

"That is interesting that you suggest that my friend, I have thought such things myself. They are looking for us in these mountains, but if we move to Islamabad and find a safe haven they would not find us as easily." He stood and stretched his long frame hitting his head on the cave ceiling.

Finally he turned to his friend and said, "Ayman, they would not think to look for us in the center of a city. Perhaps we should go to New York City and live within blocks of that World Trade Center site."

"I think that may be pressing our luck, Osama, you are a tall one in a crowd and I am rather rotund. No, I think New York would be imprudent, mainly because we hope to again blow it up. But Peshawar, or Islamabad would be a good site and safe. We have many friends in Pakistan, people who believe as we do. We would need to find a large compound that we could move freely within. We will continue to use couriers to talk with our brethren."

"I agree," Osama said, "let us start a search for such a place, but I would like it to have high walls so we could move about freely, and exercise."

"I will look for such a place. It will be safer than we are here, my brother," Zawahiri said.

"I trust you brother. Islamabad is the capital of Pakistan. They won't think we would be hiding there. Make such plans."

Ayman reached behind him and pulled some rolled maps from the shelf. "Again, I agree. I was thinking we should perhaps build our own compound and design it to give us security, while at the same time blending in with the neighbors."

"Interesting, the cost would not be a factor, we could get someone to front it for us, so we would not be on a record." He thought that through and finally nodded his approval of the concept. "I agree, we should try to blend in with our neighbors. But I would still like to be able to see people and the neighborhood if I could."

"I will start looking for such a place. If we can't find one already available, then we will build one, and get off this infernal mountain."

November 2006, 44th & Broadway

More than four years had passed and Meredith had aged considerably. He had worked on tucking the anguish and hurt further back in his brain, but in his heart he still felt the loss. It was never too far from his thoughts. It still caused sleepless nights. His son's dreams were never going to be met and his dreams of seeing grandchildren had vanished in the rubble of the twin towers.

His son's body had never been found, not even a trace. From the official 9-11 Report issued by the government, Meredith had learned that the first jet aircraft had flown almost squarely into the north windows of the 93rd floor right where he probably would have been working. Meredith was always reminded of the fact he had spoken to him an hour before on his first day of work. Will had said he was going into a meeting at 9:30 am. Why had he picked that Tuesday to start, he thought for the hundredth time.

As he walked down the street on his way to counseling the flood of memories poured into his brain again. He decided to stop and grab a cup of coffee at the McDonald's on the corner of 44th and Broadway across from Schubert's Alley, before going to Dr. Hensley's office. The Doctor's coffee was usually old, stale and burned, and he'd found McDonald's coffee was passably good.

The twice-weekly counseling sessions had dropped down to just one per week and not everyone was attending religiously anymore, but they still relied on each other when the need arose. It was kind of like an AA meeting in that sense. The participants showed up when they needed to get some support, perhaps when a birthday or an anniversary came up. They helped each other through the day or missed event.

Meredith sat there sipping his steaming coffee at a table by the window when he heard that bastard's name on the TV hanging from the ceiling. He looked up and stared at the television. Bin Laden had surfaced again on another tape and it was being shown on the evening news. As Meredith watched, his anger and frustration grew, to the point that he involuntarily squeezed his paper coffee cup so tightly, the liquid shot straight up in the air and all over his hand and the table.

At that moment Michael Pappas walked up. "Bill, hey, relax buddy, don't let that son-of-a-bitch get to you." Michael pointed at the TV above him and gave a one-finger salute to the bearded man being shown on the screen.

"Your blood pressure will go through the roof if you let him get to you like that."

Bill looked up at the words being directed at him by name and saw Michael Pappas standing there, still in his police uniform. He looked back down at the table and realized that he had coffee all over his hand, and his hand was burning from the hot liquid.

"He is a son-of-a-bitch," he growled. "And my blood pressure is already shot. Hell, I'm on three medications now." And with that he calmed down, grabbed a wad of paper napkins and began mopping up the milky coffee running all over the table.

Eventually Meredith looked up at the policeman and said, "I'm glad you can join us for a change Michael, you haven't been around for a couple weeks. Have a seat."

With that welcome, he went back to mopping up the mess. When he had pushed the liquid around awhile, he looked out the window and seemed lost in thought, so Michael just sat there quietly.

"You know," Meredith said to no one in particular as he stared out the window, "If I could, I would personally kill that bastard with my own two hands. I can't believe they can't find him and take him out."

"Stand in line Bill, ... and I think it would be a long line. I'd gladly help you wring his neck until he was blue in the face. But then you would have to hold him so I could also kick him in the balls, eight times for each one of my friends he killed. But what are we going to do, if Bush and his entire Administration can't find him with all the resources he has, then how can we?"

"That's the problem in a nutshell, the government's hands are tied by the Congress, and President Bush can't just go after the son-of-a-bitch. Instead, he's going after Saddam Hussein. What's with that? If I were him, I would just send out a hit squad for bin Laden and make him pay for what he did to my son."

"Again I'm with you, but I don't think the government can just do that."

As soon as Meredith said what he did and heard Michael's response, he was ashamed that he had again personalized his anger. He knew that Michael had lost his fiancé and all sorts of police and fire friends in the 9-11 terrorist act. Michael was dealing with the very same issues as he was, but he still couldn't let go of his personal hate for the bastard.

In the months and years after 9-11, it had been proven that bin Laden and his al Qaeda henchmen had organized the attack. They had trained 20 young 'jihad' terrorists in their foreign camps. These individuals had come to America, set-up their plan in motion, trained themselves to fly planes, and carried out the most diabolical terrorist attack known to mankind. Osama bin Laden had masterminded the whole plot and now he had a target and a bounty on his head, but he was nowhere to be found. To make matters worse he kept popping up on the evening news every few weeks and months to crow about his so-called victory over America.

"Come on Bill, cool down, let's go upstairs, maybe we can all get together and heal our wounds. Maybe we should come up with a plan to get the bastard ourselves."

With that Michael Pappas and Bill Meredith left McDonalds, walked a quarter block east and turned into an office building just off Times Square, where Dr. Hensley's office was located, just as they had been doing for the past two years.

Upstairs, the Doctor asked everyone to report on how their week had gone and what may have been a problem for them in dealing with the past events of 9-11.

While the two Pakistani brothers had been quiet for the first couple months of these therapy sessions, learning what such things were all about, they were now almost always the first to speak at the sessions. And they always had interesting stories to relate because their taxi driving gave them a window to Manhattan and the people of New York.

They would talk about the many memorials that had been set up to honor the fallen of 9-11. Often they reported on conversations they heard about loved ones that had died, and lives that were changed because of the tragedy.

This night, the two brothers started talking almost in unison reporting that another bin Laden tape had aired on television on the evening news. They had seen it on a TV in the garage as they were turning in their cabs for the night. This news set off a tirade of hate and venom from the assembled group.

The noise level in the room went up considerably and the Doctor was glad that most of his neighbors had already left the building for the evening. Everyone quickly weighed in with a comment and a few choice expletives and the room turned into a free for all. And with that Dr. Hensley realized his counseling session was over before it really began.

Whenever this happened the good Doctor knew that he had lost whatever progress hoped for the evening, but he also had learned from past outbursts that it was important for this group to vent their anger because they each had lost so much. He allowed them to vent and get it out of their system.

While the raving ratcheted up with a number of competing discussions going on at the same time, he noticed William Meredith was strangely quiet. He sat there staring out the window and rubbing his right palm, which was all red from the hot coffee that had exploded on his hand a half hour earlier.

Dr Hensley slowly stood up and vacated the circle. No one even noticed. He knew that he wouldn't be able to rein in the group until they had exhausted themselves, and walked towards William, motioning him to come over to the window.

"Bill," he said, "you rarely miss a good argument like this one, what's up?" When he got no answer he tried a lighter tack hoping to pull the man back into the same room and conversation.

"As we say in the trade, what's bothering you bunky?"

With that comment, William snapped out of it, looked up with a questioning look on his face and said, "bunky? What the hell is that?"

The Doctor smiled remembering that most of these folks had limited understanding of American slang. He said, "It's an old saying that was popular way back in the 60's, I think it was a comedy routine at the time, and even made it into a song back then. My compatriots and I have adopted it as a starter conversation. It usually gets people to react. And I guess it worked. So what's bothering you Bill?"

Bill didn't really know what to say in response but he kept thinking about the thoughts swirling in his head. He wasn't sure it was really a thought that could be explained, or even verbalized, but he was wrestling with the thread of an idea in his head and he wanted to finish the mental exercise. But the noise level in the room was too much and he needed some time to work through his thoughts.

"Doc, I'm not feeling so well this evening, so I think I'll check out a bit early and call it a day."

The Doctor disliked his charges leaving in mid-session, or on a sour note, but he recognized that William was not mentally depressed, just troubled about something he didn't want to talk about. That he understood. So he nodded and walked him to the door, said goodbye, and rejoined the fray to see if he could possibly regain order.

William took the elevator down, went out the front door of the building just off Broadway, and went back to the McDonald's for another cup of coffee. Hopefully this one he would get to drink. After he bought a large coffee with double cream, he found a seat in the front window, and aimlessly watched the pedestrians flowing by.

As he watched the people filing by, he realized he wanted to think through an idea that was festering in his mind since he had spilled the first cup of coffee. An hour later, after a second cup of coffee, he had progressed to scribbling notes on napkins.

He was engrossed in thought when someone pounded on the window and he looked up. It was Ralph Behar and Michael Pappas, standing outside, both giving him a 'What's up?' look. They didn't wait to be waved inside; they just pushed through the revolving door and walked to the counter. They both got coffee, with Michael adding two chicken sandwiches, and came over to the table.

"What's with you Bill", Ralph asked as he poured some cream into his coffee, " all of a sudden you weren't there anymore? Doc said you weren't feeling well so you went home. So this is home now?

In between bites of his sandwich, Michael chimed in. "You have more money than God and you're spending your quality time at McDonald's?"

Bill smiled and slipped his napkin notes in his pocket. "No, I wasn't feeling well and with the brothers new outburst tonight, I thought I'd prefer to have some quiet time down here instead. The coffee is better."

"I agree with that." Michael said.

"Did the two brothers ever calm down upstairs? Talk about two guys with a perpetual hard-on. Boy, they do get passionate, don't they?"

"Yeah, but after two years at least now we can understand what they are saying", Ralph offered as he laughed about the situation. "When I first met O his English was a pretty lousy, but when you hear him now he makes New Yorkers sound like choir boys."

The group had decided early on to call the older Pakistani brother named Osama just O for short, because no one in the counseling group could bring themselves to say the name Osama without spitting it out. They had learned early on of O's tragic loss of his entire family, and his brother's equally horrific loss, so they did not hold the name Osama against him, but they just couldn't stomach saying it.

Osama for his part gladly accepted the name change and readily appreciated their effort to give him a new nickname. He liked being more American. After 9-11 he had also quickly learned that the name Osama was a cross to bear as people upon hearing it, would refuse to speak with him. People would get out of his taxi, throwing their sodas at the cab and swearing at him. He had even changed the name on his license in the back seat of the cab.

The only good that came from all this anger was that he had learned a whole new vocabulary, and now used the words liberally to malign that dog bin Laden.

Both Ralph and Michael realized that William had something else on his mind and they knew him well enough after a couple years of counseling that he would share his thoughts when he was ready. So both of them sat back and waited.

Finally William broke the silence and kind of just blurted out, "So why don't we get the son-of-a-bitch?"

Michael stopped chewing on the last of his sandwich. Ralph set down his coffee and they both looked at each other. Then they both turned back to William and said almost in unison, "What was that?"

"I said, why couldn't we go after Osama bin Laden ourselves? Hell, the government can't seem to find the bastard and they have all sorts of assets out there looking under every rock. But no one can find him, so I say again, why don't we do it ourselves/"

Ralph and Michael again looked at one another but didn't say anything. Ralph did a quick scan around the restaurant and saw that almost no one was within earshot, and said quietly, "You left our session this evening to plot the assassination of Osama bin Laden? What, are you out of your fucking mind?"

Ralph leaned in and took a look at Meredith's coffee cup and said. "What have you been drinking in there?"

"Coffee if you must know, maybe three cups, and the last two were decaf. I'm serious, what's to prevent us from taking this asshole out? God knows that Bush and all his soldiers can't find him, and now we are all tied up in a war with Saddam Hussein in Iraq rather than going after bin Laden. I think we have an open playing field, and our government won't even notice if we go after him."

"Again, I ask, are you nuts?" Ralph whispered it this time and gave a quick glance around the room, "We can't just kill him, we don't even know where he is; Unless you have some magical potion we can sprinkle around and get a genie to show us the way?"

The young cop Michael sat there with his mouth open and finally weighed in, "I actually kind of like the idea, it wouldn't be easy, but it's an interesting thought."

He looked up at the blank television screen and thought some more, and then he said, "I'm in, I know it violates everything I stand for as a policeman, but what do you want me to do?"

Ralph turned to his right and now his mouth was hanging open, "What are you crazy too? What have you guys been smoking? You can't just decide to kill someone while sitting here in a restaurant in the middle of Times Square? I don't think we should even be having this conversation," he said looking around to see if anyone was in the vicinity.

William fished into his coat pocket and pulled out the two napkins that had some notes scribbled on them. He waved the napkins at the two guys and said, "I was making some notes before you guys came in here. I don't know how to do it, but I for one, sure would like to give it a try. I want that guy on a spit, driven right up his ass and out that big fucking mouth of his."

Ralph looked at the napkins, leaned back in his chair and let out a loud laugh, drawing a bit of attention to the table from the few people in the fast food restaurant. People looked over for a moment, but then quickly lost interest. Ralph decided that Meredith was being serious. He tried another tack.

"OK, I'll agree, I'd like to get the bastard too, and all of those al Qaeda nutcases, but come on, this is absolutely crazy. What are we going to do, get us some guns and go charging up the hill in Pakistan like Teddy Roosevelt charged up San Juan Hill?"

"I don't think that would be very prudent." Michael said, as he grabbed the napkins and tried to make sense of the scribbling.

"I don't think we'd get that far. We'd do all the planning and Bush and his FBI guys would nail us before we got to Kennedy and hopped a plane for the Middle East."

Ralph still couldn't believe they were even talking about such a thing.

"They probably would throw us in jail as terrorists and throw away the key. I don't want to spend the rest of my life mourning Kathleen looking through bars." Ralph said quietly to the people at the table.

William started to say something still clutching the napkins in his hand. Before he could get out a word, Ralph continued.

"Come on, stop even thinking about such nonsense and let's get out of here before the FBI comes swooping in. Hell, now I want a stronger drink than this coffee. Obviously they've put something in yours, how about at least letting me catch-up."

William smiled at the comment and decided to stop pushing. He stuffed the napkins in his pocket as he stood up. Ralph was right, this was nuts and a drink did sound like a good idea.

→ ←

On Broadway, Times Square

William Meredith's car pulled to the curb at 11:45 am. He jumped out telling his driver to take a break for a couple hours, that he would call him when he needed picking up. He was across the street from the huge Sheraton Towers on 7th Avenue.

For the better part of a year after 9-11 the Sheraton Hotel had become headquarters for many of the federal agencies that descended on

Manhattan to coordinate the aftermath of the 9-11 terrorist attack. These federal bureaucrats had commandeered whole blocks of rooms to set up command centers. The hotel had top federal agency personnel coming and going, thus it was often ringed by convoys of black suburban SUV's used to move the Homeland Security, FBI, NSA and other agencies around. It had been like an armed camp for a year after that fateful day.

Another large block of rooms and whole floors in the Sheraton and its sister property across the street had been leased by various investment houses and companies that had lost space in the Twin Towers. They had moved into the Hotel and other business buildings in mid-town in less than a week after the buildings had been destroyed.

Many hotels still served as offices for companies after the collapse as they were starting over almost from scratch. This was where Ralph Behar's company had relocated its offices.

Meredith took the elevator to the 9th floor and went down the hall to Ralph's office – room# 910-A noting the room numbers were in sequential order. As he knocked he noticed that the room number plate had a second plate on top of it. When he looked across the hall and saw room 912, he wondered if this room actually had been 911, and been changed. That would make sense. He wondered if it bothered Ralph every time he came to work. Damn he thought, he would have changed the number too.

He heard Ralph's voice invite him in so he took a deep breath and opened the door prepared to layout a plan. "Hi Ralph, I'm sorry to bother you at work but I wanted to apologize for my behavior last night. Maybe I was a little too caffeinated."

"You think? Really? No apology necessary, the group got to blow off some steam at the session in Doc's office last night, and all you got was McDonald's, so I understand. What's up, your not going to start in again are you?"

"No, I was thinking we should have lunch and forget about my ranting last night. How about we try that lobster place, just down the street with the checkered tablecloths. It'll be my treat."

Ralph looked skeptical but knew he had the time to spare so he shut down his computer and pushed back his chair. He stepped into his bathroom, which was one of the perks of having a hotel room for an office, washed his hands and combed his receding hairline.

"This is a pretty nice set-up for an office. Your own bathroom, is that a sleeper couch?" he said, pointing to the sofa near the window.

"Yeah it is, and let me tell you, a couple years ago I spent many a night up here because I was just too miserable to go home to that empty house. I'm not doing that quite as much anymore, maybe the therapy sessions are actually helping. So now I'm getting the house ready to sell because it just has too many memories I don't want to re-visit every time I come home."

"Ralph, I know what you mean, my son didn't even live with me anymore but I still don't like to go home. I leased a place here in town just so I wouldn't have to go home as often. Come on, let's go."

As they entered the hallway, Ralph pointed and said without being asked, "Yeah, I had the number changed. I couldn't believe that I drew this room. The Hotel was actually very good about it when I asked."

Meredith didn't say anything but knew he would have been devastated if he had to look at that number every day. Leaving the hotel they crossed Seventh Avenue and walked to the restaurant, just a long block east. The restaurant specialized in lobster and had dark wood framing and ceramic floors, and bright wide windows. The tables had red and white, checkered tablecloths that created a nice casual atmosphere for the business world. No longer a three-martini lunch crowd, the two guys ordered iced tea and two lobster lunches. Both willingly allowed the waiter to put on the lobster bibs when the food arrived. Over the food they engaged in small talk about their jobs and personal interests although they knew each other pretty well from counseling sessions for the past three years.

After lunch, William casually started in on a new conversation by saying, "Ralph, I know you think I was crazy last night but I would like to re-visit the concept for a moment if you would allow me to."

Ralph groaned knowing he had been hoodwinked, but decided that he liked William enough that he didn't want to fight with him. So he said, "If you can keep your voice down, so we don't draw the feds to our lunch table, go ahead, knock yourself out."

William reached into his breast pocket and pulled out a neatly typed sheet of paper. He had spent most of the night converting his napkins to some orderly notes. He joked that he must have looked a bit crazy waving his scribbled napkins the night before.

Ralph just rolled his eyes back in his head and listened, motioning with his hands to cool the volume down. He didn't want to go to jail just for thinking about killing someone.

"You have to admit the feds have been completely lost in their efforts to find Osama bin Laden," he began, "Now we're tied up fighting this war in Iraq when everyone keeps telling us bin Laden is hiding out in some mountain cave in Afghanistan. So I think that we should form a team and go get him ourselves. Maybe we hire some mercenaries, or we draw him out in the open and then shoot the asshole."

He was silent a moment reflecting what he had said, then went on. "All I know is that I would sleep much better, and I think you would too, if we knew he was dead. I bet all the entire group would sleep better. I also think if we were to propose we go after bin Laden, they would all join the team."

They talked quietly for another twenty minutes arguing the merits of what had been suggested. The waitress stopped at the table to refresh their coffees, and left the bill in a shiny black leather portfolio. Meredith quickly reached for it and dug for his wallet.

"All right Bill, I'll agree that we would all like to see the bastard pay for his crimes, but what the hell could we do? We're a bunch of old men who don't know a thing about war and terror.

"I agree with you there, although we do have some young people, but that's also what makes the idea so workable. No one would expect us to do such a thing and go after him. We're a bunch of amateurs. We could do it and stay under the radar"

"So what would we do, just march up there, somewhere, wherever up is, and just shoot him? Hell, up until recently, I haven't shot a gun for years. Kathleen didn't like the thought of guns so I never had one in the house. But now since she's gone, I've taken up trap shooting as a way to vent my anger. I shot last Saturday morning, and hit 23 out of 25 clay targets on the range. But I figure we aren't going to get close enough to him to use my shotgun, so I'm no help in your quest."

"That's cool that you're a deadeye with a shotgun." William said, making a motion as if cocking a pump shotgun. " I took up shooting too, same reason. I may have to join you some Saturday and see if we can have a little competition?"

"Works for me, but you won't need to rent one or buy one, I've built up a little arsenal at home. I just bought a rifle, have two shotguns and even a pistol. I guess it was a reaction to my frustration." Ralph said as he stared out the window. "See…I'm frustrated too. Let's do it some time."

"I've got a small arsenal too and joined a shooting club up north. It's a nice club too. You'd be welcome to come out there anytime. Your right, it does help to vent the anger." He went on seeing an opening.

"What I guess I'm saying is why can't we quietly explore our options and see if there is some way we could get bin Laden. As you've said numerous times, I have more money than God. I couldn't think of a better way to spend all of it than going after him. Hell, I don't care what it would cost, and if I spent all of my money, so what, I don't have a son to give it to anymore, so who gives a damn. I guess I'm just saying we should talk more about this. Maybe the group could help us think about options."

"Well, we would have to keep it from the Pakistani's because they can't seem to keep their mouths shut about anything." Both laughed at the comment but realized there was a potential leak that would certainly have to be thought about.

Ralph thought a moment and then said. "Maybe Josef and Michael would be interested in exploring the idea. I'm not sure what Courtney or Kate could do to help, but hell we don't even have a clue as to what we could do at this point."

"That's true, but it could be more therapeutic than these sessions that don't seem to be going anywhere." William said. "Sometimes I come to these meetings just because I want to see you people, even O and Malik. You are all my family now, and I care about you." With that William went silent for a few moments and toyed with his coffee cup.

"Ok, I'll agree that the concept might actually do this group some good. But...."

Meredith saw this as his final opening and quickly said, "That's what I'm saying, let's not kick this idea to the curb until we explore it a bit more. Hell, the others may think we're nuts too, but we won't know unless we ask them about it. And some of them could come in handy if we were to try to get him."

"I don't know about that with Michael being police and Courtney former ATF. We may get ourselves arrested for even talking about such a thing." Ralph cautioned.

But Meredith was persistent if nothing else. "Let's ask them anyhow, let them tell us we're crazy about such a thing. How about we get them all together after Doc's session next week? After our session, we'll ask everyone to re-assemble here at our favorite McDonalds. Dinner will be on me." He put away his wallet and started to grab his coat off the chair.

Ralph began getting up as well but said. "If Doc walks out of the building with us next week, how do we explain our need for a post meeting? We may have to split up as we leave and then come back to the restaurant from the other side street door."

Meredith smiled and said. "See this is getting covert already."

Ralph just shook his head and said, "I think we're both crazy to even be talking about this stuff, but yeah, let's ask them what they think. Maybe they will be smart enough to talk us out of it. You know Bill, I thought you were a little bit off the wall retiring at such a young age, but now I'm sure of it. You're certifiable, and maybe I am too."

With that William called his driver and offered Ralph a ride back to his office but he declined stating he needed to clear his head. He walked away deep in thought.

→ ←

A Week Later, Dr. Hensley's Office

The session had gone well because the Doctor hadn't opened the floor at the beginning of the session, allowing O and Malik to go off on their usual rants about life in a cab. The group had a solid discussion about moving on and dealing with what life was handing them. Everyone seemed to be participating well and Dr. Hensley suggested breaking a bit early so that everyone would leave on an upbeat positive note. Little did he know that William had been hoping the discussion would keep moving along a little faster.

The group broke up with everyone heading for the elevators. Doctor Hensley stayed behind to clean up the dishes and turn off the lights, so when everyone got on the same elevator, William announced that he would like to pop for a late night fast food dinner. Everyone quickly said yes, until they heard he meant the McDonald's around the corner. Ralph intervened and said it would be fun. He asked if anyone wasn't hungry? They all agreed they were.

Because it was a fast food joint, everyone ordered more food than they could possibly eat just to teach Meredith a lesson. Even he marveled when he saw the cash register showing $101.35. They had ordered everything they could see on the menu. Even Josef, Uri and the Pakistani brothers had ordered more American food than they could possibly eat. And then he realized that some of these folks were taking food home to others and he was privately pleased they were doing so.

They sat in the back of the restaurant at a couple of four-tops pulled together. It was after 9:00 pm so there was absolutely no one around them in their corner of the restaurant. They had the place to themselves. Everyone tore into their Big Macs and fries with abandon.

After the eating frenzy had slowed down, Meredith gaveled the impromptu meeting together by rapping on the table. He made sure there was no one anywhere close to the group before speaking.

"We have all known each other for a long time now, more than five years, and while we came together under horrific circumstances, I want you to know that I now consider you my family, even you, O and Malik." Everyone laughed and slapped the two Pakistanis on the back.

"You have all helped me immeasurably through a most difficult time, and I hope that I may have helped you a bit too. No one should have to go through the pain we have all experienced these last few years." With that he raised his milk shake and proposed a toast to the group. Everyone understood and grabbed their paper cups as well.

"To my fellow survivors who have made my life livable again, I say thank you… May we all have a chance at peace sometime in the near future. I'm thankful that you have all come into my life. Cheers!"

Everyone brought their cups together making very little sound at all, but then followed with loud slurping noises as they sucked on their straws, and laughed, smiling at one another.

Outside the McDonald's window, Dr. Hensley happened to be passing by on the way to his car. He glanced into the restaurant and saw the entire counseling group sitting at a couple of tables. He stopped and stared in the window. He saw that they were all eating and seemed to be having a good time, as a group.

That's interesting, he thought, with all the pain this group had experienced. Perhaps the healing process was working better than he thought. He stood there staring in the window and watched the scene. He was pleased with their bonding relationship.

He was tempted to go in and join them to see if he could use the impromptu meeting to help them move forward even more, but then he checked himself and decided perhaps they should work on their own. He was pleased and walked past the storefront window towards his car a block away.

Inside the restaurant Meredith raised his cup a second time and waited until everyone at the table had a chance to join him.

"I just said that no one should have to go through what we have all experienced in pain over these last couple years. But that's not entirely true. I can think of one person who should have to deal with such pain, and I for one would like to inflict it on him myself." He raised his cup further and said, "May bin Laden rot in hell, and may we all have a chance to show him the way."

The group erupted in cheers slamming their paper cups together. Drinks were spilled on the table but no one cared. Everyone agreed with the sentiment. At that moment, William looked at Ralph and nodded that he was going to bring up the subject right here and now. He let them settle down, and then went on.

"I'd love to get that bastard and would go to the ends of the earth to do so. Hell, I would spend my fortune to make it happen."

"I'll drink to that too." Ralph said, as if endorsing Meredith's decision to move forward. "That would give me some of that closure the Doc keeps talking about. If I could find the bastard I would personally pull the trigger without a bit of remorse."

Josef normally sat quietly through the meetings absorbing the talk and dealing with his pain in his own silent manner, but now he too spoke up.

"William, I too would go to the ends of the earth to see that man dead. Why can't this huge country of ours find the bastard? At the U.N. everyone talks about how he has just disappeared, but still, he is on the news every other day. I know that Elena would be here if that devil had not ordered those planes flown into the Towers. If you will have me, I would join you in this hunt."

His comment initiated a firestorm of support. Everyone agreed the United States was not doing enough to find the terrorist. Meredith let the talk go on without interrupting because he knew from his years in the financial business world that new ideas were developed in informal sessions like this.

These folks needed to voice their concerns and help each other build some consensus on what could or should be done. He had gone through this process hundreds of times. Now he was hoping their discussions would lead them to a similar consensus. So he waited as all of them spoke of their hate and their desire to cut off bin Laden's balls, to gouge out his eyes, and kill him a hundred different ways.

After another ten minutes, everyone seemed to have satiated themselves in their hate for this monster and were settling down when Meredith intervened and simply said," So why don't WE go get the bastard ourselves?" He emphasized the word WE.

At that moment all talk ceased. Everyone tried to process and comprehend what William Meredith II had just said. Ralph Behar looked around the table and saw the same looks that he and Michael must have had a week earlier, when Bill first raised the concept to them in the same restaurant. He looked at Bill and saw that he too was searching the faces at the table. He was looking for a specific reaction from the group, waiting to see what would be said.

The silence was broken by Michael Pappas, who said, "Bill, I told you before, I'd follow you to the gates of hell to get my hands around that bastard's neck. I meant it then, and I mean it now. Give me a job that will help with the cause, and I'll start right now. But if we do try to get him, I personally want to be the guy that gets to beat the shit out of him."

Everyone listened carefully as Michael spoke and tried to absorb his words. Each person became lost in their thoughts for a couple of moments, but then one at a time, they started talking and pledging their support for the concept.

Kate who was the youngest person at the table spoke up. "I would join your cause, even though I don't know what I could possibly offer or do to help. Unless you need some crack graphics or printing." She laughed at herself.

"Kate we may need your graphic and printing capabilities. But at this point we don't have a plan yet. All we have is desire! But I'd be honored to have you join us."

Uri Navroz, the Egyptian spoke next. "I have long wondered why I am sitting in a circle in a Doctor's office, when I should be avenging my son's death. I may be old but I still have a deep desire for revenge for my son. Ali was even Muslim and the bastard did not care. As a Muslim myself, I want revenge for my son's death. I want to cut his heart out and feed it to the buzzards. William, I would join your holy mission if I can?"

Josef said, "I don't know what I can offer either, but I'm willing to help anyway that I can. I don't speak Arabic, but I know people that can. I can assist if we need any Russian or European language translated. And perhaps I know some people that could be of use at the UN."

Malik and O looked at one another and each placed their hands on the table in a fist.

"As a sacred oath to our children," O said as he looked at Malik, "we will take bin Laden's terror to his own house, or his cave, and we will bury him in it. This must be done and we join you too. Can we be a part of this plan? We have even been to the mountains where he is hiding, like a rat in a cave."

"O, Malik, that would be very important to us, to actually get close to him. Thank you for your support. We must talk more afterwards." Meredith said this as he bowed thanks to the two Pakistanis.

Courtney spoke up and said," I'm glad I've resigned from the Bureau because if I hadn't, I would be sworn to turning all of you lunatics in. This is the craziest idea I have ever heard. You can't be serious?"

"Courtney, I'm as serious as I can be. No one else seems to be going after this guy. They are too busy going after Saddam Hussein and his weapons of mass destruction in Iraq. Well, screw them, lets go get the bastard ourselves."

"Ok, your right, God knows no one else seems to be interested in bin Laden. But I'm not sure what we're all talking about here yet. I won't turn you in, but we need to think this out carefully before we all get thrown in jail."

Ralph cleared his throat gaining some attention from the group at the table and said, "I think we are all certifiably crazy to even be talking about this. What I think we are all agreeing to participate in is a completely illegal act. But I have thought about it long and hard, and I would some day like to sleep again. If you all feel this is something we should do as a group, then I'll join too. But God help us!"

With that everyone sitting at the table quieted down and turned their attention to Meredith at the end of the table looking for some direction. He looked around the table at each person and noted the resolve in their eyes.

Finally he spoke up. "I've felt this way for the past few months, but I wanted to know if anyone else felt as I do. Doctor Hensley keeps promising us all peace and perhaps it is there somewhere down the road, but right now all I still feel is uncontrollable rage and anger."

A number of people acknowledged they too felt the same way. But they quieted quickly, allowing Meredith to continue.

"It drives me crazy that bin Laden is laughing at our misery, our murdered loved ones, and our country. I came to this current state of mind, because of my utter frustration that the bastard has gotten away with his terrorist act. I keep feeling he is looking at me every time he broadcasts one of those damn tapes and the Middle Eastern world glorifies his act. He is laughing at me, and all of us."

Meredith put his head down for a moment and then said, "I don't know how we can accomplish this task, but I do know that if we put our heads together we can come up with a plan of attack. I will personally finance this entire effort even if I need to spend every last dollar I have. But before we even utter another word I have to ask for your complete secrecy on this quest." He stopped talking and looked around the table again.

"I can't emphasize this enough. We can't breathe a word of this to anyone." He looked specifically at Osama and Malik Tarkan. "And Malik and O, I mean anyone! Not your family, not Dr. Hensley, not your mothers, your children, not anyone. If we let this get out, we will all go to jail and then he wins a second time."

He looked into the Pakistani's eyes again and saw that they were listening and understanding what he said. "Can I get everyone's promise that not a word about this will be spoken to anyone, except to the people at this table? If one word gets out we will be thrown in jail and we will have failed."

Josef said, "William is right. At the U.N. everything is secret, yet everyone knows what all the secrets are. And people die because the secrets are spoken and passed around. We must make a sacred pact."

The Russian looked across the table at the Pakistani brothers and continued, "O and Malik, you have regaled us with your taxi stories for the past few years telling us about all the gossip in New York City. Our discussion here must not be spoken about, ever, to anyone if we are to make a plan and then carry it out."

Both Osama and Malik shook their heads in agreement. They understood. They had a burning look in their eyes that said they could be trusted.

Meredith looked around the table searching everyone's faces and asked, "Can we all promise on the souls of our loved ones that we will keep this secret, tonight, tomorrow and forever?"

Michael Pappas interrupted the long silence at the table when he threw his big hand into the center of the table with his palm spread down. Before he could even ask the rest of the group to follow suit, Josef and William joined him. O, Malik and Uri looked confused but realized that they too should throw their hand in the middle. Ralph, Courtney and Kate looked at one another and slowly added their hands to the pile. Michael then placed his other hand over the mound of flesh on the table to seal the pact. From the focused look in everyone's eyes, a sacred bond had been consecrated.

→ ←

Baggem, Federal Territories

"Osama, I have identified a place where they will never find us. It is north of Islamabad about 35 miles in one of the nicer suburbs. The city of Abbottabad has about 500,000 people, mostly middle class, with peaceful surrounding farmlands. It is on the Karakoran Highway N-35, on the northerly route to China."

"Tell me more, why there?" Osama said putting down his Koran to offer his full attention to Zawahiri.

"Abbottabad is a military retirement town and has many universities and schools. It is even the home of the Pakistan Military Academy, where they train the Pakistani military officers. It is like West Point, the Army's Military Academy in America. They will never think that we would be in such a place."

"That is interesting. I like the irony of such a location." He accepted the map of the city that Zawahiri was handing him and started scanning the noted features on the map. "There are many mosques as well. Might we be able to hear the call to prayers?"

"I have tried to find a suitable existing house that would meet our needs, but I haven't been able to locate such a residence. So that we would have security and the high walls you suggested, I think we should have one built on the eastern edge of town." He pointed to a spot on the map slightly northeast of the central city. "You can see the site I have outlined here."

Bin Laden pulled the area maps over and began scrutinizing them. "Ah, yes. The site is pretty much surrounded by farm fields. That would give us some security and perhaps we would be left alone which would be a good thing, as long as we didn't draw attention to ourselves."

Zawahiri pulled out some additional drawings and spread them out on the table. "I have designed a compound that will offer us security with high walls surrounding a central building that shall be three stories high. That will give us a commanding view in all directions. We will top the walls with barbed wire and we will only have a single gate for outside access. This will make entry difficult and easy to protect."

"Again, I like what I see. There is space to move about unseen by the outside world. I will relish that movement and freedom. What do you propose here?" He pointed to the layout and surrounding areas within the compound.

"We will have a separate building for any guests we have, and out here we will be able to burn our trash so that nothing will leave the compound. When we need supplies and food our men will do the shopping and deliveries will come through the single access point."

" You have done well, Ayman. When could our new residence be ready?"

"We have local workers putting up the perimeter walls right now, and they will start on the interior buildings in a couple weeks. The builders are pleased that their client is paying them as they go." He could see that bin Laden liked what he was hearing so he continued, "Our cover story is that the house is being built for a retired college professor who is looking forward to solitude so that he can write a book."

"Perhaps I will write my memoirs there. Some day we will need to write down all of our triumphs, and chronicle the downfall of the decadent west. I look forward to this new journey. It will be good to sleep in a real bed again."

"The compound should be ready in about three months, Leader. The Pakistanis are slow workers and we don't want to rush them, nor show up early. We should be there by May."

"You take good care of me Ayman, thank you. Now tell me of today's news from the couriers. Tell me we have killed more Americans. That is always a good day!"

Times Square, Dr. Hensley's Office

The session had gone well, but rather quickly by Dr. Hensley's estimation. He sensed that the participants, all of whom were present for a change, were pre-occupied and not really paying attention. Perhaps that was a sign they were healing, he thought. That would be a good thing. Thus, he announced that they would end the session early, and he got no arguments from his patients.

Everyone seemed eager to leave, so he noted the next week's meeting time and said good night. Everyone cleared out, almost as a group, gone in a flash down the hall to the elevator. By the time he turned off the coffee pot, flipped the lights off and looked for his keys, no one was in sight.

A few minutes later he exited the building. Walking past the McDonald's, he again saw his whole counseling group sitting there, gorging themselves on burgers and fries. He stopped and stared at the group sitting in a corner of the restaurant, eating, laughing and talking, as close friends would do. He decided this must be some homegrown, self-therapeutic, post-session they dreamed up. He saw that they were helping each other and acting like a team. Satisfied, he continued on to his car and thought maybe he was making a difference.

→ ←

McDonald's, near Broadway

Meredith smiled to himself as he realized this was going to cost him a lot of dinners. At least it wasn't Sardis, just a couple blocks away. He could readily afford this.

The group was enjoying their Big Macs and fries, especially O and Malik, and he could see that all of them had a gleam in their eyes. They wanted to talk about a plan. They all had committed to a mission and now they wanted to know what that entailed. They wanted to get on with it.

"So everyone, you have had a week to think about a concept. Anyone have a great idea on how we get the bastard?" he looked around the table, "Hell, I would settle for just finding him at this point."

Ralph took a sip of his drink and cleared his throat. "I think he is in Pakistan or those mountains near Afghanistan, just like the news reports keep saying. He's probably buried in some cave so deep that we would need a nuclear weapon to get him, or one of those bunker busters they used in Iraq."

O decided to speak up. "My brother and me came from those mountains... we hid there when the Taliban and the clerics persecuted my families, before we come to America. You are right, there are many, many caves in the mountains and they are deep. How would we get him out of there?"

"I think that's the problem," Michael said, "he is not coming out and we have no idea where to go in, even if we could get close. Ralph, I agree with you, we may need a bomb to stuff down one of his rat holes, if we want to get him and his crazy followers. I hope the damn mountain caves in on them."

Josef listened quietly to all the talk as they discussed how they could get bin Laden. He was doubtful that it was even possible unless they could just drop a bomb on top of his head. That would require a bomb and a delivery system, and then it would be impossible to even get close without tipping them off and without getting shot. He bit his lip and continued to listen to the talk at the table.

Meredith always tried to find some consensus in these talks and he asked everyone to think about possible scenarios that could be used.

He said, "We have to think about a whole series of options and maybe we can come up with one that would work. " There has to be a way. I'm willing to pay for any good idea you guys come up with!"

He looked around the table, saw the two ladies and immediately apologized,

"Courtney and Kate, I apologize, I say guys out of force of habit, and I certainly am not excluding you two."

Kate said, "No apology necessary, my Dad always said that too, bless his soul. I always thought I was a guy!"

As long as she had Meredith's attention she thought she should offer one piece of advice. "All I ask is that as we talk about this plan we don't always meet here because my diet can't take it. Once in a while is fine, but I don't have the strength to eat salads every time we come in here when you're all chowing down on burgers and fries."

Meredith laughed and made a mental note to change the cuisine next time, even though he noted Malik and O were enjoying themselves immensely with this American food. "Kate, duly noted, I agree that we will all look like fat Americans if we keep meeting here each week. I'll come up with a new place where we can talk and save the waistlines."

He then suggested that perhaps there was a way to get bin Laden to come out in the open. That if they could get close, they would just shoot him, even though they might die in the effort.

Uri responded by saying, "I would gladly pull that trigger, and I'd be willing to die for the revenge and satisfaction I would feel for the effort." Find him and I will personally do the deed. I only hope I can take out a lot of them with a Kalashnikov. I used them when I was younger. We kept a stash of such guns in a locker on my ship. It was a way to fight off the pirates and to protect our cargo. Get me near him and I will shoot him between the eyes."

"Stand in line Uri," Michael said, "I want the bastard too, and I'll gladly take the chance of getting killed if I could get to him. That just gets me to Michaela sooner, so I am ready to march up that mountain too."

Malik put his hand on the table and said, "I will lead you up that mountain in my homeland, but I want to shoot too. Maybe we all get him shot at the same time. That way we don't miss."

Osama patted his brother's arm and said, "If we can find him, we will, and then perhaps we all shoot him, I shoot for Vispy and Sonji and Pasha. Malik is right, we know that mountain area of Pakistan and we have relatives in the Warizistan. You find where he, and we find him. I will gladly die to do so, my family is killed, and I have no one to go home to. Let us get him."

Meredith felt that enough had been said on the need, now they needed a plan of action. He then said, "So how do we make this happen? As I told you, in addition to these dinners, I'll pay for the entire plan and anything that we need. Money is not an issue. Give me a plan and we will go after him one way or another."

Courtney, the former ATF agent cautioned everyone about secrecy again.

"People, we can't talk about this on the phone, there are government agencies who listen to all phone calls, and if they get wind of this we will all be in trouble."

"What is this wind you say," O looked confused and asked what the term wind meant. "I am not hearing wind at all?"

"O, I apologize, I should not have said 'in the wind' without explaining." Courtney apologized. "I think we all have some need to be careful what we say as so many cultures are represented at this table. What I meant to say is that the U.S. government can listen to any and all phone calls, and they do. Ninety-nine percent of them are just phone calls, but that other 1% is what they are looking for."

Meredith joined the conversation. "I'm told that this NSA sits in a building in Washington, D.C. and has super computers that listen and record conversations all day, every day. They are specifically listening for the talk and chatter of terrorists, especially since the Towers came down. They have access to all messages in this country and probably other countries as well."

Following up Courtney added, "The NSA computers listen to all calls, even the boring ones, and then there is human analysis if they hear anything they think sounds interesting or dangerous. If we were to talk about this on the phones, I guarantee someone at NSA would become interested. Thus, no one should use your own phones, in fact I would not use any public phones at all because they will find you and us as a group."

"Courtney, I agree. We have been talking about our own secrecy and not talking about this to anyone but ourselves. But that means we can't even talk about it on the phones. It should only be face-to-face and then very quietly and make sure that no one else is listening. Otherwise we will all be in jail."

"How about we use those one-time use phones and then throw them away? Michael asked. "The vice guys at the precinct are always complaining that the drug pushers are using phones for selling and then they get tossed after being used."

"Michael, that's a great idea. To maintain security, I want all of you to go buy a pre-paid limited minute phone somewhere. But be cool about it. And make sure that you are not being videotaped when you buy it," Meredith suggested.

He thought for a moment and then dug his billfold out from his breast pocket and pulled out a dozen one hundred dollar bills.

"In fact, here is a $100 bill." He handed them out. "Each of you should go buy as many of those phones as you can, but only buy one phone in each place and try to be casual about it. Buy some other things as well so you don't attract attention."

Ralph Behar spoke up as he was handed a bill. "Trac Phones are a name brand I just saw last week at a Wal-Mart. They were just $10 units with a limited number of minutes on them. They can even be used internationally."

William then quieted everyone as they looked at their hundred dollar bills. "I suggest we will only use them when we have to and then our messages will be short and possibly in code. Then you wipe the phone clean so you don't have any fingerprints on them and destroy them. And I do mean destroy them, not just toss them in the garbage. Take them home and bang them with a hammer and then dump them in different trash cans around the city."

"If we go this route, Bill is right. We can't minimize this security," Courtney said, "tripping up on the basics is how the police catches bad guys all the time. While we are not the bad guys, no one will be able to know that, so his suggestions are right on the money."

The whole group looked at the $100 bills and quickly stuffed them in their pockets. Then Meredith said again. "Remember, buy the phones one at a time at different stores, preferably not where you usually shop. People will remember if you buy five phones…. you want to blend in, not stand out. Make a few trips in the next week to different stores and just be casual about it. The store will activate the phone and you can take it home and store it in your underwear drawer until you need it."

He continued, "I'd also ask you don't use them to call anyone until we have something to talk about. For now I suggest we keep talking face-to-face. Kate, next week we will meet in a Poet's Restaurant up on 52nd St. just north of the cheap tickets booth in Time Square. We will leave the Doc's office after the meeting, split up and re-meet at Poet's. This time I'll pop for steaks if you want them. But I want you all to come with some idea on how we go after this bastard."

The group broke up with O and Malik fingering their hundred dollar bills as they walked out the door. Michael eased in behind them and told them to be careful with the money. That Courtney and William knew what they were talking about. Otherwise this effort would be stopped before it even got started. The brothers agreed and promised to keep their mouths shut and not use the phones they were about to buy.

→ ←

11:00 pm Brooklyn

Josef went home that night and stayed up late waiting for a call from his brother-in-law, the General, in Russia, This was his semi-annual call from his wife's brother who would be calling in his early morning hours prior to going to work. He would try to catch up on family matters.

General Dimitri Gralashov was an older brother who had loved his little sister Elena so much that he was beside himself when he had heard the news from Josef. His sister had died in the 9-11 tragedy and her body had never been found. They both thought that when the Towers came down, they must have fallen on the Marriott, which sat between the two towers.

Since the tragedy, they had tried to comprehend the terror she must have felt, and they hoped that it had been an instantaneous, crushing blow that had killed her and that she had not suffered. They also were very frustrated that the North Tower had fallen close to an hour after the planes first impact, and wondered why she had not escaped the hotel.

Dimitri expressed anger and frustration every time they talked and Josef knew that he would have to re-visit that horrible day again as his brother-in-law worked through the rage of the memory. It was like the anger that he was dealing with in therapy. Josef almost wished his brother-in-law could join in the counseling sessions, but that was a fantasy because Dimitri was still a General in Russia.

He was a senior General in the Army, a decorated veteran of the Cold War years, and had been an in-country commander of Soviet ground troops in Afghanistan. He had shown great valor and bravery in that theatre of war and had been rewarded with an important General Command of a major base in Russia, very close to the eastern coast of the Black Sea. He was an influential man in the new Russia.

Josef and Dimitri talked for over an hour about Elena and her untimely demise. Dimitri expressed great remorse that he was not there to honor her memory. Josef explained he held a wake in New York with his and her friends, and Dimitri said he held a funeral service for Elena back in her hometown, even though there was no body to be interred in the ground. Both again expressed anger and frustration that a proper burial could not be had.

Josef wished his brother-in-law well and suggested that perhaps in his powerful position he could secure some time to come to the US and New York, to honor Elena's memory.

"Our countries are no longer at war, Brother, you can come and visit now. Perhaps you can find a way?"

"That is an interesting thought Josef." Dimitri said, "I do have a possible trip I could make to Washington DC, for some military matters with your Pentagon. Perhaps I could also come to New York and make pilgrimage to the 9-11 site. That would be a good thing to honor Elena. I am getting ready to retire and with little family here, maybe I should come just to see if the US is all that everyone says that it is."

"I would like that Dimitri, you would be welcome to stay with me although the apartment is not much. I don't clean like Elena did. God I miss her!" Josef exclaimed and sighed again, "I would like to have you come over."

"I will check my schedule, Brother. I have to meet with your nuclear people about matters that concern both of our countries, so I will see if I can arrange a couple extra days to travel to New York. While I have been to Washington DC, I have never seen New York. I'll see what I can do."

He continued, "Come to think of it, I would also like to see the 9-11 monument that Russia sent to the people of America after this tragedy. I believe it is near your harbor. It is so like you people, you fight and squabble about a tribute and monument to the 3,000 people who died in the terrorist attack, and meanwhile my Russia quietly builds a huge monument to the 9-11 victims. You know we lost people there too! Yes, I would like to see that Russian Memorial, if possible."

"I was not aware of it Dimitri, but I will find it and we will do that together. I look forward to hearing from you about such a trip."

They finished the call. The General said goodbye and went to work. Josef hung up the phone and went to bed.

→ ←

11:30 pm, Upper Eastside

Meredith sat in the Upper Eastside Condo he bought since he couldn't stomach driving to the country anymore. He was staring at the television without really watching it, having finished a delivery pizza and his third scotch. He was stewing about the meetings he had organized with his fellow survivors. Now that he had assembled the group to general anarchy, he had no idea how to proceed.

The TNT television program he had on went to commercial and the announcer promoted a new movie opening in theatres in a week. It was called Troy, starring Brad Pitt. The movie trailer showed Pitt dispatching soldiers left and right with the swing of his mighty sword. It showed the lovely Helen of Troy, and an image of the Trojan horse, the famous horse of Greek mythology.

He stared at the movie images flashing across the screen and then in a moment of clarity sat up as if hit by a thunderbolt. That was it! The Trojan horse was the way to get bin Laden. They would entice the son-of-a-bitch out into the open with a gift that he could not refuse. They would offer him a bomb, or a missile, and then use it on him to blow him to kingdom come.

He sat there staring at the screen not watching the program but letting his mind work through the concept. It worked for the Greeks and it was working for Brad Pitt, so why wouldn't it work for us. He jumped up from the couch and went to his desk and computer. Connecting to the Internet he googled references to the Trojan Wars, the Trojan horse, and Greek mythology. His desk printer began spitting out paper as fast as he could hit the print button. In minutes he knew more about Greek history and mythology than he ever had learned in school. The Internet certainly made it easier to study and research than when he was in school at Oxford.

He even found a reference for a 1962 movie starring Steve Reeves and John Drew Barrymore. He vaguely remembered that Steve Reeves was one of those 60's sandal and sword actors who had made a career out of the public's love for big budget Greek and biblical films that were hitting the theatres every week back then. He decided he would need to rent that film just to make sure he had the story right.

He got up and poured two more fingers of scotch, added a couple cubes of ice, and congratulated himself on coming up with an idea, even if he didn't exactly know what he was going to do yet. But at least now he could suggest something to the group and maybe they could all come up with something even better. He downed the drink and fell into bed. He thought he might sleep for a change but all he did was dream of a big wooden horse parked on a mountain in Pakistan.

→ ←

September 2008, La Guardia Airport

Josef waited at the bottom of the steps near the baggage claim area for his brother-in-law Dimitri to exit the security area. Why they still had stairways at La Guardia always mystified him. Even in Russia they had gotten rid of such problems in the major terminals. Why did New York still have such narrow chokepoints? People struggled down the flights of stairs, dragging luggage, pull carts, and children.

He saw Dimitri start down the steps carefully holding the handrail and noticed that he was aging, as each step was labored. He had a well-cut black suit on and locked like any elderly businessman. With him were two big men who were obviously bodyguards as he was an important General traveling incognito in a former enemy country. They both had on long trench coats although they too looked pretty fashionable.

He thought things must have been improving in Moscow. Josef wondered if they were along for the ride to protect Dimitri or to prevent him from going off the reservation. Either way he expected that they would be attached to his brother-in-law's hip for the duration of the trip.

He waved and his brother-in-law waved back. At the same time the two bodyguards slowly scanned the large baggage area looking for any threats to their man. Seeing no apparent threats, one of them re-focused his attention on Josef, while the other stood back and continued to scan the crowd behind dark glasses.

The General gave Josef a big Russian bear hug and a kiss on both cheeks. He said, "It is good to see you Brother, this is not for the usual European tradition, but the second kiss is for Elena, who should be here too."

"And good to see you Brother. My heart aches that Elena is not here, but we will celebrate her life this weekend in her absence."

Since they were traveling unannounced, the two bodyguards relaxed when all looked safe, and one of them fetched the bags. As the guard bent over, his sport coat rode up and Josef wondered if he had a weapon on him, and then remembered he had just gotten off a plane.

They loaded the car, which was at the curb right outside the baggage claim area. It was parked illegally in the bus and cab lane, but it had a UN plate on it. Josef knew he could get away with such things, in fact a policeman was watching the car for him. When the bodyguards saw the policeman they went back on alert out of habit.

Loading the car, they quickly drove out of the airport. One of the guards in the front seat turned to the General and mouthed the word Consulate, and as if on cue, Dimitri turned and asked. "Josef, I have some papers I have to deliver to the Consulate on Fifth Avenue. Could we go there first, before we do anything else?"

"Yes certainly, that's not a problem. It is close to where we are going. I thought we would have lunch at the Russian Tea Room just to show you we have a bit of Russia in our fair city."

Josef turned towards the city and decided he would take the Brooklyn Bridge above ground rather than the tunnel or the Causeway to the north. This way he could show his brother-in-law the city that had broken both of their hearts.

When they got to the Consulate, the two bodyguards got out and started to walk to the gate, when Dimitri called them back. "Sergei, please see that these papers are given to Colonel Melenkov, the Military Attaché.", He handed him a large envelope. Both men looked mystified but took the folder and walked through the Consulate Gate.

"They are morons Josef, and I wish I could rid myself of them, and all this nonsense. I am tired and I wish I could just retire now. Perhaps one day we will have some of the freedom that you have here. I do long for that day to arrive. Now that you do not have Elena, maybe you and I should plan on retiring together to leave all these things behind, yes?"

The two guards quickly came out and one was twisting about as if he had a back problem. At that moment it occurred to Josef why they had come here first. Now the two bodyguards were armed. While they could not travel on a commercial flight with a weapon, the Consulate had provided them each with a weapon upon arrival to protect their charge. Yes, Josef thought, this would be a difficult visit with these two agents tagging along. But at least, he thought, he too would have bodyguards and be safe in the city for a few days.

→ ←

Wal-Mart, 83rd St. Brooklyn

O and Malik drove the taxi across the bridge to Brooklyn to find a Wal-Mart where they could buy a throwaway phone. As they turned into the big parking lot, they saw a store security car with a yellow light on its roof slowly cruise by and the man inside looked at them. Malik wanted to turn around immediately but his older brother said to relax, that is just their job to look at all people.

They parked the cab away from the building and walked inside separately. Malik thought he looked guilty and that the greeter at the door already had his number. Osama told him to relax. They marched over to the electronics area and started looking at phones. They had used such phones in the cabs to call the dispatcher but had never had a personal phone because they had no one to call other than themselves since their families were no more. Just that thought made Osama tear up and question what he was doing.

As he walked up to the counter he saw that the man behind the counter was of south Asian background himself and that made him relax a bit. Malik on the other hand thought that this man must be a government spy looking for them already. Malik was rather excitable.

"May I help you?" said the clerk in heavily accented English. He smiled and showed a white set of teeth unblemished by American sweets.

"Yes, thank you," Osama answered, "I'm looking for a phone for my brother and I. We can't spend much as we don't have but a few dollars. We have heard that there are pre-paid phone services that can be buyed," he proudly said trying to use his English skills. At the same moment he looked up and saw that a store camera was aimed right at him. He quickly looked away.

"We have such phones but they are of limited use", said the clerk, "because they don't have many minutes on them. I would suggest you try some of these phone plans as they will give you a lot more time and cost less in the long run."

"But we do not wish many time, just a few short minutes," Osama said, and realized that he was saying more than he should have. This was going to be more difficult than he thought. But he recovered quickly and said, "May I buy this one trac phone and have the brochures for some other phones, so I can make study of what my brother and me can afford."

"Certainly, let me ring this up and I'll pull together a number of options for you."

The clerk pulled some brochures out from beneath the counter and sorted them by style and make, and he threw in other pre-paid phone brochure without Osama asking for it. Osama thanked him and he and Malik quickly moved out of camera range.

"Malik, this is going to be hard to do if you look guilty like a terrorist. Let's go before they throw us in jail." And as casual as possible with their hearts pounding they walked out of the store. They again saw the security guy making another sweep of the parking lot. As they got into the cab they also noticed that there were all sorts of parking lot cameras all pointed at them. They were so spooked that they took a different way back to the city.

→ ←

Russian Tea Room, 34th Street

Josef had made his brother-in-law and his two security people very happy on their trip to New York City. He took them to the most traditional Russian place he knew in town, rather than all the shady Russian mob restaurants. They had a great meal of borscht and red cabbage, stone ground bread and some vodka to wash it all down. Everyone looked stuffed now and the two soldiers had finally relaxed, moving over to an adjacent table near the waiter's station. They were not paying any real attention to Josef. There minds were on the waiter and waitress that had served them lunch. Obviously Sergei was gay and he wasn't trying to hide it. The two body men had let their guard down and were enjoying speaking their language to the Russian staff. The fact that they had each consumed a half bottle of vodka didn't hurt either.

Josef and Dimitri talked about all the family back home. Josef had found out his youngest niece had married a foreign banker she had met in Kiev and had moved to Switzerland. Dimitri admitted that the family was for the most part all gone or had disbursed to the far corners of the earth. Only he was left and holding down the honor of the family. And he did so in a very big way as he was the General of a large mysterious military base in eastern Russia on the Black Sea.

As he was also feeling no pain, he leaned over to Josef and whispered. "You know what they have me doing now don't you? I am a babysitter, but my babies are nasty children that cannot be left out of my site."

"What does that mean Bother, you aren't really babysitting, are you?"

The General went on again slurring his words. "These children are so nasty they even scare me, an old man with no one to love," he said as he eyed an older waitress two tables over.

Josef rolled his eyes up and cursed having ordered the full bottle of vodka, and then said, "Brother, what children do you have, this is a surprise to me, Elena never talked about such things. How can a General be bogged down with such responsibility?"

"Josef," he whispered again, "I thought you knew about my job since Afghanistan. They gave me a whole base to manage with thousands of troops, in my old age, but they also saddled me with sitting on their arsenal, do you know what I mean," he slurred. "I have more bombs than I know what to do with. And I have to slowly get rid of them, tit-for-tat, whenever your government decides to get rid of some of theirs. That is why I have come over here; we have agreed to get rid of another thousand nuclear weapons. Your people will come monitor our destruction efforts and we will come and watch theirs. Tit-for-tat," he said as the older waitress walked by again.

Josef sat there, stunned, his brother-in-law was a nuclear weapons guy who babysat the bombs. What a way to end a career. He didn't know what to say but he realized why all three of them drank like they did.

Josef decided that today was not the day to take Dimitri down to the World Trade Center site. He was unsteady and the two bodyguards looked as if they were in no shape to be walking around carrying weapons. He would save the Ground Zero tour for tomorrow and would readily remember to get all the vodka out of the apartment.

➔ ←

Poet's Restaurant, 51 St.

The counseling group assembled in a dark corner of the second floor restaurant in the Theatre District, between Seventh Avenue and Broadway. It was 8:30 pm and those attending the plays on Broadway had long departed. Again, they had this part of the dining room all to themselves.

Meredith had been good to his word and everyone had ordered off the menu. Most had ordered up steaks, as they all knew William Meredith could afford it, and most of them couldn't. So they enjoyed themselves.

While waiting for the food, Ralph suggested they wait to talk until after dinner so the waiters would not stumble into their conversation. But O could not wait and asked if he could ask some questions.

"Malik and I tried to buy some of those paid phones last weekend, and we run into trouble at the Wal-Mart. The security guys look at me, and Malik when we come in store, and the clerk, who was from Pakistan I think tried to sell me expensive phone, and I was looked at by a camera, up in the ceiling. "

He was excited to tell his story and continued. "Malik was very nervous in store, and he did not have that poker face you talked about, I think. So we did buy only one phone. I still have my dollars."

Courtney frowned and spoke up. "This is what I was afraid of. We have to be careful. I think it would be wise not to have Malik and O do this again or we will have the law on our backs in no time. O, don't buy any more phones for now. I will get you some. That way you can stay undercover." She winked at the brothers and smiled so that they knew she was not upset. She was becoming protective of them.

Malik and O looked at one another and seemed pleased that they would not have to try the exercise again.

The others quietly reported that they had indeed purchased some of the phones. Uri showed the group his phone and so did Michael, in fact, they were identical. They each said they had four more at home, all purchased at different places and none of them near their homes or apartments. Both Michael and Uri had even used the phones talking about the group.

Dinner was served and everyone enjoyed the meal quickly, hoping to get on with the discussion. Meredith felt as if everyone had given much thought to the task at hand. He was excited to hear what they had to say, but he thought he might be able to trump them with his idea. But they all needed to have a chance to participate.

Everyone skipped dessert so the discussion could begin. Meredith asked for the bill and a large pot of coffee, and asked the waiter if the group could use the table and corner of the room for a quick meeting. The waiter had cleared most of the dishes and when he saw that he was getting a $200 dollar tip he said no problem and cleared out.

"Well folks, anyone have any bright ideas?" Meredith asked and a couple people raised their hands.

"We should find out where he is by sending some people up there and then when we know we should tell the government and the President. Malik and O both know that country and I think they could find him."

"They could probably get to Pakistan with our help, but they would never get all the way up the mountain without being killed in the process," Courtney said, " My sources tell me that he is squirreled up in some mountain caves and moves around a lot. His people don't even know where he is because they don't trust anyone. It's a good thought Uri but we won't get far."

"I say we just steal some bombs and find a plane that we could hire someone to fly up there and bomb the crap out of him," Michael said, "and I will lead the charge if you need someone to go up there."

Ralph got into it this time, and said, "Michael I'm with you but there are a bunch of mountains up there, hundreds of crossing points, and we don't even know what country bin Laden is in. It could be Afghanistan or Pakistan. Hell, it wouldn't surprise me if he were actually hiding out in Kenya with all those tall Swahili guys. He'd blend in there. We just don't know where he is, and until we do, all the missiles in the world won't get us anything except a lot of blown up rock."

"What we need is some good intelligence that could tell us where he is." Courtney chimed in. "If the government can't find him with all their assets with the CIA, NSA and the boots on the ground, how the hell do we find him? Maybe we could buy the intelligence from someone. Bill, here we go again, spending your money."

"Don't worry about the money, Courtney, that's the least of our problems. After watching the World Trade Center coming down, I'll spend everything I have to get this guy. I know I can't take my money with me. I would love to spend it on something like killing Osama bin Laden. If we can find a way to do this, I'll pay for the entire enchilada without blinking an eye.

The group talked and threw out a number of other ideas, but every one of them presumed they had a good idea of where bin Laden was located. It quickly became clear there were no good ideas coming from the group. After exhausting themselves, Meredith decided it was time to offer his rather novel idea.

"Last week I couldn't sleep, which I'm sure you can all relate to, so I had the TV on to keep me company, but I wasn't really watching it. It was TNT, I think, and a commercial came on for the new Brad Pitt movie, it was called *Troy*."

Before he could say another word, Kate chimed in. "I saw that movie last night. God it was brutal, but what I really went to see was Brad Pitt in leather shorts and bare-chested. That alone was worth all the blood and guts. I know why Jennifer Anniston is such a fan of the guy."

"Thanks for the movie critique Kate, but that wasn't my intention to review the movie." He said this with a laugh. "What I was intrigued with in the movie trailer was the image of the large wooden Trojan horse. Anyone here know its history?"

A few nodded their heads yes; Ralph and Michael both initially looked confused but then it dawned on them what William was talking about.

"Let me explain," Meredith said, "This movie is based on stories from Virgil's epic poem the *Aeniad,* way back in the Bronze Age. Whether it was fact or fiction is still argued, but in the story, the Greeks were at war with Troy and had laid siege on their primary fortress city for ten frustrating years."

Everyone listened closely trying to comprehend what Meredith was getting at. Michael and Ralph had it figured out already but they let him continue.

Meredith continued, "One day the Greek forces that numbered in the thousands just disappeared from the beaches near the fortress of Troy, leaving behind a giant wooden horse that had been built from the keels and wood of several ships."

As Meredith told this story the group looked confused but figured he must have a reason for the story, so they did not interrupt. O and Malik looked thoroughly mystified, as they had no idea what Greek mythology was about. While confused they sat there quietly and tried to understand.

"The leaders of Troy were jubilant they had outlasted the Greeks for ten years. They thought this massive wooden horse must have been left behind as a concession and tribute to the people of Troy. With the attacking Greek army having completely disappeared, the people of Troy were overjoyed with their victory and moved this magnificent trophy of the war inside the walls of their fortress city, and celebrated the victory long into the night."

Meredith stopped talking for a moment. As he looked around the table in the semi-dark corner of the restaurant, he could see that he had their attention. Michael and Ralph were nodding their heads and encouraging the others to listen carefully. Courtney and Kate had figured out where Meredith was going.

Meredith continued, "After all the celebration and revelry was concluded that night, the Trojans retired to their homes and beds to sleep off the drunkenness, leaving the huge horse statue sitting as a victory trophy inside the walls of the city. But inside the hollow belly of this wooden horse were Greek soldiers, kind of like our special forces, silently waiting for the city to go to sleep. Eventually, these warriors climbed down from their hidden perch, overpowered the few guards remaining, and silently opened the gates to the city."

Everyone was listening intently. Some still looked confused as they tried to understand what Meredith was saying. But they remained quiet. So he continued trying to get them to see what he had seen watching the movie.

"Outside those gates, the entire Greek army had silently crept back to the fortress. As they were let in, they attacked the soldiers and residents in their homes and beds. It was a complete massacre and the invaders sacked and completely burned the city of Troy. The city was lost, all because they had trusted the gift of the wooden horse, and brought it within the very walls the Greeks had been unable to penetrate for ten years."

At this point he stopped to look around the table. Osama, Malik, and Uri continued to look confused, but he definitely had their attention. Courtney and Kate were nodding their understanding of the history lesson. Ralph and Michael were broadly smiling and waited for Meredith to continue.

"While this may be a legend in Greek mythology, this story has been told and retold, now even in this current Brad Pitt movie. This story has been past down through the ages as a pivotal war battle. The 'Trojan horse' has come to signify a devious trick that would cause an enemy to let down his guard, to believe all is well and relax enough to invite his foe into his house, or into his protected fortress," Meredith paused for a moment for dramatic effect and finished the sentence with, "or perhaps even into his own mountain cave!"

The table participants were silent. Each person sat there trying to put this Greek war story into perspective, in relation to the insurmountable task they had all agreed to undertake.

Meredith just waited. He would be patient and let them embrace the concept. He admitted he was getting good at this waiting for the right moment to tactically move the group forward.

Then, as if a buzzer had gone off, everyone started talking at the same time. Ralph put out his hands asking everyone to tone it down a notch, noting they were still in a public restaurant, even though only a waiter was wandering about.

Ralph got everyone's attention by asking, "So all we have to do is build a big fucking horse and give it to bin Laden? That should be easy enough. Who wants to hide inside?"

Meredith frowned at his tablemate with a look that silently conveyed, 'what's wrong with you', and then he tried to regain everyone's attention. "Come on Ralph, you know what I mean, if you all think about this

Trojan horse concept, why couldn't we use it for our own advantage, and come up with some way to get bin Laden to let us into his circle. I'm not saying I know how, but if no one else can find the man, including all the governments on earth, why couldn't we see if we could entice him to come to us?"

"I apologize, Bill, I was just being facetious." Ralph offered this and then realized as he looked at the Middle East guys, he had used one of those words they didn't have a clue as to its meaning. He reminded himself that he needed to pay attention to them as well. "I'm sorry guys, what I meant was I was kind of making a joke on the simplicity of the concept." Turning back to William he said," I actually like the concept and as soon as you mentioned the Trojan horse, I saw the possibilities.

Turning to everyone at the table Ralph said, "What I think William is suggesting is that we need to find a way to encourage bin Laden to come to us, or call us. Now how we do that would be the next question."

Courtney jumped into the fray and said, "I get the concept Bill, and you're right, it might be a great way to draw him out from whatever rock he is living under, but the $64,000 question is how do we do that?"

Josef spoke next and said, "This scenario reminds me of a joke I heard from a Jewish friend at the U.N. just last week. Meredith looked frustrated with the interruption, but let him continue.

"A little 1st grader comes home from school and tells her father they learned about Valentines Day at school that day. " Dad, since Valentines Day is a Christian celebration and we're Jewish, will God get mad at me for sending someone a Valentines card?"

Her Father thinks a moment and says, "No, I don't think God would mind at all. Whom do you want to send the card to?"

The little girl smiles and says, "Osama bin Laden!"

Her father looks at her in shock and asks, "Why would you possibly want to send him a Valentine?"

The little girl says, "Well, I thought that if a little American Jewish girl could have enough love to give Osama a Valentine, he might start to think that maybe we are all not so bad, and maybe he would start loving people a bit more. And then if other kids also sent him Valentines he'd love everyone a lot more and come out to be friendly."

He had their attention so he continued, "With her response, the Father's heart swelled, and he looked at his young daughter with great pride. "Young lady, that's a wonderful idea, I am proud of you."

"Yes, Daddy, and when we get him out in the open, our Marines can shoot the mother fucker!"

Everyone laughed, and slapped the table. They also began to see the parallels to the Trojan horse, everyone except Osama Tarkan.

"I am still confused. I don't think we can build such big horse here. People would not like this big thing in even Central Park. But I not understand why we want such a horse, or why he would want such a horse?"

Again everyone laughed, even Malik who seemed to be getting and understanding what everyone was saying.

"O, were not talking about a horse at all. What I mean is that we need to find some way to get bin Laden to want to talk to us. We want him to invite us over to his cave. If we can get him to do that, then we find out where he is, and then we kill the son-of-a-bitch."

Josef had been sitting quietly since his joke contemplating the analogy that William Meredith was trying to make with the Trojan horse, so he again spoke up,

"What I think William is suggesting is we need to offer bin Laden something that he would want. If he wants this something then he will show himself and then we go after him. Once we know where he is we could tell the military or the CIA and they would get him. Is that right William?"

"That is it perfectly Josef. We need to draw him out, make him want to talk with us, and then once we have found him, we come up with a plan to kill him."

Kate jumped into the discussion, "So what does he want from us besides a Valentines card? He only wants to kill all of us, and short of inviting him to do so, I don't think we are going to get his attention."

Michael then jumped in, "Well, let's think about that. He wants to kill all of us and his al Qaeda are hell bent on coming at us again even worse than 9-11. We keep reading about their bombings and terror attempts all over the world. So why don't we go undercover kind of like our CIA does, and plant someone who could make believe they are interested in helping him create more terror? We could offer him something that he wants, like drugs or weapons or maybe, a missile."

The CIA and all the Federal Agencies have all sorts of undercover agents trying to do that all of the time." Ralph offered, "Maybe we could get one of the Agency people to help us out?"

Courtney jumped right in and said, "I can tell you from personal experience at ATF that the FBI and CIA won't even talk to you about what they're doing, so why would they even think about helping a sorry lot like us. We try that and we will all be in jail in a New York minute. No, asking for help from anyone is a mistake. If we do anything, we have to do it ourselves."

William decided to take control of the conversation and asked a question, already knowing the answer he was looking for. "So perhaps what we need is to get bin Laden to think we want to help him. Maybe we offer to become a terrorist cell right here in New York. That could work, but I don't think that it would get him here and I doubt we could go to him without pulling some slight of hand."

Bill Meredith immediately realized he'd lost the Middle East guys with his use of slang. Looking at Uri, Malik and O, he said, "I apologize, what I meant is we probably couldn't get him to believe we're on his side."

"I like Michael's suggestion that we offer him a bomb, or missile. And then shove it down his throat. Maybe we could buy one of those things on the black market." Ralph offered, "How hard can it be to buy that stuff, it's in the newspaper all the time about these military gun runners. Let's find some missiles and sell them to him. Maybe that will draw him out."

William thought he saw a new nugget of an idea, so he suggested, "Well, if we thought that would work, I'll front the money, I don't care what it would cost to buy such a thing. Anyone know anybody that sells this kind of stuff?"

Josef, always the introspective one, quietly said, "I know someone that perhaps could point us in the right direction. My brother-in-law, Elena's brother, is a Russian General and may be able to suggest a name or two."

Everyone looked at Josef. So he went on. "Dimitri has been very hurt by what happened to his sister Elena. He talked about the need for revenge."

Josef cleared his throat and went on. "He fought against bin Laden in Afghanistan many years ago when the Soviet Union was trying to take over the country. He has no love for the asshole. Ironically, at that time the Americans were actually helping Osama bin Laden and the Afghan militants. Because of that Russian war, he hates these terrorists as much as we do." He paused for a moment and looked at Meredith. "Perhaps he could suggest how we get to an arms dealer to see about some weapons. Might that be something of interest?"

William let out a low whistle and said, "Maybe we should all explore our backgrounds a bit better to see if we have any other possible connections we could use. Josef, is your brother, I mean brother-in-law, someone we could trust to get such information from?"

"I know that he would do anything to revenge his sister's death, if that is what you mean. He is tired of war and would like to retire right now. He says he is tired of babysitting Russia's bombs."

"What do you mean by that, babysitting bombs?"

"I should not say, but he is the Commander of a military base that protects all sorts of weapons, missiles and big bombs. He has even told me he sits on thousands of these big bombs. He was just over here a month ago working with the Pentagon on plans to destroy equal numbers of these weapons as part of the non-proliferation treaties the US and Russia has jointly agreed to. The United Nations is encouraging this destruction of weaponry that should never be used to protect the earth from devastation."

William sat there stunned. Everyone agreed a Trojan horse scenario was plausible, and in thinking about a gift to Bin Laden, everyone agreed it would need to be pretty spectacular to get him to show himself. And then he had it. He slammed down his fist on the table and said to everyone, "I think I may have an idea, but I need some time to think it through before we talk about it. How about we call it an evening."

He looked at the bill the waiter had presented an hour before and said, "Whew, you guys, and girls, sure know how to eat. This one will set me back a little, so next week its back to McDonalds. Just kidding, but I do think we should alternate our meeting locations. Anyone have an idea?"

"How about the Broadway Deli, on Seventh Avenue?" Ralph said. "It's just a block up from my office and I eat there all the time. Can't you tell?" He showed his belly profile. "They have the best kosher beef in town. They have a nice quiet back room and if we meet there after 8:00 pm, while all the plays are going on, it will be slow enough to talk. But we will have to finish by 10:00 pm because the theatre crowd comes back after the plays let out."

"Ok, how about the Broadway Deli at 8:00 pm. That means we have to be out of Doc's office by 7:45 pm. Is that ok with everyone?

They all nodded yes and start saying good night. William gently tugged on Josef's arm and asked if he would hang back for a moment. He wanted to talk with him about his brother-in-law the General.

→ ←

Sheraton Towers on Seventh Avenue.

When everyone left, William and Josef crossed Seventh Avenue and turned north up a couple of blocks to the Sheraton Towers. William knew they had a very quiet bar just off the lobby that would allow them to continue their conversation.

The Bar was around the corner from the main entrance of the Hotel on 50th St. It was a small lobby bar enclosed with dark smoky glass to convey the theme. It was an ideal place to not be seen or even noticed. It was the last cigar bar that William knew of in the central city. The City Council was legislating away the right to smoke in public buildings. Postings were already up. William ordered a Glenlivet single malt scotch, knowing they would not have his preferred brand, and Josef asked for a Napoleon Brandy. William asked the waitress to bring over some quality cigars and they both lit up. He noted Josef handled his cigar and cut it expertly when he offered his cutter. William asked Josef if they could talk some more about the Trojan horse.

"If we were to entice bin Laden with something that could draw him out in the open we could perhaps get a bead on him and take him out. That would indeed be a great day," he mused to get Josef on the same page. "Josef, when you mentioned your brother, sorry, brother-in-law, was a high up General in the Russian Army, I had no idea. Does he really have responsibility for all those bombs?"

"He doesn't like to talk about it but yes, over the last few years he has shared his duties with me. I have mostly pieced this together on my own. As you would guess, he doesn't willingly talk about the bombs. But he was just over here for meetings with the Pentagon on the subject of destruction of nuclear weapons."

William took his cigar and dipped the end of it in his scotch, then took a long drag on his cigar and enjoyed the co-mingled taste that the single malt offered. He exhaled quickly. He had learned years ago that he didn't want to inhale the cigar smoke if he wanted to live past 60. It was a foul habit but it also relaxed him, especially when it was matched with scotch. "That's astounding about your brother-in-law, Dimitri, is it?" Josef nodded and sipped his brandy.

William waited a moment to not look too eager, and then continued, "Your revelation has given me an idea. If you will allow me to suggest a scenario, perhaps we could actually make this work."

Josef nodded, but already had an uncomfortable knot in his throat, because he too had connected the dots, and he thought he knew where William was going.

"Josef, how upset was the General when he heard about Elena's death at the hands of terrorists? Has he really had a hard time with this loss of family? I know you have tried to deal with Elena's death, but has he tried to make sense of it?"

"William, Bill, if I may, I think I know where you are going with this. And I think rather than beating around the bush we should just get to the point and ask the tough questions."

"Bill is fine, after these past three years, I feel that you have become one of my dear friends. I have come to know all of these people, including Osama and Uri and Malik, as if they are my brothers, so yes, I would like you to use Bill."

Josef smiled, leaned back in his chair and said. "I too would like that Bill. In the last three years, you and the others have become an important part of my life. You have been the glue that has held it together. It's probably not a good thing to be dwelling on our personal losses, the anger, the hate and the frustration, but I think everyone has helped me through this ultimate trial. I only hope that I have been some comfort to all of you."

"Josef, I could not have said it any better. You too are important to me."

The waitress returned to the table, capped the ashtray now full of cigar ash, and replaced it with a clean receptacle. William asked for two more drinks and she quickly retreated to the service bar on the opposite side of the main bar.

William waited until she departed and then continued. "I also appreciate that perhaps you can see what I am seeing. I am an old man who no longer has a son to cherish. His loss has been devastating, just as much as Elena's loss must be for you. I keep coming up with angry thoughts in my head. These thoughts of revenge just don't go away. So with that said, I will more directly ask a couple of questions. Josef, do you think you could persuade your brother-in-law to join us in our quest for revenge? But before you answer, let me lay out what could be a possible plan of attack on Osama bin Laden."

"Using this Trojan horse concept, we try to obtain a weapon of mass destruction, a WMD I think they call it. I am hoping that we could talk to the General, to help us, and avenge his sister. If we could get such a weapon, we could offer it to bin Laden and al Qaeda. Maybe that would allow us to figure out where he is."

"Bill, that's what I thought you were leading up to and contemplating. While my brother-in-law has been devastated by the loss of his sister, he would never go for such a far-fetched plan. It would be his head to even consider such a thing. He would be in a gulag an hour after they found out what he did. And he would not survive, as he is sick and getting old. No, he would not cooperate, and if I were to ask him he would have to turn us in himself."

"Josef, I understand, but what if we made it worth his while? Does he still have family in Russia?"

"Most of his family is not in Russia anymore," Josef said. "When the USSR collapsed many of the family started migrating to other states and countries. He was in the Army and had to stay. He was a hero of Afghanistan and became a General. The army was his life. So no, he has very little family back in Russia. In fact when he retires he hopes that he can visit all the family that is spread all over the world."

William thought a moment and then suggested. "So why don't we ask him to retire early and I will pay him enough so he can retire anywhere he wants to. If he could get us a bomb, and even make it inoperable until we wanted to use it on bin Laden, I would pay him anything he wanted and help him relocate anywhere, even here if that's what he wanted.

"Dimitri was just in New York and Washington, D.C. last year and I took him to see the Trade Center site." Josef admitted. "That was when I first found out that he actually guarded the bombs at his base back in Russia. He was here to talk with the Pentagon about the destruction of all sorts of nuclear weapons."

Josef thought for a second as if he was remembering the day they had ventured to the deep hole in Lower Manhattan. He then continued, "When he saw the site he was moved by the destruction and realized how Elena must have been crushed by the buildings coming down. He said he wished he could get bin Laden himself."

"I also took him across the river to New Jersey to see the Russian Monument that was given to the people of the United States to commemorate 9-11. Have you seen the monument? It's beautiful and much larger than I thought it would be. It is a huge teardrop hanging in a framework, overlooking the World Trade Center site from the Jersey side. My brother thought it was ironic that we're still squabbling about a fitting monument to 9-11, and the Russians go ahead and build one in just a short time. They even have a wall with every known name of the victims inscribed in granite. The Monument is a gift from the people of Russia to show their solidarity with our tragedy."

"I wasn't even aware it was there! It figures our own government and the press would brush such a thing aside. Probably because it shows that someone is capable of accomplishing something rather than just fighting about a memorial. I'll make a point of visiting the site."

"He loved that his country was a part of the effort to honor the dead, and his sister. He was proud of the fact that the Russians were first to do something for the victims."

Meredith leaned forward and quietly said, "So Josef, why can't we ask him if he would be willing to help us? I would gladly pay him for a bomb. He could help us avenge Elena, use the money to retire anywhere he wanted, and even get out of Russia, all with one bold action."

"I don't think he would look at it that way. If he were to consider such a thing, he would be in prison or killed as soon as they knew a bomb was missing." Josef started shaking his head and took a long sip of his brandy.

"But you said they are dismantling most of these bombs now, with the cooperation and assistance of the U.S., so why couldn't he just keep one of those bombs off the records, sneak it off the base, and let us have it?"

"I think that is much easier to say than to actually make happen."

William continued with his thought. "He could even make it a dud, so we wouldn't actually give a real bomb to bin Laden. Josef, your brother-in-law is the key to the Trojan horse approach of getting bin Laden. If we had that bomb, as our horse, we would be able to find the bastard. Actually, I think he would find us. All the work would be in getting the bomb to him, and then blow the asshole up."

Josef took a couple drags on his cigar and looked out the large window. Traffic was lighter due to the late hour, but there were still people walking up and down the street near the Hotel just off Broadway.

"I understand the concept Bill, I just don't think we could talk him into it. He has too much to lose."

"We all have lost a lot already, our loved ones, families and in his case, his sister, but most of us don't care if we lose because we have to do this to have some peace. We have to try this. This is our best chance to make this happen."

William realized that Josef was actually trying to work out the scenario in his head so he continued. "Didn't you say that you wanted to go home to Russia? How about I fund the trip and you go ask the General if he would help us. If you want, I'll go with you so he knows that we mean business?"

"I did want to go back one last time because Elena was the last tie I had to mother Russia. It would be good to see home again." Josef waved his cigar butt as if flying north. I tell you what, let me think about this some more and figure out how I could ask Dimitri to do such a thing, and then perhaps we could go and see about getting this package."

"Josef, take your time. That is one thing we have, God knows that our government isn't going to beat us to the guy. I'll gladly help you get over there. You could even use my jet if you would like, but I don't think we should fly all the way to Russia. Too many people might take notice of our travel."

"Maybe we could go on vacation to a neighboring country so as not to draw attention, and then drive over the border to see my brother. We should have no problem getting across the border and I have a number of passport entries to Russia with my business travels.

Trying to encourage him to think the visit through Meredith readily agreed. "That sounds like a good idea. Think about it and let me know and I will set it up."

With that they finished their drinks, paid their bill and went home for the evening.

When William got home he fired up the computer and started to type in a search for nuclear, but as he started to type the word 'bomb' he thought better of doing such a search from his home computer and instead typed energy. Once the search engine found the 3,000,000 related items he wandered about for a couple of minutes and then signed off.

He realized that the need for internal security within the group would also have to extend to use of the computer, especially when the Internet was being used, as he was sure that the government agencies were monitoring the Internet for terrorist activity. He kept reading that was how the FBI was catching terrorist cells all over America, and the world. He made a mental note that he needed Courtney to instruct the group on what they should and should not do on the Internet. Maybe he thought she could set up some sort of code that could be used.

He decided that he would buy a number of portable laptops with Internet cards for everyone and that they would use them remotely from different locations just like they had done with the cell phones. He took out his laptop and laid it on the table. He would do his nuclear weapon search from the Starbucks down the street the next morning.

→ ←

McDonald's, a month later.

Most of the group were again gorging themselves on Big Macs and fries. But William noted a few of the members were restraining themselves and had just ordered coffee, like he had. Calories added up.

There was a full Agenda to be covered this evening, so he interrupted the feast. "People, some interesting developments have come up in the last week. Josef and I have been talking and we think we may have a means of getting bin Laden to show his ugly face."

"Remember that Trojan horse story, well we have something better than a horse to drag him out of his cave. Josef's brother-in-law, Elena's brother, is a Russian General and responsible for nuclear weapons storage," William whispered, and then let the sentence hang for a moment.

Before he could continue further Courtney spoke up. "Hold on a minute. Were not going to try and steal a bomb are we? If that's your plan, I just can't go along with that. I'm not in the government anymore but that would go against everything that I have stood for in my former job."

"Courtney," Michael said, "hold your horses, Trojan horses if you will, let's at least hear what he has to say. I kind of saw this coming but I would at least like to hear what he is proposing. I'm a cop just like you, but at least I am willing to listen."

Courtney bowed and apologized for cutting off William. "I just think that we are biting off a bit more than we can chew without getting our ass' in a wringer. As I said before, if we aren't careful we'll all be going to jail just for talking about such stuff. But I do apologize Bill, go ahead."

Uri, Malik and O just looked confused but they had been around this group long enough to keep their mouths shut, they would figure it out eventually. They just listened and tried to understand all the U.S. slang that was being used.

"Courtney I understand your concern, but I truly think this may be the way to get him. It is truly what he wants." William suggested to everyone. "If we can get a bomb, which we'll make safe and inoperable, we can draw that asshole out of his cave, or at least we can find him and go in after him."

"OK, I'll listen, but I am still leery of this whole scenario. This is a lot to comprehend in a few moments."

William noted that everyone was intently listening to him and he had become the leader of this mismatched group of foreign nationals whether he wanted to be or not.

"After talking with Josef last week after our group meeting, I asked him if we could ever talk his brother-in-law, the General, into joining our little band of counter-terrorists. We decided that it was worth a trip to Russia to visit the General to see if he would join us. We leave tomorrow and we will be gone about a week. When we get back, maybe we will have our own little Trojan horse to offer to the enemy."

Everyone looked at Josef who just sat there quietly as he normally did. Then they looked at one another. Malik brought out an article he had printed off the computer that was all about the Greek mythology of the Trojan horse. He passed it around the table and everyone took a look.

That reminded William that he needed to talk with everyone about computer security and how to use the Internet if they were doing any background work for the group. Before the meeting he had asked Courtney and Kate if they could assist. "Courtney and Kate, could you talk to the group a bit about security and the computer?" William asked.

Courtney took a quick sip of her milk shake and said, "We talked about phone use a few weeks ago and I think you all know how important it is that we limit our talk about this subject on the phone, but we also have to be careful when we are using the computer and the Internet."

She hated to always be chastising the team but someone had to raise these subjects.

"Believe me when I say that there are government agencies that monitor the Internet. They are looking for bad guys and terrorists and pedophiles all at the same time."

Kate chimed in and said, "I work with the Internet all day, every day. What I think Courtney is saying is, the government could be looking for messages that suggest bad activity, or searches on the Internet that would suggest someone is planning on doing something bad, or about to do something bad. When Bill came up with the bomb idea, he was about to search the Internet for nuclear bombs, when he remembered that someone would be able to determine that he made that search, and they could trace that back to him if they thought he was a bad guy."

"It's kind of a big-brother thing. People may be watching everything that is on the Internet, and all of our communications. I know that the government and the NSC listen to every phone call made in America, and probably all those overseas," Courtney advised everyone.

"They don't actually have someone listening, but a huge computer records every conversation, every email and probably every text message, and records every computer Google search. The computer program then scans all these conversations and searches looking for certain words that could be a problem. Words like 'murder' 'bomb', 'terror cell', 'jihad', 'poison' and such. They look through millions of messages on the Internet and when words like this, and many more, are found the entire conversation is kept and sent over to a person at NSC who analyzes what is being said."

She went on because everyone was listening intently. "Just about 99% of everything heard is harmless, calls with innocent people talking to one another, and the calls and searches are ignored and destroyed."

Courtney took a sip of water and continued. "But that other fraction of a percentage is analyzed and looked at carefully to see if bad guys are trying to harm someone or blow up a building. This is how many of the terrorists are caught before they can hurt anyone. The government was listening, heard plans being made and sent in teams to get the bad guys before they knew what hit them."

Kate took them the next step by saying, "So what we are asking you is to be very careful in anything you say when on the phone or using the computer. In fact it would be better if you never used the phone and computer at all, but I think we all know that is impossible."

William jumped in at this point. "So we want you to limit your conversations only within this group. You must never tell anyone about our plans." He looked directly at O and Malik again and then continued, "Anyone can prevent us from succeeding to get Osama bin Laden if we let them know what we are doing. Thus you cannot talk with anyone outside this group unless you talk to me or Courtney first."

Courtney offered some additional comments, "You also shouldn't use the computers for anything directly related to our plan. If you need to do some research you will have to use a public computer in a library or in an Internet coffee shop where you can rent a machine. Just be extremely careful not to do it from your home, or from your own computer, or phone."

"I know that you will have times when you have to use the computer and the Internet. When we finish I'd like to have you all come back to my Condo. I went out and bought each of you a small laptop and loaded them up with Internet service cards. Kate here will help you all learn how to use these units and then only when you have to, from neutral sites like public buildings and Starbucks and such."

"So what are we going to call ourselves when we do all this talking in code?" Uri asked. "I am confused already."

"Uri, that's a good question," Kate said, "I have been thinking about that and it's something that we should talk about because we can't start blurting out our intentions without drawing great attention."

William spoke up, "Kate your right about needing a name and some code language. I have some thoughts, but what do you suggest?"

Well, as you know my job is to create graphic design and artwork." Kate said, "Once you have a project concept the next step is to visualize it so you can tie everything together graphically. Using that approach I think we should work with the Trojan horse concept. I would normally design a logo based on the concept, but I don't think that is what we need at the moment."

"Kate I agree, William stated, "What we need is a coded name that will tell us we are talking with our inner circle. We must never use our names when we do talk to one another on the phone, Internet, or in emails. I was thinking we should call ourselves THCT."

Everyone sat there quietly and mulled that over for a moment and then Malik said, "What is a THC, I don't know this?"

William turned over a piece of paper that he had taken out of a folder and on the paper was a photo image of the Trojan horse and the words 'Trojan Horse Counter Terrorists' - THCT.

"If we were to use this as a name for our little group, we could talk to one another and always know who the other person was, without ever having to identify ourselves. All of our messages would have this as an authenticator so we know who is on the line."

Ralph spoke up and said, "I like it, it carries the theme without giving the horse concept away, and its simple enough they will have trouble trying to figure it out. But we also need to have a code –authenticator that changes each week, so we know it is us talking to one another."

Courtney continued. "Actually, it is a innocent sounding series of letters that won't draw any great attention like the al Qaeda terrorist cell names 'American Jihad' and "Death to America' do. This will keep everyone guessing as to what it may mean. The secret will be to make sure we never make a reference to the actual Trojan horse. We will just all know that is our objective. Actually this will keep the NSA busy trying to figure out what THCT actually means. My guess is that they won't put it into their greater scrutiny files until they make a terror connection. They will just think it is some lettering of no importance. All we have to do is keep all correspondence and messages very simple."

Michael spoke up for the first time. He was usually always in the thick of things. "I like it too and I like the fact that we will be able to trick bin Laden into showing himself. But that's where I see all sorts of problems. How will we contact him?"

"Were not sure how all that gets worked out yet," William offered, "But we are working on it. If we can get a bomb and then get some sort of message to al Qaeda, I think we will hear from him or his people. But first, we have to get the bomb. That's' is why Josef and I are planning to fly to the Ukraine, adjacent to Russia next month."

"So let's all head over to Bill's Condo on 74th and Second Ave." Kate suggested. We should all go in a couple of cars. William said we should park in his garage and use the freight elevator to get up to the Penthouse, so we don't draw so much attention. The class starts in an hour. I always wanted to see how the rich live."

With that the group broke up, some going out the front of the McDonalds and some cutting through the building to exit on the next street to the south. William watched and noted that while they were a rag tag group, in a way they were becoming soldiers in a most holy war. They were committed to a cause. He too hustled out and waved for a cab. He needed to be home before they got there just so that slacker working in the garage beneath the building would allow them all to park for a couple of hours.

→ ←

April 2008, Over the Atlantic Ocean

Josef sat in the left captain chair facing the rear of the plane and William, with a small table between them. They had finished an early breakfast after an overnight flight from Teterboro and were both nursing coffees. They were discussing how they would approach the General.

"Bill, I think I should go alone and spend some time with him to get him in a good frame of mind. I think if I can get him thinking of his sister again, maybe he would again say how much he would like to kill bin Laden like he said at Ground Zero. Then perhaps I could ask him and tell him about our group."

"Well, that makes sense and I'll gladly stay out of the picture until you think I'm needed", Bill stated, "But at some point he will want to know if your serious, so at that point I think you should introduce me. And it might be a good idea that the meeting site be somewhat neutral away from the army base. Is there any place that he could take you that might be a neutral site?"

"Yes there is, now that you mention it. Last time we talked about Elena, he said that there was a small memorial in town for her remembrance. Even the Russians were shocked with the horrific terrorist attack. You know they have also had their fair share of terror attacks in Russia."

"Maybe you could ask him to take you there on a morning excursion after you broach the subject. Then I could meet you there and we could show him we mean business and have the money to make him safe after he gets a bomb smuggled out."

"That's OK with me if he doesn't throw me off the base right away." Josef said as he looked out the window at the approaching coast of Ireland. It truly is the emerald isle he thought.

Josef, one more thing, you will think I am too security conscious, but when you talk with him, you should not be in his house. It may be bugged, especially since there are such sensitive things on the base. I think you should talk outside away from the house, or when you are walking. Once you broach the subject, he will probably want to talk outside as well. He too has a lot to lose if someone is listening."

Ryan Younger, the pilot of the Bombardier Global Express came on the intercom and announced that they were just leaving Ireland's airspace and would be crossing over the English Channel shortly. He said they would be landing in the Ukraine in a few hours.

→ ←

Novorossiysk, Russia

It was a great homecoming. The General welcomed his brother-in-law with open arms, bear hugs and a sharp slap on the back in the Russian way. The General drove him throughout Gelendzhik, a town south of Novorossiysk, famous for its seaside resorts and its beautiful circular deep-water port on the eastern coast of the Black Sea. He pointed out that the Winter Olympics were even coming to Sochi in 2014, just down the Black Sea coast about 70 miles.

This area had a rich history with the czars and the commissars who had their dachas on the Black Sea and in the forested mountains above. It was also wine country because of the temperate climate and the mountainous region. The General showed him the entire area and how much life had improved in Russia. The farms and fields looked healthy, with newer farm equipment working those fields, and the local peasants looked as if they were eating well and prospering. Much had improved since the cold war ended. Josef realized that he should have come back more often, and brought Elena to have seen such vast improvements.

The General showed him the entire area and they visited the surrounding towns for some wonderful Russian meals and a sampling of the local Dyurso wines, and the vodka.

After the long sightseeing trip and such good meals, Josef was tired, but he wanted to broach the real subject of his visit. As they sat on the front porch of the General's very comfortable home on the military base, they sipped vodka and smoked cigars as they watched the sunset. Josef realized it was the perfect time to talk. But as he was about to start, not quite knowing what he would say, his brother-in-law asked him a leading question.

"So Josef, you tell me you come to visit and see your homeland, but I cannot locate you on any airplane manifests. I wanted to pick you up as you did when I came to New York. I was unsure how you got here, until you called from the hotel in town. And then I found out with a little checking that you flew over here in a private jet aircraft, and crossed the border from the Ukraine by car, with another man. Yet no one but you shows up, and this other man sits in the hotel in town under what I think is a false name. What is with all this intrigue?"

Josef sat there stunned that the General could lay out the whole itinerary that had brought him here. He didn't know what to say and felt that he was already compromised. As he sat there staring at his cigar he tried to control his first instinct to just get up and leave. As he thought more about the General's comments he felt that it actually might give him an opening to start the conversation.

"Dimitri, you have very good sources as I should have expected you would have as General of this large military base. You're right; I did come with a friend who was kind enough to help me make this visit. He did not think you would want to meet with someone else, so he has stayed at the hotel for a few days."

The General arched his considerably bushy eyebrows and thought perhaps his brother-in-law was actually a gay man who had taken on a new lover. The thought immensely troubled him, but he knew how much Josef had loved Elena so he dismissed the thought as silly. Yet he was troubled by this turn of events.

"So he is a friend with a big jet plane that has traveled with you to the Ukraine and Russia, that is fine, but why, is my question?"

"That is a difficult question to answer my brother, but I will try to explain. Perhaps we could take a walk and smoke one of those cigars. You can show me more of this huge base. I have never seen such a large facility in Russia."

The General understood the code words and started to rise. He reached for their coats to ward off the evening chill, and started down the steps walking towards his black military-issued sedan parked at the curb. The General signaled his driver that he would drive himself and sent the young soldier on a well-deserved break. They climbed in and the first thing the General did was turn on the radio announcing that they now had many stations they could listen to. Josef saw that he was signaling to remain quiet.

They drove around the perimeter of the base, which was more than six square miles around. The General acted as a tour guide showing him the more public areas of the encampment. As they drove Josef noted that the base was set up much like what he thought prisons must be like. There were outer perimeter fences, three sets at least 20 feet high, topped with tight spools of concertina razor wire. Each fence was spaced about thirty feet apart with crushed stone perimeter roads on the inside. Between one set of fences there was a field of sand raked smoothly so that any footprint or traffic could be noted. From the exterior fence line there were clear-cut fields for at least 1,00 feet in every direction.

Along these fence lines, at 1,000-foot intervals there were guard towers with clear views over all three fences. Josef noted that it was formidable barrier for anyone trying to get in or out. It was indeed like a movie prison.

Josef felt that Dimitri might be trying to tell him something, but dismissed the thought and asked if they could stop and get out when they came to the large parade grounds at the rear of the encampment. The General was already pulling over by the time he asked. He parked at the edge of this massive parade ground area, stepped out and started walking into the field.

The General pointed out a number of buildings and monuments and acted as if he were a tour guide. They continued walking towards the middle of the parade grounds and finally the General turned to Josef and asked a simple question.

"Josef, it is wonderful to see you and return the hospitality you showed me when I was in New York, but I know you have come here for a reason, perhaps to ask me something. Thus, we stand here away from prying eyes and sensitive ears. What is it my brother? What do you need from me? What does your friend need?"

Josef again was shocked! He realized he needed to close his mouth. Were his actions that obvious to his brother? As he thought, he was reminded that his brother was a General in the Russian Command. Certainly he would have the ability to read people and see that they have something in mind. And he wondered if he could dare ask the question he had come all this way to ask. It was an audacious request with mind-boggling ramifications.

He decided he had come this far with the conviction he would avenge his wife because no one else would do so, so he would ask. But how should he do it? Should he just ask him? "Can I borrow a bomb to kill bin Laden?" He just didn't know what he should say.

"Dimitri," he finally said, "I do come with a mission in mind, and yes the man who came with me is also on this mission. He too lost a loved one in the 9-11 terrorist attack. He lost his son who was just starting a Wall St. career. In fact it was his first day of work when the planes crashed into the buildings. His name is William Meredith and he is like us in that he lost a loved one, just as we have lost Elena."

With that Josef steeled himself to tell the whole story, as if that might make sense of his formidable question he was about to ask.

"I don't know how to explain what we have in mind, but perhaps I should start at the beginning to tell you why we have come here."

"The beginning is always a good place to start, Brother. I am listening."

With that opening Josef told the General the entire story about the tragic day on 9-11, the anger and frustration in the days following the tragedy, and the eventual three years of almost weekly grief counseling in small groups.

It was at this point that he explained that the majority of the people in his group were naturalized or foreign-born citizens. The caregivers had theorized similar people would be better able to help one another and deal with cultural differences. He explained that over time this diverse group had banded together, as if brothers and sisters, all trying to help one another deal with the utter sense of loss they felt for their loved ones. He said they became friends in grief they also commiserated with one another about their anger and frustration for al Qaeda and Osama bin Laden.

At that point the General said, "I understand and even agree with your considerable efforts to secure some closure, but how could I be of service other than to grieve with you?" As he said it he had an ugly feeling about what it was that Josef had come to ask.

Josef laid out the rest of his story. He said that the frustrations of the group drove them to talk about getting bin Laden themselves. He explained that they had money and felt that they could do at least as good a job as the U.S. government had thus far done, which was mostly nothing, wasting their assets chasing other tyrants rather than focusing on bin Laden and al Qaeda. The General listened and then slowly began to realize why Josef was there and what he had come for.

When Josef was finally done the General sighed, took his old arthritic fingers and passed them through his grey hair. He pulled his coat tighter around his considerable girth, looked at his brother-in-law and said,

"So what do you want from me? Do you want me to give you a gun, a missile, or perhaps a bomb? Is that why you have come thousands of miles to see your brother-in-law?" He let the question float in the cool, moist air of the parade grounds for a moment, and then sarcastically said, "Let me check in the trunk and see what I have available." He waived his hand across the large parade field grounds and asked, "Or do you have a trailer hitch? Because if you do, we can hook up an old ballistic missile I have behind my quarters. You could take it with you." With that he laughed so loud that a group of soldiers jogging in formation a hundred yards away all looked over to see what could be so funny. Seeing the General, they averted their gaze and jogged on.

Josef waited until the squad of soldiers had passed. He steeled himself, looked the General grimly in the eye and quietly said, "No brother, I don't want a missile, we want a bomb, perhaps a small nuclear bomb, I think they call them suitcase bombs in the U.S."

He let that sink in for a moment and then continued. "I know what you are going to say, but you can make it inoperable, in fact, we want you to do that because we don't want to actually give bin Laden a real bomb. "

"Give him the bomb?" he said incredulously. Now his mouth was hanging open. "You are all out of your minds."

"We just want it for bait to get him to crawl out from whatever rock he is hiding under. If we make him an offer of a bomb, something that he wants dearly, maybe he will show himself and then we will kill him."

Dimitri threw his arms in the air, and then around his brother-in-law's shoulders. He steered him towards the road where the car was parked a few hundred yards away. As they walked on he said, "Josef, I am literally shocked that you are talking this way. This is unbelievable; it is inconceivable what you are saying. You know that America has been looking under every rock already." He stopped walking short of the roadway, and turned to Josef.

"For that matter, so have we, and if we found him I think we would share that information with the U.S., so why on earth would you think that a bunch of amateurs like yourself could find him, and then would have the means to actually kill him?"

"Brother you know the story of the Trojan Horse don't you, in Greek mythology?"

"Yes, the Greek and Trojan wars are taught in the military classes. What of it?"

Josef stopped walking and pulled out a frayed Classics Illustrated comic book copy of 'Helen of Troy', the Trojan horse story from his coat pocket. He handed it over to the General.

"We will do the same thing, entice him to let down his guard with this bomb, just like the Greeks enticed the people of Troy into bringing the Trojan horse into the walls of Troy."

"So now were building a large wooden horse? And reading comic books? Brother you have gone mad."

"We will try to sell the bomb to bin Laden, and if need be take it to him directly through the underground. And we will insist that we take it personally to him, and him alone."

"You are issuing your own death warrant. This is a comic book for God's sake! Josef, I'm pretty sure you have lost your mind." He hit him over the head with the rolled up paper.

"Do you think bin Laden would just invite you into his house, or even his cave in Pakistan, just like an old friend? I think not. They will kill all of you and take the bomb from you and blow up New York or Moscow. And then what would we have done?"

"That is why we need a smart bomb, that will be of interest to him, and can also be 'safed', I think that is what they say. We need a bomb that we can make safe and that cannot be tampered with until we give them the codes. We would deliver the basic bomb but not the codes."

The General just kept shaking his head and walking towards the car.

"Why would he believe you, if you had such a weapon?"

"We would prove to him that we have the weapon. We would tell him we obtained it on the black market. He would see actual photos of the bomb and its inner workings. His people would understand what they are looking at."

"And then he just says yes, give me the bomb?"

"That would not be believable. We would demand a huge ransom so that they think they are truly getting a black market weapon being offered to the highest bidder. We will say we are willing to sell the weapon for $2,000,000 Euros. And the codes would be delivered after payment is completed. And then we explode the bomb and kill the son-of-a-bitch."

As they arrived at the car, the General motioned for Josef to stop talking. He made eye contact and held up his finger to his mouth. Josef understood and the discussion stopped. Josef decided that if they were being monitored, utter silence was just as telling so he started a completely new conversation.

"Brother, it has been good to see you and I know that Elena would have liked to be here with us. Please know that she loved you dearly and wished she could have see you more often."

The General looked over to his brother and said, "Josef, she was a good woman and you are lucky to have been married to her. I know that you still love her beyond all reason, just as I do. Let me think about when we might be able to visit again."

With that Josef nodded and reached over and patted his brother's hand. He thought that the General's words were a good omen that perhaps he was considering the proposal that had been asked of him. Time would tell whether he got through to Dimitri, he thought, time will tell. With that, they drove to the house and then the General took Josef back to the hotel in town.

→ ←

Borosjkav Restaurant, Gelendzhik

Meredith was waiting for his thick toast to pop from the ten piece commercial toaster when Josef walked in and sat down. He ordered coffee and then came over to the breakfast buffet to see if he could find something that would settle his stomach. He had not slept the whole night, wondering what his brother-in-law must be thinking after their discussion on the parade grounds.

"Good Morning Josef, I trust you had a good night sleeping in these coverlet beds. I was so hot that I had to sleep on top of the quilt." He waved his hand over the breakfast buffet and said, "The herring is especially good this morning, and I can't get enough of the caviar, even if it is breakfast."

Josef just rolled his eyes. He reached for two hard- boiled eggs and two pieces of course Russian bread. He silently walked back to the table in the corner of the room. He was slavering on the butter and preserves when William returned.

"I had a good time reminiscing with my brother-in-law last evening. I guess we shouldn't be surprised, but he is aware of you and that we are traveling together. Russia is still a society that has eyes and ears everywhere." He put the knife up to his lips to suggest silence. "We will need to take a long walk after breakfast to work off this meal. I see that you are enjoying the caviar again."

William took the signal and kept the conversation light, on the level of a tourist visiting his first Russian town. He explained that he had wandered the small village they were staying in the prior afternoon visiting the sights and the Russian Orthodox Church at the center of the town.

Josef decided the eggs and bread, had settled his stomach enough that he too would try some Russian caviar as a treat, noting that it would have cost an arm and a leg in New York. They both enjoyed their coffee and breakfast.

Afterwards they turned in their room keys at the desk and headed out the door to stroll into the center of town. In the cool morning air flowing down from the adjacent mountains, they found an isolated bench near a fountain making enough noise to drown out their conversation.

"I called New York last night just to report we are here. I kept it short and sweet and signed off THCT. They didn't respond." He splashed some water from the fountain and stared at the distant mountain. "So does your brother-in-law think we are certifiable? I can tell from your looks this morning that you broached the subject of our little mission."

"Oh, I think he thinks we are nuts, crazed and certifiable. I think that too. But at the end of the evening he gave me a signal that perhaps he was willing to think about the concept. Hell, I even gave him my comic book about the Trojan horse. Maybe he read it last night."

"That was probably a mistake. He won't take us seriously looking at a comic book."

"Perhaps it was. Sometimes I feel the same way. I don't think he will throw us in jail or anything like that, but I doubt he will assist us in any way. I just don't know."

"So where does that leave us? Should we stick around or maybe pack it in and see if we can buy something on the black market?"

"I would say we should wait a day or so and see if he comes back to us. By the way, he knew that you were with me, that we had traveled together, and had a question to ask of him. I think he actually put it all together before I laid out the plan for him."

"How did he know about me? That's why we flew into Odessa in the Ukraine, and drove across the minor border checkpoint. I figured it would draw less attention."

"I guess that knowing I was coming he assumed I would fly into Novorossiysk and then need a ride from the airport. Well, I wasn't on any plane manifest, so he must have started to look elsewhere and then saw my name crossing the border by land, with you. He probably thought I had turned gay and you were my new partner. Anyway, he knew you were back at the hotel, so, so much for security. "

"Maybe we are in way over our heads?" William offered. "Well it's too late to panic now."

At that moment a black sedan pulled up next to the fountain with a young soldier driving. A middle-aged officer got out of the car and approached the two men. He snapped off a salute.

"Gentlemen, good morning, I am Sergeant Major Shostakovich, Aide to General Gralashov. The General would like to meet with you both at his dacha. He wonders if you might like to do some Russian fishing?"

Both William and Josef looked at one another, back to the Sergeant, and Josef said, "We don't have any fishing gear. Will this do?"

The Sergeant nodded and said. "The General will provide all provisions. Shall we?"

He walked back to the car and opened the back door for his guests. Both men again looked at one another, slowly got up, and silently entered the vehicle. Perhaps they had their answer.

→ ←

The Forest above Gelendzhik

Driving along a well-kept two-lane asphalt highway, they looked out over vistas of farmland and forests, and snaked their way up the hills. They traveled about 25 miles without a word being spoken by themselves or the Sergeant and driver.

They turned off the highway on a crushed rock road that wound through a conifer forest and proceeded another two miles to a small home in a forest clearing, overlooking a rather large lake. This was the General's dacha, a residence hidden in the forest for the proletariat and the movers and shakers of Russia.

Waiting on the front porch was the General, dressed casually in a plaid shirt and fishing vest, along with a floppy hat with fishing lures stuck in the brim. He waved.

"Brother Josef, welcome to my home. Please introduce your friend,.... as I have not yet had the pleasure of meeting Mr. Meredith."

Both Meredith and Josef looked at one another and tentatively advanced to the porch. Josef hugged his brother in the traditional manner and then turned to introduce his companion.

"General Dimitri Gralashov, I would like to introduce Mr. William Meredith from New York. He is an associate of mine."

The General reached out a large hand and shook with strength and a show of friendliness. He then turned to his driver and Sergeant who stood at attention near the car and yelled, "Sergeant, thank you, you are dismissed for the afternoon. We have some fish that want to jump into our boat! Please return at 8:00 pm to retrieve my guests."

With that the Sergeant and driver jumped in the vehicle and left the same way they had arrived. The General turned and led the way into the house. In the small parlor he stood before them and pointed out the window at the lake a hundred meters away.

"Gentlemen, I know that you have already had breakfast, so I think we'll pack some lunch and do some fishing. The temperature is right and they should be biting." He seemed to say this more to the walls, more than to his two guests. "I look forward to spending the day with you two and showing you some real Russian hospitality. Let's see if we can catch our dinner. I'll cook them myself on an open wood fire. Josef, I know that you will enjoy some good Russian fish. It's been years I think."

With that he placed a finger on his mouth in the universal sign for silence and waived them towards a side room, "I have some fishing gear for you in the bedroom, choose what you want, it may be a bit cold until the sun gets higher. Then join me in the kitchen. I'll prepare us some lunch. Have you had any Russian herring while you have been here? It's very good. And how about some caviar?"

Josef and William exchanged a knowing glance and advised that the herring and caviar sounded fine. They went into the bedroom to find casual slacks and thick plaid shirts that would come in handy on a windy lake. Both kept looking at one another not saying anything. But they were uncertain about their immediate futures.

➔ ←

Newark, New Jersey

Uri sat in his son's apartment in Hoboken overlooking the Hudson River. He had taken responsibility for the large apartment after his son's death when the Twin Towers had crashed to the ground. He stared at the phones that he had in his hand. He had four of them, each purchased at a different store just as William and Courtney had suggested. He'd activated them at the time of purchase for cash, again not using any credit cards. He had even pre-screened the purchase points to make sure there were no cameras taking his picture. Each phone had ten minutes already built into the memory.

He sat there debating if he should use one of the phones to acknowledge he was coming to Dr. Hensley's weekly session, and then the group's meeting afterwards. He thought about that and decided if he mentioned the counseling sessions he would compromise the whole group if someone were actually monitoring the call, as Courtney had said the government could readily do. He was unsure how he would use these phones that would not be compromising.

He picked up the cheap Trac phone and dialed Michael's new Trac cell phone number, the one he had just obtained for his similar throwaway phone. He left a message very simple and said.

"This is U. I'll be there for the two meetings. THCT." He ended the connection, hung up, and thought what a waste to now throw away the phone. He decided he would keep it for a few more short messages or calls, and then he would take a hammer to the cell phone and deposit pieces of it in the throughout Manhattan.

Uri got up, looked over at Ari's photo that showed the whole Windows to the World Restaurant staff standing in front of the Manhattan skyline, and walked out the door and down the hallway. He had a new job in

Manhattan at another restaurant. This one was on the ground floor. He had decided that he wasn't going to work in any high-rise buildings anymore.

→ ←

Lake Dyurso

The General had perfected his casting and was able to hit a specific spot with regularity. He had already caught a number of keepers, two walleye pike and a bony Northern that had a vicious set of teeth. He was using a variety of plugs depending on the vegetation level that he was casting in. He used surface baits that he could retrieve quickly working them across the surface when the vegetation was thick. He would use deeper water plugs that would dance and twirl when the water allowed for it. He had caught fish in both deep water and the congested vegetation areas. He looked like he had been in this element all his life.

The other two showed that they were fishing novices and after a number of poorly executed casting efforts which had created danger for everyone in the boat, they had settled for some straight poles, with simple bobber action. They were using large night crawlers and the fish seemed interested. The fluorescent bobbers were dancing enough that they had to pay attention.

An hour later it was time for some lunch, just as the General had promised. In a metal container that passed for a cooler, the General pulled out some jars of creamed herring and caviar, fresh bread and some wafers that did not look store bought. The creamed herring was very good. Heaped on the crackers, it was a complete meal all by itself, in the middle of the lake. This simple meal, plus some Russian beer made for a solid lunch while the fishing continued.

But then the General stopped talking about fishing, he lowered his voice as he looked about the lake, and then started a conversation carefully by saying, "Mr. Meredith, first let me offer my condolences to you on the tragic loss of your son. He seemed like he was a good boy and would have made you proud. We have all lost loved ones with this Trade Center devastation. In that we are comrades in arms."

Meredith having looked up from his earthworm when the General spoke, realized that the General had great empathy for his loss, but he was again dumbstruck that this new fishing buddy already knew so much about him. That was an important thing to remember especially if this crazy plan was to proceed forward. If he could access that type of information so quickly, so could the bad guys.

The General continued as he cast his line again, "I understand you have more money than God, and that you have convinced my Brother here that he should try to help you spend a little of it over here in Russia?"

Meredith looked at Josef and thought carefully about how he would respond. "General, as you have said, Josef and I are somewhat comrades in arms, but we are so, because of our personal tragedies. No one should lose a loved one in the manner they were taken from us."

The General bowed his head in agreement, so Meredith continued. "I also offer you my sincerest condolences for your sister, no one should die as an innocent bystander just doing a job. From what Josef has told me over the last three years, Elena was an extraordinary woman, and I am sorry that I did not get to meet her."

Casting his line, the General slowly reeled it in and with a wave of his hand he encouraged the two men to continue to mind their poles and bobbers.

"While we are talking, I ask that you make an attempt to look as if you are fishermen. You can never tell who may be watching us from shore. While you don't see them there is a security team out there assigned to protect me, and I think also to keep an eye on me. Some things have not changed here, thus we will talk while we fish. I hope I won't be the only one catching our dinner."

With that Josef lowered his pole and bobber back into the water and said, "Dimitri, we thank you for the opportunity to fish with you, but as you know we are on a specific mission, and we have to move forward with or without your help."

Having reeled in his lure, he raised the rod and cast again, hitting the same exact spot as before. He let the lure settle in the water a bit and then started slowly retrieving it.

"Josef, I did not bring you out here in the middle of this lake to teach you how to fish, although some lessons would certainly be in order. No, we will leave that for another time, perhaps when I am retired and living in the northern woods of Wisconsin, which I hear is as remote as we are here."

Meredith wondered what he was saying, and decided he would try to clarify the situation, " General, retirement is a wonderful thing and if you have a passion like I think you have for fishing, Wisconsin would be an ideal place to retire and get lost in the woods. I've been there myself."

"That is what I have heard. I am told that it is God's country. It must be a good place, no?"

Meredith decided to play out the conversation to see where it might go. "Yes Sir, it is that kind of place. For years I went on an annual fishing trip with a bunch of guys to Northern Canada to do some real fishing, and then one year for no particular reason, we switched to Northern Wisconsin. I think some of the guys couldn't string enough days together to make the Canadian trip."

He cast his line, or tried to, and continued. "It was the best trip we ever went on and we caught more fish than ever before. We were on one lake, Lac Vieux Desert, which is right on the Wisconsin – Upper Michigan border, with half the lake in each state."

"Yes, William I would like that someday. Now that I am alone, I have little to hold me here except for this frustrating job. And as you saw at the base Josef, sometimes it feels more like a prison then a major military base that I am responsible for. So let's talk about your plan, there is a plan, No?"

Josef looked to Meredith and waved his hand to let him have the floor, "William, you should talk about this because I am very busy fishing." Just then his fluorescent bobber went down below the surface and Josef yanked the pole up to set the hook. A second later he could tell he had something on the line as it continued to bend the pole. He lifted his pole and saw that he had a nice little keeper on the end of the line. He hauled it up and into the boat in one easy motion.

"Ah, we have a fisherman after all. You have a nice Russian crappie that looks like it could start a meal. But we will need many more. You fish while William and I talk."

The General reached out with his callused hand and cleanly grabbed the fish holding down the sharp fins. He reached up and gently wiggled the hook out of the fish's mouth and then held up the hook with the worm still on it. He smiled and said, "The fish paid the ultimate price and he is still hungry."

Meredith decided that comment was perhaps a perfect opening and quietly said, "General, that is what we want to do with bin Laden, we want to hook him and not give him the satisfaction of a meal, if you know what I mean. But we need your help to bait the hook. And Josef tells me that you have the right kind of bait right here on your base."

The General hooked the crappie on the fish line that also held the walleyes and the northern, by feeding a closed hook though his gills. The line was attached to the boat and thrown overboard where the fish would stay fresh and perhaps alive a bit longer.

"So William, you do not beat around the bush, do you? I like that, but for what you ask I could throw you in prison here in Russia and throw away the key. Or I could turn you over to your FBI and they would put you in a prison over there and throw away the key. Either way you are like the fish, caught on a hook."

Meredith just stared at the General not sure what he could say, contemplating that perhaps he was going to jail. But he continued anyway, like a fish nibbling at bait.

"General, we have both lost loved ones to a madman, who now hides from the world in a cave, in a third world country out of our reach for any kind of revenge. I cannot go about my life and go fishing when this man breathes, while my son, and your sister doesn't. If I can go after him and get him, you can do anything you want with me. I just want to put that bastard away once and for all."

The General softened his tone and continued, " I too would like to see the bastard dead. I fought against him in Afghanistan long before you Americans knew him to be a terrorist. He and his followers killed many of my men and he has been a thorn in the side of the civilized world for over 20 years."

The General continued casting with almost mechanical precision.

"I know why you are here, and my heart says that I should help you, but my position says that I must not. I would be thrown into a gulag for the rest of my years, if not killed outright for doing what you suggest. Yet, I understand your quest, I too would like to exact revenge for my sister and the many men that have fallen to this twisted man."

Josef dropped his line over the side and watched the bobber drift out about ten feet from the boat. He cleared his throat and in a quiet voice said to his brother-in-law,

"Dimitri, we are only asking that you give us a chance to flush out this terrorist, with one of your small nuclear weapons, one that you could make harmless, so that it could never actually be used against anyone else. But we need a real weapon to get him to take the bait. We have assembled our own little band of counter-terrorists who are crazy enough to actually pull this off, if we have a way of getting to him. And one of your suitcase bombs would be the way and the bait," he said as he held up a hooked earthworm squirming on a hook.

Meredith threw his bobber and line in the water to keep the façade of fishing going, and quickly added, "General, we know that giving us such a bomb, even if it was neutralized, would be the end of your career, perhaps even your life, thus I am prepared to help you disappear completely off the face of the earth, even to Wisconsin if you like. I can make those kind of arrangements, get you a new identity, and fly you anywhere you want to go."

"I am aware of your jet aircraft across the border, and as such, I am sure that others are aware as well. Thus, I don't think that we will pack our bags just yet, and take a holiday in God's country. No, this will take some considerable planning."

Meredith and Josef looked at one another and marveled that they had accomplished their goal, in the middle of a lake, in the southern forests of Russia. Just then Meredith's bobber went under water and he too had a bite. Now they were all fishermen, in agreement that there was a bigger fish to catch.

The General helped him land his first crappie. He placed a hand on top of William's and said, "We will avenge our sons and sisters my friend, just give me some time to think how we can do this. And perhaps later on when I lose my job here as Commandant, perhaps there is a lake in Wisconsin where we can fish together."

With that, the General turned to the water and cast his line again. He was silent as he thought about what he had just said. "My God", he thought, "what have I just promised to do?"

Meredith and Josef just looked at one another with bewilderment as they realized what had just been transacted in a boat, in the middle of a lake, in the Russian countryside. They were silent for quite a while as if lost in their thoughts, still fishing and pulling in their dinner. The two caught a number of other fish with the General landing another large walleye that gave him fits on the line. But he fought the fish and tired him out netting it after a couple of minutes.

Once the fish was on the stringer, he reached into the metal container and pulled out three more beers and handed them to his two guests. "We will toast this crazy idea. I will fulfill my part and I will meet you in Hell for what we are about to do!" They brought their bottles together and looked into one another's eyes with resolve. The deal was done.

"I will need four months to make this happen on my end. In the meantime you must decide how to move this dangerous package from here to wherever bin Laden is hiding. I do not recommend that you try to fly the package out of Russia. Security in my country has improved enough that they could find the bomb and end this drama before it begins. I would suggest that you plan on using a ship."

Meredith thought for a second and said he had shipping interests that were in the Mediterranean that could make a run into the Black Sea for a trans-shipment out of Novorossiysk.

The General interrupted. "That is being made into a huge larger Naval Port for the Russian Fleet now that the Ukraine is kicking us out of Sevastopol in 2017. Billions of dollars are being spent to bring that port up to speed. I would not suggest that you plan on berthing there. Come to Gelendzhik. While it cannot take a large ship, it would draw less attention and scrutiny being a tourist city."

"General, I have shipping interests that work the Aegean and the Black Sea. The ships are called 'coasters' in the trade, shallow draft ships that can get in where the large ones cannot. I could get one of my ships into Gelendzhik, no problem."

Meredith mentally started thinking of arranging some shipments that could be made to various ports on the Black Sea. He would come up with a plan.

"I don't want to know how you do it, because if I am caught, they will make me tell them what has happened to this little package. So you must do your planning and keep me out of it."

"General, we will do so," Meredith promised with a handshake. "All we need is the transfer of the package and we will be responsible from there on."

"At the same time, I would ask that you do create a new identity for me, one that could perhaps take me to Wisconsin someday, maybe soon if this crazy plan of yours does not work. In fact I would suggest that you all should have new identities as you play your spy game. Because it is not a game!"

"That is good advice. We are already developing first class identities and documents for our group. If I could have a photo or two before we leave I will have good foreign documents made up for you as well. And I will personally assist you in finding that lake in Wisconsin where no one else will find you. I will need more fishing lessons after we conclude this effort."

Meredith turned to Josef and said. "We will need to work out some sort of code that will allow us to communicate when you, and we, are ready to move. I will ask Josef to set up a regular monthly call to you and we will determine the necessary codes."

With a line full of fish, to prove their fishing success, they pulled in their fishing gear and prepared to call it a day. The General started the engine for the quiet trip back to the Dacha. Each man was lost in their own thoughts as they plotted their part in this odyssey that was about to unfold.

➔ ←

Pizza Hut, 53rd St.

The group had finished their meeting with the good Doctor for their now once a month sessions and had gathered at a different pig-out place for another covert meeting. There were remnants of five pizzas strewn about the table. The group had done justice to the pies. They were all sitting around a back table and Meredith started the conversation by clearing his throat. Everyone quieted down.

"What I am about to say is important and must never be spoken outside this circle. In fact, it should not be spoken at all if possible."

He looked around the table and then said. "We will shortly have a suitcase bomb at our disposal."

He let that sink in for a moment, noting everyone had sucked in his or her breath and not exhaled. "It is one of those suitcase sized weapons. It will not level a city but it will do a healthy amount of damage to a mountain." With that he smiled and looked at each person. Everyone still held their breath, and then as a group exhaled. They stared at Meredith and waited for him to continue.

"Please don't ask how we got the weapon or ever speak about it to anyone, even your families. Just know that it will be entirely safe for us to handle. It will be neutralized while we have it in our possession. But the bad guys will not know that."

"So how are we going to advise them we have something they want?" Kate asked. "How do we get to them?"

"We are working on that now. And you will all be involved." Meredith said.

He continued. "Bin Laden will be offered access to this bomb. Hopefully, this will get us closer, and if we play our cards right maybe we will meet the bastard, and then kill him with the weapon he wants to buy. Live by the sword and die by it."

Ralph Behar jumped in, "To make this happen we will all have to take on some assignments as part of the team effort. We have to compartmentalize each assignment so no one knows what the others are doing." Everyone gathered in closer to make sure they understood the assignments. Ralph continued.

"This is for security, so bear with us. We don't want to leak this thing, nor do we want anyone of you to know the total plan, so you can safely deny any knowledge of the plan should you be compromised."

Josef raised his hand to gain everyone's attention and said, "People this is serious stuff. William and I both found that out on our trip. We need your commitment and support. We think we have devised a good plan and each of you and your background and skills will definitely help us to accomplish our goal."

"Thanks Josef," Meredith interjected, "Kate, I'll need your expertise to help us develop new travel documents, passports etc. Do you think you can do that with your contacts in the graphic industry?"

Kate looked at William and said, "I was wondering how I would be able to fit into this anarchy, but sure, over the years I have come to know people, who know people, who do that kind of work. Yeah, I can help."

"Great, don't worry about the money, I can cover that. We just want the best documents money can buy and we will need them relatively quickly, so please figure out whom you can trust to assist you.

"Malik and O, you are both critical to this plan on the front end, and at the end. I will need to talk separately with you about ways to get to al Qaeda and eventually to bin Laden. You have been to the mountains so your knowledge will be critical. We'll talk later."

The brothers felt proud of their importance and participation in the plan.

"Uri, and Michael, I know both of you have not been to sea in a few years, but I need you to brush up on your shipping skills as we may need you to assist with one of my ships in transporting the weapon. Michael, I would also ask that you brush up on your shooting skills as they may come into play as well. For that matter, everyone should learn how to handle a gun."

The group seemed startled by Meredith's statement. As if they hadn't thought about the whole plan, and the end game. They began to realize that this was not a game at all. "If you don't have a license to own a gun, get one at your local sports store. When you sign up for a gun license, just tell them you are interested in sport shooting. It will take some days to be approved, but do it now so that we can all get some practice on handling guns safely and shooting straight. Courtney, if you could coordinate getting this effort organized that would be a big help."

"I'll be happy to assist, but do we really want everyone to be armed? Doesn't that seem a wee bit dangerous?"

"Yes, I know what you are saying. We won't be carrying guns around here. This is going to be for when we are traveling, to protect our package. We can't let that thing fall into the wrong hands. I assume that most of you will want to participate in as much of the plan as possible?"

Everyone at the table nodded their heads in agreement.

"We won't be carrying weapons around, but I think we should all learn how to be comfortable around them, if we ever need to use them along the way. I want everyone prepared for any eventuality, how to fire a gun, and how to defend yourselves. A little practice will go a long way to making everyone more comfortable."

"I agree with that approach and will be happy to help." Courtney stated.

"I belong to a private gun club north of the city and I can reserve it on weekdays for some private target practice. After everyone is legal, we can all go out there and do some shooting instruction. You don't even have to buy a weapon, I have all sorts of them and when we actually do this I will have a whole assortment of specialized weapons that we could use if need be. Courtney will coordinate."

Meredith looked to others sitting at the table. Eyeing Ralph working his laptop he said, "Ralph, I'll need you to coordinate finances for this entire operation. We will need all sorts of operating capital that I will supply. The money can be in dollars for the time being. But everyone will eventually need working funds, so I think we will need Euros, Russian Rubles, Turkish Lira, Saudi Riyals, Indian Rupees, and Egyptian Pounds for starters."

Ralph nodded and started making some notes. "We may need other currencies as well. While the dollar is accepted almost everywhere, it also draws attention to you like an American tourist, so we will try to go native when we can." Ralph gave a 'thumbs up' sign. He opened his laptop and started creating some Excel spreadsheets as Meredith continued moving around the table with assignments.

Looking across the table, he said, "Josef, you will lead the research team and I think a number of people can assist you in these endeavors. Once we zero in on a specific plan we will need research, maps, etc. I would like to know more about bin Laden than our own government has on him, which can't be much because they can't find the bastard." Josef nodded his agreement, fully knowing where this effort was heading.

After Meredith had handed out assignments he again asked everyone to understand the gravity of what they were embarking on. He advised they would be breaking the law in many countries, they would be evading their own government and they would need to become very careful if they were going to survive.

He again asked them to clear any thoughts they had about adding people or asking for outside assistance with him and Ralph before they expanded any circle. "Loose lips will sink ships." As he said it the younger people gave him a weird look not understanding the comment.

Meredith encouraged everyone to keep the end game in sight, and perhaps they would someday sleep again at night. Everyone agreed that would be a good thing, to sleep without nightmares of that fateful day. That simple thought seemed to give everyone purpose and satisfaction they were doing the right thing. With that, the group disbanded, except for Malik and O, who Meredith asked to stay behind. He asked them how difficult it would be to make contact with al Qaeda.

O looked to Malik for a moment and then said. "I know people in Pakistan that know tribal leaders in the mountain areas, who know others, who know Taliban and al Qaeda. But these people change every day and we have been gone for a time from Pakistan. But we still have family there, and I will see if help be got."

Malik thought for a moment and then offered. "My brother and I came to America by way of boat from France. In France, we stayed at a refugee camp in Calais on the English Channel. It was an Afghan and Pakistani camp. There were tribal men there that could help us contact the Taliban and al Qaeda. Maybe we could find a way to talk with these men and offer them a trade."

O agreed by nodding his head and interjected additional thought. "I know of people in the 'Jungle', that is the camp's name in Calais. They could carry messages to the right people. We could go there and try to make a contact with them if you want."

Meredith was pleased and sensed that Malik and O understood the importance of what they were volunteering to do. "That would be good my friends. If we could make contact with the bad guys in a place like that it might make the potential offer much more believable. If you would be willing to try, I will fly you two to France and we will see if we can make a contact with al Qaeda."

"We are ready to do what it needs to be done." O said in his broken English. "I think we can find the terrorists we need in the Jungle camp. And then they can send a message to bin Laden."

Meredith asked them if they could go to France within a couple weeks and made a mental note to get them new travel documents through Kate, to protect their identities. He promised a full briefing on what they would be asked to do and suggested they ride out with him to the farm to go over the plan.

→ ←

Book III – Amateurs

June 2008, Times Square, 7th Avenue

Meredith, Josef and Ralph sat in Behar's small office in the darkened office building on Seventh Avenue. They knew that the only person moving about on the floor was a janitor and he had already been to Behar's office. They were looking at a world map trying to talk through how they would move the package from point A to point B, without getting caught or killed in the process.

They were starring at Russian and Middle Eastern maps at the moment. Underneath, a second map of Afghanistan and Pakistan also lay open with a number of notations on them. They knew that Point B, was bin Laden's location, somewhere in the mountains between Pakistan and Afghanistan in the lawless tribal lands between the two countries. Government experts and reporters had offered countless theories in the newspapers and magazines about the whereabouts of the elusive terrorist, and most theories said he was hunkered down in some caves in the North Waziristan Tribal lands, west of Peshawar and east of Kabul.

So they had identified their package delivery area and agreed that they would need to get better intelligence than they could find from newspapers. They needed first hand knowledge of what was going on in those mountains and caves.

They also agreed that any of the THCT group other than Malik and O would be dead meat if they ventured into these areas on their own. They would instead have to order up the best aerial photography that was available on the Internet to allow them some level of intelligence.

Meredith realized that Malik and O would not only be traveling to France to try and establish some level of contact, but they may have to also go back to Pakistan to be the eyes of the group on-site. He decided he would broach that subject with them later. The small group turned its attention back to Point A, the initial delivery point for the package and talked about how such a package could be moved.

"When we spoke to the General he suggested that we take the package out of Russia by boat on the Black Sea. With the amount of shipping that goes into this area since the cold war ended, it would be difficult for anyone to know that such a package was moving."

Ralph asked a question that was bothering him. "Just how big is one of these dirty bombs anyway? They call it a suitcase bomb but is it really that small or are we talking about a Volkswagen size bomb, like in the 1945 Nagasaki photos?"

Josef spoke up and assured everyone, "My brother-in-law assured me it truly is about the size of a suitcase. That's why he thinks he can get one off the base."

Meredith also chimed in. "I was wondering about that as well, so I made a casual inquiry to a military friend in England and asked him the same question. I mentioned an article I saw in the New York Times on the subject. He said the same thing. I asked him if he had actually seen such a bomb and he said that he couldn't actually say, but wink, wink, yes, he had. I also asked if the Russians had similar bombs and he said yes. He said they wanted miniaturized versions back in the 80's."

"The General said they had a whole series of such weapons at his base scheduled for dismantling this year as part of the joint disarmament with the US. That's why he has been over here talking with the Pentagon."

"Well ok, we can assume this thing is small enough to move around once we get a hold of it. But how will we transport it?" Ralph asked.

"I've been thinking about that since the day we went fishing with the General," Meredith responded pouring another three fingers of scotch in his tumbler.

Josef pulled the map forward and noted, "The closest deep water port to the General's base is actually in Novorossiysk, seventy kilometers from his base. It has become a major military installation for the Russian Navy. He said it is a beehive of military activity. My brother suggested we should look elsewhere."

He pointed to a smaller port down the coast. "It is called Gelendzhik, with a natural harbor in a circular Bay that could handle a small commercial ship. It is a big tourist region with lots of beaches, so we wouldn't stand out if we were there."

Meredith traced his finger over the map and said, "It can't be that easy to spirit a bomb away from a heavily guarded military base and just drive to the sea, can it?"

Josef, looked at the map with a magnifying glass and said, "Yes, I think it is that simple, if Dimitri can actually get the package off the base without raising suspicion. The secret will be to get out of town silently without raising any alarms."

Josef continued. "I'm prepared to do the actual driving if you want me too, because I can speak the language and will not draw attention to us. I drive as bad as the next Russian, but I would make every effort to do a good driving job for this trip."

→ ←

Mid-Town Manhattan

Uri and Michael Pappas sat across from William in his limousine parked a half block from the Central Park Zoo entrance. William opened the privacy window in the car and advised the driver to be back in an hour. He, Uri and Michael got out and walked to the Zoo, where William bought three passes and they entered through the old Arched Entrance, and headed for the bear cages off to the left. There were some benches and tables there, and it was not crowded since the bears had already been fed.

William pulled out a number of newspapers and underneath them he had map of the Black Sea that had a casual line drawn on it, starting at the Black Sea port of Gelendzhik, down the eastern coast of the Black Sea, skirting the Turkish coast all the way to Istanbul and the Bosporus. From there the line went into the Adriatic Sea and the Mediterranean south to the Suez Canal. The line went down the Red Sea, navigating between Egypt and Saudi Arabia, through the narrow Gulf of Aden, and then into the Arabian Sea.

Michael and Uri studied the map for a couple minutes and William just waited to see what they would say. Finally Uri said, "You have certainly taken the most direct route if we will do this by water, but you couldn't have picked more powder keg countries to go past if you had tried to do so."

Michael agreed and said, "But I guess this might also be the best way to look innocent and be left alone. We take it right past them. Who would be crazy enough to do that?"

"That is somewhat how I came to this route myself," William offered. "I have a number of ships that ply these waters in the Med and through the Suez Canal so it would seem normal to the average observer. And we do want to look average. Wait until you see the rust bucket I have in mind for this special trip. I hope you aren't looking for a modern ship?" He handed them a photo of an old merchant marine ship that had seen better days. It name was the Majorca and it was 200 feet long with a width of 45 ft. and a shallow draft allowing her to get into most ports of call.

"All we need is something that will float, with a good engine." Uri said.

"Yeah, it has to have good engines and screws," said Michael, "so we don't have any breakdowns and have to pull into unscheduled ports. That would be a problem."

Uri agreed, "I have been on the worst ships afloat so that is not a problem at all. Just get me a sound engine and people that can make it hum and we can do the rest."

Michael pulled the map closer to him and said, "William, I do have some questions concerning the route. There may be some problems with the route you have chosen."

Meredith looked from him to the map and asked him to continue.

"I have some friends in New York that are with Homeland Security and they have mentioned that the U.S., Russia, and even NATO have set up monitoring stations at various pinch points around the world that can monitor any nuclear radiation materials that are passing by. The U.S. has been covertly monitoring the Bosporus and the Straits going through Istanbul for years to keep an eye on the Russian Navy and any nuclear materials passing through the straits. We have these monitors here in New York harbor because this city is such a target."

"I've heard similar things about this in Egypt at the Suez Canal." Uri said and dragged his finger down to the Red Sea. "This could be a big problem if the Egyptians, the Saudis or Iranians also have such monitoring equipment that could pick up the nuclear materials in our small suitcase package as it passes by."

William looked surprised and concerned. Obviously this was not something he had considered. He stared at the map to think of an alternate route. "Maybe we could haul some legitimate nuclear material on the manifests so that they would assume that is what is setting off the monitors?" William offered hopefully.

Uri said, "It has been my experience that such an approach would only bring us greater inspection requirements, and then we would have our papers scrutinized, our passports checked more carefully, our destinations and ports of call reviewed, and they might notice that we are not whom we say we are."

Michael jumped in and said, "There is something else we could try. What if we off-loaded the package before entering these pinch-points, took the package overland and re-boarded at some point on the other side."

"That would be a great idea if we could do it without getting caught? What would you suggest?" William said.

I know I could come up with a plan for the Bosporus." He traced a finger along the Black Sea on the Turkish coast. When he found what he was looking for he pointed and said. "Here at Sile, just 20 kilometers from the Bosporus entrance we could anchor temporarily. It is a small seaport and the ship could pull in, and we could declare a medical emergency and say we needed to offload a deckhand, me. Once I'm off the ship with our package it pulls out and passes through the Bosporus and the Sea of Marmara, clean as a whistle."

All three men were staring at the map and nodding their heads. "That could work."

Michael continued, "I have actually been to Sile with my Father years ago and know my way through that part of Turkey. With someone to meet me with a minivan, and assist in the driving we could head south through Turkey and meet up south of the Canakkale Straits, about 250 kilometers overland. We would get there faster than the ship."

As he looked at the map he smiled. "This might be a great place to meet up." He stabbed the map. "This is Truva, where the ancient walled city of Troy was supposedly built. The ruins are actually a tourist destination. I'd like to see the place that has given us this crazy plan."

Everyone thought about that for a moment and then nodded their agreement, Truva it would be. William was impressed that Michael did indeed know his homeland as well as Turkey "Perhaps we get one of the ladies to meet the ship and then you two would drive south as a couple on a sight-seeing tour?"

"That would work. How heavy is this package. Will it be difficult to move around?"

"I haven't seen one, it's not like they're readily available for viewing. I was told they weigh about 40-50 pounds and could fit inside a larger suitcase. With wheels, it shouldn't be too hard to maneuver."

Michael smiled and said. "Hell, it's just a heavy suitcase then, all I'm worried about is drawing attention to what we are doing."

"Moving on down the route, the Mediterranean along the Turkish coast shouldn't be a problem as it is heavily traveled as a tourist destination with cruise ships and pleasure boats all along the coast. Syria, Jordan and Israel may be a bit more troubling."

Uri again agreed and said. "We will need a good cover because the Israeli's patrol their coastal waters religiously, and they often board and inspect ships. But we should be able to make it past them, without incident if we stay further out in the Med. But let me raise another challenge. When we get to Egypt we may run into the same nuclear sniffing problem in the Suez Canal."

"I guess that makes sense, another pinch point." Meredith said again scrutinizing the map.

"Perhaps I should be the one to offload the package in Egypt." Uri offered, "I too would have no problem driving the package through Cairo and then back to the ship downstream."

He pointed further down the map along the Suez Canal and said, "We could pull into Damietta, which is just down the coast from Port Said at the mouth of the Suez Canal. With a minivan we could drive south through Cairo until we got to Suez at the other end of the Canal." He pointed to the southern port city on the Gulf of Suez. "There is a lot of ships stacked up at this point and we could sail south through the Red Sea with no problems. I have done this many times."

"Gentlemen, this sounds like a good plan. To be safe I think we should also build a lead container within the ship to minimize any radiation detection. I've got some people working on the ship in Marseilles right now. I'll send instructions to add a lead container box or room somewhere in the bowels of the ship. They are also completely rebuilding the engines. The ship will be as good as new on the inside. It will look like a piece of junk on the outside, but it will run like a shark."

"So how many crew will we have on this ship, William? I am nervous about extra people and prying eyes. You know there are no secrets on a ship." Uri looked concerned.

"Fair question, Uri, I have a good Norwegian Captain on the Majorca, his name is Derek Brinkmann, and he is trustworthy. I'll personally talk with him. We may need to bring him into our confidence. He will work with you and Michael, I'm sure of it. But he will still be the Captain to his men. He knows how to stay out of trouble and he is being paid well, like the rest of the crew, to keep their mouths shut."

"That is fine. Will any of the rest of the team be joining us for this excursion? We could use some company and some backup if we do run into trouble."

Meredith nodded and said, "I think a number of us will be coming along, mainly because we all want to be in on the end game, I'm just not sure yet who that will be. I'm having the ship re-configured so we will have a few extra cabins. It may be that everyone will want to go on this cruise."

"Well my concern is that we will also be passing through pirate waters off the Somali coast." Michael said. "I just read about them again in the paper this morning. I wouldn't mind having a few guns available if we have to defend the ship and the package from those one-eyed crazies."

"I have thought of that as well. One of the things my engineers are adding to the ship, are some very unobtrusive defensive positions. In effect we will have some machine gun nests on the bow and stern, and the sides of the ship. They will build them to blend in and they will give us some shooting ports to ward off evil spirits."

"I'm also sending a full complement of weapons in concealed storage lockers that will be loaded. When we are on the open sea we can even do a little practice to ward off the bad guys."

"In the paper this morning they said that their favorite tactic is to attack from the stern and board the boat in the middle of the night," Michael said. "How do we defend against that approach, short of posting a stern night watch?"

William put his hands up and cupped his eyes and said, "Night Vision glasses and some night vision cameras should do the trick. We can also post watches while we're in the dangerous waters off Somalia. I am putting in some state-of-the-art low level sweep radars that should pick up just about anything on the surface including small inflatable boats so that we would know they are coming."

Both Uri and Michael looked at one another and seemed satisfied with the preliminary plans. They knew there would be time to tune the plan once we had contacted the quarry. With that William scooped up the maps and said, "Who wants to see the lions and tigers and bears?"

→ ←

51 St. and Madison Avenue

A few days later, William and Ralph flagged down a cab that had two Pakistanis in it and climbed in. They drove to Battery Park and found a parking spot close to the park leading to the Statue of Liberty boats. It was late in the day and few tourists were boarding to go out to the monument, so when they boarded they pretty much had a stern bench all to themselves

William started the conversation by saying, "O and Malik, your task is a major one. It is critical for the rest of the plan to work." I have been thinking about how we get to bin Laden and al Qaeda and there is no direct route we can employ. We can't just call them up and say Mr. bin Laden, we have a bomb for you. May we bring it over about dinnertime?"

Both O and Malik smiled but said nothing. They understood the gravity of the situation.

"So we would like to ask you to take a trip back to Calais and see if you can make some contact with al Qaeda in that Afghan camp you visited when you came to the U.S. You may be able to plant some seeds that will allow us to make more direct contact. Remember the Trojan horse story that I told you. We need to make them want to talk with us. We need to make them believe we have what they want, a bomb that they have wanted for many years."

"Mr. William, I think we can do this thing and believe us when we say there were al Qaeda people in the encampment. I think they send terrorists to London and the U.S."

Malik spoke up. "So I think we can find these people quick enough. I am just worried what we tell them, and what they will do to us?" As he thought about what he just said he straightened up and continued, " But I am not afraid because I want bin Laden's head on stick, and I have nothing to lose. He has killed the babies. So we do this thing and get us to bin Laden." That was all he wanted to say.

"I have been doing a lot of research on this so-called package that we will be getting soon. On the Internet you would be surprised what you can find about nuclear weapons and suitcase bombs," William offered as he opened his laptop and showed them some images he had saved.

Ralph said. "We will show you how to call up these encrypted images once you have made contact with someone at the camp in Calais. You can say that you represent people who have one of these bombs in hand and would be willing to sell it for $2,000,000 dollars. That should get you connected to the right people."

"I can handle the computer equipment well. My brother and me sold electronics in our business in Peshawar before they made us leave our home. We can handle the laptop and we will get us to the men we need to see."

Ralph continued, "This computer cannot be traced to any of us. It will have blind contact information should they choose to contact us. If they do we are off to the races."

With that comment, both O and Malik again looked confused and Ralph realized he was truly more American than he was Iranian. He corrected himself by saying. " I apologize, what I meant to say was, you can make this whole plan work if we find the right people to carry the message to bin Laden."

"We do it," they both said.

→ ←

Belmont Park, NY. August, 2008

It was the dog days of summer and the group assembled at Grand Central Station at 11:00 am. They loaded into two rented vans and drove over the Williamsburg Bridge into Brooklyn and headed east on the Cross Island Parkway. Everyone was excited Meredith had thought up a new meeting place. A day at the races at Belmont Park would be a nice change of pace. Everyone agreed they'd been gaining weight meeting at the fast-food joint all the time, so this was a welcome departure.

Meredith had given them directions from Manhattan, and two executive parking passes so they pulled into the Executive Parking Gold lot close to the Clubhouse entrance. Most of them had never been to a horseracing venue. He had also distributed Suite Level tickets for them to get into the Race Track.

Entering the Clubhouse gate they looked up and down and all around like children in a candy factory. The main building loomed above them. It was a long Grandstand with all sorts of levels offering expansive views overlooking the Paddock and Stables where the horses were kept between races. There was a festival mood around the grandstand area, with people milling about checking racing forms, watching the horses as they were exercised, and grabbing food from all sorts of vendor stands. Seeing all the food, the entire group thought, here we go again!

They were soaking up the atmosphere when Meredith walked up. "Hello gang, I see you got here safe and sound. So what do you think?"

Michael was the first to say anything and it was very appropriate for the venue. "Where are the betting windows? I already have a horse in mind."

"Whoa buddy, to use a horse term. Let's get settled first. Here, I have racing forms for everyone." Meredith said as he handed out the Daily Racing Guide showing all the scheduled races and horses running that day. " Let's head upstairs, I have a private suite that will allow us to see all the races in comfort…and privacy."

His raised eyebrow sent everyone the right message and they all fell in behind him as he walked towards a private elevator.

The elevator operator was a beautifully coiffed mature women in a red sports coat. "Good afternoon Mr. Meredith, were glad to have you join us today. Do you have any horses running today? I haven't had time to look at the form yet?"

"Hi Margaret, I have three horses on the track today in the second, fifth and eighth races, if the trainers don't scratch them. He said they looked awfully sluggish this morning, so we will see."

Hearing Meredith's comment the entire group started looking through the forms, looking for his horses as they rode the elevator. The group passed the Suites level and went on to the Penthouse level. As the door opened, another red-jacketed Steward stepped forward and introduced himself as Carlos. He also welcomed Mr. Meredith by name, and escorted them down a short well-appointed hallway with some red leather sofas and upholstered chairs lining the walls. There were multiple framed paintings of famous horses on the walls. At the end of the short hallway another large red door was unlocked for the group. Everyone poured in.

Inside was a large private suite of comfortable leather couches, tables and chairs all facing floor-to-ceiling windows overlooking the track. Just outside the Penthouse level windows was a private veranda that could accommodate the entire group for the actual races. On one sidewall there was a marble bar that was fully stocked and along the opposite sidewall there was number of chafing dishes with all sorts of food on display.

The entire group stood there with their mouths open, and then slowly started moving to the large windows in front of them, to look out over the entire oval racetrack. They were right above the finish line and from this vantage point could see the entire track, including the backstretch and the far turns.

Meredith turned to the steward, slipped him a tip and said, "Thanks Carlos, the bar and food look great. We won't need a bartender today with this small group. We will take care of ourselves. Just have the mutual teller step into the room about 10 minutes before each race and we will place any bets that we have. Who is on duty today?"

"Hutch will personally handle your group today and he will be pleased to offer advice, as I think you may have a few novices with you. I'll let him know you're in the Suite now." With that Carlos departed and shut the door.

With the steward logistics handled, Meredith turned to his guests and welcomed them to the track a second time.

"I'm glad you could all make it today as we have some important work to discuss. But that will be a bit later, first let's have some recreation. Just before each race a mutual teller will step into the room to take your bets, and I am sure that he would be pleased to help you place your bets. And here, to grubstake each of you, here is $100 in $5's so you can all bet on the ponies."

Meredith handed out a stack of $5's to each person. He waved at the bar and encouraged them all to fix themselves a drink and get some food. He then said he would be pleased to show them how to read the forms so they had a fighting chance of winning something. Everyone looked excited and the two Pakistanis just stood there dumbfounded looking at the bills in their hands.

They looked as if they were fish out of water. Meredith put an arm around them and steered them to the bar offering them bottled water, as they were Muslims and alcohol could not touch their lips. The others poured themselves drinks and dove into the food with relish.

While everyone got comfortable, Meredith held up the racing forms and started explaining the finer points of reading the forms and betting on the horses. He explained there would be ten races scheduled about every half hour, and each race would have anywhere from seven to twelve horses running.

"Each race in this daily form shows you the names of the horses scheduled to run, who the jockeys are that will be riding them, what kind of race history the horses and jockeys have had, what kind of track they will be running on, dirt or grass, and the distance to be run. Some horses are sprinters, and some are distance runners, some have a great pedigree and others have none, but can run like the wind. The secret is to figure this all out in a few minutes, place a bet and then hope your horse is a winner."

The newcomers looked confused already and Meredith remembered how overwhelming all this data could be when you were trying to absorb it all at once, so he realized he didn't want to frustrate them, rather he wanted them to enjoy themselves.

"I know it all seems confusing, so let me tell you what a lot of people do. On each race, there is a commentary section where knowledgeable horse racing professionals offer comments and insights on who is running, what to look for, and who may have a good chance to win. You should take a look at that."

With everyone following his every word, he then pointed out the front window down at the track and said. "You can read those summaries and also review the race odds by horse down there on that big electronic tote board. If you look you will see the odds are changing as people are placing bets."

Courtney spoke up for the first time and said, "Or you can look at the names and choose one of the horses that interest you because it sounds good. You would be surprised how many people bet that way. As a chemist,

I'm looking at the first race and love the name ' Chemically Hot ' so that's who I'm going with. No analysis, no form review, just gut. And I have a lot of fun approaching it that way, and more time to drink."

"Come on Courtney, that's no fun." Ralph Behar offered. "Back in Iran hundreds of years ago, I went to the Shah's tracks with my father and he taught me to scrutinize the jockeys and see how they had been doing on various horses, and various tracks. We would examine what their win-loss ratios were, and you can find that info on Page 4 of this racing form. At least that gives you a little edge. I think the jockey makes the difference."

There was a knock at the door and a tall, big man with a well-trimmed beard stepped into the room. He introduced himself as Hutch and said he would be pleased to take their bets. He stepped over to a computerized betting window near the bar.

Once the betting window was set up he asked if anyone had questions and sat down to see if he could help the players understand the forms. The true novices went over and tried to pick up some tips on wagering as they intended to break the bank. Michael and Ralph were huddled near the front window going over their forms and making notations about the horses they would be betting. Everyone looked as if they were enjoying themselves.

After the first race was over most of the group had lost their $5 and $10 dollar bets. But Courtney had bet $10 on her 'Chemically Hot' horse to "win/place/and show, and the horse came in second just missing a photo finish. When Hutch returned, she presented her ticket and her $10 bet had turned into a $23 payoff for a solid start. She waved the winnings around and announced she was now playing with the track's money.

The second race had one of Meredith's horses running ' My Son's Pony' in a $40,000 Claiming Race of just six furlongs. The horse was a sleek black colt of a 2001 Breeder's Cup winner named 'Macho Uno' and was having some success as a juvenile on short courses.

This was a short turf track race. A jockey by the named of Hector Alverado was driving in this race. He was a very successful jockey with 487 starts in the past year with 117 wins, 93 – 2nd place finishes, and 70 - 3rd place finishes.

When Hutch returned again to take the individual wagers almost everyone placed $10 to win on William's horse out of respect. Once the bets were laid down, everyone grabbed a drink and some food, and headed out onto the balcony to watch their pony run, and hopefully win.

The track was crowded on this Saturday afternoon. Once the horses were lined up and placed in their starting chutes, the Announcer yelled, " And they're off", the atmosphere became electric. Everyone quickly got into it. Because the race was a short distance starting on the back straightaway everyone was immediately standing up and yelling from the call. The group in the Penthouse was no different, they hooted and hollered the entire race willing their horse to break away from the pack.

On the Clubhouse turn that is exactly what 'My Son's Pony' did. He surged ahead of the other horses and moved to the rail to maintain his position. The jockey had his whip out but he was only tapping the horse on his flank with a light stoke, leaning in to talk and whisper him to the finish line.

The horse knew it was his turn to win. He set the pace for the rest of the tightly grouped pack who could do nothing but try to play catch-up. 'My Son's Pony' crossed the finish line by three lengths and the Penthouse crowd erupted, so much so, that the people in the private suites below them all turned to look up at the rabble rousers above. They could see that the festive group of high rollers were indeed enjoying themselves, dancing around like children. Obviously they had a winner.

Ralph and Michael encouraged everyone to watch the electronic board on the field beyond the finish line, to see what the posted winnings would be. The horse had left the gate at 6-1 odds and would probably pay off quite nicely based upon the volume of bets placed for the race.

A few moments later the race posted as official and the scoreboard showed that a winning bet did indeed pay 6-1 odds. That meant the better won $14 for every $2 that he had bet, and each person in the group had just won $70 with their $10 bets.

Ralph Behar raised a glass and said, "William, here's to you, how many more horses do you have scheduled today?"

Everyone toasted Meredith who was also beaming because he had just won over $14,000 on the horse that was named to honor his son. Just then Hutch came into the room and re-opened the window. He already knew that he was making a bunch of payouts on this race.

Everyone seemed to be enjoying the afternoon, and Meredith made a short announcement.

"I can see you are all enjoying yourselves, so rather than pulling you away from the ponies right now, lets talk after the races. I have this room as long as we want it, and it will be a lot quieter then."

With the win under their belts and some capital in their pockets the group broke into smaller groups and began analyzing what they planned to do for the next race. They ignored the food because they now had a mission. But they didn't ignore the drink except for O and Malik. By the fifth race everyone fancied themselves as pros at making bets and picking the horses, although everyone seemed to have a different approach to picking the winners.

Ralph and Michael were boxing their bets working the Exacta's and Trifecta options, which seemed to be working for them. Courtney had picked up a convert in Kate for her method of picking by the cool name. Kate had added the jockey's colored silks as another factor but they were not having much success with that approach. By the time the seventh race was announced, everyone had made their choices and were looking ahead to the last three races.

"I have my horse for the eighth race!" Kate announced as she waived her racing form above her head, "and this time, I think you'll all join me on name alone. Check out horse number 3. This is a real winner."

Everyone looked up and then flipped their books to the next page of the Daily scanning the Eighth Race. It was a full mile turf race starting on the backstretch in the far corner, almost out of sight except for the penthouse crowd.

"Son-of-bitch, William, is that your horse? I thought we were supposed to be secretive and not draw attention to ourselves?"

"I'll be damned, your right Kate, that's my horse too!" Ralph announced, "I don't care who is riding him."

Osama and Malik had gotten into this horseracing thing, and had even made some money, which they were sharing and protecting like greedy bankers. But they had a hard time comprehending what everyone was talking about. They looked at the forms, pointed at the name listed as the number three horse and silently mouthed the horses name, repeating it three times before they got it right.

"I'll be, Osama's Dead2, that's a name I can bet on." Josef exclaimed. He smiled at Meredith and shook his racing form. "But why the two William?"

Meredith saw that everyone had the same question, so he offered some comment.

"After 9-11, I was distraught and lost. I left the city and the only thing I found I could do was work the farm, alone with the horses and manure. I had lots of time to think about life and how fragile it is and about the loss of Will. In 2002, I bought a horse with a great pedigree, mostly for breeding purposes, and he sired a wonderful young stallion that I named 'Osama's Dead' because even then, I harbored a desire to get the son-of-a-bitch. I wanted to show the world my sentiment and determination."

"Well, the horse ran well and in a year of racing at a number of tracks, a lot of people bet on him. As you can imagine a lot of people around here are still pretty raw about 9-11. I think betting on that name for a horse, they were venting their frustrations as well. Once the horses running days were over, I studded him out and he produced another great runner. Named him 'Osama's Dead2', because I didn't want to forget. Hence, the second generation #2. He is a good runner and does well on the regular turf, not quite as good on grass."

Just then Hutch knocked on the Suite door and opened the betting window. Everyone crowded around him to place their bets for the seventh race, but they all were slapping down an extra $40 or $50 on horse number 3 in the eighth race as well.

Hutch worked Meredith's Penthouse Suite all the time and he knew this would happen, once people saw that 'Osama's Dead2' was running. On days he wasn't working he bet on the horse too. He liked Mr. Meredith and cringed at the thought of he having lost a son in such a tragedy.

In the Eighth Race the odds at post time were 9-2. The bet volume was high with people betting for and against the horse. The jockey was again Hector Alvarado and his silks were black and white. Most silks were colorful with reds, greens and yellows predominating, but Meredith insisted on the black when this horse ran, again carrying a theme that he would carry with him for the rest of his life.

The commentary written in the forms that day suggested that 'Osama's Dead 2' was a solid performer and was an above-average juvenile sire. He had won a number of claiming races, was rated as a closer, and had finished well on turf tracks, but not grass. He was well thought of in mid-length races and the commentator suggested that he should do well today against this competition.

Everyone placed bets with Hutch and the betting pattern changed; everyone was placing big money on Meredith's horse. Just before post time, everyone made his or her way to the balcony rail six stories up, overlooking the track. Because they were so high they could see the starting gate way back in the far corner of the track, and could even see the horses being loaded into the starting gate. Just then over the P.A. system, the announcer said,

"The last horse has been loaded into the chute,....... and they're off!"

Running from the third gate, 'Osama's Dead2' took off quickly but was sandwiched between the number two and four horses as they closed the lane to the rail. Forced into the role of stalker, a horse that holds back in the second flight just off the pace, Meredith's horse stayed with the pack and bided his time eating dirt and searching for some daylight.

On the extra long straightaway, due to the back stretch start, at mid-point to the Clubhouse, the jockey Alvarado squeezed the reins to the right just a slight bit and the horse recognized the signal, easing off a notch, and moved to the outside as the field widened a bit. Now the horse had some running room and that's all it needed to take off and run his preferred race as a closer. He started shooting through the competition.

In the Penthouse Suite everyone watched silently gripping the glass rail as if they were riding the horse themselves. At the far turn, the horse was now clear of the pack, on the outside and moving up. On the balcony rail there were some whispered comments spoken so softly you would think they were leaning into the horse's ear. Then the noise level on the balcony started to slowly ramp up to a loud murmur. Eventually this turned into a much louder crescendo as people throughout the racetrack found themselves yelling and willing their horses to run.

In the Clubhouse turn, 'Osama's Dead2' was still second to a horse by the name of 'Bosco Rules' who had posted at 4-1 odds and was the pre-race favorite to win. But 'Osama's Dead2' was possessed this day, and pushed Bosco to the limit, tiring him out as they ran down the last few furlongs. Neck and neck the two horses traded leads three times in the last 300 yards sending the entire day's attendance into a frenzy.

On the balcony overlook the group was screaming, except for Meredith who had a grim look on his face. He was always distraught when this horse ran, but it was something he needed to do and he was glad the group was into it as well. He watched in silence and promised himself the horse would help him achieve his true goal.

In the last 100 feet, 'Osama's Dead2' gained the upper hand and lengthened his lead to a full head. Alvarado looked to his left and could see Bosco snorting and steeling himself for one last lunge to the finish, so he brought his whip up and violently stroked his horse's flank to gain the last second advantage. The two horses closed on the finish line with ears flattened, nostrils flaring, and eyes bulging, both seemingly flying to the finish with nary a hoof actually touching the ground.

The THCT group, standing right above the finish line, saw the camera flash go off as the two horses crossed the finish line, so close together they would indeed need to see the photo finish to determine a winner. The yelling stopped and the backslapping started, as everyone presumed 'Osama's Dead2' was the winner.

But no one left the rail; they all watched the scoreboard to see who would get the win and what the payoff would be. They had learned how to play the game and now waited to see if they would see another payday. And this one would be meaningful if the horse did win.

Meredith was a bit more casual about it and walked back into the Suite and poured himself another scotch on the rocks. He sat down at the bar watching the group through the window. He was proud of this ragtag group, as they had come together. They had a goal that would carry them forward out of their individual grief and despair. And he was proud of himself for finding a way to help them along, even if this crazy plan did not actually come off. Hopefully they would come to grips with their personal losses.

He looked up when he heard them roar and saw them giving high-fives to each other. Even Osama and Malik were jumping up and down. The horse must have won again and the group had bet heavily enough that some money was going to be made. He raised his drink and saluted the group through the window as a knock came at the door and Hutch stepped in to pay off the bets of the Eighth Race.

Everyone crowded around Hutch, with their winning tickets in hand and watched as everyone turned in a winner. Finishing first with 9-2 odds, the horse paid $11 for every $2 dollars bet. Most of the group had placed a $50 bet to win, and that meant they were getting $275 for their efforts.

Ralph and Michael each turned in $200 tickets as they had fared better on previous races and had decided that this time the name approach would be the plan. The bet earned each of them $ 1,100 and Hutch paid it out with a smile.

Meredith looked over at Hutch in the crowd of winners and shook his head saying no. It was a signal to not say anything about his own bet, which he had placed a moment before post time as Hutch was getting ready to leave the room. Meredith had booked his usual $5,000 bet on the terrorist horse and he was going to earn a $27,500 payoff. He would collect later.

Meredith clinked a glass with a serving knife and everyone looked up from the revelry. "Folks, I think we all had a good day at the races, but now we need to have that short meeting." In a heartbeat the group all remembered why they were there and assembled around Meredith.

Looking at Hutch, Meredith handed him a couple hundred dollars as a tip and said, "Hutch, I think were done betting for the day, as winners! Would you let the staff know that we will be having a meeting in here for a couple of hours and that we would prefer not to be disturbed. They can clean up later and I'll take care of their extra time."

"You got it Mr. Meredith, have a great day everyone and I hope we see you here again." With that he locked up the betting window and left the room.

"Michael, would you mind pulling those glass doors shut, if everyone would grab a drink and sit down at the table, we have some assignments for people, we need to discuss a number of things, and some of you will be making a trip."

→ ←

Police Sub-Station, Times Square

Michael Pappas was sitting in a corner of a small office away from other officers taking a moment from Times Square duties. He was looking at a number of maps Meredith had sent over. They were maps of Southern Russia, Turkey and the Greek Islands in the Aegean Sea. He was trying to not draw attention to himself but with the maps out sooner or later someone would come over and ask what was up.

He was prepared to move the Greek map on top over the others and advise he was thinking about going back to Greece for a while. Everyone knew he had lost his fiancé Michaela in the World Trade Center terrorist act. They would cut him slack, but he was worried they might see he was actually involved in something else.

Just then a big burly cop in his street blues came into the office and plopped down in the chair on the other side of the report desk. He took off his police baseball cap revealing a head of sandy red hair that matched his bushy eyebrows. He pulled his baton out of his equipment belt and laid it on the table. Kevin Geary was one of Michael's closest friends on the force.

"Mike, what are hiding in here for?" It's really nice outside and the tourists are back in Time Square in force. You should see all the babes. We should both be out there soaking up the visual stimuli. You need to get back in the saddle, buddy."

"Yeah, I know Kevin, but my heart just isn't in it yet," Michael said. He held up the Greek map and brochure and said, "I'm thinking of taking some leave and taking a trip back to Greece to visit the family. Maybe that will pull me out of this pissed off state of mind."

The cop smacked his nightstick on the edge of the desk and said, "Now that sounds like a plan, I could see you relaxing and getting some on those Greek beaches. Hell, I may want to come along. How much time you got coming. Think you could swing it?"

Michael looked up at the mention of Kevin coming along, as he hadn't factored that into his cover story. But then he thought about it for a moment. Kevin was as pissed off about 9-11 and terrorists as he was. He had lost a bunch of friends on 9-11 and he had known Michaela well. He had shed tears of rage and sorrow for her and his fellow officers. He had the same anger and frustration. Plus he could shoot the crap out of anything. He was on the waiting list for the SWAT team and had served in the Marines as a sniper in the Kuwait - Iraq war.

But how could he even bring up the Trojan horse plan. He had promised to hold the plan very close and not bring anyone else in. "Kevin, That would be cool, us catching some rays on the Greek islands, and chasing the dollies. You know what they say about Greek women, but I will be seeing family for much of the trip. Hell, I'm not even sure I am going."

With that Kevin got back up, grabbed a soft drink from the cooler under the table, slid his nightstick back into its slot, adjusted his belt and holster and said, "Well little brother, it still sounds like a great time. If you decide to go, let me know. I have a ton of off time still hanging around my neck, and I can put up with family. Have any sisters?"

"Get out of here before I use that stick on you. I'll let you know if I decide to go." With that the burly officer walked out and Michael watched thinking that adding a new team member to the THCT group might be a good idea. That might be something to bring up with Meredith as the group could certainly use some more muscle.

He went back to his maps and re-arranged them so he was looking at the Black Sea coast from Gelendzhik all the way down to Turkey. He followed a line south along the west coast to a natural resort town harbor of Sile, only a short distance of 20 nautical miles from Istanbul and the Bosporus.

If they made landfall in Sile, he would drive the package through Turkey and meet up with the ship again on the other side of the Canakkale Straits leading to the Aegean Sea and the Mediterranean. He could move the package no problem, just as Meredith and Ralph had suggested, going around whatever NATO and U.S. nuclear monitors might be set up in the Bosporus.

He also liked the idea of meeting the ship again in Truva, the city near the ancient ruins of what was said to be Troy. Most of the team would be on the ship or with him by that time, and seeing the ruins might help inspire them to get their man.

He reached into the pocket of his protective vest and pulled out his current temporary throwaway phone. He had kept this one for a few extra days, as his calls were short and coded. He'd get rid of it after this message when he went back on the street for the rest of his shift. He called Meredith's temporary phone number advising that he had come up with another idea. He would share the plan tonight. He signed off saying THCT.

→ ←

Soho, New York

Kate Shanahan was in her office preparing all the data she would need to get everyone new identities. She already had personally taken all of their photos against blank white walls and had interviewed them all to better understand their ethnic background. It had been agreed upon they would have papers that were not of U.S. origin, to minimize exposure for all of them. U.S. passports would draw additional scrutiny in other parts of the world. Instead, depending on where they needed to go, they would have passports from those countries.

A few weeks earlier she had made some quiet inquiries with her vendors and peers in the graphic design field. After a good number of false starts, she had finally been directed to some people, who knew people, who had specialized skills in making the kind of travel documents she was looking for. She had been vouched for, and vetted by a number of people, and then after meeting with a number of what they called cutouts, she eventually was connected to the right creative people. Once she proved to them that she had the financial resources to pay for these special travel papers, passports, and various supporting documents, she was on her way to get what she needed. Obviously money spoke a distinct language in this shadowy world.

Her most important concern was they had to be discreet, and for the hefty price she was paying, she found them to be very much so, as well as quick and reliable. They had already produced documents for the Pakistani boys, as they had been sent on an early assignment overseas. She had been told to get them Pakistani passports and documents calling Islamabad home, and to also produce French documents for them as well. She didn't know why, but the request had come from Ralph Behar and William Meredith, so that was good enough for her.

She was now assembling all the information, photos and back-stories for the others, as each would have distinct responsibilities in other parts of the world if they were going to pull this off. She also made herself a number of identities because she didn't want to just be the forger, she wanted a piece of bin Laden's head as well, to avenge her father. Giving it some thought, with her olive complexion, she fancied herself to be Italian and Turkish as she hoped to have a part in the transfer of the package through the Mediterranean Sea.

The 14 double and some triple sets of documents had been promised for three weeks from now and the cost for all the various passports and overlaying wallet type documents was going to exceed $70,000 dollars before it was all over. Meredith had said he didn't care and expected such expense for good documents. He wanted the best money could buy, so they had a fighting chance of passing judgment before they left New York. That had made her as determined as ever. She didn't know who was doing the work, but she was confident that quality work was being done. She used her new throwaway phone to advise Ralph Behar that the papers had been ordered. She signed off THCT, but couldn't bring herself to throw it away. It still had most of its pre-paid minutes loaded.

Central Park Zoo

Michael and Ralph assembled almost the entire group at Noon, near the Zoo entrance in Central Park. They were all excited because they knew what today's meeting was all about. They were going shooting. Some were anxious because they had never shot a gun before. For obvious reasons they would have to go elsewhere for this exercise.

They loaded up in a rented 12-passenger van and headed north through Harlem to catch the NY State Thruway. When they got to the Bronx, Michael drove past the New York Botanical Garden and pulled over to the curb at Kazimiroff Boulevard. Ralph got out of the front passenger seat, and moved into the back with the rest of the group like he had a plan. Everyone grumbled because it was now crowded as they had all settled in.

Someone yelled at Michael from across the road and waved. He crossed the street walking over to Michael's side window, and offered his handshake. Michael shook back and motioned him around to the passenger seat.

Before pulling away from the curb, Michael turned to the group and said. "Everyone, I would like to introduce Kevin Geary to you. He's a fellow officer with me on the NYPD force. He is a certified firearms instructor with the department. I asked him if he would be willing to come along to help you all learn the finer points of handling a variety of weapons."

Kevin turned around and waved to the entire group sitting behind him. He noted that it was quite an eclectic group of individuals. They included young and old, male and female; some with accents he thought were Russian. He wondered what Michael was up to and what was going on.

Michael had told him all would eventually become clear before the day was out, to just play along and have a great day shooting guns at a fancy Gun Club upstate.

Everyone said hello and a number of people asked Kevin about his job. He responded by saying, "I keep Mike here out of trouble and that's almost a full time job."

155

Josef sitting in the mid row seat said, " I can believe that. I still can't believe they gave Michael the right to carry a gun and arrest people."

"Well, they did, but only after I showed him how to use that gun safely. Believe it or not, he is pretty normal on the job. It's afterward that we should all be worried."

Everyone laughed and those within reach of the drivers seat punched Michael in the arm as he pulled away from the curb and headed north on the Major Deegan Expressway, eventually merging with the Thruway.

The group carried on, making a casual but thorough investigation of Officer Kevin Geary's background. They asked him more about the force, how long he had been there, what his background was, and was he married or single.

Kevin played along and answered the questions but kept thinking to himself what an odd array of people Michael had hooked onto. He wondered why the hell he would be teaching these folks to shoot a gun? Michael had just asked him to come along as a favor not really explaining why these folks needed to learn how to shoot. He had said it would be therapeutic for these people to let off a little steam. So Kevin had said yes.

They drove north On I-87, and then crossed over to I-684 North driving past the Westchester County Airport. Turning onto Highway 35, then Lake Street, and then another hard right on King St, the two-lane road led them up Cooney Hill Rd. into the Kensico Lake area.

The van turned into a private gated drive that looked as if it was a private estate. It was the Kensico Gun Club and looked as if no one was around. As they drove past a rather ornate clubhouse building towards the gun range, they saw William Meredith standing up ahead waving them in.

Everyone piled out, walked over to Meredith, shook hands and started looking around. The gun range was a large oblong fenced area. On one end there was an open roofed enclosure lined with table height shooting areas. In the center of this roofed area there was a well-built log cabin building that stored weapons, ammo, and was the Range Captain's office.

Downrange there was a 300 foot long corridor with designated shooting lanes and target boards staggered at different 50 foot intervals. At the far end of the enclosure behind all these targets was a large dirt hill that rose some thirty feet high, obviously designed to absorb all the bullets that missed their targets.

Michael introduced Kevin to Meredith and explained that he would be assisting with the training exercise with a variety of weapons.

"Kevin, it's a pleasure to meet you. Michael has told me a lot about you. I'll look forward to getting some lessons myself."

"Mr. Meredith. Also a pleasure, Michael has said similar things about you. You have a beautiful place here. I wish I could belong to such a club. You know we never get to use long guns at the police range in the city. I hope I can shoot a bit with the long guns today. I need the practice."

"Be my guest. We have the place to ourselves today. I rented the entire facility for the whole afternoon. Let me show you around and then I'll show you what we have available to shoot. Everyone walked around in a group as Meredith pointed out the whole facility, how the shooting lanes worked, how the targets were attached and could be sent downrange and retrieved at the push of a button.

"That's great Sir," Kevin said to Meredith, "The one thing I hate at these long ranges is walking downrange when there are loaded weapons on the firing line. This setup makes for a much safer range."

Meredith then showed everyone how the range warning strobe light and klaxon worked. If the emergency light and horn went off, everyone stopped shooting immediately, no matter what stage of firing they were in. "If the klaxon goes off, you stop, immediately, not one extra shot. You put your weapon down and unload immediately. Understood?"

Everyone agreed listened carefully and nodded their heads in agreement.

With the range rules explained, Meredith led them over to one of the shooting tables and pulled off a blanket covering the weapons he had assembled. Everyone looked down at the table covered with an array of handguns, shotguns and long guns. Michael and Kevin glanced at each other.

Kevin whistled like it was an exclamation point, "Mr. Meredith, What are we doing here, starting a little war or something?"

"Well no, we aren't planning on starting a war, but later on today, after we get some of these rookies trained in basic gun safety, and squeeze off a few rounds, you and I will talk a little about what we are doing. Fair enough?"

Kevin picked up a Kimber 8400 Advanced Police Tactical rifle, one that he readily recognized as being a custom build. He passed his hand over the polished stock and turned it over lovingly, took hold of the bolt action, opened the breach, made sure no cartridge was present and sighted downrange through the heavy-duty scope that was mounted on the rail. He whistled again and gently set the weapon down on the table.

"Fair enough, Mr. Meredith, fair enough." He said and reached for another weapon like a kid in a candy shop.

There were a couple of very mean looking Legacy 12-guage Aim Guard pump shotguns, and a new Mossberg 500 Road Blocker, a no stock, sawed off shotgun that would be useful in tight quarters. With the pump action they were both capable of firing off five shells with one in the chamber. These so-called defensive shotguns were built to intimidate without having to pull the trigger.

Both weapons had muzzle brakes that looked like weapons all by themselves, but were actually meant to spread the combustion gases quickly when the gun was fired, minimizing the weapon's kick. Again Kevin whistled quietly and said, "I want one of these too. These are outstanding."

Michael was staring at the handguns on the table with the same awe that Kevin had exhibited. He picked up a Kimber .45 Caliber Tactical Pistol, capable of handling 9mm. loads, recognizing it was a top of the line law enforcement model. He ejected the clip from the handle and slid back the slide to make sure the chamber had no cartridge loaded. He sighted it with a locked full arm extension and took aim downrange. Then he carefully set the weapon down.

"Yes sir, I'll look forward to that meeting," Kevin said. He couldn't take his eyes off all the beautiful weapons that were lay in front of him. Finally he turned to Meredith and said,

"May I dare ask where you got access to this outstanding array of weapons, Sir?"

"You may, Kevin, after 9-11 I took up shooting as a way to blow off some steam and frustration. I thought it might ease some of my pain." Meredith pointed downrange at the targets. " See those targets down there? I like to think of them as big, fat, Osama bin Laden targets. I find that my aim is always a bit better when I have him in my sights. I've gotten pretty good at shooting, so much so that I started looking at munitions companies as a potential investment opportunity."

Meredith reached for a handgun on the table and lifted it up open palmed towards Kevin. "My first exposure was with this Kimber Raptor. I was shooting it one day out here and the instructor asked me if I liked the gun."

"What's not to like?"

"He advised me it was manufactured right here in New York. I was surprised. He said they were a top-notch firearms company just down the road in Yonkers, New York. So I investigated the Kimber Firearms Company and eventually bought some stock in the munitions manufacturer."

That was a few years ago, and since then I've shot a lot more and bought more stock. I now have enough investment and interest in the company that they asked me to sit on their Board of Directors. Thus, I have access to some pretty impressive weaponry. And I like testing their products seeing what they handle like on the range. These aren't all mine, but they are all available to me, and now you too for today, and any other practice times we schedule."

Kevin and Michael both looked at one another still looking like kids in a candy store with lots of pennies to spend. They both grinned at Meredith. Michael spoke for them and said, "Bill, we're pleased to assist you in breaking these puppies in, and getting this crew up to speed, without getting anyone killed."

"That's what I was hoping for Mike." Meredith said. "As you know these people are important to me."

The whole group had gathered around and watched the exchange between Meredith and Kevin and Michael. They too were ogling the impressive array of formidable weapons spread out on the table. And they too wanted to touch and feel the pistols, it was like candy, they just had to have some.

"Alright everyone, gather around so we can start this little gun safety class." Kevin raised his voice and took command of the group. "If you don't listen and learn, you will not be shooting today."

Michael glanced at Meredith, with a told you so look, and then took a step back so the others could step forward for their first shooting lesson.

The first thing Kevin distributed to everyone was a set of ear protectors to muffle the noise from the guns. Like cold weather mufflers, they fit nicely over the ears to form a seal, and muffle the sounds of the gunfire, yet still allowed a person to hear someone talking nearby. Kevin demonstrated how to put them on, and then showed everyone how to cock one ear flap up somewhat higher on the head so that the instruction part of the gun safety course could be heard better.

"When we are actually firing on the line, I want these protectors down on both ears. The crack of a shot in close proximity can be deafening and also disorienting. So everyone should wear these ear protectors religiously, or you'll not only have a hell of a headache, you'll eventually have some hearing loss. OK?"

Everyone nodded and tried to adjust their mufflers so they could hear more clearly.

Kevin picked up a .45 caliber silver handgun with a three-inch barrel and held it high so that everyone was looking at the weapon.

"This small gun can kill you in an instant. Drill right through you. It will kill you,…. if you don't handle it carefully and respect its power. Learn that lesson right now, and I will make you an expert marksman in no time at all." With that he showed the group where the safety was on each weapon. He said the safety was to be kept on at all times, unless they were actually on the range, and authorized by Michael or him to actually shoot.

→ ←

Teterboro Airport

The private WM Industries hanger was a massive unit housing three planes, two large jet aircraft and one large dual engine prop plane, all registered to the company. And there was still enough room for additional planes. In one corner there was two-story structure that housed a number of offices on the lower level, along with a map room, rest rooms and weather computers clustered around some large drafting tables. Upstairs, on a mezzanine level was a large living room setup with a large picture window overlooking the field. It had comfortable sofas, with a number of smaller sleeping rooms down a hall for emergency use by the pilots, crews, and passenger/guests.

Ryan Younger sat on a stool at the large drafting table studying maps and weather printouts. He was chief pilot for the company and exclusively flew William Meredith wherever he needed to go. With Meredith's diversified business interests, this took them to all corners of the earth.

Ryan liked this job much better than flying for the airlines which was boring and frustrating after having been in the Air Force flying fighters for 15 years. This position made flying much more exciting then jockeying big lumbering passenger jets back and forth. Here, he was flying fast, sleek jet aircraft that could run rings around the passenger jets. These planes held his interest. And his boss always gave him great places to fly.

Ryan had flown A-10 Warthogs for the past 10 years, seeing action in Iraq, and Korea. After these extended foreign tours he had become a training pilot, at the Air Force's Fighter Weapons School at Nellis Air Force Base, just north of Las Vegas to finish out his career.

He held dual citizenship in the United States and Canada. His parents had met while both were vacationing in Hawaii back in the 70's. His father, Tony had been a long haul independent truck driver hauling loads from eastern Canada all the way west to Vancouver. He would work for about 10 months of the year and then take off on holiday because from a tax standpoint he would only be paying the Canadian government taxes during the last two months of the year. So he went to Hawaii and met his future wife, Susan, in a pizza parlor, where she was working so she could stay in Hawaii longer.

They eventually fell in love and when they returned to the mainland they got married and set up shop in Vancouver. For the first couple years Susan rode shotgun with him as he made his cross-country journeys, but then they settled down in White Rock, BC, just over the border from Blaine, Washington.

A short time later Ryan was born and because of his parent's two-country residency, he automatically received dual citizenship status. This was of little consequence for him as a child growing up, other than allowing him easy access to visit his grandparents, Ralph and Peggy in Milwaukee, Wisconsin, in the States.

As a young man he decided he wanted to fly jets. After high school in Canada, he tried to get an appointment to the U.S. Air Force Academy but didn't have the clout to get any official notice in the U.S. But that didn't stop him. He joined the regular Air Force as a grunt, and after basic training with top-notch grades, was able to secure a position working on the AWACS, Airborne Warning and Communications Systems, reconnaissance jets, patrolling the skies over Iraq and the Middle East.

By the time he was nineteen years old he had earned a bunch of theatre of war battle ribbons, had attended jump school, survival training, and had even served a stint as honor guard to the President of the United States. So when he re-applied to the Air Force Academy he had no trouble getting an appointment based upon his Air Force credentials and grades.

On his first day at the Air Force Academy in Colorado Springs, he was told he had to wear his dress uniform and all earned insignia and decorations, even though he was a lowly plebe. This caused some complications the first few days as the upper classmen were confused that a plebe could outrank them and had a number of earned classifications and theatre of war insignia on his chest. But the earned decorations also showed him to be a committed leader, someone that his fellow classmates could look up to and emulate.

This got him noticed. With his practiced discipline learned as an Air Force non-com, he quickly rose to various Academy leadership responsibilities, representing his unit and his class. The fact that he was also a committed student made his four-year stint a cakewalk. He graduated at the head of his class with honors and headed off to flight school to learn to fly A-10 Thunderbolts.

He was a natural on the flight line and took to driving his A-10 Thunderbolt II, also called the Warthog, with gusto. He liked the close quarter action, as the plane was designed for low level ground support and this would put him directly in the action. The jet aircraft was known for its tank killing capabilities. It had excellent maneuverability at low air speed and altitude, and had a highly accurate weapons delivery platform.

Because the jet flew low to do its job, the pilot sat in a titanium-armored cockpit making him less susceptible to enemy ground fire. The plane's munitions included general purpose, cluster, and laser guided bombs, Maverick and AIM 9 sidewinder missiles, rockets and illumination flares, plus a 30 mm cannon capable of firing 3,900 rounds per minute. It was an ugly looking, nasty, no-nonsense military craft that packed a punch.

Ryan's call sign at the time was "Clicks" although he refused to tell anyone how he had gotten the nickname. While there were some possible reasons, he wasn't talking. He learned how to fly his craft well and served with distinction, rising to the rank of Captain, and then Major. He had served overseas with distinction and then became a Fighter Weapons School training pilot for a couple of years at Nellis AFB, with the new call sign "Chips". He put in his twenty years of military service and then mustered out, to fly the big jets for American Airlines. But he quickly grew weary of those boring flying machines although he was always in awe that the monsters stayed in the air at all. He started looking for a different sort of challenge.

Then "McGruff", one of his former wingmen from Korea, called one day to say he had heard of a possible cushy job flying a rich guy around the world. It was based out of New York and it was a top-notch aircraft with all the bells and whistles. Ryan jumped at the chance to investigate and met with William Meredith the next week.

With his military credentials he got the job and was now piloting a Bombardier Global Express ultra long range, twin engine, jet aircraft, capable of making trips of 6,200 nautical miles between fuel stops. It had a luxury cabin seating over 10 comfortably and could be outfitted to sleep 6 for overseas flights. It had state-of-the-art navigational aids, SATCOM, a full data array and full satellite phone capability.

Ryan often said the Bombardier Global Express jet was sweet and flew like a bat out of hell. It was almost as much fun as the Warthog. The only thing missing was the sidewinder missiles and the 30 mm cannon, but such armaments were frowned upon at Teterboro and over the eastern United States.

Ryan was checking his flight plans because he was ferrying a couple of gentlemen and a woman to Paris for the boss. He had seen these guys with Meredith before but was unsure why the boss was so intent on assisting them. His instructions had been to get them to Paris, assist them getting in the country, arrange for a nondescript vehicle for transport, and then move the plane to Calais and wait for their return which could take a number of days.

They would stay in touch with each other through some satellite phones they were bringing but all the conversation would be minimized throughout the trip.

Ryan thought that was a good bit of drama for the week but decided a trip to Paris was always a good thing and he would play along since the boss had never steered him wrong. He would do anything for this guy since he felt he had been almost adopted by him. Ryan knew the story about Meredith's son death on 9-11.

He had been in the air over New York City that fateful day flying Meredith back to the city. He strongly felt that had they known what was going on they would have used their own jet to crash into one of the planes before it hit the Trade Tower. He knew Meredith would have approved such a move and he would have done it, perhaps saving thousands of lives. While he understood that he could never replace the son, Ryan felt a strong allegiance to William Meredith II and would always assist him any way he could.

Just then the door to the hanger opened and two olive skinned men and a pretty young woman stepped over the threshold built into the door, which was cut into the larger hanger door. He figured they were South Asian and in his mind determined that they were either Indian or Pakistani. The three adjusted their eyes to the darker interior of the hanger and seeing Ryan at the drafting table, waved and walked over to introduce themselves.

He could see the two men accompanying the lady seemed uncomfortable. They looked to be wearing ill-fitting suits that looked like they had just come off the rack. And each was carrying an ominous looking old duffel bag slung over their shoulders. The shoddy bags sent a chill up his spine.

The woman on the other hand was young and beautiful. She had a confidence about her and looked as if she could take care of herself. She was Ryan's kind of woman. She was dressed well, like she had just stepped out of a fashion magazine. She pulled a small-wheeled overnight bag and walked forward extending her hand.

"Captain Younger, I'm Courtney Ranker, an associate of Mr. Meredith. I'd like to introduce you to Mr. Osama Tarkan, and his brother, Malik Tarkan. They are both businessmen that have had some business dealings with Mr. Meredith." Ryan shook her hand and noted that it was a strong handshake, which he felt was an important indicator of personality. She continued, "It is good to meet you, Mr. Meredith has spoken highly of you."

Ryan returned the handshake and turned to the Pakistani gentleman and extended his hand in greeting to them as well. "Mr. Tarkan it is good to meet you," he said as he shook hands, and then he repeated the welcome and handshake with Malik as well.

The pilot waved his hand in the direction of the jet aircraft that was parked behind him and said. "Welcome to the WM Industries aircraft hanger. Mr. Meredith said you would be coming today. I am pleased that I can be of service."

The older of the two men said somewhat formally, "We appreciate your seeing us and transporting us to Paris, at the request of your employer. He has asked us to do some work for him over there. It is important enough that he thought we should fly."

He looked at Ms. Ranker and the two men, and said. " Well, if you are ready, the plane is fueled, and I've filed the flight plans, so we are good to go whenever you wish." He pointed to the jet aircraft behind him " If you will board, I will open the bay door, and we will be on our way."

"Thank you Ryan, I have to make a quick call to Mr. Meredith to advise we are on our way. It will only take a moment."

She reached for a cheap looking cell phone, which Ryan thought was odd. He turned and walked towards the hanger door electric panel.

Courtney punched in a phone number and left a short message in a matter of 30 seconds. When she finished, Ryan observed her out of the corner of his eye casually breaking the spine of the folding cell phone into two pieces, and then observed her discarding the pieces in two different trash bins in the hanger. That too was odd, he thought, what's that all about?

The three passengers then walked to the plane's steps and boarded. The two men did so somewhat tentatively.

Standing by the panel of red and green buttons near the office door, he pushed the green UP button and a low-pitched buzzer sound went off as the large 40-foot wide, hinged door began opening. It folded upwards into itself and rose twenty feet in the air offering full clearance for the jet aircraft tail fin standing some eighteen feet off the ground.

Ryan then boarded the plane and retrieved the hatch door in one fluid movement. As the door closed and locked, the co-pilot already in his seat, started spooling up the starboard engine, and then when a programmed level of rpm was attained, spooled up the second engine.

Ryan took a quick look about the cabin, made sure his three guests were securely seat-belted in and stated that he would advise when it was safe to unbuckle and move about the cabin after attaining altitude. He pointed out where the lavatory was, and advised that the refrigerator was well stocked with various liquids and sandwiches that they could help themselves to during the less than six-hour flight.

He then stepped into the cockpit but left the curtain separating the cockpit from the main cabin open, so he could occasionally keep an eye on his guests. The plane started rolling out of the hanger and turned into the alley between another hanger building. Ryan pointed what looked like a garage door opener out the window and the hanger door started closing.

Courtney settled in and took a quick look about the cabin and mumbled to herself that this was how the other half lived. And then adjusted the thought by saying how the other 'one percent' lived.

Osama and Malik just sat there stunned, having never been in an airplane much less a luxury jet. They were so scared that they had not said a word. They had figured out how to click the seatbelt by watching Courtney but now they had no idea as to what would happen next. The sound of the engines spooling up were getting louder by the second and they were looking about and at one another wondering what they had gotten themselves into.

The narrow alley causeway was large enough to accommodate the wingspan but O and Malik were still unsettled as they could see the wings out both sets of windows were only ten feet from the two buildings. The jet picked up a bit of speed as it got to the end of the alley and turned on to a wider approach to the taxiway. Once there the plane turned again and lurched ahead picking up speed as it began its run up the taxiway.

Out from between the hangers Malik and Osama looked out the windows and also looked straight ahead at the cockpit window, which was just fifteen feet in front of them. Both were gripping their armrests as they watched the plane move quickly down the taxiway approaching some trees a couple hundred feet away. Then without warning the plane abruptly turned to starboard and started a fast roll as it hit the main runway. The engines spooled up to a high-pitched whine and the two men looked at each other panic stricken.

Then they heard the pilot speak some words to the air controller, and then offer a loud, " and we're off ", as the Bombardier Global Express raced down the runway faster than they had ever traveled in their lives.

The two brothers hands were white with the tense grip they had on their armrests when the nose suddenly went up, the plane leaned back and they shot into the air. Except for the whine of the engines, Courtney would have heard both of them whine as well at the moment of takeoff. The jet stayed on its 35-degree upward angle for the next three minutes and then began leveling off to a slower, more moderate rate of ascent. In less than 15 minutes they were at Angels 40 above sea level and cruising at a speed of 450 kts.

Courtney had silently watched the two men ahead of her and noticed they had white-knuckled the entire ascent and were only now relaxing a bit. They were staring out the windows and their mouths were open. She looked out but realized they were already way out over the Atlantic and there was nothing to see but ocean blue.

All three looked up when the pilot unbuckled his harness and climbed out of his seat, and walked into the cabin. Osama and Malik looked quite concerned that the pilot was not up there flying. Ryan smiled and offered a casual comment.

"I hope you didn't mind me catching the wind back there on takeoff. I still love to soar as straight up as allowable in these planes. It reminds me of my Air Force days when we had to take off fast and take a 45 degree angle to get as much lift as we could." He used his hand to show the rate of climb he wished he could have taken.

"Gentlemen, you look a bit pale, I'm guessing you haven't flown much, huh? Maybe a drink and a sandwich will help settle those stomachs. Please help yourself in the fridge in the galley here."

Both brothers tried to relax and looked back to see if they could spot whatever a 'fridge' was. They continued to look confused.

Ms. Ranker, could I get you anything, a drink, a pillow, any thing?"

"It's Courtney and I'm fine, but you may need to show these gentlemen where the restroom is and what you meant by 'fridge' she laughed and smiled at the pilot. "I would guess you just knocked off a couple of virgin flyers, Captain."

"Oh hell, sorry, I didn't even think about that. I'm always glad to be back in the air and I never think about rookies. My error." He turned to the brothers. "Gentlemen, I apologize, I may have taken that lift-off a bit steep."

He asked the two Pakistani's if they would like to move around the plane a bit, hit the head, or get something to drink." When he said head they just looked even more confused, thus he led them to the back of the plane and showed them 'the head'.

He returned to Courtney's seat and asked, " So what is so important that we are flying to Paris, the City of Love?"

Courtney rolled her eyes and said, "I'm just assisting them because they were novice travelers and could use the directional help and international travel expertise. They are doing some contract work for Mr. Meredith that required their particular expertise."

"Which is what? Ryan asked, "It's certainly not flying."

"I'm afraid you would have to get those questions answered from Mr. Meredith. I am not even sure what they are doing." She lied and started looking at her magazine again. "All I know is that they needed the ride, we will get them a rental car while in Paris and that we will pick them up in Calais at some point a number of days later."

"That I knew because I had to file the flight plans. Well, if the boss wants me cooling my heels in Paris, I can't think of a nicer place to settle in. Could I talk you into dinner in Paris or are you off with the twins?"

"I am not," she said, "after I get them to Paris and into a car, they are on their own. Thus, I intend to spend a day or two shopping and saying hello to some old friends that I know over there."

"So it's a date," Ryan said with a smile on his face. He was confident this could be a very good layover.

Courtney rolled her eyes again for effect and said, "A date may be a bit strong, but we both have to eat, and I know a number of restaurants on the Champs Elysees and on the Left Bank that are spectacular."

"So you're a frog? Is that it?"

"No, but my former work brought me over here a good number of times. That's why Meredith thought I would be useful to the brothers."

"So what do you do?" Ryan asked.

"I am actually semi-retired and do investigation work for a number of clients." She looked over her shoulder at the two brothers and said, "Your concern about them can be put to rest. You needn't worry. I vetted them for Mr. Meredith and they are two very nice gentlemen who can offer him valuable services for an important job he has undertaken. Its our job to make sure that they have the help to succeed."

"That's good to know. Now, I can shut the cockpit curtain and not worry what is going on behind my back. I hope they didn't notice my concern like you did?"

"I'm sure they didn't, they were too busy gawking at the planes to notice. Look at them, I'm guessing this is there first time in a jet and a pretty fancy one at that!"

Just then O and Malik came forward from the head. Their color had somewhat returned and they'd found bottled water. They looked a lot calmer than they had 30 minutes earlier. Ryan said, "Gentlemen, I see you're feeling better, that's good. We should be landing outside Paris in about five hours if the winds are with us."

Both men looked up when they heard that the winds needed to be with them, and Ryan realized that he would need to be careful in his words or he would have two basket cases on his hands.

"What I meant to say is that the blowing winds will help us arrive faster. That's a good thing. For now, eat whatever you like, those chairs fold down into beds and there are blankets and pillows in that locker. Enjoy yourself and let me know if you need anything."

O and Malik said almost simultaneously, "Thank you Mr. Ryan. We appreciate your hospital."

Ryan nodded figuring out what they really meant to say, he winked at Courtney, and went back to the cockpit. This time he drew the curtain closed satisfied there was no danger lurking behind him.

> <

Louis Breguet Airport, Paris

The Bombardier landed effortlessly and the brothers dealt with the landing much better than they had with the take-off. They had both moved to window seats and watched the entire final approach looking down at the French countryside, the busy highways and the houses and villas spread on the hillsides. They still gripped the armrests as the plane closed the last twenty feet to the runway but Ryan brought the plane down with hardly a bump.

On the ground but still racing down the runway the brothers felt the speed with which they had been moving and again became terrified. Courtney looked over and signaled with her hand that they should just relax and enjoy the ride.

When the plane came to a stop at the charter facility, the three passengers exited the plane and went to Customs in the airport terminal. All three knew that this would be the first test as they were carrying false documents. Courtney had practiced with the brothers on how they should act, what they should say and how they should answer the business questions they might be asked. The French Customs Officer looked over their documents, scanned the passports, asked a simple question about duration of stay and waved them through.

As Courtney marveled at the brevity of the review, she noted that Ryan was with them and was a regular business professional passing through this private airport portal. Perhaps they were familiar enough with him and Mr. Meredith that there was no reason to be concerned or extra vigilant.

They walked over to the car rental desk and quickly obtained a 2- year old Peugeot with GPS. They advised it would be returned in Calais at the airport four or five days later. They also got some maps, as a backup as there were too many century old roads to have everything mapped well. They exited the airport as a group and drove into Paris driving to the center of the city.

The GPS worked well and they were able to find the Hotel Marignan, between Ave. Montaigne and the Avenue de Champs-Elysees that Courtney and Ryan would stay in while the brothers went on their mission. The Hotel was central to many of the sites of Paris including the Eiffel Tower, the Arc de Triomphe and from the higher suites you could see the Sacre Couer Basilica in Montmarte, and Notre Dame Cathedral across the Seine River. It was a perfect location for tourists.

Courtney and Ryan pulled their bags from the boot and Ryan started to carry them into the hotel before the hotel staff could react. Courtney came around to the passenger side and leaned into the front window. She smiled and offered a simple but heartfelt "good luck" comment to the brothers, stating that she, Ryan and the plane would be waiting for them in Calais on the Charter side of the airport. They nodded in agreement, turned the engine over, and pulled away from the curb.

Courtney then stepped to the curb, pulled out another cheap looking phone and made another call. This phone had international calling capability. She left a short message for Mr. Meredith and signed off whispering some initials that Ryan thought sounded like THC something. Again he thought it odd but his job was to be the flyboy. At least this time she did not throw away the phone.

→ ←

North of Paris

The two brothers drove up the wide tree-lined Champs-Elysees towards the Arc de Triomphe marveling at the sights. They had not seen this part of Paris when they had been in France a number of years earlier. The buildings were ornately designed, with expensive stores, shops and restaurants lining one side and a very formal park lining the other. After circling the Arc two times just trying to get off the circle they crossed over the eight lanes of traffic to the park side and found a spot to pull over in the shade of a tree. They needed to study their maps and GPS before driving north. They were confident they could handle the traffic, as it was the equivalent of the New York madness they were used to, but the French road signs and number systems would still be a challenge. Once they were settled on their route, they drove north out of the city on Highway A 15. They drove carefully, the only car actually doing so. They made sure they maintained the speed limits to limit the amount of interest they might draw on themselves.

Courtney had briefed them on what they might run into with the Gendarmes and various constables they would see along the road. She had suggested the best way to avoid problems was to be good citizens at all times. If they were stopped, they were to maintain their cover and simply state that they were businessmen in the electronics business and they were making calls in the north of France. Their bags included electronic catalogs and order forms for their electronics company with offices in New York and Pakistan. All they needed to do was be careful and stick to their cover.

The trip north was uneventful and they covered the distance in less than two hours taking their time. The two brothers talked about their task and how they would each handle the situations that they thought they would find. They went over and over the plan making sure that they could do what Meredith had asked them to do.

Once they got to the outskirts of Calais, they drove through the city towards the industrial shipping port and then north a bit back into the country and the northern farmlands paralleling the port and the English Channel. This was where the immigrant encampments were located.

Just short of their destination by perhaps two miles, they parked their rental car in an old shopping strip that had seen better days. The lot was large and their car would not look suspicious parked there for a few days. It was a considerable distance from the actual encampment, which was down a couple roads and then some dirt paths and through some woods and farm fields. They would walk the rest of the way.

Leaving their suit jackets neatly on the rear seat of the car under a blanket they took their duffel bags, and one at a time, walked to an adjacent petrol station men's room to change into their Pakistani traveling clothes. Some of the clothes had been salvaged from their first trip to New York. They were worn and tattered much like they would have been had they traveled a great distance on their trip. They even smelled like they had been worn for days.

Once they had both changed and all vestiges of their New York life had been washed away, they stowed their city clothes in the car, locked it up, and started walking towards the Afghan / Pakistani encampment they had left ten years earlier. On the way in, they left the old roadway and walked into the high grasslands surrounding the forest and fields, all within eyesight of the English Channel and harbor areas.

As they walked they searched for some potential hiding places to bury some things. They found some rock outcroppings that would offer cover from rain and prying eyes and hid their computer equipment under the ledge inside one of their duffel bags. It would be safe there until they needed it once they made contact with the right people.

Moving back to the dirt roadway they started walking again towards the ragtag encampment. They wandered in past some blue-tarps stretched between trees that seemed to be empty, and then past a number of hastily assembled shanties of metal and cardboard that lined a well-worn path. This was the Jungle. There seemed to be no one about as they looked for signs of life, but knew that people were probably watching them approach. As they made their way further into the encampment an occasional man would appear here or there, and then another a couple of meters ahead. They would step out from behind a partial stonewall, or piece of metal siding, and just watch them. They were sending a silent message that both O and Malik understood. It had been the same way years ago when they passed through this same area looking for passage out of Europe.

As they walked forward the slum dwellings opened up a bit, and they saw a number of people gathered around some lighted oil drums that burned wood and offered some warmth from the English Channel chill. Malik and Osama stepped forward and offered a greeting in their native pashtun language of the North-west Frontier Province in North Waziristan.

With the greeting uttered, the assembled people all turned and returned the greeting, showing a warm willingness to allow these two men to step forward and into their midst. They were welcomed to the fire to warm their bodies, and a veiled woman stepped forward offering some course bread and bitter coffee. Pleasantries were exchanged, some small talk followed, and eventually some questions were asked to determine who these two men were and why were they here.

Osama and Malik introduced themselves and then basically told the true story of their travels from Pakistan, only leaving out that it had occurred years ago and that they had moved on to America. They spoke the native language well enough that no one doubted where they had come from. While they were being gently interrogated by this ragtag assembly they knew the process was critical to being accepted by them. This would allow them free reign in the encampment and hopefully a chance to identify who they were looking for.

This talk went on for an hour and ceased only when Osama asked if they could have a place to sleep after their long journey. The group showed them to an empty shanty and they were given some blankets and a lantern to heat the small area. There was a teapot on a small butane burner sitting in a corner. They were left to themselves.

→ ←

Kensico Gun Club, Westchester

The group had progressed well in a couple of hours. With Kevin and Michael taking the lead, every one was now comfortable with the safety issues of guns. Using the short range, shooting at 25 feet and 50 feet, the group had learned how to handle the weapons carefully, how to factor in the safety, load the clips, and how to chamber a round. They had all learned the hard way how to avoid getting 'clipped' in the soft tissue between the fingers and the thumb, when the slide rushed back to eject a round while pulling another one into the chamber.

Michael had distributed unloaded weapons to everyone and many were surprised at how heavy the handguns were. They learned how to safely hold the weapon with a standard two-hand grip. One hand would grip the pistol and the other hand would grip the wrist to steady the shot. They learned that full extension of the arms in a locked position would minimize the recoil and would also improve accuracy, especially if multiple rounds were being fired.

When they stepped to the firing line, each of them picked up an unloaded handgun. They checked it to be sure of its empty status, slipped in the pre-loaded clip, chambered a round, flipped off the safety, and steadied their aim at full extension at the target just 25 feet away. The target was a silhouette of a man's body with a sweet spot target on the torso. They were told to take a breath, exhale and gently squeeze off a round.

On their first shot all the first-timers were shocked at the recoil of the weapon and understood why they were only chambering a single round and using a full extension, locked arm firing position. More than one of them let the gun fly up, or turned to their sides without thinking where the gun was now pointed.

Both Michael and Kevin patiently explained this as gun safety 101, and why they needed to experience that first shot on their own, so that they understood the power and the danger of the weapon they were handling. They were then asked to reverse the process of shooting, first putting the safety back on, then ejecting the clip, and finally pulling back the slide to make sure the chamber was empty. Then they were allowed to place the gun on the table.

This first go-round went slowly and the group was initially impatient. But as each person took their turn, they began to realize the power of the weapons they were holding. They ran this drill one more time and then everyone was invited to select a handgun and a box of shells. Each was carefully instructed on how to load a clip the right way so that the cartridges would not jam when they were being shot in succession.

Then they all lined up on the line with a handgun in front of them. On Kevin's call, they picked up their weapon, made sure it was pointed downrange, inspected it to note the gun was safe and in good shape. They were told to slam home their clip, chamber a round by pulling the slide, and click off the safety.

With all nine weapons pointing downrange, they took their stance, locked their wrists and elbows in the classic shooting stance, and were told to fire just two rounds at their individual targets. In a matter of three seconds all the guns roared. Before they could even begin to move, Kevin bellowed. "Safe your weapons, eject the clip, and slide the chamber open. Make sure your chamber is empty."

Everyone did as they were told. They all stared downrange at their targets. Of the seven targets before them, five had at least a single shot somewhere in the torso drawing. Two targets were completely empty and Katie and Uri were scratching their heads. Kevin explained what happened and why everyone missed on their second shot.

"Your first shot recoil will make the weapon rise when you fire and many of you pulled the trigger the second time before leveling your aim. That's why they have a thirty-foot dirt wall behind the targets. Let's try it again, and this time, don't just pull the trigger twice, re-aim after the first shot, then squeeze off the second round. Ready?"

"Ok, pick up and inspect your weapon. Make sure the safety is on and locked, examine and load your magazine clip. Pull back the slide and chamber a round, flip off the safety once you are aiming downrange, aim using a two handed grip, and then gently squeeze the trigger."

This time there were two distinct successive roars of the weapons with a second in between rounds. They had listened and taken the time to readjust their aim. After reversing the shooting routine and placing their weapons on the table they looked downrange. This time everyone had hit the target at least once and four people had hit their targets twice although most shots were high, but on the target.

Meredith heard his new temporary cell phone ring in his pocket and debated taking the call. He decided to let it ring and the caller would then leave a message. He knew who it was but thought minimizing the back and forth conversation would be a good security measure. He waited a few minutes to let the message get recorded and then wandered away from the group, to hear the message he was waiting for.

The message was from Courtney in Paris. She acknowledged they were safely there and that the others were heading north. She said all was well and that she would call again in a few days. She had signed off THCT almost in a whisper. Meredith thought that she must have been close to Ryan when she made the call. He thought that he would have to bring his pilot into his confidence sooner or later. Meredith walked back to the group and found a spot on the line to try his hand at shooting. He knew what he was doing.

The afternoon proceeded well, with everyone falling into a solid gun safety routine and improving their shooting with each round. By the end of the afternoon, five of the shooters were consistently hitting their targets and their groupings were getting tighter with each round. The rookies were still struggling but they were developing good habits and their aim was improving. Since almost everyone except Michael and William had received a good scrape on their soft tissue between the finger and thumb from the slide recoil, Kevin decided to call it a day to everyone's frustration.

"Kevin, thanks for the lessons," Katie offered, "I have a new respect for what you guys do every day. But before we leave could we see a little demonstration of how well you and Michael shoot? And then I would like to see what those shotguns do and maybe that air rifle."

"Katie, its not an air rifle but a real long distance weapon that can shoot the eyes out of a gopher at 500 yards. And I would like to give this baby a try, if its alright Bill?'

"Kevin, be my guest, here's the ammo, and I have the targets set up at 100 yards, so let her rip. I'd like to see how you handle the rifle as well. I'll spot for you."

While Kevin set up the sniper rifle, William pointed to Michael and said, "Michael, you may want to show these guys what one of those shotguns can do as well."

Michael didn't need an invitation. He grabbed both types of shotguns and moved over to the short range at 25ft. He took out a box of 25 shells, loaded five, 3½-inch target rounds, after showing everyone that the safety was engaged.

Meanwhile Kevin inspected his long gun and sighted in the target before loading a single .308 two-inch cartridge into the chamber. He carefully wrapped the sling around his arm, settled his grip and shoulder into the weapon and stepped to the firing line. With a wide stance for balance, and leaning just a hair forward, he gently squeezed the trigger and the shot went downrange.

Everyone watched the target as it registered the hit with a small puff of smoke. He had hit the target at 100 yards on his first shot. With a spotting scope, Meredith announced that the shot was five inches off center, up and to the left.

Kevin reloaded and took his stance again. Sighting through the large scope mounted on the rail, he made a minute adjustment that only he could feel and gently squeezed off another round. This shot also hit the target and those with good eyesight could see that it was closer to the center mass of the human outline.

Meredith checked the shot through the scope on a table tripod and said.

"Bull's-eye Kevin, you nailed it dead center. Nice shooting. What did you say you did in the military?"

"Thanks, I didn't say what I did over there, but suffice it to say that I did a lot of shooting with weapons like these. Bill, this is a mighty fine weapon. I would like to do more shooting just so I can keep my ratings."

"You will Kevin, you will, as my guest as often as you like." He turned to Michael who was waiting a few tables over with the shotguns. "Michael, how about demonstrating one of those monsters over there?"

The group slid over to stand behind Michael as he prepared to shoot the shotgun. They all adjusted their ear mufflers. He loaded five shells into the storage chamber mounted under the barrel. As each shell was shot, it would automatically eject as the next round was pumped into the chamber.

He demonstrated he was flipping off the safety, took aim at the targets hanging just 25 feet away and squeezed the trigger. The shotgun roared and people thought they saw fire coming out of the muzzle as the super-heated gases belched from the barrel.

Down the line the target was shredded like Swiss cheese. Michael moved slightly to the left and signaled that he would be shooting multiple rounds this time. He aimed at a new target, pulled the trigger, moved slightly left, chambered a second round using the pump action and fired again at the second target. He did the same again and again, shooting another total of four rounds downrange. All five targets were shredded hanging by a thread in a matter of seconds. Everyone applauded the shooting effort not readily understanding that it was pretty hard to miss with a shotgun. Michael made a show of clicking on the safety and laid it on the table.

"Show off!" Kevin said. The group turned and followed the voice back to Kevin.

Kevin took aim and nailed another target as if he had been doing it all morning. But this time he immediately opened the breach, reached down for another shell sitting in the box of 100, reloaded and squeezed off another round hitting the target as well. He repeated this four more times, hitting the target each time, as if he was matching Michael shot for shot. He set the weapon down and looked over at Michael.

Not to be outdone, Michael picked up the Mossberg shotgun. It had no wooden stock, just a short handgrip, making it a much shorter weapon. He loaded five shells. Moving down the firing line to some fresh targets, he announced that he would be firing.

Everyone put on their mufflers and watched. He proceeded to shoot and for the most part obliterate the new targets as quickly as he had the last ones.

This time he whistled and looked down at this deadly weapon, still belching smoke out of the nasty looking barrel. He silently wished he had this type of equipment in his own squad car. Damn this was one fine weapon, he thought.

Being late in the afternoon, Meredith signaled that the demonstration was over and everyone could remove his or her ear protection. He said they would return in a few weeks to work on the next level of shooting and to take a crack at the long guns.

The group thanked Kevin for his instruction. He felt as if he'd done a pretty good job of instructing these first time shooters.

As the group was congratulating one another on their target groupings, Meredith leaned in and spoke to Kevin. "Come on up to the clubhouse. Michael will get the group home, and I'll drive you back to the city myself. Let's have a drink and that talk I mentioned."

Kevin and Michael finished putting all the weapons away. Michael slapped Kevin on the back, pointed him towards the clubhouse and said, "Bill is really a good man, he's become like a father to me. Have a drink with him and I think he will share with you what is going on. Make sure you ask for the good booze and let him know you like a good cigar. Thanks buddy. I'll see you back in town."

→ ←

Jungle Encampment, Calais

It was very early with a damp mist still hanging in the lowlands along the English Channel. The sun had not yet broken through the gray cloud cover. Malik and Osama had slept fitfully, being unsure how welcome they really were in this refugee camp. The two brothers sat huddled together sharing a blanket and drinking tea to ward off the ocean chill.

Out of nowhere a bearded man appeared and knocked on the tin sidewall of their small tent, which had been pieced together with various scraps of wood and metal, and covered with a large blue tarp to divert the rain. He asked if he could enter and Malik said yes in his native language and offered him greetings as he would any guest.

The man was a tall, dark complexioned Afghan with long hair and a short-cropped beard. He wore western pants with a loose cotton shirt that hung over his belt. A leather satchel was strapped across his chest. He stepped into the room and reached up to pull his long hair back and away from his face. In so doing, both O and Malik saw a small curved knife tucked into his belt. They presumed he did that on purpose just to set the tone for his conversation.

He sat down on the edge of the blanket and offered his hand as a sign of friendship.

"I am Tasneen Akbar, from Jalabad in the mountains east of Kabul. I was not here yesterday when you arrived in our camp of squalor and frustration. As you can see we live like barbarians in filth, but we have no other place to go. How did you find us?"

Osama knew this line of questioning would come as it had years ago when they had first arrived. "We are from small village in North Waziristan, I think close to where you come from, just across border. We have been traveling for many weeks. We caught a ship to Marseilles, and there we were directed to this 'Jungle' place. So we came here across France to see if you can help to direct us. We hope to find a way to England where we hear that we can make a life," he said in good conversational Pashtun.

"I see, many have come before you, and this is in fact a place where we have had some success in getting people to other places. Perhaps we can be of assistance. Tell me more of home, what is going on? I have not been in the mountains for three years now, as I am a senior here helping others."

Osama recognized he was being tested and offered, "We have also been traveling for the last four months getting here. Everything is in disarray back in the homeland. The Americans are changing the governments in Kabul and in Islamabad and they chase the Taliban and the al Qaeda all over the mountains between our countries."

Malik offered some insights of home as well. "They fight and they bomb us everywhere. It is an unsafe land. While we side with our brothers, we are looking for safe passage so we can carry on the cause in England."

They exchanged stories for a few minutes. Osama and Malik were happy they had read the Pakistani local newspapers in New York before leaving so that they could talk about their country and local news.

"So you side with the Taliban and Al Qaeda?" O noticed that his body language changed slightly and that he looked more relaxed. His hand moved to his leather bag and he opened it to offer some food and water as the conversation continued.

"We have been sent to meet with some people in England. We are supposed to join in their efforts there but we are unsure what it is that they are doing."

The man nodded as if he understood their quest and said he would try to help arrange passage. He asked what kind of money they had left, as such transportation efforts would be costly.

"We have a few Euros left but used most of our money getting to France. We are prepared to work our way there as we did on the ship that came from Karachi. We can work hard."

The man nodded again saying he would see what he could do. They talked about home and the mountains for another half hour. Tasneen looked as if he was satisfied as to whom they were. He encouraged them to stay in the camp but to be useful as there were hundreds of people who were trying to survive here and in other camps nearby. He left and Osama and Malik exchanged glances wondering if they had set the right tone in this first meeting. Time would tell.

They got dressed and left the encampment to see if they could scrounge food, useable clothing, or wood for fuel from the surrounding area to help out. They had done this on their earlier visit and they knew that would put them in good light with the people running the camp. They walked through the farmer's fields and along the roads leading into town but did not go anywhere near where their car was parked or where they had hidden their duffel bag of computer equipment.

→ ←

Fort Meade, Maryland

Bill Dalde sat at his desk in one of the many buildings within the 5,000-acre complex known as Fort Meade, in Maryland, closer to Baltimore than Washington D.C. His job was not a very exciting one, but he knew that it was important, and he tried to maintain vigilance even though the work was often monotonous. He was on the front line of Homeland Security's terrorism watch and his job was to analyze data that the super computers spit out each day from millions of telephone and data calls being monitored.

He and hundreds of other analysts just like him worked for the National Security Agency, the NSA, in what was sometimes called Crypto City, a large top-secret federal facility charged with the responsibility of finding terrorists before they found us.

The NSA complex at Ft. Meade was like a fortress and he was reminded of that every day when he drove in and had to go past a number of checkpoints with armed guards. The base had its own top-notch security forces and they made sure they knew each and every employee that had access to the site. While they were north of the Washington D.C. corridor, just off I-295, and the Baltimore Washington Parkway, they were still a highly confidential facility.

Ironically, these mysterious buildings backed up to the Fort Meade Golf Club with a number of the fairways running within 50 feet of the perimeter fence. The joke was that terrorists and bad guys must not golf.

The NSA super computers focused on listening to all sorts of communication information from phone calls, email and text messages, financial data and satellite transmissions. The many buildings on the fenced campus had huge dish antennas pointing to satellites floating in space collecting all this data and sending it back to NSA for analysis. Surrounding many of the multi-story buildings were huge radar domes and all sorts of antennae pulling in signals from around the world. If there was information moving anywhere on earth, the NSA satellites and computers were capturing it and transmitting it to Ft. Meade for review.

The complex computer system was generally known as 'Echelon', and it did the data mining, because there were not enough people to listen to all the calls and texts that came in. Most of the talk, 99% of it was benign and had nothing to do with terrorism. Most calls and conversations were simply family or business calls, texting back and forth, cell phone mothers gossiping to the neighbors, buy-sell orders being made for businesses, and porn talk at three dollars a minute. No one on staff wanted to listen to all that talk, nor would they be able to, there was just too much of it.

So these super-computers were programmed to do the work of listening to everything. They were programmed to sort calls and analyze communications based on all sorts of logarithms, looking at word association, call sequences, frequent calling, known bad guy numbers, etc. Certain words and phrases would automatically single out a call, and kick it to a higher level. Then the entire communication message would be further analyzed, by more sophisticated computers. Ultimately, if the message or information had what was deemed to be of interest, it triggered an additional review and landed on someone's desk for more focused research and human listening and analysis.

Bill was listening to such a call that had been referred to his desk this morning. It had all the attributes the computers were programmed to screen. The call was short, cryptic, and made little sense in and of itself. The person who had been called also made no sense in responding, and was just as abrupt in the communication.

The flagged word wasn't actually a word, but a series of letters - THCT, that made it interesting. But the real fireworks associated with this call came from the name that was also mentioned. Osama bin Laden was stated in the short conversation, thus it was definitely of interest. His name was a permanent trigger.

Bill listened to the twenty-second call again. He figured they would ultimately find the call came from a throwaway phone that couldn't be tracked again.

Bill reached for a notepad and filled out a red flag form on the sequence of letters THCT. Then he sent a coded email message down the line to the Echelon computers asking that the trigger word be added to all call monitoring. By doing so every other reference that might pop up, or even remotely relate to that sequence of letters, THCT, would be routed back to his desk for further analysis. He had his first flag of the morning. There would be many more.

→ ←

Kensico Gun Clubhouse

Meredith invited Kevin Geary into the plush surroundings of the clubhouse. It looked like most log cabins on the outside, but inside it was as lush as a building could get. It was designed to cater to the tastes of guys that shoot guns, rich guys that shoot guns. It had all the bells and whistles of a very private cushy club. It was a manly sanctuary. There was a huge bar that looked to have been carved out of single broad oak tree. It had been finely cut, and polished to a glossy shine, to the point that you could have shaved with the mirror finish.

There were massive leather armchairs and sofas scattered about the room, in small groupings. And you couldn't miss the mounted heads of various exotic game animals, from the north woods to Africa. Over a large stone fireplace there was a massive buffalo head that stared down at the two men.

"As I said, I rented out the entire gun club for the whole afternoon so we don't have a bartender, but I can offer you anything you would like to have. How about a whiskey, a scotch or a beer, now that we are done shooting?"

"Mr. Meredith…."

"It's Bill, Kevin, Mr. was my father and he died many years ago."

"Bill then, Michael told me you have some mean single malt scotch you like a lot, and I'd love a shot or two of that if you have it available?"

"A man to my liking, I do have a personal bottle of Glenmorangie, 18 year old single malt up here, they keep just for me. Got it in Scotland last spring. Liked it so much I had a case shipped over here. Now let's see if I can find it." He stepped behind the rugged looking bar and rooted around in a couple of cupboards.

"Got it." He walked around the bar with a bottle and two glasses. "On the rocks?"

"Yes, if you don't mind. I prefer my scotch cold. I know that can compromise the taste, but I drink it quick enough that the melting ice won't destroy the flavor."

"Again a man to my liking. Rocks it is." He dropped some cubes into both glasses and came over to the fireplace. "So Michael has told me all about you and your background. Did he tell you anything about me?" He poured and handed Kevin a glass.

"Thank you. Mike did tell me how you two met and how you happened to be in the same counseling group." He leaned forward, raised his glass and said, "My sincere condolences on the loss of your son in that tragedy. I can't imagine what a loss that must be. I lost a number of good friends that day, and I won't ever forget. And I've spent a couple years consoling Michael on Michaela's loss. She was the best thing that ever happened to him. She also meant a lot to me. She was like the sister I never had."

"Believe it or not, that is what this ragtag group is all about. Every one of those people on the range today, and a few more that weren't here, all lost loved ones on 9-11. It is our personal day of hell! You probably don't know this but I am British, I lost much of the accent being over here for the last ten years. Many of those folks you taught today are foreign born as well. That's how we all came together, to help one another grieve through this whole process of remorse, frustration, guilt, and anger. We have all been in hell for a long time now, just like you."

"I kind of figured they were mostly foreigners from their accents, but I am still mystified as to why we are all out here shooting at targets. Unless." He finished his drink with the open-ended thought and pushed his glass across the table for a re-fill. Meredith poured another.

"I'll answer the unless, in a moment, but let me give you some more background first. I mentioned the process of grieving and the many steps we have gone through. First there is disbelief that it happened. Then there is yearning for the person or persons lost. That can take months to work through. Then you eventually get to an anger stage, where you try to rationalize why such a thing happened, and wrestle with the fact that you were powerless to do anything about it."

William realized he had finished his drink and was still parched with all his talking, so he reached for the bottle and poured himself another, the ice still lingering in his glass. He continued.

"From anger you eventually fall into a deep depression because you can't do anything to bring them back. This step can last even longer the doctor tell us. This is when you try to come to grips with your loss, but as you can readily imagine, how can you come to grips with the inconceivable tragedy of 9-11."

He stood up and walked to the bar, leaned and reached over it for a moment. Then he pulled up a large, ornate Humidor, and walked over to Kevin.

"It's a bad habit, but one that works beautifully with a good scotch. Would you like a cigar? The one's on the left are Cubans and they are stronger than anything on the market, legal or illegal."

Kevin looked in the Humidor, scanned a nice array of light and dark tobacco and thought what the hell, reaching for one of the Cubans.

"Screw the ban, I never figured out why it's in place in the first place. It's probably so the price stays high. Thanks again. I could get to like this relationship."

"Getting back to the grieving process, this whole group has been working through these stages with a wonderful Doctor downtown. But we are all in a rut and having a hard time getting through the anger stage. It doesn't help much when that bin Laden son-of-a-bitch spouts off on television and Bush and his cronies can't find the asshole. Every time I see him it throws me backwards to the anger stage again."

"Bill, I'm with you there. Everyone on the NYPD force would like to go after that rag head. We even have a lottery set up that pays big bucks for picking the day they do get the guy. Having been a shooter in Iraq, I would gladly put a bullet between his eyes if I had the chance."

Meredith leaned forward and looked Kevin right in the eye. "Well, remember your 'Unless' question? In this long process of grieving, I've kind of added another phase to the process, following anger and depression, it's called revenge."

Meredith settled back in his chair for a moment and took a long drag on his cigar. The tip lit up and crackled as he exhaled the strong smoke into a big ring. Then he continued.

"All of us have been frustrated that no one can seem to lay a hand on this guy. Maybe it's because of U.S. law limitations on what we can and can't do, and then all the diplomatic nonsense, but no one seems to be getting any closer to getting him." He paused to take another sip of scotch and then said. "So this little ragtag group you have been showing how to shoot guns has decided to do it themselves."

Meredith waited for what he had said to sink in, and he watched for some reaction, any reaction. Kevin heard what Meredith said as he took a long pull on his cigar, and while he didn't normally inhale, he found himself sucking in air and deeply inhaling the Cuban smoke.

He could feel the heated smoke burning his lungs, but strangely he just held his breath for a fraction of a second longer, staring at Meredith. Then he exhaled the super-heated smoke in a torrent that shot straight across the room. And he started to cough up a lung.

"Did I really hear you correctly? You and this group are banding together to get this wacko yourselves? And I'm teaching you how to shoot guns!"

Kevin leaned forward and grabbed the bottle again, this time filling his glass, "Screw the ice!"

Bill inhaled his cigar and waited another moment before speaking. He had perfected the concept of letting a thought hang in the air.

"Everyone out there on that firing line lost someone, and two Pakistani brothers you haven't met yet lost two wives and three children between them. They all have nothing to lose and everything to gain in going after Osama bin Laden. And I have the money to fund the whole bloody scheme. Each one of those folks brings something to the table with various skills that can help us accomplish our goal, just like you could do."

Kevin sat there but didn't quite know what to say, so to buy a moment, he took his cigar butt and dipped it in the scotch to think. Meredith smiled because he often did the same thing to obtain a cooler draw.

"Kevin, we have a plan that is being initiated in France as we speak. We will be acquiring the means to get bin Laden and I am willing to spend my money, and even give my life in the effort. Everyone out there today has sworn they are willing to die for the effort. Michael thought you might like to join our little band of thieves as you too have experienced great loss on the force due to bin Laden's hand. We thought you might like to get some vengeance. You also mentioned an interest in joining Michael on his Greek island vacation. Only he isn't going to Greece, he will be sailing a tramp steamer with the rest of us going to Pakistan."

"Holy shit, you're really serious!"

" We are Kevin, we are!"

"Ok, but I'm confused. How do you possibly think you can get to Osama bin Laden when the whole fucking world is looking for his head on a stick? And no one, least of all our government can seem to find him?"

"By getting him to come out of whatever rat hole he is hiding in, or under, and letting us know where that is."

"And how, pray tell, do you do that?" Kevin said somewhat facetiously.

"By giving him something he wants very dearly, a big bomb to blow up New York City."

Kevin stared at Meredith trying to understand what he was being told but it just wasn't computing and he continued to look confused. He had stopped puffing on his cigar and it had gone out. The ice in his glass had completely melted. He just sat there.

"Ok, so you're going to give him a bomb, and then what, just blow him up?"

"Something like that, we're actually going to draw him out of his cave with the bomb as an incentive, and then once we see him we're going to use the bomb to blow him to kingdom come or his Paradise, where all those virgins are supposed to be dancing around. Maybe we get lucky and take out some of his leadership as well. Thank you very much."

He reached for the scotch bottle and said, "See, we don't have to play by the moronic rules our government has to honor. No morality issues, no ethical questions. We just find him and blast him to kingdom come. Pure and simple."

"As I said, OK, I can buy the premise, but the devil is in the details. How is the real question? Your group's pretty close to a bunch of amateurs."

"Have you ever read about the Trojan horse in Greek mythology? They offered a huge wooden horse to their enemy as a peace offering, and then once the horse was dragged inside the city gates, they had their soldiers hidden inside, sneak out and, open the gates. The Greek army swarmed in, killed everyone, and ransacked the city of Troy."

"So that's why Mikey dragged me out to see that Brad Pitt movie and keeps talking about it. Yeah. I know the story, it was a cool movie."

Meredith frowned and made a mental note to talk to the group about such slips. If it happened here it was happening elsewhere.

"We are in effect building a kind of Trojan horse that he will want more than anything else, and then when he has our horse, our bomb, we'll blow him up with it. We're in the process of getting the bomb now."

"Ok, Bill, I'm trying real hard to put my arms around this but your scenario is a lot to take in, even with good scotch and cigar. How do I fit into this Trojan exercise again?"

"Michael and I think you can help a lot. We need to train these folks in basic defense and firearms, we need good security aboard ship when we are moving this weapon, and we may need your eagle eye somewhere along the way. Just your run of the mill security job."

"Bill, I know I keep saying this, but I'm still trying to get my head in the game. I'm with you, but I guess I'm being dense."

"Not at all Kevin. I understand your confusion. This definitely isn't your run-of-the-mill conversation over drinks around the fireplace, so I understand your frustration and your questions. Michael speaks very highly of you so I am going to be very direct. But I need to know that you can keep this conversation in complete confidence. Can you do that?"

"Yes, I'll honor that confidence. Go ahead, because you got me. I hate the bastard just as much as you all do. I just want to comprehend what you are saying."

"Ok, straight talk, no bull. We're in the process of obtaining a small suitcase nuclear weapon, a dirty bomb they call it. We are going to make it available to bin Laden and al Qaeda, and then once we meet with them we're going to blow him and his mountain sky high. Pure and simple. Is that straight enough?"

Kevin choked on his last sip of scotch. He laughed nervously, and looked around the room as if someone might have heard what had just been said. He looked back at Meredith and searched his eyes to be sure that he was hearing what he thought he was hearing. He didn't quite know how to react, so he rose and walked to the bar and poured himself another scotch and drank it down in one gulp. He grabbed a stick matchbook on the bar and relit his cigar, taking a deep breath. He exhaled a cloud of grey smoke in a heated blast.

"So don't hold back Bill, just give it to me straight." he nervously said staring through the smoke.

"I just did, Kevin, as straight as I could, and I meant every word of it. This motley little group you have been training to shoot all afternoon has already committed their lives to this deadly mission. They are going through with it and have all said they're willing to die to try and pull it off. They have already lost most of what matters to them and they all have a burning desire for revenge. Same for me."

"Mikey got me out here by explaining these folks all lost loved ones in 9-11 and needed to blow off a little steam. I guess they have some more steam to let go."

"They do Kevin, they all feel they have nothing important to lose, they have already lost it. They feel like they have everything to gain."

"I know where they're coming from, I lost a lot of friends too," Kevin said as he ran both hands through his hair, "but I had no idea this was also on the agenda."

"Yeah, I can imagine this could be a little hard to comprehend. So, since I've let the cat out of the bag, ask any questions you want, and I'll try to answer them, again all in confidence."

"Hell, I don't know where to start. How did all of you come together and decide to go after Bin Laden? How did you come to this particular course of events? And how the hell are you going to get such a bomb?"

"You know that Michael has been going to therapy for a couple years now. Everyone here today is in the same group. We meet every other Wednesday night in Times Square.

Over the past few years, we went through all the stages of remorse, frustration, acceptance and anger, but found ourselves getting even more frustrated when our own government couldn't seem to find the bastard."

"I'm with you there. They're more interested in that nutcase Saddam Hussein than bin Laden. And that asshole turns up on the evening news all the time taunting us with his worldwide terror shit. Yeah, I can understand where you're all coming from."

"Since 9-11 have you undergone any therapy, Kevin?"

"No, I had all the therapy I could handle back in the first Iraq war. But I do think your current therapy sessions have had a good effect on Mikey. He seems more together lately and driven I guess."

"That's because we've decided to undertake this mission as a way to satisfy accounts. Every one of us is bringing something to the table. They are all committed to this mission."

"Ok, ok, I get it, but how the hell do you get to a bomb? And don't give me this Trojan horse bullshit."

"That was just the model we used to conceive the plan. We have access to a Russian contact that can get us such a bomb. He has no love for bin Laden either. In effect we're buying it on the black market, and right now, at this very moment, we are making contact with al Qaeda through some contacts in France to try and sell it to bin Laden. And the deal is, we'll only sell it to him."

"Your kidding me, you're just going to give it to him?"

"No, we're going to sell it to him for $2 million, because we don't want him to think this is a joke. We use the thing to smoke him out in Pakistan and when we have him in our sights we will set the thing off in whatever cave we have to."

Kevin shook his head to try and clear all the thoughts swirling in his brain. But it was apparent that he was trying to embrace the mission. He was silent for a few pulls on his cigar. The smoke made him giddy. Finally, he said.

"So how do I fit in? And, Michael for that matter?"

Meredith noted the transition that had occurred and realized that Kevin was mentally buying in even though there were still all sorts of questions swimming around in his head.

"Good question, as I said earlier, we need your expertise for weapons training, security, your marksmanship and to assist with whipping this rag-tag group into some sort of military shape. Michael will actually be assisting in the move of this special package all the way from Russia to Pakistan. We decided that the safest route was by boat, because it would draw the least attention."

"Well, I know Mike is a great sailor, I guess that makes sense. Are we going to use a sailboat or what?"

"No, I have some major shipping interests around the world, and I have a ship being readied to actually move the package and most of this group from one location to the other. I'm the money guy for this operation. I have some wealth and I'm prepared to spend it all to send bin Laden to his maker."

Kevin finished another glass of scotch and began wondering if it was all a dream. The scotch and cigars weren't helping. He shook his head to clear his thoughts.

"Bill, I must be crazy, but I'll join your little band of Trojan warriors. It's such a crazy concept I'm intrigued. I lost a good number of friends on the force the day your son was killed. I'd love to honor them by being a part of this effort."

"Michael said that would be your answer. I'm pleased he was right. As you can see from this afternoon, we are truly starting this mission with a bunch of rookies. I'm hoping you can help us whip them into shape."

"I must be out of my mind, but I'm in for a full cut if you'll have me. Now that I've seen those people out there, I'll have to stand in line to put a bullet in bin Laden's head, won't I?"

"Yeah, you may have to take a number, they are pretty driven. But we'll let you get in the line, that's for sure." Meredith rose from his chair and he took his bottle over to the bar locker to put it away. Kevin grabbed the glasses and the full ashtray, and joined him at the bar.

Meredith reached across the bar and said. "I'm glad you're willing to join us Kevin. Welcome aboard. We'll be meeting the group again in a week, after our regular therapy session. I'll want to have you there to advise the group you are one of us."

They headed for the door and William locked up the Clubhouse. As they walked to his car, Meredith turned to Kevin. "I'll put your name and Michael's name on my personal guest list for this Club. You'll always be welcome from this point forward and you can get used to all the guns in my locker, especially the sniper rifles."

Kevin smiled and said, "I just wish I personally could pull the trigger on that guy. Count me in Mr. Meredith."

With that Meredith called his driver. They were in no shape to drive. On the way back to Manhattan each of them were silent and lost in their own thoughts.

→ ←

Camp Novorossiysk, Russia

The General was at his desk working on reams of paperwork. As he worked through the pile, he slipped a signed document into the pile. It was a Commandant's Order calling for a complete inventory of all weaponry being stored at the base. This was a very important control document that would identify and categorize all weaponry on the base. These reports were sent up the chain of command to higher powers within the military, and on to the Kremlin as well. Both Russia and the United States were watching each other closely as they counted weaponry.

He recognized this inventory control review process was his best opportunity to possibly secure a weapon for his brother-in-law. He needed to determine how he could secure a weapon and have it ready for pick up, when the time came.

Since he was ultimately responsible for securing these weapons, it would not be unusual for him to be involved in this inventory process. He and his chief Executive Ordinance Officer had been the ones visiting the Pentagon to discuss disarmament procedures over the last few years. Since agreeing to reduce the nuclear numbers both the U.S. and Russia had destroyed numerous weapons and each country had monitored and verified these efforts. Yet, there were still thousands and thousands of these weapons of mass destruction on both sides. The numbers in inventory could still easily destroy all of the earth. Thus the disarmament efforts were important. It was a long and tedious process that would keep both countries on edge and vigilant for years to come.

These nuclear weapons came in all sizes and types, including intercontinental ballistic missiles, submarine torpedoes and missiles, land-to-land, sea-to-land, and air-to land missiles and suitcase weapons of small yields.

These smaller weapons were tactical weapons to attack a city or a specific part of a battlefield, rather than destroying everything for miles around. It was these very suitcase weapons that were being scheduled up for disposal at the moment, as it was feared that they could most easily fall into the wrong hands. Even the Russians were now fearful of that happening. In recent years they too had become targets for terrorists and they recognized that such weaponry was a big responsibility.

The General decided he would take a more active role in the inventory reviews for the next few months. He would look for the opportunity to divert a weapon and then replace it with a similar one so the weekly counts would not be thrown off. He would observe procedures, find weak points in the review process and determine how to pull off the switch. Once he found a way to gain access to a 'suitcase' as he was now referring to it, he would then 'safe' the weapon so his brother-in-law didn't kill himself, or other innocent people with his crazy plan.

His personal office assistant came into his office and took the files and orders of the day that were stacked up in the out box. The General watched him leave the room and wondered what he had gotten himself into.

→ ←

The Jungle – Calais, France

Malik and O had been instructed to take their time in making contact with whatever elements of al Qaeda might be present in the camp. Meredith had suggested they try to not look too eager and to delay making any mention of the computer pictures they had of the weapon. He stated that if such persons were there they would eventually make themselves visible.

Meredith had encouraged them to make their frustrations and complaints about the world known. He suggested they talk about the state of affairs in Pakistan, and to show their anger with the west, the Americans, and the British infidels. In that manner the word would get to the right people, and they would seek out Malik and Osama.

After another two days in camp, the same man as before, Tasneen Akbar, approached them as they were having some tea in a corner of the main tent in the area. Osama could see that another man was trailing Tasneen as he approached, but this man made no effort to follow him into the tent.

"Allah Akbar." Tasneen offered as a greeting. He retrieved a chipped coffee mug from a sideboard and motioned if he could join them on the carpet.

"Allah Akbar," the brothers responded in pashtu, and waved him in to sit with them.

"We have some old muffin we can offer you from the bakery in town." Osama broke off a piece of muffin and offered it to the man across the carpet.

"Many thanks my friends, I hope you have been faring well here in this dog of a place. While I have been here a long time, I still resent the fact that we must live like animals to get by."

"But here we are not dodging bullets like at home my friend, at least for the time being. I have heard from others that the French police have been threatening to come and tear down the camps. Is that true?"

Tasneen took a sip of his tea and looked out of the entrance towards the road a couple hundred feet away. "I am afraid so, thus we must be careful not to give them reason to come through the fields. We must try to be invisible and try to keep our numbers down so the locals do not complain and make the police come out."

Both Malik and O nodded and sipped their tea biding time as they felt perhaps this was a meeting that was needed to move forward.

The bearded man looked them both in the eyes and then said. " I have brought a friend with me that I would like you to meet. He may have some work for you if you are interested."

Malik and Osama looked at one another and nodded agreement.

"We would like that Tasneen, if it would help us to move forward. We cannot stay here forever, there is not enough to eat." He laughed and smiled as if making a joke.

With that, Tasneen waved his hand and another man who had been standing just left of the opening in the blue plastic tent ducked into the enclosure and walked over to the carpet. Tasneen waved his hand and encouraged the man to sit and have some tea.

"This is Abdul and he is a friend that may be able to assist you." Everyone bowed to each other and Tasneen reached for another broken mug to pour the new guest some tea. Osama poured what little tea was still left as a courtesy and asked in his native pashtu. " May we ask, is Abdul your whole name?"

The guest answered in pashtu as well, "For now that is enough as I do not know either of you, although I am pleased that your language is refined enough to speak our native tongue."

"We are from the Territories in Pakistan and have been traveling from Peshawar for the last four months. It has been a difficult journey. "

"So what do you come for, a new life? Jobs? or perhaps something else?"

It was an open-ended question that Osama knew was a good way to start the conversation that they had come for. He knew that he must not be too eager to want to join the movement, but that it was important to express frustration and see what might come of it from this man.

"My brother and I have been displaced because of the American soldiers, and the militia fighting them, and so we have decided we could participate in this war with the infidels in other ways. We have heard there are groups in America that will help us to get even with the infidels and we are hopeful that we can get to them."

Malik listened carefully all the while watching the man's eyes to see if he was buying any of this pitch. He knew he wasn't supposed to be too eager but he jumped in anyway. He would use his life experience, with just a slight twist. On this he could sound truthful.

"These American bastards have killed our families in their rocket attacks. We were away, fighting in the hills. Osama would not tell you this but I will. We have vowed to avenge our sons, to kill a hundred infidels for each of their deaths. But we do not know how to make this happen."

Osama tried not to swallow his tongue and searched the man's face for any sign that Malik had crossed the line and that they were now in trouble. But he didn't see that in the face. He saw understanding and agreement. Osama held his breath to see what would come next.

"You have found the right person to help you in your quest." Abdul offered. "I can help you to meet the people you want to meet and to join in the cause. We need good committed people. I can take your message to my leaders. Allah Akbar!"

With that both Osama and Malik relaxed for a moment. They realized that perhaps they had now found the right person to carry their real message to al Qaeda. But they would need to be careful before taking the next step. Hopefully, this was the man they were looking for to share the laptop computer with so it would get to the appropriate al Qaeda representatives.

Before leaving New York, Meredith had set up the computer with a PowerPoint presentation on the sale of the weapon for $2,000,000 Euro's. The presentation would show that the weapon was available for sale to the highest bidder, and it would offer proof that it was in hand, and that it could be delivered to al Qaeda and Osama bin Laden in a few short months if the terms of the contract were met.

O raised his cup and offered a toast to his guest. "We would like to thank you for talking with us. We are honored that you have done so. We would like to speak with you further about this. Could we meet tomorrow morning and begin planning? I will even find us some better tea and bread for the meeting."

Abdul raised his empty cup touching theirs, and said. "To our cause, may we drive the infidels from our lands. I too will bring cakes for tomorrow's meeting."

With their tea gone, the group broke up after talking more about their homeland and the need to avenge the deaths of so many of their brothers and sons. When Abdul and Tasneen departed, the two brothers looked at one another and thought about what had they done.

That evening they went into town to get some tea and bread for the following day's meeting. Since they were unsure if they were being followed, they stayed away from their hidden stash, and concentrated on getting tea and food money by panhandling the French locals for some coins and Euros. By dark they had secured enough money to make their purchases and began the walk home.

In the dark, they could tell they were not being followed and diverted into the farm fields and the rock outcroppings where the computer bag was hidden. Once there, they took out a small cell phone that was also in the waterproof bag. It had been purchased in Paris and had 10 minutes pre-paid on it. Malik dialed the number they had memorized and waited for Courtney to answer. She answered the phone after just two rings.

Malik simply said "tomorrow, O & M", and heard a woman's voice acknowledge with an "OK, THCT", and hung up never identifying himself. The call had lasted about ten seconds just as Courtney had instructed. They turned off the phone, poured water on its keys letting it seep into the mechanism and then broke it into pieces. The phone and sim card were buried in two different locations in the mud a good distance from the outcropping that had hidden the laptop for the last few days.

Malik and Osama took the small notebook computer and batteries and hid it inside their bag of groceries. Satisfied, they started walking back to camp. Upon arrival, they hid the computer in a corner under a prayer mat, ate something and settled in for the night. The next day would have to be executed perfectly.

➤ ◄

Camp Novorossiysk, Russia

General Gralashov was about to make his first visit to the ordinance bunkers in a couple of years. He had toured all the facilities upon arrival, but he had not felt it necessary to make these inspections since then. He knew the Americans would be coming to see the arsenal for disarmament review and that gave him an excuse to renew the inspections.

He knew what was down there and it always gave him a chill to know he was sitting on top of such deadly weaponry. There were enough WMD's stored in the arsenal to wipe out all of mankind, if they were ever used in anger.

In his office he had documentation on each and every weapon that was stored on the base. The records were supposed to be reviewed and scrutinized regularly. They weren't. In addition, he had access to photo and specification documentation that would probably be carefully reviewed in the disarmament discussions between the United States and Russia. With this information he'd already made photo and computer copies of the various suitcase low-yield weapons stored on base and had sent copies to his brother-in-law in New York. These documents were hidden inside Christmas presents from the homeland.

The Armaments Bunker was a large nondescript building in a remote corner of the base. It was also set behind additional multiple rows of razor wire fencing, guard towers and security patrols.

His planned walk-thru, with his aide, Sergeant Major Tristan Shostakovich, was predicated on the impending visit of the Americans to devise schedules for downsizing the various categories of WMD's, both here and in America.

While he gave the impression he was making sure that all was in good shape prior to this visit, he was really trying to determine how he would be able to secure a single small weapon for Meredith's crazed band of counter-terrorists.

He needed to obtain only one suitcase weapon from the many that were stored in the building. But that would be the challenge. There were many such weapons left over from the cold war. At one time these weapons were actually stored in special sealed storage lockers in embassies all over the world, in case they were ever needed in the event of war. It had actually taken years to bring them to these storage bunkers. The General wondered if in fact they were all back in Mother Russia.

The building itself was built into a fifty-foot high solid rock faced wall and looked unpretentious from the outside. But inside the rock face of the building was a huge three-level subterranean bunker with thick stonewalls. On the first level a large football field sized area was sectioned off into a number of different fenced areas traversed by a two-lane street from one end to the other. There was high intensity lighting in all areas and there were no shadows, except the shadows cast by the rock walls at the back of each fenced locker. Cameras were strategically mounted to afford the guards unimpeded views of all corners of the floor and all movement around it.

On this first level the larger weapons that were mounted on weapon delivery systems, flatbed trucks, military vehicles and hundreds of heavy-duty dollies were stored. These weapons were so large they were kept on the surface level of the bunker just because they would be more difficult to maneuver from the lower levels.

In the center of the bunker there was a massive set of twin industrial sized elevators that took you to the two lower levels. Level 2 was a smaller sized bunker, the equivalent of a basketball floor, also divided by a single lane aisle that traversed the large room in a circular clockwise manner.

It was partitioned off in pie-shaped fenced lockers from floor to ceiling facing the middle with cameras strategically covering all areas, and the entrances to the storage lockers. Security personnel could monitor all movement in and out.

Behind these fences were medium sized nuclear weapons, in the 1,000 to 10,000 pound variety. These weapons still required truck and flatbed support, but were more easily moved. These lockers included ground and air-to-air missiles, nuclear torpedoes, and limited yield ground shells.

As the General walked around Level 2 with his ordinance officers he kept looking for something that would assist him in eventually stealing a single suitcase nuclear weapon. But the bunker looked as if it was impregnable.

They returned to the Elevator and moved on to Level 3, which by the General's estimates had to be at least 50 ft underground. As the elevator opened he saw and remembered that this was by far the smallest level because it stored the smallest weapons. The presumption was that the smallest, easiest moved weapons needed to be protected to a greater degree, as they were more mobile.

This level did not have fenced storage lockers. Instead the room had large industrial storage racks lining the four walls. They were all facing the elevator doors. There were cameras aimed at the door and in the corners of the room that measured about 1,200 square feet. Each suitcase type package was secured to the others on the racks with long half-inch thick steel cables stretching thru various welded metal grommets on each weapon.

At first glance the General estimated there were probably more than one hundred of these weapons, as he couldn't remember the specific numbers from his last inspection. Because of their small, easily carried size, regular inventories were supposed to have been taken a couple times a year, as was the case with the other larger weapons stored on the other two levels.

As they walked about the General noticed that a plumbing and HVAC system ran along the ceiling of each level, providing fire suppressant and sprinkler systems, air, and heat for all three levels. These sprinkler pipes traversed the ceiling, converging to the center and then upward from level to level, parallel to the elevator system and emergency stairwell. At each level there were large flywheels to balance water pressures and flow rates. He noted the setup and filed it away in his head as a possible diversion opportunity.

Once they were back on the first level, the General hesitated a moment outside the elevator and looked at a large empty space outlined in fluorescent tape as if it were a reserved parking space next to the elevator bank.

He pointed to the area and inquired, "Colonel, what is this area being used for?"

"General, It's just a temporary trailer parking area used when 2nd and 3rd level equipment is being moved to another location, or out of the building. It allows us to coordinate more efficient use of the elevator on transfer of materials."

"How often does that occur, Colonel?"

"With détente, we have not been moving weaponry about as much. It is empty most of the time, Sir."

"If that's the case, and the space sits empty most of the time, I would like to have my fishing boat and trailer stored here. Right now it is buried in snow behind my quarters and I would love to have access to it to prepare for spring fishing."

The Colonel, always looking to keep the General happy, and out of his hair, readily agreed. "General, that would be fine as long as we could temporarily move it aside if we should have trailers to load or unload?"

"Yes, that's fine, my boat trailer can easily be pulled by two soldiers without any problem. I'll send Sergeant Major Shostacovich over with the boat after we knock off the snow." He thanked the officers for their time and advised them he would be back again for additional inspections in two weeks.

Paris, France

Courtney and Ryan had seen the sights, had walked the River Seine, checking out the artisans and bookshops. They had walked to see Notre Dame and the Left Bank, Montmarte, and the Eiffel Tower, which had been built by Gustave Eiffel in 1889 on the Centennial of the French Revolution.

They were now in the Marignan Hotel restaurant called Spoon Paris, having a late dinner, when the second phone she had in her purse rang quietly. They looked at each other as Courtney reached for it. She answered and said hello, allowing her voice to be recognized, and she heard the word, "Tomorrow THCT."

She nodded to Ryan and he immediately signaled the waiter for their check. His only thought was there goes another potential great evening in the city of love.

He already knew what he had to do, file a flight plan to Calais, and then back to Paris, which made no sense, and then on to New York. But, he thought, that's what they pay me to do.

→ ←

The Jungle Camp, Calais

Osama and Malik again slept poorly thinking of their task. They rose early before first light and began preparations. They knew their Taliban contact would come early so they had just a short time to prepare as Meredith had suggested. His plan would allow them to remain safe in the delivery of this offer.

In the darkest corner of their tent, they spread a large prayer rug on the floor and set up a mismatched tea service on a small table in the center of the rug. This would be the meeting area when their guest arrived. Next they pulled out the Toshiba Tough Man laptop known for its rugged ability in the field. The unit had an extra long battery pack that would provide about six hours of service before a re-charge. Malik booted up the unit to verify that it still had a full charge and then clicked on the Windows and PowerPoint software to verify the programs were loaded and ready. They also laid the secondary power adapter plug to recharge the batteries next to the unit, although without power in the tent it would not assist in the actual presentation.

Once all the preparations were finished, they pulled out two detailed instruction sheets written in English, Arabic and Pashtu. The cover sheet simply said, READ THIS FIRST. One set was placed in the computer bag, and another copy was placed on top of the laptop taped to the keyboard.

Finally they threw a large blanket over the entire assembly leaving it almost invisible in the recesses of the makeshift tent. Osama pulled out another instruction sheet and brought it with him to the front of the tent.

Since they were alone in their tent, they sat in the entrance and bided their time in the moonless pre-dawn. The sky went from a dark grey to a light grey. As this occurred Osama pulled out the simple note that said 'HAVE SOME TEA' and laid it at the entrance of the tent with a teacup to hold it in place.

"Come Brother we must go before the light."

The two brothers stuck their heads outside the tent and seeing no one moving in camp, they eased out and slid into the shadows, ducking from tent to tent and then on to the farmer's fields. Once they were a good distance from the campsite, they moved faster to put more distance between them and the Taliban messenger who would be visiting the tent. They got to the road but stayed down in the culvert walking towards town and their vehicle. Forty-five minutes later they walked up to their car parked alone in the lot. It was dirty and had a police warning citation on it for illegal overnight parking. But at least it had not been towed.

Osama and Malik climbed into the rented Peugeot and drove away casually so as not to draw any attention to themselves. They drove a few miles and stopped at a petrol station to reverse the process they had undertaken on their arrival, each taking a turn in the men's toilet to clean up and dress in their business suits. Satisfied with their appearance, they stuffed their camp clothes in a dumpster behind the station and drove back onto the highway. Instead of driving away they again drove towards the Jungle encampment. Just about a mile from the dirt road that lead to the encampment, they pulled off the road into a commuter parking lot and parked their vehicle in the midst of the other cars.

They rolled down the windows and could again smell the ocean air blowing through the car windows. They turned on the radio softly and settled in eating some breakfast sweets and coffee they had picked up at the petrol station. They would wait and watch.

→ ←

8:00 am – The Jungle

The sun was out but the wind off the English Channel still made it chilly morning for a man who spent much of his life in the southern deserts of Afghanistan. Tasneen walked towards the blue tarp tent and announced his approach by calling out the names Osama and Malik. He had muffins to share with the morning tea and he looked forward to their conversation. He was always looking for new recruits.

There was no response from the brothers. As he got to the makeshift entrance, he could see the tent was dark except for the angled morning light shining in from the east. He stood there a moment and surveyed the surrounding area to see if they were out and about gathering wood, or talking with someone at another tent. But they were nowhere in sight.

As he stood by the entrance he looked down and saw a piece of paper that said 'HAVE SOME TEA' in pashtu. It also said the same in English. So he stepped into the tent and as his eyes adjusted to the darker interior, he noted that a blanket was thrown over the usual sitting place for the tent and it too had a note attached to it.

This note said 'READ ME FIRST'. He started to sense trouble but crossed the space and picked up the note, seeing that it was a number of papers that had lengthy paragraphs in the two languages.

Before reading further, he walked to the front of the tent again and looked about to see if the brothers were anywhere in sight. They were not. So he turned into the sun, rising above the tree lines and started reading. He chose the Pashtun as his native language was preferred over the infidels' language.

As he read the summary document, he kept looking up to see if the brothers were playing a joke on him and they were laughing behind a tree. They weren't. He went back to his reading and then read the summary again, this time in English. Once he finished he looked to the back of the tent and slowly walked to the blanket that was draped over some objects.

He slowly lifted the covering blanket not sure what he would find underneath. Once it was up sufficiently to see what the objects were, he ripped the rest of the blanket off and stared at a small table that held a laptop computer.

He was familiar with such electronic things because of his job searching for lost souls who wanted to join the cause. He reached for the computer and followed the instructions but it was slow going as he searched for the appropriate keys to push. After pushing a number of them he froze for a second as he realized that perhaps the computer was a bomb and he was setting it off. He thought about that for a few minutes while the screen blinked showing the unit was on. It did not explode, thus he decided to proceed carefully.

He followed the directions and path as the papers suggested, and finally got to the screens initiating a PowerPoint program. As instructed, he pushed the Show button. The program popped open and showed that there were 15 slides assembled with written script in both English and Pashtu.

He found himself reading both languages to make sure he was truly understanding what he was reading. As he scanned them he became more confused. When he advanced to the 5th slide there was a photograph of a suitcase that had stenciled markings on it.

The stenciling was in a language he did not know but perhaps was an eastern European language or Russian. The next slide showed the same suitcase opened up. Within the case was a complex metal machine that filled the space and had a number of computer ports and digital read-outs. As he read the corresponding information, he realized he was looking at a photograph of one of those suitcase bombs that he had heard al-Qaeda members talk about. He stopped reading and just stared at the photograph image.

"What the hell is this," he said out loud to no one but himself. He again looked out the tent entrance and wished that the two brothers were here to explain what this was all about. But they were not and that troubled him.

He advanced the next few screens and read that some sort of proposal was being offered, and it was directed to Osama bin Laden and al-Qaeda. His first thought was why was he holding this computer, and why had these two brothers brought this message here, to him? Why hadn't they taken it to bin Laden?

As he thought about that, he realized that would have been impossible because even he had no idea where the leader of al Qaeda was located. As the slides progressed he found that this computer was making an offer to sell such a suitcase bomb to bin Laden. The second last slide showed the price. It was $2,000,000 Euros.

The final slide started with "For Osama Only - Let's Talk!" It gave a series of instructions for making contact that involved some innocent email addresses, and some international phone numbers, that would lead to other messages and more directions. It was a complicated process for anyone to make contact.

Tasneen sat there staring out at the morning sun. It burned his eyes as he tried to digest what was going on. He called over to a tent that was fifty yards away for one of his fellow countrymen, who stuck his head out of the tent, located Tasneen and came running.

"Kasir, our two brothers seem to have disappeared. Take some men with you, spread out and make a search throughout the camp, and then check the other camps nearby. If you see them, come back here and tell me. Do not let them know you are interested in them, just let me know where they are."

The young man turned and gathered a couple of other men from the fire pit in the center of the camp. He gave them some instructions and they spread out looking in all the tents and the surrounding fields for the two Pakistani brothers.

Tasneen continued to reflect on the morning's events and decided to review the computer program one more time. After a careful review, he again confirmed in his mind what the program was suggesting. He closed the laptop, gathered its cords and battery charger and walked back to his hut on the other side of the camp. Once there he went into his things and pulled out a cell phone and made a call.

Without identifying himself, he listened for a moment to identify the person answering, and then said, "We must talk now, it is important." He waited for the response, which was simply, " Yes, at 3." and he hung up.

He sat in his hut entrance a long time and waited to see if Kasir had found the brothers anywhere in the surrounding area. When the young man returned, he said an old man relieving himself in the woods at dawn saw two men quietly walking out of camp and down the road. This confirmed what he thought would be the case. He dismissed Kasir telling him to keep an eye out for the two men. After Kasir left he gathered his leather satchel, slipped the laptop into it and hung it around his neck. He then started walking out of camp to the dirt road that eventually led to the city and the train station. The laptop was going on a journey.

Out on the paved road leading to Calais, Osama and Malik parked in a commuter lot. Their vehicle was parked two rows in from the exterior of the lot, with a number of other vehicles between them and the road. They hunched down in the seats and quietly watched Tasneen walk past the commuter parking lot and flag down a bus that went to the city. Once the man was on the bus, they started their car and casually followed the bus at a distance. They were interested in knowing where he would be taking the news of a bomb that was available for a price.

Calais Airport, Charter Terminal

Ryan landed the plane without any trouble on Runway 3L and followed taxi instructions to the Chevron Charter Terminal that was situated across the field from the main Calais Passenger Terminal. He had already ordered a re-fueling truck to meet him with the aviation fuel he would need for the short trip to Paris.

As they were still in France, there was no customs review to worry about, thus he and Courtney decided to wait in the cockpit scanning the roadway leading into the charter side of the airport. The co-pilot disembarked and verified the fueling was handled correctly, and that the flight plans were filed and in order. Ryan also asked him to do the walk around inspection now so that when their passengers arrived they could be wheels up as soon as possible.

Landing at 8:00 am they hoped the two Pakistanis would be coming along soon. They were prepared to wait as long as it took for them to get to the airport. They had risen at 6:00 am, gone to the airport and flown to Calais, the flight only taking 20 minutes in the sleek jet. They had not even reached cruising altitude before they began their descent into Calais airspace.

Courtney was lost in thought when Ryan called her attention to the roadway.

"I think that's them, and it looks like no one is following them."

She grabbed binoculars from the cockpit dashboard and trained them on the car as it made its way into the Charter parking lot.

"They even have their suits on, so I guess they've accomplished their mission." She said this and realized her comment would confuse Ryan even more than he was already confused about all this covert travel. And it did.

"What? What would they have been wearing, swimming trunks? I still don't understand what we're doing here. Way too much intrigue, Lady! But if the boss wants me to ferry you guys around and spend a couple days in Paris with a beautiful woman, who am I too complain."

Courtney gave him the tenth deadpan look of the trip and suggested the same thing she had offered the other times.

"Ryan, as I've told you a number of times, I am not at liberty to explain all this to you. You will have to ask Mr. Meredith for any explanation. Which I believe he might be willing to give you, since I think you will be a pivotal part of this whole escapade."

With that she exited the plane and walked across the tarmac to the entrance of the Charter service building. She walked towards the single car rental booth that was in the building and got there just as the brothers came through the door and headed for the desk as well.

They settled the rental car bill with an alias credit card and headed for the door leading to the tarmac. The nice part about private charter service was there were hardly any security issues and flight delays to deal with. When you were ready, you went. Often if there was security, it was just a matter of walking through a chain link gate just outside the building that led to the tarmac and planes, the presumption being that all parties using private planes and charter facilities were known quantities and the owners of these planes knew who was flying with them.

As they walked out to the plane Courtney asked. " So gentlemen, did we accomplish what we hoped to do?"

Malik was the first to respond almost shouting a response as another jet was taking off on the main runway. "We found our man and I think he is carrying our message for us. We're able to follow him as Mr. Meredith planned. Tasneen took our computer and he went to the Calais train station. He bought a ticket for Paris, a train leaving about now. " He was excited that he was the message bearer.

"That's great Malik. Let's fly to Paris quickly and see if we can catch up to him on that end. If one of you can point him out to me at the train station, I'll follow him and see where he goes, before we fly to New York. Remember, we can't talk about this on the plane for the moment, both pilots are not aware of our work. Perhaps when they get off the plane in Paris we can talk as we go to the Paris train station. I am pleased that you were successful and that you are back safe." She reached out and touched both of them as they walked, and they blushed and then smiled.

Station Paris du Nord

Courtney and Malik had arrived at the Paris du Nord train station just a half hour before the train from Calais was to pull in. They found the right track and then found a somewhat hidden position on a mezzanine that offered a clear view of everyone getting off the train and entering the station waiting room.

At the appointed time, the train arrived on Track 3 and disgorged its passengers. The crowd flowed towards the central waiting room like lemmings. Malik spotted Tasneen casually walking through the entrance still clutching his leather bag tightly to his chest. He identified the man to Courtney. She followed his movement and then advised Malik to head back to the airport and wait for her arrival.

Courtney descended the stairs and fell into the line of passengers about ten people behind her man. Her old surveillance skills would come in handy as she shadowed him to see where he might go with the THCT computer offer. As he left the station he walked over to the taxi line and waited just a moment for the next taxi to pull up and take him into the city.

Hanging back behind two people in line, Courtney watched him enter the taxi and pull away from the curb. She stepped forward and grabbed the next taxi ignoring the two in front of her, acting like an ugly American. She instructed her cabby to follow the green Peugeot taxi and settled back in the seat but never took her eyes off the vehicle ahead. The taxi maneuvered through the streets of Paris paralleling the Seine River. It crossed over to the Left Bank and pulled up to a five-story office building facing the River.

Her quarry paid the driver, stepped out of the taxi, never once looking around. Courtney asked her driver to pull over to the curb a block short of the building, paid her tariff and got out, all the while watching the man on the sidewalk ahead. As she expected, he did not think he was being followed and went right to the building entrance he wanted. She casually walked down the other side of the street and scrutinized the building without even turning her head towards it. She pulled out a camera and took some photos of the Seine River and the ornate bridge they had just come across. Then she swung around and took some photos of the building he had entered. A half-mile away she could see the Cathedral of Notre Dame and noted these guys had some pricey real estate digs as part of their cover.

→ ←

South Asian Imports, Paris

A well-dressed Arab man sat in his office on the Left Bank staring out the window at some barge traffic on the Seine River below, watching tourists snapping photographs left and right. It was a beautiful day and he wished he could be out there himself. But he had to work to do, and he was waiting for someone.

The third floor office was nothing special, but that was by design. The entrance marquee downstairs simply said South Asian Imports Ltd., and the third floor office door had a similar name on it. This import company did in fact import products from the Middle East, primarily from Jordan and Turkey.

Zohair Joshi actually had two jobs; one was importing products of interest to the European marketplace, and the other being the eyes and ears of al Qaeda in France and the Netherlands. Both jobs paid well, but it was the second one that truly gave him his reason for being in Paris. His job was to do anything that needed to be done for the terrorist organization.

This work included covert fundraising, money laundering, assisting operatives as they moved through the area, and occasionally doing the dirty 'wet' work for his terrorist organization. No one knew it but he had personally assisted in the funding and physical movement of the 9-11 terrorist cell as they planned their attack on New York.

Today, he stared out the window pondering what he should do about a confusing call he had received from a contact in Calais. It had come from Tasneen in the Jungle encampment on the English Channel. In the past, Tasneen had proven to be reliable as a field agent and in moving people north to Great Britain. But his most recent call had been troubling. So troubling Zohair had cut him off so as not to verbalize the words on the phone. He had asked him to come to Paris right away.

His thoughts were interrupted by a knock on the door. Tasneen walked in carrying a computer in his shoulder bag. Zohair rose and placed a finger on his lips signaling quiet. He said. " It is good to see you Tasneen. I hope you had safe travel. Here, let me take your jacket. Can I offer you some refreshment?"

Tasneen took the cue and responded. " It is good to see you too brother. The trip was uneventful. The train is slower than I thought it would be with the name bullet train. I must have been on a slow one." They both laughed. As he spoke he took out the computer and opened it up. He turned on the power and called up the PowerPoint program that he needed to show. He went on.

"I have some new products that I think will be of great interest to your clients here in France. We have done some preliminary market testing and they seem to be priced right. I think you will like them and I can have supplies moving in a matter of weeks."

Zohair relaxed as he realized that Tasneen understood the challenge of this conversation when others could be listening in.

"Excellent, I've been hearing about these new items for a long time. Give me a moment to look through your on-line catalog. Perhaps you would like to use the restroom? It is right down the hall on the left."

"I would appreciate that. The train ride was a long one. Take a look at the catalog summary and let me know what you think. I'll be a few minutes." With that Tasneen stood up, walked to the door, opened it and then shut it again. He then silently returned to his chair.

Zohair, observed the man's movement, waved him to a chair, and started in on the PowerPoint, clicking through the screens quickly. At first he could not comprehend what was being presented, and he went back to start over, much the same as Tasneen had done in the Jungle in Calais.

As the man read the various PowerPoint screens he kept looking up over the computer at Tasneen searching for some acknowledgement of what he was reading.

Tasneen just sat there quietly, acknowledging the silent inquiry with arched eyebrows. He raised his arms in a gesture of mutual confusion and surprise at what was in the presentation. Both men kept looking at one another seeking some sort of clarity. After Zohair had finished reading the documents twice, he pointed to the door and the other man walked over to open and shut the door again.

Tasneen started the conversation at the doorway across the room by saying, "So my friend, what do you think of these products? Do they have a potential market here and perhaps in other countries as well?"

"I am really impressed with the quality of these items. They should sell well, here and abroad. But we will need to talk more about volume and delivery schedules. Might I suggest that we break for an early lunch? We can structure a deal over some pasta and red wine. I always draw up better contracts when I have a full stomach and a clear head. Let's go my friend."

Tasneen understood completely. He shut down the computer and stuffed it into his bag. He looked forward to a good lunch.

Once outside, Zohair walked to a sandwich stand and bought some bread and wine and took a couple of paper cups out of his bag. Tasneen looked crestfallen as he had hoped for a good hot lunch, something that was rare and far between in the Jungle. They walked across the street to a small park and found a bench that would afford them some privacy.

"Tasneen, I apologize for all the intrigue, but I am concerned that my office may be bugged, by the French, the Americans, or both. Thus, I like to do my import business there, and my important business out here. I hope you understand?"

"I do Zohair, I knew that this would be a difficult concept to discuss anywhere, so this is OK, even though I would have liked that wonderful lunch you described."

Zohair laughed out loud and promised to take him to a good luncheon place right after they talked. Tasneen fired up the computer again, using battery power and Zohair pulled apart the French bread and began tossing it to the pigeons that were milling about. Soon he had a crowd of birds swarming the scraps of French bread. If nothing else it was good cover should they be watched.

They both watched the PowerPoint again and scrutinized the photos of the suitcases as well as the contact information. Eventually they closed the laptop and sat there staring at the birds.

Tasneen started. "So what do you think? Am I crazy to even bring this to your attention?"

"Well, I am astounded by what is presented here. And I am unsure if such an offer is legitimate, but I am pleased that you brought this to me. Let me ask, what did you think of the two brothers you received this from?" Zohair said and continued to toss out bits of bread to the pigeons. They fought for the scraps. French bread was obviously tasty even to pigeons.

"If you are asking, were they really Pakistani, I would say yes. They spoke the pashtun language as natives would. They said they were from the territories and that they wanted to join the cause. I was actually going to meet with them again to see if they would be willing to go to London when they disappeared."

The Arab businessman thought about that for a couple seconds, and then said, " I think they used you to bring this message to us. Thus, I wonder if they are really who they said they were."

"I agree, I think they sought me out in the camp because they knew there was a good chance al Qaeda sympathizers would be located there. They hoped I would open some doors for them, and I have. That is why they left this computer to make this astounding offer rather than being killed for making such inquiries."

"Yes, that is my thought as well. That is why I am pleased you have brought this to me. I would think that someone higher up in our organization would very much like to see what is presented here? I think we must pass it along. You have done right Tasneen."

He continued, "I will pass this along to my superiors. Who knows, maybe we will have a chance to use this on the Americans and have a bigger terrorist act than they have ever seen. Now let me buy you that lunch for your train trip north, huh?"

→ ←

Paris, on the Seine

Courtney had vacated the taxi and crossed the street just a half block down from the building where the man had gone in. She continued to use the camera as cover. Approaching the building entrance she looked at the marquee, listing tenants. She took a photograph of all the listings and noted a South Asian Imports business located in the building on the Third floor. That sounded promising so she took the elevator to the third floor and looked for a women's toilet, in case someone asked her business. No one was about so she slipped into the ladies room and kept the door slightly ajar, so she could see the offices down the hall.

She had hardly settled in when the office door of South Asian Imports, just two doors down and across the hallway, opened for a moment. She spotted her man within. He did an unexpected thing. He opened the door and announced he was going to the restroom, and then didn't leave the room, instead quietly closing the door again.

That was odd, she thought. But Courtney had what she had come for, the location of an al Qaeda contact in Paris. She quickly moved out of the restroom and to the elevator.

Once down on the street, she crossed over and found a park bench a half block up from the building entrance. She sat down and took some more photos. A short while later she noticed her quarry and another well-dressed Middle Eastern man came out of the building and looked as if they would cross the street. She quickly took a picture of both of them and put her camera away so as not to draw any attention.

They crossed over to the park and found a bench just four benches down from her location. She got up and started walking in that direction, with her hand raised as if hailing a cab. When she came abreast of the two men seated on the bench she took a single good look at them through her sunglasses and then turned into the street between two cars. She hailed a taxi driving by, jumped in and quickly took a photograph of the two men. Then she looked in the other direction as the cab pulled away.

She instructed the cab driver to head for the airport and the private commercial terminal. As she sat there she jotted down the al Qaeda address she had just visited and reviewed the photos she had taken.

→ ←

Soho, Lower Manhattan

Kate met the short, rotund man in a Starbucks in Soho. She knew it was the right person because he carried a large red Macy's bag that had a green ribbon tied to its handle. That was the signal that she was to look for. They each ordered latte's, with Kate's being non-fat with skim milk. They silently waited for their drinks at the pickup counter. Once they had their coffees in hand, the two walked to a corner of the small coffeehouse near the front window and sat in two comfortable black leather chairs. This spot still gave them a good view of everyone in the room.

While their coffees were cooling, the man placed the red bag in Kate's lap as if he was presenting her with a gift from Macy's. She played the part and pulled the pink tissue paper inside apart to see her gift, and noted a large number of tissue-wrapped documents in the bottom.

She reached in and casually pulled one from the bottom of the stack and set the bag on the floor under the table and between her legs. Looking around and seeing no one was paying any attention to her or the man, she carefully unfolded the tissue enough to take a look at the assorted documents within.

This set of documents included an Irish passport, a driver's license, a number of city documents including some rail passes, and a few business cards with an Irish woman's name on them. Opening the passport a bit more she saw that the photo was of her. She also noted the documents were well worn, even frayed as they should have been, if carried in a purse or pocket. She re-wrapped the documents in the tissue and reached for a second one.

The man sat there quietly looking out the window enjoying his latte. He was comfortable and composed as Kate continued to inspect the merchandise.

Kate scrutinized two additional sets and was impressed with the quality of the work presented. Satisfied with the documents she too sat back, sipped her coffee, and watched an elderly man pass by on the street.

Enjoying her latte, she reached into her purse that was still strapped across her shoulder, and pulled out a Business Week magazine that was folded in half. She had glued the top and bottom of the magazine together forming a deep interior pocket. In the pocket was an envelope with $40,000 dollars in it, all non-sequential bills of varying denominations. She slid the magazine over to the man.

He casually glanced into the hidden pocket of the magazine, and then pulled out an industrial sized rubber band wrapping it around the entire magazine. Then he carefully tucked the periodical under his arm, smiled and said thank you for the coffee. He got up, threw his partially empty recyclable paper cup in the trash bin and walked out the door, raising a hand to hail a cab.

In less than 30 seconds he was gone down the street.

Kate remained seated for a couple more minutes, watching the crowd pass by, enjoying her beverage. She then casually stood up and threw her empty cup in the recyclable container, grabbed her bright Macy's bag with the green ribbon, and walked out the door. Before she could start to hail a cab, one pulled to the curb dropping off another coffee addict who looked to be in a hurry for his caffeine fix. As the man vacated, Kate offered a smile and jumped in asking the driver to head uptown.

Kensico Gun Club

Kevin and Michael made two more trips to the gun club with their student soldiers. Meredith rented the facilities in the middle of the week so that no one else would be around. Money talked and the club was vacant except for the close-knit band of counter-terrorists.

The group learned how to shoot safely and accurately and some were getting pretty good. If nothing else, Meredith knew that it was a good teambuilding exercise. He also knew that not everyone would actually be going into the field. Those decisions would come when they had a better plan. In the meantime they practiced.

The group finished their handgun shooting practice. They were now watching Kevin and Michael shoot the rifles with a great accuracy. The two policemen were using full body targets at 300 feet with their custom built, Kimber Advanced Police Tactical rifles, drawn from Meredith's gun locker. And they were getting comfortable with the powerful weapons, consistently tearing the hearts out of the targets.

"I would hate to be down range of you guys when you are pissed off," said Ralph Behar who was squaring up with a Mossberg 500 pump shotgun. It was the sawed off version, with a pistol grip stock, a nasty looking weapon. He let loose with five consecutive rounds aimed at targets 30 feet downrange. The gun belched fire as the first shell exited the massive brake fixed on the end of the barrel. Ralph moved left with each shot pumping another round into the chamber. He fanned his shots, the targets literally exploding and torn from the clamps holding them in place.

Kevin watched and offered a comment, "Nice shooting Ralph, you've done this before. I like a close-in guy watching my back." He turned back to the sniper rifle sitting on its tripod. "But I prefer to work at a distance so the bad guys don't get close enough that we would need that bad boy."

"Yeah, but if they do get close, I'll take care of business and cover all your asses."

Josef laughed and said, "What about me, I think I could handle that monster. At least let me try."

Kevin agreed they should all get a crack at the Mossberg if they wanted, and a couple of other shotguns as well.

Ralph and Michael clipped some new targets on the rail and sent them sliding downrange. Everyone put on their protective eye and sound gear and watched as Josef and Uri did justice to their targets, each coming away with a good appreciation for the power they had unleashed. They were also rubbing their shoulders realizing why planting the weapon deep in your shoulder was a smart thing to do. They would remember that next time.

Kate went next and after some instruction from Ralph, she too peppered her target at 30 feet. Kevin smiled because they were all using good gun etiquette without being reminded. Safeties were being clicked on and off at the right times, they were mindful of where the weapons were pointed, they checked for bullets in the chamber when unloading, and they respected each other on the firing line. His little army was shaping up.

"People, we will continue to practice with all these weapons every week until we are rolling. Once we're on the open sea we can practice some more because then the targets will be moving and so will you as the ship rises and falls on the surface."

Michael then announced to everyone. "After we finish shooting today we are going to show you how to break down these weapons and clean them. Keeping these guns in perfect working order means you will have less jams, more accurate shooting, and you'll have more confidence in the gun. That could save your life. Any soldier will tell you knowing your weapon is the most important task in the shooting process."

Gelendzhik Bay, Black Sea

The General walked casually with Sergeant Major Shostakovich, his key aide, along the beach enjoying the January air. They were savoring some cigars and sharing a small bottle of vodka that was in an unobtrusive flask, to ward off the chill coming off the Bay. The large circular Bay leading to the Black Sea was an inky black color that made the water look frigid and foreboding.

Being January they were alone on the beach and in casual clothes. If it had been summertime, the beach would have been crowded with holiday vacationers, and they would have gone elsewhere. But today they would have to settle for a walk on the mostly deserted beach of Gelendzhik Bay.

These two old soldiers had been together for over 20 years, going back before Afghanistan. They had watched each other's backs for years. The Sergeant Major thought of the General as his father. The General thought of him as a son.

They knew each other well. The Sergeant Major knew of the General's displeasure with his current assignment, he knew of the tragic loss of the General's sister in the 9-11 terrorist attack, and he knew of the General's brother-in-law's visits in recent months. He knew that something was up and hoped that his boss would share it with him.

He would do anything he could to assist the General. He just didn't know what it was that he needed to be done. As they walked enjoying the cold crisp air and the strong Cuban cigars, the General talked about his desire to retire soon, before he died with his boots on. He talked about his family having disappeared, and even his sister having been killed by the terrorists.

That made him remember the many tragedies that he and his troops suffered at the hands of the Mujaheddin in Afghanistan. Both agreed that many of their fellow soldiers died in that godforsaken land. His Aide hated them as much as he did.

He brought up the subject of his brother-in-law's visits and stated that he had come to ask a favor, a big favor. The General stopped walking and faced out to sea, looking at the twin peninsulas that came together to form an almost perfect circular bay. Even though it was very cold, the waters were calm, just as he was.

Without any preamble he said, "Tristan, Josef asked me to give him a bomb, a suitcase bomb. One that he intends to use to find bin Laden and then kill the son-of-a-bitch!" He paused for a second and then turned towards the soldier to see what reaction he had to the statement.

The Sergeant Major didn't flinch, he slowly looked at the General and said evenly, "I knew that he didn't come half way around the world to go fishing, he's as bad as I am in that category, I figured he was here for another reason. He and that partner of his," he said with a smile and a raised eyebrow.

The General laughed out loud and said, "I thought the same thing. But I have determined they are not gay lovers, and that they both came here for the same reason. We think alike my friend, but I am shocked that you have no reaction to the bomb part of this scenario?"

"Oh, that threw me for a loop alright, but I figured if you were telling me this, there must be more to the story. And if I have learned one thing as a soldier, it is to be patient, and not rush to conclusions. I figure you will tell me more when you are ready. And I presume you would like my assistance."

"As I said, you are perceptive Tristan, that you are. I would indeed like to ask your support as I think that together we could actually do some good for this crazy world we have created."

"So, hand me that flask and lead on my General. I'm listening. Mostly, I am intrigued with the concept, as I can't quite see how your U.N. translator brother could pull off what most of the western world has been trying to do for years. If nothing else I like a good story, and this has got to be a cluster fuck."

The General laughed and took a swig out of the flask, passed it to the soldier, and started walking. He started at the beginning and they were able to walk almost to the southern tip of the peninsula before he was finished. The Sergeant didn't interrupt other than a few times to try and understand what was being said. He listened and became more interested in meeting this little band of warriors.

"So, how can I be of service and help with this cause? I think I would actually like to be a part of this escapade. If they were to succeed and their plan is crazy enough that it could, I would like to know that I had a hand in it."

"Well, that's how I made a decision to buy in as well. If you are serious, I need to secure one of those suitcase bombs we have on Level 3 in the Ordinance Bunker. Just one, but as you well know from our inspections, they are well guarded and counted often. In our walk around getting ready for the American inspections coming next month, I think I could get one out of the building, but I would need your subterfuge and assistance in creating a massive diversion."

"General, does this little caper involve your fishing boat that I have just been ordered to move into the bunker for winter storage?"

"Yes, as a matter of fact, it does. I was hoping that we could create a hidden locker in the bait box next to one of the seats that would hide one of those suitcases. Then we'd create some sort of emergency on Level 2 and Level 3 that would force us to move all the weapons from 3 up here."

Tristan thought a moment and then said, "When we were down there inspecting, I noticed you looking at the pipes and HVAC running

212

up the stairwells. I think we could use them to create some sort of flood happen."

The two men started developing the concept. The General's mind was working overtime.

"If this flooding occurred while we were actually in the building, on our inspection visit, we could mobilize all the security people to join in the rescue effort, even those monitoring the cameras. That would create all sorts of confusion and that would be our chance to grab a bomb!"

"General, perhaps we could actually get in there and assist them, in the spirit of saving the weapons? I'm willing to get my boots wet for the cause."

"Yes, that would be good, if we got everyone helping, we could have them stack the suitcases next to the 1st Level elevators, which is where my boat will be stored for the winter."

"Which I can place there next week," Tristan stated, getting into the design of the scenario. "It is almost too simple."

The General continued. "So with a little slight of hand, perhaps we could switch out a real bomb for a fake case weighing the same. And then slide the real unit into the large bait box under the boat's seat."

"It does seem a little simplistic, but I have always found the simplest plans usually work best. Once the bomb ordinance has all been brought up, we let the soldiers haul the boat out of the way so that ordinance trailers can be brought in to secure the weaponry. We actually don't even have to retrieve the boat until spring, In fact, we may not want to pull it out, we could just leave it there."

"Sounds like a plan. Next week we will scope it out. In the meantime, can you fashion a compartment on the boat. Also we would need to find a suitcase container and match the weight so we have a dummy case ready. …. So do you think I'm crazy or what?"

"Your not crazy Sir, maybe dazed, but not crazy. But, I can see where this is probably leading. Either we are successful or we are dead."

"Unfortunately, that may indeed be the case my friend."

"We have been together through many wars General. I have shared my life with you long enough to be able to live with that. But if we pull this off, I would ask a favor. You have mentioned this Wisconsin place; I would like to join you if we could make this happen. Might that be possible? I too don't have any family left and any reason to stay here. I have earned my retirement. Could I get passage to this Wisconsin too?

"Tristan, that is entirely possible, but you would have to learn to fish, that's all they do up there."

"I could learn to fish, if you would show me, but I hear they also have great hunting. And I have always wanted to open a shop and sell those eggs that telescope inside one another and Russian bobble heads. Enough of this soldier nonsense."

The General laughed heartily in the wind. He turned up his collar to the cold and then upended the flask, and found it was empty. The cigars had long gone out and he stubbed his into the sand as the sun was going down. They called it a day and walked back to the car.

The Sergeant Major drove the General home and immediately walked around the house to take a look at the boat. He pulled back the snow-covered tarp enough to note the seats were wide and could easily conceal one of those suitcases under a large bait storage tank. He realized all he had to do was improvise a bit and come up with some sort of a cover to drape over the whole thing. He decided he would use the life preservers that could be thrown over the seat and act as a blanket. What could look more natural he thought. This should not be a problem.

NSA, Fort Meade, Maryland

Bill Dalde arrived early at his desk because he was working on an advanced review he had been monitoring for weeks. It had started with a series of red flag calls intercepted out of Great Britain. The intercepts suggested that some homebred Pakistani nationals were making plans for a series of bombings in and around London. In recent weeks the chatter had become more focused and seemed to suggest their target was the London Underground and the Red Bus System that made up most of the public transportation in the city. It had become a priority analysis and review and was his primary responsibility.

The voices and conversations on the cell phone calls were not that sophisticated, suggesting they were not well-trained terrorists, but that made them even more dangerous and less predictable. These amateur terrorists obviously did not think their conversations were being monitored. They had been using the same cell phones for weeks now.

As this call activity was analyzed, it was shared with the British desk over at the CIA. They in turn were talking with their counterparts at MI-6. Everyone was paying attention on this one. Having flagged the activity weeks ago the British were now deeply involved in an investigation and had the suspects under constant surveillance. The intelligence being sent over now was more goodwill than anything else.

One by-product of the global terrorism war occurring all over the world was that many governments were now sharing more and more of whatever intelligence they were picking up. Even the Russians were sharing, when they thought it was in their best interests. They too had terrorist problems.

Bill picked up his phone and hit a speed dial number for an analyst friend of his at Langley on the south side of the Potomac River just outside Washington D.C. The encrypted call went to the British Section, Terrorism Desk and was answered on the first ring, by Bede Long, an Australian working for the spy organization. He had been working this case since the beginning. Matching updated files were sent electronically. They would be analyzed again by the CIA and then forwarded to the British.

"Bede here, hi ya mate, get any lately up there in the north woods?"

"For Christ sakes, Bede, I'm only 35 miles north of you. Shopping centers, office buildings, twelve lanes of traffic, and a golf course surround me. What do you mean north woods? I just saw a guy hit a golf ball to the perimeter fence and security was on it before the guy could even find his ball. Only place I know where your golf ball gets thrown out on the fairway all by itself."

"What's up? Oh, I see you have more on our Pakistani idiots. Well, that will be over today. The Brits are taking them down, in fact they will have them locked up before the sun sets over there. So another victory for the good guys, huh?"

"That's good to know, we need to string a couple of victories together. With what I've been monitoring, I thought they were ready to pull something soon. It's in my report. Let me know if we are truly closing this one and I can move on. Otherwise I have to hold the file open."

"You got it mate. Now comb your hair and go make some lovely sorry she didn't meet you earlier. That's what I am doing this afternoon after I close this bugger."

"Bede, I do have something I would like to run past you. Have you heard the call letters THCT anywhere before?" Bill hoped that his friend could make some sense of the letters.

"Sounds like a drug or some chemical to me. Been listening to the druggies again have we? You have too much time on your hands. No, it doesn't sound familiar to me. Can you give me any kind of reference? I'll run it through the computers over here and see if we get a pop."

"I would appreciate it." Bill agreed. "I flagged it a couple of weeks ago up here. It came in with bin Laden's name mixed into the conversation." He hit send/receive on his secure email program and saw that a number of high priority flags were in the queue.

"And I see." Bill said as he updated his email. "that I just picked up a couple more flags on the computer just now. Don't know if it's anything yet, but I guess I have my next major file opening up. Have a good day Bede. You try to get some."

"I bloody well will my friend, that is definitely on the agenda."

Hanging up the encrypted phone, he reached for a Langley house phone and called upstairs to inquire about any information the CIA might have picked up on a terrorist cell going by the name, or initials of THCT. The terrorist analyst upstairs said he would run a complete check on anything even close to those letters and get back to him within an hour.

The analyst then made a call to the CIA's Covert Operations Officer and the Assistant Director's Office and asked if they were aware of any terrorist chatter in the New York area relating to something called THCT. Both desks personnel said there was nothing on their radar but they took notes, started files and asked for all follow-ups to be passed along with priority.

The next day the CIA's Director's daily morning briefing with to the President had a footnote there was some new cell action in the New York area. The international city was still considered a prime target and anything even remotely related to it got a priority rating that eventually made it all the way to the West Wing. While it was routine at the moment, there would now be a whole bunch of homeland security people listening for anything THCT.

→ ←

Camp Novorossiysk, Russia

The General and his Sergeant Major arrived at the appointed time to do another inspection of the Ordinance Bunker. They knew the American Disarmament team would be coming for their inspection in two months to the day, so they now had a clear timetable. They met the Lieutenant Colonel in charge of Ordinance and his Officers and advised of the new schedule of inspection.

The tour followed the same path as before. As they were finishing Level 1 and walking to the elevator, the General walked over to his boat parked in the empty space next to the elevator, and pulled back the tarp to see that all of his equipment was safe and secure, just as he had left it. He was not worried about any pilferage, as everyone knew it was the General's boat and messing with it would be a bad thing. He left the tarp pulled back and walked to the elevator entrance. They inspected Level 2 and then moved on to Level 3.

On Level 3 as they walked around the room looking at the various bombs and other ordinance stacked on the tall shelves, the General came to a realization. All of these weapons were strung together at multiple points with heavy steel cables that were then bolted to the heavy duty metal racks.

"Colonel, when these weapons need to be moved, what is the procedure for making that happen? How will our American guests and our soldiers be able to move these weapons out of here?"

"General, a good question. As you can see the weapon cases are all bolted and woven together with steel cable through these eyelets. The cables would have to be removed to move the suitcases."

The General stepped forward and looked at the steel cable and the locks that bound them to the metal racks. "How often are these locks opened and checked, to be sure that they do open?" he asked.

The Colonel and his aide seemed flustered for a moment and looked at one another as if saying, they had no idea.

"That's what I thought. Does anyone have a key for these locks? Do we even know where the keys are?"

The Sergeant Major saw this as an opportunity to test a theory he had developed walking about the shelf lined room. Without any warning to the General, he walked over to one of the cables running thru the cases and picked it up as if weighing its strength and thickness. He followed the cable to the end of the rack where it was double looped and strung around the thick vertical metal shelves. All of this was locked together with a massive padlock.

Before anyone realized what he was attempting to do, he picked up the lockset and wrapped his two meaty hands around it, giving the lock a tremendous pull. Everyone in the room was drawn to his movement and the sharp noise from metal on metal. To everyone's surprise, the double loop of the cable pulled itself out of the clamp eyelet that held the cables bunched together. The security cable was obviously not tightened up to the point it couldn't be pulled through the lockset. He turned to the others and held up the loose cable, which now could be snaked back through the many suitcase bomb eyelets allowing each case to be free of its locking mechanism. He didn't say a word.

The Colonel and his aide stood there shocked, and then a crestfallen look came washing across their faces. Finally he stammered. "General, I am shocked that padlock did not hold." The Colonel's voice betrayed that he was quite bewildered and dismayed by the incident.

"Sir, no more than I am." The General responded sternly as he looked at the Sergeant with a how did you know that was going to happen look.

He turned his attention back to the two Officers and growled. "And think what the Americans would say should they decide to give those damn cables a tug."

Before, the Colonel could speak the General stepped forward and grabbed the padlock. He held it up and said. "It's not even the padlock that failed, it's the clamp that was supposed to be holding the cable tightly."

He continued to play-act his fury and anger. "Well, I guess we won't be needing those keys after all." With that he waved his hand at the Sergeant Major who recognized he was being encouraged to try another lockset.

The burly Sergeant Major walked to the other end of the shelf. He grabbed the long cable and yanked as hard as he could. The short part of the cable slipped almost effortlessly through the steel clamp and through the lockset, and it too was loosened. Again the Sergeant held up the cable and separate lockset. Everyone just stood there in silence.

Then the Sergeant decided to take the ruse further and grabbed one of the nuclear bomb suitcases off the shelf pulling the cable through the attached eyelet. He stood there with the case in hand, and noted that the weight was identical to the dummy case he had hidden in the General's fishing boat on Level 1.

➤ ◄

Bank of America, Grand Central Station

Ralph Behar sat patiently across the desk from the international banker as he gathered the correct denominations of the three currencies he had requested for a business trip. He had asked for $9,000 in Russian Rubles, $9,000 in Turkish New Lira, and $9,000 in Egyptian Pounds. He was exchanging U.S. funds from a numbered Swiss account that had been set up by William Meredith for the mission.

He would collect these currencies and then repeat the process at a few other New York banks for other denominations they would need for the trip. By staying under $10,000, which was the transaction amount banks, were required to report to the government, and spreading out the withdrawals at a number of different banks, hopefully they would lessen the attention drawn to the financial transactions.

The plan was for team members to have local currencies with them when they flew to meet the ship in a number of different ports. Other currencies would be also packaged and flown to the ship on Meredith's plane for use in the various ports of call.

The group would be traveling as if they were tramp steamer tourists looking for a different experience off the beaten path. It had been decided that the bulk of the group would fly directly to Istanbul, Turkey and then travel as tourists to the archeological sites in Truva, just 50 kilometers to the south on the Aegean coast. This was the historical site where the legend of the Trojan horse was supposed to have occurred. Michael thought it would be a great rallying place for the group to assemble for the second phase of the mission. Meredith had readily agreed.

After signing various documents using his false identification, which seemed to be working well and not causing any undue interest, Ralph gathered his currency denominations in a locked briefcase, thanked the banker for his time and effort and left for his waiting car.

→ ←

Pier 3, Catania, Sicily

The Majorca, registered as a Greek ship, was tied up and off-loading on Pier 3 in Catania. The pier jutted straight east into the Ionian Sea. Technically it was the Mediterranean, but sailors felt the need to separate their bodies of water, into more definable spaces whenever they could, since water covered three-quarters of the earth and greater definition was a good thing. Captain Derek Brinkmann was reviewing his manifest and looking ahead to see what the shipping line had organized for him for the next couple of months.

He was taking a mixed load of cargo from here to Athens, and then on to Odessa in the Ukraine, with a large shipment of steel and oil machinery parts. As he scanned down the manifest, he saw they would be picking up farm machinery parts in Odessa, and tons of wheat in Gelendzhik, Russia, on the east coast of the Black Sea.

He was pleased he would not have to go to the port in Sevastopol, in the Ukraine, or to Novorossiysk, in Russia, both places being ports for the Russian Naval Fleet. He knew the Russian Navy was in a foul mood, having to relocate all their naval facilities from one place to the other because the Ukrainian government was invoking the end to their long lease of the Port of Sevastopol.

The Russians did not like being pushed around and they seemed to be taking it out on commercial shipping interests within the Black Sea, a body of water they considered their own personal bathtub. It also didn't help that there were problems brewing in the Republic of Georgia and it looked like Moscow was try to pick a fight with its neighbor to the south. The Black Sea was not a friendly place at the moment.

As he scanned a cable, he noted they would be picking up some of his owner's people in Athens and they would be part of the crew for the duration of the Black Sea trip, and perhaps points beyond. He respected Mr. Meredith immensely. He was a good owner that cared about his fleet and personnel. He had bought the shipping line about 15 years ago and had made a success of it by investing in the business.

The cable stated there would be three coming aboard in Athens and they were seasoned sailors able to pull a full load as part of the crew. They were to be given every courtesy and they would have important documents for him to read after they left Athens. That sounded like intrigue, but he trusted his owner's judgment.

He liked Meredith because he was a hands-on owner, but still smart enough to allow his captains to manage their own ships while at sea. He understood that if he allowed his ship captains their authority over the crew, they produced efficient and timely results, meeting shipping deadlines. He understood time was money and an unhappy ship would not maintain its schedule.

The Captain stepped over the hatch door and looked over the rail to see that the last of the pallets were on the pier and they could be underway in a couple of hours. He walked back inside and gave his First Mate the manifest summary so he could chart the next leg to Athens and Odessa and then on to Gelendzhik, Russia.

→ ←

Camp Novorossiysk

The General walked over to the cable in the Sergeant's hand and held up the frayed loose end for the Colonel to see. "Colonel, I think we, I think you have a serious problem here! We, you, have some work to do before our American guests arrive. Either you fix these locks or you find a better way to secure these cases, before they arrive."

He threw down the frayed cables and the faulty padlock in disgust. "I think I've seen enough for today."

The Sergeant recognized the signal and positioned himself to be the last one out of the room. The General pointed to the stairs saying he would walk up so he could vent his frustration with the day's events. The Colonel and his aide followed meekly behind like beaten dogs having peed on the floor, and started up the stairwell.

The Sergeant started to follow, but intentionally lagged a few steps behind. When the three officers had gone up the half flight of stairs and turned on the landing, he slipped back into the bunker and quickly grabbed the suitcase weapon he had pried loose from its fetters. Then he quickly went back to the stairwell heading up. He called ahead and projected his voice.

"General, perhaps you should reconsider using the stairs, your heart isn't used to this level of stress anymore."

His booming voice gave the impression he was on the stairs right behind the officers. This bought him another few seconds. At the half stair level between 3 and level 2, he stopped next to the flywheel attached to the water pipes. He silently put the suitcase down, and pulled a pair of gloves from his tunic. He slipped a wrench out of his uniform sleeve. Twisting the clean-out valve cover as silently as he could, he loosened the valve cap completely, and then rewound it a couple of threads so that it would hold in place. He thought that once the water pressure built up it would blow. He turned the large flywheel in a counter-clockwise direction opening the flow of pressurized water pouring into the pipe. He picked up the suitcase and quickly moved up the stairs. Again he called ahead to let them know he was right behind them.

At the next half level he repeated the process almost unthreading the purge valve cap and opening the flywheel. It took just a few seconds and as he moved upward he could here the officers just a half-floor away. The General had slowed down and was taking the stairs with a labored effort.

The Sergeant maintained the half-floor separation distance because he still had the bomb suitcase in hand. He took off the gloves, sliding the wrench up his sleeve again. Being out of view, he conversed with the officers ahead. Once he heard them exit the fire door at the top of the stairwell, he rushed up and hid the metal suitcase in a dark corner of the stairwell behind a trash bin. As he came through the door, he walked over to the General who was standing next to his boat making a show of trying to catch his breath. He asked if he was ok.

As he bent over the General to check on his condition, he whispered, "Done, I actually brought it up with me. It's behind the trash bin inside the doorway."

The General looked up with a contorted face, but kept his composure. He directed his gaze at the two officers standing ten feet away. As he continued to catch his breath he realized the slight change might actually work even better. He straightened up and pulled his uniform tunic taut, turned and addressed the Officers.

"Colonel, I believe we have some security issues that need to be addressed here. Your office, now!" He sternly looked at the two officers and then at the command bunker across the floor.

The General, his aide and the Ordinance officers walked across the Level 1 tarmac and headed for the Command and Security office. As they entered the cement block building, they passed the security room being staffed by a by a number of soldiers monitoring the cameras. The General signaled the Sergeant Major to wait in the security room.

He directed his two ordinance officers into a small conference room and shut the door. As they stood there, the General waved them to chairs and took a seat at the end of the rectangular table, so he could see the security monitors across the hall.

He sternly eyed his two officers sitting across from him. They were staring at the table obviously aware they had a big problem on their hands. The General gave thought to dressing them down loudly enough for the whole building to hear, but thought better of it.

His focus was to complete the real objective, so he chose a more restrained approach. He also wanted to draw out the reprimand long enough so he would have a reason to be in the building for the next calamity about to occur. He calmly spoke to the two officers.

"First, I will tell you that while I am very upset, I am glad that what happened with the security cables actually happened today, and not when the Americans are here next month. Colonel, can you imagine if one of their Generals or technicians grabbed one of those cables and gave them a good hard pull. We would be the laughing stock of the disarmament community, and Moscow would have our heads." He let that sink in for a few seconds.

"Thus, while I am angry, I am grateful the problem presented itself today and not when they are here. That being said, I am still shocked that you have not checked such things yourself? What kind of security do you have around here?"

"General, I apologize for this lapse in security protocol. While I have not personally checked the cables we have in place, we do have personnel that should be checking and testing such things. I will personally deal with each of them immediately."

The General noted his words were contrite but he wasn't going to let him off with just a tongue-lashing. He emphatically said, "You're damned right you will check every protocol we have in place. You will be personally involved from this day forward, reporting directly to me, that everything has been checked and double checked, before the Americans come into this bunker."

"Yes Sir, I will personally lead the review starting today. This problem will be dealt with quickly and all other protocols will be reviewed and tested as you have requested."

Just then a klaxon started bellowing in the adjacent security room. It was loud and meant to get everyone's attention. As all three officers looked towards the window, as the Sergeant Major burst into the room.

"General, I apologize for the interruption, but I think you should see what is happening out here. We have another serious problem with the weapons!"

"Now what? My heart can't take this crap!" With that the three officers pushed back from the table and exited the room with the General leading. The other two officers were terrified that another problem had arisen.

When all three got to the wall of security monitors, they saw personnel looking at the Level 3 monitors. As they stared at the monitors, the cameras showed that Level was flooding with water, and the room had at least two feet of water already on the floor.

"What the hell is going on?" the General yelled above the din staring at security monitors. Everyone in the room turned to the voice and seeing the General standing there, immediately went silent.

The Sergeant Major decided to break the silence.

"General, that flooding will compromise every one of those weapons unless we get them out of there now." His voice conveyed it was indeed a serious problem. The General responded accordingly.

"Damn it! One problem after another." He threw his hands up and turned glaring at the Officers. They again stared at the floor. "Colonel, organize a crew, we have to get those weapons out of there and now. Gather everyone you have on duty. Damn it, lets go!"

With that he led the charge out of the office and across the Level 1 tarmac. The bunker commanding officer ordered everyone to follow, including the security personnel monitoring the cameras. Everyone was being drafted and took off running for the elevators.

The Sergeant Major held the door open while the General led the charge to Level 3. After everyone followed him out he went to the security office equipment locker and kicked it open to see if there was any kind of bolt cutters inside, and found one. He too charged out of the office and caught up with the group at the elevator. The security klaxon kept ringing incessantly, creating general chaos among the troops.

When the whole group got to the elevator, it would not respond. The water levels on 3 must have shorted out the power. The General pointed to the stairs and led the way charging down the steps. Everyone followed. The

Sergeant caught the Ordinance Colonel before he went down the steps and handed him the bolt cutter.

He sarcastically said, " In case you can't pull out all the cables with your hands. We don't have time for the keys. Go!"

As the soldiers rushed down the stairwell, the Sergeant Major did a quick search on Level 1 to be sure that all personnel were engaged. He ran back to the Security room and verified that all personnel had left. Then he ran back to the General's boat, put on his gloves and pulled the life preservers off the seat in the boat. He unlocked the latch to the compartment under the seat.

The Sergeant Major took one last look around to make sure no one was watching and then quickly pulled out the perfectly identical suitcase bomb casing. He walked to the stairwell doorway, made sure everyone was on the lower levels, and switched out the fake suitcase for the real one hidden behind the trash barrel. Returning to the boat with the real weapon, he slipped it into the hidden compartment under the seat, latched the lock, and reburied the seat with the mountain of life preservers.

Stepping back to the stairs, he heard the first soldiers coming up the stairwell with the weapons in hand. He decided he'd act as traffic cop and direct activities topside. As they exited the door he orchestrated the stacking of the weapons side by side next to the wall of the elevator shaft. Then he sent the soldiers down again for another trip.

The downward and upward flow of the soldiers carrying the bomb suitcases created gaps in time as one group would stop and let the opposite group pass going the other way. During one such gap, the Sergeant Major quickly retrieved his fake suitcase from the stairwell and placed it in the midst of the others. It was nestled in the middle of the stack and looked and felt like the real thing. Once this was accomplished he too followed a group of soldiers down the stairs.

Last in line, as he got to Level 2 he noted the flywheel was still wide open. The blown valve cover was hanging from the pipe by a chain. With a break in traffic on the stairs, he closed the flywheel valve and clamped it to prevent slippage. He did the same on the next half level above the swamped room. The water shooting out of the purge valve slowed to a trickle.

When he got to Level 3 he found the water had risen to just about three and a half feet and completely covered the bottom racks. But the cable cutters he'd sent down had done the job and the weapons on the lower racks had been stacked on the higher shelves until they were carried upstairs. Only the higher shelves now held weapons, and they were still high and dry.

The Sergeant sloshed his way over to the General who was in the middle of the room with water up to his hips directing the soldier's assembly line moving ordinance up the stairs. He leaned in close and whispered. 'Done'. The General acknowledged and turned back to his command efforts. The Sergeant turned and lent a hand to cut another set of cables, working side by side with the Colonel. He felt sorry for the career officer, but knew the General wouldn't kill his career.

In a matter of ten minutes the entire bunker was emptied and all the weaponry was stacked on Level 1. All the personnel involved in the equipment rescue stood around catching their breath. Their uniforms were soaked to the hips.

The General appraised the overall situation and gave another dire look at the Colonel standing near the elevator. He was out of breath and beside himself with the mess that he'd witnessed on Level 3, and now had on Level 1. The General walked over to him.

"Colonel, we are not having a good day here, are we? I am at a loss for words. We will talk later. Let's get this cleaned up and organized. Get some armed guards around this ordinance and try to figure out what the hell happened." He leaned in closer and quietly added. "Again, if this was going to happen, it was better today than in the future, but then I said that already, didn't I."

The Officer looked completely shaken, seeing his career flashing before his eyes. The General made a mental note not to be too hard on him, since he had caused the mischief to occur.

"General, I too am at a loss for words. I'll get on this right away. Sir, May I move your boat away from this mess to begin the cleanup process?"

The General simply waved his hand and nodded in feigned disgust. He turned and walked away with the Sergeant Major towards his car at the other end of the bunker. His mission had been accomplished.

→ ←

Aegean Sea, east of Sicily

The Majorca was a good ship, but a bit small, which made her very useful. She was a shallow draft Coaster, able to get into all the small ports that the larger ships couldn't access. As a small ship in the Tramp-Tanker class, she was a coastal workhorse vessel plying the shallow waters of the Mediterranean, the Aegean Sea and the Black Sea on a regular basis. She occasionally had ports of call that took her through the Suez Canal and down the west coast of Africa, and even east into the Indian Ocean.

Her registry was Greek with the Iolcos Hellenic Maritime Enterprises Company, out of Piraeus, Greece. A British Financier, Mr. William Meredith, II, owned that shipping line. He also had controlling interests in the Ascape Shippers Line, in the UK, and the G.C. Reibsner Shipping Company out of Norway.

Captain Derek Brinkmann loved his small ship and he was pleased that the owner had just put in substantial improvements, just a month ago. The ship, out of commission for three weeks, but substantial improvements had been made to its four-stroke diesel engines. The yard had also added a new state-of-the-art twin screw, and propeller /rudder assembly that would make the ship much faster and very maneuverable. In the pilothouse, there was new over the horizon radar, surface radar and gyroscopes added. They had even done some work on the few cabins that were on board, which might explain why they had some passengers coming aboard in Athens. While the Majorca wasn't much to look at, underneath it was a ship-shape vessel that could do the job well.

Maintaining a steady easterly course through the Ionic Sea the ship was headed for the Isthmus of Corinth. One of the advantages of being a small ship was she could still make passage through this narrow manmade Canal, built through sheer rock in the 1880's. This route saved some 400 kilometers of passage around the Peloponnesus Islands, and offered an almost direct route to Piraeus, the Port of Athens, from the west.

Because the Canal was only 21 meters wide at its narrowest point, large commercial vessels could not utilize the passage. But the Majorca had just a 45-foot beam for its 200-foot length and could slide through the deep canyon of rock without a problem as long as the helmsman knew what he was doing. It was a claustrophobic passage with walls towering over the ship on both sides for the 7-kilometer run, but time was money and this shipping channel cut hours from tight schedules.

Approaching the Canal, the Captain radioed ahead his position and was placed in line with two others ships heading east. There would be no delay, waiting for ships heading west. The Canal had sheer rock walls rising to over one hundred feet on either side of the cut. As a ship passed through the Canal, crewmembers could look straight up and see people above them looking down. It was quite an extraordinary experience.

Captain Brinkmann had to pay attention to this passage because there wasn't much room for error. So he personally manned the wheelhouse and stationed lookouts with radios along both sides of the ship to monitor and maintain separation from the walls.

Upon arrival on the far side, breaking out into open water, Captain Brinkmann followed the two ships in front of him straight east. It looked as if they too were heading for Athens some 100 kilometers away.

→ ←

NSA, Fort Meade, Maryland

Bill Dalde got his fourth and fifth hits on the THCT letters in less than two days. They were all phone calls and were short and to the point. No names were used, and the words seemed disjointed. Anyone listening to the conversation would not be able to make any sense out of it. Yet all of those factors made this a high priority message worth additional analysis.

He looked at the phone records and time stamps, and noted that they were all coming out of the Tri-State New York area according to the satellites, primarily from Manhattan and a couple coming from New Jersey across the River. That too added a level of concern because New York was usually thought of as a permanent terrorist target. Perhaps a new terror cell was forming.

That same afternoon he received another scrambled email download, this time from overseas listening posts that identified two very short calls from both Calais and Paris, France. The Echelon computers had picked up the call letters THCT again in the cell phone communications. Now the questionable call letters had officially gone international. That changed the game and raised the ante. They elevated the red flags to the next level. He listened to the calls a number of times and verified locations. While the conversation was innocent in nature it still had ominous implications. Something was going on and it would need to be investigated further.

He realized it was time to bring this to the attention of his NSA supervisors. They would determine what level of scrutiny would be attached to the calls. He created a red flag file on THCT and gathered the few materials he had accumulated. He called his boss and made an appointment for 11:00 am the next day.

→ ←

Piraeus, Greece

After another leisurely day of sailing, the Majorca turned north into the Port of Piraeus, the shipping seaport for the city of Athens, just a few kilometers to the north. This harbor had been the busiest seaport in the Mediterranean Sea for over 2,500 years.

Piraeus had been the center of shipping and commerce for the entire known world back then, and today it was still the most dominant commercial shipping port in the Mediterranean. It was home to more shipping companies than all the rest of the Med., the Aegean Sea, and Black Sea put together.

As the Majorca entered the outer harbor, a pilot boat motored up on the starboard side and matched the speed of the ship for just a moment so the port's pilot could board. He climbed to the bridge and said hello to the Captain in Greek and English. The Captain turned the ship over to the pilot fully confident in his ability to bring the ship to the dock. He walked over to the bridge window to enjoy the scenery.

The pilot took control with practiced ease and gently drove the ship into the Harbor. The Majorca passed numerous large container and bulk carriers at anchor, waiting their turns for the limited dock space available for off-loading, or accepting cargo. As a small Coaster, the Majorca could always find dock space between the larger ships. It's parent company, Iosco Hellenic Maritime was based in Piraeus and prided itself on its tight scheduling and cargo handling efficiency.

In the channel it passed a number of large and small cruise ships tied up at the passenger piers. Athens was a major stop on the cruise ship itineraries and they came all the way into the Harbor for the convenience of the tourists. In addition, there was constant ferry traffic coming and going to all the outlying Greek Islands. Thus, the Captain welcomed the assistance of a harbor pilot.

In less than a half-hour the pilot had carefully weaved through all the shipping traffic and was nestling up to the pier with little effort. As soon as the cables were extended and tied to the pier bollards, the cargo boom was engaged and put to work moving cargo to a number of trucks that had pulled beside the ship. Everything was in motion like a fine tuned watch. A gangplank was put in place to allow the port authorities access, and for the crew to disembark for a few hours after unloading was complete.

At the other end of the pier, Michael Pappas, Kevin Geary and Uri Navroz sat in their rented van with their luggage and gear, waiting for the appropriate time to board the ship. They had just flown in that morning on Meredith's jet to a private charter airport in Thrakomkedones, north of the city. Passing through Customs was not a problem and again, no one asked to look through the baggage and boxes they carried. Obviously, Meredith had pull here as a shipping company owner.

Michael had rented a van with his new traveling documents, and driven the group south through the city of Athens on Highway 1, heading directly to the Port. While driving, he pointed out points of interest and the historic sites that could be seen in the hills above the highway. Kevin was eager to absorb all of the history around him, but Uri seemed bored, perhaps having seen the famous sites numerous times before as a sailor.

Once they were near the Iolcos Terminal, they parked and had some lunch at a small pub just outside the commercial pier. The place was nothing to look at, but Michael did the ordering and the food and Greek beer were terrific. Having a beer, it occurred to Kevin that he needed to check what the ships protocol was on drinking. He made a note to ask the Captain before they departed.

After a leisurely lunch of lamb and rice, they saw the Majorca's off-loading activities were winding down at the other end of the pier, so they climbed into the van and drove over to the gangplank.

The Captain saw them coming and walked down the gangplank to welcome his guests. He was intrigued to see who these people were, and why Mr. Meredith had them boarding.

"Good afternoon Gentlemen, I'm Captain Derek Brinkmann, welcome to Athens, and to our ship here, the Majorca."

He extended his hand in greeting and looked each of them in the eye, appraising them. Two were relatively young men and had strong handshakes. They gave him the once over as well. The third man was older and more weather beaten, perhaps Lebanese or Egyptian, he thought. He knew he was a sailor as soon as he shook his hand. It was callused, and hard as rock.

"Captain, it's good to meet you, I am Michael Pappas, currently hailing from New York City, but originally from these Greek islands." He turned towards the other two men and introduced them as well. "I would also like to introduce Kevin Geary, also from New York, and before that from that Emerald Island to the far north. And finally, I would like to introduce Uri Navroz, also from New York, by way of Cairo. As you, he has been a sailor all of his life and has plied many of the same routes you have."

"It is a pleasure. Mr. Meredith advised me you would be joining us in Athens. He asked that I extend you every courtesy that is available on this old boat."

Michael spoke up and said. "William Meredith sends his best wishes. He hopes he might be able to join us somewhere down the road. He asked that I give you this envelope. He'd like you to read it carefully, after we leave port. He hopes it will explain everything to you about us mysterious travelers."

The captain raised an eyebrow, but trusted Meredith's wisdom to explain this course of events. He took the sealed envelope and tucked it under his arm, and then waved his free arm towards the ship.

"Welcome to the Majorca! How about we get you loaded and I'll show you to your cabins. This is an old ship so please don't expect too much in the way of luxuries. Although we have had a number of improvements added recently. Maybe you know something about that, huh?"

He held up the envelope again and said. "Or perhaps this will shed some light on the many improvement to our ship? Let's board shall we?" The Captain had a couple of deck hands assist with the baggage and boxes, but Kevin and Michael personally handled a large footlocker that seemed to be quite heavy.

As they boarded amidships, Michael noted freshly welded half-inch thick metal boxes next to the gunwale that were on the starboard side of the ship. On closer inspection, he noted that each metal box would comfortably accommodate a man or two and had cutouts that he recognized could be shooting ports for weaponry.

Meredith had indeed made some changes to the ship. As he crossed the deck he noted a similar metal pillbox was in place on the port side as well. He presumed that there were similar additions at the bow and stern.

They entered the superstructure stepping over the hatch fiddley, to a midlevel deck, just two decks below the bridge. There were a total of four cabins on this deck, two on each side. Each cabin had two wall bunks and a single scuttle porthole for fresh airflow. The cabin size was much smaller than on a cruise ship, and didn't offer any of the amenities. The head and shower were shared and down the hall. A small locker for clothing and personal items was attached to the bulkhead.

Michael and Kevin paired off in one unit and Uri took a bunk in a second cabin across the hall. He would get a roommate later. Michael took the locked footlocker and shoved it under his bed leaving it locked. He placed a small ashtray with seven marbles in it on top of the locker far enough under the bed that it couldn't be seen. If the locker were disturbed he would know about it.

Once they'd hung up their clothes, they changed into t-shirts and jeans and headed out on deck to see the rest of the ship and to see if they could be of service in leaving port. Michael wanted to check out the other changes that had been added to the ship and headed for the stern. He found another two metal pillboxes on the stern. Standing over them he realized they offered a clear line of vision over the taffrail. They could see anything that would appear behind the ship. He knew what that might be.

He walked forward and found a similar set-up on each side of the bowsprit gunwales.

"So gentlemen, I see that you are inspecting our fine ship." the Captain called out as he came forward. "She may look a little old but she will surprise you at sea. Mr. Meredith just paid for a complete engine overhaul in Marseilles, just a month ago, and since then, she has been purring like a kitten."

He placed his weather beaten hand on top of one of the pillboxes. At first he didn't say anything but as he rubbed his hand over the new welds he said, "There have been all sorts of changes on board. Even I don't know what they are all for."

Ignoring the unasked question, Uri said, "She looks to be a fine ship, Captain. I have spent my whole life on Coasters just like the Majorca. I feel as if I have come home again and we haven't even weighed anchor yet. I will look forward to riding the open sea again. Can I be of service as we leave port, Sir?"

"Meredith said that two of you have had experience at sea, thus I'm guessing it's you Uri, and Michael? We can always use knowledgeable help out here." He pointed a finger at Kevin sizing him up. "And you must be the muscle?"

Kevin laughed and said, " Blame the size on my Mother, bless her Irish soul…. Actually, I told Mikey here that I always wanted to go to sea, and before you know it, son-of-a-gun, here I am standing on the bow of a ship about to cruise the Greek Islands. He promised sun, sand, and women, so I'm staying up here on watch if that's ok with you Captain?"

Everyone laughed and the Captain decided he wasn't going to get anything out of these guys. "Well Kevin, if you're willing, I think we'll make a seaman out of you before we get out of the Greek Islands. With a guy your size we can always find you work on board. Gentlemen, we are just about ready to get underway. Why don't you show this landlubber here how we prepare to cast off the lines, and I'll go see if the motor will turn over."

"Aye, Aye Skipper." Kevin saluted and followed his partner's starboard.

→ ←

Cairo, Egypt

Zohair Joshi made some innocuous phone calls from Paris and advised a business contact in Cairo he would be coming by to talk about some new products he had identified. He used a key code word that told the listener it was critical he come to Cairo as he had important news. It would be news that could not be discussed on the phone.

The person responding heard the code word needed and encouraged the import business manager to schedule a flight. He would be met at the Borg El Arab Airport in Alexandria and driven to a meeting site in northern Cairo.

Zohair set up the one-way non-stop flight from Paris to Alexandria on Egypt Air, and was on his way early the next morning. His return flight would be arranged on the other end. It was expensive to get a flight on such short notice but the cost was unimportant. His employer had a limitless supply of money to do the work of his superiors. He arrived in Alexandria at 11:30 am as scheduled and passed through customs without incident. He was traveling light with only a small rolling bag and a computer case. He was met at the curb, escorted by a professional driver, and driven south towards Cairo.

As they drove on the modern highway angling towards Cairo and the Nile River, he noticed how lush the countryside was near the Nile River. On each side of the Nile the land was lush and green owing its existence to the life-giving waters that flowed through this desert land. In the distance, he could see the Pyramids rising above the low buildings lining the highway.

A half hour later the driver pulled off the highway and drove to a small local restaurant on a dirt road spur a few hundred meters off the road. It was not much to look at, thereby insuring that tourists going to the pyramids and museums would not be stopping for lunch. The driver opened the door and pointed towards a man sitting in a small courtyard under a wide European café style umbrella.

Zohair got out of the car taking his laptop with him, but left his small suitcase in the backseat. He walked towards the man in the courtyard. The driver rolled down the windows of the vehicle and settled back listening to some local music playing on the radio.

Zohair embraced the man in the courtyard, Mustaffa Haqqani, who was actually the covert head of al Qaeda in Egypt. He had been Ayman al Zawahiri's second in command before the Doctor had left to be at Osama bin Laden's side in the battle for Islam.

"Greetings Mustaffa, it has been a while since we have seen one another." He waved the man to a chair and offered him a toke on a shisha water pipe, as was the custom in cafes all over Cairo and Egypt. The smoke rings emanating from the water pipe hung under the umbrella

"Zohair, you look well, Paris must be treating you well. That, or the women perhaps?" he smiled a knowing smile as if he too enjoyed the sinful thoughts of western women. "It is a good day here, Cairo's smog has cleared with these desert winds, so we should have a good meal and talk of these products you mentioned." Again he smiled and picked up a black fig, tossing the whole thing in his mouth.

The guest looked around to verify they were alone and said. "Mustaffa, I have a truly remarkable thing to show you. It is something that I presume you will know what to do with, and perhaps can carry on a journey to our other customers." He raised his very tangled bushy eyebrow and looked at the computer.

He signaled a waiter to bring him some tea and then opened the laptop unit and turned it on. Pushing a number of keys he eventually got to the Power Point program he was looking for and turned the unit towards the man who was sitting with his back to the wall. No one else could see the program.

Zohair hit the play program button and the screen began telling the story he had come to Cairo to discuss. He sat back and grabbed a fig for himself and signaled the waiter for some bread.

Mustaffa watched the program in silence occasionally looking over the screen at his guest. When the slide presentation had run its course, he sat quietly for a minute thinking and then signaled Zohair that he wanted to see the Power Point again. The program was started again with the push of a button, and the courier settled back for a second look sipping his tea and eating another fig

At the end of his second reading, Mustaffa looked up at his guest and said, "You believe this offer to be real?"

"I do believe it's real because of the way it came to me. The Pakistani men who brought it to my friends in Calais made everyone there believe they were real. They spoke Pashtu and did so as natives. That is why I came to you so quickly."

The waiter came up and took their order. When he left, Mustaffa expressed his pleasure with what had been brought to him and said, "You have done well in contacting me with this new product news. I think we may have some special buyers that would be most interested in this product line. Do you know if there are multiple products available?"

" That I do not know. I thought this was something I should share with you as soon as possible. It is an exciting sales opportunity, is it not? I believe this could have a very big impact on our projections and numbers, especially in the west. But it must be taken to market carefully and correctly. I don't think we are talking about a big volume, I think it may just be a prototype at this point, but who knows, once we talk to these people, perhaps they will have more."

"You have done well my friend. I think I have the right kind of buyers who will be very interested in becoming involved. I will take this information to them immediately and they can make contact as we have been directed to do. They are better prepared for this type of negotiating."

"That is what I thought as well. I was tempted to make a call myself, but I realized I did not have the ability, or the money to make such a deal, thus I brought it to you. I will leave this computer with you to take to your customers. I hope they will be excited?"

Mustaffa reached across the table and patted Zohair's hand to show how pleased he was and then reached for a date. "I will make plans tomorrow. They will indeed be pleased if such products are truly available. Let us eat. My driver will then take you to Cairo airport for your trip back. You have done well Zohair. Allah be praised!"

They shared a meal in the soft breezes of the small courtyard, and did not speak of the computer program again. After the meal Mustaffa signaled the driver his guest was leaving and they drove to the Cairo airport. As he passed the pyramids and drove through Tahir Square in the center of Cairo, he knew that he had done the right thing in bringing this to his superior's attention.

Mustaffa sat still, but his heart was racing with the information he had read on this laptop computer. He used a one-time use cell phone and made a call He knew this important information would work its way up the chain of command, eventually being hand-carried by Osama bin Laden's personal courier to the terrorist leader in Pakistan. This was big, really big.

→ ←

The Aegean Sea

Once the lines were cast off and pulled in, the harbor pilot again took the controls and eased the ship away from the dock. In no time at all the ship was steaming past the fishing fleets, cruise ships and ferries, and headed south out into the open Aegean Sea. In fifteen minutes the pilot boat came along side and picked up the pilot, who saluted the Captain and took the stairs to his boat. It quickly peeled off and moved over to another ship waiting for its temporary skipper.

The Majorca pulled into line in the primary shipping lane and picked up speed. In a hundred kilometers it would turn to port and the east, and eventually north passing through the Greek Islands of Ceos, Andros, and Lesbos off the Turkish coast.

Captain Brinkmann advised his First Mate he would be in his Cabin. He tucked the manila envelope under his arm, grabbed a cup of coffee and walked through a hatch to his cabin just behind the bridge. He closed the door and opened his porthole. The cabin was small but offered a large single bunk, a private head and a full size desk for his personal use situated at one end of the room. The porthole did not offer much light, but it did offer fresh air and for this alone the Captain was grateful. His one personal item was a first class captains chair that had wheels for mobility in the small space, but could also be locked down in inclement weather.

He sat at his desk, turned on an old-fashioned green accountant's light and adjusted his coffee cup on a heated pad that kept the brew hot and steaming. He reached for a letter opener, noting that the envelope was sealed tightly. It was from William Meredith II, owner of the shipping line. He pulled out the small sheath of papers that were clipped together. The first sheet was a letter addressed to him as Captain. He put the papers aside and read the letter.

Dear Captain,

By now you are steaming south into the Aegean Sea and I wish I were with you. This letter and the enclosed documents are for your eyes only. I will explain fully. I am sure you are mystified about the three guests I have asked you to take on board the Majorca. These gentlemen are doing an important task for me and will be with you for the next couple of months. Their responsibilities are difficult ones that will be dangerous for them, and ultimately for you and your crew.

I ask your indulgence and patience, as I will try to explain the challenge I am placing before you. I know you are a man of principle and I hope you will agree to assist me in this challenge. If not I will completely understand and we will seek alternative means of accomplishing this formidable task.

I have enclosed a sheath of important papers that must be held in strict confidence regardless of your decision to participate or not. I am confident that you can give me that assurance, as you have been a faithful Captain and employee for many years.

Please read the documents I have enclosed carefully. After you have finished, please read them again if necessary and then I would ask that you have a private conversation with our three guests. These gentlemen are committed to the cause I will lay out for you, and they can answer your many questions, as if I was there myself.

In fact, I will be joining you in about a week when you arrive in Odessa, Ukraine. If you should still have questions then we will talk more.

My friend, I know that I can trust you with this classified information. Remember, my guests speak for me and you can trust them to better explain what we are undertaking.
With the utmost respect,
William Meredith, II

The Captain looked up and reached for his coffee. He then looked back at the letter. He was intrigued but a little confused. He hoped Meredith was correct, that these papers would explain what was about to happen.

He took the papers and started reading. The first part was background that reviewed the tragedy Meredith had experienced losing his son in the World Trade center destruction. He spoke about the horrific events and his personal loss on that fateful day.

Captain Brinkmann was aware of Meredith's background and the tragic loss of his son but this helped him to fill in some of the blanks. The story went on to explain Meredith's long road back from the despair and anger of the 9-11 tragedy.

Then the narrative explained that Meredith had been in counseling for these ensuing years and had met a so-called band of brothers and sisters that had all experienced similar losses. They had come to think of themselves as a close-knit group and had bonded to help each other heal and get on with their lives.

He thought about that for a second and then realized his three guests must be a part of this so-called band of brothers. He filed that away and kept reading the document.

Meredith slowly presented the whole scenario, from the weekly sessions to the first spilled cup of coffee, to the initial plotting, to the eventual commitment of the group to a cause they all bought into and believed in.

The Captain decided he needed another cup of coffee, perhaps even a pot might be necessary, to fully comprehend where this might be going. He stood up, stretched and walked out to the Bridge, noting that everything was in order. He looked at the ship's plotline on the map table and saw they would be making their turn east within the hour. He nodded to the First Officer, reached for the coffee pot on a small table bolted to the floor, just behind his Captain's chair, and took it with him as he retuned to his cabin.

He settled into his reading again and when he got to the part about them hatching a plot of revenge he had an " Aha" moment. He also decided the head needed a visit before reading any further. As he stood there staring at the wall, he started thinking ahead and wondered what it was that the three men had brought on board in that large, locked trunk. He shook the thought out of his mind, as he shook the other end, and zipped up his khaki trousers.

He returned to his desk, threw his feet up on the desk, locked the chair's wheels, leaned back and continued reading. He had a foreboding chill running up his spine even though the cabin was warm and there was little island breeze blowing in.

As he read he matched the script with what he already knew. The Majorca had been mechanically updated and improved with unusual fittings in Marseilles, he had received shipping orders that would take him to Russia, and he had picked up three mysterious passengers in Athens boarding with locked trunks. And now Meredith would be joining the ship in Odessa.

They planned on moving a special package that would be picked up in Gelendzhik, Russia, in addition to freight and tons of grain consigned for shipment. The grain shipment and the special package would be going to Karachi, Pakistan as part of an international earthquake relief effort on the part of Lions Clubs International.

Finally Meredith's letter asked that he should have a private conversation with his three guests to talk more about the plan. Meredith's asked for the Captain's patience and allegiance, promising he would share more when he boarded the ship.

Captain Brinkmann got up and walked out of his cabin directly onto the bridge. He stepped out of the side hatch scanning the deck fore and aft, and saw that all three guests were sitting on storage lockers a deck below. They looked up and waved to the Captain inviting him to come down and talk. The Captain got rid of his cup, reached into a corner of the pilothouse and grabbed four cigars, four more cups and a bottle of Old Turkey, and headed down the steep stairway to the deck below.

"So Gentlemen, I'm sure you can see I'm even more confused than when we left port. Mr. Meredith suggested you would be in a position to help me sort out this confusion. So I've brought a few cigars and a bottle of whisky. How about we walk out on the fantail where we can have a private conversation and enjoy a smoke and drink? Huh!"

Michael, Uri, and Kevin smiled and reached for a cigar and cup.

"Now we get to enjoy the good life," Kevin said as he reached for a large Cuban. Perhaps this cigar will lead us to wine and women?" he said wistfully.

"Down boy, we have nothing but blue water to look at for a solid week my friend, unless you have brought some good binoculars. We will be passing close to the Island of Lesbos by tomorrow afternoon and you may see some bathing beauties on the shoreline." Michael said.

"Lesbos, you're kidding, right? Don't tell me there's an island dedicated to women only out there?" he pointed out to Sea. "I don't want to hear that. I'm a growing boy with needs for wine, women, and sin!"

Everyone laughed, as Kevin was being true to form. The Captain said. "Kevin, in addition to being the muscle, you must also be the comedian. I have some good binoculars if you don't, but I'm guessing you have that kind of stuff in that trunk of yours."

Just before they got to the stern rail, the Captain ducked into a hatchway so he could light his cigar. The wind was blowing hard enough on the open sea he would never have gotten it lighted at the rail. He passed his cigar around so they could all light theirs off his. He grabbed some deck chairs and they settled around a new metal box welded to the deck. The beat of the engines produced a rhythmic cadence and the ships screws were rotating fast enough that the water churned beneath them creating a four foot rolling wake that spread out behind the ship.

"So tell me, what illegal acts will I be committing on this trip to Russia?" the Captain said, and took a long drag of his cigar.

Michael spoke up. "Captain, Mr. Meredith advised you would probably be quite direct and not pull your punches. He encouraged us to do the same, and said you could take it. He has great faith in you, Sir." He continued and decided complete honesty would work best.

"Well Sir, to be direct, we are picking up a suitcase bomb and we're going to sell it to Osama bin Laden and al Qaeda." He let that sink in for a moment and then said, "Direct enough?.... And once we know he is holding this bomb in his lap we are going to blow the son-of-a-bitch off the face of the earth!"

The Captain didn't know quite what to say, so he thought he'd be honest and asked.

"You aren't kidding are you? That was certainly quite direct Mr. Pappas." Again he paused gathering his thoughts. He was trying to connect all the dots but the pencil he was pushing in his mind kept breaking. Finally he said. "You really expect to just take a bomb to him and blow the thing up?"

Uri decided to jump in. "Yes, Captain that is exactly what we plan to do. We're going to kill the son-of-a-bitch and then laugh at him the way he has been laughing at us for the past couple of years."

Michael continued pointing at his partners in crime. "We have all lost loved ones in the devastation of 9-11, as Mr. Meredith pointed out in his summary. We've all been grieving and trying to find some comfort and closure. In a couple years the hurt still hasn't gone away. We believe in this plan and it has drawn us closer together."

Kevin jumped into the conversation. "Captain, I'm like you, I didn't lose any of my own family in the Twin Towers terrorist act, but I did lose two-dozen police and fire buddies that day. I also knew Michael's fiancé as if she were my sister, and thus when she was killed in 9-11; I was readily willing to join this little band of amateur counter-terrorists. Believe it or not, they, we are going to do this thing."

"That package we're picking up in Russia is the suitcase bomb. Let's say we acquired it from someone who also has a vested interest. It was determined the best way to move such a weapon, under the radar, would be to move it by ship," Michael said.

He pulled out a pocket map of the Black Sea, the Aegean Sea and the Mediterranean and laid it on the pillbox they were standing around. He dragged his finger from the eastern shore of Russia in the Black Sea, down through the Bosporus, through the Aegean Sea and the Med, through the Suez Canal and Red Sea and into the Arabian Sea.

"We figure we pick it up here in Gelendzhik and then just take our time delivering it to Pakistan and whatever mountain rat hole bin Laden is hiding in. We have a separate delivery team once we get to Karachi, Pakistan."

The Captain kept looking back and forth to the men as they each added details as if they were planning a boating regatta. He still didn't know what to say.

"What is in those locked cases you brought on?"

"Those are just handguns, rifles and a shit load of ammo for defensive use. And yes, we do have binoculars and night vision goggles. Uri here thinks we may run into pirates when we clear the Red Sea, so we decided we'd deal with that if need be. So yes, I guess I am the muscle you spoke about earlier."

Captain Brinkmann didn't know what to say. He was incredulous. These guys must be nuts, he thought, as he took a long pull on his cigar. The tip bristled bright red as the wind blew off the dead ash onto his shoulder. He brushed it off. "And I'm guessing Mr. Meredith is financing this whole charade, am I right?"

"Yes, again." Michael said. "Our little group here, has assembled a whole lot of expertise in all sorts of critical areas for us to be successful, and Meredith is financing everything."

Past the point of no return, Michael realized that he needed to explain the whole plan just as they had done with Kevin and the General.

"We have a person handling document forging, a chemist and former ATF agent, translators, a police sniper," he pointed to Kevin, " And even some very dedicated Pakistanis who lost their whole families in 9-11. We have a committed group and we have been planning for months. More important, we are actually going to pick up the weapon that is waiting for us as part of this ship's itinerary in the next month."

The talk went on for another half hour as the Captain asked questions and the three men tried their best to answer honestly and candidly. By the time the Captain had exhausted himself, the cigars were gone and they were all parched from the extended talk.

The Captain held up his hand signaling a stop to the conversation.

"Gentlemen, you all may be crazy, but I'll give you credit, you have thought out answers for everything I have thrown at you. Enough for tonight! I promise I will not speak of this to anyone except you three. Let me gather my thoughts and questions. We'll have dinner late tonight after the rest of the crew is finished and on watch. We can then lock the mess room and continue to talk. I have to get back to the bridge as we are about to start our turn east and we're in a major shipping lane."

Uri nodded and said. "Captain, we appreciate your time. Please remember Michael and I know our way around a ship like yours, and if we can be of assistance, please let us know. But until then we will stand aside unless called upon by you."

"Uri, let's not wait. Both of you should join me on the bridge and let me introduce you to my crew. They need to know you will be part of my command. And you, Muscle, you should polish your binoculars, as we will also pass some other islands in the morning."

Michael, Uri and Kevin took these comments as good signs that they had a new member of the THCT team.

➜ ✦

Teterboro, WM Industries Hanger

William Meredith sat on the mezzanine upper deck inside the hanger swirling a glass of Scotch watching the on-going flight activities at the busy charter airport. He was waiting for his pilot to come up the spiral stairs.

Ryan Younger had just deadheaded home from Athens, Greece with an empty cabin after dropping off three guests and a boatload of gear. He was exhausted but he came bounding up the circular stairs two at a time.

Meredith thought, *if only I could do that.* He waved Ryan into a chair and tossed him a beer. They sat for a moment looking out the reinforced glass picture window that overlooked the North-South Runway 27 L in the distance.

Meredith took a pull on his drink. " I'm guessing that you have some questions for me Ryan. Questions about the trips to the Ukraine, to Calais, France, the overnight trip to Athens and the scheduled return trip to Russia. Am I right?"

"Well Sir, yes, I'm a bit confused by all the international travel especially when you have only been on a couple of the flights. We have been ferrying a bunch of people I've never met before all around the globe. Some rather interesting people I might add!"

"That we have Ryan, that we have. But it is all for a good cause. One that I think I should explain to you, as you will be involved in a number of additional flights in the next few weeks and months."

"I would like that, Sir. I have all sorts of thoughts and questions on what is going on. Lots of bits and pieces, but nothing I have been able to string together."

With that, Meredith started telling the story again. He was getting good at the delivery. He knew that Ryan knew all about the loss of his son as he had been with him that day as they watched the Towers come down. He also knew that Meredith had been attending counseling sessions for years now. He had even met some of the group participants when he had offered to fill in driving Meredith's car on some of his counseling session nights.

Meredith told him the whole story. He told him about the Trojan Horse parallel, the band of brothers and sisters who had committed to the plan, the seeking of the bomb, the shipment strategy, and the ultimate end game plan.

Ryan sat there quietly, whistling once and then getting up to grab another beer and bring the bottle of Scotch to Meredith from the bar. He listened intently, and occasionally nodded as another thought fell into place. Eventually Meredith stopped when he thought he had completely covered the subject.

"Ok, so now our earlier trips to Russia and Paris and Calais are starting to make more sense." He sat quietly for a few moments as if searching for what to say. He nodded his head slightly and then said. "So how do I say this, I'm in, if you will have me." His eyes said even more. He wanted to help this man that had been good to him, almost like a Father. "How can I be of service?"

"Ryan, you already have helped and I'm pleased that you would be willing to join us. But please consider that this might go counter to what you have stood for in the past."

"I understand Sir. I thought about that as you were talking. But I think your cause is admirable and God knows the bastard deserves to go down.

So, don't worry, I have thought that part through and I still want to be a part of it."

Meredith looked pleased and raised his glass. "I hoped that would be your reaction, but I didn't want to presume anything. Whether you realize it or not I have thought of you as my son for a number of years already. I'm glad you're joining us. With our worldwide corporate interests and the plane, we can move our people around as we need to. That's why you just came back from Greece, and you will be taking some team members to Odessa, and to Turkey in the next couple weeks. This plan will work with your help."

"Mr. M, you give me the flight assignment and I'll make it happen. With your approval I'll get the Jet overhaul completed a couple weeks early. Sounds like we will be making a number of long-haul trips. What do you want me to tell our co-pilot, Rick?"

"At this point I would say nothing other than we have some far-flung runs to do positioning some people and managing some new business accounts. He will probably figure out some of the intrigue, but let's keep him out of the circle for the moment."

"Done, Sir. I do have one question though. Will I be flying this bomb around in the Bombardier?"

"No, we will be moving the package by ship once we get it in Russia. We are still establishing contact with our terrorist friends. Eventually we will deliver it by boat. But you will be moving people to support that effort, and me too for that matter. I'll keep you posted."

"Yes, Sir. As I said, I'm in, and will do whatever I can to support your mission. I wish I could do more. Maybe I should get a gatling gun added after all," He smiled and then said. "I want a piece of the bastard too!"

→ ←

Sea of Marmara, Turkey

The Majorca took its time sailing north through the Aegean Sea and had already passed through the Canakkale Straits and was now in the Sea of Marmara, the major shipping lanes approaching the Bosporus and Istanbul.

The three THCT members had bonded well with the Captain and now were considered part of the crew even though their quarters were somewhat better than the rest who were below deck.

As they entered the narrow Bosporus channel, requiring expertise to navigate, all three were on the bridge with Captain Brinkmann checking out the passage. They were lined up in single file with ten other ships heading through and into the Black Sea and could see that an equal number of ships were steaming in the opposite direction heading for the Mediterranean. It was one of the world's tightest pinch points.

Captain Brinkmann signaled he wanted a word with Michael Pappas and they stepped out onto the starboard side of the bridge housing.

In a low voice meant only for Michael he said, "As I've thought about your package, I was reminded that NATO, the Russians, and the US all have monitoring stations here in the Straits to sniff for nuclear material. Are you aware of that?"

"Captain, we are aware and have made plans to deal with that situation. We have the same monitoring capabilities in New York harbor. I was aware of the sniffing capability as a policeman. We figured on it being the case here too, so when we come back through here, I'll be getting off the ship before the Bosporus, and then I'll re-board after the Canakkale Straits near Truva. I grew up in Greece and Turkey, and know this land well enough to drive the package overland. You just sail through with your regular cargo and I'll re-board after we clear the Straits."

The Captain was impressed and said so. "I'm glad that you considered this, and that you have a plan or we would have the U.S., NATO, and Mother Russia breathing down our necks before we even get started. But how do you suggest that we get you off the ship in Turkey without drawing attention?"

"We thought that through as well. I'll just get violently sick in the Black Sea and you'll have to declare a medical emergency. Using my fake Turkish passport, I'll be taken off the ship, with our dangerous suitcase."

"I think we could arrange that, I've had to do it before." The Captain said.

"If we can dock the Majorca in Sile northeast of the Bosporus, we'll have one of our people meet us and then instead of driving to the hospital, we will hightail it through Istanbul and meet up with the ship on the other end of the Straits near the ruins of Troy. William suggested that we have the entire team get a feel for our namesake before we try to complete this mission."

"OK, I think that could work. We can pre-announce the illness while still at sea, and ask for access. Sile is a small seaside village and you should be able to disappear easily enough. How big is this package you'll be taking off?"

Michael held up his hands and boxed out a square about the size of a mid-size suitcase. " I've been told to expect that size. We will actually have it in a special suitcase, and I'm told it will weigh about 45 pounds, so we will move it just like luggage in a rolling suitcase."

"OK, that works for me. Glad you thought of it before we pull back through here. I have been stopped a number of times for inspections and luckily we had no contraband to get them too excited. I can only imagine what they would do if they found our little package on board."

They walked back onto the Bridge and the Captain took command of the ship. In two hours they would be in the Black Sea and charting a course to Odessa where they would pick up William Meredith and a few more passengers.

→ ←

Abbottabad, Pakistan

Ayman al Zawahiri quietly walked into the sitting room in the three-story house. There was fire burning in a fireplace with all the smoke venting up the flue as it should, rather than wafting to the ceiling like it would back in the caves. Osama bin Laden was diligently making notes in his personal diary seated in a gold fabric chair that supported his lengthy frame. He looked up as he saw his cohort approaching and removed his spectacles.

"Good evening, Ayman."

"Osama, I apologize for interrupting you, but I have some news that I think you would want to hear. My best asset in Egypt called our people in Damascus yesterday. While the message was coded as always, it had some interesting words that were spoken. It seems that we may have a seller who would like you to pay them big dollars, for something you have wanted for a long time."

Osama had listened only half-heartedly up until this point but then he had heard words that made him pay full attention.

"Again, Ayman, I am getting old and the hearing is going. I think you said someone wishes to sell me something? And it is something of great value? Did I hear that it is what we have been praying for, for many year's? Do you speak of my ultimate gift? Tell me again, the words I have long wished to hear."

"That is what I have been told, Leader. A European arms dealer has offered us a suitcase nuclear bomb, I believe. This proposal has come to us in such a way that it leads me to believe it is not some western trick."

"And how did this come to us, Ayman?"

"Osama, I have been told that one of our field agents was approached in France at the Jungle encampment where we send people to get into Britain, and on to the U.S. Our people did not know what they should do with the proposal. It was delivered on a computer, so they passed it up the line to our Paris contact. He went directly to my personal agent in Cairo. He in turn called our people in Damascus, and they sent coded messages to Islamabad and then Peshawar. From there our courier brought it to us. I will have the actual computer proposal in hand in two more days so we can see this proposal with our own eyes. I think we may be dealing with some Eastern European arms dealers."

"I am awed by this news,.... if it is real. As you know, we have wished for such a weapon, since we took down the buildings in New York. This could change everything if it is for real. We can take down the whole city, or we can take Washington and hurt them even more."

"I apologize, Osama. I have only heard of it yesterday. I think we must investigate further. I have sent a return message by courier to make further inquiries. In a few days we will know if this vision is real."

Camp Novorossiysk

The General finished the call with his superiors in Moscow. He was concerned that the THCT plan to get bin Laden might not actually see the light of day. Upon finding out from his Ordinance Officer they had another significant security breach and problem, he had called Moscow immediately to report the issue, as it was his responsibility to do so in such a serious situation.

In the Colonel's considerable efforts to make amends for all the Ordinance Bunker bungling that had taken place two weeks before, he had every weapon inspected in preparation for the eventual visit by the Americans on the disarmament efforts. In doing so, he had identified that there was one tactical weapon unaccounted for, a limited yield suitcase weapon.

As they went through the weapon stockpiles on all three levels, noting serial numbers, categories of ordinance, and verified supporting documentation, they had found a suitcase container that had no bomb in it at all, just a similar dead weight to the other suitcase weapons that were all accounted for. This was a grave situation, especially with the Americans coming for a visit soon.

The General had reacted as he should have and flew off the handle demanding a personal review of the situation. Again he thought about this

TOM RENK

poor Officer's career. In his personal review of the new crisis, he verified and agreed that a single weapon was indeed unaccounted for, and following protocol he would immediately have to notify his superiors with the news, as this would be a major problem for the military. Needless to say Moscow was very upset and were sending investigators down to Novorossiysk immediately. At this point it was only a military issue and they hoped that it remained that way. They were on their way and would be on base the following day.

The General went outside and signaled his Sergeant Major to join him on the sidewalk, away from the house and from the car.

"Tristan, we may have a problem with our little fishing package. Our zealous Colonel has inspected every weapon and he found the empty case. He immediately reported it to me, and I have just reported the issue to Moscow. They are furious and will be sending a special FSB team down here immediately. I would think they would be here as early as tomorrow."

The Sergeant looked concerned, but was also thinking about options. Before he could speak the General offered a temporary solution.

"Thus, I think we should move the boat out of this area. So that we may do some fishing on the Bay in the near future, I suggest that we take the boat down to the water and moor it at the pier in town. Then after the inspection team comes down, if we are still employed, we may want to do some salt-water fishing. I am tired of fresh water fish and I think it would be a good time to teach you how to fish."

The Sergeant liked the idea. Again simplicity was probably the best course. "Sir, the boat is ready to go and I will look forward to learning this new fishing experience. I will move it down there this afternoon. Perhaps you would like to come along to make sure we are given safe passage off the base?"

The General leaned in and in a quieter tone said. " That may bring suspicion to us. You take it down there and make sure the harbor Master knows it is my fishing vessel. He will keep an eye on it. Then after FSB's investigation we can start taking a couple of fishing trips out into the Bay so we can establish a new pattern. Then when our ship comes in, so to speak, we can get rid of the package while fishing one day."

"Perhaps we should wrap the package in an air-tight container and latch it onto a marker that they would sweep up as they are in the Bay."

"I like that. Let's see what we can do to seal this little monster up in an airtight package. Then we will have to teach you how to fish Tristan, you do like worms, don't you?"

246

"Not since survival camp Sir, but we don't have to eat them do we? I thought that is the fish's job. I'll have the boat hooked up in about 30 minutes. Once we have it off base we shouldn't have any problems."

→ ←

Teterboro Airport

The small THCT group started assembling at the airport. They'd been encouraged to arrive by mid-afternoon so they could have one more meeting concerning assignments and run through the plan again. As each person arrived at the hanger, they unloaded their gear and suitcases and then drove back to the extended stay parking lot at the charter service building. Meredith had suggested the cars could stay there for an extended period of time without raising any suspicions. Osama and Malik used one of the golf carts in the hanger to shuttle everyone back and forth.

In the upper level sitting area, Ralph was counting out various currencies for traveling money depending on where people were going, or where they would be joining the ship. He had Russian Rubles for Josef and William Meredith who would be flying to Odessa, Ukraine to join the ship that evening. He was also making up packets of Turkish Lira for Michael, Uri and Kevin who were already on the Majorca cruising through the Black Sea.

Kate Shanahan was there to make sure everyone's documents were in the right hands and that they were well briefed on the back stories relating to the bogus travel documents. In some cases multiple credentials were being distributed because the travelers would be in a number of different countries. She sat down with each person, grilling them on their identities and back-stories that went with the documents. She explained what every piece of paper was, down to receipts from local stores, ticket stubs from rail lines, family photos of girl friends and grandchildren. Each piece had a purpose even though they were dog eared and frayed as if they had been carried for months.

Everyone had been briefed on the need to have non-U.S. made clothing in their bags, preferably from the countries of their documents so as not to raise suspicions with the border crossing agents and the officials that would meet the ship as it entered various ports of call.

The excitement level was palpable and everyone seemed to be nervous enough that they were walking about, making believe they were interested in exploring the various aircraft that were in Meredith's hanger. Some of them were seeing a corporate jet for the first time and were interested in looking it over from top to bottom. Pilot Ryan Younger, now a full part of the THCT team, was accommodating and patient as he answered various questions and showed them around the aircraft.

The door inside the much larger hanger door opened and William Meredith walked in nodding to everyone and headed for the upper level. On the way he stopped at the map table and asked Ryan a number of questions about the flight.

"Ryan, are we good for the flight tonight? What's our weather going to be?"

"We have a perfect evening Sir, even the winds will be working in our favor." He pointed at the Bombardier sitting right in front of the hanger door. " She is already fueled and I have a flight plan filed for London's Gatwick Airport for a re-fueling stop."

"That's great, I see everyone is here so maybe we can even move up the ETD an hour or so."

"That would work for us. We will need a couple hours on the ground in London and from there we can fly straight into Odessa. If we get off the ground at 7:00 pm this evening we will be in London easily by dawn, and then I'll have you in Odessa by Noon or 1:00 pm, depending on European air traffic and how they vector us in."

"I have an important call and meeting to take upstairs, but let's plan on wheels up by about 18:00." He headed for the circular staircase and asked where Ralph Behar, Osama and Malik were. He was told Ralph was already on the upper level playing with his monopoly money and that O and Malik would be sent up. Meredith went upstairs for the next email interaction with the terrorists.

He found Ralph counting and stacking the various currencies and Osama was there as well, watching intently.

"Gentlemen, we got our bite on the bait."

"Mr. William, I do not understand this word bait? What does it mean?"

"O, my apologies, the bait is what you left in Calais on the computer program for the al Qaeda's contact people. The computer was the bait, and now we must reel it in, like fishing. Since that bait left your hands they have become very interested in what we have offered them."

"I see, you mean bait like a fish? I thought we were talking about a very large horse."

"We are my friend, we are. You will see. I need you here in case they ask a question I cannot answer."

Malik bounded up the stairs and joined the small group. "You asked for me Mr. William?"

"Have a seat Malik. We are about to receive an email message from the people you talked with in France."

Ralph looked pleased and asked, "So how will we know it is them and how will they know we are for real?"

"Good question. We will authenticate by using the code word and they may ask something that only Malik and Osama could answer. Thus, we wait to talk with them. My IT guy is bouncing our email back and forth to Europe and South America a couple times to throw the dogs off, but we are actually going to talk with these assholes. The email should be coming in around 4:00 pm our time although they will think we are in Russia."

"I knew those guys would bite. Do we know who we are talking to?"

"No, all I know is that we received a solid response to our PowerPoint offer. They came back by email as we directed. They said they would like to buy the entire shipment of archeological artifacts, and that they would be emailing instructions to confirm details. Hopefully we acknowledge and make arrangements for payment and delivery."

"Unbelievable, these guys mean business. Didn't they even ask if we were serious?"

"Believe it or not, no. I guess they have wanted this for so long they are willing to take some chances. Reminds me of Troy pulling the horse in. But I am guessing they will have all sorts of conditions. We will let them set their conditions and then we will tell them ours. Bottom line is that we want the suitcase to be presented to Osama bin Laden, if he is willing to pay the two million dollar price."

Ralph considered that and said. " I think we shouldn't play too much hard ball on the bin Laden thing, at least for now. It could scare them off. If we insist on these things too early, they will smell a trap. Maybe we should just say that we have the capability to deliver the weapon to Pakistan and we will bring it to them because we have already set the apparatus in the works."

Meredith gave that some thought and agreed. "Your right Ralph, if we look to eager they may back off. I think we will insist on payment of 25% now in an unmarked account I have in the Cayman Islands, and 25% in an account in the Maldives. That will show them we are thinking mostly about the money."

"Ralph nodded and said. "Those accounts are already set up? Are you sure they cannot be identified by anyone?"

"Over the years the one thing I learned how to do as an investor was squirrel away money where no one can find it if you don't want them to. Ask my former wife about that. Yes, the numbered accounts are all set up and as soon as such funds would be deposited, I have standing orders to disperse the funds again to other Swiss accounts that have the same security capabilities. They won't get to us that way."

"So let's take this slow so we don't spook them. We should let them nibble on the bait a bit. If they like what they taste, they may take a bigger bite and then we can set the hook and make some demands. I think it is a good idea that we say we will deliver it to Pakistan, that way they will know the apparatus is already heading their way."

"I agree, so let's sit tight and see what we have." He hit the send receive button and six emails downloaded from the central server. One of them was the one they were hoping for. "Here it is, *Subject: Persian Artifacts for sale.*" He clicked on the email and a short message appeared.

The email was short and to the point but said all that they wanted to hear.

"Subject: Persian Artifacts for sale.
Dear THCT,
We are most interested in the artifacts you have available. We have wanted these for many months. If authentic we will pay as asked. Interested in early deliver by Fed Expr. Will pick up at mutually convenient location. God speed.
The Relics Division
Persian Institute

Meredith stared at the computer screen and reread the short message. He looked at the others and smiled saying, "It can't be this easy can it?"

Ralph brought him back to reality by saying, "We haven't even got the damn weapon yet, so don't count your eggs too soon. But this is a really good step. So how do we answer?"

Meredith acknowledged the comment and fixated on the email message. He hit the reply key but did not start typing. "Well, they did use the code word we asked for by adding the pr to Fed Ex, so I think we should acknowledge and suggest down payment terms. What do you think?"

"That makes sense, but we should keep it short and neutral. You have to figure that big brother will see these emails."

Meredith nodded and said, "Yeah, that why I have the emails going out through a half dozen cutouts on different servers and email accounts. Hopefully it will be innocuous enough that the NSA and that computer in the sky will be bored by the transaction."

He continued and started slowly typing a response.

Subject: Persian Artifacts for Sale

We too are pleased. We are packaging the items now and they will be on their way soon. Terms are 50% down and the remainder on delivery after determination of aging and authenticity. Please send 25% to Account #1 and 25% to account #2 as stipulated in the Proposal. Once received and verified, additional information on a delivery schedule will be sent. Expect arrival of early shipment Fed Expr as soon as one month. 6-3-8 9-2-2

Regards,

THCT

Meredith read the return message to the group and asked if it was ok. He looked at everyone noting that Osama and Malik were trying to grasp what was being said.

"Sound good to me. Might I suggest that you ask them to verify immediately when the money transfer is handled, so we can check as well."

"In the PowerPoint, I gave them the account numbers leaving off the first, middle and last digits on both accounts. They will know that is what I have given them and they will get back to us quickly. I'm guessing the money is the least of their problems. I heard that bin Laden and Al Qaeda has millions of dollars socked away, so I'm sure they will get back to us soon if they are truly serious."

"Well then, I think its fine,…. send it, and lets see if the fish is really nibbling."

With that Meredith hit the send button and the message disappeared through a maze of blind email accounts in Europe and South America. His IT guy had told him it would bounce back and forth from a number of servers that had been set up for this eventuality.

Just then the computer announced another email had arrived. He opened the email document and it amounted to a couple of words. *Agreed - Money being transferred Fed Expr -thct*

Meredith and Ralph Behar looked at one another, smiled and stood up to shake hands. Malik and Osama did the same but weren't sure what had just taken place. But they too joined in the handshake recognizing that it was cementing their resolve to see this through no matter what the personal implications might be. They had all agreed that their objective was worth dying for.

They went downstairs to tell the others about the good news. Everyone took a moment to savor the thought of being closer to their objective and then went back to packing the plane with the materials that would be going to Odessa.

The plane left for Europe right on time with William Meredith, Josef Veronin, and Ralph Behar on board. The others would be coming on a later mission flight and would meet the ship on the far side of the Bosporus, and the Canakkale Straits in Truva, Turkey. Truva was the original site of Ancient Troy.

→ ←

Amman, Jordan

Mustaffa Haqqani sat staring at the computer before him. He was in a vacant office that temporarily had an Internet connection that had been hooked into the building grid by one of his people. The connection went out the window and into a rat's nest of electrical and Internet lines in the alley. The Internet connection would be removed as soon as he was finished.

He adjusted his necktie so that he could breathe. He hated playing the western business agent. He had already taken off his grey pin stripe business jacket in the heat. His eyes kept darting from the computer screen to the window hoping that a breeze would blow in to cut the heat and humidity within the room. He watched the dust and sand blowing across the rooftops of the city and then looked back to the screen. He kept thinking that it couldn't be this easy to gain access to a bomb. They had been trying for years, and now one was actually being offered to them.

While he was elated, he felt that this whole venture could still be something that was just too good to be true. He would have to go slow, but felt that he should take the next step. He would transfer the deposit money because it was only money, and the leader would want him to do so, no matter what the cost.

He sent back another email with the same salutation and authenticity code word and simply said. '*Agreed – Money being transferred Fed Exp r -thct.*' He hit the send button and closed down the computer, disconnected the connection from the wall in the unmarked office, and walked out of the building.

He turned left towards embassy row and went down the street four blocks walking through the local bazaar shops that had cropped up near the embassies. He turned into an import export building and walked to the third floor, entering an office that had no markings on the door. The male receptionist looked up and nodded at him as he walked by and down the hall to a private office.

Once there he used the same laptop to send a more detailed message to Peshawar, Pakistan advising that the purchase of new products was going well and he hoped to have good news of a confirmed sale in the next few days. He advised he was waiting for proof of product availability and had gone ahead with deposits to secure the product shipments. He sent the message and then shut down the laptop as quickly as he had fired it up. He disconnected the computer, tucked it under his arm and then went out the door again, past the receptionist without a glance, and left the building.

He headed for the bank where he could initiate a wire transfer as two deposits needed to be sent. The transfer path would be through a number of coded accounts, before arriving at the required depository. At the back of the bazaar he found a trash bin, opened the computer, broke its spine backwards and smashed the hard drive against a side of the metal bin. He tossed part of the drive in and walked on until he found another bin for other components. On his palm he had two sets of the three numbers written in ink. He had the other part of the account numbers written down in a briefcase. He walked into the Bank of Jordan and asked to see an International Banker.

→ ←

Lubyanka Square, Moscow, Russia

The FSB leadership had organized the meeting in their headquarters building, which was only five blocks from Red Square, the Kremlin and St. Basil's Cathedral. They sat in a fifth-floor conference room in the imposing yellow brick structure, built at the beginning of the 20th Century. The building had once housed KGB headquarters during the Cold War, and also housed the infamous Lubyanka prison. Many a Russian soul had disappeared from the face of the earth while a guest in this building. The building still instilled fear in the Russian citizens of Moscow.

The Ministry of Security leaders sat around the large table with their military counterparts and discussed what they would need to do now that the missing nuclear weapon had gone from possible loss, to identified loss, and possible theft. Their faces showed anger and frustration over the disappearance of a limited yield nuclear weapon, under their control. All of their departmental efforts to determine what had happened to it had turned up nothing.

The FSB, formerly the KGB and the NKVD, came into being in 1995 as the Federal Security Service in the Russian Federation. It handled domestic security much like the FBI did in the United States. The Foreign Intelligence Service, the SVR conducted intelligence activities outside of the Russian Federation just as the CIA did for America. In 1998 Boris Yeltsin appointed as its Director, Vladimir Putin, who was a KGB veteran. He later succeeded Yeltsin as the Federation President.

In 2003, President Putin expanded the authority of the FSB taking on all sorts of intelligence gathering responsibilities, both internal and external control of intelligence, and all counter-terrorism matters. A number of major appointments and reshuffles of key personnel occurred in recent years due to the increasing amounts of terrorism that were being experienced in Russia.

Thus, this group of FSB leaders and military liaisons were strategizing on what they needed to do. There was a bomb out there and no one knew where it was and who actually had possession of it. The presumption was that it was perhaps already in the hands of home grown Chechen terrorists or would be shortly. All of Russia's covert agencies had already been given limited information on the situation and they were trying to identify how such a weapon had been lost. Everyone was looking for any sign of the weapon before they found it beneath the rubble of an explosion.

The weapon's paperwork was available and showed that it had been one of the many suitcase weapons that had been deployed in the late 80's. This one had been in a hidden storage locker, in a locked closet in the basement of the Soviet Embassy in Cairo, Egypt. Many of these weapons had been placed around the world to give the Soviets a retaliation strike capability if it was ever needed. Only two people in the Embassy would have known that such a weapon even existed, the lead KBG Agent, and the Soviet Political Officer stationed at the Embassy. They would have taken direct orders only from the Kremlin, and that would have involved all sorts of safeguards.

Extensive review of the background of the KGB field agents responsible for the weapon in Egypt had determined that the two men had passed away a few years ago. They had led frugal lives in retirement after the fall of the Soviet empire, both returning to Egypt to live out their lives. Their financial records had been checked and they had not benefited from the sale of such a weapon.

When the Soviet Union came apart in the early 90's, these weapons were all pulled back to the homeland, where they were stockpiled. All of the known weapons were accounted for although it took some time to get them all safely back to Russia. The paperwork records were unclear whether they were each inspected upon their return to Russia. At the time, there were so many weapons deployed, that the physical assembly of such weapons may have just been counted on a numeric basis, and the suitcase code numbers verified against the manifests, and then stored away.

While these weapons were in the field they had been upgraded with computerized triggers, digital clocks and updated wiring. Only three agents had done the on-site work. These individuals had also been questioned carefully and had been eliminated as suspects.

The records noted these weapons had been brought back to a number of military gathering sites based upon the continents they had come from. Once all the weapons were accounted for inside Russia, they were aggregated in Novorossiysk, on the Black Sea, under lock and key, with a complicated system of overlapping security protocols.

"I think we are all coming to the same realization," the Director stated, "We do not know where this bomb is. But I think we must presume that it is out there and will be used by terrorists, if they have it. Since it is one of ours, we have a responsibility to find it and get it back, and I would suggest that we do it before the Americans come for our next set of disarmament talks. These suitcase weapons are scheduled to be part of that process, thus we will not be able to hide the information that one is missing for much longer."

"I agree General, but I think we have exhausted our internal search efforts…. But, I do have some good news from our search efforts. We have all sorts of people out there looking under every rock and in every back alley. We have picked up a number of terrorist suspects in our sweeps for information and leads."

"That is good, God knows we have too many terrorists in our own country now. I think we have created our own problems. We will be sorry for stirring the terrorist kettle all these years." General Mirov said disgustedly. "We must now fight the very terrorists we encouraged."

"Well, our sweeps have produced results. Two days ago we picked up Ali Taziyev from Ingushetia Province in the North Caucasus region. We have been looking for him since 2004 when he killed all those police officers in Nazran, and blew up that Interior Ministry Building that killed 92 civilians. We are hoping we have more such luck as we press the underworld and our terrorist contacts for information."

"That is good Sergei, but I am more interested in this bomb at the moment. This could do a hell of a lot more damage in Moscow's subways or in Red Square."

Another officer spoke up. "Director, I think we are at the point we should advise the Americans of this issue, and encourage them to get involved, with all their assets. That way we can at least show them we are concerned enough to bring them into our confidence. It may blunt some of the anger and finger pointing they will have if we wait to tell them when they are here."

"You're right, but that decision is above my pay grade. I am not terribly excited about taking this news over to the Kremlin. President Medeyev and Putin will have to make that call. But I agree, I think it would help to have the Americans snooping around as well. I'll make that recommendation."

Everyone was taking notes. The General continued. "In the meantime, let's send word down that General Gralashov, at Novorossiysk will be retiring from duty immediately. I want him out of there. He may have to be our scapegoat."

"General, I have reviewed his file and he is a real war hero that fought many years in Afghanistan, so I suggest we retire him, but with a good pension. We just need to get him out of town before the Americans arrive. Then we need someone to replace him and take command down there, someone who can tighten up the security issues. This new person will have to deal with the Americans and try to make a good situation out of a bad one. If this situation gets any worse and a terrorist group has a hold of the weapon we will have a whole new set of problems."

"Unfortunately, I agree. Let's make it happen."

→ ←

NSA - Ft. Meade, Maryland

The NSA Echelon computers worked day and night and didn't need to take any breaks. The massive data banks sorted through millions of bits of information that came in from all around the world, from phone calls, emails, text messages, and some said even thoughts that were in the mind.

The people that backed up these complex building sized systems were the ones that needed to take the breaks and occasionally sleep to recharge their batteries. Analyst Bill Dalde was just returning from a morning break when his computer signaled that another one of his flags had popped up in the prior night's chatter.

Bill sat down and placed his coffee cup on the warmer on his desk. He hit the flag button and watched as a series of downloads dumped on his computer. He saw that they were THCT references.

He took a sip of his Starbucks, grabbed a pad of paper and started reading the various references. None of them really made sense, but he expected flags to be confusing and out of the ordinary. That is what made them flags. As he scanned the information he noticed that the THCT circle was expanding again. He saw that additional hits were coming out of the Tri-State area of New York, but he also had hits coming out of Cairo, Egypt, Amman, Jordan, Islamabad, Pakistan and Moscow, Russia, with a couple of bounces even passing through South America. And he noted with interest, these were not phone conversations, they were emails.

He even noted that two of the emails had gone to a courier they have been monitoring for months. This particular courier was a known liaison with bin Laden. Osama bin Laden did not use electronic means to communicate but rather some trusted couriers who often had to cross mountains and move from country to country to convey command messages.

Bill thought, this added development ratcheted up the concern level even more. Perhaps this group was talking with bin Laden. So he started running various search engines and programs that would try to track origins and connection paths. He presumed whoever was sending these messages was routing them through various blind cutouts and dead end alleys, bouncing them around to hide the real senders. But that too was revealing in itself as it suggested the senders were up to no good and hiding something.

Laying out the message threads he noted the messages were referring to vague merchandise sales and artifact offers. He snickered to himself and wondered why the bad guys always referred to contraband as merchandise and presumed they were covering up their true intent. They obviously had little understanding of what the U.S. was capable of monitoring, but that was good because hopefully he could figure out who they were and what they had going on that involved all these volatile locations.

He tried to piece together a scenario but the information was too scattered. He decided that something bad was definitely happening, and that he would need more information and analysis if he were to make any sense of it. For the moment this monitoring would remain at his level until he could gain a more focused analysis. An hour later he gathered all his materials and stuffed them in a file. He noted that the file was getting thick and wondered if something might happen before he could put all the clues together.

Then he got a special top-secret flag notice advising that the Russians had just advised they have a nuke missing. Here we go, he thought.

→ ←

Black Sea, 50 kilometers from Odessa

The Majorca, being a shallow water Coaster, hugged the western coast of the Black Sea passing by Turkey, Bulgaria and Rumania without incident. The ship would make landfall in Odessa's harbor in the Ukraine before nightfall to pick up various shipments and passengers. The next day they would be taking on tons of wheat and barley that were destined for relief efforts in Karachi, Pakistan.

Lion's Clubs International had donated this huge shipment of basic foodstuffs for earthquake relief in the mountain regions of West Pakistan. The distribution area included the Federal Tribal Territories. William Meredith had seen this as an excellent opportunity to chart a course to Pakistan and then have an excuse to have a contingent of western people amongst the group of relief workers. It would allow them to transfer the package all the way to their ultimate target.

In addition to the tons of bagged barley and wheat stacked on pallets, they were also picking up a number of passengers including William Meredith, the owner of the shipping company. The Captain knew what this was all about and having had many conversations with his current three passengers, he was ready to do what he could to make the plan work. He actually was impressed with the level of planning that the group had undertaken and he thought they might have a chance at succeeding.

The Captain was watching his new radar screens, compliments of Mr. Meredith, tracking a number of ships that were entering and leaving Odessa's harbor. He walked out on the bridge deck and whistled down to Uri Navroz and Michael Pappas, waving them up.

The two men came up the stairs, Michael taking them two at a time, with Uri following at a more practiced gait. He was enjoying his return to the sea and was in his element. He had Meredith to thank for that and looked forward to seeing him the next day.

"Gentlemen, we are an hour out of Odessa, so I suggest that you make yourselves presentable. I would make sure you remember who you are and have your papers in order if we should get a visit from one of our friendly customs officers. They will want to see our Manifest, but they may also want to check out the crew."

"Aye, Aye Captain. We will probably make ourselves pretty scarce until the group arrives tomorrow." Michael said as he saluted.

"You better stop saluting me or you'll make me a target. We are a bit more casual aboard these small ships. Last thing I need is pomp and circumstance."

"I hear you Skipper. By the way if you do get a visit from the authorities, we have all the good stuff well hidden away and we even made those four pillboxes looked old and stressed just like the rest of the ship. I doubt anyone will even notice that changes have been made."

Uri spoke up saying, "Sir, speaking of changes, you've added some great improvements below deck. That engine is purring like a kitten, and will give us the speed we need should we have to really get moving. You also have the best electronics I have seen in years on an old ship."

"Again, thanks to my boss and your leader, Mr. Meredith. I'm looking forward to seeing him tomorrow to thank him myself. He bought this ship another ten years of sailing with the improvements we added in Marseilles and I want to thank him in person. We should be tying up at the pier in about an hour. You can see the city on the horizon now." He pointed north.

➔ ←

CIA Headquarters, Langley, Virginia

NSA Analyst Bill Dalde drove down the I-495 Beltway through Maryland on his way to Virginia. Once across the almost unseen state border he turned east onto the George Washington Memorial Highway paralleling the Potomac River. He was on his way to a meeting at CIA Headquarters, tucked into the woods above the Potomac River and just south of the GW Parkway. The large, two thousand acre complex was built on the former Claude Moore Colonial Farm, purchased by Thomas Lee, in 1719, fifty years before the Revolutionary War. He called the land Langley. Today it was one of the most secretive places in the world.

Turning off the Parkway at a rather nondescript sign, he drove towards the well-protected entrance to the George H.W. Bush Center for Central Intelligence. He followed the winding roadway and eventually stopped at the Guard shack set up to block all entry to the complex.

The CIA campus entrance had formidable gates and vehicle barricades to prevent entry of any unauthorized vehicle. This checkpoint building was fortified and had well-armed guards checking all who entered. He passed his credentials over to a uniformed guard while another did a visual walk-around the vehicle with a long handled mirror to see under the carriage of the vehicle.

His name was on the guest list for the day. His credentials were returned to him and he was given directions to the next checkpoint. He knew he was being watched every step of the way. He parked in a close-in visitors lot. The lot was still far enough away from the buildings to prevent a suicide bomber from doing any serious damage to the CIA complex that rose in the forest. As he drove to the parking lot he noticed that there was a large black aircraft parked over on the lawn west of the building. He thought that it looked like one of those very secretive spy planes that had been used 40 years ago. That made sense, as this was the CIA.

He parked his government issued car in a guest spot, grabbed his files, locked the doors, and walked towards the Visitors Entrance. He could see Bede Long, his CIA counterpart, waiting for him at the door.

"Glad you could make it William, from the far, far north woods to God's country here in the south." Bede Long stuck out his hand to greet his guest.

"Here we go again. I told you, I'm just 35 miles up the road from you. Next time you can visit me so you know I'm not within the Arctic Circle." Bill said showing his frustration.

Bede laughed and held the door open. He escorted his guest over to a Visitor's desk where his credentials were checked again. After a moment the necessary badge work was presented and he hung the name badge around his neck. He already knew that he would be escorted by CIA personnel every step of the way. It was the same at NSA in Ft. Meade. He was used to it.

"You've been here before, mate, haven't you?" Bede asked as he pointed the way through the main lobby. They skirted around the CIA crest that was imbedded in the floor of the massive hallway. The official Seal of the Central Intelligence Agency was sixteen feet in diameter and was made of granite. The crest was comprised of an eagle's head, symbolizing strength and alertness, and a large shield that stood for strong defense. On this shield was a sixteen point compass star that represented the gathering of intelligence data from points all over the world, all converging on this central gathering point within the CIA.

As the NSA Analyst looked at the large ornate Seal, he noted to himself that the NSA also had a big stake in that intelligence gathering and he took pride in knowing he was a part of the effort.

They crossed the hallway and walked past the Memorial Wall that stood as a stark reminder that they were involved in serious business. The wall had no names, just simple stars carved into a white marble. There were ninety stars on the wall, each signifying a CIA Officer who had died on the job, and an inscription,

" In honor of those members of the CIA who gave their lives in the service of their country."

Beneath this passage was a Book of Honor listing the names of fifty-five of the ninety CIA Officers. The other 35 names remain secret after their death because of the sensitive intelligence work that they had done.

In recent years, each star was hand engraved by a single artist Tim Johnston of the Carving and Restoration Team, out of Manassas, VA. He had taken over this solemn job for the past few years from the original carver, Harold Vogel, after his death. Each star precisely measured 2 ¼ inches by 2 ¼ inches by ½ inch deep. The carved out star was then painted black and as it slowly aged and weathered on the wall, the star slowly took on a grey sheen. Some of the stars dated back to the 1950's.

Bede Long did not interrupt his guest's thoughts. He knew the impact these memorials had on visitors coming to the CIA. Further on they past a large statue of Major General William J. Donovan. He was known as the 'Father of Modern American Intelligence Gathering'. General Donovan had been the head of the OSS during and after World War II, and from that beginning became the founder of the modern CIA. Bill also saw the CIA Motto engraved on the wall and recognized the passage from the Bible, John 8:32,

"And Ye Shall Know the Truth and the Truth Shall Make You Free."

Suitably impressed with his surroundings, he followed Bede into an elevator where he pushed the button for the top floor for a private meeting between their clandestine agencies. They entered a medium-sized interior walled conference room without windows. There was a slightly discernable white noise humming in the background and he presumed they were in a soundproofed room. That was actually good because the information he needed to discuss was getting rather interesting and ominous. It was time to get the CIA involved.

Once they settled in, the Assistant Director of Field Operations, Karen Lee, joined them. She had spent much of her career as a field agent, working primarily in Eastern Europe and had distinguished herself as a top-notch spy helping to end the Cold War. After many years in the field chasing down leads, handling spies, and turning agents, she had come out of the cold and returned to headquarters to oversee covert operations for the Agency. Bede Long introduced the Assistant Director to Bill Dalde and she offered a strong handshake and some pleasantries. Then she got right to the point.

"So Mr. Dalde, you believe we have a new terrorist cell that is up to no good?"

"Yes Ma'am, and it's Bill, I do think we may have a new potential terrorist group operating in the New York Tri-State area."

"Ok, Bill, it works both ways, I'm Karen. What makes you so sure these guys are for real?"

"Well, at first I thought it was just another home-grown bunch of dissidents. You know, just blowing off steam. The intercepts that I have been monitoring were typically disjointed, innocent type messages that rarely had any real context. Up at NSA, that's a red flag in and of itself. Once we noted some repetition and identified some key words we flagged them, and all of a sudden Echelon started spitting out all sorts of related references. Then we started getting picks from various points in Europe, the Middle East and even Russia that may all relate to this THCT group."

"So you think we have a live one?"

"Yes, Ma'am, I do think this could be serious. I'm concerned that they may have interacted with our on-going courier investigation. If so, we will definitely have something to talk about."

"Yes, that is of concern. The bin Laden couriers are the best leads we've had in years. If your group is meeting with them, it will be game on!"

"Yes Ma'am."

"You say Ma'am one more time and I'll shoot you." And she smiled.

"Yes Ma...., Karen, the interesting part is such contact will take this to a whole new level. That's why I'm here sharing what we know."

" So what does THCT stand for?"

"I'm not sure what it stands for. It's nothing we have on record. While their chatter is cryptic and innocent enough, there are veiled references to sales efforts, large packages, and much desired antiquities. And these calls are coming from one-time use phones that are never used again. The email messages are coming from places that drew my attention. And, I presume you got that flag notice about the Russians losing a nuke?"

"We got it and are already working on it. I can readily see why you are concerned. Let's see what you have?"

Bill Dalde pulled out his files and started spreading the data out on the table in front of Karen. He slid a second set of documents over to Bede.

"I've arranged the phone conversations and messages by date from last October through this week. As you look at them, they all seem innocent enough, but when you look at the whole enchilada, you begin to see something."

The Director crossed her legs and leaned back, slowly reading through the seventy-three notations, noting the dates, location, and destinations of the conversations and emails. Just as Bill had said, the trail started innocently enough in New York, but then had blossomed out to places like Cairo, Amman, Jordan, Paris and Calais France, and from a number of cities in Russia on the Black Sea and in Pakistan in Peshawar and even in the Federally Administered Tribal Areas where Osama bin Laden was supposed to be hiding out. Since they had a repeated thread about selling antiquities and packages, and involved both Pakistan and Russia, this NSA inquiry was indeed warranted.

After a second careful review of the NSA data, she looked up, removed her glasses and said. "I think your right, Bill. This is certainly something worth looking into. I assume your people have started working the New York angle?"

"My Director has already put an FBI field team together and they are trying to get a handle on the New York side of this equation. We were hoping you could ask your people to take a look overseas in a number of places and make some inquiries?"

"We can and will do that. As you said, it's the package references and the Russian nuke that has me concerned. I always hate it when we hear these kinds of words whispered by unsavory types. It's never good news when they're whispering."

"That's why it was time that we developed a joint approach to this one," Bill said, feeling more confident that he had come down and asked for the assistance.

"I would like you to keep Bede in the loop and he can keep me appraised. If we can pick up anything overseas, we will feed it back to NSA through you. Let's hope it's nothing, but I always get a bad feeling when we get this kind of chatter going."

She stood up, shook Bill's hand with a firm grip, picked up her files, nodded to Bede, and walked out the door. The analyst stood there a moment watching her exit the room and then said. "That was fast. You guys don't fool around. My coffee's hasn't even cooled down yet."

"She doesn't waste time. But she's the kind of partner you want on this side. If there is something out there, she is the one to put the wheels in motion to figure it out. Our people will get cracking right away and ferret out anything we can on our new friends." Bede said, as he too gathered his materials in a top-secret file folder.

Bill Dalde decided he'd get another cup of coffee out on the Beltway and joined Bede in moving to the door.

➔ ←

Odessa Harbor, Ukraine

The Majorca eased up to the dock under it's own power, gently handled by the harbor pilot without incident. The lines were thrown to the pier, the cables were pulled through the chocks and secured to the dock bollards, and the on-board crane was already being fired up to take on the many tons of wheat destined for Pakistan.

When the gangplank was put in position amidships, Captain Brinkmann met the Customs Officer as he came on board. The Officer readily conveyed that he had a job to do, and he seemed to have an edge on his inquiry. Normally these officers would be bored and passive in greeting a small ship entering the country. This official was different; he was very interested in scrutinizing the ship's manifest and wanted a complete rundown of all the cargo going on and off. He even showed interest in where they had been and where they would be going.

After a careful scan of the documents he announced everything seemed to be in order as far as he was concerned. A couple pieces of official documents were stamped, signed and exchanged, he said good day and he turned around and walked back down the gangplank loosening his tie as he went.

The Captain smiled to himself about his luck, since he did in fact have some cargo and special passengers that would have been of particular interest to this Officer. But the travelers had stayed out of sight as they entered the harbor and when they tied up, no one even thought to ask to see the crew manifest and passenger lists. We will have to use this approach at all the future ports of call, he thought.

He looked down the pier and could see a van parked on the side of a warehouse building two hundred yards away. He presumed that it was Meredith and whomever he was bringing aboard. He had been smart enough to hang back while the Customs Officer did his business.

He waved his arm from the bridge walkout and a moment later he could see the van's engine came to life and it drove slowly down the pier. It stopped at the gangplank and a number of men got out of the vehicle. He recognized William Meredith and again waved him aboard.

As Meredith and some other passengers arrived on deck, Captain Brinkmann shook his boss's hand and then ushered him and the group following him through a hatch into the interior of the ship. While it was a bit cramped with his new guests holding their bags and duffels, he wanted to minimize the number of people standing out on the deck.

He again threw out his hand and shook Meredith's hand saying, "Welcome aboard, Sir. I have been looking forward to seeing you since I got my orders in Sicily. It's good to finally meet you, Sir."

"Enough of the Sirs, Captain, I'm Bill from now on, and I am glad to meet you as well, I've watched you from afar for a long time. You've been an asset to this shipping company. I have been looking forward to this meeting. Now that I've dragged you into this little escapade, I'd like to introduce you to the rest of my team here."

In the tight quarters of the gangway, Meredith introduced Ralph Behar, and Josef Veronin. They all shook hands and the Captain offered to take them to their cabins so they could get settled. He announced they would remain in Odessa for the evening, that they should be loaded by noon the next day and on their way shortly thereafter. He showed them the way to the cabin deck.

"Sir, I was hoping that you and I could have a private conversation in the near future?"

"Captain, I presumed that you might want to do that, so would I. You suggest the time and place where we can speak in private and I'll be there. I'm sure you have questions about this entire operation."

"I do, Sir, I do, ah, Bill. How about we meet on deck aft in an hour. There will be all sorts of crane noise out there and our conversation will not be heard by anyone, probably not even by us. I'll bring a bottle of scotch and some cigars. Your other friends already on board mentioned you liked a good Cuban every now and then."

"That I do, Captain, that I do."

Just then, Michael Pappas, Uri Navroz and Kevin Geary came up the stairs from the lower deck. In the tight hallway it was like old home week with everyone shaking hands and slapping backs. The Captain noted they were all obviously committed to this plan.

→ ←

FBI Field Office, New York City

Two young FBI agents, Brian Jones and Steven Olson had been assigned the boring duty of watching tapes collected from the Best Buy stores spread out all over the suburbs north of Manhattan. They were to try and identify any persons seen purchasing limited-minute or pay-as-you-go cell phones in the last six months. As new agents assigned to their first field office, they drew the assignment because the SAC, the Special Agent in Charge, had assigned everyone to this new THCT Task Force that had just come in from Homeland Security.

They had been staring at tapes for two days with hardly a thing to report. Except on a tape over five months old, they had seen two young women buy at least six phones. This was at different times, but at the same store, and on the same day. They thought that was an odd coincidence, but the women didn't look like terrorists. Still, they were trying to track back to see if the women could be identified. They re-recorded the sequences on a control tape noting day and date, and went back to watching the overhead camera recordings that were meant to catch shoplifters.

Late in the afternoon, they were looking at the five-month-old grainy tapes from a Best Buy store on Long Island, when they saw two Middle Eastern men step up to the Phone counter and ask to see some limited minute phones. They seemed nervous and one of them kept looking around as the other asked questions of the store clerk. The one scanning the store eventually noticed the sky camera bubble in the ceiling above them and looked directly at it for a second, before realizing that the camera light was on. With that realization, he pulled his partner aside, and whispered something in his ear. The two men quickly thanked the clerk for his time and turned and walked out without buying anything.

Both agents looked at one another, realizing this was what they were looking for. They re-spooled the tape and ran it again, recording it with the time stamps on their control tape.

Steven Olson rummaged through the many boxes of tapes on the floor and looked to see if they had parking lot tapes for that store on the same day. "Maybe we can spot them in the parking lot and get a license plate."

"I'm on it, Steve… here, I think this is the same store and day." Brian pulled a tape out of a box and loaded it into the machine, fast-forwarding to thirty minutes before the time stamp on the first tape. They settled in and started watching as cars came and went from the massive parking lot for about fifteen minutes. They were getting bored again when Brian pointed and said, " There, roll the tape back a minute."

Steven hit the reverse button, rewound the tape. And then hit the play button.

"There, see way back in the parking lot?" Brian yelled in the small office attracting attention from agents on the other side of the glass wall. See, the two guys that got out of that yellow car, now they are walking towards the store entrance."

As they got closer to the store entrance camera, Steven said. "That's them alright, that's the guy at the counter. We got them! We got them!"

Brian picked up the clicker and slowly advanced the tape to see if they could see them leaving the store as well. About fifteen minutes into the same tape they saw the two men walking out of the store, and moving quickly. Their backs were to the camera but the tape showed them going to the far side of the lot.

"They're actually pulling out of the lot coming right towards us." Steven said as he inched closer to the monitor. "It's a taxi, that's why it's so yellow. Maybe we can get the license number?" As they continued to watch the tape, the taxi pulled to the front of the parking lane almost directly in front of the store entrance. A mother pushing her child in a stroller cut in front of them and they had to stop for a second, then they made a quick turn and drove out of the lot.

"Brian, I think we got us a smoking gun. Let me have that tape. I wonder if the lab downstairs can lift the license of the cab medallion off the hood of that car. If we can get that number, we can track down the taxi's owner. Hey, maybe we can get out of this crappy duty and get some real street time."

"Let's go." Brian pulled the tape from the machine and they gave each other a high five, and headed for the door, and the FBI lab two levels down.

→ ←

On the Black Sea

The Majorca pulled away from the dock at 1:15 pm and was out of Odessa's harbor by 2:15pm. The Captain had had his meeting with William Meredith and was confident that he could accomplish what the boss was asking of him. After a couple of drinks and cigars, he was more confident that this motley group of people could perhaps pull off the impossible.

As they headed east, they saw on the radar a number of ships ahead of them tracking across their bow. The Captain explained those were probably Russian warships going in and out of Sevastopol, which had been the Soviet Union's primary warm weather naval base. Since Sevastopol was now part of the independent country of the Ukraine, the Russian Fleet was being moved as they had lost their lease on the port city. The Russians were now moving their Baltic Fleet operations to Novorossiysk and had to do so by 2013. And they were not happy about it.

Meredith and the Captain were standing out on the Bridge wing looking east. The Captain pointed and said,

"We will be seeing quite a few Russian ships out there for the next couple days, mostly destroyers and frigates, maybe even a submarine or two. The subs run on the surface more now after all their accidents. I guess they aren't built as well as they used to be. The ships move back and forth between Sevastopol and Novorossiysk getting ready for the big transfer of the naval base. That may actually work in our favor because who would be dumb enough to carry a nuclear bomb in the midst of all this military hardware."

"I had not thought of that but you may be right." Meredith said in response to the Captain. "Let's hope that they don't pay any attention to us at all."

The Captain nodded and said, "Once I knew what you were up to, I was pleased that you scheduled a number of different shipments here in the Black Sea. That way at least we have an excuse for being here if we are stopped."

"I thought that might make sense, so I had the shipping office look for a number of shipments which would give us some extended work time in this body of water," Meredith said.

"Well if we are looked at we can show a healthy number of manifests and consignments that will warrant our presence," nodded the Captain.

Directly east off the bow they observed a Russian naval vessel of about 250 feet in length, stem to stern, crossing their path about a mile out. It had a sleek, low superstructure, suggesting some sort of corvette or destroyer. The Captain went into the wheelhouse and checked his green radar screen, and saw an identification listing it as the Admiral Chabanenko. The Captain went to his map table and pulled out an issue of Jane's Naval Directory and looked up the ship by name. Jane identified the ship as an Udaloy II Class Destroyer, christened in 1995. It was part of the Black Sea Fleet stationed out of Sevastopol and obviously heading into port.

An hour later they saw another large Russian salvage vessel off starboard about a mile out. Again radar identified it as the VMF Kommuna. The Captain said that it was an old ship, perhaps as far back as World War II, or earlier. He again reached for his Jane's Directory and began looking for the name.

"Wow, it is an old ship, first christened in 1915 during World War I. The summary here says the ship is the oldest naval vessel still in service in the Russian Navy. You're seeing a bit of history. That ship is almost 100 years old."

"As long as they stay at a distance, I'm fine with that, Captain." Meredith said. "After we stop in Gelendzhik and pick up our little package, I'd like to give wide berth to all their ships if we can. The last thing we need is for one of their coastal boats to want to board us."

"Agreed. We will make every effort to be good international citizens and mind all the rules of the road, or the sea, as the case may be. But that also means you and your fellow passengers should probably minimize any deck time whenever any ship is within a couple of miles. They always have lookouts posted. No sense giving them a reason to want to come over and say hi!"

"Definitely, I'll remind my guys to keep that in mind. I presume that target practice would not be prudent in this bathtub either?"

"Michael and Kevin did some shooting off the stern in the Aegean before we got to Turkey, and they also brought out the weaponry in the southern part of this bathtub, as you call it, but that was before we got anywhere close to Odessa. I asked them to store their guns while we were up here. Once we get the package and go further south out in the Med, we will be able to pull out the weaponry."

"I'll remind them again. Last thing we need is for anyone to come snooping."

→ ←

New York City FBI Field Office

The two first year FBI agents had come up with a good lead on the pre-paid phone angle, and after running it past their supervisor, they were allowed outside to run it down. The taxi medallion had indeed been visible when the print was blown up on the videotape. They had a medallion number, #1949.

Making initial inquiries and checking the city cab records, they found that the vehicle was registered to a Mohammed Bathur, a New Yorker originally from Syria. He had purchased the medallion over ten years ago from a New York driver who retired. He actually had two cabs in service in the city.

Agent Steve Olson and Brian Jones ran the cab owner's name through the databases and found that he had no criminal record in the city or the State and had actually earned citizenship just two years ago. They decided to visit Mr. Bathur's house in Brooklyn and see if they could get a rise out of him.

The house was on a nicely kept side street in the middle of the block. It had a small well-manicured yard, some bright flowers in a window box and a welcome sign on the doorstep. The two agents approached the door, not really knowing what to expect, as this would be their first field interview. A young woman answered the door and after seeing their badges, looked troubled, but invited them into the small foyer, calling for her father.

Mohammed Bathur came around the corner in a wheelchair. He was a big man overflowing the chair, with a pleasant smile. He said hello to the agents, and they to him. He could see that they were surprised he was in a chair, so he explained.

"I was in an car accident six years ago in Little Italy. A truck making deliveries barreled into me, as I was about to pick up a fare on Mulberry St. The truck hit me broadside and almost rolled completely over the cab crushing the roof in on me. They had to cut me out of there, and here I am, stuck in a wheelchair ever since."

"I'm sorry to hear that sir. So you're not driving a taxi anymore, I presume?" Steven said as he pulled out a notebook.

"Hell, I can hardly get out of this chair to go the bathroom, no, I' haven't driven since the accident. I got a fair settlement from the delivery company, and a new cab out of the deal, but I'm not driving anymore. Now, I'm an absentee cab owner, not a driver."

"I see. The city records say you are still the registered owner and you actually have two cabs. Do you have regular drivers that work for you?" Brian said.

"Well, yes, I normally do. Since the accident I've kept the cabs rolling on the street to maintain the medallion, so I hired a couple of brothers who have done a good job for me for a number of years. They had been with a different company, but had a rough time after 9-11 and needed jobs, so I hired them."

"And they would be whom?" Brian poised his pen to write down the names.

They are two Pakistani brothers, Osama and Malik Tarkan, good men that work hard. They both live in a small apartment on the lower Westside near the Javits Center."

"Where might we find them, Mr. Bathur, we have some questions for them?" Steven said.

"What's this all about? Did they do something? Did they wreck one of the cabs?"

The man in the wheelchair was clearly concerned.

"No Sir, they didn't do anything like that. We would like to talk with them...... about an investigation we are doing. They may have seen something that would be helpful to our case." Brian said, congratulating himself that he had thought up the non-answer so quickly.

"Well, it's interesting that you ask about the brothers, because I don't think they are here at the moment. This is the second time that they have taken off for an extended period of time."

"Could you explain that, Sir. We would really like to talk with them." Brian said anxiously.

"It was about four months ago, I think. One day they came in and just said they needed to take a couple weeks off. Later on, I heard they had been in France. Then, about three weeks ago they told me they had to take a month or so off, because they were going home to Pakistan."

"To Pakistan? Did they say what they were doing on either trip?" Steven said, getting more excited because they obviously had something here.

"On that France trip, they mentioned they had flown for the first time on a private jet to do some work in Paris and in Calais, I think they said. I've never been to either of them places."

"So what would they have been doing in France if they are New York cab drivers?" Steven said, to draw out any additional information.

"Oh, they were electronic retail store owners when they were back in Pakistan. In Peshawar, I think. They were driving cab here because they couldn't get any other jobs. So maybe they were trying to get back into electronics. I don't know." Mohammed said rolling his chair back and forth. He was confused about what this was all about.

"So can you tell us anything else about these two drivers?" Brian said, hoping to elicit any other information.

"Yeah, they had a real tragedy come out of 9-11. It took a long time to hear this but they both had wives and children that were killed when the buildings came down that awful day. I guess their wives worked at a day care center in the Towers and the children were with their mothers. Everyone was lost in the collapse of the buildings. As you can imagine, they took it real hard. I can't imagine what I would have been like losing my family."

Both Brian and Steven looked at one another trying to understand what they were hearing. The information wasn't what they had expected. The comments did not make sense if these two brothers were terrorists. This sounded more like they were victims. They both took all sorts of notes so they could try to explain to their supervisor what they had found.

"So you don't think they are around here now? Do you know when they might be back?" Brian asked.

"No Sir, I don't. I wish I did because they were good boys and did their jobs. I've had a hell of a time keeping the cabs on the streets since they left. I hope they'll be back soon enough."

"Thank you, Sir, we appreciate your time and the information you've given us. If they should call you, would you let us know? Here's our contact information. Have a great day. Thanks for your time."

With that the two agents left the house. When they got in their car, they sat there trying to figure out what they'd heard. They figured they should have some answers in mind before they went back to their supervisor.

They decided they would track down the two Pakistani brothers first, so they drove to the office and started a new thread of investigation.

Gelendzhik Bay, Russia

The General and his Sergeant were rolling in the gentle swells about three hundred yards off shore, enjoying an afternoon of fishing. It was a warm day with a bright sunshine beating down. The heat was offset by some gentle breezes blowing in from the Sea. There was one small ship tied up at the commercial dock just east of their position. The two fishermen were marking time as they had received a coded message stating the ship would be arriving this afternoon.

As they rolled in the gentle chop, the Sergeant Major was smiling and enjoying his fishing lessons, even though he was sitting on top of a small nuclear bomb tucked under his bench seat. On the horizon, they noticed a small ship approaching the harbor and wondered if it was the Majorca. Both of them wanted to get rid of the hidden package because the heat was on at the base. A number of Russian FSB Security officers had already arrived and another group was arriving the next day. It was not the place to be.

The officer in charge of the investigation had taken command of the entire military base and had in effect told General Gralashov his services were not required at the moment. The General had known this would happen once Moscow found out about the missing bomb. Thus, he presumed his time as a Commanding General would soon be over.

He advised the lead investigating officer he would stay out of the way and would be fishing on the Bay. The FSB security agent said that was fine as long as he was within contact should something come up. At this point, they were not thinking of him as a suspect. He presumed they would instead make him the scapegoat.

As the small ship came into the Bay, it headed straight for the commercial dock and in the process passed the two men sitting in the small fishing boat. The Captain was at the helm as no harbor pilot was required in this small port. The General recognized the man standing outside the bridge housing as William Meredith. He nodded acknowledgement but did not wave or even give much of a glance at the passing ship. He knew this was the Majorca before the stern name came into view.

The small boat drifted in the water just a couple hundred feet off the starboard bow as the ships engines reversed and the Majorca slowly eased itself against the dock. Once the lines were thrown and tied down on the pier, the ship's cranes came to life to unload the cargo, mostly oil rigging equipment destined for points east.

From their vantage point, the two Russians could see the gangplank was put in place, and a Custom's Officer boarded and approached the Captain. While the Officer was standing there inspecting the shipping manifest, the Captain ordered a small boat over the side to make some repairs as the ship had been taking on water.

Shortly thereafter, a small workboat was lowered over the side of the ship. Two men descended to the craft and started inspecting the ship's water line and hull. A matter of three hundred feet separated the two small boats.

In the fishing boat, the General continued his fishing, casting away from the ship, while the Sergeant Major casually opened up the sealed compartment below his seat and dragged out a package. It looked to be the size of a medium suitcase and was wrapped in plastic and sealed almost completely with industrial tape. With some of the tape wrapped around the package he had fashioned a large strong loop that could accommodate a rope. He attached a long line and then picked up his fishing rod and went back to casting. He already knew that the water's depth at this point was 25 feet.

In the workboat, Michael Pappas and Kevin Geary were working their way along the water line inspecting the metal plates and the rivets holding them together. Working with black pitch they were painting small areas where they noted cracks in the plates.

With less than a couple hundred feet separating the two boats, Michael looked over to the other boat and casually asked. "Ahoy there, how are the fish biting? Maybe I should get my gear out so we can have a good fish dinner tonight."

The General looked up and acknowledged the question, noting the voice was that of an American. He also glanced up to the bridge and saw that Meredith was watching and nodded his head as a signal.

"It is a good day for fishing, Majorca." He made a show of holding up a line that had four large fish on it and smiled. If anyone were watching him this would be an innocent conversation. "I think the Bay would be good to you as well, and I can't take them all home. Join us when you have finished working."

"I think we will." They waved and went back to their respective fishing and work efforts. With neither party quite sure how they would accomplish a covert transfer without drawing any undue attention from anyone watching on shore, they bided their time looking for an opportunity.

The General asked his Sergeant. "So what do you think we should do. I don't want to go over there. We may be watched as we are speaking." He cast again and slowly reeled in his line. They both thought about this for a few minutes. The General looked up at the ship's Bridge and held up a hand to block out the sun in his eyes and could see that Meredith was casually leaning on the railing, without a care in the world.

"I think I have an idea." The Sergeant said with a grin on his face. "How about I stand up to try and land a big fish, a really big fish, and I lose my balance. I could fall over board and swim with the fishes. Then you can try and drag me out of the water. You're an old man and would obviously have difficulty dragging me back in the boat. We could make a commotion. Because I'm not the lightest guy in the world, maybe we could ask them for assistance to help you get me in the boat. Then we just pass them this line and once they go back, they can drag the package back to the ship still under water. They can pull it up this evening in the dark."

"Not bad!" The General thought for a moment. "That could actually work, but are you sure you want a bath? This water is not as warm as you might think yet."

"No problem, it will give me a reason to make a lot of noise as I thrash about."

"That would certainly make anyone watching think it was a simple emergency. I think it could work." The General slowly turned in his seat and quietly called over to the other boat while he cast his bait again. "Gentlemen, don't look up, but in a moment we're going to have a bit of an emergency over here, and we would appreciate your assistance...... Ok?"

"Sounds like a plan. We'll be there. Give us a holler when you're ready. We'll just keep fixing this blessed boat, I mean ship, until then. This pitch stinks."

The Sergeant took the 40-foot rope he had coiled at his feet and tied it to the package loop that he had crafted from the wrapped watertight package. He then eased the package into the water on the far side of the fishing boat away from the shore and any prying eyes. The weight of the suitcase took it straight down into the dark blue water without any difficulty. The line played out over the gunwale and when it touched the sandy bottom of the Bay, there was still about 10 feet of line in the boat. He tied it off to a boat strut with a simple slipknot.

"Ok, here we go," he whispered. He stood up with his fishing rod pointing towards the water as if he had a big fish on the line. He made big deal of trying to set the hook on his fish. He jerked the rod up and in doing so he lost his balance and crashed back against the side of the boat.

He tried to recover but his weight carried him over the side and into the cold blue water of the Bay.

He hit the water with a big splash. He went completely under for a moment and then came thrashing to the surface, clawing for the side of the boat. He was quite the actor. "Damn that's cold!" he said in Russian.

The General jumped up throwing his fishing rod into the well of the boat. He stepped across the middle seat and worked his way over to the man in the water. Leaning over the side of the boat he threw out a hand to help him grab onto the gunwale. The two of them struggled to get the Sergeant Major even half way out of the water, almost causing the boat to tip. Tristan slipped back into the cold water. He again put on quite a show splashing about and making a commotion as he went under a second time.

In the workboat, Michael and Kevin looked up as they heard the splash. They looked at one another in a way that acknowledged they too were actors in this farce. Then they looked at the man in the water about 35 yards away from the ship. Kevin turned to the stern and started the old 10 horsepower motor with a single pull of the ripcord. Michael yanked in the oars they had been using to move along side the Majorca. They quickly motored away from the ship and headed straight for the fishing boat.

Kevin cut the outboard engine as they came closer to the fishing boat and expertly eased next to it with the man in the water between them. He immediately grabbed the sides of each boat and steadied himself and the two boats.

"Good afternoon, General. Mr. Meredith sends his best wishes." Michael said this looking from one to the other unsure which was actually the General, the man in the boat, or the man getting a very cold bath. He figured it was the older man in the boat.

"Gentlemen, any port in a storm, I think you say. Let's get my Sergeant Major out of the water shall we?"

"Ok, big fella, give me one of those massive paws."

With that the three men all made a showy effort of pulling the Sergeant out of the water, heaving him up, and into the fishing boat. As they did so, the General very casually handed the rope to Kevin who immediately tied it off on one of the seat struts in the workboat.

With the Sergeant Major making a show of hopping around and stripping off his fishing gear, boots and shirt, Kevin picked up a sealed envelope that had been sitting on his bench seat and casually threw it into the well of the fishing boat.

"General, Mr. Meredith wanted you to have that package, Sir. I suggest you bury it in your tackle box for now."

William Meredith and Captain Brinkmann had been drawn to the bridge railing when they heard the splash, and commotion. They casually watched as the two Majorca sailors lent a hand to pull a man in distress from the sea. They also noticed the covert passing of the rope and the envelope. From their high vantage point on the Bridge they scanned the surrounding area and up and down the nearby pier to see if anyone else had noticed the commotion. They couldn't see anyone. Meredith wondered if they could really make the transfer this easily, and quickly went on to consider whether they could also get out of port without anyone being the wiser.

As the two small boats bobbed in the dark water, the General offered his hand to say thanks for the help and said, "Thank you gentlemen, please give my regards to Mr. Meredith. Tell him I am already persona non-grata here and will shortly be out of a job. If they don't throw me in prison, I will be doing more fishing than even I want to. I may need his help later on."

"We can appreciate that, Sir." Michael said. "In that envelope there, you will find some new identities for both of you. Moldovan, I think. Mr. Meredith said he'd personally come and get you with his plane once this is over, wherever you are. I guess he promised you even better fishing back in Wisconsin. And he said he wants some more fishing lessons. But right now we better push off before someone notices this international terrorist act."

"Thank you, young man. Haul up that line later tonight and you will have the package that Mr. Meredith so dearly wanted. It will be fine down there for a few hours. All the instructions and discs are inside as he requested."

Tristan reached over and also shook their hands. He said simply. "Get the son-of-a-bitch for me, will you? He killed a whole bunch of my soldiers too! I wish I could be with you."

"We will try, Sir. Take care and get some clothes on before you turn blue."

With that the two boats separated. Kevin started up his motor and slowly turned back to the ship. They traversed the 200 feet rather slowly because they were now trying to gently drag a nuclear bomb behind them, 25 feet underwater. Once they arrived back at the ship's side, they casually went back to work on the waterline pitch painting, in case anyone was watching.

The two fishermen quickly hauled in their fishing lines and stowed their gear planning to call it a day. The Sergeant was soaking wet and the ocean breeze would bring his body temperature down unless he got into dry clothes rather quickly. They started their engine and made for shore.

"Tristan, you are one crazy Bolshevik. If anyone was watching that escapade, I think we will be honest and tell them you are one lousy fisherman. But a very resourceful one. Thank God we are done with that thing. Now, let's hope they get away with this and complete their mission. Then our efforts will not be for naught."

The General started his motor and steered towards the shore and docks off in the distance. He never looked at the ship beside him.

→ ←

CIA Headquarters, Langley

Assistant Director Karen Lee stared at the new reports that had been sent over from NSA. She had received a number of updates since her last meeting. The THCT call letters had not stopped, rather they were popping up again and again, in all sorts of problematic places. Places like Russia, Egypt, Lebanon, and now in Pakistan, and with one of the couriers bin Laden used. That was not a good sign and she now had field teams in all those places snooping about and making inquiries to see if she could put some names and faces to this threat.

Everyone agreed that these THCT people were a real threat now, especially with the unofficial news about the missing Russian nuke. While this THCT threat had its roots in New York City, there could be more sinister connections in bad places that harbored and protected terrorists.

Just then Tim Lavstik, an analyst from the Russian sector knocked on the door and asked if he could have a moment of Karen Lee's time. He had been with the Agency for twenty-five years and looked like your classic white-haired college professor with rimless glasses. He was carrying a dispatch in a top-secret file casing.

Karen Lee looked up from her papers and waved him into the office. She noted that he shut the door and she instantly dreaded whatever news he was bringing.

"More good news Tim? That's all that I need. Why do I get the impression that whenever you visit, I get more work out of the deal?"

"Ma'am, that's never my plan, but I thought you should see this. It just came in from our guy in Moscow. His people verified the military cables and dispatches between the Kremlin and a military base in Novorossiysk, on the Black Sea are for real." He handed her the file and papers and sat down while she read it.

The Director scanned the document, and then reread it carefully as she recognized what was being suggested. She looked up and smiled at the man who was cleaning his glasses. He did remind her of a college professor.

"Just as I thought. Why can't you ever bring me news about your wife's gardening club activities, or where you're going on vacation this year." She waved the document in the air and then opened it up again to re-read the dispatches.

"Sorry, Karen, but I knew this would be something you'd want to see right away. A missing nuke is a bad nuke. Over here we call them a broken arrow, but I don't know what the Russkies call them. We have verified their efforts haven't turned anything up yet. We just received these so I thought you should know."

"Thank you, this is of great concern. Novorossiysk is where they keep their nukes, if they are not active. This may relate to another flag were working on. Tim, do me a favor and stay on top of this. I'll make some inquiries, too. We have some good assets on the ground over there. They can monitor the base comings and goings and all those WMD's. Maybe they can get us some more information quickly."

"You got it Karen, by the way, for vacation this year I'm hunting Red Stag in Argentina. Jane isn't going. She hates to travel that far to kill something, so I'm batching it. I'm hoping for another trophy for the wall." He headed for the door. "I'll see what else I can dig up on this."

Karen Lee reached for her phone to call Bede Long. She asked him to set up a scrambled conference call with Bill Dalde, and his boss at NSA, as soon as possible.

→ ←

Gelendzhik Bay, Russia

The members of the THCT group on board the Majorca were quite nervous all through dinner, and afterwards paced the decks as if waiting for a baby to be born. None of them ventured to the starboard side of the ship because they were afraid someone would see them looking down at the small workboat bobbing in the Bay next to the ship. The boat with a nuclear bomb attached to it. They waited until it was past midnight to fetch their weapon of mass destruction.

"Ok, let's go get our nuclear device," Meredith said almost comically.

It was a cloudy night and the moon was not a factor. The lights of the commercial docks were bright, but they cast deep shadows on the waterside of the ship and anyone moving on that side would be almost invisible.

It was decided that Uri Navroz was the lightest person in the group, and that he was the best candidate to be lowered into the workboat to haul up the weapon. Only Michael and Kevin were on the deck when they lowered Uri over the side, again to minimize the activity should anyone be watching the ship. He went over the side with a harness jacket trailing 30-foot length of rope behind him.

Once in the vessel he tried to minimize his profile by sitting deep in the boat well. He tied the line he'd brought with him to the bomb rope with a strong sailor's bowline knot. Making sure it was secure he gave the line a tug and the two men on board started slowly pulling the line up over the gunwale.

The weight was lighter than they thought it would be with the drag. Michael and Kevin hoped they still had their fish on the line. The package broke the surface with hardly a sound and Uri signaled a halt so the package could rid itself of the seawater. Once he was satisfied the dripping had ceased, he silently signaled for continued upward movement and the package crawled up the side of the ship in the darkness. The sealed package rose to the rail without effort and Kevin quickly reached over and gently wrestled it to deck away from prying eyes.

Letting the package drain on the deck, they turned back to the rail. With a tug on the harness rope to signal Uri, they hauled him back up to the deck as easily as the first package. As he cleared the rail he fell onto the deck next to the black plastic wrapped package.

Just inside the deck hallway, Meredith and the Captain stood watching the effort. They had resisted the desire to be on the bridge pacing about and looking over the side. Now they were staring at a nuclear bomb. They watched the three men gather their gear and gingerly pick up the weapon. Two of them carefully carried it over to the cabin door and stepped in.

The package was immediately carried below deck two levels and back through the engine room to a small but very secure room that had been recently fortified in Marseilles. It had been lined with lead two inches thick. Heavy-duty locks and pins had been added to the door to protect whatever was placed in the room. The locks and pins had been aged and beaten to look old and worn. It was stocked with food and water as well as oxygen and waste disposal. It was a self-contained safe room that could protect a crew in danger.

In recent years, ship owners concerned about pirates, had been adding safe rooms for their crews and valuable cargo. The rooms were secure enough that rescuers could even fire on the ship and know that they were not endangering the crew. This would be where they would keep the WMD for the duration.

The team members pulled out a couple of knives and started carefully cutting into the many layers of plastic wrap that protected the package. They were careful not to cut the case within because other than the photographs, they had never handled such a bomb. In a matter of minutes they had all the wrappings cut away and they found that the suitcase was bone dry, just as the General had said it would be.

"That's a relief, the last thing we needed was a water-soaked, corroded bomb that won't work," Meredith said folding his pocketknife and placing it in his pocket. He carefully turned the suitcase towards him. It had Russian Cyrillic markings and numbers on the casing. There was also one number in English; it read RA 155. He examined the locks and noted that they were in the closed but unlocked position.

"Thank you General, just as you said it would be." He pointed at the numbers and said, "That RA 155 number is the Soviet code for this class of weapon, first built in the 80's. I did some Internet reading, and it said this weapon has about 25 pounds of very high-grade plutonium in it."

"So convert that into the amount of Pakistani mountain rock it will move?"

"Well, I'm told it would yield about five kilotons, and that's about half the explosive power that was unleashed on Hiroshima in World War II."

"Holy shit. This small thing can do that much damage?" Michael said as he mopped his brow even though it was rather cool in the sealed room.

The Captain, Michael, Kevin and Uri all watched silently as Meredith reached to pop the locks. As he touched the locksets he made eye contact with each one of them.

"Open it up for Christ sake!" Kevin said. " If it's going to blow, I want it over and done with. This waiting is driving me nuts."

Everyone smiled one of those nervous smiles that came with unknown territory. Most of them hadn't even thought about it blowing up. But they were thinking about it now. Meredith hesitated another second as if he was weighing the same thought and then he flipped the locks and opened the case, carefully laying the cover back on the table. Everyone stared at the suitcase, not saying a word.

Before them was a small but complex looking machine that had a number of metal cylinders, the obligatory wires, red white and green, a digital timer, a numeric keyboard almost like a calculator, a data entry port for a floppy disk, and a small computer monitor screen. It was obviously a complex machine jammed into a small box. And it could kill everyone within miles if it went off.

"Now what?" said Michael Pappas searching the others faces around the table, "Are we sure this thing can't go off on its own?"

Meredith waved his hand over the suitcase and said. "I've done a lot of reading about these things since we started. It's in what we would call 'safe' mode. Once we met with the General, he sent us all the specifications and photo's by diplomatic courier, in gifts for Josef."

Meredith reached for a number of plastic sealed envelopes that were marked with Russian words and numbers. They were taped in the suitcase cover.

"The General said he'd send these. Josef, I think you should do some reading tonight." He handed Josef a set of the documents and a manual. He immediately stepped to the other end of the table and started reading.

"Hopefully these directions will assist us in becoming familiar with our little monster. I don't think we're going to tamper with it until we've all read the spec books carefully. Plus we have to off-load and re-load this thing a number of times, so I think we shouldn't tinker with it at all for the early part of our journey."

"What do you mean WE have to unload and re-load?" Michael said. "Not to quibble, but its Kevin and I that get those loading honors!"

"Sorry, Michael, I meant that, I was just thinking collectively. That we are all in this."

"I know, I know, I'm just yanking your chain, just a little deadly nuclear bomb humor. No problem," Michael said

"That's easy for you to say. I'm still getting use to the fact that this baby is capable of blowing us all out of the water, in fact probably out of Russia," Ralph said this gently patting the suitcase cover as if it were a baby.

"Yeah, but if you think about what will happen when bin Laden is stroking this little baby. That's the image I want to take to bed with me tonight," Meredith said. "I think I'll sleep well tonight. I hope you will, as well."

Captain Brinkmann had kept his mouth shut up to this point but now spoke up to the assembled group. "Gentlemen, since we have this special locker all made up, let's put our baby to bed in a nice soft blanket, one that will keep it warm and not allow it to get cold down here. I want to keep my ship in one piece too."

"Agreed, Captain. Let's get this thing squared away. But first, a re-commitment for our plan." He put his hand out over the bomb and everyone knew the drill. Meredith was big on commitments. They threw their hands in upon his.

"May this weapon find its mark with Osama bin Laden, the bastard, and give us all the peace that we have been searching for. We dedicate this THCT effort to our loved ones, past and present."

With that, everyone gently reached down to touch some part of the suitcase, vowing they would carry out their mission.

→ ←

NSA, Ft. Meade, MD

Bill Dalde finished his burger and fries lunch in the cafeteria courtyard. He threw out his paper wrappings and utensils and grabbed some extra napkins to wrap up a couple of chocolate cookies. He went back to his cubicle to dig deeper into his primary project. The THCT questions were still mostly unanswered.

Walking down the hallway on the 5th floor, he looked out the back windows of his building and could see military personnel golfing on the adjacent course just one hundred yards away through the trees. That is where he wanted to be rather than listening to countless telephone tapes and reviewing pieces of disjointed information that seemed to lead nowhere.

He entered his cubicle and noted some additional dispatches had been downloaded from the Echelon computer. As he opened the confidential files he saw that a number of new THCT calls had again come out of the New York area. This time a couple of calls were traced to a private gun club north of the city, and the calls had originated on a number of different days, and then the numbers never used again. There were also a number of calls emanating from Teterboro Airport in New Jersey, and a bunch of calls coming from Times Square.

While there was no direct linkage between all these calls and locations they were ominous because they involved airports, a gun club and a huge tourist area in the center of New York City. The fact the calls all used the letters THCT in some way linked them as a common thread. And that different phone numbers were being used for each of the calls was textbook terrorist cell activity.

The gun club calls came from the Kensico Gun Club, in Westchester County north of the city. Bill Dalde scanned the Internet and ATF records to secure a list of gun club members. Everyone on the club's roster had gun permits on file. Perhaps one of the terrorists was actually a member because it was an exclusive private club.

Once he had that list of a couple of hundred names, he decided to try the same thing with airplane owners using Teterboro. But the Teterboro Airport list was less fruitful because a lot of the plane ownership information was buried in corporate listings, multiple time-share ownership, not individuals' names.

He filed away the information and tried to find another way to break the THCT puzzle. He pulled up his call and cell phone usage charts, which plotted every one of the related calls in the Tri-State area. Adding time and date stamps for the gun club and Teterboro he recognized certain patterns. The next heaviest concentration of calls, to or from someone, came from the 44th and Broadway area in Times Square. He thought about that and wondered if this could be the central headquarters area for the THCT terrorist group. He had already decided he had a live one. His job was to find them. He reached for a phone.

He called up a fellow analyst in the NSA Geography Department, in another building on the campus. His name was James Becky. He had degrees in Geography and Engineering and had come to the NSA right out of the Milwaukee School of Engineering fifteen years ago hoping for a life of intrigue and covert operations. Instead, they had him work in the Cartography Department, studying maps from all over the world. In the last ten years he'd only left the NSA buildings in the evening, when he went home for supper. So much for the life of a secret agent!

Bill Dalde asked him what kind of map support he could offer on the Times Square, specifically in the triangle area. He said it was an urgent matter of national security. James excitably said he had all sorts of information on the whole area because it was deemed to be a high value target for the bad guys. He advised he had a pretty comprehensive list of every building, restaurant, store, business and the tenants in the buildings. He could advise who owned what, and he had detailed floor plans of almost every skyscraper in Manhattan. He asked what Bill would like to see?

James saw a chance to get out of the building, and offered to come over to help decode the information. He'd built the Times Square files himself after 9-11. Bill Dalde asked him to come over at 10:00 am the next day with whatever he had for a six- block area around 44th and Broadway. James gave himself a high-five and said he'd be there.

Teterboro Airport, NJ

The remaining members of the THCT group still stateside began arriving at the airport and entered the WM Industries Aircraft Hanger. Those who had driven dropped off their luggage and then parked their vehicles in the long-term commercial lot so as not to draw any undue attention to the WM Industries Hanger. Malik used a golf cart to collect the drivers at the lot.

Ryan Younger was now a full partner in the THCT group and everyone knew they could trust him. He checked them all in verifying they had brought the necessary equipment, clothing, documents and travel papers. He encouraged them to relax upstairs or to take a nap in the pilots' rooms that were on the upper level.

Checking his list, he verified he had Courtney Ranker, Kate Shanahan, Osama Tarkan and his brother Malik all checked in. They would be departing at 6:00 pm for an overnight flight to Europe. That would get them to Belgium early the following morning. Once they were re-fueled they would fly on to Istanbul, Turkey later that day. In Istanbul they would make like tourists and enjoy the sites for a day or two. Then they would rent a minivan and Courtney and Kate would drive north to the Black Sea town of Sile, to await the arrival of Michael Pappas and Kevin Geary. They would then become two tourist couples driving south through Turkey on their way to the ruins of the fabled City of Troy, located in a the Canakkale Straits, south of Istanbul.

The other group members would loiter an extra day or two in Istanbul. Both Osama and Malik had heard about the Blue Mosque in Istanbul and hoped to go there for prayers. They would then rent another minivan to join the others driving south to Truva, Turkey. It was a popular tourist attraction, especially so since the two recent movies about the Trojan War and Helen of Troy. The THCT group thought the meeting site would inspire everyone.

At 5:45 pm they all loaded up and settled into their seats. Ryan made sure everyone was comfortable and welcomed Courtney back for another flight. She just rolled her eyes. So he turned to Kate.

"Kate, you haven't flown with us yet, so please let me know if there is anything I can get for you. We loaded up on sandwiches and drinks, so please help yourself. I'll be back after we are at flying altitude to see if there is anything else we can do to make this trip a good one."

"Thanks Ryan, I think I'm fine at the moment." As the pilot turned and walked forward, Courtney looked at Kate, rolled her eyes, one of her favorite expressions, and smiled. "I told you so. I wasn't the most pleasant person on our previous trip, so I'm now off his radar screen, but you have just been sighted. Have fun. Maybe this time I will get some sleep."

"Listen, I'm nervous as hell. If he can take my mind off this mission for a while I'll welcome the diversion. Hell, he's a former fighter pilot isn't he? That should be an interesting conversation in itself."

"Fine by me, just don't talk too loud if you hear me snoring over here.

"I'll enjoy the attention. How's it feel to be a has been?"

"I can live with it. He was a gracious host in Paris and he is a dedicated guy. He respects the hell out of Meredith and I'm glad he's on the team. We may need him and this jet to pull us out of a jam, so be nice. It's your turn to entertain him." She buckled her seat belt and looked forward to make sure that the brothers were settled. She was reminded of their first flight in the jet.

Ryan was thinking the same and he walked forward to check on the brothers. This trip Osama and Malik sat in the first row of passenger seats directly behind the pilot. They felt as if they were old hands at flying now having made two trips over the Ocean back and forth to France. On their return trip they had gotten comfortable enough to sleep and even eat a meal. This time they wanted to watch and see how Ryan Younger flew the craft and what actually made it go.

Recognizing he now had two flying converts, when he started to step through to the cockpit, he pinned back the drapes so his two passengers could get a clear view of the controls.

"I'd let you guys up here if we had the room but it is pretty tight. Looking through the hatch will have to do for the moment. Maybe Rick will allow you to sit second chair when he needs a rest. I'll show you how to fly."

"Ryan, Sir, I am not yet ready to steer this aircraft I think. But I would like to see the cockpit."

Fair enough Malik, I won't make you fly, you can just keep me company so that I don't fall asleep."

Both the brothers looked horrified when they heard that and then Osama said. "We will most certainly talk with you to keep you awake Mr. Ryan. I think this is necessary."

Ryan laughed out loud and then turned to do his final pre-check. The electric hum of the large hanger door opening waffled through the air as the co-pilot boarded and sealed the hatch. He jumped into the right cockpit seat, buckled himself in and started his final pre-check. Both brothers watched through the door with rapt attention trying to understand why the plane would actually fly.

The Bombardier Global Express slowly rolled out of the hanger and made a right turn in the alleyway between the hangers. As he reached the tarmac he received ground instructions and turned right again heading for the runway. Ground Control gave Ryan approval to move onto the north – south runway. As they taxied into position he leaned through the curtained doorway and asked the Pakistani brothers.

"Ready to take off guys? How about a fast climb, even steeper than last time?"

Both brothers stared ahead and offered a slight nod. They both gripped the armrests and Ryan could see they were white-knuckling it already and they were only rolling down the approach to the end of the runway.

He laughed one more time and said. "Take it easy guys. I may need some help so be prepared to flap your arms if we can't get this bird off the ground."

The brothers again looked aghast. Neither was prepared at let go of their armrests, no matter what. Both stared straight ahead out the cockpit window. But neither closed their eyes. They were about to have another love hate experience.

Ryan received his clearance from the control tower, powered up the twin jet engines, released the brakes, started rolling and said. "And we're off."

➜ ←

Gelendzhik Bay, Russia

The Majorca spent another half day loading its cargo of farm implements destined for Pakistan. Twenty Russian made tractors, wrapped in clear plastic and stacked on large wooden pallet containers were the last items lowered onto the deck. They were too large to be placed in the hold. The fire engine red machines were strapped down for a long, open water journey. After the port officers inspected the final shipment papers, the Majorca was cleared for sailing at 1:00 pm.

At the appointed time the lines were quickly cast off from the moorings, and the ship proceeded out into the Bay under its own power. No pilot was required, thus Captain Brinkmann was at the helm. He wanted a fast departure, but without giving any impression that he was high-tailing it out of Gelendzhik. He just wanted to get moving.

Once out in the Black Sea he ramped up the speed to 15 knots and set a course due south for the Turkish border. He had pre-plotted the course and made sure the shipping company was aware of his plans so no one would be surprised to see the Majorca in these coastal waters. He would hug the coastline just as expected and would hopefully draw less scrutiny. If he had ventured out into the Black Sea's major shipping lanes, he would have saved time, but he would have also had a greater chance to run into Russian naval vessels. He wasn't sure what kinds of nuclear sniffing equipment they might be carrying, and he didn't want to find out. Thus, he would be a good 'coaster' vessel, and follow the coastline maintaining a twelve-mile distance from shore. His new side-look radar equipment would automatically maintain that distance making slight adjustments as necessary. He handed over control to his First Officer and went below.

When the ship was in open water, Meredith and the THCT group gathered in the ship's mess at the two long tables that were wedged into the space. The cook had brewed a strong pot of coffee at Meredith's request and had retired to his bunk for a couple hours rest before the evening's supper was to be prepared. There was a knock at the door and Captain Brinkmann joined the group.

"Ralph, would you throw the lock on that door and Uri, please turn on that radio and see if you can find us a gypsy channel for some background noise." Meredith pulled out a briefcase and took out the documents that had been in the package a day earlier.

Josef started the conversation. "I've tried to review all of the manual and documents to see what we actually have here. It is not as sophisticated as we were led to believe. I think it actually is more in the class of a limited yield weapon, that will be devastating but in a limited area. It's the radiation exposure that comes from the bomb that is the real weapon of mass destruction."

"Just tell me that it will do the job if we put it in the right place?" Ralph asked as he returned to the table with the pot of coffee and a fist full of mugs.

"It will do the job well, and will kill our target and anyone within a mile of him. If he is stroking it on his lap in his cave, it won't level the mountain, but it will kill everyone within the connecting caves as the explosion rushes through them. Don't worry, it will do the job."

Captain Brinkmann asked the next question. "How safe is it as we transport it from here to Pakistan. Do we have to be very careful?"

Josef spoke up. "From what I have read in the manual, it is very stable and safe until it is armed. It can be moved around as a piece of luggage would be moved, and can't just detonate on its own."

"That's my read as well." Meredith said. " But it is stable as it sits here now. Once we alter its capability to detonate, then I think we must take extra precaution. We need to figure out how to make it safe and harmless, until we need to arm it and make it dangerous. Before we mess with anything, I want Osama and Malik involved in the process."

Everyone around the table looked a little surprised. Noting the reaction Meredith spoke up again. "The Brothers have computer expertise, especially with these older components, from when they ran electronic stores in Pakistan. Remember, these weapons were made in the 80's and don't have a lot of high tech in them. It is armed with floppy disks and some pretty basic programming. O and Malik sold both Russian and U.S. equipment and serviced components like these for years."

The small group standing around the bomb thought about what Meredith said about the two Pakistani brothers. None of them doubted their sincerity, and they knew that they had an instrumental part in even getting al Qaeda on the hook, so they accepted that Meredith knew what he was talking about.

"William, after reading the manual, even I could understand the component parts involved, thus I agree they are pretty rudimentary. With my present day translation computer capabilities, I think we can re-work this bomb to do as we wish. Osama and Malik can make this work for us," agreed Josef.

"Then it's settled. We wait for the Brothers." Meredith said. "They will join us in a couple days in Turkey along with the women. Let's put this thing back to bed under lock and key. Michael, lets get you ready for your medical emergency."

"We should be pulling into Sile, Turkey tomorrow." Captain Brinkmann said. "Once we get close, I'll radio ahead that we have an extremely sick sailor that needs to be off-loaded. We will ask that a fellow sailor accompany him to the hospital and that we have a shipping company van meeting the ship. The harbormaster won't let us dock because we're too large for this tourist resort town. But they will come out to us with a pilot boat and we'll offload Michael and

Kevin that way."

"If our timing is right, Courtney and Kate should be there to pick you two up," Meredith continued. "Then the four of you will leave and be able to get out of town with hardly anyone noticing."

Meredith pointed at a map on the table and followed a general line from Sile through western Turkey leading to Truva. "Once you're out of town you become two tourist couples. You'll join up with the rest of the team in Istanbul and then we will all meet in Troy after we clear the Straits. So everyone go about your business. Michael, get ready to be sick. I have some special pills here that will give you some real stomach discomfort so you won't have to act. You'll have some very real moans and groans, but it will pass in a matter of hours."

"I'm looking forward to it," Michael said feeling sick already.

"I am too. This should be fun," Kevin said as he slapped Michael on the back.

"Kevin, were hoping that they will allow you to disembark to take care of our sailor, but it isn't a given," Meredith said. "Michael, can you brief him on some Greek phrases to assist you?"

"Will do boss. But he has trouble with English, how am I going to get him up to speed on the Greek language?" He punched Kevin in the arm.

"Just a few choice words should do the trick. As soon as you're away from the seaport, you can handle all the translation chores. Both Kate and Courtney will need help too. In Turkey you can act like American tourists, backpacking your way through the country."

"No problem, let's go lover boy."

→ ←

Black Sea, Sile, Turkey

The Majorca was sailing on a peaceful sea, maintaining a steady course west at a solid rate of 15 knots. When they were about 25 kilometers north of Sile, the Captain got on the ship's radio and called the Sile Harbor Master. He announced that he was a merchant ship making way to the Bosporus and had a very sick seaman on board. He knew it would be more difficult to stop in the channel, thus he asked if they could have someone meet the ship to offload him for medical treatment. The Captain advised he had already called the ship's owners in Athens and they had dispatched some employee assistance from their offices in Istanbul. They would be meeting the sailor and would transfer him to a hospital for treatment.

The Harbor Master advised they could provide such assistance. He asked that they stand off outside the harbor. He said a Customs Officer would need to inspect their papers as they were arriving from Russia into Turkey, but he didn't feel that would cause any delay since they were not docking nor bringing any shipments in or out. He said he could assist and allow the ship to continue on its way. The Captain advised he would be there within an hour and would call to bring out the pilot boat.

As the Majorca approached Sile they could see the natural harbor was nestled between three large cliffs with jutting rock formations. While it had once been a major shipping port dating back hundreds of years, it was now a resort village that secondarily supported a small fishing fleet.

Captain Brinkmann had gone on the Internet and found the port city went all the way back to Roman times and the Byzantine era. Its one claim to fame was a tall lighthouse built on one of the cliffs that beckoned all sea travelers from near and far. It was said to be the second tallest lighthouse in all of Europe. Built in 1859 by Sultan Abdulmecit, it utilized steel paneling and glass crystals manufactured in Paris. Eight lenses were first illuminated with burning oil, and then later by electric lamp.

Dropping anchor about a quarter mile outside the breakwater, Captain Brinkmann and William Meredith watched a small boat as it motored past the harbor entrance. The Captain signaled one of the crane operators to fire up the bow crane. They would fasten lines to a wooden pallet that would allow the sick patient to be lowered over the side.

"I think we should get our patient out there so he can get comfortable on the pallet, supported by our nuclear bomb," Captain Brinkmann said facetiously and then smiled nervously at his boss.

"Well, we won't have any trouble making them believe that Michael is truly sick. He has turned green and been throwing up all over the place. I think they'll buy it," said Meredith. With that they left the Bridge and made their way to the deck surface where Michael was being tucked into his temporary gurney on the pallet.

As the two men walked up they heard the motorboat pull along side the ship and cut its engine. The captain leaned over and signaled the Official to come aboard.

"Kevin, take care of our boy, and take care of our package. I'd prefer it if you would handle it personally when you get back to the dock. Make it look light and easy to handle. We've packed clothes all around it so even if someone actually asks to see it you should be ok."

"Will do Sir. I just hope Mike here doesn't barf on me. What the hell did you give him, anyhow?"

"It's nothing that will hurt him unless he barfs up his intestinal tract," Meredith said as Michael's head weakly bobbed up from his bed. He looked as if he was in great pain, but nodded to signal he was taking one for the team.

The crane went over the side with an empty pallet strung to the lines and a half-minute later brought a Port Official back onto the deck. He wore a Turkish police uniform and had a pistol on his belt, but looked bored as the Captain approached and offered his handshake.

While the shipping papers and passports were being reviewed by the Official, Ralph, Uri, Josef, and Meredith, dressed in sailors' jeans and faded t-shirts made a show of saying goodbye to their fellow sailor, wishing him a quick recovery. The document review took less than a minute, as the Official flipped through the papers. The Captain explained that the shipping line would have people at the dock to meet the sailor and his mate for transfer to the hospital.

The Official, looking bored, handed back the papers, shook hands with the Captain and returned to the pallet. He stood opposite to Kevin to help balance the load as the crane carefully lifted the human cargo over the side and down to the pilot boat.

Once there, the boat's pilot helped Kevin wrestle Michael's gurney onto the boat. Kevin then reached onto the pallet and grabbed the suitcases before anyone else could. He made them look as if they were light as a feather and he deposited them in the back transom of the boat.

As soon as they were all clear of the pallet, the crane operator lifted the empty pallet back onto the ship. In a moment the motor was started and turned towards shore.

The Official never looked back. He took a seat in the small pilothouse and put his feet up on the dashboard. Kevin sat at the back of the small boat near Michael who was lying on the makeshift gurney in the stern well, looking green in the gently tossing sea. Kevin looked up and waved goodbye to the crew. The Captain and Meredith walked up to the bridge and casually watched the small pilot boat make its way into Sile Harbor. Through two sets of powerful binoculars that Meredith had brought with him, they watched as the boat pulled up to the commercial dock in the calm harbor.

Scanning the dock, they noticed a white van parked just one hundred feet away that actually had the shipping company's name on the side of it. Two young women in white blouse and skirt uniforms stepped out of the van and walked to the dock. They greeted the Port Official, showed him papers as to who they were, and took charge of the sick man and his companion mate. The boat's pilot assisted Kevin in carrying the sailor's makeshift gurney to the van. The Port Official ignored them and walked away for the comfort of his air-conditioned office. Kevin quickly ran back to the boat to get the luggage, again making them look light and full of clothes.

From the Majorca's bridge, the two men watched until the van drove off the pier and was seen turning onto the highway leading away from the port. "That went better than I expected," the Captain said, and offered a handshake to Meredith.

"It really came off without a hitch, didn't it? It's kind of scary if it's this easy to move people and contraband around. If we can do it, the bad guys certainly must be doing it too. It was a nice touch - the uniforms and the shipping company logo on the van. I bet that was Kate's idea. I may have to hire her for all my graphics work."

"So how about we turn around and make our way through the Bosporus, the Sea of Marmara and the Canakkale Straits. Hopefully our sick sailor will be better when we see him on the other side."

"Sounds good to me, Captain. Let's weigh anchor. I always wanted to say that."

The Captain leaned over the Bridge rail and yelled out. "Haul in the anchor. Let's get under way." He turned to Meredith and said. "Weighing the anchor takes too much time."

➔ ←

Moscow, FSB Headquarters

"So what can you tell me Major? Have we figured out what happened to that damned weapon yet?" The General and various Kremlin agency leaders were sitting in plush leather chairs at the large mahogany table in the middle of a very ornate room that was once part of a palace of the Czars. They all looked to the Major sitting at the end of the table. He was very uncomfortable.

"No Sir, we haven't. All we have been able to determine is that a switch was made some time ago. We have had forensics check out everything. We have interviewed everyone on the base and we have checked out all camera tapes for the past six months. Our records show that particular series of weapons dated back to the mid-80s. These were weapons we covertly deployed at a number of embassies around the world. When all that changed in the 90's, the weapons were brought back home for fear they would wind up in the wrong hands."

"Which is exactly what seems to have happened, Major." Another General said, contemptuously, to no one in particular. Everyone at the table was intent on passing blame to someone else.

"Yes Sir. These limited yield weapons were all brought back to a secure Sevastopol storage facility on the Naval base. Records were meticulously kept to count and record the types of weapons, their yields, security code numbers, and to establish security protocols for these weapons. They were carefully secured in bombproof bunkers since the mid-nineties. Then about five years ago when our Ukrainian friends started complaining about our Naval base in their country, it was determined that the weapons should be moved to a more secure facility somewhere in Russia. That is why they were sent to Novorossiysk."

"Well, aren't we lucky that we stored them there." The head of the FSB said sarcastically. "Have we truly exhausted all options to find this weapon, or can we ascertain it is in safe hands or destroyed?"

"No Sir, we still have concerns that this nuclear weapon is out there somewhere. There was a bomb suitcase that was sitting in its appropriate place, locked and catalogued with a perfectly weighted mass inside. We believe someone deliberately made a switch and the real bomb was spirited away. We have undertaken an exhaustive search, and we believe that the bomb is still out there. We just haven't been able to get a lead on where." The Major didn't know what else to say. He was the bearer of bad tidings and he hoped they would not take it out on him.

"So what do you recommend Major?"

"Sir, with the Americans coming to inspect our nuclear armaments in one week, and with all these suitcase weapons scheduled to be destroyed, I think we must advise them that we have this single weapon unaccounted for. If we do not advise them, they will ultimately find it for themselves and that would not be a good. We must bring it to their attention before they stumble upon the missing weapon."

Another General sitting across the table spoke up for the first time.

"Major, I think we are all in agreement that we should share this problem with the Americans, but I also think we must continue our search. The last thing we want is for our enemies in Chechnya, Georgia, and all the 'Stans' to get a hold of such a weapon. We think we have had problems in Moscow in the subways, and at the schools, but those tragedies would pale in comparison if one of those terrorists got a hold of a suitcase bomb."

"General, I too agree." another man said sitting at a chair on the wall away from the table. He was dressed in an impeccable suit and had not said anything up to this point.

"The FSB is putting everyone on the task, here and abroad. We are yanking every person we can off the streets to get information. We have already pulled in suspected terrorists, the local criminals, and the Russian mob to see what we can learn."

"And has that produced any good leads, Yevgeny?"

"I wish we could report good leads on the whereabouts of this bomb, but we are getting nothing at the moment. We are being very careful and non-specific in our inquiries because leaking this information will only complicate matters. If this gets out we will have every potential terrorist group snooping about looking and competing for this bomb."

The General turned to his cohorts and said. "Unfortunately, I agree. I don't want to do this, but we will have to share this information with the Americans. They need to know there is something out there that could cause them major problems. They can bring all their assets to the task. Hopefully if this bomb is out there, together we can get a lead on it before it is used by a terrorist organization. And let us hope it will not be used here in Russia."

"Major, stay on task and keep me posted. I will be talking with the Americans by tomorrow and I'm sure they will have questions that I have no answers for."

The Major sensed his portion of this meeting was over. He pushed back his stiff wooden chair, saluted, and marched out of the room. On the other side of the massive door, he reached for his tunic collar and opened the button to let some air in. He ignored the people sitting along the perimeter of the chamber and marched out the door.

→ ←

Bosporus Straits

The Majorca sailed east from Sile heading for the Bosporus Strait. It had already requested its passage slot 48 hours in advance and fell into line with other shipping traffic heading southwest. After registering its position with the Traffic Control Center managing the Strait, Captain Brinkmann brought the Majorca to port into the primary southern shipping lane. They were the eighth ship in line, directly behind a Russian submarine, the Alrosa, a Kilo class boat running on the surface. It was less than 1,000 yards ahead of the Majorca.

On the bridge Captain Brinkmann pointed forward and said, "Their position in front of us may be a blessing as we pass the monitoring stations. I don't know how they do their sniffing but if they smell any nuclear material, that sub could throw the scent off."

"I hadn't thought of that, but that makes sense. Still, I'm glad Michael and Kevin are heading around this whole narrow passage."

Just then Meredith happened to look behind the ship. Another ship was lining up that had come from the other direction. It was a much larger vessel and you could see five-inch guns mounted on the bow. "I'll be damned," Meredith said pointing to the stern. "The Russians are behind us as well. Now I know what a turkey sandwich feels like."

Captain Brinkmann smiled at the reference and grabbed his binoculars, walked out the bridge hatch and checked out the ship behind them, about a 1,000-yards back.

"I believe that's the Admiral Chabanenko again. We crossed its path on the way to Gelendzhik a few days ago. It's one of their Udaloy II Class Destroyers. It has nuclear power generators as well. That may be a good thing. We have nuclear material in front of and behind us. As you said, now we're a nuclear turkey sandwich."

"Yeah, the Russians are all over the place," Uri said to no one in particular. "They just keep following us."

The Captain returned to the wheel. He would personally take the helm through the passage. He had done it many times before. The narrow passage was one of the busiest canals in the world, with some 55,000 vessels passing through each year, three times the number passing through the Suez Canal, and four times more than the Panama Canal.

As they motored at a steady 10 knots into the Strait maintaining speed and distance with the vessel in front of them, Captain Brinkmann offered his passengers a crash course on the Bosporus and its importance to the shipping world.

"The Bosporus, coupled with the Dardanelles Straits further ahead, is an international waterway connecting the Black Sea with the Aegean and Mediterranean. It literally divides Europe from Asia and has always been a major shipping channel since the dawn of man. Many wars have been fought over its strategic importance."

"This northern Strait we just entered is over 30 kilometers long with varying widths from 3,700 meters down to as little as 750 meters at its tightest point up ahead. That is where I would think NATO does it's sniffing for radioactive materials. The depth of the channel was carved out first as a river way in the Tertiary Period. Don't ask when that was, it was thousands of years ago. The depth varies from 36 to 124 meters in midstream."

Meredith jumped into the impromptu education lesson. "I've also been doing lots of reading on our passage route. The Greeks referred to this passage as the Thracian Bosporus, and it is unique because it divides the City of Istanbul almost perfectly in half, with major portions of it's 11 million citizens living on each side."

The Captain was enjoying this little history and geography lesson, and continued, if for no other reason than to entertain himself.

"While Istanbul is an enormous city spread out on both sides of the channel, here's the kicker, there are only two major bridges that connect the whole city. A third bridge has been talked about for decades but hasn't been built yet. In its place there are hundreds of scheduled ferry services that cross the busy waterway. You'll see them buzzing back and forth across our bow all day, which makes it a dangerous trip for large oil tankers and container ships that can take miles to stop."

As the Majorca maintained its speed and separation between the submarine and the Russian destroyer behind, most of the crew lined the decks to enjoy the views of Istanbul. The portions of the city in the hills along the Channel were obviously beautiful places to live and work because of the views, cool breezes and Mediterranean climate. The huge homes, businesses and Mosques could be seen all along the rolling hilltops.

As they approached one of the massive bridges crossing the channel, they marveled at the height of the suspension bridge strung between two towering 165-meter piers. Ships passing under the 8-lane Sultan Mehmet Bridge had 65 meters of clearance. This bridge was part of the Trans European Motorway linking east with west, connecting Europe with Asia.

"Wow, look at that castle, it's huge and looks like it was built way back," Josef said to no one in particular, as he pointed to the shore on the starboard side of the ship.

"Josef, that's Rumelihisari, built back in the 1400's." Meredith said this as he brought out a book he had brought along all about the historic passage. Looking around, he continued. "I think right about here is the tightest point on the Strait, the book says just 660 meters wide. That Castle on the European side of the channel helped control the shipping traffic that came through here. There used to be another fortress on the Turkish side as well. They controlled all shipping from those two vantage points. As the Captain said, they've been fighting wars over this important passage since the dawn of man."

"It says here a Sultan built that huge fortress in just 4 months using thousands of workers. You don't see that kind of work effort anymore," Meredith said as he stared at the shoreline."

"Yeah, but they didn't have unions back then and they were probably all slaves that died in the process of building that thing," Uri said, "That's how the pyramids got built too. On people's blood, sweat, and tears."

"Still beautiful to look at. I wonder what we'll find in Troy?" Ralph Behar asked as the Majorca started passing under the massive suspension bridge.

"Again my reading says there is not much there other than ruins and the bases of some walls."

"I don't care. I'd still like to see the place. It'll keep me motivated and on point! That's what were doing here," Uri said this as the ship passed under the 8-lane highway more than 100 feet above them.

The Majorca continued its southerly route matching speeds with the submarine. On their right an almost continuous line of ships were passing them in the opposite direction, heading north, much like a busy, two lane highway. The separation between these two shipping lanes was less than one hundred yards in some places.

At the southern end of the Bosporus Strait, the water opened up again into the Sea of Marmara, some 30 miles wide and fifty miles long. This was a very large body of deep water with all sorts of towns and fishing villages dotting the shoreline. The shipping traffic kept in line for the most part, right down the middle, maintaining distance and speed between ships. This would prevent a bottleneck when they all entered the next Dardanelle Straits.

→ ←

Istanbul, Turkey

Having pulled out of the Port of Sile, with Courtney driving, Kevin changed into his tourist outfit, while Michael continued to groan and look sick. They encouraged him to relax while they put some miles between them and the port.

"Welcome to Turkey, gentlemen," Kate said. "It is really beautiful here, the little bit we've seen thus far driving up from Istanbul. You wouldn't believe how big Istanbul is. It's on both sides of the Canal. I have a whole bunch of tourist brochures in English on the dash. You might want to take a look, since we are now tourists."

"Kate, the last thing we are is on a tourist vacation. Remember we have a rather large firecracker with us, and I don't mean Mikey."

"You may still want to take a look, in case we're stopped by any of the local constables. We'll want to look the part of married tourists. Say, that raises a good question, who is suppose to be mated up with whom, now that we have this little charade going?" She raised an eyebrow in the rear view mirror.

Kevin never missing a beat said. "Ladies, I'm man enough for the both of you. I don't think old Mikey here will be much company for a while yet. Green is a handsome color isn't it? But in fairness you ladies get to pick."

"Kevin, I may be turning green and doubled over, but I could still kick your ass, from here to Karachi. Ladies it's your choice."

"All right, macho man. I'll decide then," Courtney said as she made a left turn onto the multi-lane highway going back to Istanbul. "Michael, you'll be my husband, and Kate you get Kevin as yours. But don't get any bright ideas boys."

"So let's start using our new alias' so we respond to the right names if we do have to talk to anybody along the way," Courtney said. "I'm Jane from Naperville, Illinois, and a travel writer out to see all that Turkey has to offer."

Kevin spoke up and said, "I'm Jeff and a legislative director from Wisconsin, taking a trip to get away from all the politicians."

Kate was next. "I'm Susan, and I work with special needs kids at a School in the Chicago area. The school is called Little Friends. Kevin, I mean Jeff, and I have known each other for years and decided we should make this trip of a lifetime together."

"Love you Babe." Jeff /Kevin said as he blew Susan /Kate a kiss from the passenger seat.

Michael propped himself up against the sidewall of the van and said,

"I'm actually starting to feel a bit better. Anyone have some water to help move this crap out of me." He was handed a bottle and took a big swig. "I'm getting thoroughly confused, but I'm a newly retired cop from Chicago's suburbs, named Rick and I have a passport to prove it."

He threw off the blanket and got up, still somewhat wobbly on his feet. "I want to feel like a tourist again and get out of this sailor suit." He managed to strip off his clothes ignoring the two women in the vehicle. He pulled on some khaki cargo shorts and a tee shirt with Naperville PD stenciled across the front.

"And now Jane, I believe it is Jane, right? Could you please stop the van, as I have to throw up one more time? But it's the last time, I promise."

They were now out in the countryside amidst farm fields and orchards so Jane pulled over to the side of the road. Michael stumbled out and barfed again. Kate jumped out too and when there were no cars coming she tore the Iolcos Shipping magnet logos off the doors of the van. Kevin walked around and took over the driving duties as the two women climbed in back with Michael. He lay down again and the girls changed from their white sailor uniforms into more touristy clothing, paying no attention to the sick man groaning beneath them on the van floor, or the guy driving, who kept looking in the rear view mirror.

They drove southwest towards Istanbul. On the outskirts of the city that straddled both Asia and Europe they spent an afternoon seeing the sites of this large very westernized city. After a leisurely lunch everyone enjoyed except Michael, they piled back into the van and utilized the rented English speaking GPS to get them pointed to the E-80 Highway that would take them around the city proper and towards the Sea of Marmara, and eventually to the Canakkale Peninsula and Troy. This route would take them the rest of the afternoon and would get them to Bursa where they could get some rooms for the evening. The following day after a good night's sleep, they would have a leisurely drive on the E-90 expressway west to the Canakkale coast and wait for the ship to arrive.

→ ←

Pentagon, Washington, DC

Just across the Potomac River from the city proper, the Pentagon is one of the world's largest office buildings with over 17.5 miles of office corridors within the five-sided building. The complex has more than six million square feet under roof, three times larger than the Empire State Building in New York. The entire site encompasses 29 acres and has six zip codes within its framework. It also has a subway system running through its lower level helping to move the thousands of soldiers and civilians that work there as part of the Department of Defense.

On this particular morning the Joint Chiefs of Staff had gathered in a heavily guarded suite deep within the bowels of the Pentagon. It was in Ring 3 of the five circular rings of the massive government building. It was also three levels below ground, in a bombproof, soundproof bunker like room, safe from everything except perhaps a direct nuclear attack on their specific location. No one wanted to test the veracity of that claim. The Pentagon had already experienced a deadly attack on 9-11, with a great loss of military and civilian personnel.

Gathered around a large oval conference table, that gleamed even though it was scarred with old coffee stains and cigar burns, these high ranking military leaders were immersed in a nuclear arms discussion about the news they had just received from their Russian counterparts. Through unofficial back channels, they had just been advised that a Russian suitcase tactical nuclear weapon was missing. The Russians had done a comprehensive search, but had not been able to identify its whereabouts. They sent the coded message as a high priority dispatch, to honor the importance of the nuclear disarmament talks that were ongoing.

The dispatch stated their full investigation documentation of the missing weapon was being forwarded through official channels but would be in their hands before the end of the day. In effect this advisory was a clear indication that the Russians were asking for assistance, something the Russians did not typically ask for.

When the complete files had been delivered, they were copied and distributed as top-secret documents to the Joint Chiefs and their key staff in the room. Everyone in the room reviewed the details about the missing weapon, the Russians efforts to find it, their search process parameters, and the ensuing investigation. The assembled warriors scrutinized every detail of the report.

After a thorough review and assessment of the documents before them, with heated discussion by everyone in the room, Dan Bishope, the Chairman of the Joint Chiefs settled the matter by advising that this issue would become priority one until the threat could be neutralized.

He ordered that Homeland Security be advised, along with all the clandestine U.S. agencies, that they had a probable 'broken arrow' in the wind. He wanted it understood it was not one of ours; rather the Russians had lost one of theirs. He wanted the appropriate people brought into the equation, and quickly. He invoked the highest level of secrecy on the subject and dismissed the soldiers to their required duties.

The room emptied in a few seconds as everyone ran to their posts and started making secure calls to their counterparts at NSA, Homeland Security, the FBI and CIA as well as another dozen agencies that would put people to work. A terrorist threat had been identified and the most likely target was the United States of America.

→ ←

Canakkale Straits, Turkey

The sea traffic moving south towards the Mediterranean maintained its designated distance between ships, if for no other reason than there were hundreds of small craft darting back and forth, including ferries, pleasure craft and working boats. The Majorca maintained its speed as it entered the Dardanelles Straits, once known as Hellespont, which was Greek, for the Sea of Helle.

The crew and the THCT members not actively working within the bowels of the ship were at the rails sightseeing as they cut between the two continents. The Captain explained the waterway had been named the Sea of Helle because it actually had extremely turbulent waters moving in both directions, from the Sea of Marmara south to the Aegean Sea on the surface, and the reverse direction north as an undercurrent at varying depths. The Strait itself was some 61 kilometers long, about 38 miles from end to end, and very narrow, often less than three-quarters of a mile from side-to-side. It was also 180 feet deep; hence the water currents and movement in both directions could be fierce and unpredictable. For centuries it had challenged shallow draft shipping. As in the Bosporus Strait, there were two shipping lanes in the canal and shipping traffic was constant in both directions.

The Captain enjoyed giving his geography and history lessons and told his students the Dardanelles also paralleled the Gallipoli Peninsula on the European side, opposite the Canakkale District on the Asian side of the channel. This was the land of Greek Mythology and where wars had been fought through the centuries. The Greeks had fought the Persian armies of Xerxes, and later others had fought the Greek armies of Alexander the Great. The ancient walled city of Troy was located near the southern entrance to the Strait on the Asian side of the channel. This fabled City State had been the focus of the Trojan Wars.

In Byzantine times in 400-500 AD, the Strait was an important defensive position for the entire Turkish Empire. It was a strategic crossing point for all of the Crusades and in the 18th century it was strategic in the Napoleonic Wars and the Ottoman Empire's defeat in the Russo-Turkish Wars in the 1820's.

The land and sea approaches also played a critical role in 1915 during World War 1 when a massive British, Indian, Australian, and New Zealander invasion force tried to secure the Straits. Their attempt was unsuccessful and over 200,000 casualties resulted in the Battle of Gallipoli. World War II also generated tremendous concern over the strategic passage.

Passing through this strategic passageway, the Majorca maintained its sandwiched position behind the submarine and the destroyer. At the southern end of the Strait, where it meets the Aegean Sea, the Majorca sailed out into open water and signaled its plan to pull out of the line of ships heading for the Mediterranean. The Captain casually waved a goodbye to their temporary travel mates and headed to port and the small town of Kumburum, Turkey. Meredith was happy the Majorca had been decommissioned from the Russian Navy.

Kumburum was a small tourist harbor town on the Aegean Sea just a few miles south of the site of the Trojan ruins. There was deep water almost to the concrete breakwater perimeter according to the sonar so the Majorca eased itself in close at almost a drift. It was a protected harbor that mostly catered to tourist site-seeing boats and the pleasure boat crowd sailing up and down the Turkish Gold Coast.

The Captain used the ship's radio to talk to the single port official on duty and asked for permission to dock for a couple of days, as they had tourists aboard who would like to visit the ruins of Troy. They stated they had already entered and registered in Turkish waters, having passed through the Straits, thus the port official waved them in, but asked that they moor on the outside of the breakwater so as not to bottom out inside the protected harbor. The Captain readily thanked him for the access and agreed to come over to share a cup of coffee, and to pay the bribe that would be required for the mooring spot. He said he would stop by while the tourists were running around.

Within the hour the ship's anchor was firmly drag planted on the sea floor and the ship faced into the southern wind. The forward crane came to life and lowered a small passenger boat over the side for transport to and from the dock. A security watch was set up and the Captain encouraged the rest of the crew and his guests to take some time off in town. The ship would be departing in two days.

Meredith and his team dressed as tourists and brought out their cameras and backpacks for the day in town. They boarded the small tender and took the five-minute ride to the city dock. When they stepped off the boat they saw their THCT teammates had arrived and were waiting for them close to the dock area.

They had agreed not to look too chummy with one another because there were other tourists and townspeople nearby, so Meredith gave the impression that he was hiring the van for a site-seeing tour. To make it look even more realistic if anyone was watching, they exchanged Turkish lira, and maps. In a matter of a few minutes the whole team had loaded into the van and pulled away from the dock. Everyone crowded in and sat with their feet gently planted on top of the nuclear weapon. Gently was the operative word.

They took a local two-lane highway a short distance, out to the E-87 Highway, a modern expressway traversing its way through the historic Canakkale District of Turkey. They backtracked the route Michael, Kevin and the girls had just come from. Heading north about five miles, they followed the various signs pointing the way to the historic site of Truva, the small tourist trap near the ruins of Troy. This Village had grown up because of the ruins and mostly served the tourist trade, greatly advanced by the Hollywood movies, and more recently the Brad Pitt blockbuster on the Trojan Wars.

Troy had originally been built as a fortress state on a long flat plain just south of the Canakkale Straits, about a mile inland from the beaches and the Aegean Sea. It had been built there for it's strategic location to give the walled fortress commanding views in all directions. As they drove towards the historic ruins, the land around the area had numerous farmer's fields, orchards and gently rolling hills. In the distance they could see forests rising up to the mountains in the east.

Approaching the village of Truva, the team saw a gigantic wooden horse towering over the countryside, rearing its head above the surrounding trees and buildings. Obviously, there was indeed a Trojan horse to be viewed. The team seemed excited about this diversion from their ocean voyage and Meredith was pleased that he had made the stop.

They drove into the center of town and then went to a large dusty parking lot filled with buses and tourist vans. They got out and carefully locked the vehicle. The ladies had been smart enough to get a van that had a security system wired in that would sound an alarm if the vehicle was tampered with. Satisfied their vehicle was safe they ventured through the dusty parking lot towards a series of low-lying buildings. Turning a corner they ran into a small, commercialized tourist bazaar with shops selling miniature Trojan horses, photos of Brad Pitt, various trinkets and all sorts of rubber and tin metal swords and shields. It was like a miniature Disneyland, but without the rides.

"So much for biblical authenticity," Michael said before anyone else could say it. "Kind of cheapens the whole Troy story doesn't it? I wonder if Brad Pitt saw this when he was filming?" He laughed out loud as he looked around.

"Yeah, it wasn't biblical, it was mythology way before Christ, but this isn't quite what I expected either." Courtney said. "I thought we would see some sort of dignified archeological site, like the Roman Coliseum."

"Hang on guys, these are just the trinket shops that prey on people like us. I believe the real archeological site is a decent walk over in that direction. See the Horse over there?" Meredith said this pointing over the many one-story shanties that lined the street.

"Let's walk over there before we spend all our lira on this crap," Kate said. "But I would like to get a Brad Pitt poster for my cabin before we leave." She looked sheepishly at everyone and continued, "It's going to be a long journey and you can only read so much!"

Everyone laughed and started walking towards the giant wooden horse that dominated the view, towering over the trees to the west. Noting the heat, Ralph stopped at a beverage stand and in Farsi purchased a six-pack of Coca-Cola and bottled water, which he carried in an iced plastic container towards the site. The group joined the rest of the tourists and started taking photos of one another to blend in.

When they got there, the Trojan horse replica was indeed huge. It was probably eighty feet tall at the head. The tourists were snapping photos as if they were standing at the gates of Troy. The THCT members joined in as well. Everyone stood around gawking at the horse and the scene wondering if the tourists actually thought that was what the Trojan horse must have looked like, even though this horse had a large viewing room built on the horse's back where the saddle should have been. There were even windows in the sides of the horse's flanks so the tourists could look out and take photos.

Pointing at the towering horse Kevin said. "So the Trojans took this huge gift horse that looked something like this into their city and didn't think to look inside? Come on, I don't buy that at all. Hell, it even has windows, which would suggest someone was inside. Were these people stupid, or blind, or both?"

"Perhaps they did want to look a gift horse in the mouth," Michael responded.

Meredith decided that he better discourage the negative comments before they transferred back to their mission. "Remember everyone, this was Greek mythology, and written about centuries later. There is historical documentation that much of this may never have actually occurred. There is even a school of thought that the legends written about in Homer's Iliad actually took place in Scandinavia with the Vikings, not the Greeks. But I'm sure these legends sell all sorts of trinkets. Let's go see the actual ruins and then if you want to climb up the horse we can do that later."

As a group, they all started moving west towards the archeological sites that were off in the distance. Once they climbed the hill and looked over the countryside they could see what once were massive perimeter walls and the destroyed foundations of many buildings. As they looked out they could see the Aegean Sea off in the distance, where the Greeks must have come across the Sea to wage battle on the Trojan city-state.

Meredith decided to be the historian today in the absence of the Captain. He explained, "This site dates back some 4,000 years when Troy was an important city-state trading European and Asian goods. It was the cultural center of the times located in a very strategic location. All sorts of wars were fought for this land at the junction of the continents."

"The ruins here weren't even discovered until 1822 by a Charles McLaren, and then after that were mostly unexplored, except by thieves who stole whatever artifacts may have still been intact. It wasn't until the 1870's that a German Archaeologist named Heinrich Schliemann excavated further exposing deeper ruins. He and his people took whatever else was left. Today there are protected archaeological digs going on. They have discovered nine distinct layers of civilizations built on top of prior ruins."

The Team walked around in small groups and took photographs. They read the historical markers presented in a number of languages including English to get a better feel for the historic site. But after an hour in the sun and heat, they signaled each other they were ready to head back to the Trojan horse.

When they returned, Kevin was the first to climb up as high as they would let him go. In a flash he was in the small room built on the back of the horse hanging out one of the windows.

He yelled down to the group. "You should come up here. You see the Aegean and you can see the massive site of the ruins. It's worth the climb."

"Susan, let's go. You can't let your boyfriend go up there alone." Courtney turned to Michael and said. "Come on Rick, let's go see the sites." With that they entered the base of the horse and found the interior stairs leading up through the flanks of the animal.

The other members of the group were scratching their heads trying to figure out who Sue and Rick were, but then realized the two were using their new identities. Osama and Malik just looked confused until Meredith pulled them aside and explained what was going on. Once they were told, they too started calling themselves by their new identities.

Everyone in the group eventually decided to climb into the horse and they found themselves in the largest viewing area. The size of their group scared off the other tourists from the room. They looked out the windows and could see the Aegean. Meredith pointed southwest and noted you could see their ship off in the haze about four miles away moored at the edge of the harbor breakwater.

Meredith seeing they were alone decided to utilize the moment. "People, put your hand here for a moment, you know the drill. Let's think about our mission. We can do this? Agreed?"

The group was used to Meredith's constant reinforcements. They had come to expect it. Everyone threw their hands into the center of the small room like they had done that first night in the McDonalds restaurant. They mouthed a quiet commitment to one another, as they stood in a replica of the Trojan horse. A moment later they broke the bond and headed down the stairs and out into the bright sunlight.

Ralph offered to buy everyone another soda or water. Kate ran ahead and said she was getting her Brad Pitt poster no matter what before leaving. Everyone went back to the bazaar and bought various trinkets and snacks because they knew they would be on the ship for a couple weeks crossing the Mediterranean and Red Seas.

A couple hours later they boarded the van and headed back to the pier with all their purchases. Kevin, Michael, Osama and Malik had even bought shields and swords for some swashbuckling pirate dueling on the ship.

➔ ◂

Aegean Sea

The following morning the Majorca left port early before all the pleasure craft started moving about, cutting back and forth in front of the ship. The ship got out a couple miles to the southern shipping lane and settled into a casual pace as they cruised past Lesbos Island. Kevin was begging the Captain to pull into port but Meredith insisted that the ship continue on its southerly journey.

"Kevin, I promise we will come back here some day."

They made good headway all through the day passing large and small islands and absolutely beautiful beaches, mountains and cities that looked as if they were on postcards. Everyone was enjoying the sights and wishing they were sitting on those beaches, or were bobbing in the gentle surf of the various inlets and bays they passed. In no time they were told they were officially out of the Aegean Sea and now were heading east in the Mediterranean Sea, where they would pass north of the Turkish Republic of Northern Cyprus. They were not stopping but being a traditional coaster ship, the Majorca would follow normal shipping lanes for their craft the entire trip.

That evening Meredith called the group together for dinner in the ship's small galley after the rest of the crew had eaten. As a joke he got them all seated and brought out a number of large McDonald's bags to the table. He had packed them just to remind everyone of their early meetings. Everyone started groaning.

"I kind of wish these were real," Kevin said. "Remember, I'm a growing boy and I've been on this ship two weeks already. And I'm still angry we didn't stop in Lesbos."

"It's just a very beautiful island Kevin, not a way of life," Kate said as she slugged him in the arm. "What do you think you would see lesbians on the beaches?"

"Well, I was hopeful that I would see something. But from out here all I saw was mountains and beaches," Kevin said as he got up to assist Meredith in bringing in the real dinner.

There were large plates of steaming lobsters and thick steaks. No one needed an invitation and they dove into the food. Meredith gave the cook the rest of the night off.

"Thanks boss, at least we aren't going to starve on this trip," Michael said as he reached for a steak. "We'll all look like very well fed Americans when we get to Pakistan."

Osama was relishing his steak and lobster. "Michael, I never eat this way. I will be a fat man by the time we get to Pakistan. My family there will not recognize me. We will be fat together." He stuffed a morsel of lobster meat in his mouth.

"I have sailed for years and we never got steak and lobster. The food was always good or we would have mutinied, but not this good," Uri said, smiling to the others.

"Captain, I might want to go back to the sea again if it has changed this much."

"Uri, you are a good seaman, but I can't promise such fare unless Mr. Meredith is traveling with us. But you would be welcome on my ship anytime," Captain Brinkmann said.

"I promised you I would foot the bills if we took this journey together. I figure the food is the fuel that will get us all there," Meredith said as he poured a pitcher of cold beer into the glasses across the table. "I think I had them lay in enough food to feed us well, and the rest of the crew too. Cheers."

"This is a hell of a lot better than McDonalds," Ralph said as he put his beer down and cut into his steak. "After dinner some of you haven't seen our little firecracker yet, so I thought you should all see what we are taking to our mutual enemy."

"Good idea, Ralph. With that said, all of you should be careful with what you might kick under the table. Space is at a premium around here you know," Meredith said.

That got everyone's attention and they all froze rethinking what Meredith had just said. Then like lemmings they all leaned back or sideways and took a look under the table. All conversation stopped and everyone stared at a large suitcase that was leaning against the center pedestal of the round table.

Both Ralph and Meredith laughed out loud. "I didn't mean to put a damper on things people. It's completely safe and not armed. Too valuable to be playing with, but I thought that since we have the whole team assembled now, we all should get a good look at our Trojan horse."

Ralph held up a couple of computer floppy disks and said. " Hey, really guys, we didn't mean to scare you. It's just a big paperweight right now. Enjoy your meal. Who wants more lobster?"

The conversation re-started but it was a bit more subdued. People tried to relax, but everyone scooted back a bit on the bench seats and made sure they didn't extend their legs too far under the table for the rest of the meal.

After the dishes were cleared Ralph gingerly lifted the 45-pound tactical nuclear weapon up on the table. He flipped the locksets and opened up the casing. Again the room was silent as everyone stared at the components.

Josef broke the silence. "William, I've looked over all the documentation and the manual and I was able to translate all the Russian instructions and procedures quite well. As far as I can see this thing is ready to be armed and should function as it was designed to do. I'm confident that we can make it go boom when we want to. In fact, I have some ideas about how we can make that happen."

"Excellent, Josef. I want you to sit down with Osama and Malik. They can assist with their computer skills," Meredith said and everyone listened intently.

"Hopefully, we will see if we can make some safety adjustments to this thing so it will only go off only when we want it too. These are older components that were readily produced in the late 80's so I am hopeful that it isn't too sophisticated."

The new travelers who boarded at the Troy stop stepped forward to very tentatively reach out and touch the casing. Osama and Malik reached out and fingered the Russian lettering that was stenciled on it. They looked over at Josef and nodded they would take on the responsibility.

Meredith pulled out his digital camera and said, "I just remembered that we're due to send a new message to our al Qaeda friends. This time we'll show them the actual weapon with Osama and Malik in the photo. Uri, you should be in this photo as well. You guys are the best hope we have of getting this package to the right person."

Ralph and Michael took a white sheet and stepped behind the three men and stretched the material out to neutralize the background. Uri stepped forward and joined the Pakistani brothers. "I look forward to personally delivering this gift to him, if I have to carry it up the mountain myself."

Ralph asked everyone else to step out of the camera range. He placed a recent Ukrainian newspaper on the table with the day and date prominently shown. The three men leaned into the picture and placed their arms over the edges of the bomb suitcase making sure the newspaper could be seen. Meredith took a couple of photos making sure that the Russian numerals were visible and the bomb components were clearly shown. He also made sure that the photos were neutral enough to not show they were on a ship or that other people were in the room.

Josef sat down next to the Pakistani brothers and started sharing his translated information with them. They looked at the schematics, the wiring plans and the computer manuals that were laid out on the table. Both brothers analyzed the schematics and made comments that suggested that they did indeed know what they were looking at and how they might make some adjustments to the weapon.

→ ←

The Mediterranean Sea

The Majorca made good time knifing south through the Mediterranean on even seas and under bright sunlight. It maintained a standard 12 knots and stayed on the far western edge of the international sea-lane heading south passing Lebanon, Syria, and Israel. The Captain wanted to give wide berth to Israel, thus he tried to blend into the shipping lane traffic and look as innocent as possible. He was aware that Israeli gunboats monitored all traffic passing by the country to prevent any rogue ship from making a turn east and bringing danger to the small country. If they were boarded by such naval craft, the Israeli Intelligence Services could scrutinize them. That would effectively end their mission.

They did not need that type of trouble and made every effort to sail past without so much as glancing towards the east. As they closed the distance to Egypt in the south, they turned slightly west so that they could approach the Port of Damietta, just ten miles west of the Suez Canal. They were again concerned about possible nuclear material scrutiny in the tight Suez Canal.

Having had good luck off-loading and re-boarding their package in Turkey, Uri was enlisted to repeat the slight of hand by going around the Suez Canal, where they again thought NATO and the Americans could be sniffing.

Uri, the Egyptian, would be handling the getting sick honors this time, and Ralph Behar would be his escort, as he too was of Middle Eastern origin and could more readily pass in this part of the world as a sailor. They planned to use the same ruse Michael had used in the Bosporus.

About twenty miles out in the Med, Captain Brinkmann got on the ship radio to report a very sick seaman needing assistance. He asked if the sailor could be off-loaded in the deepwater Port of Damietta. He advised they only needed to drop off the sailor and a second sailor to assist him getting to the hospital. The Captain asked if the port's pilot boat could be used to transfer him to land, and then on to a hospital by company van.

The Port Authority responded positively stating that they could assist the medical emergency and would meet the ship outside the harbor for the transfer. They also advised a customs officer would be sent out to review the seamen's papers before they would be allowed ashore. Since both men had false papers, and Uri's papers were in fact Egyptian, there was no concern about the added scrutiny.

A half-mile outside the Damietta Harbor, amidst numerous container and oil storage vessels waiting for their turns in the harbor, the Majorca dropped its bow anchor to await the pilot boat. A half-hour later they saw the small vessel rounding the breakwater. The pilot dropped a harbor pilot at a nearby container ship, and then it motored over to the Majorca. As it was pulling up to the starboard side of the ship, the forward crane was engaged and a pallet was again employed to move Uri and Ralph Behar over the side. The transfer was completed in a few minutes. The lines were quickly released and the crane pulled its winch back up and away from the vessel.

In the pilot boat Ralph Behar presented the two men's travel documents. The sick man was lying there groaning and looking quite ill. The customs officer didn't want to get anywhere close, so he quickly checked the papers, entered a hand stamp on each, and then moved to the bow of the pilot boat as quickly as he could. Mission accomplished for a second time.

Captain Brinkmann yelled down to the pilot boat captain and offering his thanks for the courtesy of the transfer. As soon as the pilot boat backed away from the Majorca, the Captain ordered the anchor pulled and the ships engines re-engaged. As he had promised the Port Authority and Customs Office, he set sail and headed east towards the Suez Canal entrance.

The pilot boat re-entered the breakwater in a matter of minutes. Ralph sat quietly in the well of the boat keeping his eye on the old sailor who really looked quite ill. He thought that stuff Meredith gave Uri must be pretty potent since Uri was groaning and clutching his stomach and it didn't look fake at all. As they approached the docks, he scanned the area and sure enough spotted a white van waiting for them. Meredith had ordered it through the shipping company.

310

At the dock, the sick sailor was carried off the boat by a couple of dockhands. Ralph Behar wheeled a rolling suitcase behind him and steered the men to the waiting white van. They loaded the sailor into the rear of the van and went back to work.

Ralph gingerly lifted the suitcase into the back and wedged it into the space between Uri and the van wall. He took the blanket that was covering Uri and threw it over the suitcase, slammed the door and trotted around to the passenger side.

The driver from the rental company was instructed to turn the vehicle over to the two sailors and asked for a ride back to Alexandria. Ralph said yes and encouraged him to drive. From the back of the van Uri spoke up. "I'm down but I'm not out, just feeling really queasy. Hand me some water will you?"

The driver headed for Alexandria and twenty minutes later he turned the vehicle over to Ralph who took over the driving.

"Head south on this highway for El Mansura about ten miles down the road," Uri croaked from the back of the van. "I just need some water and a bit of rest. I'll be fine in a little while, and then I'll give you a driving tour. We have at least a half-day to kill before catching up with the ship in Suez on the other end of the Canal."

"Here's that water. William said you should take a couple of these pain pills now and they'll make you feel a whole lot better." Ralph handed back the pills.

"I hope so." He propped himself up and was able to see out the window. Eventually he said, "The Canal is just over there about ten miles. In between are the ruins of ancient civilizations at Tanis and Ismailia. I've mostly seen them from the water."

"So where are the pyramids?"

"As we head south towards Cairo, you'll seem them off to the right in the distance. I'll point them out as we drive. Now let me rest for a few minutes. Without the boats movement anymore I am feeling better already."

"Uri, I'll try to drive carefully and nurse you back to health."

➔ ←

NSA, Ft. Meade, MD

The Conference room was completely secure deep within one of the main buildings on the National Security Agency campus. The diverse group of security bureaucrats, from the FBI, CIA and Homeland Security, had assembled and they were helping themselves to sweet rolls and coffee when the door opened and Karen Lee, Assistant Director of the CIA, walked in with Bill Dalde.

"Good morning, everyone. Thank you all for coming. Please take a seat." Everyone found a leather chair around the mahogany table and settled in.

With a nod Karen Lee said hello to those in the room that she already knew, and asked that the others identify themselves and their agency. Everyone in the room quickly gave their name, agency and title. Almost everyone was involved in homeland security in some way, shape or form, and everyone had top security clearance. All the important players were assembled.

"In front of you is a red file concerning a possible nuclear threat to the United States that is starting to look pretty real. It started out innocently enough, but now has taken on some sinister ramifications with the Russians acknowledgement that they have misplaced, or had stolen, one of their old suitcase weapons, that was still functionally capable. Bill, I'd like you to bring everyone up to speed on this situation, from the beginning, please."

"As you know, I'm one of the Echelon Analysts here at NSA, and my job is to analyze all your phone calls, emails, computer files and Facebook pages that Echelon reviews on a daily basis." He smiled and said. "Its 99.99% pretty boring stuff, although some of your Facebook photos are rather interesting."

"Can it Bill, were not here to scare them with your big brother machine, let's move it along."

"I apologize, Karen, couldn't resist." He looked back at his notes and started in. "About five months ago we started picking up on some abbreviated phone chatter in the New York Tri-State area. Calls that were short, out of context, and kept including some code, or name that sounded like THCT."

"What are those initials exactly?" someone said from the other end of the table.

"THCT. We aren't sure what they stand for, but they haven't disappeared, in fact those same letters are starting to appear in our overseas messages as well. And in some troubling spots like France, Lebanon, Egypt, Russia and Pakistan. That got our attention and we started a file and did some investigating. A couple weeks later I spoke to my counterpart at CIA, Bede Long and he set up an appointment with Karen's Division."

"That's when the CIA, FBI, and Homeland Security got involved to do some domestic and international snooping and see what this THCT acronym actually stands for." Karen Lee picked up the file sitting before them and asked Jeff Madison, the SAC in the FBI New York Office to continue.

"Thanks Karen, our New York guys did some investigation and didn't find much initially, but we did stumble on a real run on Trac phones at all the discount stores and Best Buys in the Tri-State area, all within a two week period about four or five months ago. They checked through a mountain of store camera tapes and found some NY cab drivers that looked middle-eastern buying the phones. They tracked down those leads."

"Don't you love field work? And everyone thinks it's glamorous!" another person said from the far end of the table said.

" We're also trying to match those specific phone numbers to Bill's data at NSA, and so far twelve such calls have already surfaced as THCT related. The phones were used once and must have been tossed because they haven't appeared again. That alone is pretty hinky. We now have a dozen agents tracking any and all leads in the New York area."

"Thanks, Jeff." She turned to the other side of the table. "Bede and Perry, could you comment from CIA's standpoint?"

Bede looked at Perry Clarke deferring to him as the senior Agency person in the room, second in rank to Karen Lee.

"We've had some people do a look see at a number of locations overseas that keep popping up on the NSA computer. We also didn't find much initially, but Bill's tracking and posting site references in France led us to the 'Jungle' refugee camp for Afghanis near Calais. It is a known transfer point for al Qaeda. We have someone that is pretty close to that situation and he advised there has been some al Qaeda activity in recent months and that he heard the letters THCT whispered by some suspected terrorists in conversations. Nothing really concrete but the field agent's information blended nicely with the raw data Bill has accumulated. We're expanding our search to some of the other sites in Egypt, Lebanon and a new contact we just had in Turkey."

Bill Dalde thought that the discussion needed summarizing. "These call letters keep popping up in various phone conversations, emails and even some encrypted satellite calls that we are monitoring. Just a couple days ago we picked up conversations coming in from Pakistan, from people that we think are very close to bin Laden. All things seem to be pointing to something very bad."

"Which is why you are all here." Karen took the floor again. "As some of you already know we've determined the Russians have indeed admitted to losing one of their old 80's suitcase bombs, and thus this situation is going to the front burner. A couple of those THCT referenced calls emanated from Novorossiysk, Russia, where their nuclear arsenal is kept under lock and key, or so we thought. Thus, we think we have a real terrorist threat on our hands, and New York may be the target again. We need to go active."

With that preamble the discussion broke into a number of small groups. Like people from different agencies were comparing notes, suggesting plans for getting better information flowing, and trying to clarify what they were going up against. Every known element was dissected and looked at from different viewpoints.

Each Agency took on certain responsibilities and assignments. The CIA would get their field agents to explore every international angle. The FBI would do the same domestically, centering their attention on the New York Tri-State area. The military advised they would add additional people to the roster going to Novorossiysk, Russia for the disarmament talks. The CIA asked if they could be part of that team as well to get a different kind of insight about the nuclear encampment.

CIA Director Karen Lee asked everyone to maintain a high level of security for this investigation and requested daily reports be funneled to a special Task Force office that was being set up in her office. She asked that Bill Dalde and Bede Long act as coordinators of all the information being gathered and distributed. She closed the meeting by asking everyone to make this a priority. A terrorist group was planning a strike!

Suez Canal, Egypt

The Majorca, headed east passed a number of large, shallow brackish lakes on the Mediterranean coastline, home to all sorts of small boat fishing fleets. Port Said was next on the western side of the Suez Canal, and Port Fouad was on the eastern shore. The Majorca radioed their position and ship's name for the Canal Zone authorities. The company had already filed the necessary paperwork to traverse the Suez Canal. The Manifest stated the cargos that were being shipped, ports of call that were on the itinerary, and the timing of the Canal passage. The ship was given a position to transverse the Canal, and pass through the desert land known as the Ancient Cradle of Civilization.

Since the earliest days of humanity, the Nile River Valley has drawn traders and travelers from around the known world. The area has known civilization for over 5,000 years and was the crossroads of the Asian, African and Mediterranean worlds, where trade took place and helped the world to grow and diversify. From space you can see a seventy-five mile strip of lush fertile land running north and south. It is nestled between deserts and wastelands east and west. This fertile greenway is fed by one of the World's greatest rivers, the 4,000-mile Nile River, providing fresh water and turning desert into farmland.

The Majorca entered the Suez Canal, which was wide and expansive at the entry point. The ship easily passed between numerous freight docks with large gantry cranes loading and off-loading containers, between bulk carrier ships being top loaded, and oil storage and refinery facilities that could be seen on both sides of the Canal.

"Captain, why didn't we just stop here and off-load Uri?" Kate said as she watched the passing dockyards and piers on both sides of the ship. "Seems like we went to a lot of trouble down the coast dropping Uri and Ralph."

"Well, I may be a bit overly suspicious, but had we pulled in here we may have had the scrutiny of those nuclear radioactive watchdogs on us in no time. I'm guessing they have such sniffing efforts here as well. And this isn't even the tightest area yet. Wait until we get another mile down the Canal. It narrows down to about five hundred feet from shore to shore and ships pass in both directions within fifty feet of one another. We decided why take a chance on someone smelling something radioactive and singling us out."

"I see, I guess that makes sense. Remember, I didn't pass through the Bosporus." Looking ahead and pointing downstream, Kate said. "It does get narrow, up ahead doesn't it?"

"It does indeed young lady, and now if you don't mind I've got to concentrate. I'm not worried about hitting anyone. I'm worried they may hit us."

"Aye, Aye Captain. I'll be quiet as a mouse."

The Majorca kept its pace with the ship in front of it by about two thousand yards. The Captain knew that bringing a ship to a halt in these tight quarters would take a good distance, short of changing course, and then evading other ships going the opposite direction. He needed to pay attention to the spacing and speed of the ships around him as he traversed the Canal.

The water was calm and small commercial fishing boats gave leeway to the larger shipping vessels that ran down the channel. A bit further and the main channel split in two with an industrial island in between allowing the ship traffic to separate. As this was a more open area, many ships were in the channel at anchor.

Everyone was on deck taking in the view. Off in the distance they could see the tops of the Pyramids of Giza and Saqqara through the desert haze and ozone of Cairo. Focusing downstream they passed under a highway bridge that actually crossed over the Canal and they could hear the traffic above their heads. Then further down the Canal the ship actually went over a highway tunnel that passed underneath the deepwater passage. While the Canal had few crossings, they saw a number of man-made water canals that traversed the ships Canal, bringing water to the fertile farm fields on the Cairo side. They then went under a single rail bridge that easily spanned over their heads.

The Captain expertly maneuvered the ship into Great Bitter Lake, which was a shallow, large body of water more than a mile across and a couple miles long. This was home to a huge fishing fleet that plied the waters of the Gulf of Suez to the south and provided seafood to all of Cairo.

Cutting straight through the middle of the lake was a well-marked deep-water channel that was constantly being dredged to keep the passage open for shipping. The channel took them safely into Little Bitter Lake, which was still twenty miles from the southern entrance to the Canal. The rest of the Canal trip was uneventful, which was exactly what everyone wanted.

An hour later they pulled into Port Tanfiq, which was a scheduled stop for delivery of the oil rigging and processing equipment that had been picked up in Russia three weeks earlier. Meredith had specifically set up this industrial shipment to allow the ship to have a reason to dock for a day and a half, offloading the equipment. He knew the equipment would just sit in this warehouse until he sent another ship to pick it up, but it served the purpose he wanted. Once the equipment was off loaded there would be little activity on the dock and the two radioactive travelers would be able to re-board without anyone paying any attention.

From his small cabin, Meredith made a short satellite phone call to Ralph Behar and Uri Navroz traveling somewhere in Cairo. He stated they were at the rendezvous point. He signed off THCT. The call bounced off three commercial satellites floating one hundred miles in space, to a front company shipping office in Panama, and from there went through another satellite to a storefront travel agency in Athens, and then back to Egypt and Cairo.

Ralph Behar answered the satellite phone with a nondescript "Yes?" and listened to the short message from Meredith. Without giving any name he responded with an "Excellent, THCT," and cut the connection. He turned to Navroz. "They've docked in Tanfiq as planned and expect us tomorrow. So we have a couple hours to kill. How about seeing Cairo and the pyramids?"

➔ ◄

Port Tanfiq, Gulf of Suez

The day following the transfer of the package, the unloading process was finished on time, and the local dockworkers wandered off to another job over on the next pier. Driving the van along the dock frontage road, Uri saw the dock was completely empty, so he drove through a chain link gate and into the yard. He was prepared to stop if challenged by anyone, stating he was just returning to his ship after a day of drinking in town.

As he pulled up to the Majorca gangway, he stopped and Ralph jumped out in the shadows of the afternoon sun and casually walked up the gangway. He was pulling his 45-pound suitcase behind him.

Once Ralph was on board and out of site, Uri pulled away from the gangway and drove over to the side of one of the storage buildings. He parked the vehicle in the deepest corner of the building, and wiped the last of his fingerprints off the steering wheel. The vehicle would be abandoned because it had been rented in Alexandria with a false passport, in an office without cameras that recorded the comings and goings of customers.

He sauntered over to the ship and up the gangway stopping only to casually flick a cigarette into the water. As he stepped on deck he saluted the Captain and Meredith and said. "Reporting for duty, Sirs. I had a wonderful time seeing the Cradle of Civilization."

"Welcome back sailor. Did I notice a bit of a bounce in your step?" Meredith said. "Glad to see those pills wore off and you're feeling better. We're ready to cast off."

"Aye, Aye Sir! I'll not volunteer for that duty again. Someone else can eat their own intestines."

"Hopefully, that will be our last group sickness, until we give some hurt to bin Laden."

"But that hurt will be instantaneous," he snapped his finger. "I thought I was going to die for 12 hours."

"I'm glad your feeling better. Ready for some good food again?"

"Aye, aye Sir."

The Majorca eased away from the dock and followed the channel markers back to the deep-water trough in the center of the lake. As he went to half-speed, Captain Brinkmann found the gap he was looking for and pulled into the line like a thoroughbred easing to the rail for the sprint to the finish.

In no time they were back in the deep blue waters of the Gulf of Suez heading southeast with the Sinai on their left and Egypt's Eastern Desert on the right. The Gulf opened up as a much wider body of water allowing substantial separation between ships moving in both directions. They were now sandwiched in between two oil tankers that were riding high in the water, obviously empty and returning for another quarter million gallons of the black gold.

Captain Brinkmann was now much more relaxed and it showed. He was smiling and pleased that they were clear of danger for the moment. Meredith joined him on the bridge and they lit up a couple of cigars. As soon as the cigars were lit and producing a rich aroma, the rest of the THCT team came running to join in. Courtney and Kate even reached for the thick Cubans and decided to give them a try. It got so crowded on the bridge the Captain suggested they all go aft for some air.

The group of counter terrorists assembled on the bow in the fresh air and attempted to blow smoke rings but the hot windless air wrecked their efforts as soon as they exhaled. They sat with their legs on the rails and watched the late afternoon sun dance off the desert shores. As they looked to the southern Sinai, Captain Brinkmann pointed to a couple of tall mountains far off in the distance and asked if anyone knew what they were called.

"I don't know my biblical readings very well, but I do remember that Sinai was where Moses went up to a mountain to get the Ten Commandments," Courtney said. She had allowed her cigar to die a graceless death and was now using it as a pointer.

"That was a good guess, Court," the Captain said. "The highest peak on the left is where St. Catherine's Monastery is built, the biblical site of the burning bush that spoke to Moses. After centuries in this location the Monastery is still an active and important religious center venerated by a number of religions."

Kevin Geary was perfecting the art of blowing perfect smoke rings and decided to add a bit of levity to the conversation.

"All I remember about the burning bush was from the movie, the Three Amigos, where Steve Martin, Chevy Chase and Marty Short, get lost in the Mexican desert and Chevy Chase shoots a burning bush for talking back to him."

Half the group had no idea what he was talking about, and even those that did, let the statement stand without any comeback. Kevin smiled at everyone and went back to blowing smoke rings.

"The peak on the right is actually Mount Sinai, otherwise known as Mount Moses, the biblical scene of the Ten Commandments, so you were very close. I'm told you can walk up there, if you're fit and in good health. The climb is pretty steep, and the peak is just about 7,500 feet above sea level." The Captain looked over at Geary and said, "That leaves you out Kevin. You'll be dead by this evening if you keep sucking in all that smoke."

Everyone laughed. Meredith had wandered away for a few minutes but came back bearing a couple of six packs of cold beer and two orange soda soft drinks. "This always helps me when I'm eating smoke." He passed the six- packs around and handed the soft drinks to the Pakistani Brothers. Everyone broke off a can and eagerly popped the tops.

Meredith raised his beer to call for a toast. "I would like to thank you all for the parts you have played in getting us this far. Truth be told, I didn't know if we would get this far. Hell, I wasn't even sure we would ever get our hands on the little monster."

"Well we did!" Osama and Malik chimed in, "Cheers!" The two Pakistanis were getting into these western self-congratulatory parties, even if they were only drinking pop.

"Thank you boys, you have been instrumental in getting us this far. Josef, you produced our weapon when we had no idea of how to accomplish such a thing and the rest of you have each played an important roll in our quest for bin Laden's head. We can make this happen. The next few weeks will tell the story. Let's drink now, so that we can keep clear heads in future days."

He again raised his drink in salute, and the others brought their beers together so violently that there was a small explosion of froth, beer and orange soda.

The group downed their drinks and then began drifting off to their responsibilities and some to an early dinner. Michael and Kevin offered to hold a handgun class in the hold below water level where no sounds would bellow into the desert. They reminded everyone that the ship would soon be in pirate waters off the coast of Somalia. Courtney, Kate and the Pakistani's all jumped at the chance to shoot a few rounds. The Captain returned to the bridge and Meredith asked Josef to walk with him around the ship.

"Josef, I was checking my email and heard that Russia has advised the U.S. privately the loss or theft of a small nuclear device. Might you send a message to your brother-in-law and find out if he has been affected by this discovery?"

"I'm concerned I might not reach him now, but perhaps I can at least find out his status by going through family. Are you sure that an email can't be traced to us?"

"My IT people tell me my calls and email are safe from all over the world. They don't know why they are bouncing my signals around the world, but they say I am safe. I'd like to know we have not caused problems for Dimitri. That would take a load off my mind for the moment."

"I understand William. That would be my concern as well. But please remember, he agreed because he lost a sister in 9-11, just as I lost a wife, and you lost a son. He hates bin Laden as much as we do. He made his decision and I am proud of him for it. Plus we learned how to fish."

Meredith laughed. "That is the reason I want to know he is safe. I promised him I would get him out of there if necessary and set him up in Wisconsin as a fishing guide. We gave him good traveling documents to get out if he needs to, so if he is in trouble, I can send Ryan and the plane anywhere he wants to get him out of there. He should know that. After dinner, we will craft a carefully worded email that perhaps your family could send on to him. Let's see if we get any response. It would make me feel better, rather than hanging him out to dry, after all he has done for our cause."

"I like that, I'll send a message after dinner."

➔ ◄

The Red Sea

The Majorca cruised steadily south along the 1,440-mile long Red Sea, a tropical body of water just north of the Equator, with a depth of up to 7,000 ft., and some 200 miles across. The Red Sea has been a major seafaring waterway connecting the Mediterranean to the Indian Ocean with some 21,000 commercial ships traversing yearly. There are 3,000 miles of uninterrupted desert coastlines with soaring cliffs, sandy beaches. The azure waters are teaming with marine life, coral reefs and over 1,200 species of fish. It's a diver's paradise, with such clarity you can see underwater 100 feet at night with a full moon.

The deep blue body of water was crystal clear. There was nothing but desert on both sides, Africa and Egypt to starboard, and Saudi Arabia to port. But with the Majorca sailing south out in the center of the shipping lanes, the shorelines could not be seen without the powerful binoculars. While shipping was still moving in both directions, the traffic was now spread out with 10-20 miles between vessels. The Majorca's radar tracked the coming and going of all the commercial traffic.

It was a peaceful day at sea for a change, the group was not evading Russian ships, slipping past Israeli gunboats, or trying to sneak people and bombs off and back on the ship. Almost everyone was relaxing, catching some extra shuteye, shooting target practice off the stern, or just spending time lounging on deck in the hot sun.

The Captain had advised them not to lower a boat to go swimming because the Red Sea was known for its voracious sharks. He shared this shark information in another one of his many national geographic moments that he took such joy in presenting. Taking the shark threat seriously, the THCT team kept them selves cool by hooking up a fire hose on deck, and setting a fine spray to cut the heat. It did the job.

But not everyone was able to enjoy the weather. Josef, Uri and the Pakistani boys were holed up below deck, in the windowless galley pouring over the weapon manuals, searching for some way to alter the bomb to their advantage. They had come up with some ideas and discussed the merits of each. After careful reading and discussion they were pretty confident in understanding the bomb's makeup and mechanics. They were ready to test some arming and disarming sequences, following the manual directions. Meredith came down to see how they were doing.

Josef having scrutinized the Russian language manual, written for field personnel use, felt comfortable suggesting that they could be armed by almost anyone that had read the manuals. "This class of weapon was built so an agent in the field, in some embassy, could pull it out of a closet, arm the thing and then set the bomb off. The mechanics were kept pretty basic. Luckily they were never used."

"So what you're saying is even we should be able to set this thing off when we want to?" Meredith asked hopefully.

"That's about it. We set the codes and then stand back and it goes boom," Josef responded throwing his arms up and out.

"How far back?" Uri said already aware that he planned on being on the delivery team.

"Way back, I think," Meredith said. "We were told this thing could level a medium sized city."

"So how do we live through the boom, especially if we are in some cave at the top of a mountain?" Malik asked. "While I'm willing to pull the trigger myself, if I can live to see him dead, that would be even better!"

The men continued to discuss how they might make that happen and finally settled on a rather simple solution. The THCT team would deliver the suitcase weapon, collect their final payment, and verify the monies had been wired to a safe location. While waiting for these financial matters to be taken care of, the team would offer to demonstrate how to arm and disarm the weapon. They would readily share the instructions, both Russian and with subtitle notes in English. They would also demonstrate the sequencing procedures any number of times, proving it to be safe from premature detonation.

To complete the mission and detonate the bomb when they wanted to, the key was in the arming and detonation procedures. The question was whether they could alter the sequencing, deliver the bomb and then leave the area before detonation?

To do this they decided they would need to adjust the Russian manuals, and the English subtitles that Josef had been working on for two weeks. They would build in a special trigger code that would change the arming and detonation sequence. The al Qaeda terrorists training on the weapon would actually make the change themselves, and they would actually detonate the bomb.

Once bin Laden had his weapon, he would start to devise a plan for its use with his terrorist leaders. And they would begin the process of training their field personnel to deliver and detonate the bomb. In preparing for such a terrorist act, a calamity far bigger than 9-11, the terrorists would routinely test the firing mechanisms and when they did, it would blow up in their faces, taking Bin Laden and his terrorists to meet the virgins in paradise. The only question was how would the delivery team members get safely out of harms way?

Osama, Malik and Uri had already volunteered to be part of the delivery team they would blend in the best, being from Pakistan and Egypt.

"William, I will carry this bomb on my back, up the mountain, if I need to," Malik said, and his brother nodded his head in agreement.

"I too will carry the suitcase up the mountain to bin Laden," Uri said quickly. Pointing to the brothers, he said. "You are both young and should live to start new families. I am old, and I'm prepared to die to get the revenge we all seek. I will be the one to stay and see the thing through."

"Gentlemen, your enthusiasm is remarkable. If I could blend in better, I would go with you as well, but I have another idea I've been toying with that may get all of you off the mountain without a scratch," Meredith said, and then went on. "We just received word the Russians have very quietly advised the Americans that a nuclear weapon is missing. We heard that from our General friend. I would think that information will eventually be picked up by the bad guys as well," Meredith said this while still organizing his thoughts. He went on with a statement he thought to be true. "But the Russians have not acknowledged how many weapons are missing. Perhaps, we could make bin Laden think we have more than one bomb in our control." He said this as he picked up the photos of the bomb that they'd sent to the terrorists.

"What if I also came along for the delivery, playing the role of the international weapons dealer, that we have said we are? I would be the one who secured this suitcase weapon, or is it weapons? I could advise bin Laden that we may have more weapons that could be made available for an additional tariff. I would think he would jump at the chance to obtain additional bombs, and he would gladly pay for them, once he sees we really have the first sample. And I think it might also prevent him from biting the hand that is feeding him."

The Pakistani's looked confused with the hand biting reference, but said nothing. Uri looked as if he understood what Meredith was suggesting, but he too remained silent.

"I think with the promise of more weapons, bin Laden would want to treat us well. We may have to sit up on the mountain for a while, but I could stomach breaking bread with the bastard, knowing he would be dead soon enough. What do you think? Could we pull it off?"

Josef, had been quiet up to this point, but now spoke.

"I think that scenario could work, but, I would also like to come along. I could be your Russian bomb expert. I could show them that we know what we are doing with the weapon. I could help them translate the Russian training manual and show them the sequencing procedures, including the code changes that would later trigger their demise. I want in too!"

"Hold on Josef, before we know it we'll have the whole damn team traipsing up that mountain, and we don't even know where we're going yet," Meredith said, although as he thought about what Josef had said he admitted it would complement the scenario he had just dreamed up.

"Before we go charging up the hill like Teddy Roosevelt, let's get some additional opinions. How about we broach this subject to the rest of the team at dinner and see what they think of the plan?"

Everyone in the galley thought that was a good idea. They carefully closed the small but deadly thermonuclear devise casing and locked the latches. Josef and O carried it back to the lead lined box in the engine room. Meredith went to spread the word about a dinner meeting with the rest of the THCT group.

→ ←

Bagram Airfield, Kabul, Afghanistan

Most of the air traffic had ceased for the day at the United States' largest air base in Afghanistan. The daily log of combat missions and related activity was winding down when two UH-60 DAP Blackhawk's, and one Boeing Chinook helicopter were rolled out of their steel fabricated bunkers and prepped for departure. The sun was setting in the western sky dipping behind the mountains of west Afghanistan. In the waning twilight twenty-five soldiers walked out of the bunker with full battle gear in tow. They nodded to their superiors standing to the side, and started saddling up for a mission.

SEAL Team Six was one of the best counterterrorist units in the world. Part of the Joint Special Operations Command (JSOC), they had been training for two months for this Operation code-named Geronimo. Until they were airborne, they would not get final confirmation what the target would be, but many had strong suspicions about what their mission was all about. At least they hoped it would be Him. They had been training for this for many years and everyone was professionally excited about the prospect.

Battle tested, these highly trained soldiers carefully packed their gear, each responsible for various battlefield specialties, while at the same time all qualified deadly killing machines. The group split into two almost equal units and loaded into the two Blackhawk attack helicopters. With that many bodies plus the two pilots and two crew chief/gunners, it was a tight fit. But everyone found a place because no one wanted to be left behind for this covert operation.

Given clearance to depart, the helicopters moved out onto the tarmac, following direction from flight control. The pilots saluted and elevated their machines, immediately rising north heading into the Afghan mountains.

Their ride was the military's workhorse helicopter. The UH-60, Direct Action Penetrator (DAP) was a fighting machine that had seen battle all over the world. With more than a dozen adaptable platforms used by all the branches of the U.S. military and many of its allies, it could fly attack and penetration missions, support ground troops, act as transport ships, coordinate rescue efforts and handle field medical evac.

The Sikorsky Aircraft Company had been building them since the 70's adapting them as military needs changed. The four-bladed, top-rotor craft could move fast exceeding speeds of over 180 mph. It could reach a ceiling height of some 19,000 feet (5,790 meters). The sixty-five foot length and eight foot width gave it a long narrow profile. With the 25 foot rotors folded, the craft could be easily transferred anywhere in a C-130 Hercules Transport to any theater of war in the world.

As the Special Ops Team Six flew north into the darkness at a cruising speed of 170 mph they received the confirmation they were hoping to hear. The Team Chief clicked his throat mic once signaling both crews in the two choppers and said, "I think you all know what were doing here tonight.

But to make it official, we are going to collect, or kill Osama bin Laden. We have a green light, direct from the White House Situation Room, to get the son-of-a-bitch."

There was no hurrah or applause. Each operator knew what was coming. The Chief looked at his SEAL Team crowded into the helicopter shoulder-to-shoulder. He made eye contact with each operator. He saw they were ready, and confidently excited. He knew the fires were burning in their bellies, as they were about to participate in their own military version of the Super Bowl.

"You've practiced this for months, so I have no doubts we will be successful. Remember, this will be for every person who died on 9-11. Let's make it count, because we may never get a second chance."

Looking at one another with determination, they realized they were going to be making history, ridding the world of one of the most heinous terrorists ever encountered. They knew what they would be facing, and now they knew who they were after, dead or alive.

With a ferrying range of over 1,300 miles with ETS stub wings, and External Stores Support System (ESSS) mounted, they could fly north into the mountains and then east into Pakistan over very lightly populated areas to minimize early warning. Once they were there they would go in hot and with guns blazing.

Turning south out of the mountains they dropped below all searching radars and raced down the Swat River Valley hugging the terrain a mere 35 feet off the ground. With the lights of the small town of Mingaora off in the distance, the two craft turned east and started a climb over another range of mountains. Ten minutes later they bridged the peak and settled into the Indus River Valley again heading south towards the TarBela Dam Project, which provided much of the electricity for northern Pakistan. They stayed west of their target city of Abbottabad. If they had gone further north and circled around to approach from the east they would have entered airspace over the Kashmir region, which has been a hotly contested border dispute between India and Pakistan for decades. This so-called Line of Control had armed camps on both sides with thousands of troops facing one another, always looking for a fight. It was not the place for two military helicopters, that weren't supposed to be there, to wander through their airspace. Any unusual activity on the ground, or in the air, would start another border war.

Thus, the two helicopters stayed west of Abbottabad flying at tree top level. Flying over the Khyber Pakhtunkhwa Region and the black waters of the massive Tarbela Dam, the pilot's signaled they were 20 miles out from the target. The SEAL's silently made final preparations checking weapons and equipment, and crosschecked their seatmates. They already had their game faces on.

A third of the operators would be carrying M4A1 Assault Rifles. Another third would have HK MP5 9mm Submachine guns as their primary weapon. Others would carry Benelli M4 Super 90 Tactical Shotguns used to breach doors, and get hostiles attention. The Team also had M14 Sniper Rifles available for perimeter coverage and M203 Grenade Launchers if walls needed to be breached. Every SEAL also carried a personal MK23 Model O .45 caliber, or M11 Sig Sauer P228's handgun. That was their choice. They had the firepower necessary to do the job.

Red Sea – Bab-el-Mandeb Straits

The Majorca was still sailing south in calm weather and making good time. It would reach the narrow southern mouth of the Red Sea, the Bab-el-Mandeb Strait, in less than a day. At that point the waterway narrowed to less than twenty miles across. While this was one of those natural geographic pinch points that ships past through, there would not be any monitoring station because it was mostly desert and uninhabited land masses on both sides of the Strait. There had been a military installation on the peninsula years before, and even an airstrip, but the Yemeni government had abandoned them years ago. The government had their hands full fighting the rebels and tribes in the northern and eastern mountains.

Once through this desolate pinch point, where there were only a few small fishing villages, the ship would enter into the Gulf of Aden, in more recent years known as Pirate Alley, and eventually the Indian Ocean.

At 6:00 pm, 18:00 military time, the THCT group met for dinner in the ship's small galley. They had fresh fish caught off the side of the ship. Everyone enjoyed themselves but noted there was no wine and beer on the table this evening. That meant that an official meeting would be following dinner. Once the meal was done and the cook cleared out of the galley, they locked the door and the meeting started.

Meredith stood and said, "People, I'm pleased to announce that we've come up with a solid plan to deliver the bomb and get it to detonate once it's in bin Laden's hands. And we're also working on getting the whole team out in one piece. I've grown to like you folks, you're family, and I'd hate to leave anyone behind. What is it the Marines always say? "Leave no man behind!"

Kevin spoke up first and said, "Yes Sir, and the Marines mean it. It should be our solemn pact as well, Sir."

"Stop with the sirs, Kevin. I agree, we will not leave any man, or woman, behind! To continue, we've got the bomb set-up now so we can kill the bastard. It's ready to go. It's just we all want to get off the mountain to savor the day, so, here is what we have come up with."

Everyone listened intently, because this was the payoff, what they all had traveled across the earth to do and dearly wanted to see to completion.

Meredith continued, "We already know that O, Malik and Uri are willing to carry the weapon up the mountain to bin Laden. Because they speak the language and will pass for natives, they volunteered for the delivery duty early on. I can't argue that concept. But we also want them to come back down the mountain, and not in little pieces."

Ralph interrupted, "Don't you think bin Laden and his boys are going to be a bit suspect if they try to leave. I would think they'd insist on them staying."

"I agree, Ralph. My guess is they may even feel they are expendable once the weapon is delivered. These bastards could just try to kill them."

"So how do we prevent that from happening? Kate said, all of a sudden very concerned about the welfare of the two brothers and Uri.

"That's the challenge. Once they have the weapon, they could kill the delivery team, unless......" he trailed off so he could grab everyone's attention. "Unless, we make them believe we can deliver additional weapons of mass destruction,......for future terrorist acts! If we could do that, they wouldn't want to mess with any of us. They'd want to nurture the relationship."

"And not bite the hand that feeds it," Osama said this beaming with pride because he had figured out what Meredith had meant when he made the same comment earlier.

"You got it O, if we make them believe we have more weapons, they'll treat us like the international arms dealers we're supposed to be. So I think we should play up the arms dealer angle completely."

"And how do we do that?" Courtney said playing her traditional skeptic role to the hilt.

"Well, I would go along on the delivery team as the international arms dealer, to offer an even better deal to bin Laden."

And so he wouldn't get cut out of the developing plan, Josef quickly piped in, "And I'd go along as his Russian translator and bomb technician!"

All of the team readily saw what was going on and jumped into the conversation.

"Well then, I'm going too, as the arms dealer's financier, because that's how we do it in this gun-running business," Ralph Behar said this smiling smugly. He wasn't getting left behind. He had a score to settle.

"Hold on, hold on, before we know it we will all be riding donkeys up the mountain," Meredith said as everyone started to find themselves a job on the team.

"So what do we get to do?" Michael said, pointing to himself and Kevin Geary.

"You two could be our muscle, as the Captain often calls Kevin. Any self-respecting international arms dealer would have a crack security team with him, to act as bodyguards, and give us some firepower if we needed it, although I doubt they would allow us to keep weapons in the camp anywhere near bin Laden."

"That's fine, as long as we get to see the whites of his eyes just like you do," Kevin said and relaxed, knowing he would get to be a part of the delivery team.

"So what are we, chopped liver?" Courtney and Kate said almost in unison as they sat at one end of the table.

Meredith looked down the table at the two women and said, "I figured you would say that! But the facts are, in that part of Pakistan in the Federal Tribal Territories, swarming with angry Taliban and Muslims, wherever the hell it is, women would just not be acceptable. You would draw all sorts of unwanted attention to the team. It would just incite the hell out of them, making everyone edgy and trigger-happy. If you two came along, we might be defeated before we actually get up there to see the bastard."

"I know you're right, but it's unfair us two women have to be relegated to the peanut gallery," Kate said, "I came on this trip because I wanted to be a part of the effort, and look the asshole that killed my Father right in the eyes, just before we blew him up."

"I understand Kate, and you too Courtney, you have both been instrumental parts of this operation. Courtney, you been flying all over the place putting pieces in place. Kate, your documents have gotten us this far and I still have important tasks for you to accomplish on this boat if you're willing." Meredith knew he had to sell this. "In order to pull this off we'll need some crack electronic tomfoolery, to make them believe we have more of these little monsters up our sleeves. Do you still have all your computer gear with you? Can you take our bomb photos and multiply them, add new serial numbers, and make them all look slightly different? What we need is something that will make them believe we have more bombs stacked up somewhere that may be available for sale."

"That's not the same as going up the mountain, but yeah, I can do whatever you want. We could even stage a whole cache of weapons in some locker, take photos from different angles and make them believe we have a warehouse full of these bad boys. I can do that stuff, but I'm still not going to be there am I? Damn!…… Yeah, I'll be a good girl and do my job. But I won't like it."

"Ok, that leaves little orphan Annie here, "Courtney said, pointing to herself. "You pulled Kate in but I'm still watching from the peanut gallery and I want something to do."

"Court, that's fair, and I've been thinking. We need someone that could be on the other end, back in the office so to speak, to respond to our inquiries from the mountain and from al Qaeda, send whatever we may need to carry out the charade, and be our eyes and ears once we are up on the mountain. If anyone could do that and be creative when I don't quite know what we may need, it would be you. I also think we need you to coordinate with Ryan, and have the jet positioned somewhere nearby. If we actually pull this off, we may need quick extraction."

"Yeah, yeah, yeah, I get it, someone has to live to tell this story," she said as she held her hands up conceding she would be a team player too, "Just kidding! I'll play the role of Chief Bottle Cook & Washer and keep an eye on all you Indians. But I expect you all back on the reservation."

"What Indians? We aren't going to India are we?" Osama asked confused as usual.

The Pakistani's were completely lost on the reference to the Chief and Indians but they had learned to just accept all the crazy American talk. Everyone else seemed to be satisfied with all that had been said.

"It's agreed then," Meredith said to the table as a whole. "The whole team now has new assignments to get used to. "

He looked from one person to another. " Ralph, I think some financial spreadsheets are in order. Let's figure out what we could charge for five additional suitcase weapons. Maybe we can come up with some two-for-one sale concept. Let's talk."

"Josef, I like your idea of being my Russian counterpart. You can allude to how the weapons have been secured, how we can secure some even larger ordinance in the future. You should probably think through how you would explain all that."

"Michael and Kevin, I need you two to be the muscle guarding us. I think we brought along enough hardware to put on a good show. I may ask you to demonstrate the weapons if need be, so let's come up to speed on all the toys we have in the locker before we depart the ship."

Meredith continued scanning the room, O, Malik and Uri, you and I will need to talk through how we present ourselves so we have a solid story. You will still be the front men, but once we get there, I will take over with you assisting in translations and such."

"Kate and Courtney, let's meet tomorrow and get the graphics worked out. We will need to set up some cut-outs for the satellite phones we will use for the trip so that we can communicate."

"Ok people, it's a wrap. Thanks for all your help. Tomorrow we sail into the Gulf of Aden where the pirates have been operating and causing problems for shipping. This afternoon the Captain spoke to some container ships and a tanker heading north. They said there was a lot of small boat activity out in the middle of the Gulf. Small boats out in the open sea are unusual, because they are so unstable in the rolling sea. That could mean they are pirates working the shipping lanes, looking for an easy target. Once we pass through the Strait, I think we will set up 24 hour watches, especially at night."

→ ←

Abbottabad, Pakistan

Hugging the terrain on their approach, the helicopters made a hell of a lot of noise passing over Abbottabad, but there was no other way to get boots on the ground quickly. As they passed over the last few housetops the pilots spotted the compound ahead in the moonlight and made their run. The plan was to go in hot and fast, hover over the compound and have the SEAL Team rappel down to clear any hostiles, and then secure a landing zone.

Because of the full throttle rotor wash racket pounding off the surrounding area buildings and walls, bodyguards were awakened and quickly came to the defense of their compound. Pouring out of the three-story house in the middle of the complex they started firing assault rifles at the approaching helicopters. The Sikorsky on the right took some hits and started losing power and systems control. The pilot wrestled his stick as he lost altitude and the craft started to counter rotate sending the tail rotor into the perimeter wall. Sensing he could not wrestle it into submission, the pilot calmly announced they were going down. Because they were hovering just twenty feet above the compound yard he cut power and let the Blackhawk drop hard into the dirt yard.

The SEAL's were out both doors firing at unseen defenders before the wheels touched down. They laid down a withering spray of fire back and forth as they advanced on the building in the center of the complex. The guards were driven back to the building they had just come out of.

At the same time, the other Blackhawk continued hovering and the SEAL Team unfurled their lines and rappelled down as planned, joining the firefight. Overwhelming firepower was the order of the day. Joining up, the SEAL's assessed their situation and set up perimeter protection. Part of the Team cleared the grounds looking for any other hostiles. In seconds, they had taken control of the entire outside compound. A sniper position was established on the roof of an outer building with a commanding view of the entire lot.

The rest of the Team advanced on the first floor doors of the residence. Two shot gunners stepped forward and without a word, blew out the hinges of the door knocking it out of its frame. It crashed inward from the concussion. Two other soldiers immediately threw flash bang grenades into the dark hallway to clear the entrance. Knowing the intense flash and disorienting bang was coming, the SEAL operators handled the startling loud noise well. Anyone inside would not have been so prepared. Before the smoke had cleared the elite fighting unit poured into the entrance preparing to do battle.

The main residence hallway was dark and ran the length of the house leading to a stairway going upstairs. There were a number of side rooms off this hall on both sides. Hugging the walls the SEAL's moved fast and silently as they searched for the bad guys, scanning and clearing each room and then moving forward. If they encountered another doorway entrance inside a room they advanced that way as well. The first two rooms were sitting rooms and were empty. Before they had a chance to clear the next two rooms they encountered more gunfire, and this time more weapons were being fired by the defenders of Osama bin Laden. The rest of his defense force must have awakened and joined the defense.

Taking fire from the end of the hallway, the SEAL Chief silently gave a cease-fire command, and every SEAL stopped shooting without a word. He listened carefully to the sounds of the return fire. Knowing his weapons, especially the Kalashnikov, and its very recognized spitting cadence, he counted and thought that he heard only four or five weapons actually being fired. He signaled the rest of the crew his count and they opened up again. Less than two minutes had passed since boots had touched the ground.

Noting the defenders were hunkered down at the end of the hallway, he again brought the tactical pump shotguns forward. With solid heavy-bore slugs loaded, he had the two soldiers lay down a cross-field wall of fire aimed at the two sidewalls framing the end of the hall. The slugs tore into the wallboards at waist and knee level, passing right through them like butter. The defenders, using the walls as shields never knew what hit them as the slugs tore through their bodies. They went down. Return fire stopped for the moment and the Chief signaled his crew to advance. They moved down the wide hallway ready for action. Reaching the staircase they saw several downed defenders, while at the same time, they heard others running up the stairs to the upper levels of the residence.

Verifying the status of the defenders lying on the floor, they saw that two were dead, one a woman. The third was alive, but most likely would not be in a few minutes. He had caught two rounds in the thighs and was bleeding profusely, probably from a severed femoral artery. Clearing away their weapons the bodies were turned over and a SEAL stepped forward and took digital photographs of the bloodied faces to be sent back and analyzed.

During this momentary lull in the fighting they looked at the faces hoping they would identify their quarry among the dead, but the face they all knew so well was not among them. They re-focused on the upper levels. The staircase was more industrial than decorative, not like the wood staircases you would see in a suburban home.

Silently creeping up the stairs expecting fire from above, they gained access to the second level. They carefully searched and cleared each room and closet to be sure none of the bad guys would get behind them, and started up the stairs for the third floor. They were confident the rest of the house had been cleared. In addition, all potential exits and windows were being carefully monitored from the outside. Their quarry, if he was in residence, had to be here. The CIA and satellite tracking had eyes on the house for months and he had never left the compound. He had to be here.

The lead soldiers carefully climbed to the third floor and found a number of bedrooms and bathrooms. In the two closest to the stairs they found some non-combatant children hiding in a closet and carried them out of the building. The other bedroom and sitting room were found to be empty. The SEAL's inched down the hall, passing a framed photograph of the crumbling World Trade Center building on the wall. It was a grim reminder of what they were doing and who they were after. Before they could reach the last bedroom, they heard voices quietly arguing from within. Because of the narrow hallway two Team members loaded fresh clips and took point prepared to open fire.

As they approached, the point man closest to the door did a snap glance around the corner and pulled back. He held up two fingers signaling his partner there were two defenders standing together at the far corner of the bedroom. Acknowledging, the two soldiers quickly entered the room with guns up and tracking.

Two people stood across from them near a large bed. One was a woman in flowing robes and the other was a very tall man with a beard, dressed in a traditional dishdasha, the loose-fitting tunic that looked like a long nightshirt. The woman was standing in front of the man and when the soldiers entered she moved towards them aggressively. The SEAL didn't hesitate and shot her in the leg. She went down. In the next half-second the second SEAL tracking the man shot him twice, once in the chest and another in the forehead. He fell forward onto the corner of the bed and then rolled off crumpling to the floor. The rest of the Team secured the bedroom and the rest of the floor.

The SEAL Chief entered the room and walked over to the lifeless body pooling in blood. He turned the body over and inspected the face of Osama bin Laden very carefully. He wanted to make sure it was him and not an imposter. He had his other Team members in the room do a visual too. Getting on his satellite radio he sent a coded message and simply said, "Geronimo, E- KIA."

Once they were sure they had cleared the entire house, the Chief threw down a large duffel bag and said, "We have ten to fifteen minutes before the local cavalry arrives. The back-up chopper will arrive shortly. Let's make good use of the time. I want all the intel we can find. Tear it apart. I want everything that isn't nailed down. Hell, I want that too, if its info! Grab any and all phones, electronics, computers, hard drives, DVD's and disks. I don't care if it's Michael Jackson tapes, or Koranic hymns. We can sort it out later." The men began spreading out into the various rooms.

Pointing to his cameraman he said, "I want photos and video of every square foot. I doubt we will be invited back here for a post-mortem."

Two SEALS grabbed linens from the bed and wrapped the body of Osama bin Laden in it. They hand carried the lifeless body down the stairs and out to the waiting Blackhawk helicopter. They yelled to the flight crew, "Got a present for you, keep an eye on it until we get back." Both pilots and their crew chiefs gave thumbs up signals and then went back to their pre-flight check.

Outside, the perimeter guards heard the Chinook coming in from the West and signaled the landing zone inside the perimeter with their laser lights. They resumed scanning the area surrounding the compound for any advancing hostiles. The neighborhood had been awakened and lights could be seen, but few people had actually ventured out yet to see what was going on. That would soon change.

The Team completed its sweep of the entire house. They gathered at least ten hard drives, five laptop computers and hundreds of DVD's and thumb drives. Coupled with all the papers and files they had gathered they were taking a ton of fresh intelligence back to America.

Once the Chief was satisfied they had all they could collect he personally cleared his Team from each floor and room and had them assemble in the compound yard. The perimeter guards were pulled and the operators split up pouring into the Blackhawk and Chinook. Counting heads one more time, SEAL Team Six lifted off. Once clear of the disabled helicopter, multiple C-4 charges were detonated in the twenty million dollar disabled bird that had brought them, reducing it to a very expensive pile of aviation rubble.

The helicopters rose quickly attaining height to get away from any ground fire. Stealth was not an objective anymore. Now they just needed to get the hell out of Dodge. They headed west flying right over Abbottabad, moving as fast as they could without overheating the General Electric T-700 engines. Clearing the city, both helicopters returned to the deck to evade radar. They passed over the Tarbela Dam again, but did not turn north following the Swat Valley path they had come in on. Instead they continued west and flew through the Khyber Pass between the mountains and into Afghanistan. On the Afghan side of the border they knew they had air cover and headed for Bagram. Mission accomplished. No casualties for SEAL Team Six.

→ ←

FBI Office, New York City

Agents Steven Olson and Brian Jones, still grateful to actually be working in the field, followed their leads and verified the two Pakistani brothers were nowhere about, not in jail, not at their apartments, nor their usual taxi garage on the Westside near the Javits Center. At the garage, the dispatcher couldn't say where they might be; neither had been seen in more than a month. Because they were gone, the dispatcher had removed them from the roster.

The two rookie FBI Agents were now joined by another two senior Agents. They were to work together and follow all leads on the two brothers. Invoking the Patriot Act with a federal judge, the lead Agent obtained a search warrant for the small apartment they had on 34th St., above an industrial heating and cooling company.

The apartment had two other Pakistani families living in it. All of the people in the apartment were interviewed and asked about the Pakistani brothers. They all willingly spoke and said the brothers were pretty quiet, did their jobs well, and contributed their share to the monthly apartment costs right on time. They said the two brothers kept to themselves, ever since their families had died in 9-11. They rarely spoke about the subject but everyone knew they had lost their wives and children. They mentioned the brothers were in some kind of therapy, ever since 9-11. They were committed to attending the sessions.

The agents got what information they could about the grief counseling and the two rookies went to track down the lead, presuming it would lead nowhere.

Steven Olson made some phone calls to the 9-11 Commission offices and tapped into their database. He found there were hundreds of grief counseling sessions that had been functioning since the tragic event, all over the Tri-State area. Many of these groups were still functioning.

In checking the 9-11 database records, the two Pakistani's names turned up. They had made counseling inquiries a few months after 9-11, and were assigned to a special group that was made up of foreign nationals and other naturalized citizens who had lost loved ones in the terrorist act. They were assigned to a therapy group headed by a Doctor Peter Hensley. His grief counseling sessions were held in the city, in his office right in Time Square.

Brian Jones looked at the address and remembered that numerous phone messages had been cross-referenced coming from the Times Square area, close to the Doctor's office address.

'Gotcha!' he thought, and pulled Brian away from the counter heading for the door.

They made the trip cross-town in about 20 minutes and found the Doctor's building right on Broadway. They parked in the loading zone for the McDonald's Restaurant and went into the building.

They took the elevator up to Dr. Peter Hensley's office and stepped into his waiting room. The receptionist was talking with a man in a long lab coat, with a name stitched on the breast pocket, Dr. Hensley.

The two Agents introduced themselves and showed their badges, something they didn't get to do much until they got into the field. The Doctor had a gap in patients so he invited them into his office and asked how he might be of assistance.

"Doctor, we are looking for some men that we believe may be part of one of your 9-11 grief counseling groups."

"I actually have about seven groups that are still active. Some of them have disbanded, worked through their grieving if you would. What are their names?"

"We would like to talk with an Osama Tarkan and his brother Malik." Both Steven and Brian held their breath waiting for the Doctor to respond.

"Yes, I knew both men. They were part of one of my immigrant groups, but they aren't meeting anymore. It's funny that you ask about them. This group started way back in 2002. There were ten people in the group and they had all lost loved ones in the 9-11 terrorist act. When they started therapy, they were despondent, lost souls, looking for answers that no one could give them. They met as a group almost twice a week in the beginning, then a couple years later cut back to once a week and more recently to once a month."

"Sorry to interrupt Doctor, but you said funny? Can you elaborate?" Brian said, getting more used to doing interviewing. He was learning how to drill down.

"Well, I was about to get to that," the Doctor responded. "These folks were diligent about getting together and I think we had made great progress. But, then, just a couple months ago, the whole group kind of disappeared. They just stopped coming to sessions. I called them a couple of times but no one returned my calls."

Both Brian and Steven recognized they had stumbled on another anomaly. Not only had the two Pakistanis disappeared in the wind, now their whole therapy group was missing as well. They again knew they had found something.

"Doctor, we're looking for the two Pakistani brothers because we are concerned with their safety. We'd like to see if we couldn't find them by checking out the rest of the therapy group. Could we get that list of names and addresses?"

The Doctor raised his eyebrows and started to invoke the doctor-patient privilege.

"Doctor, it's for their own safety. We're concerned about them.

"Well, I guess I can share that list with you. I'd like to know what happened to them as well. I thought we were making real progress."

"We appreciate that Doctor. Hopefully we can get you some answers." Brian said, pleased that they wouldn't need another search warrant.

The Doctor started rummaging through his files. "We have been meeting for years. You know there is another funny thing about this group. A couple months ago when we would finish our sessions, they would all leave this meeting and then re-congregate downstairs at the McDonald's. I saw them a couple times and they were laughing and bonding, like a tight little group. I chalked it up to my bringing them together, but maybe they decided they didn't need me anymore. Here is that list."

The list had ten names and addresses on it. Brian and Steven thanked the Doctor and told him they'd be in touch. They walked down the hall with their next lead, not quite sure what they were looking at. But everything seemed a little hinky!

→ ←

Monday morning, Bab-el-Mandeb Strait

As the Majorca was preparing to pass through the deep blue waters of the Bab-el-Mandeb Strait, they gave wide berth to some ships heading north through the passageway, riding closer to the coast of Djibouti, in North Africa, perhaps a half-mile off shore. Captain Brinkmann was on the bridge with Meredith. Both had their long distance binoculars out and were scanning the Djibouti coastline.

"Captain, take a look at 11:00 o'clock to the west, and scan up on that large bluff overlooking the Strait. There seems to be a turbaned gentlemen looking at us with big glasses mounted on a tripod."

"Ah,....ah,....yeah...OK, got it. Interesting! Yeah, I think that son-of-a-bitch is watching us pass by. He looks like he has better binocular equipment than we do."

He continued to watch the man on the hill over looking the Strait. "Now it looks like he's on a cell phone, and a few seconds later, " now he's packing up, see?"

"Looks like he saw us watching him," Meredith said as he continued scanning the coast. He set his binoculars down on the railing. "The fact that he didn't bother to wave a hello may mean trouble! My cynical mind says he's probably a spotter for them one-eyed brigands that are working these parts, checking what kinds of goodies may be coming through the Straits. If he does works for those guys, he probably saw the farm equipment stacked on deck. My guess is they'd love to get that stuff, if they could. I bet it would sell quickly on the black market."

"I agree, William. The ships I talked to yesterday, said there was a lot of small boat activity out in the Gulf, a lot further out then they expected. That could mean they must have a mother ship assisting them somewhere out there. The small boats couldn't stay afloat for long in these ocean swells. They probably have a well-organized little ransom ring going. We'll need to keep a watch for the next few days, until we get way out in the Indian Ocean. How about we get the team together to set up a four points watch."

The Captain and Meredith called everyone together. They were about to talk about the need for greater security as they were entering pirate waters when Ralph and Josef came running into the galley.

"Bill, you gotta see this!" Ralph said excitedly as he ran up carrying his laptop. "Holy shit. You won't believe what just happened!

William sat down on one of the benches and stared at the screen. He took a few moments to read the screen and from his eyes you could see him scanning back up to the top of the document to read it again.

"Son-of-bitch!" was all that came out of his mouth. He looked at Ralph and Josef and his jaw hung on his face and looked as if it might fall off. "Osama bin Laden is dead! A U.S. SEAL team made a raid in Pakistan and killed him last night. It's all over the news."

Everyone crowded around the laptop and read the information that was on the screen. Ralph gave everyone a minute to read the screen and then started driving the machine to search for more stories. The news was on every news Website and was being updated by the minute. Courtney and Kate retrieved their laptops and fired them up. They started scanning articles as well. The entire group clustered around the three computers and read all that could be found. No one said anything as they tried to absorb what had just happened.

Fifteen minutes later Meredith decided to try and regain control of this ship before it sank in its own disbelief. He tried to get everyone's attention. "My first comment is it's about time. We and America have been waiting for this day for almost ten years."

Everyone was nodding their agreement but they still had their mouths agape from the news. Meredith continued, "My second thought is now what the fuck do we do? Our mission is in effect over."

Courtney, ever the protagonist, interrupted and said, "And with a stolen nuclear weapon hidden in the hold. What the hell do we now do with that?"

The entire group thought about that for a second, some of them visibly considering that fact for the first time. Everyone started speaking to one another trying to make sense of the situation as they floated along in the Red Sea. There was no consensus.

Meredith again tried to regain order so they could talk about what to do. "I see us with a number of challenges and problems. We have been doing illegal things. We have obtained a suitcase nuclear bomb by illegal means, and we have actively been trying to sell it to Osama bin Laden, may he rot in hell! We have been using fake ID's and we have circumvented the law in a half dozen countries. Have I missed anything?"

"Yeah, we're fucked," Michael said. "But I'm still pleased that someone got the mother fucker. I can live with what I've done to tray and accomplish this end result. I just think we have to reintegrate ourselves back into society."

"Easier said than done, Michael. What do we do with our favorite piece of luggage sitting in a lead box below deck?" Kate said. "It's not like we can take it home as a souvenir."

" Maybe we wrap it up like we originally found it and weight it down and toss it into the Red Sea. Isn't this supposed to be a very deep gorge? It sinks to the bottom and is never seen again."

" I wonder what happens when saltwater eats away at the box and the components?" Ralph said thinking of a horrible outcome some years down the road.

The group kept searching the Internet for additional news but it was spotty coverage as the story developed. What they were getting was repetition on the facts as they were being shared with the World. The President had made a formal announcement from the White House and every news media outlet had taken the shocking information and run with it. All that was consistent was that Osama bin Laden was dead and the SEAL assault team had removed his body from Pakistan. They tried additional sources, plugging into CNN, the BBC and various news broadcasts coming out of Europe. But it was all basically the same information. Their quarry was dead.

The entire group sat in a blue funk trying to understand the facts of the matter. They discussed options on what to do in light of the mind-boggling news. They readily admitted this was the ultimate result they had wanted all along, for the better part of ten years, but in the most recent past year and a half they had always factored themselves into the revenge equation. It was what had motivated them. They had molded themselves into a team, a team for retribution. And now it was over with them sailing in the Red Sea with a nuclear bomb in the hold.

Continuing to monitor the Internet, sopping up every bit of news they could find on the shocking outcome, Ralph took a moment to check on the special email account that had been their primary link with al Qaeda. He looked there more to take a break than anything else.

"Holy shit again. Speak of the devil. Guess who has just sent a new message?" he said to the group as he turned his laptop so Meredith could see what he was looking at.

Everyone looked up from the computers they were huddled around.

Meredith read the abbreviated email and said, "Just when we thought we were out of the game, we get sucked back in. Al Qaeda wants to talk with us and soon."

"They must be seeing the same news we're seeing on the Arab news channels." Josef said trying to type in one of the Arab Websites. "I'm guessing they are very pissed off right about now."

"So why don't we accommodate them and see if we can knock off a few more of their top guys." Michael offered. "Why couldn't we do business with whoever is stepping up to the plate?"

Meredith reread the coded message from the al Qaeda contact they had been dealing with.

"Perhaps we could do that. You're right they do sound as if they are really interested in meeting up with us. I think we may be back in business, people. Let's respond and see what comes of it."

Courtney sat down at the laptop and started typing a response as Meredith dictated the words.

Subject: Persian Artifacts for Sale
Dear Relics Division:
We are still very interested in completing the antiquity sale as before. In fact, we have some new items of exceptional value now available for sale that your principals may be interested in. Terms of sale would be the same as before. We look forward to a response Fed Expr.
Regards,
THCT

"Let's see if that gets their interest. Go ahead and send it," Meredith said. " If they bite we may be back in business."

Everyone went back to scanning the various Websites that were covering every angle of the death of Osama bin laden. As the minutes passed new information kept being added as the story unfolded about the daring assault on the bin Laden hidden hideout somewhere in Pakistan. They all voraciously read each new post, still incredulous that the object of their anger had been found and killed in the midst of their journey for revenge.

Twenty minutes later Courtney snapped her finger and got Meredith's attention, pointing to the computer. "I would say we have some interested fish on the line. They're back already with a response."

Everyone jumped up and crowded around the laptop and read the coded message that had just come in.

Subject: Persian Artifacts for Sale
THCT,
We are indeed still very interested in the antiquities you have identified. We are also very pleased that there are additional items now available. We would like to set up a time to view these artifacts at your very earliest convenience. We would like additional photographs by Fed Expr.
Sincerely,
The Relics Division
Persian Institute

"Well I'll be, so much for cutting off the head and watching the snake die. This must be a multi-headed Medusa snake that intends to move forward whether bin Laden is dead or not," said Meredith/

Malik spoke up trying to comprehend all that had taken place in the last hour. "If I understand correctly, the al Qaeda terrorists are the snake, and while the head of bin Laden has been cut off, the body still wants to continue to do what it does?"

"You got it Malik. What I think their saying is they are continuing on in battle even though their boss has bit the dust, so to speak." Ralph said. He looked at Osama to make sure he was on the same page as well.

"So I say let's fire up the engines and go deliver this bad boy to the next big shot in al Qaeda." Kevin said rubbing his hands together. This is what we came for. Even though that asshole is dead it doesn't mean we can't try to do some additional damage."

Meredith looked around the galley and saw that everyone was nodding in agreement.

"Let's play this thing out a bit further before deciding whether we keep going. I'm concerned that if we have to go up the mountain in Pakistan, we may run into a greater amount of hostility than we ever thought we would. I like the idea of completing our mission, I just don't want to put us all in harms way unless we think we can still pull it off."

With that everyone agreed that it would be prudent to take this slow, because events were now moving fast and a lot was out of their hands. Everyone was intent on searching the Internet for more information. No one wanted to shut down the laptops; they were interested in any and all news that heralded the demise of their most hated enemy.

Captain Brinkmann asked to be heard. "Just before we got this news we were about to talk about pirates and the dangerous waters we're going to be entering in a few hours. I talked with a number of ships entering the Red Sea. They advised there was quite a bit of pirate type activity in the

Gulf of Aden. We may need to be ready if we are attacked. Whatever our new mission is, we can't let our cargo get into the wrong hands."

"Captain, I fully agree," Meredith said. "Michael and Kevin, I'd like you to establish a watch that we'll all participate in. I also think we should break out the weapons and position them around the ship in case we do have to defend ourselves"

"You got it boss, we can be locked and loaded in an hour. Kevin will draw up a continuous watch schedule for everyone on six hour shifts," Michael said as he pointed to Kevin. They both got up and headed for the weapons locker.

Gulf of Aden

The Majorca came through the twenty-mile wide Bab-el-Mandeb Straits without incident and turned due east heading out into the Gulf of Aden. This body of water sat between Yemen to the north and Somalia to the south. Over a hundred and fifty miles wide it could be rough, but on this evening the waters were calm and placid. The ship made good time.

On the deck the two police officers broke out their defensive weaponry. They put the heavy-duty rifles, a shotgun, and a grenade launcher on the stern figuring that any attempt to board the ship would come from the rear. But they also placed some small arms, Ak-47's, and shotguns in the side bunkers and at the bow.

The ship's radar scanned the Gulf ahead of them and showed no traffic other than identified ships that were in the sea-lane. A duty roster was developed. Michael, Kevin, Meredith and Courtney took the first night shift from midnight to 6:00 am. The others penciled themselves in for various daylight shifts. Captain Brinkmann stayed on the bridge and monitored the low-level radar screen as a first line of defense.

Kevin was moving around the ship making sure everything was prepared for any unexpected guests. He was quietly singing the Marine Fight song because Meredith had reminded him that the lines "from the shores of Tripoli" referenced the birth of the Marine Corps when they fought pirates in defense of American shipping interests. He knew his Marine Corps history. In 1801 – 1805, in the First Barbary War, the United States took on the pirates operating out of the Barbary Coast in the Mediterranean. The Barbary States harbored these roving bands of pirates who terrorized all commercial shipping interests plying the north coast of Africa from Gibraltar all the way east to Algiers. He was proud of his Marine Corps and couldn't get the song out of his head.

After the sun had gone down off the stern, the four scheduled THCT members dragged some lawn chairs to their respective guard posts and settled in for the night. Kevin was spoiling for a fight and actually hoped it would come, but all he saw was a calm sea and a couple million stars in the moonless night.

By 3:00 am, all four of the team members on the dogwatch were bored, getting more tired by the minute. They were starting to nod off. Courtney was at the bow position leaning against the bulwark, staring out into the darkness. She was marveling at the millions of stars in the southern sky, seeing shooting stars every few minutes. It was an extraordinary light show. Back home she would have been lucky to see a couple hundred stars in the night sky. There was just too much ambient light from cities, streetlights and buildings. It reminded her of her parents favorite song from the 60's, 'Up on the Roof' by the Drifters, where they sang, "and the stars put on a show for free."

Suddenly, her eyes were drawn to a slight movement in the shadows to her left. As her eyes focused on the deep shadows, she saw a tall man materialize and then slowly step out of the shadows. He was holding what looked to be an AK-47 automatic rifle, and it was pointed directly at her. His dark as chocolate features completely blended in with the night. He was wearing a dark t-shirt, jeans and black sneakers, against the black night and the dark gray metal shadows of the ship. She could hardly make him out until he smiled wickedly and his white teeth blazed like a beacon in the darkness.

He put up a bony finger to his white teeth and signaled her to remain silent. She did not make a sound; and frantically tried to figure out where he had come from. Standing silently, he looked around to see if anyone else was close by. She saw him look back, looking her up and down. She could see that his eyes and mind were making some mental adjustments to whatever his initial plan had been, now that he had run into a woman. She understood that look.

Recognizing she was in jeopardy in a number of different ways, she tried to minimize her movements, but slowly, almost imperceptibly, she turned her body so the .45 automatic handgun holstered on her belt was not visible to the grinning idiot. She hadn't been asked to raise her hands yet, so she let them dangle free at her side, and ever so slowly edged one hand around her hip so it slipped out of sight in the darkness.

She waited and he continued to grin at her as he sized up his next move. He continued to look about the ship, trying to determine what he should do next, claim his unexpected prize, or go back to his plan of overtaking the ship. He looked back and grinned at her again, as if making a decision.

Recognizing the look, she knew she would have to act soon. Seeing that he continued his casual head movements looking around, Courtney realized she might have a chance to quickly draw and fire if he looked away again. She figured firing her weapon would do a couple of things. She would first be defending herself from his impending physical assault, and the shot would also raise the alarm, bringing immediate help from the team.

She calculated she would have to take a quick shot and then dive for cover. Luckily, she was standing next to the thick metal pillbox that had been fitted on the bow of the ship. If she could get to the side of the metal box, she could protect herself from the automatic fire of the AK-47 pointed at her.

The young man, no more than 17 or 18 years old, looked more nervous than she was as he wrestled with his personal desires and his original mission. She remembered the AK- 47 was not known for its accuracy, rather it was known for laying down a lot of lead in the general direction it was pointed. She knew she needed to move quickly or a lot of slugs would be flying her way in a few seconds.

At that moment, a rope lanyard clanged against a metal pole from mid-ship and pulled the gunman's attention away from her for a good couple of seconds. She saw her chance and took it. With her past ATF training she knew how to handle a handgun. She drew her hidden hand up her hip in one fluid motion, and gripped the .45 semiautomatic. As she slid it out of the belt holster, her thumb flicked off the safety as it came up to a firing position. She brought her other hand up to meet the weapon, gripping her wrist to form a solid firing position.

She aimed the weapon at the interloper's chest cavity just like she had done so many times at the range, and gently squeezed off two rounds in a fraction of a second. The first shot hit him in the lower right chest cavity, and with the gun's recoil, the second went high and hit him in the left arm, high in the biceps. As she finished pulling the trigger sending the second shot down the barrel, she rolled to her right and ducked behind the thick metal pillbox. In doing so, she actually ran into her second cartridge being ejected and it burned her arm with the hot piece of brass.

The gunman heard the first crack of the gun before he turned back to the woman. He looked at her with surprise and felt a round hit him in the gut, and then another caught him in the arm, his gun arm. The reaction was immediate. His gun went flying across the deck and slammed into the port gunwale. He stood there in shock, not understanding what had just happened. No one had ever shot at them; they just gave up their ships, and did as they were told. He crumpled against the metal bulkhead behind him and slowly slid down the wall.

Courtney crouched behind the metal box, and took a quick glance over the top. The pirate was not there. As she slowly inched up she saw that he was lying against the wall in a heap. He was gripping his waist with his good arm. And she could see he was in shock and didn't have his weapon close at hand. That will teach him to have bad thoughts about a woman for a while, she thought. She stepped out from behind her cover with her handgun cocked and ready to fire again.

She hoped her two shots had sounded the alarm, but decided a few more wouldn't hurt. She raised the gun in the air, pointed out over the rail and fired off two more rounds for good measure. Then she heard the cavalry coming, with boots thumping on the deck. Michael was the first to get to the bow and Ralph arrived a moment later. Both had their handguns drawn, but were also carrying rifles and shotguns.

"Courtney, are you alright? What the hell happened?"

"I'm fine," she said, and then pointed downward towards the shadowed wall to her left. "But he's not. I think we got us a pirate."

Both men looked towards where she was pointing and pointed their weapons. Michael went over to the black man and turned him around. His police training kicked in and he made him roll into the wall and use his one good arm to support his weight. He patted him down and found a good- sized knife in a rope belt around his waist, which he pulled out and threw on the deck. He made the man kneel down and put his good hand behind him. He then brought the injured arm back as well and tied them together using the rope around his waist. He looked back at Courtney.

"You sure you're OK?" When he saw her nod, he smiled and said, "Nice shooting but I guess you missed twice."

"The second two shots were to wake you guy's up. I can't defend this whole stinking ship by myself." Again, she smiled and leaned back against the pillbox.

Ralph walked over to the rail of the ship and looked over. He couldn't see anything in the inky darkness. "Well, if there's one of them, there has got to be more. We need to do a search. Now!"

As he said that, everyone else on board came running up to the bow, having heard the two volleys of shots. They crowded around Courtney to make sure she was ok, and then walked over to the cringing prisoner to take a look at him.

When the Captain arrived he immediately assessed the situation and said to everyone, "If there is one on board there could be others, they don't work solo. He may have been their point man and the others are still coming. He had to get way the hell out here somehow, so look for a boat in the water, look for grappling hooks, and spread out to search the rest of the ship."

Meredith shouted another command, as everyone started moving.

"Work with a partner. I don't want any of you wandering around alone. Let's be careful so we don't shoot one another. Kevin, get back to the stern, if there are more bad guys coming, that's where they'll try to board. Michael, you lead the search team. If we're clear, then join Kevin. Let's go."

Just then Uri came running up with a rubber coated grappling hook in his hand.

"I just found this on the port rail, pretty close to the bow. I cut off the rope but there may be more."

"That explains how our young brigand here got on board," the Captain said. "Maybe he was the point guy who was supposed to bring the others on board."

The Captain looked up as the First Mate came running forward. "Captain, the surface radar is picking up a bunch of small boats about a mile out. There's also a larger ship about five miles south of here, paralleling our course."

Kevin pulled out his binoculars and searched the southern horizon, but it was too dark without a moon. He searched for running lights on the ship but could see none.

"Nothing out there, Cap."

"All right folks, I think we may have a full assault coming our way. Hopefully they don't know we're on to them. Let's do a quick sweep and make sure there aren't any others on board, and then man the battle stations. I'll be on the bridge and I'll call out any boats that I see coming."

"Captain, what are we going to do with him?" Courtney said.

"I don't know, my first instinct is to toss him overboard and let the sharks get him. But I know you'll all get crazy on me. So get someone to stop the bleeding, bind his wounds, and then lock him up somewhere for now."

"I shot him, I'll take care of him and lock him up." She grabbed the prisoner by the good arm and dragged him towards the superstructure. "Let's go partner!"

Everyone else took off searching the ship for additional intruders.

→ ←

CIA, Langley, Virginia

The Joint Task Force meeting had been called quickly and moved to a much larger conference room because of the Osama bin Laden raid. A lot of intelligence was coming out of Pakistan. It was a treasure trove of terrorist information. There was a heightened level of concern there might be fallout over the death of the terrorist leader aimed at America. There were now about one hundred different people tasked to this THCT inquiry, chasing down leads, and trying to make sense of all the bits of information that had been found.

"So people, what can you tell me? I understand we're getting some good information on these THCT people." Karen Lee said from the head of the large conference table.

"Ma'am, Jeff Madison from the New York FBI Field Office. We stumbled on some interesting information in doing our phone canvassing in New York. Rather than try to repeat the Agents findings, I brought them along to share what they found. Agent Olson and Agent Jones."

Looking like lost schoolboys both young agents were still trying to figure out how they had got to the CIA's Headquarters in Washington, D.C.

"Yes, Sir," Agent Brian Jones said, turning to the woman at the head of the table.

"Ma'am. My partner, Agent Steven Olson and I were assigned to track the phone purchases and messages and cross-reference them against triangulated call locations in New York City. These were a whole bunch of pre-paid throwaway phone call leads that we got from the National Security Agency."

"The NSA identified the phone numbers used and we tied those back to the phone purchases. We found the stores they were sold at and then we watched mountains of videotapes looking for the purchasers. After two days we got lucky. We saw two Middle Eastern types trying to buy throwaway phones on some of the tapes. We then looked to see if we could see them leaving the store and again we got lucky. They got in a NY City taxi and it drove right past the camera. We got a cab medallion and a license number." He looked to his partner to continue.

"Ma'am, we then tracked down the medallion taxi owner and he told us the two men were his drivers and they were Pakistani immigrants. We asked to see them, but he said he didn't know where they were as they hadn't been to work in about a month. He also told us they had disappeared once before, five months earlier. He said he later found out they had been in France on business. We checked those cell phone numbers again and found a couple of them had originated in Calais and Paris, France. That made us hungrier to follow the leads."

"So we tried to visit these men in their apartment and found out they were missing. Didn't find anything at all incriminating, but we did get one very interesting fact from neighbors. These men, both had loved ones that were killed in 9-11. They lost their wives and their children in the terrorist attack. That seemed to be odd, but with their names and addresses we went to the 9-11 Commission and verified they were survivor family members of victims."

Agent Olson took over the narrative again. "The 9-11 Commission records also showed that the two men joined a grief counseling group to deal with their family losses. They were assigned to a group of mostly foreign nationals that all had similar losses. They met with a Dr. Hensley in New York City on a regular basis going all the way back to 2002."

So we looked up the Doctor in charge of this counseling group and paid him a visit. His office was on 44th Street and Broadway in Time Square and when we checked the phone logs of our mysterious calls we found they all originated in that immediate area. The good doctor was very helpful and confirmed much of what we had already discovered. These two guys had suffered a terrible loss, dutifully attended therapy sessions, and then about a month ago just stopped attending. The Doctor said that everyone else in the group stopped attending as well. The Doctor tried to call them but no one was ever home. He assumed they decided they were over their grief and were moving on."

"So how many people were in this counseling group?" Bede Long asked. " Have you tried to contact any of them to corroborate this information?"

"Yes Sir, we did." Brian answered, finding he enjoyed being the deliverer of all this investigative data. "We got a complete list of all the therapy group patients from the Doctor. He was as mystified as we were."

"And I bet all the other people have disappeared and are in the wind? " Karen Lee said from the head of the table. "I'm guessing that no one has seen any of these individuals in a month or more?" again a statement, as much as a question.

"You are correct Ma'am. We have a group of agents tracking them down as we speak. They have homes and jobs in New York City. These individuals include a wealthy financier, a Wall Street investment banker, two cab drivers, a graphic design firm owner, a translator from the United Nations, a former ATF agent, a NY Cop, and an Egyptian from Hoboken. But they all have some thing in common, they lost loved ones in the 9-11 terrorist act."

"Well, this is a start. I want all those names and the information shared with the other agencies. Let's coordinate talking to their families, to their business associates, and to their neighbors. I want in depth profiles prepared on each of them. And I want it yesterday! With bin Laden taken out of the picture these guys may be even more rogue and we have them inside the border. Somewhere in there we will find a clue on what they are up to, how to find them and stop them from whatever they are planning. Let's get busy." Then Karen Lee turned to the young FBI novices. "Agents Olson and Jones, thanks for the great fieldwork. I understand this was your first outside assignment. You did a good job dogging the details. Keep up the good work."

"Yes Ma'am, we will." the two agents said almost in unison. They gathered their findings and gave copies to Bede Long with the CIA, and Bill Dalde with NSA. They in turn would prepare summary files for distribution to all the Homeland Security agencies working on this THCT Task Force

→ ←

Gulf of Aden

Continuing straight east in the primary shipping lane, the Majorca maintained its speed, with everyone having a heightened awareness of the dangerous waters they were in. The Captain made sure the running lights were on and that the ship looked mostly bedded down for the night. Only the dim lights from the helm and monitoring equipment could be seen from the sea.

The THCT group quickly swept the ship from bow to stern looking for boarders but found none. Michael had distributed nine headset microphone/intercoms so that each person could communicate with the others. Everyone was awake and nervous and took up pre-assigned defensive stations in case there were more pirates about.

Keeping low profiles they scanned over the gunwales out into the black seascape but could see nothing on the almost moonless night. There were four people on each side with Kevin and Michael holding down the stern access. Courtney had earned the right to protect the bow from all interlopers. No one questioned her ability to defend her position.

Everyone kept their heads down below the gunwales so they didn't become a target and watched for any telltale grappling hooks announcing an attack. The presumption was the pirates would sneak up in small boats, throw up some lines with rubber-tipped grappling hooks, and then shimmy up to take the ship by surprise. They waited.

The Captain was monitoring the radar screens. He noted the other large ship was maintaining a three-mile separation; and when he slowed to half speed or deviated his course, the other ship did likewise. It was definitely the mother ship for the smaller boats.

As he watched the low-level surface radar, he saw a number of small targets coming towards the Majorca from three different directions, almost like a pincher movement. In the green glow of the radar he could see that the two boats approaching the bow would arrive before the one coming in from behind the ship. He presumed the forward boats would come in and create a diversion, while the stern boat would creep up and board the pirates. He clicked on his microphone and walked to the bridge window.

"Attention, people. It looks like we have two fast boats approaching the bow at 10 and 2 o'clock. We also have one boat approaching from the stern. Kevin, you keep your head down. My guess is the front boats will make a pass and draw everyone's attention to them. Then the stern boat will quietly swoop in. I'm betting they're the boarding party. If you're patient, you can catch them with their pants down."

"Roger that, Captain. Patience is a virtue and did me well in Iraq."

"Kevin, I'm on the starboard side mid-ship at the moment, and can assist if you need me." Michael said.

"I'm fine partner, I can't let Courtney do all the shooting."

"That's what I thought you'd say," Michael said as he peeked his head over the starboard rail to see if he could spot anything. "Everyone else keep down. They may come in shooting and bullets could be flying. Anything hitting the ship's superstructure is sure to ricochet."

The various team members remembered their communication lessons and responded with a simple 10-4, without cluttering up the system. They hunkered down. The team members in the side pillboxes had pretty good vision through the shooting slots. They checked their weapons and watched the black water below.

Soon there was a low buzzing sound in the sea air that gradually got louder. As it did, the defenders recognized the sound of outboard motors, and large ones at that. Then two small craft appeared in the dark, coming directly at the ship. They were actually military type, rubber inflatable boats, with large twin outboard engines, that angled in and passed the ship from front to rear. They circled away from the ship and then angled in again at a slower pace. In each boat there was a driver and three or four young men, all armed with automatic rifles and handguns. They were standing and waving their weapons, but did not say anything. The drivers revved the engines as they slowed mid-ship and then bobbed in the water about fifty feet off both sides of the ship.

"People, I'm standing up to acknowledge their presence. Ralph, you do the same on the port side, but be ready to hit the deck. We might as well play their game and see what's up," Michael said this as he stood up at the rail, ready to dive for cover if needed. He didn't say anything or make any threatening movement; he just silently watched the boat as it bobbed off the starboard side of the ship.

"Alright everyone, here comes the stern boat, very slowly and quietly." Kevin said into his microphone, as he crouched down behind one of the pillboxes. He wasn't inside it; he didn't like the enclosed space and he was a big guy who wanted to be able to move about. He had been the same way in Iraq always moving from position to position, never allowing for a fixed target.

"Looks like they intend to quietly pull right up and throw a line on board. Have to give them credit for planning, if nothing else. I'm going to let them make the first move, before I start letting them have it. They may just be a welcoming committee."

Kevin put down his sniper rifle and grabbed the large Mossberg pump shotgun with the huge, evil looking brake fixed on the end of the barrel. He made sure five shells were loaded and two boxes of ammo were nearby. He chambered a round and waited.

The small boat slowly pulled in tight coming right up to the stern and he heard a grappling hook fly up and connect with the deck railing missing him by only a few feet. He could see it had hooked tightly in a metal cleat and was now being pulled tightly by someone below who was obviously pulling himself up.

He duck-walked over to where the grappling hook was, still out of sight, and took out his military knife from a sheath belted on his chest. With a single strike the sharp serrated blade cut through the very tight line, and he heard a yelp and a scream, then a loud splash as the weight fell back into the dark water. He stood up and quickly looked over the taffrail at the black man thrashing around in the water next to the small boat. One of the other young black men in the inflatable boat looked up and saw him and started shooting with his AK-47 pointed almost straight up. Kevin leaned back quickly out of harms way, as the continuous stream of bullets came arcing up and into the night. He bided his time and held his position.

He could hear the pirates pulling the man from the water. Then the boat engine was thrown into reverse, the engines whined and the boat started backing away from the ship. As it did, two pirates on board opened fire and laid down a stream of tracer bullets aimed at the stern deck.

Kevin ducked behind the pillbox, pulled up the Mossberg and fired the weapon down at the back-peddling boat. He fired, and pumped another shell into the chamber in one motion, firing again and again. Because the target boat was now 40 feet away and backing up, the shotgun pellet array was spreading out as it traveled to the target, and everything in the boat was showered with shotgun pellets. The pirates went down in the hail of pellets and their firing ceased. Kevin could hear them screaming and could hear the air deflating out of the boat from the pellet punctures.

The driver hunkered down in the boat well, and frantically tried to back away. In doing so he increased the amount of water breaching his stern. Kevin reloaded the Mossberg, this time with slugs, and stood to see if they returned any more fire.

They did as soon as they saw him again. They opened up with three AK-47's, sounds that he knew well from Iraq, and the stern was raked with bullets ricocheting off the metal plates. He waited behind the pillbox, and then in a moment of quiet, raised the shotgun and fired five times hitting the small boat with slugs that tore into the rubber and two of the pirates. He realized they were drifting out of effective shotgun range so he flipped on the safety, and pulled out his .45 semi-automatic sidearm, which he knew would do the job if they opened up again.

On both sides of the ship, the other two inflatable boats heard the commotion, looked to the stern of the ship and saw the tracer shells arcing up into the black sky. They opened fire on the ship from both sides, while gunning their engines, and raced away from the ship angling for the stern. One boat raced in to the crippled craft, now half submerged and capsized in its own wake. They pulled in and quickly hauled the three wounded men into their craft. Then they pulled away into the darkness.

Kevin kept a low profile and switched to the sniper rifle, which had a night-vision scope on it. He scanned the darkness. He wanted to try this long gun under battle conditions and this was it.

Just then Michael came running up and dove for cover next to the pillbox.

"You OK? Just as the Captain thought. They attacked from the rear."

"I'm fine, I think I nailed all three of them with this bruiser." He reached down and caressed the Mossberg 500 Road Blocker leaning on the pillbox. It was hot from the firing. "I think I have a new favorite gun if we ever get back to the mean streets of New York."

The other THCT members came running even though the Captain was yelling for them to hold their positions.

"People, hold your positions, stay where you, they'll be back. Now they know they have fight on their hands and they'll come hunting for bear with missiles or grenades."

"He's right everyone," Michael said. "Nothing to see here anymore other than some blood in the water. Back to your positions."

The Captain came on line and said, "We won this skirmish, but now I'm guessing they are pissed and will be coming in force for a real battle. That means we need everyone under cover. Let's get more ammo to each station. I understand we have a ton of that. Make sure you have more than you think you will ever use."

"Kevin, Michael, how about you take those sniper rifles and the night vision equipment and get up above the pilothouse. You should have a pretty good field of vision up there and you could cover all directions. It wouldn't surprise me if they come at us with RPG's. Maybe you can get them way out before they get close. Once they are in close I'll shoot some flares to light up the sky, but I'll let you know before I do, so I don't blind you."

"You got it Captain, Ralph, how about you come on back here and take over with the Mossberg if they come calling again?"

"I'd like that Kevin, how did it handle under fire?"

"It tends to buck every time you pull the trigger, but once you get used to it, and make an effort to hold it down, it's a hell of a crowd control weapon. I used the pellet loads when they were close and then switched to slugs once they were further away. Both handled nicely. You got a ton of ammo in the pillbox. Good hunting."

"You too, be careful up there. You'll be exposed."

"I spent my whole tour in Iraq on my belly looking through scopes into the night. From that height we should be able to catch them well out there before they get close. I'm looking forward to it. Let's go Mikey."

With the two cops going high, the others re-distributed themselves along the deck. They quickly restocked the ammo they needed for their weapons. This time they readily took to the metal pillboxes realizing the boxes would protect them from ricochets and any shrapnel coming off all the ships metal. They took their firing positions and settled in to wait.

→ ←

Socotra Island, Yemen

Within spitting distance of the Arabian Sea on the very eastern end of the large Island, Ayman Al Zawahiri, sat in the courtyard of a small house and contemplated the view of the ocean with the sun setting behind him.

This new place was not much to talk about but it was quiet and peaceful and no one would know they were here. He was sick that Osama bin Laden would not get to see this place. If the reports were correct, the Americans had dumped his body somewhere out in the Arabian Sea. Zawahiri mentally kicked himself for not getting bin Laden to move here earlier. After five years in Abbottabad, Pakistan they both had known that their time was marked before someone would slip, or word would sneak out that Osama bin Laden was living in a suburban house running al Qaeda from a bedroom. If only they had made the move from Pakistan earlier, he would not be sitting here mourning the loss of his close friend and leader, instead they would be enjoying the ocean breeze and plotting to destroy America. They would have been able to run the terrorist organization for another five years. He was angry and vowed to get even for this tremendous loss.

He had read all the reports coming from a variety of sources, and he now knew they were true. There was too much detailed information being revealed to believe his friend had not been gunned down.

Anwar al Awlaki walked up to the terrorist and sat down quietly. He didn't want to interrupt the thoughts of the now number one terrorist. Finally he said, "Ayman, I apologise for the interruption, but we must not forget about the devil Satan country. We must strike back for what they have done to us."

"I agree Anwar, I agree, but my heart is just not in it yet."

"I have good news that I believe you will want to hear. I just received word that our special package will be coming soon. We have now re-directed them to meet us in Yemen, although we have not yet told them where we are located. I think we must hold that secret, in light of what the Americans have done. And I have more good news... Once we complete our transaction with this Russian arms dealer, he has advised he now has five more special packages available, for a price."

Zawahiri turned away from the ocean view and digested what had just been said. "There is always a price, my friend, but the costs of our holy war are of little consequence. At this point I would pay whatever price is necessary to strike back at the Satanists. We need to reawaken terror in the minds of the infidels again. As we did in 2001."

"That is my hope as well, Brother, and perhaps we can, with this new development." Zawahiri gave some additional thought and then continued, "We have only had limited success in recent years. They have prevented us from attacking a number of times and I think the Americans are less fearful of us again. We must change that. We must strike again, even harder to get even for our loss. Thus, these additional weapons will be important. I don't care how much they cost. We need them to win our holy war. How can we make this happen?"

"We received a coded message this afternoon from the weapons dealer. They promised they'd deliver this nuclear weapon to us soon as a show of good faith. And after payment is satisfied, they would be willing to sell more, if we are interested," Anwar offered.

"I definitely want to show that interest, Anwar. We must get that weapon and the others as well. We must strike back and avenge Osama. Make whatever deal you have to! If they insist on coming here we will accept them, although my first desire would be to kill them. But if they truly have something we want, I think we will have to be good hosts for the moment. Let us not scare them off. If we could get five or six of these small nuclear devices we could take out all of America, and avenge Osama's death. Then we can bring Islam to its rightful place as Mohammed and Osama wished. We will give them whatever they want for their bombs. I have been told these weapons could crush a city."

"That is what I have been told as well. They are Russian devices I believe, very small and easy to transfer, but very deadly. I have read they could kill a half million people in the actual explosion and then another half million in the aftermath because of the radiation," Anwar said.

"That would teach the Americans a lesson. I want New York and Washington blown from the surface of the earth. I may want London leveled as well. After that, I think we must scare the rest of America, and go after their centers of the people. I think the sin city Las Vegas would be a good target and tell the world Muslims do not cherish their depravity. I would suggest we also look at Chicago, and then San Diego, where they have many military installations." He counted on his fingers the six bombs that would be used.

"That would be good Ayman. I will send a message advising them to come to Yemen. From there we shall check them out and then once we are sure of them bring them here as partners. I will also prepare the finances so that we could initiate another larger purchase. It will be done!" He bowed to the new leader of al Qaeda, realizing his stock in trade was going up again even with the death of Osama bin Laden.

→ ←

Gulf of Aden

A half hour later the Captain announced, "I have something on radar,…. here they come on starboard, and it looks as if there are at least six, maybe seven boats in the water tracking this way. They are coming fast. They aren't even trying to be covert."

He reached up on the console and told everyone to turn off any remaining lights. He killed the running lights as well. "Here they come, straight in about 1,000 yards out. Kevin and Michael, see if you can pick them up a bit further out and give them a what for. Once they get close they may hit us hard. I won't put up any flares just yet."

"Roger that Captain. We will engage before they are close and see if we can get the drivers. That should cause some problems for them and maybe they'll find some other ship to bother."

Meredith came on line and offered another one of his rallying speeches. "We've come a long way together people. Let's make sure we get through this in one piece. No heroics. Just remember what we talked about at the gun club. Remember the mission. We have to get through these guys to get there."

Both topside shooters swiveled around to starboard and started scanning the waters with their night vision equipment. They didn't have to wait long. In a matter of minutes, they saw one inflatable, and then a second came into view. Michael aimed at the boat on the left and Kevin sighted at the one on the right. Using their Kimber Model 8400 M LPT advanced tactical weapons, and .330 ammo, with a tactical load, they tracked their targets, waiting until they had the rhythm of the bobbing boats figured out bouncing over the swells. Almost simultaneously they both gently squeezed off a round.

Michael's shot hit the boat's driver in the shoulder and he went down falling on the wheel, causing the boat to turn violently to the left, narrowly missing the other boat. Kevin's shot missed its mark when the boat dipped in a trough, but the shot clipped a pirate standing behind the driver, and took him right out of the boat. The second boat kept coming, and the first boat recovered enough to stay in the game.

"The water is a factor that takes some getting used to," Michael whispered to his partner lying beside him.

Both shooters calmly reloaded, working the large bolts with practiced ease. The second set of boats came into view and the two men sighted their scopes and 24-inch barrels at the next two targets. This time they decided to try shooting at the rubber boats to see if their slugs could penetrate the heavy rubber rendering the boat useless. They again aimed at the black bobbing boats as they drove towards the ship. The two bullets hit their targets.

"Damn," Kevin said, "they bounced right off the rubber inflatable, they must be Kevlar-protected. Let's switch back to those one-eyed pirates."

Two more inflatable craft came into their night vision glasses and they started tracking the boats. These boats, having seen their fellow pirates being fired upon, were weaving back and forth in defensive maneuvers. Kevin noted the tactic and said these guys are good. The pirates had already taken up their weapons and were preparing to open fire on the ship. Kevin and Michael saw the pirates armoring up.

"We have RPG's coming in! Get your heads down and under cover!" Kevin yelled over his microphone.

Both he and Michael loaded cartridges and adjusted their aim to the guys shouldering the rocket propelled grenade launchers in each boat. As these fighters pointed their RPG's over the roll-bar frames of the inflatable boat, Kevin and Michael fired trying to take them out. This time Michael missed, Kevin didn't. He caught his target in the chest and he went down pulling the trigger of the RPG, which flew into the boat's cowling and exploded. The entire boat was blown out of the water by the concussion.

The other boats had now closed the distance to the ship and were racing by raking the superstructure with gunfire. The Captain and Meredith decided they should add some light to the situation and give the THCT team a fighting advantage. They advised their snipers they were going to light up. The riflemen switched off the night vision scopes.

Meredith and the Captain each grabbed a flare gun and a number of illumination rounds that would light up the sky for at least a minute. The Captain went to starboard, stuck the weapon out of the pilothouse door and pulled the trigger. Meredith went the other direction and stepped outside shooting a flare to port. As he stood there a tracer arc of bullets marched along the metal plates on the superstructure heading right towards the pilothouse hatch. The Captain saw it coming and grabbed Meredith's shirt collar, yanking him into the bridge housing as the bullets flew by. Two of the bridge windows were blown out showering both men with glass. On the floor they could see the flares arcing up into the pitch-black sky.

The two flares climbed a couple hundred feet in the air and burst like fireworks. Then a superheated light wand slowly drifted in the sky illuminating everything in a bright light. Meredith and the Captain both pulled out their handguns and using the bridge housing for cover started returning fire at the pirates and inflatable boats zipping by.

All of the boats attacking must have had additional RPG's on board because all of a sudden there were a number of shells incoming. Three HE, high explosive shells, hit the Majorca superstructure and rained shrapnel all over the deck. One came dangerously close to the pilothouse landing inside the dodger shield that protected the ship's bridge from rain and spray in a violent storm.

The explosion shattered half the windows on the bridge and made the Captain and helmsmen dive for cover. The other two shells landed midship scarring the quarterdeck. Everyone hunkered down in their pillbox bunkers, thankful they were still alive after that barrage. Seeing new light above, they came up shooting at the boats, which were now running parallel to the ship, circling almost as if they were Indians circling the wagons.

Kate and Uri were sandwiched in the starboard pillbox and were using the gun ports to advantage. Both had their earmuffs on in the close quarters and the smell of gunpowder filled their lungs. Kate used her handgun to lay down a consistent volley of lead at the attackers. She worked her way through two clips before she thought she actually hit someone. She wasn't pleased to be shooting at people but rationalized they had shot at her first and she was defending herself and her shipmates. She loaded another clip, pulled back the slide, and chambered a round, just as Kevin had taught her back in New York.

Next to her, Uri was using a rifle with a sight that made the bad guys seem real close. He could see their eyes and he looked into them as a sailor who had been here before. He had traversed these waters many times over the years and had been menaced by these thieves more often than he cared to remember. Back then, the ships he crewed always capitulated to the brigands. They would give up without a fight and were overrun for their cargos and ransom. One time he had been held as a prisoner on a container ship for three weeks, locked in one of those 40-foot container coffins, while the ransom was negotiated.

This time it was different and he was ready to dish it out for a change. He sighted his rifle at a boat that seemed to be sitting about 50 feet straight out and chambered another round. He gently pulled the trigger and watched as his round caught a black man high in the torso, spinning him around. He watched as the pirate fell backwards into the outboard motor screw. Then he was called to move over to the other side of the ship leaving Kate in her position alone.

Courtney was still at the bow. Seeing that the attack was initially centered at mid ship, she leaned out over the gunwale and used a shotgun on an inflatable making a turn near the bow. She peppered the boat as it made its pass. As soon as she did the pirates opened up with their AK-47's on her position.

She ducked instinctively; pulled out her Kimber .45 tactical handgun, and not even looking, shot the entire clip over the side. Then she dove into her metal pillbox presuming that a grenade might be coming her way. And it did, hitting just below the gunwale and exploding up and over her position. With her ears ringing she used her shooting slot and emptied another 15 shot clip as another boat made the turn. She thought she caught another one of the bad guys in the effort.

Osama and Malik were holding down the port side and felt left out because all the action was on starboard at the moment. But they held their positions and were awarded for their patience in the next minute when the pirates circled the ship to spread out their attack. They were like swarming bees attacking from all sides.

The brothers were both grateful they had spent hours at the range learning how to fire a weapon. But they had forgotten something. When they used the shotgun from inside the pillbox the first time they thought they had blown out their eardrums with the retort within the closed space. They had forgotten their ear protection and inside the box the gunfire seemed even louder. They improvised and shoved some wadded up tissue in their ears. They also switched to their handguns, sticking the barrels out the ports and firing as the boats came by. The noise was still very loud, but bearable. As they fired, they encountered a new problem. Being in the tight space, Malik's handgun ejected the spent cartridges right into Osama's face and shoulder. It was raining lead, so they decided to take turns shooting with the other leaning back in the box, changing clips in the handguns. They each took turns and laid down a constant stream of fire at any of the boats that would come within range.

Just as Courtney was doing on the bow, Ralph stayed in the action by using his shotgun to confront every boat coming past the stern. Josef had joined him in defense of the stern and he was hunkered down in the pillbox, using a handgun to advantage, shooting out the narrow ports.

Ralph had listened when Kevin suggested that slugs would have a better effect on the Kevlar rubber boat floors. Ralph waited until a boat came close and then he shot almost directly down hopefully piercing their rigid floors. That earned him withering fire from the AK-47s, but he maintained his position and continued menacing the attackers.

One boat hung back in the inky black waters identifying where the defenders were located on the stern and pulled off into the darkness. In the slowly fading light of the flare, they zeroed in on Ralph and Josef's position and prepared to make a run. Two hundred feet out they aimed their RPG's at the stern and let a volley go just as they were hit by sniper fire from Kevin and Michael in the crows nest. Both attackers went down.

The two RPG rounds covered the distance in less than a second, and one hit above Ralph's position; he had wisely sought cover diving into the pillbox almost on top of Josef. As the grenade exploded above them hot shrapnel rained down on the pillbox. The explosion took out the rear railing and dropped it into the sea below. As the debris sunk, it got sucked into the prop wash and the railing disintegrated as the spinning propellers ground up the metal.

The second shell was a HEAT round, a high explosive anti-tank load with a rocket motor for speed and penetration. It came in low and smashed into the rudder assembly of the ship ten feet below Ralph and Josef's metal box. Upon impact the shell exploded ripping up the mechanism that guided the movement and direction of the ship.

The Captain, still coordinating the ship's defense from the bridge, heard the two explosive charges that went off on the stern and hoped that Ralph and Josef were able to survive that assault. At that same moment his attention was drawn to the ship's instrument panels. They were covered with shards of shattered plate glass from the direct hit the bridge had taken earlier. Underneath those shards he saw red damage lights blinking suggesting there was considerable damage that had occurred to the drive shaft and the rudder assemblies. His helmsmen advised he had limited, sluggish control of the ship. The rudder was not responding correctly.

Kate was feeling awfully lonely defending her midship position but she was pretty pleased with herself, having thus far prevented any of the brigands from making any real effort to actually board the Majorca. Still the lead was flying and she had her hands full as she continued firing at any boat that came within view.

At that moment an explosion caught the side of the pillbox she was hunkered down in. While the blast primarily hit the side of the defensive position, it rendered her momentarily deaf and knocked her completely off her feet. The explosive charge came blowing through the gun port and would have scalded her with hot gases and lead had she not already crumpled to the deck from the concussion. The bulk of the blast missed her. But she was down and she knew it. They would be coming now if she stopped shooting.

The gases and fumes cleared inside the pillbox in a few moments but she saw she was bleeding from shrapnel wounds on her scalp and both arms. Bleeding or not, she was determined to defend her position. Her weapons were intact so she grabbed the AK -47 and started looking for a target. Just then a boat pulled up to the side of the ship and a grappling hook was thrown up almost catching her leg just outside the door. Instead it caught one of the foothold cleats on the wooden deck. The hook immediately went taut with a heavy weight on the other end and she could see that someone was coming up the rope to board her part of the ship.

She aimed her weapon at the grappling hook line and waited as more bullets ricocheted off her defensive position. In a matter of seconds a large hand came up over the edge of the deck grabbing around for a handhold.

She fired before the rest of the person appeared. The weapon was on a three-burst auto fire and literally cut the hand in half, and the person fell back into the sea next to the boat bobbing near the hull.

Just as Courtney had suggested earlier, Kate grabbed her shotgun and made sure she had a slug and not buckshot loaded. She leaped up and angled the barrel over the side, took a quick glance and aimed at the center of the boat directly beneath her. Kate pulled the trigger and the gun roared almost wrenching the weapon out of her hands because of the sharp angle she was holding it at. The slug tore into the plywood floor of the boat sending a geyser of water shooting up towards the sky. She pulled back just as a hail of bullets came arcing up from the gunman in the boat below. After the burst of fire, she heard them yelling and gunning the engine to get away from the ship before their boat sank.

Kate then loaded two shotgun pellet shells. Crouching on the deck, she again leaned over and aimed at the departing inflatable. She fired, and as fast as she could, pumped another shell into the chamber, and again fired downrange. Both shells hit their mark raining pellets on the shocked occupants as the inflatable was trying to back away. She had beaten them off for the moment. She crawled into the pillbox and nursed her wounds for a second keeping an eye out for any other approaching boats. She wondered how the rest of the crew was doing.

Still fighting from the bow of the ship, Courtney was trading fire with the swarming boats. She had just risen to empty another banana clip salvo when she took a round in the shoulder that spun her around and knocked her to the deck. Her Kalashnikov rifle slid down the deck out of reach. She crawled beneath the protective railing and rolled herself up against the wall somewhat protected. She groaned in pain with each movement. She had never taken a bullet before and she couldn't believe how much it hurt every pore in her body. She tried to assess the damage while fumbling for her sidearm to stay in the battle. She didn't want to compromise her position. She was determined to defend the ship from anyone coming aboard.

Captain Brinkmann saw her go down and came running to her aid in a hail of bullets. He dove for the deck, popped up to scatter a few rounds from his .45 pistol to let the bad guys know the position was defended, and then knelt down to attend to Courtney. He stripped off his shirt to staunch the bleeding that was oozing out of her shoulder and drenching her Grateful Dead t-shirt. Pulling her forward as gently as he could, she winched in pain and her eyes rolled back in her head, he saw that the bullet was a through and through. It looked like it had missed any vital organs, but had clipped the muscle pretty good, and the wound was a bleeder. He still thought that was probably good and hopefully hadn't done any permanent damage. He gently set her down, and then jumped up to shoot a few rounds downrange to keep the pirates at bay.

The Captain had taken a liking to this strong, no-nonsense woman. He found her to be beautiful and brainy, a combination that attracted him. He bound her wound as best he could and laid her in a protected bulkhead corner, while he continued to defend the bow. He reached for her Glock, made sure a round was chambered and handed it to her for protection. He said she should take it easy and not move so the bleeding would slow up. She smiled her thanks and he assured her she would be fine. Then he turned, grabbed her other weapons and took up her firing position shooting at the swarming pirates.

The rest of the Majorca crew was fully engaged for another ten minutes and fought like mad men inspired by the fact that they could indeed fight back. For years they had been made to cower in these pirate infested waters because the owners of these commercial ships were afraid of fighting for their cargos. They'd rather let the insurance companies pay ransoms to free the impounded ships and kidnapped crews. The Majorca crew laid down an accurate stream of fire that took a toll on the Somali pirates in the various boats.

The Captain popped up glancing over the rail and saw that four of the attacking boats were completely out of the fight and three of the remaining boats were fighting with a smaller number of shooters. He took careful aim with his Glock at the closest boat and sent a .303 bullet downrange at the driver of one craft. He caught him in the shoulder just like Courtney had been hit. The inflatable driver spun around causing the boat to veer sharply left. With the rapid change in direction another shooter went flying into the sea.

The Captain knew the ship was in trouble and they would very quickly need to end this assault, or they could be literally dead in the water. He advised Meredith using his throat microphone. Meredith understood the gravity of what he was saying, and after a few questions, pulled his microphone forward to talk to his THCT team.

"People, we have some control problems with the rudder. We have to end this thing now, or as soon as we can. I actually think we've taken them by surprise. They didn't expect the firefight we've given them. So now is the time to pour it on. In the next thirty seconds we're putting up new flares. I want everyone to come up shooting as soon as we light the sky. Let's give them everything we can throw at them and maybe we can scare them away. Flares in 30 seconds!"

The Captain pulled out two flare guns and loaded cartridges. He fired them to port and starboard. For good measure he loaded two more and fired them out over the bow and stern, putting up four points of light over the ship. The night sky was bright for at least a minute.

On his head microphone he said, "Open up and keep hammering away. I want them to think all we're carrying is ammo!" Both Meredith and he drew their side arms and started blazing away at the floating targets.

The entire team saw the sky turn to daylight in a circle around the ship, searched for possible targets and unleashed a withering blast of lead from all their positions. There were four inflatable craft still in the fight bobbing in the sea. Once the lead started pouring in from a number of positions, the leader of the Somali pirates realized that the ship wasn't giving in and actually seemed to be gaining advantage. With limited ammunition and only a couple of RPG rounds left, he realized they weren't going to be boarding this ship. He signaled the other boat drivers to pull back before anymore were lost. All four of the inflatable boats turned tail and retreated into the darkness.

Kevin and Michael tracked them for a few moments but because the illumination flares were still hanging up there their night vision apparatus wouldn't function and their long guns wouldn't be able to pick out the departing targets.

Noting the fight was abating and the few boats still floating were undermanned and unable to continue the battle, he called for a cease-fire. Everyone on the Majorca started standing and watching the departing pirates. One inflatable turned towards the Majorca and slowly motored toward some of their compatriots that were thrashing about in the water. Signaling they had no aggressive plans, the Captain allowed them to pick up their own, rather than having to do so himself.

Once the pirate boat had searched for their survivors, the remaining boats turned and limped back to their mother ship that was just a few miles away. The Captain came on the closed circuit microphone and said, "People, I may be a bit optimistic, but I think we may have broken their spirit and we have them on the run. At least we took the fight out of them. I suggest we stay on alert and keep moving out of the area."

The crew celebrated their victory for a few seconds, and then tended to the wounded, assessed damage to the ship, and got underway to re-establish their forward movement.

→ ←

Teterboro Airport, New Jersey

The Bombardier Global Express landed on the north-south runway within five minutes of its scheduled arrival from Wisconsin, to deliver shipping parts. Captain Ryan Younger quickly taxied over towards the WM Industries Hanger on the commercial side of the field. Younger and his co-pilot noticed that a black SUV with tinted windows fell in behind the plane as he turned on to the secondary approach and rolled towards the W.M. Industries Hanger. As the Bombardier rounded the corner into the alley next to its hanger, Ryan saw an additional black GMC SUV parked in the aisle at the opposite end of the hanger blocking his way. Out of the corner of his eye he saw the SUV behind him pull into the alley as well.

Sandwiched he thought, and quickly realized they were government vehicles and that the jig was up. They were probably looking for his boss on the plane. He laughed as he thought about their effort to lock him into the alleyway. There was no way he could have tried to turn the plane around in these tight quarters.

He gave a moments thought to opening the hanger door, and the door on the other side as well, and then just throttling up to shoot right through the hanger, but he realized they would catch up to him before he could take off and then they would send the Air Force after him.

He dismissed the thought about becoming a fugitive from the law and making his co-pilot one too. Ryan thought about the questions he would be asked about William Meredith. He presumed they had linked Meredith to this THCT group and would have all sorts of questions. But what could they say, and what shouldn't they say about their boss. Ryan thought about telling his co-pilot to play dumb, as he was a recent new addition and actually knew nothing of what was going on. While they were still in the cabin out of earshot he turned to his co-pilot.

"Rick, I think we are about to meet the FBI, or at least some national government agency. I'm guessing once they realize Meredith isn't on the plane, they will want to interview both of us, probably separately. They probably will want to know where Meredith is. My suggestion is to be honest and answer their questions to the best of your ability. We fly the boss wherever he wants to go and don't ask questions. The last trip we flew him to Odessa, Ukraine a couple weeks ago for a holiday trip. We also made a trip to Turkey. He has business interests in both places. That's all we know. We aren't his business partners. I'd suggest sticking to that story."

"That is all I know, so I'm good with that," Rick said looking out the cockpit window.

At the moment they were still law-abiding citizens coming home from a trip overseas. He hit the remote hanger door opener he had in the cockpit. The claxon went off making the agents standing next to the door jump at the noise. He signaled he was going to turn the plane into the hanger, and the guy in charge waved him in walking adjacent to the cockpit to maintain eye contact.

Ryan stood on the brakes and pushed the throttle forward a hair to obtain a last burst of power to ease the plane into the hanger. But he let the engines spool up a bit more than he had to. They whined loudly between the two hangers creating quite a ruckus. He looked down at the agents and knew they wished they'd brought earplugs. A moment later he eased off the brakes and the plane made a fast turn in, nestling itself into the allotted space on the hanger floor.

Looking out his cockpit window he could see the government guy holding up his leather identification, with a shiny badge and the letters FBI on it. He was being told to shut it down. Ryan raised his hand and waved in compliance but decided he would take his time so he could think.

They finished spooling down the first jet engine and then started the procedure to shut down the second engine that was still idling and whining with the roar now bouncing off the enclosed walls of the hangers. Maybe these guys wouldn't be able to even hear his answers. He continued to take his time and thought through his options.

Eventually he killed the second engine noting that one of the agents had climbed the stairs to the open second level and was staring in at him. They took their time and made a show of shutting down switches and turning dials, and then unbuckling his rig and climbing out of his seat. His co-pilot was mystified but played along because he had no idea about what was going on.

Eventually they opened the fuselage door and lowered the stairway. Before they could descend, an agent flashing his FBI badge came up the stairs and made a thorough search of the jet craft, declaring it clear to the man who was at the bottom of the stairs.

"Captain Younger, my name is Agent John Sedwedel with the New York Office of the FBI. I see that William Meredith is not aboard the craft? We would like to ask you some questions about where your employer might be?"

"Good afternoon, Agent Sedwedel, was it? What can I do for you now that you have forced me into this hanger, which is actually where we were going? Thanks for the close quarters escort. Glad to see you guys are on the job."

The agent ignored the pilot's tone and said, "We would like to know where Mr. Meredith is at the moment?"

"Well, why would you like to know the whereabouts of Mr. Meredith?" Ryan parried, trying to not sound too smug, as he knew it would just piss the agent off. He was just buying himself some time to determine what he would actually say.

"We need to talk with him about matters of national security. And we need to do that as soon as possible."

"Well, Sir, if I knew his whereabouts I would be able to tell you, but I haven't seen him for a good couple weeks now. I believe he is traveling in Europe on a well- deserved, long overdue vacation. I dropped him off in Odessa, Ukraine where he was attending to his shipping interests. From there he didn't file an itinerary with me. He said he would call when he needed to be picked up. I came home and have been making a number of other runs for the company these past couple of weeks, until he calls."

"Well let's sit down and talk about where you and Mr. Meredith have been flying for the past few months." He pulled out a stack of flight manifests from a briefcase. "You seem to be flying all over Europe, Russia and the Middle East?"

"Yes, Sir, I didn't know that was a concern to the FBI. Mr. Meredith has business interests in all sorts of countries in Europe and the Middle East. He owns a number of shipping companies and oil equipment interests. That's what rich guys do with their money; they buy companies and fly around the world to manage their money. And I get to fly him there. Like I said what's the crime?"

"I didn't say that it was a crime, Mister, I would just like to talk with him to resolve some questions we have on an open investigation," Agent Sedwedel said trying to keep a lid on the interview so he could continue the discussion in a less combative manner.

"About national security you said?" Ryan decided he would continue to stonewall until there was no alternative.

"Yes, that is why Mr. Meredith is needed for an interview."

"Well, I guess you'll have to speak with him then, which may be difficult, because he left his satellite phone in the plane when he departed a few weeks ago. That was so like him, sometimes he would leave his own wallet if I didn't remind him."

The Agent realized he was getting nothing out of the pilot. So he decided to take him downtown to continue the discussion. Maybe that would warm him up a bit.

"Mr. Younger, I would appreciate it if you would go with these agents to discuss this further." Looking at the co-pilot he asked if he would go with two other agents.

"We would also like to search the premises of this hanger with your permission?"

"Got a warrant?" He smiled and said, "I've always wanted to say that! But it's never come up! I can't give you access to this hanger, or the plane for that matter, which is not mine to give. I suggest you talk to Mr. Meredith. I'm sure he'll consider the request."

With that statement, Ryan walked over to the office door and made sure it was locked and then walked to the hanger door and hit the down button. The claxon went off again and everyone jumped. They now had a half-minute to slip under the slowly closing door that automatically locked when it touched the ground. Ryan made sure the door within the framework of the hanger door was also locked before getting into the black SUV.

➜ ←

5:00 am. Gulf of Aden

The Captain returned to the bridge once he knew Courtney was being cared for. He flicked the broken glass off his chair and turned to Meredith saying, "I wouldn't have thought we could defend ourselves as well as we just did. But I'm proud to be Captain of your ship and this crew, including your people. You are one hell of a fighting team. Your people really want this don't they?

"I think they just wanted to survive these past few minutes, but yeah, I'm proud of them too!"

"Sir, we will complete this mission; I'll do my part to get us there. Your crew is welcome to join me any time they want." He waved his hand across the somewhat destroyed pilothouse, smiled and said. "You now own a rather scarred ship, but one that is still floating….. So let's go see how bad it really is."

"Aye, Aye, Captain." Reaching for his mic Meredith spoke to his team, "We hope the brigands are gone for good, but let's proceed as if they haven't. I need everyone to verbally check in." Each THCT member verified they were in one piece.

Michael came on line and said, "Let's re-stock the gun positions with ammo. The Captain is heading for the stern. We may have some serious damage back there. Uri, could you join them as well. Everyone else stay on alert at your stations. We should have first light in less than a half-hour. Daylight should keep them away."

Meredith and the Captain arrived at the stern. They met Ralph who was hanging over what was left of the rail system trying to assess the damage below. Josef was sitting on his legs to keep him from going overboard.

"Captain, we took a couple of RPG rounds back here and one hit in the housing below," Ralph said with his head below the stern rail. "The rounds were aimed at me. I pissed them off with this shotgun, but they were lousy shots."

"Ralph, they weren't that bad of shots considering." Michael said as he climbed down the metal ladder rail from his snipers position. "Kevin and I both shot the two dudes pointing the RPG's at you. We figured they were about to blow you guys off the stern. We shot about the same time and hit both of them as they were pulling the triggers. Kevin's target sent his RPG round high and my guy's round went low, but we still hit both of them."

"Well then, thanks for saving our hides," Ralph said crawling back from the edge so the Captain could take a look.

"From the ripping noise of the explosion, it sounds as if it may be really messed up down there, Captain," Josef offered.

The Captain tied a line around his waist and threaded it through a rail of the metal ladder. The others understood what he was trying to do and grabbed the line to anchor the Captain's descent over the stern. They eased him down a few feet to assess the damage firsthand. He spent a full minute hanging over the side. Then he called for them to haul him up.

"Yeah, the round tore off the metal plating enough that the rudder assembly was exposed. All sorts of crap is in the housing and all ground up. They fucked up the entire control assembly pretty good with that shot. We aren't going anywhere fast. Looks like we are still moving in a relatively straight direction, but I don't recommend that we head out into open water with the limp we're going to have."

The Captain looked over to port, pointed and said. " Aden, Yemen is over there about 100 clicks to our northwest. I think we will be ok with daylight, although I would keep the watch out and armed. If we start whatever turn we can get out of her right now, we can then bring her around and aim for Aden. Plus we need to get Courtney looked at. Once we get close we can ask for tug assistance to get us towed into port and to a dock for repairs."

"Isn't that the deep water port where the Navy's destroyer, the U.S. S. Cole was attacked by terrorists?" Josef asked

"That's the one. Al Qaeda took responsibility for that one too, and blew a hole in the side of the destroyer, killing eleven sailors in the process.

Ever since then the Navy has had a different approach to port security in any foreign port of call."

"Captain, can we get repairs there without too much fanfare? How long will it take?" Ralph asked as he kept scanning the sea to the stern. The dawn light was brightening the eastern sky but the western sky still held the night.

"Aden is a first-class deepwater port. It has a lot of container and bulk carrier capability, and it has the kind of equipment and parts we will need. I would say that once we are in port, we might be able to make repairs and be on our way in about five days."

"Well, that throws a crimp in the schedule, but it has to be done or we'll never be able to outrun Captain Hook and his merry band of pirates." Meredith said this as he stared out at the field of battle they had just left, noting that the swamped wreckage of one of the pirate's boats was still visible in the early morning light. "Let's do it Captain, straight away. Send a message to the company and make sure they know we are coming. And see if they can get a line on an entire new rudder assembly down here as soon as possible."

"Alright, Aden it is. Let's see if we can come about and head north. I'll call ahead and maybe they can send out a tow to speed up the process," The Captain said as he headed for the bridge.

Meredith asked Ralph and Josef to meet him in the galley. "We're going to have to send some additional encrypted messages to our terrorist buddies. I'm not happy but we have to keep them updated if we are going to keep them interested. This may also be a good time to mention we have a bunch of us coming."

Ralph and Josef retrieved their computers and headed for the galley. They would need to construct a very carefully worded message that would buy them additional time.

→ ←

FBI Headquarters, Washington, D.C.

The THCT Task Force, as it was now officially code-named had centralized their Washington operations downtown in the FBI Headquarters Building on Constitution Avenue. They met in a secure tenth floor conference room named after the first FBI Agent ever killed in the line of duty back in 1926, the Edwin C. Shanahan Conference Room. As they all settled into their seats the security professionals read that Edwin Shanahan, had a young son when he was killed. That son went on to become a 30-year veteran of the FBI. After retirement he was doing security work in the World Trade Center on 9-11 and lost his life when the buildings came down.

The many security agency professionals went around the room introducing themselves and offer various pieces of information about the THCT suspected terrorist cell.

After reviewing all known facts, the groups' consensus was that they indeed had a homegrown domestic terrorism plot on their hands. The FBI and Homeland Security would take the lead from this point forward.

FBI Director Logan Taylor presided over the meeting. "Thank you all for changing your schedules." Looking to the other end of the long conference table, he said, "For those of you not aware, Ms. Karen Lee from the CIA and NSA Director Brent Eichalberger have been gathering Intel on this new terrorist cell for a couple of months now. With bin Laden's death we are concerned with a homegrown terrorist cell right in our own backyard. Karen, I appreciate all the work you have done thus far, and I'm pleased you will stay with us, should we have to cross over the water again in our investigation."

"Thanks, Logan, I still believe there may be an overseas connection, so I thought Bede and I should stay in the loop. Plus I don't get downtown much anymore." Karen Lee said and smiled. "If I may, I'll bring everyone up to speed. In trying to track this THCT group over at NSA, Bill Dalde, one of the NSA Echelon analysts, started tracking all communications that mentioned this series of letters. Bill would you summarize for us?"

"Thank you, Director. These letters T H C T started popping up in all sorts of communications and phone messages, in rather strange places in New York City at first, and then the same letters began appearing in messages from overseas in many of our favorite troublesome spots."

"Bill, I know how Echelon works, but why does a series of random letters stand out when they don't spell any particular word?" a Homeland Security representative asked from across the table.

"That's just it. The computer notes that it doesn't fit into the message or conversation. It stands out because it doesn't make sense. It seems out of context. If the bad guys were smart they would write lovely prose and make sense of their conversations and their sentences. We wouldn't notice that as much."

"Anyway, there was enough oddity to the lettering, so we started a Red Flag inquiry and started tracking down any and all mention of these acronyms in any form of message, phone call or communications we came across. Most of the initial stuff came out of New York and when we dug deeper we started getting some small leads. To make a long story short the FBI NY Office did some old-fashioned legwork tracking down these calls and the throwaway phones used by these callers. They eventually identified a couple of Pakistani brothers who were operating in New York City as cab drivers. But we couldn't find them anywhere in the city."

Bede Long couldn't contain himself, so he said, "The interesting thing about these two men was we found they both were victim/survivors of 9-11. Their wives and children had perished that Tuesday, in a day care center in the WTC North Tower."

"That confused us a bit, but then we also found out they had both left the country for France a few months back. CIA did some digging and placed them in Calais at the Jungle immigrant camps, so we decided to dig a little deeper. We had the NY FBI office look further into these guys and found they had been involved in 9-11 grief counseling sessions for the past five years. So we checked with the Doctor leading their group sessions. We learned the two Pakistani brothers disappeared about a month ago."

Most people in the room had already read the growing files and were familiar with the investigation but they all listened patiently. Steven Olson and Brian Jones sat there quietly knowing it was better to let the Director play out the story.

"The Psychiatrist spoke highly of the two foreign gentlemen. He said they had eagerly participated in the group dynamics for a number of years. But he couldn't say where they currently were. In fact, he said, the whole counseling group had disappeared, and stopped coming to sessions at about the same time. The Doctor presumed they were just tired of the routine, and had decided to move on."

Director Taylor looked over at his two rookie agents, and decided they should tell the next part because they had done all the legwork.

"Agent Olson, would you and Agent Jones continue." Steven looked at all the eyes focusing on him and took a deep breath.

"Yes, thank you, Director." He repeated his first fieldwork story. "We obtained the complete list of the counseling group and thought we'd interview the others to see if we could follow the two brothers. We had a good list to work from."

"If I may?" Brian Jones passed around the list of names. "These people were from all walks of life, rich guys, an investment banker, business owners, a UN translator, a NYC Cop and a former ATF Agent. There was even a dish washer in the group."

Steven continued, "So we tried to track all of these people down to interview them. We found information and addresses for all of them in and around the Tri-State area. But they too had disappeared off the face of the earth. We interviewed family members and neighbors, fellow workers, anyone we could find that knew these people, but no one could give us any good leads on where they were. One neighbor said the New York cop had said he was going to Greece on vacation. A woman business owner said she was going to Turkey on holiday. The Russian translator said he was going home to Russia to visit his dead wife's brother."

Brian summarized. "Everyone we interviewed told us these people were upstanding citizens and that they had endured incomprehensible tragedy in losing loved ones in 9-11, but they couldn't tell us where they were now. They hadn't seen them for weeks, nor had they talked with them."

"We found out the rich guy, William Meredith has a private jet he keeps at Teterboro. So we checked it out, too." Steven explained. "As you might have guessed, it's missing. We pulled the flight logs and it showed the plane has made a number of overseas trips to, get this, Paris and Calais, to the Ukraine, and to Greece and Turkey in recent months. The current manifests booked with the FAA say the plane is due back later today, so we're going to sit on the pilot when he returns."

CIA Director Karen Lee interrupted, "So maybe the CIA should get involved again. Can we get those flight logs? We can put some people on the ground chasing down that end in Europe and see if our friends have turned up over there?"

"There is definitely a pattern here, and I think these folks all have something in common, besides the loss of loved ones. But it still doesn't make sense." Director Logan Taylor said this as he scanned the list from the grief-counseling group. He was silent for a moment, and then he slowly exhaled a lung full of breath, and said, "What if they were actually part of the terrorist group involved in 9-11 and something went horribly bad for them? What if their loved ones were actually terrorists on the ground and in the buildings when the buildings collapsed? What if they are involved in plotting a follow-up act of terrorism, perhaps even bigger?"

Everyone thought about that for a minute, but couldn't seem to get their hands around it.

"According to Dr. Hensley, they were all legitimately referred to the counseling group and he assured me that they had indeed lost loved ones," Agent Jones said this as he scanned the faces at the table. "We wondered if it might be just the opposite. That this group has bonded together to seek revenge for their personal losses. Maybe they are going after terrorists?"

"That is a theory the CIA had as well," Karen Lee said, and Bede Long nodded in agreement. "We did some modeling with the known facts. Since these people all suffered tremendous loss, maybe they bonded together to get even. That may be worth asking the Doctor if he discerned any such anger focused on the terrorists."

"Hell, Karen, all of us would have liked to get even with that bastard bin Laden and his al-Qaeda henchmen. But we aren't running around in the desert or looking in caves. We talk about it, we don't act on our anger." Director Taylor stated to the group, looking for some agreement.

Karen Lee thought about what the Director had just said, and offered another insight, which hadn't been articulated up to this point.

"I believe you all have clearance to hear this, so what about the missing Russian briefcase bomb? Could that be a factor in this case? That issue flared up a few weeks ago, right about when our friends here went missing? Might they have it? Heaven forbid!"

Perry Clarke, the Joint Chief of Staff Liaison to the Task Force had sat quietly through the entire discussion, but now leaned forward. "Karen, I'm not sure everyone did have clearance for that bombshell of a comment. With bin Laden's announcement we've had a few too many bombshell announcements this week. But now that the cat's out of the bag, the Russians do have a small tactical device in the wind and advised us of it over a month ago. We have all sorts of assets out there looking into the matter."

"Sorry Perry, perhaps I shouldn't have blurted out that fact, but with all that has gone on the past couple of days, I think it may be more than a coincidence that these folks and a suitcase nuke both went missing at about the same time? It's conceivable that this Russian nuke could have crossed paths with our missing New Yorkers? The timing is about right."

Their seemed to be general agreement around the table that such a scenario could exist. Director Taylor tried to bring the focus back to the most immediate investigation.

"Perry, I think it's worth sharing files. Maybe there is a connection. Karen, maybe you could get some people looking where they lost their bomb and see if that crosses paths with our THCT group.

"Done, Sir, but everyone also has to sit on Karen's news flash. The missing nuke information can't leave this room; if it does we will have much bigger problems. The last thing we need is the press picking up on this. We'll have a stampede in New York and Washington on our hands!"

"Mr. Dalde, I want you to have that whiz-bang computer of yours do a word check on every conceivable word that could be utilized in the acronym THCT. I know that's a tall order but that is what your big brother snooper is supposed to be able to do isn't it?"

"I'm already working on that Sir, I should have a short list of possibilities in another day. I'll bring them along. I'm guessing the first T, or the third T is for Terrorist, so that's a starting point."

"All right people, let's meet here Thursday at 1:00 pm and I want answers. This one is making me nervous," Director Taylor said this as he waved Perry Clarke into a side room.

Brian Jones and Steven Olson headed for the door. They were pleased they were being kept in the loop. Once outside the Conference Room and in the elevator alone, Steven said.

"Brian, I still say we can break this case wide open. Let's get that pilot to talk."

➔ ←

Gulf of Aden, Yemen

Heading in a northerly direction with limited ability to steer the ship, Captain Brinkmann got on the ship's radio to call Aden and ask for assistance. He explained that the Majorca, making its way to Karachi, Pakistan, had been attacked by pirates in the Gulf of Aden and was having steering problems. The Aden Port Authority responded positively, as if they had heard the story many times. They advised a tug would be sent out to assist with entry into the Port of Aden for the required repairs.

The Captain was further advised that the pirates of Somalia, in recent months had become much more aggressive and were attacking ships with greater frequency. He admitted these attacks had created a cottage industry for repairing ships and it was probable the Majorca could be repaired relatively quickly, depending on the extent of the actual damage.

Two tugs were dispatched immediately and met the Majorca six miles outside the harbor. One tug lined up on the bow and extended a tow line to pull the ship, while the second nestled up to the stern, considerably improving the ship's maneuverability. Together they brought the ship towards Aden's deep- water harbor, which lies in the center of an extinct volcano's crater. It is a first class cargo facility with container, bulk and oil terminal capability dating back to colonial days.

Aden had been a major British Crown Colony since 1839, when the British East India Company landed Royal marines at Aden to occupy the territory and stop attacks by pirates. The irony was that 180 years later the pirates were still active in the Gulf of Aden. Britain did not leave until 1967 when the last of the British forces officially departed. As part of the

Indian British Empire, Aden had developed into a major international city with a considerable British influence, that could still be seen in the city's architecture, especially in its waterfront and old town sections.

Once inside the harbor, the Majorca was eased up the channel between the fishing fleets and the huge container terminal on the north side of the harbor. The harbor was large and diversified with many ocean-going bulk and container ships tied up to the many industrial docks. Deeper into the natural harbor created eons ago by an erupting volcano they recognized the military dock where the U.S.S Cole had been at anchor when it was attacked by al Qaeda terrorists six years earlier. Eleven U.S. navy personnel had been killed and the ship was taken out of commission with a gaping hole in its bulkhead. The ship had to be taken back to the U.S. for major repairs nestled on a dry dock ship.

A few hundred yards further on, the Majorca was eased up to a large ship repair dock. Lines were cast and tied to the bollards. The Captain met the port authorities to give them a summary of the pirate attack and to initiate the repair effort. The ship's manifest, cargo, destinations and papers were reviewed and accepted. The crew's documents were reviewed to everyone's satisfaction and the gangplank was put out to allow the crew a few days in port.

Down in the ship's galley William Meredith, Joseph, Uri and Ralph had been waiting for a response to the last message they had sent to al Qaeda. They had advised the terrorists that the archeology team had fallen behind schedule, but would still be able to deliver the highly prized artifacts in the near future. In the same communication, they kept the Trojan horse ruse front and center by announcing they had access to additional artifacts for a future sale, five more beautiful artifacts were available for delivery, once the first transaction was completed. They stated the archeology team would be interested in negotiating to sell these precious goods in perfect condition to the principals, once a final destination was determined.

Later that afternoon while the rest of the team was resting and licking their wounds; they received a coded response to their message. The Pakistani mountain location in the federal territories was no longer their ultimate destination. They were advised that their quarry had moved to a new location in Yemen!

The entire THCT plan was changing almost as if the quarterback had called an audible at the line of scrimmage. A new destination was designated, shocking everyone. William, Joseph, Uri and Ralph stared at the coded message in silence.

Meredith broke into an almost devilish grin and became giddy as he leaned back in his chair and contemplated the awful green metal ceiling of the galley. He tried to grasp what this meant to the plan. "I'll be damned we're there, or here, as the case may be," William Meredith finally said, turning back to the others. "If I'm reading this correctly, I think al Qaeda has come to us, rather than we to them. They are here somewhere in Yemen, and if I'm right, we were actually closer to him when we fought off the damn pirates, than we are right now. If this is for real, he's hiding out on some island in the Gulf of Aden."

Meredith reached for some nautical maps that he had brought to the galley and began tracing some lines in pencil. "Somewhere out there." He pointed to the map and drew a circle around an island off the coast of Somalia. "It's called Socotra."

Josef looked concerned with this new development and asked, "Do you think they could have figured out who we are, and where we are?"

"I doubt they know who we are and that we're here already, but perhaps we should tell them that we're close now?" Ralph Behar said staring at the laptop computer screen.

"My guess is the heat was on in Pakistan and Afghanistan and they decided to find a quieter haven. They were getting tired of all those jets bombing the mountains and those U.S. drones scanning everywhere. My reading on bin Laden says this is where he originally came from. They were probably coming here when those Seals caught him with his pants down in that compound," Meredith said in response to the question.

Ralph Behar sighed, and sat down on the galley bench. He leaned back and placed his two hands on top of his head. Throwing his legs up on the table across from him, he said, "I can't believe these terrorists are here in Yemen! Hell, we know more than the U.S. Government does! How is that for fucking luck? Those damn pirates may have actually done us a great service, even though I took some shrapnel in the ass."

"Well, if it's true we're a lot closer to our destination than I thought we would be. It's a real bonus if we don't have to navigate Pakistan and all the Taliban to get to them. I was worried about climbing the mountains without getting killed in the process," Meredith said this pulling out his computer. He activated his satellite signal and searched the words, Socotra Island, and al Qaeda in Yemen.

"I don't know a lot about al Qaeda in Yemen," Joseph offered, "but I do know that they must have a pretty strong terrorist group here, based on the attack of the USS Cole awhile back. In fact this could be where their brand of terrorism many years ago."

"William," Uri interrupted, "I think you will be surprised with Yemen once you see it. I've been here a number of times over the past thirty years as a sailor. It has been a primary trade route through the Middle East for centuries. And Aden was once an important British outpost as part of the British Empire."

"I can see that Uri, it says here it still carries a significant British influence in its architecture and many people speak the Queen's English."

"Wait until you see the city with its expressways, shopping malls and suburbs," Josef said looking over Meredith's shoulder scanning the various Internet screens. "I think this will make our plans much easier to accomplish. We may not look so out of character."

As Meredith kept reading the many hits he got on Socotra, he said, "This changes everything for the better. We are literally within striking distance, somewhere on this big island in the Gulf of Aden." He pointed at a map of Yemen showing the Island of Socotra east of Somalia and southeast of Yemen.

Josef fired up the other laptop and ran it through the satellite search that Meredith had set up for sending emails and satellite phone messages. The circuitous path, set up by Meredith's corporate IT people, bounced the messages around the globe, from server site to site a number of times before arriving at the actual destination. Josef also used the satellite phone to check messages and was surprised to find one for Meredith from Ryan Younger, his company pilot. He listened to the recorded message, and then handed the satellite phone to Meredith.

"Sir, this is Ryan Younger. Thought you should know your plane is unavailable, indefinitely. It seems your First Brother Ivan wanted to borrow it and wanted to talk to you about where you have gone on vacation. Let's talk soon."

Meredith hit the repeat button to listen one more time and turned on the speaker function so the others could listen. After the message repeated, Meredith said, " I don't have a first brother Ivan, thus I think Ryan emphasized the first letter of those three words, telling us the FBI is on to us and has confiscated my company jet. I'm guessing it won't be long before they find us here on this ship. We are going to have to get under way soon or we will be placed under arrest."

Ralph and Josef both whistled at the same time. "If they have your name and plane, they probably know who all of us are. Your right they can't be that far off." He said this without any enthusiasm, as he didn't really know what to say.

"They don't know where you are other than in Europe, so I think we're ok. Your last known location was Odessa a month ago. I doubt they will look for you on one of your working ships. So we should be fine for now. I think we can still pull this off before the cavalry comes charging in to stop us," Ralph said.

Meredith responded, "I'm glad we know they're on our trail, but we can't stop now. We're too close and the leadership of al Qaeda may be just across that water." He said this standing up and pointing out to sea through the porthole window.

"We need to have a meeting with the others and decide what this means. In the meantime let's find out all we can about this Island of Socotra and how we would get there if we abandoned ship here in Aden."

Joseph continued looking at Google Earth maps of Yemen. The satellite imagery was startling in it's clarity and definition. Looking at Aden he saw highways, a modern airport and a huge shipping port. He then tracked southeast of Aden out into the Gulf of Aden and found the Island of Socotra about 200 miles out. Looking at a satellite image he saw it was indeed a large island.

"I can see why al Qaeda would find this an attractive place. It looks almost barren and there are few roads and towns on the whole island," Josef said as he kept dragging his finger across the Google map moving the cursor from one end of the island to the other.

"So let's start building a good file on everything Yemen. I want to know the history, the terrorism connections and infrastructure. Let's get the Captain down here to see when we might be ready to cast off." He smiled and rubbed his hands together in anticipation of reacquiring his goal of avenging his son's death.

All four men got busy using their computers, searching the Internet and taking notes on Yemen and Socotra. An hour later they had amassed a mountain of yellow pad notes and information.

"Yemen looks like it has a pretty good infrastructure. It even has an extensive tourist trade with tours of ancient historic sites. They say this was the cradle of early civilization. I found a notation that Cain and Abel from the Bible are even supposed to be buried here," Meredith said this as he sorted through a number of screens.

Ralph Behar looked up and announced, "They even have mountain biking as a tourist sport and eco-tours that go to Socotra. It says Socotra is like another planet. Maybe we could try to be eco-tourists and explore the island. Once we are on the Island we could turn ourselves into the arms dealers we are purporting to be and walk up to his cave and have him invite us in. Once we get close, I suspect they will come and find us."

"How about sending Uri, Osama and Malik into Aden for some reconnaissance? They could blend in well and get a good feeling for al-Qaeda's influence around here. Uri has been in Aden before. They could hit a few of those coffee houses and maybe even some Internet cafes to get a feel for the country and see if we can get any leads." Ralph said.

"I'd like to visit again. I do know the coffee shops and perhaps can get us some leads and information. I'll talk to Osama and Malik." Uri said.

"I'll get on it." Ralph said, "What's the currency here? I don't know if I have any Yemeni whatever."

"I would think that Uri, O & Malik could use Egyptian pounds, that would be safe and would make sense," Meredith suggested.

"Done, I'll get them organized so they can slip into Aden around Noon tomorrow. It is Saturday so hopefully there won't be too much activity on the pier," Josef said this heading for the door.

→ ←

Aden Harbor

The small group of travelers wandered away from the ship and the industrial dock about Noon. Osama and Malik wanted to flag a taxi right away out of professional curiosity, so Uri let them lead the way and acted as the wise old traveler. They asked for a quick tour of Aden to get their bearings and asked to see the neighborhoods and former British part of the central city. Eventually they asked to be dropped at a coffee shop where the locals would hang out, to catch the custom and culture of the city.

In the coffee shop, they noted the stale pall of smoke from the water pipes and cigarettes. Then there was the smell of khat, a somewhat national recreational drug that was locally grown and was a major agricultural crop throughout the country. The bitter green leaves of this plant are chewed like tobacco and jammed into the cheek, like a chipmunk would store food. Then this wad acts like a strainer for the bitter coffee and produces a wet, stale fragrance in the room. This smell, plus the sweat and sweet smell of incense, made for a heady atmosphere that took some getting used to as it hung heavily in the air. A large contingent of Muslim men sat at the tables smoking their pipes and cigarettes, and drinking their dark aromatic coffee, grown in the hills of Yemen, Eritrea and Somalia.

Malik and Osama noticed some of the men sitting nearby carried a knifelike weapon tucked into their cloth belts. As their eyes became accustomed to the semi-darkness they saw that almost every man in the place had such a weapon. And everyone was watching them.

Uri directed the Pakistanis to a table on one side of the café and got them to sit down so they would not continue to stare at the many men in the shop. He leaned in and quietly explained the custom of the blade to them.

"The knives that you see are called jambiyas. They're curved daggers worn in a sheath kind of like a national weapon. They often have ornate hand -carved handles made from a rhino's horn. Almost all adult Yemenis wear the dagger-like weapon in their belt to symbolize their heritage as a warrior class. It has fueled their rebellious nature for centuries. It is their custom, so stop staring at them before they draw them on you and filet you for lunch."

"I would like for such a weapon to place in my belt," Osama whispered staring at the jeweled handle of a weapon on the elder man sitting at an adjacent table.

"I want one too. We should fit in here Uri. This will help I think," Malik piped in almost as quickly. Maybe we could get them in the bazaar down the street."

They ordered cups of thick black coffee and sat there quietly listening to the conversations around them. While Osama and Malik could occasionally distinguish some of the talk, Uri had no problems understanding the conversations. They were mostly about the death of bin Laden and Yemeni insurrection, occurring daily in the major cities. Others talked of business, western culture, the politics in general. There was general anger in everyone's conversations, as if the rest of the World owed them a living. Uri heard them speak about the Yemeni government and its political leaders with great disdain, and they talked about taking to the streets. Change was coming soon enough. Numerous languages were being spoken, often mixed into sentences for emphasis and clarity. That was not surprising as this had been a trading place for centuries. He even heard the Queen's English being spoken unapologetically and noted that was a good sign that they would be able to pass among the locals.

After drinking their brew, they casually moved on to another coffee shop across the street from a large Mosque, where mid-day prayers were just letting out. They entered the dark café and found seats at a table in the middle of the room and ordered more coffee. Osama and Malik tried some local khat but quickly found it to have a very bitter taste, and quickly went back to their coffee.

In minutes the tables around them were crowded with prayer goers who would drink and relax away the remainder of the afternoon talking and complaining until the afternoon prayer calling. O and Malik were beginning to understand more of the conversations around them and realized that al Qaeda and the Pashtun language were well settled in Aden and the surrounding countryside. All three tried to listen to the conversations going on around them without being too obvious about their eavesdropping.

The group then found a local travel agency and inquired about tours that could be taken to the holy sites in Yemen and to Socotra Island. The Agency representative was more than happy to accommodate their questions.

"We are a forward-looking country, one that is embracing change and the Western culture. You will find that Yemen has much to offer. We have many ancient sites dating back centuries that are within driving distance. We would be pleased to arrange a customized tour."

"Perhaps you could also tell us about this Island of Socotra we keep hearing about. I understand it is part of Yemen but way out there in the Arabian Sea? I have been reading a lot about it, they say it is almost an uninhabited, and a very unique place on earth. They say it is like the Galapagos Islands in that it has one-of-a-kind plants, special species of animals, and insects that cannot be found anywhere else on earth? Is this true?"

The travel agency salesman readily answered the question as he started pulling maps from a filing cabinet. "I have been to Socotra a couple of times on what I believe you call 'eco-tours'. It is indeed a different kind of place. It is a very large island and has all sorts of unique landforms, caves and hidden valleys. I heard one tourist we escorted over there and he said a confusing thing. He said "it is not the end of the earth, but you can see it from there." He thought that was funny, but it did not make sense to me."

Uri was confused by the comment as well but said, "I think we would very much like to see this end of earth place. Is it difficult to get there?"

"No, that is not a problem. There are once a week flights from Aden."

"Well, we are interested in hiking and seeing unique plants and animals. Could such travel be arranged? Might you have any brochures that we could take to our friends?"

"We could check to see about a day trip and I do have brochures. It is a pretty rough and primitive place."

"We would like that." They let him know they would check with their fellow tourists and would get back to him quickly.

By evening they were ready to return to the Majorca armed with facts, figures and impressions of the country they had been forced to visit. The taxi drove right up to the ship's gangplank, as there was little traffic around. They boarded without incident.

→ ←

Aden Harbor

Work was progressing well on the rudder assembly damage. Once the metal plating had been cut away and the housing was taken apart, the damage was less extensive than first thought. A number of replacement parts had already been shipped by the Icolos Shipping Company by air from Athens and arrived the following day. At the same time other repairs were being made to the vessel, with new rails at the stern and near the bow. The various metal plates ripped up by the RPG rounds were being torched off and replaced with new framework and fittings. The glass in the pilothouse was replaced and the ship would be sea worthy in a matter of days.

In the ship's galley the THCT team was poring over all of the information and maps that had been found in their covert trips into the city. The captain had joined the session and had brought what nautical charts he had available for the Gulf of Aden and Socotra. They discussed their options and corresponded in coded messages a number of times with their al Qaeda contacts. They had not mentioned where they were, or how they would be arriving at the final site. The al Qaeda operatives continued to encourage them to head towards Yemen and the Island of Socotra.

It was decided that when the ship was ready again they would pull out of port and make the run through the Gulf of Aden pirate waters again and head towards the Eastern end of the Island of Socotra. Once there, they would anchor off the Island and prepare to meet with the terrorists.

Captain Brinkmann searched the harbor docks and found a sea-worthy 20-foot fishing boat that looked solid. He and Ralph purchased the craft using Egyptian pounds and floated it over to the Majorca. It was then winched onto the deck of the ship. His engineer went over the craft carefully and tuned-up the engines, so it would not fail. The thought was that the THCT team could use the boat to make landfall on the island, and hopefully use it to depart as well.

As their improvised plan came together Meredith and Josef corresponded again with the terrorist contacts. They advised they would be entering the area soon.

Meredith sent a follow-up message advising the antiquities were large enough that they were traveling by ship and would advise when they were in the Gulf of Aden. The response again surprised them. Because they were traveling by boat, new instructions said to bypass Hadiboh and to instead head to the eastern side of the Island and weigh anchor. At that point further instructions would be forthcoming.

➜ ⬅

Aden, Yemen

A bearded local Yemeni sat quietly at his table smoking a water pipe and drinking his coffee. He was troubled by what he had been hearing from known al Qaeda operatives that frequented the café. He thought that he should share the information with someone. He paid his bill, dropping some coins on the table and left the café, heading for the harbor area. As he approached the waters edge, he grabbed a fishing pole that was leaning against a building and found a piling he could sit on while he sorted out his options. He sat there weighing the information he had collected from a dozen sources.

As he fished without bait he watched a ship with farm equipment stacked on deck slowly pass by. He paid no attention to the vessel. The ship left the harbor entrance and Jabir al-Fayfi opened his cell phone and dialed a number. He left a message stating he needed an immediate meeting and closed the phone.

Two hours later he slipped in a side entrance of the U.S. Consulate building, was frisked from head to toe and then escorted by an armed Marine to a small conference room. Sitting alone in the windowless room he stared at himself in the large mirror on one wall. He was actually a former Saudi citizen who had been held for years at the U.S. military prison at Guantanamo Bay, for acts of terrorism against the United States. After many years of incarceration, he had been released to Saudi Arabia in 2007, where he disappeared and fled to Yemen, quickly hooking up with al Qaeda. With his many contacts from Guantanamo and his anger for the U.S., he quickly became a part of Yemen's terrorist activities. Yet, he was actually a double agent working for the Americans.

The door opened and the one person he knew in the Consulate walked in and sat down offering him some tea and a handshake. "It is good to see you Jabir, although I'm concerned that you have broken cover. Your short message sounded ominous, so what is up?" Justin Bottos said.

Justin was a civilian attaché in the Consulate. He had been stationed in Aden for the last two years having settled in about a month before Jabir was released and sent to Saudi Arabia. Bottos was actually station chief for the CIA in this growing hotbed of al Qaeda discontent and personally handled this double agent in Yemen.

"I'm concerned with what I am hearing in the cafes and from my counterparts. Something big is about to happen, now that bin Laden has been killed. The local al Qaeda tribesmen are angry with the U.S. for what it did; they are mumbling something is up. I haven't been able to get any solid information from any one source but it is being whispered that a good number of al Qaeda leaders may be coming to Yemen in the next few days and weeks."

"That is very interesting, my friend. With bin Laden's death perhaps they are having some sort of summit?" Bottos said this as a question.

"That could very well be. Nobody has said who is coming, but I know that something is up. I have heard that al-Awlaki has disappeared as well from his mountain lair. Perhaps he has put out this call. He has become a ghost moving as much as bin Laden did."

"You were right to bring this to me. I'll kick it upstairs and see if they can offer any insights. I'll do it now. Would you like to stay here this evening and get a shower and some rest?"

"That would be good, Justin. I could use a good night's sleep without waking up every other minute to look over my shoulder."

"Done. Meantime I'll cable DC with your concerns and see what they have to say."

Justin Bottos went to the radio room and composed a carefully crafted inquiry asking what the CIA thought about this news. He hoped for a quick turnaround.

→ ←

THCT Task Force, Washington D.C.

With the death of bin Laden all the Homeland Security agencies were working overtime to insure there wasn't any retribution coming to America. The Task Force was going over new information they had identified. Slowly, piece-by-piece, additional facts were coming together. They thought they were starting to see something that didn't make much sense, but all the data was starting to suggest an unbelievable scenario.

Perhaps these people were actually not terrorists in the traditional sense. Maybe they were not intent on attacking the U.S., but instead were going after bin Laden, and now with his death, were going after the rest of al Qaeda! The Task Force had looked at the known facts a dozen different ways and they kept coming up with the same incredible scenario.

CIA Director Karen Lee kept asking questions of the Task Force members until she too was embracing the scenario. "So you all think these yahoo's have actually got that Russian nuke and were going after bin

Laden, but we beat them to the punch? Since we took that option off the table, what are they up to now?"

"Our guys have tracked some of their last known whereabouts to places like Russia, Greece and Turkey. This Meredith guy is quite wealthy and his private jet has been to all those places as well. But he is nowhere to be found. Hell, none of them are," FBI Director Taylor said.

"We have Meredith's jet locked up in a hanger at Teterboro, and we interviewed both pilots but they couldn't tell us anything we didn't already know." another Agent offered. "Since then that lead pilot has disappeared too."

Bill Dalde offered a comment, "We've also picked up a lot of chatter about the Russian nuke missing within Russia, and there has been talk of other small yield weapons missing as well. We've picked up a lot of messages coming out of Pakistan, Egypt and Yemen concerning people linked to al Qaeda. Seems a lot of them are on the move."

"Bill, I just got a cable from one of my people in Yemen about the same thing. Our guy is pressing for more but everyone's being tightlipped." Karen Lee said. "I guess it's time to suggest this scenario to the President, although I'm still confused about what we may actually have here."

"Karen, the President is at Camp David this weekend, lets schedule a meeting with him up there and not wait until next week," Logan Taylor said pushing his chair away from the table. "We can bring him up to speed together."

"Let's do it. I'm getting concerned about this in light of the bin Laden raid!"

→ ←

BOOK IV - REVENGE

Gulf of Aden

The Majorca cleared Aden Harbor and headed east through the Gulf of Aden. They had decided to leave port by mid-morning making the Gulf run in daylight hopefully minimizing any new chance of attack from the pirates of Somalia, home based on the other side of the Gulf. Even though it was quiet, the THCT members and crew were on alert with a complete over-the-horizon radar array scanning the waters ahead. Kevin and Michael had prepped all weaponry in case it was needed. Uri had even volunteered to climb the crane tower to act as lookout.

They sailed east at about twenty knots on a calm sea. Captain Brinkmann went 100 kilometers east hugging the Yemen coastline before he ventured southeast across the Gulf waters heading for Socotra.

Staying about three miles offshore the Captain then traveled east along the stark island coastline. The entire THCT team eventually came to the bridge, borrowed the most powerful binoculars on board and tried to get a feel for the barren island. All they saw were lonely stretches of white sand beaches and dunes, low lying hills and distant mountains. The range ran the astern half of the Island and was called the Haggier Range, and alternately the Skund Mountains by the Yemeni's and locals. The range rose up to 1,700 meters, over 6,000 feet.

Continuing east, the terrain got even more rugged with jagged peaks and cliffs jutting out over the water. Everyone had given up scanning for human life, as there seemed to be none. It was a barren forbidding land, just as they had been told. It wasn't the end of the Earth, but you could see it from there. They took satisfaction that this was the place that al Qaeda was retreating to because they were he was being hounded by all of western civilization.

Meredith called a quick meeting in the galley. He wanted to go over the plan of attack.

"Before we have another battle about who is going ashore, I want to make it clear the ladies have to stay on board. Courtney, your still mending and you can help more by monitoring the airwaves with the Captain and keeping tabs on Ryan Younger. Kate even if you put on the black drapes, you would stand out like foreign movie stars on this god-forsaken Island. Is that clear?"

"We hear you Bill. We kind of figured you would say something like that. Kate and I don't like it one bit, but we're team members and we'll take one for the team."

"I still think it's not fair." Kate said this as she banged the table with her fist. "We've come this far. We shot at the bad guys. I think I even hit a couple."

"I know I did." Courtney said in unison rubbing her still very sore shoulder. "And I could do it again."

"But, ladies, this whole thing is in jeopardy if we get these guys pissed off before they pull the trigger on that bomb. I'm sorry, but we're too close to let it slip away now."

"So what do we do? Just sit on the boat?"

"Captain Brinkmann assures me you will have major defensive responsibility for the ship. We need to know our exit plan is in place and this ship is still a viable way out. In addition, Ryan Younger advised they have confiscated my jet back home. They grilled him for hours and he thinks they are on to me, and perhaps all of us."

"That's great, so now we're fugitives without a country or a jet ride. How do we get home if we ever do get off this boat and island?"

"Ryan got out of New York. He drove north to Canada, flew to Iceland and then switched commercial flights to Oslo. I have a shipping company in Scandinavia that has another jet he can fly. I already sent instructions. It's a big enough craft to carry all of us. Courtney and Kate, I need you to work up a plan with Ryan and figure out how we make that happen. And be discreet in your conversations. I suspect the FBI will be monitoring everything."

"Will do," Courtney said, glad she and Kate at least had something to do.

"William, just a thought, but I believe there is a good harbor town on the Yemeni side of the Gulf that has a jet runway," Captain Brinkmann said, offering one of his nautical maps. He started tracing his finger along the Yemeni coastline heading east.

"Here, it's called Balhof. I've been past there once before. It is an oil terminal loading facility and refinery town. When we leave Socotra we could sail for that harbor and off load the entire bunch to meet up with your pilot. Then I could proceed to Karachi and deliver the farm equipment and wheat just as we are supposed to be doing."

"There you go, Courtney, looks like the Captain is willing to help with the extraction plan as well," Meredith said.

"There is another reason I suggest we go that way, Sir. If we are successful in delivering this weapon to the leaders of al Qaeda, and actually get away from them, I don't want to be heading east in the Arabian Sea when that thing actually goes off. The prevailing winds will blow the fallout drift out to sea and somewhat north this time of year. So I think we should be heading west back into pirate country to steer clear of the radioactive fallout that will be drifting in the winds."

"I hadn't thought about that. I'd been concerned about the many innocent victims that might have been in the bomb and drift zone if it went off in Pakistan. I guess we should be pleased that bin Laden's death has driven these nutcases to this remote island. If we do pull this off out here in the middle of nowhere, we'd have almost no innocent victims on our conscience. Here's to the al Qaeda for finding an even more remote rock to crawl under." He raised his coffee cup for a toast.

"Now let's talk about how we make them believe we are real gun runners."

"The way they keep paying us deposits and giving us instructions, I think they already believe who we are," Josef said. Everyone agreed.

"That's true but you have to figure we're not just walking in there, saying hello, and saying here you go buddy, bye, and we're out of there," Ralph Behar said. "I suspect there is going to be a little bit of courtship and tea passed around with a whole bunch of guns trained on us. My guess is we won't even see their leaders at first. I'm guessing they are a little spooked and gun shy. So Bill is right, we need to play the role of arms dealers well."

"Bill, you asked Kevin and I to be the arms dealers bodyguards, but do you think they'll allow us to walk in there with any weapons?"

"Good question," Meredith said. "I think we need to show up with weapons, and let them take them from us when they pat us down. We readily accept their rules, which should make them more comfortable."

"So we are going in naked? I don't know if I like that," Kevin said.

"I think we have to take that chance. We have advised them we have access to more of these suitcase bombs and I'm hoping they won't want to kill us off before we can deliver the other weapons. Kate did a good job of photo-shopping the all the pictures we sent them. They think we have five more weapons after the first delivery. That should be our insurance if we can make them believe we are arms dealers."

"So let's talk about what each of us should be doing as we visit this desolate place."

The planning went on for two more hours until everyone felt comfortable in their respective roles. Meredith would be the British arms dealer. Josef would be his Russian counterpart who secured the weapon. Ralph Behar, the Iranian, was the financier and would handle the final electronic transactions wired through a bank in the Maldives. Uri, the Egyptian, was the boat Captain who transported them to the island. Michael Pappas, the Greek, and Kevin Geary, the Irish Provo, were Meredith's bodyguards. And O and Malik, the Pakistani brothers, were the original contacts that made the offer, were his point people.

Courtney and Kate sat on the sidelines grumbling as the men rehearsed their roles.

→ ←

East of Socotra Island

The Majorca made good time and had run the pirate gauntlet waters without incident. They were now 10 miles east of Socotra in the Arabian Sea. The sun was setting in the west. As they passed the island they witnessed how remote the eastern end was. Scanning the rocky terrain with high-powered binoculars they saw it was almost uninhabitable, with a harsh, hot and dry climate, being only 13 degrees north of the Equator.

On this end of the island there was little to be seen other than some truly odd plant life. They spied small forests of very odd-looking trees growing in clusters that looked like overgrown mushrooms. Their Internet search found these plants to be unique to the Island. They were called Dragon's Blood Trees, because any injury to the bark would result in a deep red liquid pouring out of the tree. In Roman times this sap was thought to have had medicinal purposes. The limbs spread out like huge canopied mushrooms, fully green on top, with thick-veined limbs densely growing underneath. From below it looked similar to brain tissue.

There was also another odd plant that grew in clumps on the rocky plains and near the shoreline. It was called the Desert Rose, with vibrant red flowers growing out of stubby stalks that looked like elephant leg stumps stuck in the ground. It too was unique to this particular Island.

About eight miles off of Ra's Momi Point, a jagged peninsula that jutted out into the Arabian Sea, the Captain set the cruise control into a lazy figure-eight pattern in a gentle sea that would allow them to maintain their coordinates at 12.5 latitude and 54 longitude. Meredith, the Captain, Courtney and Kate were manning the computer and communicating with their al Qaeda contacts. The satellite signals were being beamed off a half dozen satellites and through servers on three continents. They sent a coded message advising they were within 50 miles of the eastern tip of Socotra and asked for additional instructions.

"The bad guys are still up this late," Courtney said monitoring the encrypted messages that were coming in on her computer screen. "They say welcome. They look forward to seeing the artifacts. They suggest arriving on the south side of the island about four miles south and east of the peninsula cliff. They certainly aren't giving us much clarity."

Captain Brinkmann leaned in close looking over Courtney's shoulder reading the directions. He reached for his computer and called up a Google satellite image of Socotra Island. Dragging the cursor over the eastern edge of the island and zooming in, he started scanning along the shoreline. The images were surprising clear and showed every cliff, beach and cove. He eventually pointed to where he thought they were directing them.

"If my eyes are reading these images correctly, they are pointing us to a small fishing village south of that massive cliff we passed. See here, it's about four miles south of Ra's Mimo Point. As you zoom in you can see the fishing boats pulled up on a sandy beach in a nice little cove away from the rough seas. I bet that is where they want us to go."

"Nice tracking, Derek," Meredith said slapping the Captain on the back. "Courtney, let's send back a message and ask if we should plan on fishing in the cove. Emphasize the word Cove."

Courtney started typing a moment later and sent the message off into cyberspace. In a couple of minutes a message came back and said. 'fishing is good in the Cove, yes.'

"Bingo, were in," Kate said. "This is all too easy. Way too easy! How the hell couldn't the government find all these al Qaeda types if its so damn easy to talk to them?..... At the same time, maybe I'm glad were staying on the ship. I hope you guys aren't walking into a trap."

"I'll take that chance. Let's call it a night and get the fishing boat ready. I think a daylight trip makes sense."

"William, in the morning I'll motor us in and cut the distance to shore to about 4 miles and then come back out here until your ready to be picked up. The sea can be pretty rough when you're out this far in a small boat. If you disembark in closer you can make the run in a lot safer."

"Alright, let's spread the word and get some rest. Courtney and Kate, if you could handle security on deck tonight that would be great."

"We were planning on it. We can sleep after you mad bombers leave," Kate said. "We have to have something to do in this crazy scheme."

"Courtney and Kate, if I may, I'll join you on deck this evening," The Captain said, "My first mate will monitor radar and let us know if we have any company coming. Do either of you play gin?"

Courtney said she did, and looked forward to spending some time with the handsome Captain. She wanted to get to know him better.

→ ←

Above Djibouti-Ambouli International Airport

Ryan Younger received his final approach instructions and banked the Citation jet he had picked up in Oslo to the left over the Red Sea and the eastern coast of Africa. With a company co-pilot who was pleased to be flying anywhere outside Scandinavia and Europe, he had made plans to fly south towards a rendezvous with the THCT team.

The jet had charted a course from Oslo to Geneva, Switzerland, and after refueling, on to Alexandria, Egypt where they had spent the night. The following day they charted a course for Djibouti, which would put them within a few hundred miles of his boss and the team.

As he touched down, he followed ground control instructions and taxied up to the charter terminal building, across from the international passenger terminal. Pulling in front of a hanger he set the brakes and popped the hatch. Ryan advised the Charter Flight Manager to do a complete servicing of the aircraft and top off the fuel tanks, advising that they might be there for up to a week.

They entered the building and passed through a cursory customs checkpoint with little hassle. The two pilots headed for the city and took a taxi down the N-2 highway to the Sheraton Djibouti Hotel on the Boulevard of the Republic. Ryan had stayed at the property before, and while it wasn't the best hotel in Djibouti, it had a great view of the harbor, a good pool with an open-air bar, and a casino on property to burn time. The hotel also catered to Western travelers. Waiting there they would not be subject to the angry fallout from bin Laden's death within the local

Muslim community. The hotel was only twenty years old but was showing its age. While the rooms were ok, the real reason he chose this property was because the air-conditioning worked around the clock.

They settled in for an undetermined stay. Ryan would spend his time studying the maps he had secured for the region. It was possible he would be flying into one of these regional airports to pick up the team. Until he heard from Meredith, there was little he could do except monitor the constant information download coming from the bin Laden take down and consider what that would mean to the THCT mission. Ryan decided to visit the pool and get one of those umbrella drinks.

→ ←

Northern Maryland

The FBI Bell Ranger jet helicopter was fast and almost silent as it cruised at 6,000 feet northwest from Washington, D.C. towards the Catoctin Mountains in a forest of oak, maple and conifer trees. They had flown northwest following I-270 for much of the way and about 42 miles from Washington had turned north into the mountains of Frederick County, Maryland. Just west of the town of Thurmont the craft began descending through the wispy clouds hanging over the rolling mountain terrain.

The pilot knew where he was going but was still being closely monitored and talked in by a Naval ground control operator. He was directed to a large open field in the forest that was to the west of a series of buildings and houses nestled in the woods. As the pilot brought the craft down the two occupants could see through the cockpit windshield they were descending into a complex that had large security fences snaking there way around a 165 acre complex. Over to one side of the large open field was a mid-sized aircraft hanger that housed two large Sikorsky Marine VH 60 N helicopters in it. These were the VIP versions of the same military Black Hawk helicopters that were used in the bin Laden assault in Pakistan. They just didn't have all the armaments mounted on their frames, or did they? The VH 60's call signs were Marine 1.

As the helicopter wheel assembly gently touched down and the main rotor started slowing, a U.S. Marine in battle fatigues standing to the side of the landing zone ducked his head and ran toward the helicopter. He unlocked the passenger door, stood erect and saluted.

"Good Afternoon Mr. Taylor, Ms. Lee, Welcome to Camp David. The President is expecting you. If you wait for a moment the rotor wash will dissipate and we can assist you out of the craft. I have transportation waiting."

Logan Taylor, FBI Director, and Karen Lee, Assistant Director of the CIA, unbuckled their seatbelt assemblies and climbed out of the quieting helicopter. They walked over to the waiting golf cart. A Navy corpsman was in the drivers seat. As they settled into the rear seat, the Marine saluted again, and they drove off.

The golf cart drove off the ball field past the helicopter aircraft hanger onto an asphalt roadway. The access road went a few hundred feet past a number of utilitarian buildings and then merged with a well-marked double lane roadway that cut through the forest. This road passed by a formal entrance building that had solid security barriers blocking all vehicular access to the site. It was obvious that the complex was crawling with security personnel, as the President was in residence.

They were driven through the forest on a winding two-lane well-marked roadway. They could see various nature trails and a number of houses off in the woods. Making a large sweeping turn they came upon their objective, a low-rise house that was called Aspen Lodge. They started up the circular driveway, passing a number of visible Marine security guards that were on the President's protection detail while he was in residence. These men silently scrutinized the visitors but knew them to be invited guests, so they went about their business.

The golf cart drove right past the formal Aspen Lodge entrance and went around the corner taking a smaller asphalt trail that led around the house. As they cleared the back of the large house nestled in the woods, they came upon a large multi-level stone patio sitting above a figure eight swimming pool with hot tub.

Below the pool area was a beautifully landscaped golf hole and the President was practicing his chipping. While the President's golf course only had one-golf green, there were three distinctly different fairways and tees set off in the woods at various angles and distances. The President took another swing, looked up and saw his guests had arrived. He set the club down on his Presidential golf bag and climbed the steps to the patio. The two guests got out of the cart and met him half way near some patio tables and chairs overlooking the pool.

"Logan, Karen, its good to see you on this beautiful day. In fact, it's been a beautiful week. Life is good, and the press is leaving me alone for a change, so what bad news do you have for me to ruin this high?" He extended his hand to both.

"Good afternoon, Mr. President," they both said almost in unison.

"What's so important that you had to interrupt my lousy golf game on a pleasant Saturday afternoon? I've had enough trauma these past few days. I came up here to unwind a bit and get away from the press and you still found me," the President said as he waved his arm across the golf hole and surrounding forest.

"Our apologies Sir, but we have some new information on that THCT terrorist threat we have been gathering information on. We are concerned this potential terrorist cell may now be organizing to avenge bin Laden. Our many sources have put together an interesting profile, one that we thought couldn't wait until Monday." Logan offered.

"Now that does intrigue me, an interesting profile? For terrorists? I thought they all had the same profile. Crazed jihadists bent on our complete and utter destruction." He smiled knowing it wasn't that simple.

"Mr. President, we think you will find the information to be interesting and surprising. Shocking may even describe it even better. We felt it was important that you hear the information right away rather than waiting for your return to DC," Director Karen Lee added.

The President raised an eyebrow and peered over his glasses, thinking about what had been said. He motioned them towards the patio table that already had been set with a pitcher of liquid refreshment. He waved off the Navy corpsman that was hovering by the door so they could talk in confidence.

"How about an Arnold Palmer?" he asked. "I wonder how you get a drink named after you?" he queried, and started pouring three glasses of the iced tea and lemonade mix, as any good host would do.

"So fill me in on all that is surprising, and perhaps even shocking," the President said as he sat down and took a sip of his drink. "I'm all ears!"

"Mr. President, as you know we have been monitoring some unusual communications for months. It took a lot of monitoring at NSA but we started to identify a potential terrorist cell up in the Tri-State area. As you well know, New York is still one fat bulls-eye on every terrorist's mind." Karen Lee took a sip of her drink and realized she had never had one before. She liked it and tipped the drink in a toast.

She continued. "Since NSA first picked up their trail, both the FBI here in the States, and the CIA overseas have been chasing down leads and trying to find out who these THCT guys are. Since we got bin Laden we have been looking at them even harder. And as we do, the findings have become more surprising by the day." Karen Lee looked to Logan and he took the signal to continue.

"Mr. President, we think we have identified all the members of this group."

"So let's scoop them up before they hurt anyone!"

"Well, Sir, it turns out they were all members of a 9-11 grief counseling group in New York. And here is the surprising part, they all lost loved ones in the 9-11 terrorist act." He stopped talking to let that fact hang for a moment.

"That is surprising," the President said as he considered the ramifications. "Hell, your right, it may be shocking! So what are these guys up to? Why haven't we picked them up?"

"Well, Sir," Karen Lee jumped back into the conversation, "they've disappeared off the face of the earth, every last one of them. We tracked them as far as we could and that led us to their therapist who had been working with the group since 9-11. These people were all in a 9-11 grief-counseling group together. They just vanished without so much as a goodbye or thank you. They haven't been seen since."

"So that's the shocking part? What are they up to?" the President asked searching the faces of his guests.

"This gets even more interesting. It turns out one of them is filthy rich and has access to a corporate jet. The jet has been tracked to the Middle East, Russia, and Europe a number of times. We talked to the pilot and he advises he doesn't know where his boss is. Now he has disappeared as well, without the plane."

"All you've done thus far is confuse me, and I don't think you have even given me the bad news yet. Is that about right?" the President said this looking at them for answers, not riddles.

"Sir, I know you've been immersed on the bin Laden take down, but you may remember that we also briefed you on that missing Russian nuke," Logan Taylor said. "We think they may actually have that bomb, bought on the black market." Again he stopped to let the President digest the news.

The President sensed a chill running down his spine even though it was warm and pleasant sitting in the woods of Camp David. He looked at both his Directors and searched their faces for a better understanding. "Now, that is truly shocking! You mean to say this group of amateurs has gotten a hold of a nuke and are planning on using it? We have to find them and get that thing back before New York is a pile of rubble."

"Yes, Sir, that's what we've been trying to do, but they aren't anywhere to be found. They have gone to ground, and thus far we don't have a decent lead on their whereabouts," Karen Lee said. "We've put all sorts of assets on the task, here and abroad, but nothing has come of it."

"So what do we do, wait until the bomb goes off and levels New York, or here in Washington? That's not acceptable at all!" The President said this and got up from his chair and started pacing the edge of the patio.

"Sir, there is another possibility," Logan Taylor said, "that Karen and I have been exploring, that we haven't shared yet."

"So explain," the President said starting to get irritated. He came back to the table and sat down.

"In all our investigations of this THCT group thus far, we have found these guys are average rank and file people who have had to deal with a devastating loss. They all have a common bond in the loss of loved ones in the 9-11 attack. They sat through years of grief counseling, moving from disbelief, to anger and frustration, and on to eventual acceptance of their loss."

"That sounds a bit simplistic to me. I don't know how I would be dealing with the loss of a loved one to terrorists," the President said this looking for more.

"Exactly," Karen Lee said. She leaned forward and continued. "We think these people bonded together in their grief, and when they got to that anger stage, they bogged down, and started thinking about revenge for the losses they experienced."

"So what your saying is this THCT group aren't really terrorists as we traditionally know them to be, but rather they are revenge minded citizens, hell bent on what?" the President asked.

"Well Sir, this is the truly shocking part. We aren't sure, but their therapist said they talked long and hard about revenge, about kicking ass, specifically Osama bin Laden's ass," Logan Taylor said, and let it sink in for a moment. He went on. "We think they're the ones that have that suitcase nuke and they were going after bin Laden, until we beat them to the punch!" He stopped talking and sat back. He had yet to touch his beverage.

"Come on! Please!" the President said as he got up and started pacing, "You mean these grief stricken amateurs went out and obtained this Russian nuke, and they went after bin Laden themselves? That makes no sense at all. Hell, it took us the better part of ten years to catch up with the bastard. How the hell did they think they would find him?"

"That's a good question. But it looks like they had made some headway and were hot on his trail when we cut them off at the pass. At least that's what we think may have happened," Taylor said.

"Well, isn't that the cat's meow!" the President stated rather angrily. "We've had whole divisions of soldiers combing the mountains of Pakistan and Afghanistan. We had spies on the ground all over the Middle East looking for him. We spent millions of dollars a day to ferret him out. We re-positioned half the world's spy satellites looking down on that region and under every rock. We've built squadrons of un-manned drones flying over every square inch of mountaintop hoping to shove a sidewinder up his ass. We've even had our super-duper Echelon computers burning the midnight oil listening to a couple billion words a day, yet we couldn't find him until last week!" The President had worked himself into an ugly frenzy, and recognized he needed to sit down. His blood pressure was about to go through the roof.

"Mr. President, I know it sounds crazy, but we think these guys were hell bent on finding him. They planned to drag that weapon up the mountain in Pakistan and blow the guy to kingdom come, or wherever they find those virgins." Karen Lee said this sarcastically, as she thought about how ridiculous the whole scenario sounded. "I agree its unbelievable but the more and more information we get, the more the pieces come together."

"I'm still not entirely buying this; what pieces have come together?"

"Well, one of the members of this grief counseling group is a Russian translator from the United Nations," Director Taylor offered. "His wife was killed in the World Trade Tower collapse, actually in the Marriott Hotel next door. Turns out she was also a sister to a prominent Russian General, who was a decorated war hero in Afghanistan, who fought against bin Laden twenty years ago. He was the primary person responsible for nuclear weapon storage in Mother Russia. Within the past couple of weeks he was relieved of duty. We are not sure why he was relieved of duty or where he is now."

Assistant Director Karen Lee carried on. "There were two Pakistani cab drivers in this counseling group. They both lost their wives and children in 9-11; they worked at a childcare facility in the North Tower. These two cab drivers are the people we traced to France, who may have made contact with al Qaeda operatives at the refugee camps. They too have disappeared."

Logan Taylor jumped in. "The leader of this so-called THC group looks to be William Meredith, a very wealthy former British, naturalized U.S. citizen, living in New York. He lost an adult son in the 9-11 tragedy. We've tracked him and his plane to France, to the Ukraine, to Greece and Turkey all places the THCT name keeps popping up. And now he too has flat out disappeared. We have his plane impounded, but all the pilot knows is his boss is on vacation somewhere in Europe. That pilot has disappeared as well."

"What I think we're suggesting Sir," Karen Lee said. "If these guys are actually the bad guys we're looking for, we think they may not be trying to attack us. We think they were really going after bin Laden? If you accept the premise, the question now should be what do they do now that we have taken the target out ourselves?"

"Heaven help us. That's a pretty wild scenario," the President said still looking emotionally drained. "I don't think we have enough intelligence to make that call or even suggest any specific scenario. But damn, you have now got my attention. I need more information to figure out what we should be doing, if anything."

He digested all that had been said and then said. "Lets keep searching for that nuke and make sure it's not aimed at us, or is already here on U.S. soil, or anywhere else for that matter. And let's not bring the Russians in on this; let's keep a lid on the whole damn scenario. First we need to find out where these mad THC bombers actually are, over here or over there, wherever over there is. And keep me posted daily, hell, hourly." With that the President pushed away from the table, got up and walked towards Aspen Lodge shaking his head.

Karen Lee and Logan Taylor looked at each other and realized their meeting was over. They stood up and excused themselves. The President disappeared into the house and a number of Marines materialized out of the woods to set up a security perimeter.

→ ←

Gulf of Aden, East of Socotra

Meredith and Josef exchanged a number of coded casual communications with their al Qaeda contacts and confirmed they could be arriving as early as the next day at the fishing village south of the Cliffs. They were given explicit instructions on how to approach the cove and beach. They were told they would be watched carefully as they entered the cove, and once on shore would be searched.

The THCT team made final plans and just after noon lowered the fishing vessel into the sea. The boat had been loaded carefully. They took only a few weapons. Michael and Kevin dressed in sand colored light camouflage military fatigues and carried AK-47s that they fully expected would be confiscated. They also had knives in their boots, which they also assumed would be found. The remainder of the group would go unarmed and trust that the promise of additional weapons of mass destruction would be their insurance card.

The rest of the team, Meredith, Ralph, Joseph dressed in British khaki-colored bush jackets, with the multiple pockets and epaulets, Michael picked up in Aden. Uri dressed as a fisherman, hopefully giving the impression he had been hired to bring the gunrunners to the island.

Osama and Malik wore more traditional Pashtun tribal garb and would act as the messengers they had been in Calais.

All of them had quizzed one another on their respective roles a number of times. Meredith would do most of the talking as the arms dealer. Osama and Malik would translate when necessary. Ralph and Joseph would assist Meredith, as a Russian bomb expert, and as the arms dealer financier.

They had talked about the possibility that the terrorists would insist on someone from the group staying behind when the others left. Every member of the team volunteered to be that person. They understood the gravity of their volunteering, but they all felt it to be worth the sacrifice.

Meredith again pulled out his maps. The group studied them carefully and agreed that if one of the team had to stay behind for insurance purposes, they would meet up on the other side of Ra's Mimo near the snow-white sand dunes, where Uri's boat would be waiting.

Courtney and Kate stayed on board with Captain Brinkmann to monitor the overall situation, communicate with Ryan Younger and the escape jet, and to protect the ship from the pirates should they decide to take another crack at the Majorca. Since most of the ships small arms cache was being left behind, Courtney and Kate had a wealth of weaponry to choose from and dispersed the various weapons around the ship. The rest of the crew had willingly taken to defending their ship once they'd seen the THCT group fight off the pirates.

The fishing boat with Uri at the helm pushed off at 2:05 pm for the hour journey to the eastern end of Socotra. As they sailed over the relatively calm waters, they reviewed the plan and their individual roles. While they were nervous about what they would find, they felt confident they were finally meeting the terrorists.

A half-mile from the eastern cliffs of the island, carved by wind, rain and turbulent waves over hundreds of centuries, Uri turned the wheel to bring the boat to a southerly course and paralleled the shoreline staying a half-mile off shore to avoid the breakers crashing over submerged reefs. He went south to another cliff outcropping a couple miles south of the first coordinate. Having utilized their maps they were pretty confident this was there cove. Meredith reminded them of the exit strategy one more time.

Rounding the second point, they saw turbaned sentries with AK-47s strapped across their chests stationed on the surrounding cliffs. They knew they were in the right place. Ahead a quarter mile was a sandy beach with a half dozen small fishing dugouts and boats pulled up on the shore. There was no pier, so Uri cut the motor to an idle and almost drifted into the shallow calm waters. As he closed in on the beach he cut the engine and hauled the prop out of the water so the boat could slide onto the sandy shore.

Closing around them were half-dozen men holding AK-47s trained on the boat and its occupants. Michael and Kevin played it cool leaving their weapons strapped across their chests and pointing down. No one in the boat raised their hands, but everyone understood that these first few minutes were critical to gain the confidence of the terrorists.

"Good Day," Meredith said in his best English accent, "May we disembark? We have come in peace."

"Mr. Bingham, I presume," a white robed bearded man said in clear English, more American than British sounding. The voice came from a man standing behind the guards holding the weapons. "Please join us on shore, but slowly, a couple of you at a time. As you might expect, we will need to check you out and pat you down before we begin our pleasantries."

He waved them ashore while the gunmen trained their weapons on the boats occupants. Michael and Kevin stepped ashore first and raised their hands in the universal show of surrender. Two Arab guards stepped forward reaching for their weapon straps and lifted them over their heads. They handed the weapons to two more men who examined them, making sure the safeties were on.

The guards patted the two men down thoroughly, found the knives in their boots and took them as well. The two men were instructed to move inland, while two more were waved ashore. The procedure was repeated for all of the boat occupants. The person doing the searching stepped back to the man in the white robe and whispered something to him.

"I see that you have come in peace gentlemen, that is good because you would have otherwise been dead by now. My name is Anwar al-Awlaki, from the United States, welcome to Socotra."

"Sir, I am Jeremy Bingham," Meredith said in the Queen's English. "I presume we have been conversing for some time now. So I am hopeful that our talks can continue and will be fruitful."

"We shall see Mr. Bingham, we shall see. But for now we must attend to pleasantries as all good Arabs do when guests arrive. We must have tea and perhaps some good Yemeni coffee."

"Thank you, that would be appreciated after a long boat journey, and very British of you."

"I have spent time in Britain too. I was an Imam at a Mosque for two years in London before coming to Yemen."

"Ten we will have much to discuss, in addition to introductions all around. But before we do," Meredith said, as he turned to the boat and pointed at a large suitcase in the belly of the boat, "May I suggest that we carefully remove the antiquity that you have been waiting for. I would not want to leave such a rare object out in the elements."

The terrorist in charge seemed surprised and was a bit taken back. The object of his desires was within ten feet of him.

Meredith did not move and spoke slowly. "We would be pleased to remove it, or your people could do so, it is your choice. It is perfectly safe and harmless at the moment, but should none the less be treated carefully and with great respect for its power."

"Ahh! You are indeed a trusting man, Mr. Bingham. What prevents me from killing you on the spot and taking the package for myself?" he said as he stood there calculating that very thought.

"A valid question, one that merits a thoughtful response. We also considered that thought before coming here, Mr. al-Awlaki," Bingham said, "But we are business people first, are we not? You have an intense interest in this object, and we are interested in selling it to the highest bidder. That is a simple business relationship. In fact, you have already paid a princely down payment for this rare antiquity. You have shown good faith and we thought we should return the favor. Isn't that what business people do?"

Meredith smiled and stared at the robed man. He then played his ace in the hole, "But we also have five more of these antiquities wasting away in a warehouse, that we would be pleased to sell you as well. Let's call this a sample of things to come. I think it behooves us both to have that tea you talked about, get to know one another a little better, and perhaps build a relationship for the future."

The team all held their breath waiting for the Arab to respond.

"I was aware of this incentive offer, but I have always been very wary of people bearing gifts. At the same time, I think I am beginning to like you. At least your chutzpah, I think the Jews say. I agree, we should have that tea. This way, Gentlemen."

He waved a guard towards the boat to assist one of Bingham's men in lifting the device from the craft. They carefully lifted it and together started up the beach.

The entire group of guests and gunmen marched in a procession in the sand, off the beach and inland a few hundred yards to a small cluster of adobe mud huts and ramshackle sheds set on a plateau overlooking the Arabian Sea. A cool breeze blew in over the rocky shoreline and cut the heated air coming from the west. While the small grouping of huts weren't picturesque in any way, they offered a commanding view of the cliffs and the Arabian Sea to the east.

About a thousand yards west of the houses at the base of a mountain ridge, there was a camouflaged cave entrance that would have been impossible to spot unless you were standing in front of it and actually looking for it. Just inside the rough-cut entrance, in the shadows created by a setting sun, a white-robed, bearded man sat in a rickety wooden chair along with some regional al Qaeda leaders from Somalia and the Sudan.

"Why is it that we always end up in caves, while others sit at tables and have tea the way it was meant to be enjoyed?" a senior al Qaeda leader said to his elder and compatriot.

Zawahiri snickered at the gentle joke. " Fazul, you are right as usual. It does seem that we spend an inordinate amount of time in these infernal caves. But it is because we have stirred the fears of the infidels in the West. They are consumed in their desire to find us, as they have cut down our brother Osama. We must occasionally hide from these trespassers, until we know they are for real, and bring us what we have desired for so long. Then we will avenge his death."

"Sometimes I wonder if what we have done to date is worth it." Jamal al-Badawi said, letting his voice betray his comment. "The Americans are stronger than the Russians ever were. Even though we have hurt them beyond their worst nightmares, they continue to hound us and chase us from place to place, from country to country, from cave to cave. And Osama has paid the ultimate price." His voice trailed off as he looked around his temporary rabbit-hole.

"Perhaps our fortunes will change with these arms dealers. And we can avenge his death and finally cripple the West so that they will fall under their own weight. We have searched for this weapon for years and will pay whatever is necessary to secure it. With such a prize in hand, we can take the battle from our land to theirs. Patience my friend."

Just then the radio transmitter sitting on the ground between them started squawking and relaying the conversations that were taking place in the house between the arms dealer and al-Awlaki. The al Qaeda leaders would listen to what was being said without giving up their covert position. The various al Qaeda leaders stopped talking and listened to the conversations from the camp. Zawahiri reached behind his chair and pulled out a thermos of tea and a couple of chipped coffee cups. He poured a steaming cup and handed it to his fellow terrorists with a wry smile.

→ ←

NSA, Ft Meade, Maryland

Bill Dalde was at his desk working exclusively on THCT, cross-referencing all the bits of information that were coming in from around the world. With its priority flag, all THCT information was being routed to his desk and to Bede Long at Langley and then on to their bosses. They were in constant communication as they sorted through the myriad of confusing and unrelated facts and bits of information. It was like a couple thousand piece jigsaw puzzle that had no reference picture to model itself on. Bill grabbed the scrambled secure line to Bede Long at Langley. A few seconds later the connection was completed and flashed - SECURE.

"Hey Bede, I'm getting a lot of chatter from all sorts of al Qaeda contacts in the Middle East. I've got reports coming out of Egypt, Syria, Iraq, Yemen and Afghanistan all talking about some meeting. I guess a lot of known terrorists are on the move and changing locations. And these are people Echelon automatically flags. My guess is that al Qaeda is organizing a mob meeting," Bill said.

"There you go again mate, always making those Tony Soprano mob references. You have a fertile mind don't you. At the same time I think you're right. Something is up," Bede said, reaching for a series of reports from field agents. He continued. "Our people in the Middle East and Pakistan have been chasing down all their reliable sources and they're hearing such things as well. Perhaps the al Qaeda big shots are planning a sit-down somewhere to discuss how to respond to bin Laden's death. The $64,000 question is where? That's a party that I'd like to be invited to, just me and my favorite cluster bomb, although then we'd be out of work!"

"Yeah, but that would still be nice. All of them in one nice little basket! And then Boom! We should be so lucky," Bill said this throwing his arms up and over the cubicle mimicking the explosion of an atomic bomb going off with a mushroom cloud billowing above it startling the guy at the North African desk in the next cubicle.

"I can see that, too. Hopefully they can sort it all out upstairs," Bede said, "I hear they just met with the President at Camp Wilderness in those north woods of yours. Karen advised our THCT friends might be behind all of this activity."

"You know Bede, it doesn't take much of a stretch to weave all these elements together, the 9-11 grief counseling, the group anger, the Russian nuclear bomb going missing, the Jungle encampment al Qaeda uses in France, and all this terrorist chatter stirring up the airwaves. Maybe our little band of zealots are actually stirring this kettle, giving us our indigestion? It makes you want to say.... Who are these guys, just like in Butch Cassidy and the Sundance Kid?"

"What does that mean? Who's Butch Cassidy for Christ sakes? These guys are just a bunch of average citizens, who have all experienced tremendous loss and pain, and they've decided to do something about it," Bede said this as he gathered up all his notes and papers. "I think I'd really like to meet these guys if we ever find them.... alive."

"Not at our pay grade buddy. If we do find them, the powers that be will throw them in a hole and we'll never see them again. I'll talk to you soon. Out."

→ ←

Eastern Socotra Island

The initial meeting over tea had gone rather well even though the THCT team could feel the enemy rifles still pointed at the backs of their heads. Everyone was working overtime to play the role of arms dealers.

Michael and Kevin were hovering close to Meredith, as bodyguards would typically do. They were silently imposing, but unsettled and uncomfortable, naked without their weapons in hand. Josef had introduced himself, using a thick Russian accent, as Dimitri, the Russian arms expert babysitting the bomb.

Ralph had spoken Farsi establishing his Iranian background, and introduced himself as the accountant, only interested in the money aspect of this arrangement.

The Pakistani brothers used their native Pashtun language to convey a sense of camaraderie, even though they were working for the arms dealer.

Overall the first meeting went well and they were still alive in the camp of their sworn enemy. They had delivered their Trojan horse to the savages and it now sat in the middle of the room like a birthday present at a party.

"So I suggest that we see this beautiful antiquity that you have brought us," al-Awlaki said, getting the attention of Josef and his lead guard. "Dimitri, would you do the honors of opening our special package,.... and, very carefully, please?" The guard handed his weapon to a fellow guard and walked with Dimitri to the center of the room. He made no move to reach for the suitcase. Josef for his part recognized the need to do everything in slow motion, or be killed on the spot.

Josef carefully reached for the case and with an exaggerated motion unzipped the suitcase, and then slowly pulled the lid up and back. Inside the traditional suitcase nestled tightly in white foam was a metallic briefcase like container that had numeric tumbler locks on it. Josef motioned to the guard to assist him in lifting the 45- pound package out of the suitcase. Together they placed it on the large hand woven carpet in the center of the room, as Meredith reached for the now empty suitcase to get it out of the way. He pulled a sheaf of papers and a pamphlet from the case.

Dimitri stood back for a moment and looked over at al-Awlaki waiting for a signal that he should continue. The terrorist nodded in agreement.

Meredith and the rest of the Team sat as casually as possible trying to convey a sense of calm, even though they had AK-47's aimed at the backs of their heads. Josef thumbed the locksets to dial the correct code and then slowly opened the case. His guard recoiled back a couple of steps as if that would help should the weapon detonate. Everyone laughed a nervous laugh when the guard retreated and picked up his weapon.

The small yield nuclear weapon didn't look like much sitting there in its case, doing absolutely nothing. There was no movement, no blinking lights, and no digital clock ticking away. It looked like a dull grey metal paperweight. Everyone in the room sat perfectly still and remained quiet.

"We have obviously not armed the mechanism," Meredith said breaking the silence. "We thought that you would like to inspect the bomb yourself and have your people take a look at it."

"Mr. al-Awlaki," Josef / Dimitri said offering the papers to the man in charge, "We also have all the instructions in both Russian and English for arming the weapon and for unarming it for transportation purposes. The bomb functions well, although you need to pay attention to the battery requirements. We have armed it and unarmed it a number of times during our journey."

Wary, but very interested in what he was looking at, al-Awlaki said almost in a trance. "I am interested in knowing more, please give us a history of this Russian weapon."

Meredith was watching the terrorist leader as closely as possible without being too obvious. In doing so he noticed there was a portable radio sitting next to his robes and it had a small flashing red light going on and off, almost invisible to the rest of the group. It seemed similar to the radio units they had on the ship and he remembered that the red light meant it was transmitting a message. He wondered who else might be listening to this conversation?

Dimitri/Josef responded to the question. "The suitcase weapon is a Soviet made device that was built in the late 70's and early 80's. It could be easily transported, hidden, and then used in the field behind enemy lines. This weapon is very much like the ones the U.S. developed at about the same time. Its numeric designation is RA 155 and it contains about 25 pounds of very high-grade plutonium. It is a miniaturized version of their much larger weapons with a 90% effective yield."

"So what does all that mean from an explosion standpoint?" al-Awlaki asked.

"The unit is set off by a well designed detonating device that has been updated since they were first built." Josef tried to sound well versed and convey an expertise with the weapon. "It will yield about five kilotons, about half the explosive power of the much larger nuclear bomb that was dropped on Hiroshima in World War Two, over sixty years ago."

"The city of Hiroshima was leveled completely. You are saying this bomb can do half of that?" What would that mean in simple language?" al-Awlaki pressed for a more quantifiable measure. He wanted something he could understand.

"Ahh, yes, I see.".... Josef said in his thickest accent and continued. "This small bomb, if placed correctly in the center of a major city like New York, could level Mid-town Manhattan," he paused for dramatic effect, "causing about a million instant deaths from the blast." He let that fact sink in for a moment, "and then, another million would die from the radiation fallout over the next six months. Is that what you are asking?"

No one said a word. The THCT team sat quietly but their eyes scanned the others in the room to see their reactions to this news. Those that understood English had a look of horror and surprise on their faces. Those that didn't understand the language looked calm and disinterested other than maintaining surveillance on their guests.

"Really? I am surprised that this small suitcase could cause that much damage?"

"Yes, comrade, this unit has that capability." Josef said.

"And that's why we are charging two million dollars a unit," Meredith / Bingham intervened. "And we have five more of these weapons we are prepared to sell you with two simple but very necessary caveats."

Al-Awlaki reacted by turning his head from the bomb to Meredith. "And what would they be, as rifle barrels are being pointed at your heads?" he said rather smugly. "I don't think you are in much of a position to bargain."

"They are simple requests. First, that you would purchase these additional suitcase units from us for $2,000,000 a piece, and second, that you would be kind enough to advise when we should take an extended vacation in Tahiti, at least a couple weeks in advance."

Anwar al-Awlaki threw his head back and laughed heartedly. "I think we could meet those terms without a problem. And we may even want to join you in Tahiti. I hear it is a very remote place on earth, much like it is here, a place to rest and enjoy the sun."

The tension in the hut eased somewhat with everyone recognizing the joke. Meredith noticed that the red light went out on the radio sitting next to al-Awlaki.

"So tell me more about this weapon. Can we handle it safely until we decide where we would like to set it off?"

Josef cleared his throat and jumped back into the conversation. "These weapons were designed for field use, to be fired by anyone with minimal training and the right instructions." He handed over the documents and small manual.

"At one time there were about a 100 of these weapons spread across the globe, many of them secreted in America. They were often stored in Soviet Embassies locked in basement storage closets. If the Kremlin did send an order, they could have been pulled out by any designated person and armed in a matter of minutes. I am sure that your people could handle this. We can demonstrate if you would like?"

"That is not necessary at the moment, Dimitri. As you said, we will have our experts take a look before anyone arms anything. For now, I think we will have some food and call it a day. I have made arrangements for you to spend a few days with us."

"We expected that perhaps you would like us to be guests for a while. We too are exhausted. The boat trip was rougher than I expected. We are glad that we hired a local fisherman to show us the way." He nodded too Uri who sat quietly in a corner.

"We will have some fish and lamb for dinner. Tomorrow we will talk some more."

The guards made motions with their AK-47s for the guests to follow them. They escorted the western visitors to another small shack a few meters away, near the center of the growing al Qaeda encampment.

Inside, the room had been set up like a barracks with some cots along the walls. It was barren, but clean, and some fresh linens and water had been put out for them. The team settled in each grabbing a bunk, but said little to one another presuming they were being closely monitored. But with their eyes they conveyed that they thought it had been a good and productive day.... thus far.

→ ←

Sheraton Hotel Pool, Djibouti

Ryan and his co-pilot were enjoying the pool and the warm sun dancing in and out of the thin cloud cover. He reached for his computer, booted it up and entered a special password to check his special email account set up for the trip. In one message from a co-worker at the Teterboro hanger he found the Feds were again looking for him for further questioning. He had used a false identity to head north to Canada and flown commercial to Oslo to pick up the Citation. He guessed he would have to do some fence mending with them if he ever did get back. He hoped that his boss had that kind of clout, but if not he still wasn't about to throw in the towel.

The next email was from Courtney. It had come to his new IP address after bouncing around the globe a couple of times. It advised she and her friends were still enjoying their cruise but were changing the itinerary a bit.

She advised that she expected the trip would be ending in a matter of days and wondered if she could get picked up on short notice. She said her friends would be coming as well. She asked him to keep a light on and to be ready to swing by and she would advise coordinates and timing once she had a better idea of what the weather would be like.

Ryan composed a response as creatively as he could not understanding what was up. He and they knew bin Laden was dead, so what were they up to. He advised her he missed her a lot and was waiting for a chance to kiss and makeup. He suggested they get together for dinner as soon as possible. He also advised he was all gassed up and raring to go. All he needed was a place and time. He shot the email into cyberspace and waited to see if she would reply immediately.

She did, responding she bet he was at the pool enjoying one of those umbrella drinks. She said she had tried an oily local drink called the Balhof but didn't like it, although she thought she would try it again. Perhaps she would try it again before leaving on Thursday. She signed off and that was that.

Ryan reached for his bag, moving his umbrella drink aside, and pulled out a flight map for the region. He started scanning for the Island of Socotra looking for a Balhof but couldn't find one. The only airport on the Island was at Hidobah. He expanded his search parameters and began following the coast of Yemen east of Aden along a legitimate highway that snaked across the plain paralleling the shoreline.

About a hundred miles east of Aden he found what he was looking for, a deep water oil shipping terminal and refinery town by the name of Balhof sitting right on the coast, nestled against the mountains. He went to his computer, called up a Google map for Aden, Yemen, set it on satellite image and dragged his way east until he found the town and the airport. He zeroed in as close as the satellite image would let him, noting their was a marked Runway 25, running west to east that would be long enough for his needs as long as he could land out of the west. The opposite approach would be problematic in a Citation because of the steep descent from the surrounding mountains.

The airstrip was probably used to ferry oil company engineers in and out. He scanned the town and seaport and presumed the Team would arrive on the Majorca, disembark and make their way to the airport about a mile away. He would swoop in, load the mad bombers and be off before anyone was the wiser.

He went back to the screen and scanned the airport in the satellite image, noting there was no terminal building, just a small square building off on a dirt side road approach. He thought about his options and wondered if there would even be any ground control. He figured it didn't matter. He would fly in on a distress call, once he knew the Team was in position, load them quickly, turn around and fly out before anyone could react.

He pulled up his email again and sent another message to Courtney. He advised he knew the Balhof drink well and would be waiting for a chance to mix a good one for her. The secret was to drink it in the dark so you wouldn't see what was in it. He advised her he would be at the far end of the ramp when they got off the boat. He hit send and signed off. He grabbed the umbrella drink and settled back into his chaise lounge.

➤ ◄

Al Qaeda's fishing Village

The THCT team ate a good dinner with the al Qaeda terrorist zealots that night, but clearly recognized they were under close scrutiny every moment, just short of being prisoners. Retiring for the evening, the group felt as if they were locked up in a third-world jail cell. They spoke little to one another except to talk about trivial things, presuming they were being monitored. They slept fitfully, knowing these guerillas now had a small nuclear device in hand.

The following morning they saw additional people had arrived in camp. Another Arab delegation arrived in Range Rovers that were covered in dust, having come to the camp overland from another part of the island. The Team members noticed these robed guests each had small entourages that remained by their sides in a loose but vigilant circle. They assumed they were additional al Qaeda leaders, although no one introduced anyone.

Breakfast was simple and spread out on a large rug. There were dates, freshly baked course bread, and a thick yogurt like mixture along with tea and Yemeni coffee. The THCT team had brought a couple cases of European bottled water and shared it with their hosts, who drank it only after the team members had consumed it themselves.

"I would like to talk more about the weapon, Bingham. We have had time to look at it over night and my people tell me it is as you say, a powerful weapon," Anwar al- Awlaki said as he finished his tea. "We have been reading the documents, both Russian and English I might add, and they are what you have said they were. This is all good, and our first impressions of you are getting better by the minute."

"Anwar, if I may, as I said yesterday, we are business people, and I know better than to come into your camp with something other than what I have offered you. I have made a good living in meeting the specific needs of my clients. I'm sure that that is true for you and was for Mr. bin Laden as well." He bowed his head to show reverence for the departed terrorist.

Awlaki ignored the comment. "I would like to talk about the trigger device and arming the weapon. I think it is time you taught my people to arm the weapon, and more importantly, how to disarm it. While I am beginning to trust you, I think we will die together should you have another plan in your mind."

The nuclear device was brought into the room and set down in the middle of the rug where the food had just been. It was opened by the same guard as the night before; this time he was much more comfortable with the weapon.

"We understand your concern and respect it," Meredith responded maintaining eye contact with the al Qaeda leader. "Please remember we too wish to leave this remote island in one piece and to set up additional paydays for the other weapons we have available. We have no plans to upset this relationship."

Meredith turned to Josef and said, "Dimitri, perhaps you could walk us through the arming procedures. I think we should talk them through first, and then when asked, we will show our hosts how to do the arming and the disarming."

Dimitri stepped forward and took the manual in hand. He flipped to the pages that instructed how to arm the weapon and showed the book to his counterpart and to Awlaki. In a good Russian accent he said, "Good batteries must be maintained to make sure you have a good electrical impulse. This is critical if you want the weapon to detonate. We checked this battery yesterday before arriving and it was good. This battery has been in the unit a minimum of six months already and we have been arming and disarming it many times in our travel here. We would recommend that you should get comfortable with the arming / disarming procedures before use, but not overuse the mechanism."

Everyone in the room remained silent. Dimitri paused to see if there were any questions. He continued, "There is a specific sequencing that must occur to arm the weapon, and then a similar specific sequence that is used to disarm it. First, you enter this series of codes using this digital keyboard, and then hit the enter button here. An approval security code must also be entered to complete the sequencing. The security code is still set for its official designation. RA 155 –1980 which we believe was the year it was built. Why it was never changed, we don't know."

A number of al Qaeda operatives took notes about the sequencing procedures. They compared notes with one another and made sure they were getting it right.

"Dimitri, I would now like you to show us this arming procedure. I have a number of people that will monitor your movements and will watch the sequencing. Please proceed," said al-Awlaki.

A number of bearded partisans stood up and walked to the metal briefcase sitting in the center of the room. Dimitri pointed to the digital keyboard and seeing everyone was watching his every move, he slowly entered the initial code, and then waited for the keyboard to register the entry. He reentered the security code and the bomb immediately came to life with the clock face lighting up blinking zeros.

"Once you have entered the start-up code and the security code, the device will request a timing sequence that could be as short as five minutes and as long as 24 hours. That gets entered in military time parameters and the bomb is armed and active." Dimitri looked up at the terrorist waiting for further direction.

"That is it? It can't be that simple to cause such destruction? So if we were to enter one hour as the time stamp, that bomb would go off and level the city of Manhattan?"

"Actually Anwar, it would level the eastern half of this island, and Manhattan would be completely spared," Meredith said and smiled. "But that is all it takes for this weapon to go off. It was built to be simple to operate and to be destructive."

"I am impressed. But now I want to see how to actually set up the timing? Can we do that right here?" Awlaki said this like a young boy getting his first BB gun.

"We can certainly arm the weapon now, but I suggest we give it a long countdown so that we can also disarm it. Remember what I said about its power. The eastern end of this island would vaporize." Meredith looked at Dimitri and nodded for him to continue with the timing sequence. "How about we arm it for two hours, 120 minutes and then we can also show you how to shut it back down?"

"That would be a good test, my friend, or we will all be vaporized, I think you say," al-Awlaki said, understanding what he was dealing with, "Proceed carefully and arm the weapon," he said without blinking an eye.

Dimitri made sure they were watching him and slowly pushed the calculator buttons for a 2-hour countdown. The digital clock blinked on and showed 120-minutes and then ... 119.59 and started its march backward. Everyone in the room stood up and looked over at the device watching the clock as it counted down. Not a word was spoken.

Anwar al-Awlaki stood transfixed, staring at the weapon, mesmerized by the clock ticking down. After a minute of watching the clock ticking down, the al Qaeda leader returned to his seat and scanned around the room. He noted his comrades were nervous and fixated on the blinking lights of the bomb as it sat innocently in the middle of the floor. The temperature in the room had risen and everyone had a sheen of sweat glistening on their foreheads.

"I am impressed, and will be even more so, when you stop the clock countdown," al-Awlaki said, coolly nodding to Dimitri to do so.

Dimitri needed no encouragement and quickly looked at Meredith for assurance to proceed. He stepped to the machine and encouraged his watchers to step in again and observe the disarming. He carefully reversed the arming procedure and this time, gave the security code to gain access to the controls of the bomb mechanism. Once that code was entered the machine stopped its countdown blinking and the clock went blank. There was an audible collective sigh of relief.

"Now I should like to see Abdul arm this nuclear device a second time. Dimitri, you have been a good teacher. I ask that you now monitor his handling of the procedure."

Everyone in the room tensed again. Abdul's breathing became a bit more labored as he stepped forward to arm the weapon. He looked into the Russian's eyes and then slowly reached down and started the sequencing procedure. Only once did Dimitri signal a misstep with the gentile wave of his hand. The operative initialized the weapon and then moved through the security arming code. He looked up and with al Awlaki's blessing reached to enter the timing code.

"Arm it this time for five hours," came a voice from the doorway. A rotund bearded man in a turban with spectacles balanced on the bridge of his nose stood in the doorway. Behind him were a number of additional Arab men who had not been seen at earlier meetings. The roly-poly man looked down the glasses at the bomb sitting before him, "Let us see our ultimate weapon at work."

Ayman al-Zawahiri, the new de-facto leader of al Qaeda stepped into the room followed by his al Qaeda lieutenants.

The THCT group looked up and saw their enemy standing before them. It took all their strength to not launch themselves across the room at the men who had killed their loved ones. They tried to mask their anger and desire for revenge.

The terrorists walked towards the center of the room and everyone in their path stepped out of the way, including Ralph Behar and Uri Navroz. Their imposing stature commanded respect from the circle of followers.

Zawahiri stood over the weapon and the operative looked up into his eyes, which were dark and black as coal. The al Qaeda leader nodded his head and the operative reached down and started the five hour entry as Dimitri watched, torn between looking down at the bomb, or up at the fat man who had helped to organize the 9-11 terrorist attack. The man was his mortal enemy. What he really wanted to do was tear the man's heart out.

The clock blinked to life again and this time showed a five-hour read-out and then immediately started counting down 4:59.59, 4:59.58. With the new men still standing in the doorway, no one was looking at the bomb counting down.

"Leader, it is good of you to join us. If I may, I would like to introduce Mr. Jeremy Bingham, a British arms dealer, who you have been having conversations with for the past six weeks..... Mr. Bingham, this is Ayman al Zawahiri, our leader."

"It has been a long time in coming, this meeting," Meredith said, not sure if extending his hand was the appropriate greeting. He chose not to. He lowered his gaze to the bomb sitting on the rug beneath them and said, "In obtaining this lethal antiquity, I could think of no organization that would have wanted it more than yours, Sir. Plus, I figured you would be willing to pay the heavy price we have chosen to put on it." He said this staring into the black eyes of the man who had planned the killing of his son. He hoped he would not betray himself.

"Mr. Bingham, I am pleased that you have contacted us, and you are correct, we have wanted this antiquity, as you call it, for a long time. It has been on our minds for years now and now it is even more important that we have such a weapon. This is an important day for us."

They both stared down at the bomb beneath them, as the timer rolled through four hours and fifty-three minutes. Zawahiri looked up and stared into the arms dealer's eyes.

"We must talk of many things." He pointed at the bomb on the floor. "I think we should allow the clock to wind down a bit and see that it works as we would like, before I pay you the remainder of your hefty ransom. I think we should take a walk in the desert. I would like to talk about these additional weapons I have been hearing about. Anwar, come and get us when we are within two hours of calamity."

Ayman al Zawahiri turned and walked towards the door. Again the people in the circle parted like Moses' Red Sea, to create a pathway. Meredith and the terrorist went through the door with a significant number of other following closely. In the bright sunlight a number of bodyguards fanned out in a circle around the al Qaeda leaders, maintaining a distance as they walked into the hills.

→ ←

Socotra Island

The small group of terrorist leaders walked towards the base of the mountain away from the Arabian Sea. Meredith walked quietly and waited for Zawahiri to speak as the host of this growing enclave of the al Qaeda leadership in the middle of nowhere. Having seen a good number of additional al Qaeda leaders arriving in camp for the past day and a half he knew that a meeting of the terrorist network had been called in honor of the special antiquity he had delivered. Each of the Arab delegations had brought armed guards to protect them. Socotra had become an armed camp and the THCT team was the only group that was defenseless. He would need to keep his wits about him, he thought.

He also marveled they had perhaps stumbled into an unbelievable bonus situation. If they could pull this off they could potentially take out the entire leadership of the al Qaeda terrorist organization. Meredith was deep in thought trying to figure out how to play his meager hand without being discovered.

"So my new friend, why was it so important that we had to meet about our antiquity?" Zawahiri asked as they arrived at the foot of the mountain.

Meredith looked into the fat man's eyes. He realized his response needed to be as sincere as he could make it. "You and Osama bin Laden were the only people I could think of who would appreciate this weapon enough to pay the price that we have placed on it. Had we tried to sell this bomb to anyone else, or any other member of al Qaeda, we might not have had the chance to sell the additional weapons that have come into our possession. I was afraid your fellow believers would grab the bomb and kill us before we could show you the weapon and develop a long and productive relationship."

"I can accept what you have said, but why shouldn't I just kill your group of gun runners and make off with this antiquity?"

"Because," Meredith said slowly for effect, "I can supply five more of these devastating weapons for you, as well as a host of other services."

"I was made aware you have access to additional 'antiquities,'" he smiled beneath his scraggly salt and pepper beard, "and I do have great interest in such things. But tell me more of these other services?" Zawahiri said, completely intrigued with this brazen arms dealer bearing gifts. He decided he wanted to explore all his options before deciding if this man, and his gunrunners would die.

"Let me explain. I suspect that with bin Laden's untimely death at the hands of the Americans, you may only get one chance to avenge his death and change the world." Meredith considered if he should drive his point home and decided to go for it.

"If you use this single bomb to blow New York off the face of the map, it will do its job, but you'll infuriate the Americans even more. If you think they have been relentless to this point, you have no idea what will happen once a nuclear bomb goes off. You will upset the balance of the earth."

"You're right, but this is what I have hoped for from the beginning, to once and for all cripple the infidels," Zawahiri said as he stroked his beard.

"But one bomb will not do that. You will kill hundreds of thousands of people, and they will come after you ten times harder than they try now."

"I see what you are saying. It would be like the Japanese when they bombed Pearl Harbor. The US went after Japan with a vengeance!"

"Exactly. But if you were to use all the bombs I offer, all at once in one major attack, you will destroy them. They will not be in a position to retaliate. You would make the entire world take notice of your supremacy and new Islamic order," Meredith lied playing to the terrorist's vanity. He looked into the glazed black eyes of the terrorist and could see him visualizing the heinous act.

"I can sell you this one-time ultimate devastation for a price, and from a service standpoint, I can actually deliver these weapons to America for you, if that is where you want them," Meredith stated, as emphatically as he could.

Zawahiri's head snapped up at the words and he peered into the arms dealer eyes trying to digest what he had just heard. He looked quizzically at Meredith.

"I can move your antiquities to North America, once we have settled the financial issues, without problem, just as I have brought this sample weapon here. Delivery on U.S. soil would not be a challenge as we have moved weapons in and out of America for years. I presume entering the U.S. has been a major problem for you and your people?"

The new terrorist leader slowly nodded his head, again saying nothing. He was trying to understand what Meredith was offering.

Meredith continued to weave his web of deceit; "I have moved weapons all over the world for years always seeking the highest bidder. That is how I make my living. And I think you are the highest bidder for these weapons right now."

"Go ahead. I am intrigued with how you would do such smuggling?"

Meredith had him. The big fish was done nibbling. He had swallowed the bait. It was time to set the hook.

"Years ago, I bought a small company in Ontario, Canada near Thunder Bay, on Lake Superior. You will find it on a map. It's a commercial fishing company in a very small town on the Canadian side of the Great Lakes. This company fishes for whitefish and salmon in Lake Superior for Canadian and U.S. consumption. The company makes a nice little profit for me and the fish are great on a grill. You would like them.

My boats fish the entire lake and make trips across Lake Superior to the U.S. side of the border all the time. We have been there so long we are rarely ever searched. We've been going back and forth for years now. I cross over this water border like you cross the desert. I've been moving weapons in and out of America for years without anyone noticing," Meredith said.

"That is good, but what is my cost to have such a delivery of artifacts to America?" Zawahiri asked, intrigued with the concept.

"Presuming we have agreed on our $2,000,000 price tag for each of these additional artifacts, I would guarantee delivery inside the United States for an extra half million dollars per unit. That would amount to an additional $2,500,000 dollars, although I would prefer payment in Euro's. I think the dollar may have some negative value in the near future." Meredith returned the wicked smile he had seen earlier on Zawahiri's face.

"Mr. Bingham, I think we shall consummate such a deal, but I will insist on making the delivery payments once my special antiquities have arrived in America."

"Ayman, if I may," Meredith used his first name for the first time, suggesting a friendship was developing. "I think we can live with that arrangement. Let's say 75% of the bomb cost up front and the remainder, along with all the delivery/transportation fees upon safe delivery. But, please remember my second condition."

"Ahh, yes, what was it, that you would like to know when to take an extended holiday in Tahiti? Was that the place?" Zawahiri smiled again, enjoying the thoughts of what was to come. "Yes, I think once we have placed these rare antiquities where we would like them, we will be pleased to encourage you and your people to seek out the beach life, like we have here. I should think a remote Pacific Island would offer great peace and tranquility."

With that response Meredith confirmed that it had indeed been Zawahiri on the other end of that blinking radio transmitter, when they had first met with al-Awlaki. He was confident the Trojan horse was now being dragged within the walls of the fortress. The enemy had taken the bait. Now all the Team had to do was get off the island.

→ ←

1600 Pennsylvania Avenue, NW

The President stepped out of his personal washroom adjacent to the Oval Office still drying his hands, "So what do we have? Where are we with these wanna-be terrorists?"

"Mr. President, there isn't that much new information since we last talked, but we are more certain we may not be the target of this THCT group," Karen Lee said sitting on a sofa across from Admiral Dan Bishope, the Chairman of the Joint Chiefs, and FBI Director Logan Taylor. She continued, "We've verified that one of Meredith's ships made ports of call on a number of the cities where we identified THCT activity. The ship was in the Black Sea where Russia stores their nuclear arsenal when the WMD went missing. The ship's manifest shows a large order of farm tractors and 200,000 bushels of wheat being sent to Karachi, Pakistan. The route has taken them through the Med, the Red Sea and into the Arabian Sea."

"Sir, we are trying to locate the ship now," the Admiral said, as the President sat in a straight-back chair in front of his massive desk. "We also received a report from Mideast Fleet Command that this ship, the Majorca, was attacked by pirates in the Gulf of Aden off Somalia about ten days ago. They sustained enough damage to divert the ship to Aden for repairs. The Port Authority verified the ship was in port for a week, and left only a couple days ago. There was no change in their itinerary, so we presume they're heading east through the Arabian Sea. I have all our assets in the Indian Ocean searching for them and we have planes up from Diego Garcia doing a grid search."

Karen Lee leaned forward in her seat and looked at the President sitting at the top of the circle. "Sir, as we suggested last week, we believe this group of amateurs is going after the rest of the al Qaeda organization with that bomb. We have been hearing about some sort of pow-wow that al Qaeda is organizing."

"I for one wish them luck. We certainly could use the help. We got the head of the snake, now we need the rest of the body," the Admiral said, slapping his sharply creased uniform trousers.

"If they could actually get al Qaeda to come out of hiding we could take them all out once and for all," the President said wistfully, "God knows we have tried for the past ten years."

"Mr. President, getting the rest of the terrorist network would be a tremendous coup for this administration, especially since we've knocked them back on their heals for the moment," Karen Lee said, trying to steer the conversation back to the facts, "but if this THCT cell uses that bomb there would be all sorts of collateral damage that comes with it. I'm told a Russian suitcase bomb could easily wipe out 100,000 people in the blast itself and twice that number later from the fallout. I see that as a troubling problem, Sir."

"Karen, you're right as usual. We need to stop them before they can set off any weapon." The President turned towards the Admiral. "Dan, lets step it up to find that ship before it docks anywhere else." Then he turned to the Assistant CIA Director. "Karen, get your people in Karachi looking for that ship, and lets get the nuke teams in place over there to handle this weapon if we can get our hands on it. This is a priority until resolved, one way or another. And keep me posted."

The President rose and walked back to his desk. The rest of the team got up and made for the door.

→ ←

Eastern Socotra Island

The THCT team spent another day being scrutinized by every Arab partisan in camp. They continued to cooperate sharing the information about the suitcase weapon. Josef/Dimitri and the two Pakistani brothers walked a number of al Qaeda crazies through the bomb safety components and the arming and disarming procedure. The Arabs, from Egypt, Syria and Saudi Arabia would obviously be used to arm the weapons at their final destinations.

Ralph Behar worked almost exclusively with Zawahiri to coordinate the transfer of funds for the deposits on the additional weapons. Ralph was able to regale him with stories about the Shah's Iran and his overthrow back in 1979. Zawahiri was almost taking notes as he harbored such hopes for other Islamic countries as well. They were getting along relatively well, even though Ralph wanted to pluck his eyes out.

The Euro's exchange was arranged and the money was wired from numbered accounts in Geneva, Switzerland to banks in the Maldive Islands. The transactions were spread over two days to prevent prying eyes from seeing any substantial amounts moving as a single unit. Unbeknownst to Zawahiri, Meredith had already placed standing orders at the investment banks for any newly deposited funds to be again forwarded to other banks in the Cayman Islands, and the Guernsey Islands in the English Channel. In those places the funding was again broken down into smaller deposits and transferred to another series of numbered accounts.

Michael and Kevin were the least utilized of the bunch. Instead of protecting their boss, they were relegated to being sullen observers. Their job was to remain silent and observant, and brood a lot having been stripped of their weapons. They didn't like it but they followed orders.

While these activities were occurring in camp, a couple of additional boats began arriving in the cove, along with a number of off-road vehicles, all bringing small groups of Arabs to the fishing village. The various baked brick shepherds huts were filling up with arriving guests. As these small groups arrived, they eyed the THCT team members with great suspicion, but Anwar al-Awlaki quickly advised the western visitors were to be tolerated as guests bearing gifts.

Once confirmation was received the money transfer for the additional weapons had been consummated, Meredith was advised his visit to the island was over. His group would not be needed any longer. That was fine with Meredith. He advised his team they would be leaving shortly.

Josef went to meet with his technical al Qaeda counterparts. He casually asked them how comfortable they were with the arming procedures. They gathered around the weapon on the rough-cut table and talked about the arming and disarming mechanisms.

Josef suggested they each take one more turn running through the arming/disarming procedures before he departed. On the fourth person's run-thru, he intervened placing his hand on top of the bomb mechanism, stating that the al Qaeda operative was not following procedure. He showed him what he needed to do and then advised he would re-set the bomb and let him try again. The Arabs all watched as he entered a code to re-set the weapon. When he got to the switch sequence number he needed to enter, he paused and then looked up at the doorway as if someone was there. As he did so, everyone in the group followed his lead and looked up too. Josef quickly entered the secret code they had pre-programmed into the machine and pressed the enter button.

As the men lost interest at whatever had been at the door, they looked back at the table. Josef advised the young man, who had been interrupted, to proceed and he flawlessly ran through the sequencing. He looked up pleased with himself. The last man then took his turn arming and disarming the bomb and did so flawlessly.

"All of you have done well," Josef said as he clapped his hands quietly together. He was excited to have entered the final code sequencing without anyone noticing, so he celebrated for his dead wife, Elena. The bomb could be armed and disarmed ten more times. On the tenth disarming the weapon would look as if it had shut down but the clock would continue counting down from thirty minutes. It could not be disarmed using any sequencing.

He tried to be as helpful and cooperative as possible. He continued, "If you follow these procedures you will be successful in arming the device. Then I would recommend that you remove yourself and get as far away as possible within the countdown time you have entered. I encourage you to be at least fifty miles away, and upwind of the blast or the fallout may affect you later."

The al Qaeda operatives nodded and said they understood. Josef went on, "Also, the instruction manual should be kept with the weapon at all times in case you are not actually there to arm the device. You will be fine with some continued practice. Let us share a cup of tea and celebrate." He shut the suitcase bomb cover, locked the device and handed it to the lead man in the room. They all went to find a cup of tea.

William Meredith sat with Zawahiri, and Awlaki in the largest shepherd's hut in the small village. There were four more senior al Qaeda leaders also in the room who had recently arrived in camp. The new al Qaeda leader cleared his throat and with a gravelly voice said, "Mr. Bingham, I am glad that you have persevered to find us. In a way that alone marks you as an extraordinary man. At the same time it concerns me that you did."

Meredith was quiet for a moment as he contemplated what that perhaps meant, but shook the thought out of his head. Zawahiri continued, "You have given us hope with this weapon to avenge our leader's life and destroy the West. I will trust you to honor our contract to deliver them, or my people will hunt you down."

"Ayman, do not worry, I'll honor my part of our agreement. I have every hope that your bankroll will underwrite many additional purchases. While I believe you will bring the Americans to their knees, I don't think the battle will be won. I am sure that you will need additional assistance. I am a businessman and you are my client."

He stood and offered a hand to say goodbye.

"I will hold you to your promise as well, and will expect some word of when we should begin our extended beach holiday. " He laughed a nervous laugh that the terrorist understood. "I would also like to ask that my few weapons be returned when we leave, you know we are in pirate waters." Meredith said this as he pointed out to sea. "Now that I have some money, I don't want to pay any ransoms if I can help it."

Zawahiri laughed as well. He extended his hand reluctantly as if touching the infidel's hand might make him unclean. Meredith accepted the proffered hand and bowed to the assembled men, and then turned towards the hut's threshold.

Before he could get to the entrance, Zawahiri spoke up and said, " Before you depart, we have one additional condition. We would like to have two of your men stay with us for a while longer, call it insurance if you will."

Meredith stopped and slowly turned around contemplating the predictable request. "That is a fair condition," Meredith said without hesitation. He knew arguing would only compromise the deal. "Which of us would you like to remain?"

"I should think our Russian friend Dimitri has the best capability with the antiquity. And then your accountant who I have grown to like."

"I will advise them they are extending their stay. I would ask that you take good care of them and get them to a safe haven in the next few weeks."

"It will be done as you request."

The meeting was over and Meredith left. He crossed the sun-baked earth between the various huts and motioned for his small group of counter-terrorists to come together. Almost as a whisper he asked, "Dimitri, are we good?"

"We are Mr. Bingham, we can and should go!" He said in his thickest Russian accent.

"As we suspected, they want two of us to remain behind. They want you and Ralph to stay with the bomb. I agreed without hesitation. Are you both still ok with that?'

"I am Mr. Bingham."

"Me too, Jeremy" Ralph said smiling. "We knew what we were getting into. We'll be fine and are prepared for the worst. But should we be able to sneak away, we'll be looking for you on the beach in the next day or so.

"We will be there waiting until you come. May God be with you!

"OK, let's gather our belongings. We'll meet at the boat in ten minutes. Don't be late. No mistakes now. We'll get our weapons back after we have boarded the boat." Both Kevin and Michael looked relieved as if they were getting their clothes back.

→ ←

Al Qaeda Encampment

The THCT team assembled on the beach. As they did so, the Arab guards also showed up with their AK-47s trained on the departing group. Bingham walked towards the shore with Anwar al-Awlaki talking quietly. When they arrived at the boat, the team members said their goodbyes to Dimitri and Ralph who were standing back with a couple of guards casually watching them.

The other team members pushed the boat off the sandy shore and jumped in. Uri went to the motor, primed it, and turned the engine over without fanfare slipping it into neutral. He waited for his boss.

Bingham extended his hand to al-Awlaki and the al Qaeda leader accepted it as if a friend. Then al-Awlaki turned to a guard and took two unloaded AK-47s and a cloth bag with four banana clips and two military knives in it. He handed the two weapons to Bingham and said they could load the guns once they left the island.

"We will talk again soon," Awlaki said. "We expect the additional 'antiquities' will be delivered within a month. Further delay is not an option. We will get your two men back to Aden and on a flight in the next couple of weeks. Meet the schedule and then you will have two weeks to begin your holiday. And I think you will want to make sure you don't miss that flight!" Awlaki said this envisioning the mushroom clouds that would blossom all over America.

"We will meet our part of the bargain, Anwar, you need not worry. Your antiquities, will be there as promised…. Please take care of my people. Just be sure the remaining funds are transferred to my numbered account in the Maldives, as we have agreed. Once we have verified payment, you will have your weapons, and we will all be able to take our holidays."

"Go then, our business is finished…. my guards will be watching from the cliffs," Awlaki stated. He turned to walk up the beach. Zawahiri was nowhere about and Meredith could only hope that he was still in camp.

Michael and Kevin manually pushed the boat off the sand beach into deeper water. They quickly jumped on board as Uri lowered the large outboard engines and threw them into reverse. They backed away from the beach as a dozen weapons followed their every move. None of the boat's occupants made any quick moves. Their single goal was to vacate the island atoll as quickly as possible.

Uri maneuvered the boat through the gentle swells of the protected bay with ease and turned to head out to sea. Around them on the hills and cliffs, Arab gunman monitored their departure. They rounded the jagged promontory and headed due east. The wave action picked up considerably and Uri worked harder to maintain a steady course.

Leaving the protected waters of the cove, Kevin and Michael reached for the cloth sack and each pulled out a banana clip for their AK-47s, checking first that rounds were actually loaded in the semi-circular clips, and then slamming them home. Both immediately felt as if they were dressed again. Kevin shrugged his satisfaction with a gun in hand and crawled to the bow, while Michael took up a security position close to the stern.

Five hundred yards out Meredith asked Kevin to break out the portable radio that was secured to the bottom of one of the seats sealed in a waterproof bag. Sitting down he dialed in a pre-arranged channel and hailed the Majorca advising they were heading out to sea directly off the eastern point of the island. He asked for coordinates and estimated time of arrival.

"Bingham," Captain Brinkmann said, "We've been worried about your fishing expedition. I hope the fishing was good?"

"Captain, you were right, the fishing was extraordinary. We caught more than we thought we would."

"Glad to hear that. I'll look forward to seeing your catch. We were worried about you. Your radio must not have been receiving."

"We had some engine problems and the batteries were low, but all is good now. We are fine, and heading directly east from the island," Meredith said, being non-specific should anyone else be listening.

"I can now see you on our radar. We are about twenty miles directly west of you. Continue on your present course and we'll be heading your direction immediately. I estimate we will be there in twenty-five minutes."

"Roger that Captain. We look forward to your arrival."

Meredith signed off and relayed the information to the rest of his team.

"The ship is steaming towards us. Should be here within a half hour. Uri maintain this heading due east. We should run into them. They have us on their radar now."

"Aye, aye Captain," Uri said, maintaining his heading. "It's good to be out of that hellhole. I still feel like a gun is pointed at my head."

"Did any of you have as hard as time as I did not flying across the table at those bastards?" Meredith said to his band of followers.

"Yeah, I wanted to stuff my fist down Zawahiri's throat," Kevin offered, "He's such a smug bastard, and all he's doing is stepping up because we took his boss out."

"I'm kind of glad they took our weapons, because I sure would have used them if we had the chance," Michael said. "I just felt dirty the whole time I was there."

"I was used to being around rag heads, but sure would have liked to take them out one by one and see their shock," Kevin said bobbing in the bow of the small craft.

Just then a fighter jet came streaking out of the west at about 3,000 ft and did a lazy turn above them, crossed their path one more time and then headed east towards where the Majorca was located.

"Let's hope they're out here looking for pirates and not us," Meredith said as he covered his eyes squinting into the sun, "and that they don't think we're the brigands out here in this small boat. Anyone see what flag or country they were flying?"

"Couldn't tell boss, but it looks like they are circling east of here where the Majorca is probably coming towards us," Michael said as he handed the binoculars to Meredith to get another eye on the departing plane.

"Now wouldn't that be just dandy," said Kevin from the bow. We've been shot at by pirates, had guns pointed at us for two days by half of al Qaeda, and now some air force wants to shoot us out of the water. I'll tell you, those Greek Islands are looking better and better every minute."

"I'm glad we're finally getting out of there as well. The Majorca is looking better and better. But we also have to go back to the point to pick up Ralph and Josef," Meredith said.

→ ←

Eastern Socotra Island

Once the arms dealer's boat left the cove and a guard advised they were headed out to sea without incident, Zawahiri relaxed a bit and called Anwar al-Awlaki to his side. He had remained in one of the small shepherd's huts a short distance from the rest of the small fishing village still unsure about these gift-bearers.

"Anwar, now that our infidel friends have departed, we should gather all the leaders that have arrived thus far. I want to discuss our fortune, and make plans for the ultimate devastation of the great Satan."

"As you wish, Ayman. We still have some arriving from Egypt and Syria within the hour. They are coming from Hodibah by Range Rover, just as we did."

"That is good. Let me know when they arrive. Our news is important enough that we will wait. In the meantime, I want to have a separate meeting with you. And make sure you keep an eye on our two guests."

"I have two guards staying with them," Awlaki said, "I will have them move into their hut this evening. I still have misgivings of these people bearing gifts."

"They are only interested in their blood money," Zawahiri said, rationalizing that he had just identified the final solution to his twenty-five years of fighting for Islam. "They would kill their own mothers if they were paid to do so. I only wish our people had found these animals sooner. We could have done this with Osama and it would have been our greatest day."

"Do you think they can be trusted? Will we ever see the other weapons?" Awlaki asked, not caring about the money, but only the results they hoped for.

"We have fought for years to bury the West. We have fought with guns and knives, we have fought with stinger missiles, ironically given to us by the Americans, and with dedicated warriors for years. We now fight in countries all over the globe. With these ultimate weapons the West will be brought to their knees, and we will bring true Islam to the rest of the world. And you, our American Imam, will be our deliverer. We will need the people you have indoctrinated and hidden in America to assist us with this massive attack."

"I will be honored to lead this effort," Anwar said bowing to the new leader of al Qaeda.

Zawahiri reached for a steaming pot of tea and some chipped ceramic cups. He began pouring tea from the pot and offered one to his cohort.

He then raised his cup and said, "A toast, as the British say, we drink to the devastation of America!" He took a sip of the hot brew and let it burn his throat. His eyes burned black as coal as he thought about what would be coming. "I would like these bombs to go off simultaneously, in all of the cities we shall choose. It will terrorize the Americans, those still alive will have fear in their hearts, and it will kill their souls. I ask that you send your best people to pick up the weapons in this Minneapolis place, when the bombs come across their border, and then deliver them to the cities we have chosen."

"I have such people in America who will do as you and I ask," Awlaki said, very pleased that he would be a part of this world-changing act. "We will only need to tell them where to go, and how to trigger the weapons. I have my technical people re-writing the Russian manual in Arabic, so we will have a backup if they have trouble with the English version our friends have provided. I have my men practicing the triggering procedures now and one of them has a clean record and can make the trip to Minneapolis without any problem. He will do the final training."

"It shall be done," Zawahiri said, again staring off at the earthen walls of the hut. "We will avenge Osama's death in a big way. America will lose its major cities and the seat of government all at once. That will bring them to their knees. They will eventually know Islam is the only religion and we will show them the truth."

"Tomorrow, I want all the leaders brought together in the main building." Zawahiri said this as he waved his hand over the table. "We will advise our brothers of our plan and tell them to be ready for the aftermath. While we will cripple the United States, I suspect those who remain alive will come after us with a vengeance that we have never seen before. All of us must be ready to protect ourselves so we can lead the revolution after the bombs."

Zawahiri finished his tea and said, "Gather the elders and our leaders. In the morning we will talk with all of al Qaeda's leadership and plan for the future. This is a momentous occasion!"

→ ←

White House, Washington, DC

Five black SUVs pulled into the White House grounds off 17th Street at N.Y. Avenue between the Old Executive Office Building and the First Division Monument. Each car passed through security and was waved into the executive parking lot tucked behind the Old EOB. In this manner the press would not be monitoring the comings and goings of the vehicle occupants.

As each car arrived, the Directors of the CIA, FBI, NSA and the Joint Chiefs quickly passed through another security portal in the lower level of the White House close to the West Wing and the Oval Office. They were escorted upstairs and brought to the Roosevelt Room, just a few steps down the hall from the President's Oval Office.

The President had just finished a private call to the British Prime Minister briefing him on the growing intelligence that had been found in the bin Laden compound. The western world was glad to see this terrorist was out of the picture. Within the office the invisible door that blended into the millwork opened and his personal secretary stuck her head in to announce the visitors. He nodded and threw his suit jacket on knowing the military would be in dress uniforms.

The men and women coming into the room nodded their hellos to the President of the United States knowing he shook enough hands every day that such a greeting wouldn't be appreciated. A steward appeared and stood at attention off to the side at a butler's table with coffee service available. Two of the Directors headed for the coffee, and then found their seats on the two sofas that framed the fringes of the ornate Presidential seal rug in the center of the room.

The President walked to his desk, grabbed his coffee mug and sat in one of the straight chairs at the top of the conversation circle. It was his chair and everyone knew it.

"I just got off the phone with the Prime Minister and briefed him on everything we are learning from our intel out of the compound. He will use everything we send him to press the al Qaeda elements within his reach. I also advised him about what we have going on here with this THCT terrorist group. He said his people have been picking up similar information about al Qaeda being on the move. He agrees we have a difficult decision to make."

"Mr. President, I know we're all pretty much up to speed on this terrorist group," Admiral Dan Bishope, Chairman of the Joint Chiefs of Staff said, as people settled down, "but I have some new information we just received from Central Command in Tampa. We just received visual verification that Meredith's ship, the Majorca, is actually sailing in the Arabian Sea and has been making lazy eight circles for the past two days off of Yemen's coast. We initially did some very high fly-bys with photo equipment. This morning we sent in a photoreconnaissance F-15 to do a close in pass. Interestingly enough, as we did the fly-by we spotted a small fishing boat with at least five men in it, and they didn't look like Somali pirates stalking the larger ship."

"Mr. President, that matches up satellite photos that NSA re-tasked to that area as well. We were looking for all his ships at sea, not knowing if he was on any of them," Brent Eichalberger, the NSA Director said. "His company only has three ships at sea at the moment and two of them just docked in ports in the Med. The third ship, the Majorca, is a coastal freighter that usually sails in the Mediterranean. We checked its manifest and cargos and it's heading to Karachi. Which would put them in the Arabian Sea, just as Dan said."

"Just so we are all up to speed," Karen lee said, "CIA has been pressing our contacts for any and all information. We're hearing that lots of bad guys are moving about and actually making trips out of their normal safe zones. The word is something is up."

"Same thing at NSA. We have all sorts of communications matching those field reports. We just picked up two al Qaeda operatives in Cairo that were getting on a plane for Aden, Yemen. That was a bonus, but it certainly points to something going on."

"Alright, what does all this mean? Do we have some crazy Americans running around with a nuclear weapon intent on blowing us, or al Qaeda up?" He looked at his Chief of Staff, Phil Kummerer, and said, "I need answers people, sooner rather than later, because I don't think later is an option. Let's connect the dots. I want you to keep Phil in the loop by the hour. What else have we got?"

Karen Lee decided she would answer. "Mr. President, these THCT guys aren't interested in us, they're going after the remnants of al Qaeda! I know it's crazy but that's what is going on. I'm sure of it."

She paused to give everyone a chance to embrace that thought and then summarized for the tenth time. "This whole THCT group has suffered terrible personal losses of loved ones, children, spouses, friends and lovers. They've grieved over their losses for years and have been frustrated with their government, who couldn't seem to get bin Laden."

The President stiffened up in his straight back chair and said, "Hell Karen, we did get him, and without the loss of a single soldier."

"I know that Mr. President, we all do, but these people have been frustrated for years watching him on the TV laughing at their misery," Karen realized she was defending these potential terrorists. She held her tongue for a moment.

Dan Bishope, Chairman of the Joint Chiefs looked in his portfolio and sifted through his information about the Russian nuke. "It's certainly possible they're the ones with the Russian warhead. We tracked Meredith's ship, and it was in the Black Sea near where the Russian nuke went missing."

"And the Russian General who commanded that camp lost a sister in the 9-11 terrorist attack, a housekeeper that worked in the Marriott Hotel when the towers collapsed, Karen said. "Her husband, his brother-in-law, is part of this THCT group. By the way, the General has been relieved of duty, and he too has disappeared." Karen Lee was just trying to get everyone to connect all the dots. "So if you take all this into consideration, what they tried to do was lure bin Laden out of his lair. They intended to kill him. We just got there first. Now I think they're going after the rest of the organization."

"They used a kind of Trojan horse approach," Dan Bishope said, as if a light had gone on in his mind. "They tried to give him something he really wanted, a nuclear bomb, and then hoped to get him to show his face in the process."

Everyone thought about that for a moment recalling their Greek mythology.

"Trojan horse? I'll be damned, talk about a gift horse. Ok, so lets say the TH stands for Trojan horse....... The other T could stand for terrorists, THT, but what's the hell does the C stand for, if anything?" Brent Eichalberger, Director of the NSA asked.

He thought about the whole case file for another moment and then blurted out, "If they aren't planting the bomb here in America, and instead are taking it to al Qaeda, then their counter-terrorists aren't they? THCT, Trojan horse counter-terrorists,.... son-of-a-bitch, ...pardon me, it can't be that simple, can it?"

"That's an interesting theory Brent, but it's still a stretch, don't you think?" the President said, wondering if it were that simple, and what, if anything, could, or would, the U.S. do.

Everyone waited for the President to speak. "I still have reservations about this whole scenario. At the same time we need to make sure that bomb doesn't turn up here. For all we know it could be sitting out there on the Mall leaning against a light pole." Everyone in the room got a chill with that comment and it registered on their faces. A few looked out the window behind the President's desk.

"Let's keep chasing these guys and see if we can't make sense of all this. Admiral, how fast can you get your people out to that ship to do an inspection?"

"I can scramble another Navy SEAL Team from Diego Garcia and they could be on that deck in about three hours, Sir."

"Do it, let's find out what is going on from the Trojan horse's mouth. Do it peacefully. These guys may actually be very misguided patriots."

→ ←

Al Qaeda's Summit Meeting

The meeting of all the important leaders within al Qaeda was scheduled to start at noon. Many of these terrorists from Middle Eastern countries and a few from far away places like England and America had not met one another before; they had taken their orders from bin Laden and Zawahiri through all sorts of cutouts. They had never been summoned by the leader and now that he was dead they were mystified why they had been called in for a summit by Zawahiri. They were excited about the rumored possibilities for revenge.

As each contingent of terrorists crowded into the largest hut in the fishing village, it became obvious there would not be enough room to accommodate everyone. Anwar al Awlaki made the decision to move the gathering outside. A large ceremonial rug was rolled up and carried outside to the large courtyard area. Once the rug was laid out the various groups of terrorists closed around the circle and quietly awaited the new leader of al Qaeda, Ayman al-Zawahiri.

From one of the smaller mud huts Zawahiri stepped out into the sunshine and shaded his eyes from the sun. He was dressed in his finest white gellebiah robe and had trimmed his beard to better frame his face. He pushed his glasses up on the bridge of his nose and took a deep breath of the arid air that was mixed with the salt of the ocean. Selfishly, he was pleased he had moved to Yemen from Pakistan before Osama, otherwise he too would have been dead. His eyes slowly adjusted to the sunlight and he straightened his frame and began walking towards the assembled group of over fifty al Qaeda leaders. When the call had gone out they had assembled without hesitation. They had come to this remote island to meet their new leader.

Zawahiri was confident that this meeting would change the world order and bring Islam to its rightful place. As he walked towards the assembled group, he mentally reviewed what he would say to his al Qaeda brothers. He would inspire them and demonstrate he was worthy of being their next leader able to win this holy war with the infidels.

As he neared the throng, there was a murmuring among the sea of robed men. They parted and made a path to let the new leader walk through to the center of the circle. Zawahiri stood ramrod straight before the group, and started turning slowly, nodding occasionally at those he recognized. Then he cleared his throat and spoke in a deep authoritative voice.

"My brothers, I am your humble servant and thank you for coming to this island to hear about extraordinary things. We have lost our leader in the last few weeks and we must regroup to carry on the jihad."

He took care to look into the eyes of every man assembled. This would be his sermon to the faithful. This would be his Islamic Sermon on the Mount.

"We have fought the infidels for many years as our forefathers did centuries ago in the Holy Wars. We have fought them on many fronts here in the Middle East. We have fought in Egypt, Palestine, Saudi Arabia, Syria, Lebanon, and Afghanistan."

The al Qaeda leaders were mesmerized with every word Zawahiri spoke. He continued.

"More recently we have fought the infidels in Iraq and in Pakistan. We have even fought for Islam in Eastern Europe, in Russia, and in Europe. But until now we have fought them on our holy ground. They have brought the battles to us and we have seen our people bleed and die from their bullets, from their aircraft missiles and from their cluster bombs. We now even have to look out for these pilot-less planes they fly and kill us with."

Zawahiri walked the fringes of the circle allowing his robes to touch those seated in front. He drew them closer painting a vivid picture of the death and destruction that had rained down on them. He stoked their anger and frustration.

"But now we come together to take this jihad to them, just as we did in 9-11. Instead of fighting and bleeding on our ground, we will take the battle to them again in a way that will make the destruction of the Twin Towers of New York pale in comparison."

He waved his hand to the outer circle and the throng followed his hand movement as he pointed to a man standing behind the circle. Anwar al-Awlaki stood there holding onto a suitcase. He started to move forward. The group automatically parted again and Awlaki pulled the wheeled suitcase behind him in the sand. Two other men followed his lead carrying a simple wooden table. When they got to the center of the circle, the men set the table down on the rug and assisted Awlaki in lifting the suitcase to the table surface. The entire group watched and held their collective breath as the suitcase was lifted to the table. Then a low murmur started as various men offered opinions on what was in the case.

"I have called you all here to show you the ultimate weapon," Zawahiri said. He pointed at the simple suitcase on the table. "Before you sits a

Russian suitcase nuclear bomb that will devastate any city we place it in. It will wipe New York City off the face of the map and it will kill hundreds of thousands of infidels."

He stopped talking and let what he had said sink in. The assembled group sat there stunned and stared at the simple case that sat before them.

"Some of you have been here for days and saw the western infidels that were in camp. They were arms dealers who brought us this weapon for a fee, a very sizeable fee, that I very willingly paid without hesitation. This is what we have all been yearning for since we fought the Russians over twenty-five years ago. This is also what Osama sought for many years."

The assembled terrorists started talking quietly among themselves trying to grasp what the new leader of al Qaeda was saying. Those on the outer fringe of the circle stood to get a better look at this weapon of mass destruction. As they stared at the suitcase they started murmuring to one another, with the buzz swelling as their questions and comments competed with one another, until Zawahiri raised a hand for silence.

"We now have the ultimate weapon to fight these Satanists. We can cripple them a hundred times more severely than we did with the World Trade Center, perhaps a thousand times more severely. And this will be done in the near future. As you can see, this weapon is small and easily moved about. We are told that once it is detonated, it will kill thousands and spread radioactivity all over the land."

The crowd got even more excited as they realized that their desire to undermine the West could be accomplished with such a small weapon. One elder who had fought with bin Laden against the Russians in Afghanistan rose and asked a question.

"Leader, this is the news we have waited to hear for years. But how will this single weapon be able to accomplish such things?"

"Khalil, it is a good question, one that should be asked. This bomb can do great damage and kill many of the infidels, but it is only one weapon. But I have secured five more of these weapons that will be put in place in the near future, in six different cities where the infidels sleep," emphasizing the word I. "With these weapons, the infidels will know the fear our families feel every time a plane flies over our villages. They will know what fear is!"

The questioning terrorist bowed his head as he contemplated what Zawahiri had said. The others all went silent as they tried to understand the carnage that such weapons would cause.

"We will use these weapons as one, on the same day, in different cities in America and one in London, England. This will break the backs of the

Americans and they will have no fight left in them. Islam will then reign supreme from that day forward."

Zawahiri continued to weave his web. "I have chosen Imam Anwar al-Awlaki to lead this mission. He has people in place in America waiting for his call to action. They will place the weapons in the cities and set them to go off, at the same time, on the same day all over America."

"Leader, can we trust these people to do our bidding. This is not like a suicide bombing. This is much bigger. How can they make such a thing happen?"

"Another good question. When we obtained this weapon," he walked over to the table and opened the suitcase latches and laid back the lid of the case, "we obtained the full instructions for arming and disarming the bomb. This bomb was designed to be activated in the field by any person who could read and follow the instructions traveling with the weapon." He waived Awlaki into the center of the circle.

"We have the detailed instructions and our people have been working with them to become familiar with the arming procedures," Awlaki said as he looked around the assembled mass of terrorists. "A few days ago we armed this weapon for six-hours, and then watched as the digital clock ticked down to the one-hour mark. We then disarmed it successfully. We have practiced this process numerous times since then. These procedures will allow our agents to plant the bombs in the cities we wish, arm the devices, and make their escape. As Ayman has said, we will time the devices to go off on the same day, at the same time all over America."

Again the crowd of terrorists started talking among themselves as they began to understand what they were looking at. Zawahiri called to a young man to step forward. He knew what the leader was asking and walked up to the nuclear weapon. He reached inside flipping a switch that turned on the battery power. The machine's lights blinked red, and the digital clock flashed to life registering zeros in the screen. The technician looked over to Zawahiri for a signal and got it, as he nodded to proceed.

The technician looked over at Dimitri/Josef, the Russian, sitting on the outer edge of the group. Dimitri smiled and gave him a nod. The young Arab reached down and started entering sequential numbers as he had done a dozen times before in training with the Russian arms dealer. He was proud of the fact that he would be traveling to the United States, to a northern city of Minneapolis, to work on the other weapons that would be delivered there. He would train the people who would then travel with and plant the bombs in the designated U.S. cities.

He continued the arming process and the machine came to life. He set the timer for ten hours and then the digital clock began counting backwards, 9:59, 9:58, 9:57. He lifted the case and showed the assembled terrorists the bomb was indeed functioning, as it should. Dimitri made note of the time. He covertly looked at his watch to verify when the unit should detonate. It was time to get out of camp.

Inside the weapons small computer, the secret code change that had been programmed by the THCT team was initiated when he entered the ten-hour countdown test. It was a very simple code change buried in the HTML language, one that simply gave an internal command to negate any shut down effort when the disarming procedure was entered. The machine would go blank, the lights would turn off, and the clock would shut down, just as it had a number of times earlier. But once the change was recorded, the internal clock would continue its silent countdown to detonation.

Ayman al-Zawahiri also watched this procedure handled by the technician. He looked out into the audience encircling him and the bomb, and marveled at how they were mesmerized by the sight of this suitcase. He needed to bring them back to the reality of what this bomb would mean.

"We expect that the Americans will be critically crippled, but we also know they will strike back with their full arsenal of weaponry. They will come back at us in anger looking for revenge, for the devastation of their cities and their economy. We must be ready to protect ourselves. We must go into hiding so that we can continue the fight after they have vented their anger and frustration. They will have their hands full dealing with the devastation in America, and that is when we will strike again, and again, in your countries and cities."

The terrorists understood what their leader was calling for. They rose to their feet as a group, and started chanting 'jihad', 'jihad' over and over again. The chanting and dancing continued as if a celebration victory was occurring. Their ultimate victory was within reach.

Zawahiri let the celebration continue for another five minutes savoring the thoughts of victory. Then he looked over at Awlaki, and then the bomb. His second in command understood the silent command and motioned the technician to shut the bomb down as it had reached the 9:28 mark.

The technician carefully initiated the shutdown sequencing, entering the control numbers, as he had done a dozen times before. The machine acknowledged the disarming procedure and its lights blinked out. The digital clock went blank just as it had done in the past. Awlaki watched him do this, and once satisfied the bomb was again inert, he had the technician close the case and latch the locks. He gingerly lifted the weapon off the table and placed it on the ground.

The assembly was over. And the crowd dispersed. It was announced that various groups would be meeting throughout the afternoon and evening with the new leader to discuss assignments to be undertaken when the Americans had been brought to their knees. The technician was instructed to take the bomb to Zawahiri's mud hut. With the nuclear weapon sitting in the corner, it would send a strong message to each of these warriors as they met with the leader.

As the shutdown suitcase was placed in the corner of the hut, the internal clock continued its countdown, 9:23, 9:22, 9:21. Another nine hours.

→ ←

Tribal Council, Socotra Island

There was a festive mood in the camp. The growing group of leaders and their bodyguards needed to be fed. A detail of bodyguards was assigned to hunt for goats for the evening meal. Josef and Ralph recognized they might have a chance to get away and asked if they could join in the hunt. The two men and their now very relaxed guards headed north of camp searching the hills for the wild goats that browsed the mountain hillsides.

They made an effort to lead the guards as far from the encampment as they could searching for the goats each carrying rope tethers to bring back their prey. Hiking north, separated from the other guards, Ralph noticed a narrow, tight rock crevice with walls rising at least ten feet above the floor of the canyon. He motioned Josef through the pass and whispered they would jump their guards when they passed through the crevice. Calling to the guards, they each picked up a large rock to use as a weapon.

"I have a goat cornered here!" Ralph shouted. The two guards came running with their weapons slung over their backs. As they passed through the narrow crevice both Ralph and Josef hit them with the rocks knocking them out. They quickly pounced on them and using the goat tethers hog-tied them and dragged them behind some rocks to sleep off their concussions.

Ralph and Josef stood up and looked at each other with a 'now what' look on their faces.

"We only have about 8 hours to get far, far away from here," Josef said again checking his watch.

"Then why are we standing here talking?" Ralph asked rhetorically. They grabbed the two AK-47s and started heading further north, vectoring east as the terrain permitted. The late afternoon sun was still high enough in the west to give them some directional assistance. They chose a path down the middle of a deep wadi ravine that looked as if it ran all the way to the ocean.

Around the next bend in the dry riverbed they saw the Ra's Mimo point far in the distance. Ten minutes later they were close and found a rocky outcropping that would give them a defensive position if the terrorists came searching for them. The position also gave them a clear view of the Gulf of Aden to the east and north. They burrowed into the outcropping trying to become invisible and began their wait.

Back in the terrorist camp seven goats were dragged into camp and tethered to a fence in the center of the village. Each goat was brought out to the central courtyard to be slaughtered for the festivities. A different tribe member would step forward brandishing their jambiya knifes and dispatch the animal with a single cut to the throat. Once all seven animals had been killed, others stepped forward to gut and skin them using the same weapon.

A huge cooking pit was prepared with seven spits set up around it. Firewood was brought from various huts to create a large cooking fire. No one seemed to notice that the two infidels were not present, nor were their guards. The festivities continued.

Zawahiri and al-Awlaki continued to meet with the various leaders to suggest ways that they could attack and take the war to the infidels in their own countries. They talked about striking hard after the bombings, attacking embassies, consulates and government offices. They all agreed that if they acted fast, they could take control in many countries because the Americans would not be coming to the rescue. They would have enough problems of their own.

In the corner of the room, the small suitcase nuclear weapon sat silently, as if a discarded piece of luggage leaning against the wall. Its internal timer silently continued its countdown, 6:32, 6:31, and 6:30. It was Six and a-half hours, and counting.

→ ←

Ra's Mimo Point

Uri's boat made a dash for the cliffs. He used his boating skills to take the small craft over the submerged reefs and breakers with practiced ease. With only Michael and Kevin along, armed to the teeth, the boat cut through the water effortlessly.

Approaching the outer point they motored to the right side of the cliffs and throttled down so they could search the cliffs for any sign of Josef and Ralph. The snow-white sand dunes ahead were massive rolling back and forth, some standing forty feet above the water's edge.

The small craft had gone about one hundred yards when Kevin noticed a movement near the base of one of the massive dunes nestled in the rock outcroppings. Two men came out of a low rock formation wildly waving their arms. Each had an AK-47 wrapped around their shoulders. Both Kevin and Michael went on alert ready to lay down a barrage of fire. As they got closer, they recognized their teammates and Uri hit the throttle and went for the shore.

Josef and Ralph didn't want to wait and started wading into the surf holding their weapons above their heads and looking over their shoulders at the dunes behind them. Michael and Kevin took the cue and started scanning the dunes and rocks looking for targets if any materialized.

Once the two got to hip deep water they pulled their weapons off and dropped them in the water and started swimming towards the boat. Uri maneuvered the boat in close to them and cut the engine so the screws couldn't cut up his teammates. Michael reached down and grabbed Josef and hauled him into the boat with ease, dropping him in a heap in the boat well. Kevin did the same with Ralph although he was a bit heavier.

"Welcome aboard boys," Kevin said. "Now let's get the hell out of here. I'm assuming our little surprise is still ticking down?

Josef glanced at his watch and said, "By my counts we have about six hours before we turn into vapor. Thanks for coming!"

"No man left behind, that is not an option," Kevin stated as he started scanning the cliffs again.

Uri gunned the engine and turned towards open water. He didn't even try and keep the engine roar down.

"Glad you're both back with us. Looks like you've worn out your welcome. Were the natives chasing you?" Michael said still scanning the shoreline.

"No, that wasn't the problem," Josef said looking at his watch which was now soaked but still ticking.

Uri steered out to sea plowing through the lines of breakers coming in. "Call the Captain and tell him we're heading due north and he should meet us north of the island. Tell him the new time parameters and that we have about six hours to clear the area. He can vector in to us and cut some time off as well."

"Done," Michael said, "So you're sure that Zawahiri asshole has armed our little bomb?"

"I'm sure. I sat there watching them arm it for ten hours about four hours ago. They'll unarm it as they have done before but that won't stop the silent countdown this time."

"Great, so how did you two interlopers get away?"

"You won't believe it, but they were celebrating and all the guards went off into the mountains to get a bunch of goats for cooking on a spit. So we volunteered to help and our guards took us up on the offer," Ralph said, excited to be safe and still alive to tell the story.

"We talked our guys into heading north about a mile from camp. They let us wander ahead down a ravine," Josef added. "We grabbed some rocks and when they came through this pass we conked them on the head. Then we tied them up with the goat tethers and took their guns to race to the pickup point. I'm actually beginning to like this spy stuff. I'm just glad you were here!"

Just then the Captain came on the radio and said he could see them on the radar screen and they would converge in about twenty minutes. He told them to remain on the same course heading and they would clear the area as fast as the Majorca could move.

→ ←

Eastern Socotra Island

The festivities went on all through dinner and into the early evening. Everyone had their fill of the goat dinner and they were lounging around talking about how the West would fall.

The al Qaeda leaders present were encouraged to attack western corporations that were exploiting the Muslim lands and natural resources. Each tribal leader came away with a specific target they would pursue once the great Satan was taken out of the game and brought to its knees.

In the last few seconds of the silent countdown, 0:04, 0:03, 0:02, 0:01, and finally 0:00, the suitcase nuclear weapon detonated, just as it had been programmed to do. A small plug of highly enriched uranium was fired into a like mass of uranium achieving criticality in a millisecond. This caused an uncontrollable chain of fission reactions, during which subatomic particles called neutrons, collided with the uranium nuclei, releasing more expanding neutrons, which collided with other nuclei. This chain reaction caused the bomb to self-destruct in a white heat reaction hotter than the surface of the sun.

When these uranium slugs collided, being one of the heaviest elements on earth, they expanded outward in a 25,000-degree heat explosion with a show of energy that defied description. In that same instant everything on the surface off the eastern end of Socotra Island vaporized, in a blinding white light of a firestorm. The explosion shot up into the sky and the expanding thermal pulse vaporized every living thing within 5 miles. Outside the 5 mile perimeter, everything else was engulfed in a raging firestorm cremating all life, melting sand, leveling and burning trees and underbrush and turning the jagged countryside into a thousand year no-man's land. One moment the temporary home of the al Qaeda leadership existed, and the next it did not.

The eastern promontory of the island jutting a quarter mile into the Arabian Sea simply vanished. While the forces of nature had created the land mass thousands of years ago, in an instant it ceased to exist. The sand and rock burned and fused together as if concrete and then vaporized in the next second. A gaping hole a quarter mile around and two hundred feet deep formed on the eastern end of the nearly uninhabited island. The tons of rock and sand that didn't vaporize, went flying in all directions, crashing into the boiling sea sending torrents of water rushing off in all directions. And then in the seconds following, the waters of the Arabian Sea came rushing back into the vacuum.

The bomb spewed its super-heated gases and radioactive dust in all directions racing into the atmosphere towards the heavens. A super-heated thermal pulse rushed outward in an ever-expanding circle from the source of the detonation in the same manner a pebble ripples the water it is thrown into. But this force was no pebble. It moved so rapidly that it became a destructive force of its own slamming into hills and mountains, tearing them apart as if they were made of papier-mâché.

Seventy miles east of ground zero, the people of Hidobah, the only major village on Socotra looked up at the intense light in the eastern evening and thought that the Sun must have crashed into the earth. The white light burned their eyes and they turned away and ran for cover. It took a half-minute for the roaring sounds of the destruction to roll in over the mountains delivering a devastating blow to the coastal area leveling mud huts, uprooting the few trees on the island and creating a sand storm that obliterated the sunlight. People ran into their crumbling mud huts to escape the super-heated blowing wind that followed fearing the world was ending.

And then it was over except for the intensely bright light in the East shining in the night sky.

→ ←

The Majorca, Gulf of Aden

The ship picked up the boat and it's occupants in a five-minute operation, with the forward crane lifting the entire boat and crew onto the deck. The ship got under way before they even stepped out of the boat. The Captain tried to squeeze as much power out of the engines as he could. They made good time east northeast plowing through the sea at 21 knots. Captain Brinkmann was glad the engines had been overhauled and fine-tuned.

"How about we get some fresh air and get out of this puke green dungeon?" Michael said and everyone agreed.

"We've come this far as a team, I say we gather on the stern and watch and see if our terrorist friends have decided to have their little show and tell pow-wow yet," Ralph said, and headed for the stern. He grabbed some deck chairs on the way.

Kevin headed the other way for the galley. "I'll get some refreshments, meaning beer. It was very dry in that God forsaken place, I've been craving a beer for days now."

Courtney said, "With all the drugs the Captain has in me for the gunshot wound, I think I'll stick to water, which right now sounds pretty good."

"Done, anyone else have any orders?"

"We would like the oranges pop" Malik said, for both him and Osama. "We are thirsty also."

They all eventually settled in on the stern deck, " So now we wait to see if our reprogramming efforts pay off. Josef, how many times did they do the sequencing while we were there?"

Josef thought for a moment and then said, "I believe we took them through the arming and disarming procedures half a dozen times that I know of, and I think I was with them all of the time. I was actually getting a bit concerned they would use up all the programmed sequences, and initiate the reset mechanism before we actually could get off the island."

"Yeah, but rushing off would have been a little suspect, don't you think? Ahh, sorry folks, we're out of time, we have to run. Bye, bye, and we jump in the boat."

"I think that would have been of concern to them. But we were polite and cool and let them tell us when they wanted us to leave. There were so many other terrorists leaders arriving I think they wanted us gone because everyone kept asking questions about who we were," Meredith said this as he stared southwest towards where he thought the Island was located.

"We were getting nervous that someone from Pakistan, might arrive and see us in a different light," Osama said. "When we were still in the Territories we would see al Qaeda and the Taliban all the time."

"So do we really think we pulled this thing off? I know we didn't get the big prize, but this would be a great second prize if we get lucky. I'm still marveling that we got them to take the horse inside the walls?" Courtney asked.

"Well, they did! Our little Trojan horse is hidden in one of those mud huts in the middle of that encampment. I'd say that's inside the walls," Ralph said leaning back in his chair propping his feet up on the metal railing.

"What if the weapon doesn't go off?" Kate said, looking very concerned. She had all sorts of questions not having been in on the delivery. "What happens then? What if they take it somewhere else that is more populated? Then what do we do? If they don't set the damn thing off, could they still take it to New York and really cause a catastrophe."

"I've thought about that too." Ralph said, "I guess we would have to tell the government where all of al Qaeda has disappeared to and they would bomb the crap out of the place. Short of killing them ourselves, that would still be acceptable to me as long as we get them."

"Yeah, but we've come this far. I still want to see them dead! I want to see a mushroom cloud." Michael said pointing to the southeast.

"Me too brother, look at the bright side, if they do shoot that thing off we may kill off all of al Qaeda in one big boom! I couldn't believe how many of those al Qaeda rag heads were showing up. And they were all giving us dirty looks!" Kevin said, grabbing another beer and popping the top on the railing.

"Yes. Let's hope they do trigger the thing." Josef said. "I encouraged them to practice the arming procedures over and over. And I believe I saw them do the arming that set off the special countdown program. I was still sitting there, so I marked the time." He again looked at his watch for the tenth time in the last hour.

"Since we offered them the additional weapons," Meredith laughed thinking about the additional warheads ruse, "and then offered to deliver them to the U.S. for an additional fee, they took the bait, hook, line and sinker."

"They wanted to practice, practice, practice. And we pressed their technicians to follow the procedures. They promised to even practice for Allah. So we will see. It should happen soon." Josef looked at his watch again.

The group sat on the stern deck discussing what they had accomplished in the past two years. They all thought that sleep would now come easier. It was therapeutic talking about the effort and they relaxed for the first time in months. They were proud of the fact that a bunch of amateurs had come up with a clever plan that had drawn al Qaeda and Osama bin laden out of their lairs. Their simple, perhaps naïve plan had gotten them closer to the terrorist organization than the US government had been in the last ten years.

The group settled back and relaxed for the first time in months enjoying the clean fresh ocean air blowing gently over the stern in the dark night sky.

At that moment there was an intense white flash of light in the east over the horizon, brighter than anything any of them had ever seen. Ralph fell out of his chair reacting to the flash. It was like lightning magnified a thousand times, so bright they had to squeeze their eyes shut. And then, they could still see the flash image burning within their eyeballs. The light increased in its intensity and continued to streak into the sky and all around. Night turned in to day. From their vantage point on the ship it looked like the light source was rising out of the ocean.

The intensity was so bright they turned away to protect their eyes, even though they were squeezed tightly shut. It was like when you were a kid and you took a glance at the sun and in just that second, your retina was seared with a white image that was all you could see, even with your eyes closed.

Ralph pulled himself off the deck and the rest stood almost in unison. Michael, Kevin and Courtney pulled out dark sunglasses they had in their pockets and continued to sneak glances at the blazing source of the light, but even with that protection they couldn't look for more than a fraction of a second.

They turned around as Captain Brinkmann came running up with another half dozen sets of dark sunglasses. He handed them out but told everyone they were meant to cut ocean glare, not to watch a nuclear bomb go off. When he said nuclear bomb, everyone looked at one another. They grabbed the sunglasses and looked over their shoulders taking quick glances and then turning their eyes away again in pain.

"I'll be damned," was all that Meredith could think to say, "What have we done? I thought I knew the power we had in that suitcase, but my God I had no idea we would see such a thing."

"I'm stunned," Ralph said. "But that is what we've been working for two years." He rubbed his eyes trying to remove the searing white image that was etched on his eyeball. "I don't know about you guys, but I can live with what we've just done. Remember those terrorists were a part of the group that killed all of our loved ones and took our lives away." Now he was angry. "I hope they all vaporized. I only wish that bin Laden had been there too! I know I'll sleep without regret."

Courtney hadn't said much for the past half hour. She took another quick glance over her shoulder at the rising mushroom cloud and agreed. "I can't believe we actually pulled this off. I remember saying we were all going to jail when we first started talking about this crazy plan. And perhaps we still are, but, I think I can live with what we've done, too."

"Me too!" Josef chimed in. "I only wish I could have been there to see them liquidate and then vaporize, but then, I wouldn't be here to savor the moment, would I?" Josef said. He said this in defiance of the guilt he was feeling with the deathly act he had just precipitated.

"I'm speechless," Kate said, "I had no idea what we were dealing with. Holy shit! We just killed a hell of a lot of people."

"A lot of bad people Kate, they were all terrorists. Hell bent on killing any of us, and all Americans, if we had let them. We just saved America. Those crazed nutcases would have blown up six cities killing millions if they had really gotten a hold of what we said we had," Meredith said, putting his arm around her.

Michael chimed in as well. "They would have bombed us to hell and back. All we did was use their crazed zealotry to get them to do it to themselves in their own backyard. And I for one don't have any remorse at all."

Meredith thought about his son getting blown up by the plane crashing into his World Trade Center office. One second he was there and the next he wasn't. Meredith's eyes burned with sorrow and satisfaction as he raised his beer bottle to the East. Then he snapped back, and looked at his fellow team members.

"What that rising cloud means is that we have obtained our revenge. That end of the island is toast. We delivered our Trojan horse and they took it inside their walls, and we have now won our personal war on terrorism," Michael said, "We just did what our own government hasn't been able to do for close to ten years. And we did it in the remotest place on earth only killing the bad guys." Michael tapped his beer bottle on Kevin's brew. They both drained their beers.

At that moment there was a tremendous shockwave that rolled across the ship without warning. The windblast literally picked up the ship in its velocity. The howling hot air seared their faces and the deafening roar blocked out all other sound. It was difficult to describe, almost like a speeding locomotive racing past as you stood a foot from the tracks. The forceful concussion slammed them backwards into the bulkhead, almost knocking them off their feet.

"Damn," this time it was the Captain mouthing the words. "We're over 70 miles away from that blast, and it still hit us like a freight train." He looked around thinking of something else. "You know we may be in for a tsunami radiating out from ground zero in a few minutes. I better turn this ship around fast." He turned and ran off towards the bridge to bring the ship about.

→ ←

Diego Garcia, U.S. Naval Weather Command

Second Lieutenant Tracy Hodges sat at her computer taking readings on ocean currents in the Indian Ocean when a bell started clanging on the Seismograph machine mounted on the wall behind her desk. She turned around and saw the needle fluctuating wildly on the roll of paper passing through the machine. The inked needle was dancing all over the sheet for almost a half minute.

She knew that meant an earthquake had hit somewhere in the Indian Ocean. She reached for her phone and alerted her shift Commander Marlena Grovis and all personnel currently on duty. In a matter of minutes, ten other Navy personnel came into the room, and were evaluating the data coming in.

Lieutenant Hodges returned to her job monitoring ocean currents and focused her attention on the North Indian Ocean where there had been considerable seismic activity in the past two years. Two devastating earthquakes in Iran and in Pakistan had caused considerable damage and loss of life. Her computer screen, linked to weather satellites circling the earth, registered ocean current activity that came off of small weather buoys that had been salted over the entire Indian Ocean. These buoys monitored currents, ocean temperatures, and wind velocities in real time. She zeroed in her screen to find the core or epicenter of the earthquake.

Commander Gravis sent alerts out immediately to all ships at sea and to all the countries ringing the Indian Ocean. Oftentimes earthquakes would cause shifts in the earths crust on land or underwater, and these massive shifts would send millions of pounds of pressurized rock moving in opposite directions. Theses sudden pressure changes could whip normally peaceful waters into a dangerous tidal wave that could race across an ocean and catch people and shipping unaware of what was heading towards them.

The Naval Station sent out Red Alert messages to all of the U.S. Navy's fleet to give them notice to brace for a possible tsunami. Priority messages were also sent to the Central Command in Tampa and the Pentagon. This information was passed along to the White House and the other agencies that needed to be aware of this just detected potentially destructive force of nature.

→ ←

The Majorca, Gulf of Aden

The Captain brought the ship about to face any impending waves and remained at half power to keep his bow pointed into the wind and current. He was in shallow enough water cruising along the Yemeni coast that if there was a tsunami, it could be very dangerous for the ship. In deep water a tsunami would pass under a ship at sea with hardly a notice, but in shallow water, the movement of the water rushing up from the deep could create very dangerous waves and currents that could easily swallow up a ship.

On his maps he measured the distance from the eastern tip of Socotra Island to the ship's present position and calculated the speed of such waves from the point of origin. He factored in a few extra minutes as a margin of error and then determined any tsunami could be arriving momentarily. He battened down everything that was loose on the ship and pulled in the entire crew. He was the most exposed person on the ship's bridge and handled the helm himself.

Looking east he could still see the extraordinary mushroom cloud rising in the evening's southwest sky. The cloud was drifting out into the Arabian Sea. Just then he felt a change in forward motion and felt the ship tremble as if being battered by something. The bow rose up ten feet in the air and then settled back down crashing into the passing wave sending a torrent of water over the bow and across the deck. A heavy torrent of spray slammed into the bridge housing and windows completely obliterating the forward view. The wave passed the length of the ship. He looked back and saw the stern rise and fall in the same manner. Then the sea became calm. A minute later a second wave half as high as the first flogged the ship from stem to stern. Anything not tied down was swept off the ship.

Remembering tidal waves were not as dangerous on the open sea, he turned his attention to the Yemeni shore less than two miles north of the ships position. He reached for one of the powerful sets of binoculars that Meredith had brought aboard and stared at the shoreline in the moonlight. With the bridge forty-five feet above sea level he could make out the mountains.

"That was definitely a tsunami that passed over us," Meredith said, as he came running up to the wheelhouse. "I thought they were supposed to be pretty devastating?"

"By my reckoning, we we're deep enough out here that it just rolled through us. The real danger from these things is when that wall of water meets shallow water and a landmass. Grab a set of glasses and look towards shore."

Meredith reached for the other set of high-powered binoculars and joined the Captain on the bridge parapet scanning Yemen's shoreline to the north. In the bright moonlight they couldn't see much except rough mountainous terrain. As they watched, the usual breakers rolling up on the beach suddenly pulled back from the shoreline at least five hundred yards. It was like some huge vacuum had sucked all the water off the beach.

The two men watched mesmerized by the power of the tsunami they had created with their suitcase bomb. The small beach area they were looking at turned into vast sandy beach with occasional rock outcroppings completely exposed. It looked like a soggy desert or what the moonscape must look like.

"My God, I've read about these things and I saw the film clips of that tsunami hitting Thailand, but I had no idea. How long does this last?"

"I don't think it will last long at all. If what passed us was the tidal wave, the water should be rushing into shore momentarily," The Captain said, staring through his glasses.

As they continued to watch in the minimal light they saw the water rise very quickly forming huge waves that raced to the shore. When these fast moving underwater currents ran into shallow waters, they first sucked all the existing water away from the landmass, and then came crashing back in to fill the void, rising up and increasing in size exponentially.

The two men watched a twenty-foot high wave rise up from the ocean, and batter the shoreline, crashing down upon the empty beach and the base of the mountain cliffs. The waters crashed into the walls of rock, with waves foaming and boiling, with nowhere to go except up. Had the mountain ridges not been right at the water's edge the waves would have raced far inland causing all sorts of additional carnage racing through the wadi's and lowlands. Denied access inland, the giant waves crashed back on the barren beaches washing them away and eroding whatever shoreline had existed.

A number of other team members arrived on the bridge and took turns looking to shore to see what the tidal waves had done. Many of them saw the second and third waves crash to shore tearing up more of the coastal plain.

"I had heard about tsunamis for years but had never seen one firsthand, I have no desire to see anymore," Kate said, as she gawked at the coastline

"Captain, might those same waves do damage to our oil refinery port? We may not be able to even dock?" Uri asked, knowing full well the destructive power of these rogue waves. "Those waves will rip up the refinery and the landing strip."

"Your right Uri, I think we'll need to consider alternatives to get you to that airport runway. Perhaps we can anchor a mile offshore closer to the airstrip," he thought for a moment, "We'll put your fishing boat in the water again. We can motor right up near the runway, eliminating the need to hike across the town at night without being seen. Are you up to captaining that little craft one more time, Sir?"

"Yes, Sir. She's a good little craft. I almost hate to lose her," Uri said looking at the boat from the bridge window.

"I'll buy you another boat Uri, with all the bells and whistles," Meredith said patting him on the back.

"The bells and whistles aren't important William, just that she be seaworthy. I'll take you up on your offer. The sea is all I have anymore."

The Captain was standing next to Meredith as this exchange went on and said, "Uri, I was hoping I could entice you back to sea with me. This old rust bucket won't be the same without you."

"I would like that Captain. I have nothing back in New York to keep me there. We've completed our mission and I have missed the life of a sailor. Maybe Mr. Meredith will still give us a sailing vessel we can use as a runabout?" He looked hopefully towards Meredith.

"You got it, I promise."

"Alright people, let's get cracking if we still want to get out of here in one piece. That radioactive drift could change course you know. Courtney, you and Kate, get on the satellite phone and hail Ryan. Tell him to crank up the plane, give him the coordinates and let's say we're going to shoot for 2:00 am for the pickup. Also remind him to fly as light as possible as we all have to get in there and still get off the ground. I think that runway can handle the plane but why tempt fate."

→ ←

CIA Headquarters, Langley, VA

Karen Lee was putting on her coat and reaching for her purse as her private line rang insistently. It was late but she knew better than to ignore the call until morning. She threw her things on a side chair and reached for the phone. The connection took a second as she heard the scrambled line activate.

"Karen, you saw the alert on the earthquake didn't you?" Admiral Bishope said.

"Admiral, good evening to you too. Kind of late for a geological call isn't it? Yes, I heard there was an earthquake, somewhere in the Middle East. Was it bad?"

"Yes it was. It measured off the seismic charts, right along the African and Arabian Plates, but it wasn't an earthquake, it was a nuclear detonation, of a limited yield small nuclear device! Similar to what might be expected from a suitcase weapon!" he said emphasizing the word suitcase.

"I'll be damned. Where, specifically?"

"Don't have an accurate ground zero yet. We're trying to figure that out now. But it's somewhere in the north Arabian Sea near Yemen. Seismic equipment at Diego Garcia called it in first, and then everyone else started reporting quake. It lit up the monitoring equipment over half the world."

"What about casualties, do you have any estimates yet?"

"Too early to tell. This thing may have gone off in a very remote area. Our people are trying to pinpoint the explosion, excuse me the quake, now. I already have planes en-route to do flyovers, with all the radioactive gear we need to get a solid estimate of what we are dealing with. We should have better information in an hour."

"Well, if everyone is thinking earthquake, let's go with that story for now. No need to escalate before we have to. Let's make sure everyone is talking in terms of it being an earthquake and not using that other word," Karen said as she considered what needed to be done next. "Ok, I'll see what our people in the area can gather on the ground. I'll send an alert right away. Have you advised the President?"

"I just put the call in. He's coming back from a campaign swing out west on Air Force One. That may be the best place for him at the moment. Once I told him it was a small nuclear device he asked if it was our THCT'ers at work. Looks like your scenario may be coming true. If so, I hope they got the entire organization."

"Damn, if they did blow up al Qaeda we won't find any pieces at all. Keep me in the loop Admiral,..... Damn!"

She hung up the phone, turned her desk light on and reached for another secure line down to the Middle East Section, hoping there were still people in the building. It was going to be an all-nighter. She called downstairs and got a hold of Bede Long. She explained the situation and told him to put the word out to agents in the field. She made sure they were to use the cover of the earthquake until told otherwise, if ever.

→ ←

Balhof Oil Terminal, Yemen

It was just after 1:00 am in the morning as the Majorca approached the Balhof oil refinery complex nestled against the mountains of Yemen. They stood off shore about a mile. A small sliver of moon was overhead, and the ship was almost invisible since they had doused their running lights. They could see that the lights on the lower refinery equipment towers had been shattered by the tidal wave. The only lights still shining were up high on the miles of pipes and rigging. That suggested that whatever crews were on-site already probably had their hands full repairing and monitoring the battered equipment.

The ship's crew silently lowered the fishing boat over the side. The THCT team prepared to disembark and said their goodbyes to Captain and crew who had helped them achieve the impossible.

Courtney decided to stay behind on the ship because of her injuries. She insisted she didn't want to slow the team down, but everyone knew she wanted to stay on board with Captain Brinkmann. The affection there had grown over the past four-week odyssey and both wanted to see where it would go. Kate gave her a kiss and a hug, squeezing gently to avoid the shoulder. She turned and climbed over the side.

The team loaded themselves into the boat and cast off waving silent goodbyes. Uri steered the craft towards shore and the flat runway that could be seen in the shadowy refinery lights. When they could hear the breakers rolling on shore, Uri cut the engine and the team took out paddles for the last one hundred yards. The ship eventually came to a halt on slick polished rocks, pushed there by the steady roll of the waves. On shore they could see massive amounts of stone and rock tossed about like piles of rubble. The tidal wave had hit the beach with a vengeance.

They worked their way inland with Michael and Kevin running point, and eventually found the end of the runway. Keeping low they worked their way down the runway finding it in relatively good shape but with pockets of slick mud washed on shore by the waves. Meredith wondered what that would do to the plane landing.

The runway was long and when they got to the other end, they hunkered down next to a small shed that offered some cover. It was 1:50 am, ten minutes before the pick-up time.

Over the Gulf of Aden

Heading due east along the Yemeni coast flying at less than 1,000 feet, Ryan Younger was flying in a rarely used commercial air corridor. The Citation had all sorts of bells and whistles that told him things he would rather not have even been aware of. It was a state of the art civilian aircraft and he was alone. His co-pilot was back in the hotel room sleeping soundly. Ryan rationalized that this way he would not be able to admit or deny anything and that could save his ass. He also figured he would need the extra space for his 'cargo'.

Having departed Djibouti filing a flight plan for Musqat, Oman, on the Arabian Peninsula, east of Yemen, he had a direct path that would take him where he needed to go to meet the team. Once airborne, the air controllers paid little attention to him when he dropped below radar. In the darkness of the night, his instruments told him he was close to where he wanted to be and he dropped even lower. He could vaguely see the Yemeni mountains rising up before him in the almost moonlit night. At two hundred feet he felt he could reach out and touch the water below him.

All of a sudden, straight ahead of him, a ship's running lights were turned on and off three times. Then they went dark again as he focused on the refinery lights ahead. He grabbed his night vision glasses and scanned ahead for the runway he knew had to be there. The aura of lights from the oil refinery threw a shadow on the black asphalt and he saw his target. He adjusted accordingly for a straight in approach.

He lined up perfectly and cut back on the throttle settling into a gradual descent, touching down in the darkness less than one hundred feet from the waters edge of the runway. He had tried to accurately measure the runway distance using his Google maps and was confident he could use the full length of the runway to slow the plane down sufficiently without having to use his reverse thrusters, which would make a ton of noise and awaken everyone in the refinery town. That would bring the cavalry. He set his flaps in a full drag position and started working the brakes to slow the craft quietly.

The THCT team watched his approach. Ralph and Josef ran out to the edge of the runway with two strong flashlights. They kneeled on either side of the runway and turned on the lights, pointing out to sea. No one on shore would see them, but Ryan could use them as end markers. They watched as he raced down the runway occasionally hitting mud patches and silently swerving back and forth. The rest of the group got to their feet and prepared to sprint to wherever the plane came to a halt.

Ryan had kept his night vision glasses on and was trying to get a good fix on what lay ahead. He kept feathering the brakes to slow the craft, trying not to overheat them. The jet's speed had dropped to less than 90 miles per hour and by his estimates he still had more than half the runway to work with. With the glasses still on, his attention was drawn to the two flashlights that were blinking on and off. He removed the glasses and used the lights to guide the craft in.

Meredith watched closely as the jet came towards him noting it looked different, perhaps he had been away longer than he thought. Then a thought seized his mind, maybe this wasn't Ryan, but was emergency refinery workers coming into assess the tsunami damage. But why would there be no running lights on a scheduled flight? It had to be Ryan. They needed to be ready to depart quickly.

Just then he heard klaxons going off in the distance coming from the small town and refinery. Then he heard a siren, the kind mounted on a vehicle, perhaps a police vehicle, and it sounded as if it was coming towards them. Would there be time, he thought. Realizing it was now or never, he gave orders to get rid of anything unnecessary, including the guns. Michael didn't question the order and quickly dug a hole with a piece of metal he found and buried the few weapons they had brought with them.

Ryan saw a number of people come running out of the shadows, keeping their heads down, trotting towards the runway. He hoped they were the good guys. Ryan continued pumping the brakes in short spurts and the craft continued to slow down. Seeing he would be successful, he now started thinking about the take-off, which would immediately follow. He wouldn't have the benefit of the lift from the wind so he would need every inch of runway to get back in the air. Then there was the added weight, so he decided he would go to the very end of the asphalt runway and then spin the craft around.

Ryan eased up on the throttle, keeping it in a low rev idle and brought the plane to almost a complete stop at the end of the runway. Then he gave it a quick goosing burst of gas, stomped on the pedals and the plane spun around as if it were a merry-go-round. He quickly set the brakes, unbuckled his harness, and jumped out of his seat heading for the access door. He pulled the lock that extended the hatch stairs and door combination.

He stuck his head out, and looked around seeing a number of dark shadows heading his way. He quietly announced, "This is your last boarding call for the al Qaeda Express! All aboard!"

Out of the dark shadows, the small group of counter-terrorists came running as if they were intent on catching the last flight out of Saigon. They didn't need any invitation and readily climbed the five steps, each shaking the pilots hand. The last person leaving Yemeni soil was William Meredith. He bounded up the stairs, and smiled at the young pilot.

"Captain, I like the new plane!"

"The FBI still has your Bombardier locked up tighter than a drum. So I decided to go on holiday to Oslo and got your other plane. Hope you don't mind, Sir, you authorized it."

"I miss the Bombardier, but lets see how this one flies, and as soon as possible. I think we have company heading our way!"

"Yes Sir," he turned to the passengers and said, "Grab a seat folks, buckle up and keep your trays in the upright position. We are out of here." Meredith closed the door and locked the hatch.

"Sir, I need a co-pilot, so would you mind riding up front, it's a bit crowded back here."

"No co-pilot? Flying like the old days in the Warthog, huh. Glad to. Just show me what to do."

"Pray Sir, pray that we can get this heavy baby off the ground."

Ryan jumped into the left drivers seat, buckled in, made sure his rookie co-pilot was secure, and glanced back to see that everyone in the rear was sitting and buckled in. He smiled when he saw Osama and Malik gripping their seats with fear in their hearts.

Sitting on the very end of the runway pointing towards the Gulf of Aden, he quickly spooled up the twin engines up to high revs, while standing on the brakes. He let them scream for a couple of seconds until they sounded right and uniform, and then lifted his foot off the brakes. The Citation started rolling with the strong thrust of the twin jet engines and quickly gained speed as they raced down the runway. Even with the new load, the jet was traveling over 100 miles per hour by the time they hit the runway mid-point. It continued to pick up speed and Ryan felt he could lift off with runway to spare.

With only 300 feet of runway left and the ocean's water just ahead, he lifted the plane off the ground, gaining altitude a little more slowly than he had lifting off from Djibouti an hour earlier. The jet climbed steadily in the still night air and when they attained 25,000, he leveled off and reached for the radio. He motioned for Meredith to remain quiet.

He got on the radio calling the air controllers managing this air route. He reported having rough engine problems and advised he would be returning to Djibouti–Ambouli International Airport. They asked if he was declaring an emergency, offering to have him land in Aden, but he said no, stating he would returning to his company's hanger in Djibouti. They acknowledged and said they would continue to monitor the flight.

Next he got out the satellite phone and called his co-pilot back in hotel room, waking him up. He told him he had to make an emergency trip with the plane, and asked him to get out to the airport to have the hanger door open and ready when they arrived. The pilot had all sorts of questions but was told to do as asked, he would explain upon arrival. Ryan said he would be there in an hour.

"So boss, tell me that you accomplished what you set out to do?"

"Well, after the news that bin Laden had been killed, it took the wind out of our sails. We were out there floating in the Red Sea trying to figure out what we should do. Most people don't have a nuclear bomb in their hold! Then, lo and behold, the remainder of al Qaeda called us back and said they still wanted the bomb, even more so, to avenge bin Laden's death."

"That's what I figured happened. I knew you weren't going to give up. So what happened?"

"Their number two guy, Zawahiri, now the new leader of al Qaeda called us in. He was willing to pay anything for that bomb. And we bluffed him and said we had five more, which is why they didn't kill us all. We promised future deliveries and they bought it."

"Son-of-a-bitch, you really all walked in there and got them to buy that story?" Ryan said.

"You bet we did. The Trojan horse thing worked. It was working with bin Laden and when Zawahiri took over he bought it too, hook, line and sinker," Meredith said as he relaxed in the co-pilot seat. " So we negotiated a price for all the additional weapons, and they paid for them as well, and then we got out of Dodge as fast as we could. All of us! You'll have to let everyone tell you their stories."

"As I was flying into Balhof, I could see the bomb mushroom off in the distance. Well, I'll be damned. Congratulations boss. I know you've waited for this day almost ten years."

Thanks, Ryan. I don't think it has really sunk in yet, but it will,…. It will!"

Once they were at cruising altitude Meredith unbuckled his harness and climbed out of his chair. He went thru the curtain to serve his guests but found they had already raided the refrigerator. They were guzzling beers and sodas, and chowing down on sandwiches, having a party of sorts. They quietly toasted one another, but it was not a celebration.

"Ryan tells me, we will be landing in Djibouti in less than an hour. My company retains a hanger there so we should be able to get in unseen. When we land we will have lights out back here, and I ask that you be ready to disembark once we are inside the hanger."

"You got it boss, how about a beer?" Michael asked as he waved a brew in the air."

"Thanks, son, but I would rather have some coffee if it's available. Perhaps some for Ryan as well."

"I'll get it for you," Kate said, "it's already made. O and Malik, do you want another orange pop?"

"Once we are on the ground we will file flight plans to fly home. Can you guys stand being in close quarters for another couple of days or so?"

"As long as we have beer on board, I'm good," Kevin said. "It'll be good to get home, even if we have to go to prison."

Everyone agreed and the somber celebration continued, until Ryan turned out the interior lights for landing in Djibouti.

➔ ←

Cairo, Egypt

Ryan picked up his co-pilot in Djibouti and after refueling they crowded in and flew north to Egypt, and Cairo's International Airport. They all badly needed some sleep and a shower, so they took taxis into the city and registered at the Ramses Hilton in central Cairo, adjacent to Tahrir Square, on the Nile River. The high-rise hotel was almost directly across the enormous square from the famous Egyptian Museum.

Upon arrival they checked in and headed for the gift shop and grabbed all the English language papers they could find, plus a local Egyptian paper. The entire group wanted to find out what had actually happened back in Yemen. Eagerly reading the headlines, they were surprised to see a massive earthquake had been reported somewhere off the Yemeni coast. The papers said it looked like the epicenter was located close to a remote and almost uninhabited island called Socotra.

In a quiet corner the group sat down and read to one another everything they could find on the topic of the 'earthquake'. There had been some tidal wave damage reported in the Arabian Sea but no large tsunamis were reported in other parts of the Indian Ocean. Large waves had hit the coast of Yemen, the Maldives, and the U.S. Naval Base at Diego Garcia where it was reported they had minor shore damage but all ships were accounted for without any loss of life.

A large cloud of volcanic dust and gases had been verified to be drifting eastward out into the middle of the Indian Ocean. Reports suggested that the volcanic cloud would dissipate before reaching India. Officials suggested there was, little cause for concern with the slow moving cloud. But as a precaution all commercial shipping and air traffic in the area was being re-routed around the island and ash clouds.

It was reported that the Socotra Island locals, mostly peasants and goat herders living on the northern coast, had seen the bright lights of the explosion, and witnessed massive ash clouds rising in the east, but they had not experienced any loss of life, just minor injuries, caused by various home and building collapses in the port town of Hidobah. Local authorities estimated the quake to have been at least seventy-five miles away on the far eastern end of the island.

All the papers basically said the same thing. Almost like someone had issued a press release, which the THCT team realized must be exactly what had happened. Some one was telling and selling a story, and everyone was buying it. It was the perfect cover for their ultimate act of vengeance against the most evil terrorist organization known to man.

It was also reported that reconnaissance flights doing flyovers and had not seen any life on the eastern end of the Island. Search and rescue teams were being sent in to help with evacuations although very few people lived on the barren rock island.

The group marveled about the earthquake story but realized that may be the best way for them to be able to return to the United States. The group talked quietly amongst themselves for another hour and then exhaustion set in and they headed for their rooms. Meredith encouraged everyone to get cleaned up, get some rest and food, and to lay low, maintaining their false identities for the time being.

As soon as everyone had loaded into the elevator, Meredith turned around and quietly left the hotel. He flagged a taxi and asked the driver to take him to the U.S Embassy in Cairo. He went up to the courtyard gatehouse and in his best American accent asked the U.S. Marine on duty if he could speak to a consular officer. Asked his name, he answered William Meredith. He was invited to take a seat and wait in the outer courtyard.

He waited for the better part of an hour, noting that two Marines were now stationed at either courtyard entrance, probably keeping an eye on him. The wait was pleasant as he too was exhausted. From the far side of the courtyard a nattily dressed embassy official walked up to him. The two Marine guards stepped towards him as well. The man didn't introduce himself but invited Meredith to follow him. As he did, the two Marines fell into step behind him. He had an escort, or were they guards, he thought.

They went into the Embassy through an unmarked side door, and then up two flights of stairs and down a hallway to a large windowless room in the interior of the building. Meredith was invited to sit down. The officer and the Marines turned and left him alone in the room. There was a large screen monitor on one end of the room and it flickered to life. Two men in suits and a pretty woman appeared on the screen.

"Good day, Mr. Meredith," Karen Lee said. "You have been a very hard man to locate. But we are not surprised to have eventually found you in the Middle East."

Well, they do know my name, he thought.

"Good day,… but to be precise, I think I have actually found you," Meredith said, offering his best Queen's English. "And I wasn't actually aware you were looking for me, …. May I ask to whom I am speaking?" Meredith said, hoping that he had found the right people.

"Certainly, we represent three Agencies of the United States Government, all concerned with Homeland Security. I'm with the CIA. This is the Director of the FBI, and on my right is the Director of the National Security Agency, the NSA. We were the first people that could be assembled over here on such short notice. You are on a scrambled secure video connection with us here in Washington, DC. As I said, we have been looking for you and your THCT group for weeks now."

Meredith wasn't surprised they knew his name and the adopted name of his teammates, it was in fact the reason he had decided it was time to come forward. He figured the jig was up and perhaps he could save the rest of his team from jail time.

"We are pleased that you have chosen to reveal yourself. Have you had a good holiday?"

"Why yes, thank you, but I wouldn't have called it a holiday,…. rather,…. perhaps a personal journey, an ultimately rewarding journey!"

The three bureaucrats reacted to his comment in unison. He could see they were intrigued so he continued.

"I wasn't able to accomplish all of my goals, but with some adjustments, I was still able to bring some inner peace into my life after many years of grief, anger and frustration. But now, I think it's time to come home," Meredith said this knowing what they were really asking him.

"That could be arranged Mr. Meredith, for you and the rest of your grief counseling group, but first we have a single question? One that we think is imperative to ask."

"There is no need to ask," Meredith offered, " Yes, I accomplished what I set out to do. You beat me to Osama bin Laden, whose death I will always be grateful for to the U.S. You finally wiped him off the face of this earth. The devil incarnate has entered his Paradise, wherever that may be. And it is my greatest personal hope that all those 72 virgins are not satisfying him in the least," Meredith said, with complete satisfaction in his voice. "Having handled that chore for me, I had to re-set my goals and I decided to go after the rest of his organization. I'm pleased to report that the entire leadership of al Qaeda has joined their former leader in hell!" He did not smile.

All three persons on screen didn't say a word but looked at one another with a sense of wonder on their faces. The FBI Director, Logan Taylor was the first to speak.

"I have a question. Was it you that obtained the Russian suitcase nuclear weapon? And then did you personally try to deliver it to bin Laden?"

"That's two questions actually, but yes, I obtained the bomb, and I personally negotiated a deal to sell it to him and his organization. When you got to bin Laden first, my plans had to change. Then Ayman al Zawahiri contacted me. He wanted the weapon even more, to avenge bin Laden, so I was back in business." Meredith emphasized the word 'I'. "Then, when I found out al Qaeda was gathering in Yemen, where I was floating on a ship, I struck a new deal with him, promising five additional suitcase bombs, which they believed I had in my possession."

Again, the three Agency heads marveled, and didn't quite know what to say. They thought they had heard it all.

Noting the questioning eyes, Meredith continued. "If I may, I would like to say that this entire plan was all my idea. And I'd like to go on record that my so-called team, as you call them, had no knowledge of this plan, until they joined me for my holiday. By then it was too late for them to not participate. I am the one you are looking for and will gladly accept responsibility for my actions."

"That is a noble gesture, Mr. Meredith, but we think there may be enough blame to be spread around to your entire THCT group. We can talk about that later," Logan Taylor said this still dumbfounded that these amateurs had actually gone after al Qaeda.

"So whom did you 'give' the bomb to? Who was there?"

"Interestingly enough, almost everyone in the al Qaeda organization, I think. Ayman al-Zawahiri had assumed control and he was calling the shots. He had brought all his regional leaders together on this remote Island of Socotra and he was intent on starting the final jihad. So I gave them a tricked out bomb and said 'Adios! I bugged out of there just seven hours before the suitcase bomb went off. I had no idea of the power that was in that small suitcase, and I doubt you will find any evidence of the organization that was hiding out there." He sat back and waited for other questions.

The three inquisitors sat there stunned. Karen Lee wondered if the story could be true. Might the CIA and FBI run out of things to do and people to spy on? She didn't know what to say. Gathering her wits she tried to speak of a few other matters.

"We will be briefing the President shortly, Mr. Meredith," Karen Lee said, "Our immediate concern is just what do we do with you and your THCT group. By the way, that THCT moniker, we presumed it stood for Trojan Horse Terrorists, is that correct? We just couldn't decide what the C stood for?"

"Meredith smiled and said, "Counter,.... Trojan Horse Counter-Terrorists. I, we took the name because the Greek war story gave us the inspiration to lure the bastard out of his hole."

"I wish we had known that early on," Brent Eichalberger said. "We thought your suitcase weapon was aimed at us and coming to America."

"That was a chance I had to take, because in all honesty, you would not have let me proceed. For that matter, who would have thought the plan could possibly work?" Meredith smiled for the first time proud of himself and his team. Even though he presumed he was going to prison.

"So tell us, just how did you accomplish this counter-terrorist plan and wipe al Qaeda off the face of the Earth?"

"If you have a few minutes, I'll start at the beginning."

→ ←

EPILOGUE

The earthquake story held. Because it was on such a remote island in the middle of nowhere, very few observers went anywhere near the place to see the devastation. There was no reported loss of life. The initial page three article, drifted to page 22 the second day, and then disappeared from print by the third day.

The radioactive fallout from Socotra Island drifted east in the winds for some 500 miles, and settled into the vast Indian Ocean to be thoroughly absorbed and mixed in the converging currents. In a matter of days only trace amounts of radioactivity were being recorded in over-flights, and by special teams flown into the zone.

On the Island of Socotra, the forty man local militia was given substantial special funding and support by the United States. This allowed them to set-up roadblocks on the two roads heading east, which prevented anyone from getting near the earthquake site.

In various parts of the Middle East the remnants of the terrorist organization al Qaeda found itself in considerable disarray. Many of its key leaders had disappeared not returning from wherever they had traveled. In the ensuing weeks various terrorist factions fought among themselves trying to establish a new leadership hierarchy. In doing so they exposed themselves to greater western government scrutiny, and were dealt with harshly and swiftly.

→ ←

Most of the THCT group returned to the U.S. and New York by private charter. They were met at the WM Industries flight hanger at Teterboro and driven immediately to a secure safe house facility in upstate New York for a well-deserved week of rest. Each individual was interviewed and all claimed they had been invited on a cruise with William Meredith through the Greek Islands and had a wonderful time. They all stuck to their story.

Eventually they were released and went home to try and re-establish their lives now that their personal demons had been vanquished.

O and Malik did not return to driving taxis. Instead they made a large down payment on prime retail space on west 49th St. and Seventh Avenue, almost in the center of Times Square. They set up a retail storefront and called it O & M's Electronics, carrying top of the line equipment, thanks to the generosity of a benefactor. As successful businessmen, they also decided to join a private club in up-state Kensico, New York.

Kate Shanahan went back to her graphics business a more focused lady. She was able to pick up a number of international shipping and trading accounts, expanding her business overseas to Norway, England and Greece. She too joined the Kensico Gun Club so she could shoot with her friends.

Michael Pappas and Kevin Geary decided to put in for retirement from the NYPD, and opened an MK Security an international company located on 5th Avenue at 50th St. in New York City. They welcomed a large number of new international shipping and trading companies as clients. Sensing changes in the shipping world, they specialized in on-board security protection for valuable cargos. Their take command approach was well received by the shipping industry and insurance companies gave encouraging signs they would reduce insurance rates.

Josef Veronin did not return to the United Nations. He instead set up an international translation company, lining up clients and first class linguists from all over the globe. While he still believed in diplomacy and compromise, he knew that often talk was not enough, and action may be necessary. He enjoyed the sport of shooting and introduced some of his compatriots to the art and science of weaponry.

Ralph Behar left his former investment company and built a solid investment portfolio working with preferred international shipping and commodities brokers. He took up horse racing as a sport and joined a gun club as well.

Uri Navroz heard the calling of the sea again and without family to tie him down, he became a Captain on one of Meredith's ships plying the Mediterranean Sea. Every morning he woke, stepped out on the bridge, and breathed the salt ocean air. He felt renewed.

Courtney had stayed on the Majorca, with Captain Brinkmann nursing her back to health. A few weeks later the couple flew to Oslo, where she met Derek's parents. They married a month later and went to sea on a completely new Coaster named Socotra that had all the bells and whistles.

Ryan Younger went back to piloting his boss around the world. He met a young woman named Alex and they settled in Manhattan. She too was a pilot and before long became Meredith's permanent co-pilot. They traveled the world together.

William Meredith spent a good number of weeks in Washington, D.C. meeting quietly with a number of Homeland Security agencies. He even met with the President in an unofficial visit to Camp David. He eventually returned to his horse farm in upstate New York to witness the foaling of a new thoroughbred racer. He named it <u>Osama's Dead 4Sure</u>, and knew it would be a winner.

➔ ←

Teterboro Airport, New Jersey

Saturday, July 8th, Meredith picked up Josef in his town car and drove to his hanger. Ryan Younger had the Bombardier gassed up and ready to roll. In a matter of minutes they were racing down the runway and headed west.

Less than an hour and a half later they were descending over the endless forests. Ryan lined up the sleek jet and approached the single airstrip in Land O' Lakes, Wisconsin. Touching down he taxied back to a series of small hangers. Ryan parked the craft, climbed out of his harness, and popped the hatch.

At the bottom of the steps a tall man with a military crew cut stood almost at attention.

"Mr. Meredith, it is good to see you Sir, welcome to God's Country," the man said with a heavy Russian accent. "The last time I saw you was from a small boat in the Black Sea. Welcome to Land O' Lakes, Sir!"

"Sergeant Major, It's good to see you as well, and much dryer than last time. It looks as if this Wisconsin weather is appealing to you, almost as much as Mother Russia?"

"It is Sir, the weather is the same, but the freedoms are astounding, and the people are open and friendly. Life is good."

"I thought that would be the case, Tristan. You remember Josef Veronin, and I think you remember Ryan Younger."

"Yes, certainly, the lousy fisherman, and my very most favorite pilot." He smiled and extended his hand to both of them.

"Come, we must not keep the General waiting." They all climbed into a black SUV. Tristan drove out of the airport, which was tucked behind a roadside hotel, and a nine-hole golf course paralleling the runway.

On County Highway B he drove down Main Street and the Sergeant pointed out a rustic log cabin storefront. The name on the front of the store was "Tristan's Russian Curio's.

"I see you've acclimated yourself very well, Tristan, and you have even brought a little of yours with you. How is the business doing?"

"It goes well, especially during the tourist season. People come up here to snowmobile, to fish, and to vacation in God's country. And they buy Russian gifts! It is a good living."

"I'm pleased Tristan, I really am."

Tristan crossed Highway 45 and took Highway B about four miles east passing an entrance to the Nicollet National Forest. At Crystal Lake Road they turned into a crushed gravel drive that led to Sunset Lodge on Lac Vieux Desert Lake. It was a resort that catered to fisherman year round, and the family vacation trade in the summer.

The SUV pulled up to the main Lodge and an elderly man came walking out before the engine died. He was dressed as a north-woods fisherman should be, with a tan fishing vest over a plaid shirt. On his head he had the traditional floppy hat with a variety of small lures attached to it.

"Josef, William, and Ryan, it is good to see you,... all in one piece."

"Dimitri, you look great for an old soldier." William Meredith said. They hugged each other like grizzly bears.

Then General Gralashov turned to his brother-in-law and Ryan, "I was not sure I would ever see you again, brother. And Ryan, it is good to see you again. Come, come inside, we have much to talk about."

"Hang on a minute, Dimitri, we have lots of time to talk. I've come to Wisconsin for a reason. You promised me fishing lessons, and I've come to collect. The last time you tried to teach me, I couldn't quite concentrate on the fishing.... Now I can!"

"Then let's fish." He pointed them towards the lake and his new top of the line fishing boat. As they walked onto the pier, Meredith noted the boat's name painted across the transom, **TROJAN HORSE**.

→ ←